The Satellite Prinz

The Trilogy: Book 2

THE RISING

By

V.C. McDade

V.C. McDade

Copyright © 2018 VCMcDade

All rights reserved.

ISBN-13: 978-179-194-0164

All rights reserved. This book or any portion thereof may not be reproduced or used in any manner whatsoever without the express written permission of the author except for the use of brief quotations in a book review.

This novel's story and principal characters are fictitious. Certain long-standing institutions, agencies, and public offices are mentioned, names, characters, business, places, events and incidents are either the product of the author's imagination or used in a fictitious manner, any resemblance to actual persons alive or dead, or actual events that occurred during the timeline this book is set in is purely coincidence.

The author has rearranged to suit the convenience of the book, space, time, location and any factual events contained within this story may have been altered for dramatic reason and although the author and publisher have made every effort to ensure that the information contained within this book were correct at press time, the author and publisher do not assume and hereby disclaim any liability to any party for any loss, damage, or disruption caused by errors or omissions, whether such errors or omissions result from negligence, accident, or any other cause.

Any similarities between the people, dialogs, event, or plot is purely coincidental. The author does not in any way endorse, condone or encourage any racist/fascist behaviour, or activities associated with Nazism. The opinions expressed are those of the characters and should not be confused with the author's.

Visit the author's website at www.sardiniaprinz.com

The Sardinia Prinz: The Rising

*To those of you who bought the first book, thank you,
I hope you enjoy this one.*

Contents

1	Chapter : The Crankbait	1-31
2	Chapter : The Dry Fly	32-80
3	Chapter : The Baitrunner	81-114
4	Chapter : The Float	115-129
5	Chapter : The Downrigger	130-141
6	Chapter : The Hook Shank	142-153
7	Chapter : The Deadbait	154-173
8	Chapter : The Steelhead Runners	174-191
9	Chapter : The Pennel Rig Spinner	192-218
10	Chapter : The Pulley Rig	219-228
11	Chapter : The Handlining	229-248
12	Chapter : The Rod	249-261
13	Chapter : The Little Disgorger	262-282
14	Chapter : The Calm Tangler	283-318
15	Chapter : The Loosefeed	319-333
16	Chapter : The Brackish	334-372
17	Chapter : The Trolling	373-397
18	Chapter : The Jigging	398-424
19	Chapter : The Blade Bait	425-446
20	Chapter : The Breaker zone	447-460
21	Chapter : The Landing	461-470
22	Chapter : The Rising	471-479

The Island of Sardinia

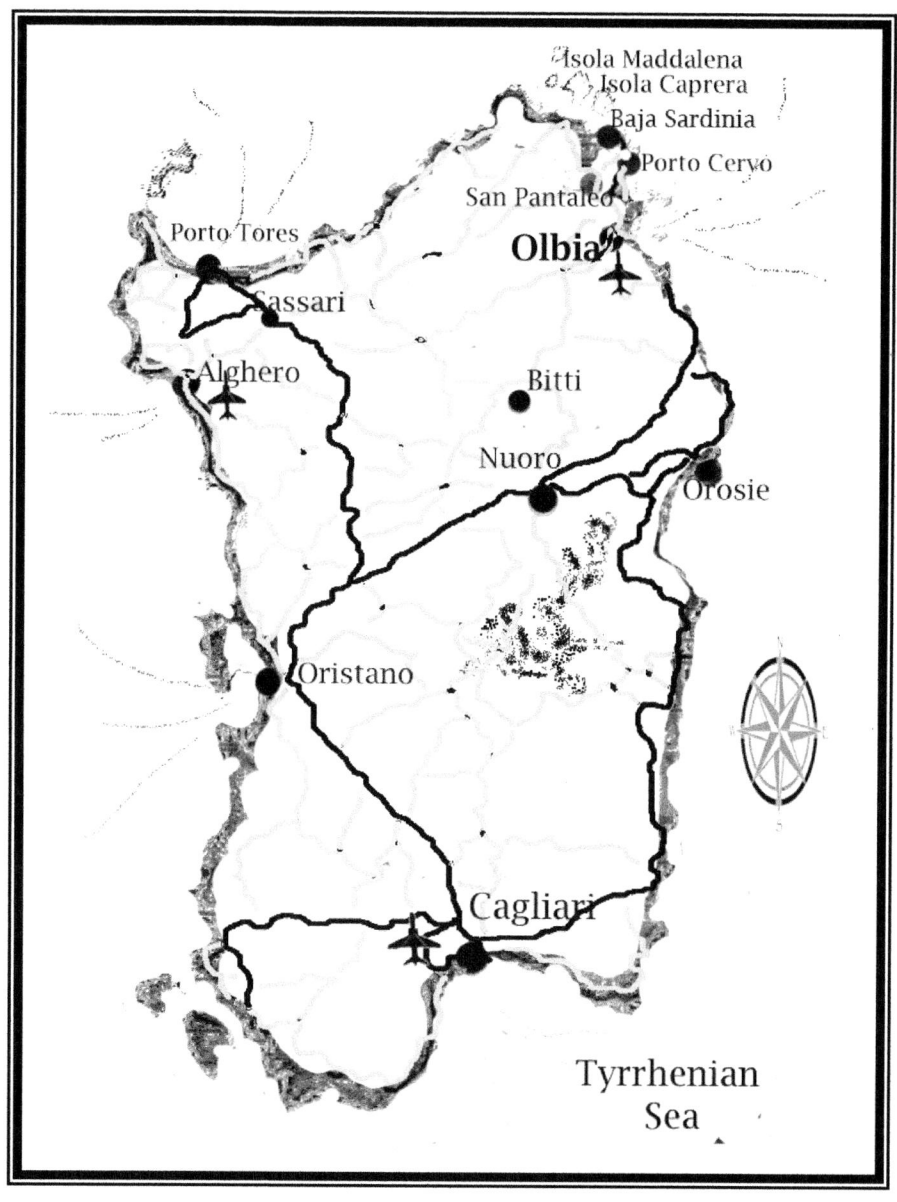

Chapter 1: The Crankbait

The British Sovereign Bases of Akrotiri and Dhekelia,
The Island of Cyprus,
September – October 1959

"Who's this new chap, Biggs?" Winston Curtiss, 19 Field Survey Regiment, Royal Engineers, thumbed the supply requisition log, trying to decipher the last scrolled signature. "Irish?"
"I don't think so Sir, arrived in Dhekelia yesterday, Major with Signals Corp. Mr Pimm. He's been set up with a bunk in the disused offices, above the garages on B.C. plot." The Quartermaster, Sergeant Biggs continued to stack boxes on the shelf.
"Things are a bit tight for space I know up here, strange he'd get a nest away from the regular officers, bit antisocial, unlikely to get a sit down to cards sticking on his own."
Turning out of earshot Sergeant Biggs muttered to himself, "Doubt he's up here looking for a bridge partner." and raised an eye.

"Bloody cheek! tinker's nabbed my Batman Gregory and Jeep. I only drove up from Akrotiri yesterday to get an early start. I was scheduled to survey the forest above Limnara beach, then Waldas and I were hoping to snatch a dive off the wreck." Curtiss frowned.
Biggs looked up at the office clock it was quarter to ten, the words *the early bird catches*, very nearly rose to his lips.
"You'd have a hard job today Sir, he booked out your theodolite and the last survey staff, I believe I saw him stow a tent pack, think he said he was heading for Kyrenia something about a freshwater well dispute." Biggs struggled to hold back a smile.
Curtiss read the list of supplies and tools Pimm had requisitioned and the site survey location.
"Odd, didn't think the Greeks were interested in that stretch, you sure Kyrenia? Thought that was the only place these buggers got on?"
Looking at the large terrain map of Cyprus on the wall, the officer traced his finger over the north of the Island.
"Oh! Well, guess I'll spend a day at Goldsmith's, I'm sure this Pimm chap will understand my landing a couple of Gin's on his tab, for the inconvenience, he's caused, what, what!" Curtis mused and made a note of Pimm's army number from the register.
"If you are going to the club, you'll need to wait for one of the duty trucks to return Sir, I have nothing spare at the moment, Sir." The Sergeant held back a smirk as he heard Curtiss flicking through the motor pool key fobs on the pegs looking for his usual assigned Land Rover keys.

"What? He's taken my Landy, my God, man! Bloody Pikey, must be a paddy." Curtiss's face flushed with annoyance.

"Don't think so Sir, sounded more Londoner to me, not that I would presume to question a senior officers heritage, such as yourselves, Sir." Sergeant Biggs had to turn away now, as he heard Curtiss return to the book to check how long Pimm had signed out for.

"Bloody hell Biggs, why is it left open-ended? Since that nasty business with Toby Morris in the Nicosia billiard hall, the chief insists all off base location times are strictly verified. How longs this bod supposed to be on his jaunt?" Curtiss slapped his palm on the counter, "and can you stop what you're bloody doing for a moment, man." Closing the logbook his frustrations nearly exploding, Curtiss rapped his leather gloves across the cover.

The Quartermaster raised his eyes to his clerk, working at a desk out of sight, listening to the exchange, and shrugged with a cheeky grin.

"Yes Sir," Biggs stamped his feet and stood at attention on the other side of the store counter, awaiting the officer next command, as Captain Peter Waldren came up alongside Curtiss, having just finished a smoke outside the store's offices.

"C'mon Winnie, what's the holdup, told the chaps we would be back for G & T'S at five and crib." Waldren looked the Quartermaster up and down and checked the register.

"This fellow's only let some newbie swipe my gear and wheels, to top it all he's taken, Bob Gregory." Curtiss gestured to the Quartermaster,"so Biggs! What did he say, when's he due back in?"

"Well, man? What's this Majors RTB *(return to base)* he must have told you, this Pimm chap? Speak up! What have you to say for yourself?" Waldren chirped in.

Sergeant Biggs took a breath and bit his lip, "I was explaining to the gentleman, here, Sir, the Major's requisition papers were in order."

The strain was beginning to tell in the Sergeant complexion, in being called to account, for carrying out orders from a visiting senior officer, to the Turkish side British army base. He had no idea who Major Pimm was but knew he was a professional. Explaining his actions, especially to, two officers who he judged from their elocution were clearly marked as the sons of wealthy parents that had bought them military rank, for having failed to secure a place within the Foreign Office and government was raising the heat to the back of his fine hair clippered sunburnt neck.

"Do you know him, Peter?" Curtiss asked, watching Waldren read the log page.

"No, says here he's in the hills near Karaman, I hope you told him that's only half a mile from the Sparrow hawk operation, there's bound to be a couple of *bubble bods* in the hills we missed. It's a dammed remote patch to get cornered." Waldren rubbed his chin while referring to an eight-day operation that captured 31 EOKA terrorists *(Greek National Organisation of Cypriot Fighters)* in the Kyrenia Hills.

"Come on Biggs, spin the dit, what do you know?" he said, reverting to army slang to coerce the Sergeant to be forthcoming.

"Permission to speak Sir's" Biggs requested, while still at attention, but the Sergeant by now was feeling he had wasted enough time explaining his purpose, bearing in mind the impression Major Pimm had made on him compared to these Zobs, *(Commissioned officers)*. He received a nod of affirmation from Waldren.
"Respectfully and not wishing to presume, the Major appeared to have made preparation for the possibility of engagement. I assisted in loading his equipment and noticed him and *the "Full Screw"* that was tagging along, sorry Sirs...Corporal Gregory, had already visited the Armoury they took along a Bren and a 3-inch Mortar, as well as one of the new Belgian, Gippies machine guns. From his manner, I believe he would be aware of the recent altercations with the Greeks, in the region. That or he's planning a party of his own Sir's." Sergeant Biggs knew he had said enough to end the conversation and carried on loading his store shelves, leaving the two officers at his counter, scratching their heads.

"Sounds fishy, like a secret squirrel to me Winnie, or green slime?" Waldren backed away as he used the army slang for military intelligence.
"Yes maybe, it could be they're looking to hang a hat on whoever cocked up Lucky Alfonso?" Curtiss looked again at the wall map.
"Only luck on that day was I was having my BCG jab, so it's not my circus, not my monkey, best stay upwind of this one, till we get the colour of his jib, what you say Sergeant?" Waldren stepped towards the door.
"Sounds like good advice to me Sir's," Biggs said and winked to his out of sight subordinate, who gestured masturbating, showing his opinion of Waldren and Curtiss.
"Come on Win. You'll get no sense here; see if the jungle drums in the mess have a word on this Pimm bod, I'll treat you to a sticky *(cake)*." Waldren said dismissively, and in closing the logbook, he flicked the chained pen, so that it dangled off the counter edge.
"Sergeant Biggs, FYI, no-one enquired about this tinker today, a couple of coffin nails *(woodbines)*, for your time" Biggs looked unimpressed at the two cigarettes Curtiss rolled from his packet onto the logbook cover and reading his indifference as a lack of substance to the bribe he added two more.
"That's very kind of you, Sir, Private Hopkin's and I will enjoy them at break." Biggs slipped them quickly beneath the counter and watched Curtiss and Waldren leave.
"I'd like to be a fly on the wall when those two decide to challenge that Major, I know who I'd put a week's pay on." The Sergeant said, straightening his counter and placing the chained pen back into its holder, before handing his clerk only one of the four cigarettes he had been given.

Standing on the south flank of Troodos Mountains, Pimm scanned across the valley to the blackened scarred hillside on the opposite side. Where once there had been a densely wooded crown, trees splintered skyward stripped of leaves and branches, the aftermath of Operation Lucky Alfonso, which had not gone according to plan.

"That's where one Para came up and got pinned with the Highlanders boxed behind getting the shit kicked out of them." Corporal Gregory pointed then wiped the sweat from his eyes.

"And you helped with the recovery, looks total TARFU *(Things Are Really Fucked Up)* from here, surprised more of your buddies got clear." Pimm said, as his eyes picked up the mortar star patterns that bespectacled the light earth and other tell-tale signs of where the British soldiers had fought their way up the hillside and back again while a forest fire raged behind them barring their retreat. The real enemy that day had been a lack of reconnaissance.

"Yes, sir, TARFU." Gregory looked up, considering what sort of an officer he had been assigned to that morning, with little expectation this one would be any different. At least he could understand this one's accent he thought.

"I understand you were on mortars." Pimm studied the soldier looking for signs of a lie or an excuse. "Your XO *(Executive Officer)* gave orders for a high round disbursement, but at the end of the day, your count was complete? You never let one rip, never fired a single shot?"

"As I stated to XO, the range guide was faulty, Sir." Gregory looked up with no remorse for his actions, but the truth was he had chosen to directly disobey his orders, realising from his vantage point their own men would be caught in the KZ *(kill zone)*. The Corporal knew better than to expand on his excuse, and Pimm already knew enough about what happened that day to challenge his word, for the record.

"Was it? It sounds more like you kept your wits Gregory, good for you." Pimm's tone had an air of disbelief, as he watched the tall, lean youth handle the Bren like it was a bag of sugar.

He had read the debriefing report, including the underlined section regarding an account of the support troop's actions that Gregory had been assigned to.

The testimony of an unconfirmed observation, a senior officer who wants his name disassociated with the disaster of the day, who was compelled, probably because he was amongst junior men, and described Corporal Gregory entering the fire to pull members of the assault team from the inferno, until he was ordered back overcome by the choking smoke, intense heat and his smouldering fatigues.

Unconfirmed? Pimm also knew it was the fact that there was a suspicion Gregory disobeyed a direct order to fire his mortar shells, and this prevented him from getting a citation for saving his comrades.

Doing the right thing, against orders never receives a reward in the army.

Pimm judged, that somehow Gregory had realised being hidden by smoke from the sight of the commander ordering the mortar barrage, the probability was high that some of those killed on the hill would be been struck down by their own mortars whilst retreating, as they tried to outrun the fire. None of which was in the base commander's report, that carried a top-secret stamp.

Looking at the young Corporal as he stood at arms scanning their surroundings, Pimm recognised in the fact each time Gregory kept his eyes lowered, refraining from looking over to the next hill the incident was still fresh in the young man's mind. Pimm flipped the Braille watch cover open at his wrist and read the time with his thumb without Gregory noticing.

"I've seen enough, you know the coast road to Kyrenia, wake me before we drop from the hills there, I'll take it then. I want to be in Agios Andronikos, on the Karpass peak, before the sun's overhead. If we do that I'll buy you two cold ones, tonight." Pimm pulled his knees up bracing himself with cap down as Gregory sped down the hillside, passing just one donkey laden with firewood on the way up, its owner cursed as he was showered by dust, as the Corporal fought the path ruts, he glanced briefly to his side, but Pimm did not stir.

As they dropped down from the hills slipping into Kyrenia horseshoe harbour it was only when the front tyres of the Jeep hit the first cobbled narrow road to the seafront that Pimm sat up. "Good job" he yawned, and stretched his arms, catching a wave from a child hanging from window, in a passing building, attracted by their engine noise.

They pulled up in front of a stack of fishing pots to the front of a low wall where nets hung on timber cross bars. Gregory took sentry position watching the street behind checking the windows of the Dome Hotel with his Bren gun laid low across the tent pack so as not disturb the few locals going about their daily routines. Taking a quick glance back to Pimm, it appeared to him as if he was searching amongst the names of the few fishing vessels and motor launches, bobbing gently in the port. It seemed he had found what he was looking for as he gestured Gregory to move from the driving seat and jumped behind the wheel.

"Well done Corporal, you made good time, enough for a treat I think." Pimm said, with a knowing smile and set off towards the north road raising an occasional salute to some of the friendlier locals they passed by as they drove out of Kyrenia.

Kyrenia town and the surrounding hills were predominantly Turkish, considered relatively safe, to those in the know and Major Pimm took Corporal Gregory by surprise as they headed out and just a couple of miles west he pulled off the main road and down the track that led into Newman's Farm, most would pass it, without knowing the treasures it held. It was here the soldiers each filled their Jerry cans with the sweetest cold vanilla milkshake Gregory had ever tasted.

"Good, eh?" Pimm said, as he tore away on the northeast road towards Agios Andronikos and along the high trail roads to the furthest tip of the island.

"Yes, they could open a dozen stores in London." Gregory licked his lips, but one thing bothered him now as his stomach sloshed with the milk, how was it this Major was so well informed to find the dairy farm, having only recently arrived on the Island.

"Better out then in," Pimm said, having made an enormous belch and both men chuckled as Gregory did the same.

The hill road became increasingly precarious at times leading along the Karpass Peninsular, but Pimm gripped and span the steering wheel like a rally driver.
It had taken them just four hours when they reached Agios Andronikos, and they continued half a mile until checking his map, Pimm steered the Jeep up a path that had only ever seen carts and donkeys. The bone-shaking ride challenged the Jeeps suspension and bracken like razor blades scratched at the jeep metal, but on a small ridge with their wheels inches from the peninsular cliff edge, hanging sharply down towards the sea Pimm stopped abruptly, much to Corporal Gregory's relief.

As the two men sat briefly staring out over the Mediterranean, Pimm offered the Corporal a Player's senior service and again brought up Operation Lucky Alfonso.
"So Gregory, if you had it to do again, anything you would change. It's just you me and the grass up here, off the record I don't tell tales," Pimm said, spitting the tiny flakes of tobacco from his lips. It was as if he had been waiting the whole journey to think of the question and he saw the Corporals hesitancy about answering truthfully. Criticising a senior officers orders could land you two on Jankers, Gregory bit his lip, catching the last taste of the milkshake vanilla and took a deep breath, "No Major, I believe I would do the same again and wish others did not."
Gregory stepped from the Jeep and began unloading their gear while keeping an eye on areas of cover he instinctively knew were likely sources of protection for an enemy attack.
Pimm understood his resistance to speak; after all, the Corporal knew nothing about him. For all Gregory knew Pimm could be a scalp hunter from Military Internal affairs looking for a scapegoat for the tragedy.
"Fair enough, maybe time will come you'll tell me what you really think," Pimm said, looking towards the highest part of the hill, crowned with a crooked olive tree.
"Well it's not the first foul-up I've seen, it won't be the last. I hear people say whatever doesn't kill you makes you stronger. Personally, I say it wasn't your day, and on this occasion, it would appear you made sure that went for some of your pals, so let's make sure that's true today, get on with this and let's be out of here."
He saw the Corporal didn't revel in the compliment.
"Yes Sir, just wished I could have got more out, a hell of a way to go, fire."
Gregory looked at his feet, not wanting to show his emotion and then grabbed his Sten gun and slung it over his shoulder.
"Yes, hell of a way," Pimm whispered, as he gave his Ordinance map a look and scratched an X and a question mark, where they had viewed the remains of the battlefield in the Troodos Mountains.

Just from his manner, Gregory could tell the Major understood what he was talking about, regarding the screaming he witnessed, as his comrades burnt to death on the hill. Then he noticed the matching scars on the inside of his wrist that appeared to continue beyond his folded back shirt sleeves, and he dropped his eyes to the kit in the back of the Land Rover sensing Pimm knew he was watching him, he was correct.

"Right then! Take the rod to the far edge of the pass break along there, on your way, pick up an earth sample every fifteen foot or so."Pimm said, handing him the earth core sampler, shaped like a giant corkscrew.

"Don't make a meal of it, enough to fill the tin, they're all numbered, you know the drill. While we're here may as well use the time wisely, save some other poor sapper slogging up here. I'll watch your back when you're down in the dirt, I need to take readings from the top, I'll set up over there, in the shade with the Bren and theodolite," Pimm said, with a hint of irony reading Gregory's expression, *Of course, you will and* passed Gregory the white survey staff, which both men knew would reflect the sun better than a mirror, ideal for a sniper.

"Remember, keep your head below the peak, no need to give them a nice skyline silhouette, with your height." Pimm could see the young Corporal was nervously alert, so far in country with no backup, even though he showed no sign of fear.

"Keep your Sten handy, any sign of trouble get back to the Jeep and let off a few pots, and this time no if's or buts, even if you have to set them at my feet, understood! With what happened over there I would expect they will steer clear of this region for a bit unless they use it as bait, in which case we will deal with it right!" Pimm said, casually fixing the 3-inch mortar base ten feet or so from the Jeep and setting three Mortar shells tail down, upright in the sand at the ready.

"Yes, sir!" Gregory said, and seeing Pimm clearly knew what he was doing, thanked him when Pimm handed him a stick of Wrigley's spearmint gum.

Watching as Gregory backed away along the ridge, Pimm then slung the Bren gun across the back of his shoulders, resting it on top of his own rucksack so that it balanced in place, holding the barrel with one hand with the skill of a circus performer, he snapped up the theodolite, tucking the tripod under his arm and climbed the slope towards the nearest peak as miniature brown crickets hopped away before each of his dusty steps, as the sun started its ascent to full glory.

Pimm crouched into the shade like some Apache scout and looked northward with an unhindered view into the wide aquamarine Mediterranean bay below. Recognising the remote beach he had seen on his MI6 assignment map, code name *"The Stable"* he followed the rocky coastline through his binoculars and the marker buoys out at sea, set as submerged rock warnings for vessels, before the water straits stretched unchallenged towards the distant shores of Turkey. To his right, the land fell away to the lowest points of the Karpass Peninsula, where outcrops of remote sandy beaches were curtained by the small Cypriot wooden fishing vessels known as Caiques, just like those in Kyrenia's small harbour.

For hundreds of years, Greeks and Turks had shared the same waters assisting each other with broken lobster pots and nets. Now the lines of division between the two races were sodden in fresh blood on this island paradise, where the British government were engaged in one of the most dangerous and complicated double dating acts since the Italians Armistice when they switched sides from the Nazi Axis to the Allies in world war II.

At stake the British Governorship and military stronghold in the region, that could easily be lost if their wooing of the Turkish Government failed.
Failure for the British would create a power vacuum allowing the Soviets to make improper advances to join the dance that would see an acceleration of the conflict, something the American could never let happen with or without the help of the emerging United Nations.

Captain Winston Curtiss was right, when he speculated on the actual rank and credentials of Major Oliver Pimm, he was not what he seemed on paper and was, in truth, an Mi6 tactical field operative, hiding in plain sight, attached to the Cartography and Topographic division assisting the 42 Royal engineers regiment at the Cyprus sovereign overseas territory bases of Akrotiri and Dhekelia.

Only a week earlier Pimm had downed tools on an existing Mi6 assignment in Saigon to be in Cyprus, having received a request from an old master of the works, the one that had taught him his craftwork and someone he could not refuse.

His cover story called for the base commander, Brigadier Geoffrey Baker to give him whatever facilities and resources he required.

Baker was informed, if he wished not to have his own name added to his investigations, to provide Pimm with a wide berth. As far as Baker knew Pimm was as Curtiss had surmised investigating the recent altercation with the EOKA, the Greek Cypriot terrorist group, during Operation Lucky Alphonse.

Local intelligence had earmarked a recruitment training camp high in the forest at an abandoned logging camp in the Troodos Mountains where General Georgios Grivas, head of the EOKA had been reported seen. Unfortunately, poor reconnaissance failed to assess that Grivas's men, a force of some 300 had come in possession of incendiary grenades and booby-trapped the trails, bordered by stacks of decaying dry tinder.
Once the engaging British troop was committed within the forest for cover, with the first explosions and tracer bullets igniting several fires, they were already well within the kill zone, with few options to retreat as the hillside was engulfed in smoke and flame. In confusion, both the British soldiers and Greek Cypriot guerrilla fighters were trapped.
Unfortunately as the timber mixture of sap and woodworm pulp dust clouds exploded and was mistaken for heavy weapons fire by the observing British officers off-site.
The reserve British support group lower down the hill deployed a ring of 3-inch mortars which killed anyone above the tree line indiscriminately. Corporal Bob Gregory was the only gunner that did not disperse his shells. During Operation Lucky Alfonso twenty-five British soldiers were killed including seven in a vehicle accident that day.
Greek Cypriot numbers are unconfirmed but were considerably higher.

However Mi6 had not sent Oliver Pimm to Cyprus to scalp heads for the Lucky Alphonse disaster, and he had no official interest in trying to find out why so many men had died, in what had been initially detailed as a straight forward surround and seizure operation. He had already seen his fair share of inane operational balls-up by some of the new wave of public school CO's hitting the ranks, in Pimm eye's it was just the same shit a different day for the PBI, *(Poor Bloody Infantry)*. And that was not his *circus,* as Peter Waldren had put it.
Pimm was in Cyprus for two reasons the first was political,

Prime Minister Harold Macmillan had finally capitulated to the realisation the escalating ferocity of the divisions between the Cypriot inhabitants would only be resolved once a hard border had been established. Agreeable not only to the island inhabitants but also their ancestral homelands of Greece and Turkey, both had been supporting their respective island terrorist groups with the supply of arms and training. So for some time there had been attempts both in the public eye, through diplomatic channels and by clandestine negotiations through military appeasement for a settlement that would see both sides withdraw from paramilitary activity, that was increasingly being directed by both sides in frustration at the policing British military force occupying the Island, who they saw as interfering in their war.
Meanwhile British Intelligence during this period ever aware of the Cold War factor and on occasion working with the American C.I.A. secretly aided both sides in turn, to propagate the necessity of the continuation of the British armed forces presence. The division between British Intelligence and the general British army had reached a complexity beyond that of the divisions of the Cypriots themselves.
Increasingly demands on Mi6 by those that walked the corridors of Whitehall placed regular servicemen in danger as the pressure in the region was fuelled by those that had their own axe to grind regarding the British presence, such as the Russians and members of the Jewish Cypriot fraction.
Since 1946 Great Britain had created a series of internment camps on Cyprus housing for the most part individuals captured and detained during their attempts to migrate illegally to Mandatory Palestine.
At its height, there were an estimated 53,000 detainees, mostly Jewish men of fighting age. However, by the time the last camp closed in 1949, around 2,000 children had been born within the camps.
There were many having suffered under British imprisonment including those who had lost loved ones, that considered remaining in Cyprus and driving the British from the island to create a free state was as much a cause to die for, as the creation of their own homeland Israel.
Some assisted the Turks, some the Greeks and some stayed to act as mediators.

The balancing act the British Military stationed as the Sovereign Bases of Akrotiri and Dhekelia were ordered to perform by their government before the U.N. interceded was an impossible task.
Operation Lucky Alfonso was only one of a number of ill-fated operations. The final tally would list the number of British forces, Commonwealth Policemen and British and European civilians dead at over 500 including many young National Servicemen. The two main combatants reported figures of over 2200 for the Turkish side, while the Cyprus high commission released the figure of 3000 Greeks dead in 1974.
However, the scale of civilian atrocities perpetrated by both sides, in their often tit for tat macabre messages of vengeance may never indeed be verified.

In September 1959, Oliver Pimm had been released from his assignment attachment to Mi6, Cook Department's Hanoi station, following a request by Albert "Bull" Gordon, Pimm's former sector chief, to undertake Operation Seahorse, (later to be known as the "Diniz incident") This was the second and main official reason Pimm was in Cyprus. In itself it was a chance by-product of his real mission, with Operation Seahorse stirring the pot of local politics, influencing goodwill internationally between the Greek mainland government and British military, by reinforcing the conception that the British army in the region were an essential non-biased peacekeeping force.

However, Pimm's primary reason for being in Cyprus was for something far more personal, which was a rarity for those in his profession, emotional sentiment, the wish right a wrong and exact revenge however deserving were not traits generally associated with a Sandman. Unfortunately what he could not know was in honouring a debt of his past, his actions would have far-reaching consequences, the catalyst of an epically, with everlasting ramifications for himself.

On the Hills of the Karpass Peninsula, Pimm stepped back into the sunlight giving Corporal Gregory a nonchalant wave of reassurance as he set up the Bren gun on the hillside with his back to a massive boulder. Then climbed the eight feet or so to its flat plateau where he began to set up the timber tripod behind him the Olive trees cut his silhouette from the hilly terrain so that at times when Gregory looked up, Pimm's image was nowhere to be seen.

The chewing gum Pimm had given the young soldier focused intent, an automated muscle memory action, allowing his brain to be distracted enough with a familiar activity, settling nerves and concentration to the task. But each time he lost sight of the Major, it increased his anxiety, as the chorus from the crickets in the long grass appeared to get louder, each time he rammed home the core sampling hand drill and began turning the handle to cut a bottle diameter width hole into the soft island soil.

When at the depth mark he pulled it out and looking up seeing Pimm still in sight, ducked low into the kit bag and fumbled for the right sample collector each identical the size of a boot polish tin.

"What the fuck are you about mate?" he whispered, his eyes flitted nervously over the brush and woods in the hills below, as the sun began to belt down, its late morning heat aiding the damp lining of his beret. Even with the stream of sweat stinging his eyes, Gregory wished he was wearing a tin *(Helmet),* as Pimm once again disappeared over the horizon this time dropping to what appeared to be the opposite side of the hill.

Gregory didn't know much, but he knew Pimm was no ordinary Royal Engineer and he began to focus more on watching his cover than collecting the samples, filling some collectors with the same dirt, occasionally offering a "Fuck" muttered under his breath.

Out of sight Pimm checked his brass Stanley London natural sine compass and noted the time and sun's coordinates, then took from his rucksack a hand-held signalling mirror. Adjusting the head prism to capture the light of the sun overhead, he tapped the trigger three times and then watched the water towards the end of the peninsular at his eleven o'clock.

Suddenly there was a group of three small flashes of brilliant white light followed by four flashes, then another two. The Morse flash spelt the code words "Dining car open."

It came from the periscope of HMS Rorqual, a hunter-killer Porpoise class submarine that had been awaiting Pimm's verification for the commencement of the operation he had been deployed by Mi6 to instigate.

"Two reservations. Playmate 4 booked, send Seahorse 0330 BP over."

Pimm tapped at the signal trigger ending with his call sign, "BP" Bad Penny, a nickname from the one who had enlisted him into the intelligence service, *Bad Penny Pimm,* coined more respectfully than derogatory.

Gregory got to the site where the path dropped away. Looking back up the way he had come Pimm was nowhere to be seen, then as the Corporal took a step back towards the Jeep, Pimm moved out into the light as he packed the signal lamp in his rucksack. Then he whistled to Gregory to raise the red and white Level staff, Gregory held it up expecting the usual corrections of how he was holding it by his superior, but with only a cursory glance through the range finder Pimm stuck up his thumb.

"All good filled the tins, excellent pack it up Corp. we'll call it a day," Pimm shouted back as he trudged down the hill towards the WIllys Jeep.

Corporal Bob Gregory had been with Cartography and Topographic's, for a little over nine months and in all that time no one had taken readings as quickly as Pimm and without making notes, but he was not complaining, he was just glad to be heading back to the safety of the camp. And little was said between them on the return journey to Dhekelia as the sun began to drop like a stone to the Med. As the

barricade sentry post dropped behind them Pimm ordered him to stow the equipment and arms back with the Quartermaster. Sergeant Biggs, studied Gregory as he signed his receipt book, having confirmed all equipment was back in place, present and correct and although he raised an eye at the return mileage reading the Corporal entered for the Land Rover they had used, aware the distance they had covered was well over the range Major Pimm had indicated they were travelling that day, Biggs held back on any questions.
"Trust the gentleman was satisfied with your conduct, today Full screw," he said, as Gregory waited for the Quartermaster to ink stamp his signature on the page.
"I believe so, Sir." Gregory snapped a salute.
"Good for you boy, you hurry along now, you've time to get cleaned up, before cook shuts the mess, you're in for a treat, liver and bacon today."
It was liver and bacon most days accepted when it was just liver.

Stepping from the store's office, Gregory noticed a group of officers who appeared to be watching as Pimm crossed the compound and disappeared in the direction of the GHQ. Gregory thought it was probably the last he would see of Pimm and after showering, lined up in the canteen for some scrum.
Two of the officer's he had seen outside, who had spent the day fretting on how their social plans that morning had been disrupted by Major Pimm, noticed him sitting at one of the long tables amongst a group of his regular squad and waited for him to visit the latrines. Outside the camp, lights were already attracting a harvest of bugs for the bats that flashed in and out from the dark.

"Look who it is Win, your old mucker" Peter Waldren flicked his cigarette butt across Gregory, setting it in his path and stepped away from leaning against the back of the latrine block wall.
"What's the matter me old mucker we're not good enough now you have found a new pal," he said, rubbing his foot in the dirt stamping out the butt.
Gregory went to salute, but his arm was caught from behind, by Winston Curtiss,
"Understand you took a yomp over to Kyrenia today with this new bod from signals or is he a nut collector?" Curtiss pressed in close to the side of Gregory and grabbed his wrist halting him in his tracks, Gregory's initial reaction was defence and to let loose with a swing, then he dropped his fist, seeing the officer's pips. There was no strength in the officer's hold, not enough to stop Gregory resisting if he wanted, but he chose not to and stepped back allowing the unorthodox confrontation, from Waldren and Curtiss who had been waiting either side of the toilet block entrance for the Corporal to emerge.
Gregory looked at the two officers now barring his way back to the Naffi, as Winston read his quizzical expression.
"So it wasn't Karaman, so where did you end up full screw, come on fess up? You were my Batman first, loyalty is a must in this man's army, without it you could find yourself, spending more time than you wish in there" he gestured back inside the toilet "cleaning the freshly decorated pans."

Gregory understood the threat, as Curtiss placed his hand on his shoulder firmly halting him.

"Come on lad what's the Gen, is he intelligence, looking into that balls up with Alfonso." Waldren barked as if giving an order.

As Gregory shook his head, he caught in his peripheral vision over the officer's heads and across the small courtyard a light as a cigarette flared once, then a dark figure emerged into the lights of the camp, and as the individual raised his head he smiled and winked at Gregory, unobserved by Curtiss and Waldren, it was Pimm.

"Get along now Corporal, there's a couple of cold Efes bottles with your name on them, waiting behind the bar. A thank you for your assistance today and not running away at the mouth, as so many do on long journeys," Pimm said as he sauntered over to the two Captains, who immediately stepped away from Gregory. "Tediously," Pimm said as he squared up to Warren and Curtiss.

"Thank you, sir," Gregory saluted the officers collectively and took one pace forward then was halted.

"Where are you off to Bob?" Pimm's tone held menace, and for a second Gregory thought he was being played as a pawn in some sort of joke by the three officers, equally Curtiss, and Waldren misread Pimm's intentions and relaxed.

"Unless I'm mistaken which simply doesn't fucking happen, gentlemen. I believe it is customary for senior officers to return the salute of a junior regardless of rank in the Queen's army." Pimm's stance had the presence of a Prop forward about to engage, as the two captains looked at each other then stood at attention and saluted Gregory, as did Pimm, then as he went past Pimm tapped him on the wrist, "How are your sea legs, Bob?" Pimm kept his eyes on Curtiss and Waldren.

"My father was a Purser, on a hospital ship." Gregory held back the feeling of importance Pimm had bestowed him and the truth about his late father.

"Good, before you turn in, let your CO. know, I'll be borrowing you for a week or so. Any problems tell them to see Brigadier Baker's Secretary, get along now, while I have a quiet word with these officers." Pimm stepped to the side allowing him to continue towards the Naffi, then swivelled back on the officers, who looked at each other, each wishing they were somewhere else at that moment.

"So gentlemen, no, please don't speak." Pimm smiled as Winston began to bluster an apology of sorts.

"As you just heard, my duties require that I remain in Dhekelia for a little while longer. I would appreciate it if our paths did not cross again." Pimm stared at the speechless pair, for a fraction of a moment Peter Waldren looked as if he might challenge Pimm, but Curtiss gave a short shake of his head gesturing no.

"Good, I'm glad we have an understanding, now unless you two bum bandits plan to do something unpleasant in there, I'd rather like to conduct my business in peace."

Curtiss and Waldren stepped away from the toilet block entrance both slain by the assault on their characters as Pimm walked forward without saying a word, they saluted his passing, but this time Pimm did not respond until standing in the backlight doorway, and he addressed Curtiss. "And gentlemen I would count yourself lucky if the young Corporal had chosen to divulge any information regarding my activities today the two of you would be on a "Fat Albert" halfway to the Falklands by morning, Consul General's son or not." Pimm waited for a response, but Winston Curtiss's mouth stayed momentarily open, not just because Pimm had threatened to dispatch them both by Hercules transport plane to the other side of the planet, but because he apparently had access to their personal files and knew his father was Sir Stephen Curtiss, Her Majesty's Consulate General in Barcelona, Spain.

"Buenas Noches Caballeros, dormir bien." (*Goodnight gentlemen, sleep tight),* Pimm said, with no hint of English accent and disappeared inside, whistling *"Viva Espania."*

Waldren and Curtiss chose wisely to spend the next two weeks in Akrotiri, the Greek side of the British base, but Curtiss made sure he had settled the drinks tab he had placed in the officer's mess, cheekily under the name and number of Major Pimm, before they departed Dhekelia.

Although there was not yet a formal hard border, security controls were already in place to prevent Greeks from crossing into the Turkish side of the Dhekelia base and vice versa as gradually they emerged as two separate entities, with additional civilian support personnel divided by race and service utilities, including even the lighting. Observed to this day, when approaching the island from an aircraft as on the Greek side the street lighting is predominately yellow, and on the Turkish, it is predominately orange.

Two nights following Pimm's dispatching of Curtiss and Waldren, at periscope depth just over five thousand yards from the shore, to the north of the Karpass Peninsula, HMS Rorqual stood at rest.

"Range established, fire number one." the XO on board the submarine ordered, as he caught Pimm's last flash and the klaxon horn began to sound,

"Firing number one," the torpedo gunner retorted having turned the final launch key and lifted the metal red protective hinge case then pressed hard on the black launch button. Deep in the bowels, there was the sound as if an underground train had just arrived at a station, then silence, except the sonar ping tracking the torpedoes progress towards Pimm.

Albert "Bull" Gordon, Mi6's outgoing Hong Kong section chief, received a quick wink from the XO, "Your fillies away Sir, running straight." he said then turned back to the eyepiece.

"Good let's hope there are no hurdles," Bull said as he watched as the submarine Captain scanned the silhouette of the northern Cyprus beachhead against the backdrop of the southern stars.

Bull with his sleeves rolled up and heavy gold watch-chain tucked inside his forest green, navy blue, white, tartan waistcoat looked as out of place, beside the white-clad naval officers, as a priest might amongst prostitutes, he flipped open his

Waltham full hunter and watched the second-hand spin and whispered the words of the engraving on the inside of the case lid *"Nemo me impune lacessit" (No one provokes me with impunity),* the Latin motto of the Black Watch Royal Regiment of Scotland of which there had been three generations from Bull's own family that had served.

Kneeling at the edge of the brush before the dunes fell toward the horseshoe beach, code-named Stable, blacked out in camouflage, Corporal Gregory held his breath as he caught the first trace of the narrow, streamlined surface wake, "There she is Sir." he whispered pointing to the incoming missile, his heart now as fast as the radar pulse on board the submarine tracking system.
"You beauty Bob knew there was a reason I brought you along, well-done lad." Pimm picked up the fine wake, just as the torpedo began to power down, some seventy feet out, he signalled his eyes indicating left and right, and Gregory used his binoculars to scan back and forth along the beachhead, as a hard thud in the sand at the water's edge could be heard, and a mound appeared in the surf that glistened in the starlight like some beached whale. Pimm immediately held up his signal light "Seahorse tied BPP out."
"Come on Bob" he said, and both men grabbed either side of a black rigger dragging it down across the sand into the water beside the torpedo.
Using a Currey Lockspike Bosun penknife, Pimm immediately began to loosen the housing cover of the torpedo, which hinged over, as Gregory waded while holding the rigger tight in the surf.
Pulling back a protective polythene cover, Pimm pull out the first AKS assault rifle, an AKA 47 version, equipped with an under folding metal shoulder stock, perfect for hiding and as lethal as a standard Kalashnikov. Passing it to Gregory, he saw the Corporal recognized that this was an enemy's weapon of choice, but he said nothing, as Pimm unloaded twenty-five from the inside of the hollowed-out torpedo. Each was already sealed in its own heavy-duty polythene waterproof bag and had an eyelet clasp that clipped onto the inflatable riggers side hand ropes. Having unloaded the contents of the torpedo that included two boxes of 7.62×39mm ammunition 30 round cartridges, loaded, Pimm resealed the torpedo and turning an external valve key, a loud hiss of air bubbled to the surface of the water, like an egg boiling, as the torpedo was made buoyant by an internal gas canister and floated free, while Pimm and Gregory began to row away with the rifles hanging down in the water. A few feet from the torpedo bobbing just below the surface, Pimm lay low across the bow and signalled with his signal torch, "Seahorse free. BPP out."

On board HMS Rorqual, the submarine Captain immediately ordered, "Pull it in!" as he caught Pimm's Morse code flashes in the periscope.
"Start torpedo retrieval!" number one announced, and deep in the nose cone of the submarine, a motor began to turn, recoiling the cable attached to the torpedo.
Pimm and Gregory saw the twang of cable in the water as it took up the strain and took a final look at the torpedo, as it disappeared the way it came. They then rowed

out towards the light of the nearest shipping warning buoy. Where they secured a leash to the buoy and laced each of the rifles onto a single cable, with the ammunition in a watertight bag acting as the anchor.

Pimm gave a last look out across the dark waves, towards the distant lights of Turkey as they made their way back to shore, swimming the last few meters, having sunk the rigger.

There was a securing clunk as the outer torpedo cover closed onboard HMS Rorqual. "Seahorse retrieved Sir." came the announcement from the XO as he folded the periscope arms up and ordered the crew to prepare to dive.

"Well done number one, Captain", Bull Gordon saluted both men. "After that little excitement, I hope you will excuse me while I get some Z's before our rendezvous with the Greek gentlemen." Bull saluted again and went to retire to his quarters as a midshipman handed the XO some lemons.

"Fresh this morning" the Captain smiled at Bull, knowing his fondness for gin.

"Well, I suppose I could manage a quick nightcap, gentleman, if you twist my arm." Bull said with a wry smile.

Oliver Pimm and Bob Gregory slipped back into Dhekelia, with no record of their departure or return recorded at the security gatehouse. The bar at the officer's mess was already closed, but Pimm walked up to the double doors and gestured towards the furthest rattan seats on the timber decking of the main porch, strictly reserved for officers.

"Park your arse Gregory I'll be two ticks," Pimm said, with a click of his trusty penknife the door lock to the officer's mess was open.

"I'll be buggered" Gregory whispered to himself, setting himself low in the furthest seat, close enough to the side rail to dive into the bushes if someone came by. Pimm emerged with four cold bottles of Carlsberg, stuck one in his teeth while clawing three in his fingers and with a click of the same pen knife in his hand the mess was sealed once again

"Don't fret Bob, I left the money on the side, no harm done," he said, placing two bottles before the Corporal.

"Can I ask Sir? You already knew my father was in the merchant and onboard the Amsterdam, didn't you?" Gregory looked across at Pimm as they sat alone on the decking drinking their second bottle of larger.

"That sounds less a question and more of a statement Bob, but yes I knew who your father was, the question is did you. Not everybody who was killed on the hospital ship in 44 when it was sunk was just a merchant" Pimm raised his glass as if in reverence to a fallen colleague.

"Here's to your dad, I never met him, but I have read some of his reports" Pimm spoke thoughtfully, as Gregory met his toast tilting his bottle, but not entirely sure of the significance of the Major statement.

"Do you know what a Lewis is Gregory?" Pimm felt, although he had only known the young Corporal for a short time, he was somewhat taken by him. Gregory was strong, keen, clearly knew how to look before leaping and more important when not to and besides he said little, but more importantly for what Pimm had in mind was that he was an orphan, like himself.

"You mean a Lewis gun, yes Sir, I saw one in basic." Gregory innocently chirped.

"No not that kind of Lewis Corporal, you see there are some establishments, the Mason's, the police force for example, where it is common to call the son of an existing or dead member a Lewis if they are to join the same establishment."

Gregory nodded his head as if he knew, taking one of Pimm's senior service cigarettes when offered

"I see Sir, so my father, you believe he was a Freemason?" he said, accepting a light from Pimm's American Zippo. It was then that he saw close up in high definition against the shadows created in the flame light the deep scarring he had noticed initially on both of Pimm's forearms when they had been carrying out the survey on the Karpass peninsula on their first day together.

"God boy you're going to have to step up your game if you wish to walk in your father's shoes" Pimm blustered the smoke from his mouth as he laughed, but questioned his original judgement of Gregory.

"Sorry Sir must be the beer I'm not normally slow" Gregory scratched his head theatrically, "It's just if I am right with what you are saying, it's probably not something I should admit knowing about, even in such good company, with respect Sir."

Pimm looked over at Gregory and gestured his agreement with a nod, understanding the young man was playing the game and realised he had chosen well, another recruit for the service. When he next met with Bull Gordon, he would have to inform him he would be returning to Mi6 with a new *"Lost boy"*. That was as long as the contents of "Seahorse" found its "rider" and the next phase of his assignment went without a hitch.

Pimm felt his Braille watch in the dark, checking the time.

"You have a way to go Bob, but clearly modesty is something you already have a handle on, good for you, let's hope you stay that way. Personally, I can't abide by an ego, even when it is deserved, and it never is." Pimm downed his drink, then threw each empty bottle into the brush, following his lead Gregory did the same, removing the evidence of their crime before they parted for the night.

The following morning a squad of men, some of whom Gregory had been attached to on previous exercise's, stood at attention in the morning sun, beside a column of jeeps. While inside the air-conditioned conference room of the Dhekelia base headquarters, Oliver Pimm introduced Corporal Bob Gregory for the first time to a pink-eyed, Bull Gordon, as they waited for their Greek VIP visitors to arrive.

There was a tap on the door, and two medal festooned Greek naval officers entered the room.

"Gentleman let me introduce Major Oliver Pimm, Admiralty Press Corp and our Foreign aid relations officer for the region. He will act as your liaison officer and security today, unfortunately I must meet with the camp commander and prepare for my return to Blighty," The Greeks' looked at each other not understanding the slang, "I am sure the Major will be able to offer you sufficient proof that we are endeavouring to live up to the agreed terms regarding the security of the exclusion zone of the islands waters. Your tour today will take in one of our MARSO flights *(Maritime aerial reconnaissance special operations)*, as you are aware we have daily sorties carry out a 360 in an anticlockwise rotation of the island, they update and offer support to the four frigates we have patrolling the waters along with the minesweeper HMS Burmaston you will be on board today." Bull introduced Pimm who was now dressed in his ceremonial marine whites and then handed the two Greek officers back to the Adjutant that had come up from Akrotiri.

"If you will follow the Adjutant, I have prepared some light refreshments before your departure." Bull gestured the door.

With the Greek's out of the room Bull, sporting his usual, Black watch waste coat and grey flannel suit, took a closer look over at Gregory, standing to attention in the corner of the room. He then turned back to the seated Pimm who was smoking, resting his arms on the table. Bull leaned forward so that his nose was less than two feet parallel to Pimm's ear.

"I know I say never go back BP, but kind of reminds me of back in the day, It was just as warm then and before you ask no it's not the same bloody waistcoat. I had a tailor on Wellington Street knock me out a dozen while in the territories, the shop was the meet I chose for your section leader, two back doors, gifted him one as a thank you for your release on my OPO Sometimes they can be influenced by the least familiar things, eh?" Bull shrugged and returned to examining Gregory, who continued to look straight ahead.

Pimm pointed with his finger "Seemed to remember the last one you wore had a gravy stain."

Bull dropped his eyes "Nice one" he realised his mistake in looking, "well moving on, my gratitude to your chief in Hanoi letting you loose for this, but must tell you. The yanks took some convincing letting you go I understand, good to hear you are getting along."

"Well, I'm here, as much for you as myself, close a chapter as it were and it's getting a little like a permanent frat party for the *G.I.'s, they are bringing in* Budweiser and coca-cola by the tanker load now, you know what that means. It's surreal until you hit the jungle." Pimm shrugged.

"Well a change is as good as a rest," Bull said, leaning back and loud enough that Gregory could hear, "So BP, all set for a good show, I know I don't need to mention, watch your range the wind whips around that side of the island, I would hate to explain why Mi6 went to all this expense to create matchsticks from the Diniz," Bull smirked.

Pimm was relaxed in his manner as he picked up his lighter and cigarette and placed them in his inside pocket, "I chose the gunner myself today, the schedule called for another. Unfortunately, he came down with the trots, as for my eye Sir it's

as keen today as when I saved your bacon in Kampala if we are not mentioning things." Pimm stood adjusting his jacket, preparing to leave.
Bull smiled reminded it was true, concerning the second occasion Pimm had saved his life with a sniper shot when covering his back in an arms exchange with a certain Ugandan General who decided he would rather not pay for the privilege of some shiny new Lee Enfield 303's.
"So this is the Lewis you want me to take back to Stirling Lines, Jock Gregory's son, well I never, a chance meet or did you know he was here when you agreed to come, I wonder." Bull went over and looked Gregory up and down,
"Your father was six-two, I remember looking down on him," he said looking up at the Corporal as Pimm watched with a wry smile, remembering Bull's first words to him before his enlistment into the security services.
Gregory stamped a salute "Yes sir, six-four."
"So you want to join the Special Air Service." Bull saw a look in Gregory's eyes of confusion.
"Bad penny didn't tell you, you're on the hop lad and you have a long way to go, my son before you can fill your father's boots working for six." Bull turned back to Pimm and winked.
"Well get this under your belt, if BPP doesn't drop you overboard, there's a jump seat on a Doris *(Hercules)* back to Blighty leaving in three days, yours if you want it." Bull stuck out his hand, and Gregory shook it, impressed how powerful the grip of a man three times his age was, and then was really surprised he was unable to control the grip, and it actually began to hurt, but he remained calm and looked ahead as the heat rose to his face.
"Don't maul the boy Bull, he's got work to do later, I won't thank you if he can't pull the trigger when need be." Pimm could see the strain on Gregory's face as he held off his hand being squashed, finally Bull released.
"That is as long as this is not what the American's call a cluster fuck, I hate them, well not all of them, but you must admit they have some truly fitting acronyms for balls Up's and if this is, neither of you needs to pack your bags." Bull winked at Bob, who continued to remain stone-faced as he watched Bull walk back over to Pimm and whisper at his ear, "Over the top or JEC" *(Just enough Clout)*
"Just enough" Pimm replied, "Now fuck of Bull before you get all emotional in front of the new recruit." Pimm then whispered
"Oh well if you are going to be like that, I will see you for debriefing, once you have settled your man in, Sardinia correct, very nice too. I visited one of the small islands once, Caprera, just after the war, to see the home of the real Godfather, Garibaldi." Through the candour Bull searched Pimm's face, knowing his mind must be thinking of the contact he would soon reunite with, an old acquaintance that was bound to remind him of darker times.

"Seriously I know there is history with your old Turkish friend, but if he turns out to be a dog without a bone, you let him rot with the others on the boat I insist. I had to promise Uncle Sam a double bonus for thanksgiving getting hold of those Russian

guns and the providence going back to an NKVD *(Soviet People's Commissariat for Internal Affairs)* General in Minsk, might come in handy one day."
Pimm saluted, "Yes Bull, I just want the list, just the list, if we get some mileage with the Greeks you want me to waltz through this panto today, then as far as I can see its win, win. If not, as you say the Turk can rot, it's not as if he has kept in touch." Pimm's tone was malevolent. But then his mood changed as he looked to his side and gestured towards Bob "as for this one, if it's a cock-up today, you'll take him anyway, no stains on his shirt sleeves, this is on me."
"Agreed, we always need a gopher, the taller the better, helps with new strip lights, when the starters go drives me mad, all the chairs are swivel at Century house these days, I'm getting too old to stand on desks and the girls just think I'm a dirty old man if I ask one of them to do it." Bull smiled.
"Bull, you are a dirty old man." Pimm watched Bull take a step to the door, and they saluted each other and Gregory stamped his feet at attention.

"Just a thought Bull, our man, are you Bobby Moore *(sure)*, it's him, the same Turk from Jerusalem, you've considered this could be a fishing expedition by the *Reds* or even Mossad getting their own back, it's some time since I last upset their plans, but they have a long memory, I still stay clear of Golders Green when back home. Why the fuck would he ask for me after all this time? He must know I know the truth." Pimm's mind tried to remember the last time he saw his intended target.

"Well he did, but maybe what you should be asking is, how we missed this one the first time around with Paper-clip. You were not much more than a Pongo, like this boy then, but you were twice as smart. Even with the shit, you went through. You were better than that, what's more so was I, so just remember your Turk pulled the wool over a lot of eyes back then, hiding in plain sight, and watch your back. I don't want to have to write a Dear June to your good lady. She'd never invite me round for Sunday lunch again, seriously." Bull stepped back in towards Pimm and held out his hand as a friend not a superior, but before Pimm took it there was a rattle on the door, the Greeks officers were already on the second bottle of ouzo, and the adjutant was concerned the operation would be over before it had begun with the Greeks to blind drunk to witness what they had been brought there for.
"Ok Bull no need to remind me, once this pantomimes over and before I go back in country you must come over, her idea, sounded like she wanted your advice, you know she's always been jealous of the strawberries and cream in your front garden, I'll pencil a Sunday lunch when I finish in Italy, that's if you can spare the time," Pimm said as they made their way out.
"My dear BP for you and your good lady I always have time, it's a date Pimm, I'll bring the Taylor's and Stilton."

Bull then turned and stared straight at Gregory who had heard most of what they had discussed, "Remember this and take it with you today, I'm not worried about this old fruit, it's you I feel sorry for son, BP here has a habit of dodging his bullet, behind fresh field hands like yourself, make sure you're not one. Then with luck, I can look forward to seeing you at your passing out in Hereford if you make the grade. On that note, good luck boys, make Bizzy Lizzy proud." Bull said, referring to Queen Elizabeth, and with that, he saluted the pair.

An hour later, as Pimm stood on deck, he could still smell the ouzo on the Greek officers' breath hovering at his shoulder. Dropping his binoculars, surreptitiously, Pimm checked his Omega brail watch and turned to Corporal Gregory, who caught his glance, he tapped his watch.

Within seconds there was the mighty roar of the low flying Shackleton reconnaissance plane on its second sortie of the day around the Island, as if God himself had just belched in the heavens above and It came up behind them with such thunder, both Greek officer's grab their caps and ducked, neither Pimm or Gregory flinched. Pimm noticed that about the Corporal, as on his cue the three gunner crew members of the forward Bofor 40/60 gun took up their stations and the forward gun lowered. Then a midshipman quickly approached Pimm from behind and handed him a deciphered radio traffic slip. The Captain had received from the Shackleton.

"The Captain asked me to pass this along Sir, a message from Playmate 4." Pimm made a play of reading the transmission and looked back across the ship's wake, towards the peninsula. Seeing the Greeks interested, he handed the communication over.

"Apparently, Playmate 4, sorry, our spotter aircraft has just buzzed a small craft coming out of Turkish waters. Could be nothing, but it appears to be heading for Kyrenia, they are not returning their squawk. As I said, it could be nothing. But bearing in mind you gentlemen are on a sightseer's the Captain has requested I ask would you mind terribly if he turned back and took a look-see?"

Pimm was a consummate actor and fawned disinterest, with a tone of apathy that would have been more at home coming from the lips of Winston Curtiss or Peter Waldren, as the midshipman waited at his side for a reply.

The two Greeks read the radio paper chit, too far away for Pimm to hear, he read their lips as they spoke to each other in Greek understanding every word.

"We have nothing out today, do we?" one asked the other obviously concerned it may be one of their own Greek arms-smuggling vessels. Pimm watched the other, shakes his head, "No."

Pimm decided to prod them along in their decision and turned midshipman.

"Let's not upset these gentlemen with some awful excitement, tell the captain to have some of our boys watch the coast, see where it comes in they'll probably get there in time if they hurry, I'm sure these gentlemen would rather get back for a spot of tuck." Pimm looked straight face at Gregory and was glad to see he stayed resolute in character as the senior Greek officer spoke up even though he needed the Greeks to act quickly, and they did, having taken his bait, hook, line and sinker.

"No!" one of the Greek officers countermanded Pimm's orders, "this would seem a perfect opportunity to see how your exclusion enforcement works. Have the Captain intercept the craft. Please inform him it would be interesting to observe, we insist." The Greek's tone was tinged with authority.
"Really? As I said, it's probably just a fishing boat on its way back." Pimm turned away and waved the midshipman away.
"Yes immediately Major if you would." the Greeks tone was now officious, but Pimm continued to play somewhat reluctant,
"Well if you insist" Pimm continued to look at the midshipman who appeared perplexed from who to take his orders from and smiled.
"Well man, what are you waiting for, you heard the General double time, tell the Captain turn around, immediately and intercept the craft!" Pimm barked, precisely like the types of officers he despised.

"Why don't we retire to the Captains wardroom until this scuffle is over unless you wish to pop up to the operation room, I mean bridge, might even get some fireworks if this fellow can't speak the Queen's, what?" he saw a scowl from the two officers then as they realised what he had said their eyes lit up
"Yes, bridge, good," they both said,
"Ok, Gregory you stay down here lad, keep an eye out, any trouble bounce on that Browning will you, if they try and start something" Pimm then directed the two Greeks up into the forward external observation platform to the right of the bridge. Inside the Captain stood with his number one as the whooping of the *Action stations* klaxon horn began, and the ship started a sharp turn seaward back towards the Karpass Peninsular and the location of the vessel reported by the Shackleton spotter plane.

Pimm held onto a wall bar as he stood forward on the bridge beside the Number one, First Lieutenant Stanton, nearest to the range gunner operating the forward deck guns, Kerrison predictor, dialling in estimates for speed and the range of the target motor vessel they were now tracking.
"There she is looks like they have seen us, Sir." First Lieutenant Stanton looked to the Captain standing before the binnacle, who flipped the brass voice pipe and sent a message to the main wheelhouse.
The ship almost immediately veered to the right at an interception course that would cut across the bow, and as they closed on the vessel he gave Stanton an order, and he pushed the throttle on the Chadburn *(Engine order telegraph or E.O.T.)* The bridge bells rang twice signalling to the engine room the ships speed had increased.
Now in clear vision of open water, the target appeared to make an evasive manoeuvre with a tight spin back the way it had come towards Turkish waters, if it reached them, the Burmaston would not have the jurisdiction to intercept, and it would be illegal for them to board.

Pimm could see the gunners beginning to direct the forward Bofor gun ready to fire as they received information from the bridge gunner whispering into a hand microphone beside him and as he continued to spin the dials on the range finder, the motorboat powered back in a northerly direction, aware it was being pursued.

"He is getting away Captain" one of the two Greek officers standing on the outer parapet began to shout with an excited exasperation as the drama unfolded, as planned by Pimm before their eyes.

"Unfortunately gentlemen it would appear they are reluctant to stop. Major Pimm in a moment I will need your decision and have to fire a warning shot or they will be shortly back in Turkish waters." The Captain looked to Pimm for guidance as if to say *is this fish worth the effort.*

Captain Mandelson had a set order of instruction for the days exercise regarding the Greek officers. In black and white it stated he was to offer Pimm the free run of the ship and if at any time they were to engage an enemy vessel or suspected vessel carrying contraband, he was to relinquish command if it was requested, to Major Pimm. The latter was a non-standard executive order stamped and signed by both the Admiralty and Cyprus command Chief of Staff.

Mandelson knew nothing of the specific details of operation "Seahorse" but was an old enough hand to recognise Pimm for what he was not, a marine Major on a public relations exercise.

"Still no response sir!" The seated signalman at the rear of the bridge announced as he repeatedly tapped out in Morse, "What ship? Where bound? Halt!"

"Sir! I have new contact off the port, north-east, bearing 20, range 1 mile, closing 60knots, looks like a Turkish frigate" the announcement by the sonar engineer behind Pimm was charged with electricity.

Mandelson looked to Pimm then checking the image of the vessel in his binoculars coolly thanked his man for the information and ordered full ahead. Pimm stepped to the side and span his binoculars to view through the side window along with First Lieutenant Stanton. Both could now see the funnel smoke of the fast-approaching Turkish naval vessel.

"Let's drop her down, give our guns a steady platform," the Captain said as he ordered the engine room to now drop their speed, preparing to fire.

"Well, Mr Pimm?" The Captain stood firm.

This could quickly turn into another MOAFU (Mother of all fuck-ups) Pimm thought and looked back to the man at the Kerrison predictor and watched the sight gunner's hands spin the elevation range finder, Pimm's concern for the man's proficiency got the better of him, he was risking too much letting another man call the aim on this target.

"Well Captain Mandelson, let's see if we can't change their minds, would you mind if I do the honours, it's been some time," with that Pimm flipped his cap backwards and stepped up to the targeting system, the gunner looked to his Captain and Mandelson remembered his orders nodded his agreement, and the gunner relinquished his headset.

"It would appear this is your show Mr Pimm, be my guest." the Captain said now entirely sure that he and his crew had been involved in a military intelligence exercise, even if the Greek observers were none the wiser.

Pimm gestured his appreciation and glued his eyes to the stereo sighting binoculars fixing the motor launch in his sights the dials clicked as they span back and forth with his thumbs,

"Target red, range 175 elevation 40, Pimm paused, fire!" His eyes lifted back to the target, and he had ended the word, the single barrel blast rocketed the vibration into the balls of his feet as an L/70 shell burst from the forward gun with a howl. In the distance, there was a massive explosion, and the motorboat disappeared into the up draught of water as it continued at pace.

The Greek officers thought Pimm had misjudged and had caught the vessel squarely, destroying it by mistake, but there was no additional explosion.

Then as the spray and mist dissipated from the air as if a phantom waterfall had just deposited a hundred gallons into the sea, the motor launch appeared from the deluge unharmed, almost at a stop and clearly heaving to starboard to be boarded.

"Well, done Major!" the First Lieutenant pushed the front of his cap up from his fringe and thrust his hand out to shake Pimm's hand.

"Lucky shot, I guess, I was always a dab hand at the arrows," Pimm said as he caught a knowing look from Mandelson. "Remind me never to play darts with you fellows" Stanton chirped

"Yesss!" Captain Mandelson muttered under his breath to himself, and from that point on, he watched Pimm ever closer.

"Sir the Turkish target has come about, returning towards the mainland." the sonar engineer confirmed, having witnessed the motorboat being halted it was no longer in a position to question or prevent any boarding of the vessel that appeared to have originated in Turkey.

"This is Her Majesty's Ship, the Burmaston, you are in violation of the exclusion waters of Cyprus, prepare to be boarded." the Captain announced twice in English, then Stanton repeated it again in Greek and Turkish.

As it came into view, below on the deck of the motor launch, four tanned men appeared to surface from different areas of the vessel, it was clear one had attempted to scuttle the boat, having an axe in hand, and it began to list away from the minesweeper. Grappling hooks were immediately thrown across by the crew of the Burmaston to prevent the vessel sinking, and as one hook was pushed away by a crew member, there was a shout from one of the Burmaston Coxswain's "Gun!"

The call to arms was met with some hesitancy by the Burmaston crew, who were not used to handling small weapons, in close proximity, but Corporal Gregory instinctively let his Sten slip to his side and dropped onto the deck mounting the Browning machine gun and let off a burst ten feet or so below the waterline of the vessel and those that had weapons dropped them to the deck and joined the others with their arms held high, signalling their surrender.

"Another lucky shooter." this time Mandelson looked sternly at Pimm as if to say *now you're taking the piss?* But more to reinforce his rank with Stanton and the regular crew on his bridge.

Pimm did not want to appear as if taking advantage of the accommodating Captain, but looking to the two Greek officers as they resurfaced from taking shelter below the platform barrier on the observation parapet, where they had been standing exposed. Pimm considered his job was not over, and things still could still go wrong, time to relax would be when they were back in port at Famagusta after he had what he came for.
He gave the Captain a casual salute of understanding as if to apologise and looked at the crew, "What that lad? They only assigned me him a few days ago, keen as mustard, little excitable, no harm done, apologies if he overstepped the mark Captain, not my intention, but probably just as well, there would have been a right ding dong if one of these bubbles got caught with a stray. That said if Bob and I clear the field as it were. Just in case the bloody things mined, then I would assume you would have no objection to the two officers taking a look at their trophy. They are after all on board as VIP Greek observers, whatever may be discovered will be unquestioned as over and above board when it's received by their superior in the Greek Government. Of course, I will insist they mention the courtesy they received on board the Burmaston to their people." Pimm held his hand out to the Captain in full view of his men, and his smile held a genuine sign of appreciation as one professional to another, and the Captain understood that.
"Apology accepted Major," The Captain stood back and saluted.

Mandelson would typically have been a little resistant, having his nose pushed out of joint. But he recognised Pimm's agenda for this exercise regarding their Greek guest was clearly above his pay grade and considered whoever this so-called press officer was, he obviously, *knew his apples* and had an orderly manner with no smugness. Mandelson liked Pimm but still counted his fingers when he released his grip and checking his wedding ring.
"Carry on Major Pimm, you landed the catch, it is only right you have the first bite, I will have the brig prepared for our new guest unless you have any further requests?" Mandelson saluted back.
"Captain, if it would not be too much trouble, I would appreciate a secure side room to have a chat with one or two of these fellows. No rough stuff I assure you, makes my life easier if I have the complete story for my CO. Helps shine my buttons, I will, of course, also mention in my dispatch the Sterling work of your crew today, who deserve a few 'sundowners' after this, my round at bar when we hit shore." He gave a broad smile and considered it an opportune moment mentioning to the Captain, he was aware that the Admiralty had a new class Type 14 Blackwood class, frigate and they were looking for a cool head to Captain it and go Soviet sub-hunting around the Norwegian Fjords, but Pimm judged the Captain would consider that

inappropriate. Still, he decided he would add the recommendation to Bull Gordon, in his Mi6 report.

With the Diniz motor vessel pulled up and supported by the grappling lines, Pimm watched as ropes were thrown to the Turkish sailors and they now cooperated as it was pulled and tied up tight alongside the minesweeper as he stepped to remove himself from the bridge, First Lieutenant Stanton turned to his Captain possibly believing he had been slighted by Pimm
"But Sir that would require the correct SBSW orders from the Major?" Stanton squawked.
The Captain held his hand up to halt his juniors advance, as Pimm reached inside his tunic and pulled out the correct warrant for interrogation of suspected terrorists under the British official secrets act and handed it over to Stanton
"I'm sure you will find this is in order, number one, quite right though, cross the T's dot the I's," Pimm said with not a hint of sarcasm as Stanton read the ordered then passed the warrant to The Captain
"It would appear, Captain, Major came prepared, even though it could still be an innocent vessel This Diniz" the name of the ship was already listed on the warrant.
"I would expect nothing less of one of the Queen's finest," The Captain said looking at the ships name stencilled in black on the side of the small wheelhouse.
"Well as I am sure your Captain has told your number one the 7 P's are not just reserved for land lovers." Pimm took back the warrant then unclipped the cover on his sidearm and went down the stairs to the deck to join Gregory and the boarding party. He paused as he saw the first glimpse of the bowed head of a man he had not seen for over thirteen years skulking at the back of the line of four men with their arms raised.
The side barrier was slid to one side, and a short roped gangplank dropped, and the crew of the Diniz were forced, single file off their vessel at gunpoint.
"That's it move along, line up, hands up! That's It" Pimm ordered, "Any of you speak English?"

As each man was mauled roughly during their search, Gregory stood high on a stow-box watching like a hawk, Sten gun panning back and forth at the ready. While the Greek officers began to converse angrily with the surly Turks as they passed by and forcibly raised their bowed heads examining their features, one even spat at the men, who looked less like fishermen and more like soldiers, with shaved heads and a broad lean structure to their frame, all except an older man at the end, last off, Pimm's contact.
The Turks were clearly unhappy to see the Greeks on board, and some began to beg, claiming they were innocent and in Turkish waters while one, possibly the senior officer, barked back at the Greeks and his crew members to stay silent.
Pimm allowed the Greek officer's freedom to move amongst their captives, happy that they would be able to confirm this was a genuine Turkish crew, which would later prove to be members of the TMT while repeating the request for an English

speaker. Finally, the older man raised his hand slowly as he began to take abuse from the Greeks "Yes, Sir me a little Sir, we are just fisherman from Tasucu!"

"Who said that?" Pimm asked, and Gregory stood above the man pointing with his hand and finger over his head,
"So you speak English, good show, tell your friends to sit, to start with." as they did each was handcuffed, and Pimm took handcuffs from Gregory and placed them on his contact, pulling the man back, towards the gangplank, he gestured over to the Diniz.
"Your boat, not a traditional kaikis design is it, where were you heading?" Pimm asked, then growled at his crewmates as they began to push and shove each other, resisting their detainment and addressing Pimm's contact to hold his tongue, shouting and jeering at the Greeks.
"Enough! Take that lot below to the brig, search them again, keep them handcuffed but give them some water." Pimm ordered, and as he spoke, some of the others began to lash out at the man that was his contact, kicking his shins with bare feet, threatening him not to talk to Pimm.
"Don't tell the English pig" Pimm understood every curse in Turkish? "I told you we should have sunk her" another muttered, under his breath.
"Enough of that, get them away," Pimm said, and turned to the older man, continuing into his second act of the play they were performing for the Greek officers, "Look, there's no point fussing, we are going to board your vessel understand? You have guns we have seen them. You were caught red-handed in the prohibited waters of Cyprus, British waters, these gentlemen are here at the request of the British Government. It would be unfortunate and carry international consequences if something should happen to them when boarding your vessel, so I ask you, are there any bombs on board, any booby traps?" Pimm then made the sound of an explosion and waved his hand while still holding his revolver.
The man looked to his colleagues then shook his head.
Pimm asked again, "So to be clear, no bombs" his contact acted dumb and begged, "Yes sir, no bombs, no bombs and no guns, we are fishermen Sir, it is my brother's boat. I assure you, Sir! No bombs"

Pimm's contact was aware of the part he was to play, but unsure of the Greeks officers' involvement and watched nervously as Pimm allowed himself to be moved aside, almost barging past they were clearly unconvinced of his claim. With the two Greeks standing either side, pinning the man to the hand rail, Pimm appeared to look on for a moment, judging the situation as they began to slap the face of his contact, shouting down his protest of innocence as they fired question after question.
"Ok, Ok! That will do gentlemen," Pimm said loudly, halting their attack,
"so no bombs, then you won't mind leading the way" he gestured the boat, looking to the Greeks, "it would probably be safer, for you gentleman if the Corporal and myself go ahead first, to make sure the scoundrels telling the truth."

But before Pimm could finish his words, the first Greek officer had hopped the rail, and his colleague immediately darted in front of Pimm, across the gangplank. Behind Gregory brought up the rear with Pimm's Turkish contract, in handcuffs

"This chaps going to get himself hurt if he's not careful, shall I send some of our men to assist the search, Sir?" Stanton appeared to become incensed at the Greeks disrespect, barging Major Pimm out of the way as he and the Captain stood looking down from the quarter deck platform watching the boarding party. "That cheeky Greek nearly knocked him overboard." Stanton tone rose excitedly.
Pimm was the last to jump down from the Burmaston onto the deck of the Diniz. Unfortunately, his muscle memory training automatically engaged as a surge lifted the boarding plank, and he landed squarely on his feet like a cat pouncing from a fence panel with his sidearm poised ready at his side, Captain Mandelson caught this and smiled contently to his second in command.
"If you think that fellow down there needs help from us number one, you are very much mistaken, if Mr Pimm is just a suited paper tiger marine major working for the Admiralty press corp. I'm a Chinaman. Have the mess send me up a black coffee with a toddy, I'm going to sit back and watch this show, better than the variety performance. But when this charade is over, insist that Major Pimm has his man their guard the weapons he finds, in my quarters and give him my key." the Captain unclipped his own small bunch of keys from his chain belt then handed them to his junior officer.
"Weapons? Those guns look like antiques from world war one, how do you know he will find more?" Stanton leaned forward, watching closely as the Greeks went through the lobster pots and began turfing out the sail boxes, while Pimm kept to one side, then within a short time, a call went up from the aft section.
"Here I have something!" one of the Greeks shouted brandishing the first Aks 47, from a hollow, false section of the back of the wheelhouse, passing out one at a time as a cheer went up amongst the British crew assembled on the deck watching the search.
"Jinkers McQuinnkers how the devil?" Stanton stood with his mouth open.
"Inform the Major there is only the one key to my office," the Captain spoke firmly, as he saw Pimm look back up towards the Bridge and raised his hand, gesturing in a circular motion, indicating the search was over and they should head back to shore. Mandelson raised his coffee mug, gesturing cheers and Pimm acknowledged his compliment, with a tap of a finger to his eye, then pushed the older Turk his contact, towards the side to get back on board the Burmaston.
"Take the one who speaks English to the hold and place him in a separate room away from the others," Pimm ordered.
There was a brief exchange between the celebrating Greeks in which one indicated that he should question the prisoner, "My colleague wished to know if we may be present when you interrogate this man?" the officer asked, passing Pimm one of the machine guns that he and Bob Gregory had retrieved initially from the hollow torpedo two nights earlier.

"These are Russian, aren't they?" Pimm said making a deal of examining the machine gun with a deliberate naivety of its features, "Light, how does this work?"
No one needed to show Pimm how to open a folded stock of a Soviet-made Kalashnikov, his personal best for stripping and reassembly was 36 seconds, but he allowed the Greek to snatch it back from him.
"Yes, Russian, here." the Greek officer's smug confidence boosted Pimm's belief his hook had struck home as he pressed down the release and unfolded the stock. "My superiors will wish to know why the Soviets are now openly supplying our enemies; they will want to speak with these men, find out how they came by these and if more are to come. This trip today could not have worked better for our two countries. I promise you, major, your name will be mentioned." the Greek officer began to stack the boxes of cartridge magazines on the deck.
"You are too kind the credit is yours regarding the decision to stop and search this boat, we would be back at base, this prize really should be yours, it is a shame they were stopped in Cypriot waters; otherwise I could have released them immediately to you."
"These men are the enemy of Greece we need to take them into custody and hand them over to our intelligence department, they will make the scum talk." the officer became agitated at Pimm's reluctance in handing over the prisoners.
"Yes, I'm sure they would, if it was up to me, you could take them. Unfortunately, general, that will not be possible this is Her Majesty's ship, and at this time we have a protocol agreement with both your government and the Turkish that must be observed if the unpleasantness in Cyprus is not too spread to your homelands. These men will be taken back to Famagusta, rest assured they will receive punishment by trial, possibly at that time your government may choose to plea for their extradition. Until then you gentlemen have the satisfaction of having thwarted a possible attack of some sort, my Government appreciates your assistance today as do I and I will ensure that they are aware of your contribution. For now, I believe it best if we get the weapons under lock and key. When I return to base, I will send communications and express your requests, once they have been satisfactorily deactivated and documented for the purpose of the trial, it may be possible for you to present a sample of them to your superiors. In the meantime, Bob take a few snaps of these Greek officers with the Kodak as a souvenir, I'll make sure we have some copies made and sent to you." Pimm said as Stanton approached with the Captain's birth key and Bob Gregory replaced the Sten in his hands with a 32mm Kodak camera Pimm had conveniently placed to one side and began clicking, staged pictures of the Greek Officers with the guns that included Stanton, making sure neither Pimm or his contact were caught in any of the images.
Pimm looked at the Captain's key and understood by offering his own secure berth. The Captain was indicating what happens from this point on until they made port was his responsibility. He threw it to Gregory and ordered him to stay with the weapons once stowed and guard them.
Lieutenant Stanton, Simon, isn't it, I wonder if you would do the honours and take our guest for *"Sundowners"*, I took the liberty of bringing along some refreshments

you' find two bottles of Ouzo and a bottle of retsina, in my cabin, I'm going to have a quick word with this chap here first and then I'll be along." Pimm said and received a salute from Stanton as he led his contact away.

"You found the buoy all right, I see." Pimm handed the old Turk now sitting at a fixed steel desk the keys to his handcuffs and placed a glass bottle of water by his side and flipped the top bottle tab on his own
"I'll get you something stronger shortly," Pimm sat down opposite with his feet on a chair as he heard the engines of the ship race and felt the movement in his buttocks, the Captain now having cut free the sinking Diniz had set a course full ahead for land. Pimm caught his bottle of water before it slid from his side.
"That was close my friend earlier, for a moment I thought you might have missed the boat, and someone else was in control of the gun shooting at us, any closer I would not need to shave." Orran Danis opened the packet of players Pimm flicked across to him, "Thank you." he said, taking out a cigarette then caught the Zippo lighter, Pimm slid across the table having lit his own cigarette.
Oliver Pimm studied the man he had not seen since he was a lowly conscript Corporal in 1946. A man who specifically requested his presence in his tactical extraction and relocation from the region. Bull Gordon had stated the Turk had insisted Pimm was the only one he trusted to verify the data he was now offering British intelligence, in exchange for his and his families relocation to a western safe haven with new identities and financial security.

"So, here I am old friend, at the expense of the Russians, they must have come at a cost, in another time I may have made a few shekels and taken my chances." Danis's voice was waspish aged by heavy smoking and dry heat, but it still had a familiarity that brought an image to the surface of Pimm's mind of the man he had first met, younger, smarter, suited, not as the unshaven scruffy Turkish fisherman, that sat across from him, hands trembling with age, not nerves as he lit his cigarette, but then Pimm knew Danis was playing a part just like him, just like he had back then in 46.
Pimm tilted his head, "Selling them to the Jews no doubt, another double-cross, it would have been your last." Danis hardly raised an eye to the comment and Pimm recognized the man appeared to have lost the will or worry about defending his past transgressions. Pimm had many questions, not least, why Danis had called for him.
"You look good, a few pounds leaner, but it has been a long time." Pimm smiled at his change of subject and nodded expressing his agreement as Danis tapped his stomach showing he also had lost weight, he then took a drink from his bottle and then poured a little of the water over his head his damp sleeves rolled back revealing some deep scars over his forearms, he felt Pimm's eyes on his skin and looked at them then gestured to Pimm's own arms.
"Do they still itch?" Orran asked.
Pimm placed his cigarette in his lips and removed his jacket, pulling up the sleeves past his elbows he held both hands out palms outstretched towards Orran, who

immediately pulled at his loose-fitting cotton shirt tugging it over his head, exposing a grey mane of chest and body hair akin to that of a silverback gorilla.

Both men had almost identically styled striped, branded scars each varying in width from half an inch to four inches in thickness that scored across their flesh at different intervals from the lower parts of their palm up their forearms to the elbows. Orran Danis had one additional injury separating them, a long brand that ran just above his nipples and almost the full width of his chest, where no hair grew as if someone had lashed at him with a flogging belt.

These wounds from their past cemented a vivid period neither man could break free from. Each of them held their own strong recollection of this period and as each studied the others markings their eyes locked, as they thought back to the same timeless memory from another land of conflict, one that almost laid claim as being their final resting place, Jerusalem, Mandatory Palestine 1946.

Chapter 2: The Dry Fly

Jerusalem, Mandatory Palestine.
March 1946

Nineteen-year-old Military Police Corporal, Oliver Pimm stepped from the WIllys Jeep and stared up at the two sand fatigued British uniformed corpse's hanging from the telegraph pole, both sporting grazes and cuts, faces swollen as if trampled by a bull. Their legs belts tied, each carried a damp stream that had begun to crystallise in the sun, from their shorts running down their bare legs to regular army socks, which flies seemed particularly attracted to.

Looking at the moist urine dirt, Pimm judged the soldiers to have been hung within the last half hour, questioning in his own mind if those responsible for the attack were watching them now, as two of his colleagues prepared to cut them down having unpacked a tarpaulin for the corpses.

"Fucking Stern Gang!" Pimm heard a voice curse from above him, as he took up a position crouching low at the rear.

Every recruit knew of the "Stern Gang" This was the first time he'd witnessed first had their work. It was the British term for the Zionist paramilitary organisation founded by Avraham "Yair" Stern, the Lehi (Fighters for the Freedom of Israel. Stern's one agenda no negotiations, get the British out of Palestine, Israel as they now considered it. Of all the paramilitary groups Stern's gang were considered the most proactive and bloodthirsty.

Pimm looked to his CO. standing up in the front seat of the lead Jeep-like some proud captain on the bow of the ship, surveying the scene, checking his map to mark their location, the wrong way up.

In the blistering heat, a shiver ran down Pimm's spine, and he looked to the man standing exposed beside him, then squatted tight into the shadow of the tailgate of his vehicle, a "Dingo", Daimler armoured car, he tapped his magazine of his Sten machine gun loosing the bullets to prevent a jamb and flipped the safety off his weapon. Catching some relief briefly by resting his forehead against the cool metal of the jerry water can strapped to the tailgate of the vehicle, he made the sign of the cross and thanked God for the fraction of additional cover it gave him.

As a bead of salty perspiration caught in his eyelash he stared without blinking towards his right as he watched the hill traffic wind slowly up Patriarchs Way, Highway 60, towards the Hebron pass. Most of the vehicles were trucks, coming up from the farming valleys, with fresh vegetables and fruit, headed for Jerusalem market.

Corporal Pimm's eyes peeled across each driver's face, considering them all a threat and noticing how some openly spat in the British soldier's direction as they leered out of their cab windows, swearing in Yiddish. He knew, even if his new CO did not, without a doubt, some of the trucks held weapons hidden amongst the produce, that could make him as "brown bread" as the men that hung above his head.

Again Pimm looked to his nearest team member, his casual familiarity to their situation made Pimm nervous, and he hunkered in tighter as he watched the soldier standing in the open as he adjusted his Sten gun top strap, resting the stock on his boot, the word "fool" rose to Pimm's thoughts, but he kept them from his lips.

Oliver Pimm was the newest replacement recruit to Amber squad, still coming to terms with the names and pecking order of the men he now served alongside. Being out on the limb gave him edginess, he not only accepted but preferred. He had already decided this squad felt out of sorts, lacking clear guidance of the potential menace lurking under every truck tarpaulin.

"You say you know this XO. You've been on patrol with him before?" Pimm asked the nearest Corporal as he watched him sling his Sten gun over his shoulder.

Ted Forrester looked down at Pimm and gave him a sarcastic smile as if to say, "What the fuck you doing down there?"

A teenager like Pimm, just six month's extra on his national service tenure and just over three months longer at the British main garrison base Sarafand, Mandatory Palestine, one of nearly a hundred thousand members of Her Majesty's armed force, sent to police and keep peace in the region.

"Yer, Amber's ok as it goes, I've been with the unit nearly four months, we seemed to be pulled, pillar to post, no two day the same, one thing you can say, you won't be bored, see plenty of country, it's ok, except for this sort of shit." Forrester gestured up to the two soldiers still hanging from the pole. "goes with the territory, but Amber, yer Amber's ok good lads" Forrester looked back down the line to the front wondering what was taking so long and then smiled, gesturing forward to Pimm, seeing the two furthest members of their squad were tossing a coin to decide which of them was to climb up the telegraph pole and cut the dead soldiers down. The officer in charge, still unfolding the map had left them to decide, not the most expeditious decision, considering the squad's exposure on the road.

Pimm could not contain the words felt that rose to his lips "C'mon, C'mon, get the fuckers down so we can get off this fucking road." he whispered to himself, ignoring Forrester's rambling.

"Yep, good lads. I know what you mean about the XO, seems a bit green, but we had a right tom-tit *(Shit)* when I first got here. This one went to Westminster, the word is he wanted to be in the Queen's, the Lifeguards," Forrester looked to Pimm to see if he was still listening and knew what he was talking about, he gestured he did, raising his eyes briefly from watching the road,

"Fucking cavalry can you believe it, as if that's a match for one of these" Forrester made a show of his Sten gun in his hands, "they all come over from Westminster, the guards, but this plonker has horse allergies, so daddy bought him the commission, and he writes like a subby, watch." Ted winked spinning on his heels

checking their rear, as in the distance he had noticed further down the road from where they were stationed, a large truck appeared, travelling slowly towards them.
"At my six!" Forrester called out.
"I see it" Pimm responded with a shout, and then heard, "I'm on it newlywed, watch your station" Pimm glanced along their column to the heavy gunner who had called out, then watched as their Commanding Officer in the third vehicle along called for an ambulance on the radio and passed a report form clipboard to the Staff Sergeant seated at his side in the jeep to note what they had found. Pimm noticed the Sergeant remained seated and like him appeared to be watching the caravan of trucks on the hill because like Pimm, he knew something felt wrong.
Most assassinations by the Israeli terrorists were orchestrated for maximum humiliation and psychological effect on the British troops. This had a feeling of something else, something more staged and the Sergeant looked forward to the road they were on, all traffic was taking to the hill rise, none was coming in their direction. He turned round in his seat and briefly looked back, past Pimm and towards the approaching truck to their rear, his stare then locked with Pimm's eyes and Pimm felt cold, gripping his gunstock, Pimm returned to scanning the hill traffic while Ted Forrester, still standing relatively exposed continued his account of his tenure with Amber squad.

"The only schizoid you want to watch is Toby Crack, he's a valley boy, same as Burton and that other actor, so he says" Ted nodded to the heavy gunner, that had shouted sown Pimm, standing braced in full view on top of the "Dingo" behind the cylinder mounted 7.92 mm BESA machine gun, chewing gum, smiling like an idiot back towards the vehicle that had been approaching them from behind, that was now less than twenty meters back down the road they had come from and appeared to have broken down through overheating the bonnet was up and what looked like dark steam plumed from the front
"Water hose has gone, idiots, they don't look after their kit." Crack tutted, and Forrester gave him a thumbs-up sign in agreement.
"Cracky's all right bit of a mong, but do anything for you, just don't call him Taff." Ted received a wink from the gunner, having heard his comment.
Pimm had already decided what he thought of the five-foot-two Welsh man "Bloody dangerous wanker, likely to get someone killed."
"Bit risky?" Pimm gestured to their XO, Lieutenant James Tilley, still standing tall looking up and down for any signs to confirm their location as he removed his cap and wiped his brow. "He knows the telegraphs are all marked?" Pimm gestured Ted to the white lettering daubed on the base of the pole the dead soldiers were hanging from.
Ted shrugged his shoulder, "He's the boss, I'm not doing his job for him....as I said plonker."
"I heard your old CO bought it in a club in Haifa, you'd think he'd be keeping his head down?" Pimm had read the camp news rag reporting the attack at an NCO billiard hall in Haifa, in which a Jewish terrorist belonging to the Stern gang, dressed

as a waiter threw a grenade beneath a billiard table. Three were maimed by the large chunks of wood and heavy, sharp slate from the table that ripped through their flesh. Aged 23, Lieutenant Duncan Taylor was not so lucky, disembowelled, he bled out within a minute, head resting on the sticky cracked melamine floor of the social club.

"C'mon, just cut the poor buggers down and let's get out of this fucking sun!" Pimm heard Crack mutter under his breath and he went to stand and speak up about the location markings on the telegraph post, but thought better of it, as the officer now stood fully exposed wiping his brow with his beret as he tried to make sense of the map, then stood up higher on his heels looking back, having noticed the broken-down truck behind.
Without the toll of a bell, the first zip of incoming fire took the top right half of Toby Crack's face clean away, exposing his shattered cheek, teeth and white jaw bone. Most of it landed on the shoulder of the driver behind, like a dropped kebab with chilli sauce. As Crack's left hand came up to feel the burning sensation to his face, another round ricocheted off the lock of his weapon then a third hit him squarely in the chest, two more catching the back of the driver who slumped quietly forward his right hand still on his shoulder from brushing the remains of Cracks face away. With his lifeless heavy boot resting on the accelerator and the vehicle, not in gear, its diesel engine plumed dark exhaust smoke then raced, increasing the tension and terror of the moment.

Pimm had already assessed it was a burst from a Thompson submachine gun, that came up along the track from the broken-down truck and let out a shout "Contact at six, ambush!" Pimm squeezed the trigger of his Sten in a succession of three-second bursts, seeing his first rounds pepper the open bonnet protecting the driver, who was firing through one-half of the trucks lowered split screen. The shooter's head ducked into the canopy, as he saw the pulse of smoke from Pimm's breach and he felt good for making their attacker go to cover, then cursed as he felt two hard ping's, like the caps of bottled beer being opened, as the Jerry water can beside him took two rounds, from new fire coming down from a group of secondary attackers hidden amongst the hillside traffic.
One of the bullets passed through the metal casing of the jerry can and slowed by the water inside pinched the metal out on Pimm's side, at shoulder height causing a blistered nipple in the metal can. As Pimm's knee began to feel damp from the water now seeping into the sand he thought at first he'd been hit and checked himself as his heart raced and time slowed above the ringing in his ears he heard Ted swearing "You fucking, fucking fucks." as he engaged the enemy.
Pimm refocused his attention on the broken down lorry and seeing movement in the cab he let off another couple of short burst from his Sten. The first caught the driver in his left shoulder and the second must-have nicked a fuel line, smoke began to appear from the engine compartment, and the driver made no movement to flee as the fire took hold. Pimm let off another burst, this time the man fell backwards and

dropped from the window so Pimm could see his hand hanging below the bottom of the cab door.

Considering him dead Pimm turned to the hillside, but poor Toby Crack, first to be hit, had not finished impressing Pimm. Already dead, his muscles spasmed as his fingers lightly twitched, squeezing the trigger, releasing thirty rounds and spitting the dirt from the ground like golf Mulligan swings. The bullet spray started just six feet shy from Pimm's position. Fortunately, Pimm was so close to the shots arch that the shells passed over his head as the barrel flayed away. But the last round was close enough it felt like he had taken a lug from a Turkish tea hooker, Ted Forrester was not so fortunate, as Pimm floored himself between the large all-terrain rear wheels of the armoured car he heard the call of the lead position to return fire, "Contact three o'clock H.A. *(heavy arms)*" as a thirty calibre browning M1919 machine gun, opened up on their position and then to his right he caught sight as Ted's headless corpse, pole-vaulted into the ditch behind the Dingo, while his Sten gun dropped inches from Pimm's hand, there was not a speck of dust or blood on it, as time appeared to stop momentarily, Pimm read the serial number on the lock, instinctively he grabbed the barrel, dragging it through the underbelly gate of the vehicle with his own weapon as he slid around, taking cover behind the rear wheel. Pimm felt a hard thrash of metal, and the Land Rover slumped down with the tyres on the opposite side hit, along with the patch of ground he had retreated from.

Looking to his left, the Officer and two other members of Amber Squad returned fire. The Radio operator Murray lay on his side, Pimm could see he had been hit, but his hand was moving as he tried to call for reinforcements from Sarafand garrison three miles away, it would take them half an hour to get there as the air filled with as many expletives from the soldiers as it did bullets,
"Fuck, fuck, fuck! Where the fucking fuck did that come from!"
He heard one of the older conscripts say, then he saw the hanging corpses of the RAMP'S *(Royal Military Police)* they had found, flaying from their noose's caught by incoming bullets like puppets that had their strings tangled.
In the broken wing mirror of the half-open door, he saw a flash of gunfire from the hill road coming from a large goods truck, its back canvas had been dropped and a denim shirt clad fighter with a red scarf was grinning as he ploughed into their position.

Something snapped in Pimm's mind, some might say training, some instinct. It was more like pure rage, with fingers on both Sten's he pulled up on the open back of the truck where poor Cracky had been standing, and over the back of the dead driver, protected to a degree by the small armoured parapet he began spraying the truck's position.
His right gun that should have been steadiest set a stream of bullets along the road edge sending dust and rock splinters up into the faces of their attackers partially

blinding them for a matter of seconds. The left gun felt unbalanced in his hand, but as its barrel rested on the opposite metal sill, it gave him stability, and it slid in a level line as he squeezed. The bullets cut into anything across his field of vision, taking in the gunner of the Browning M1919 machine gun on the back of the open wagon until it was spent. At this point there was an almighty whoosh of air as the fuel tank was hit, immediately followed by the barrel of an explosion as the spare jerry can on the back of the wagon took to the air like a rugby ball heading for a conversion.

Pimm's hits caused the attackers to check each other, and in those seconds Pimm and the XO Tilley opened up together with expert marksmanship of their targets. Pimm could not say for sure which of them got him, but the nearest of their ambushers span two feet upward, then rolled down the hill towards them gathering dirt as it stuck to his bloody wounds and clothes.

Pimm heard shouting from above and slipped back low expecting another massive assault as bullets continued to hail in their direction, but they had lost accuracy, as another truck ploughed past the one burning, nudging it from the road while remaining attackers scampered to climb aboard. Then it fled, barging and butting other vehicles on the pass, while other drivers appeared to cheer and punch at their horns, looking to support the attack. If he had been behind an 88 gun, Pimm would have probably taken out the whole column there and then, but he dropped Ted's machine gun then keeping low moved around, suddenly catching movement from their attacker that had rolled down, without thinking he pumped three slugs into his body.

"That will do Corporal." Pimm heard Tilley say from behind, with the muzzle of his gun still smoking he looked up at the burning truck, the man he had killed was on fire like a November 5th Guy Fawkes effigy resting forward against the gun in the back of the wagon. Shells pinged and zipped from around his body, exploding in the heat, while tar-black smoke from the engulfed tyres funnelled into the bluest sky Pimm had ever seen.

The horns and alarms from reinforcements that had seen the smoke returning from a search and seize raid in Bethlehem was like the call of an ice cream van to a child, and although his heart was still pounding like a charging rhino it made Pimm relax for a moment and consider for the first time, that he might survive. He watched the goods lorries and vans on the pass shunt over of the road to the edge, sometimes perilously close, allowing the British armed convoy past, staying crouched Pimm held his breath to calm his pulse.

"Pimm is it?" he heard the Officer say, Pimm turned but kept an eye on the approaching vanguard and the stationary trucks, looking to the goods trucks for a secondary team of ambushers, occasionally checking the dead, they were unnaturally still.

"Sorry, had no time for introductions this morning, James Tilley." Tilley held out his hand, Pimm looked at it, noticing it was trembling, but shook it and was surprised to see his own was as steady as Nelson's column.

Tilley gave him a reassuring pat on the shoulder as if it was something he had read a senior should do in the officer training manual. For a moment he reminded Pimm of his maths teacher at Finchley catholic school, London, a man that had survived Juno beach on "D day" only to get a ticket home when the Jeep he was travelling in overturned with a puncture, he lost two toes but it didn't stop him coaching the under twelve's rugby squad. He was the type that wanted his students to call him by his first name rather than "Sir" or "Mr" and the one they learnt more about sports with than maths.

Pimm looked back at Ted's corpse and considered straightening his legs, but stayed put, still unsure there were no snipers lurking nearby, just waiting for the opportunity, to take him down.

"Well, just you and me now Pimm, a bloody awful business, they had us hook line and sinker what?" Tilley leaned into the armoured cab past the dead driver and switched the engine off. It died with a splutter, its silence was painfully tense and amplified the approaching sound of the cavalry.

"They had you on the hook" Pimm kept his thought to himself as he watched how his CO now paid more attention to the lorries that had resumed filing up the hill road,

"Bloody shame," Tilley said, looking at the remains of the men that had been under his command.

"Yes Sir, bloody shame" the words came from Pimm's mouth, but he had no idea what he was responding to.

"If that daft Taff up top Crack, had kept his eyes peeled instead of grinning like a Cheshire cat, they may not have caught us with our pants down," he shook his head as if blaming the gunner. "But well done you, I'll make sure you get a mention back at HQ, good work Corporal sticking on the back gun."

Pimm had heard his superior's words, but it was not until he looked away from the road realising only he and the officer were left, he understood why the XO was now addressing him. Pimm looked behind the jeep, there was no movement from the radio operator, and the soldier he had seen return fire in the lead vehicle was now out of sight, Pimm could only see the back of his legs at the front of his Land Rover, toes turned in.

Pimm watched Tilley march out into the open to welcome the new arrivals and stamp a salute, a perfect target for any sniper and Pimm would have considered it a fitting end to the man's lack of judgement and leadership skills.

As soon as men from the arriving squad ejected from their trucks, a succession of concise short orders were barked by one man, setting up a secure perimeter of eyes and Pimm rose to his feet, watching in silence.

It appeared to him as if others moved around him in slow motion as he looked to Tilly, who from the hand gestures and body language he gathered was explaining the attack, for a second Pimm was sure he saw Tilley smile, and it made him sick, he felt out of place not knowing where to stand. Seeing the ambulance crew and the new squad take up defensive positions he changed his magazine, pinning himself low at the back of the armoured car where he had initially taken cover. By now the damp soil was dry, he flicked his thumb on the nipple punch that he now saw was close to eye height, its sharp burr pierced the skin, and he tasted his own blood, smiling at his stupidity he turned back out to the landscape and began scoping the hills.

The sun now felt hotter than ever, and his eyes drifted over the unfolding scene of the cleanup of the site. As they stretchered Ted away, the two crew members looking around for something Pimm went to say something about where he had left Ted's Sten believing they were looking for the weapon he had used and left up top in the parapet.

He then watched as one picked up what was left of Ted's arm and tossed it beside his body. Pimm squinted when another soldier returned from the side of the road and held at arm's length a matted meatball shape, covered in dirt, the only thing that made Pimm realise it was Ted's head was as they placed it at the top of the stretcher he caught the silhouette of his ear, then Pimm felt a hand on his shoulder and flinched, gripping his weapon.

"Steady mate, come on let's get you back, your XO's already fucked off, probably had enough excitement for one day. You can ride in with my squad, I heard your boss say you bagged the gunner in the truck and then this piece of dirt." the sergeant said with no hint of a dictatorial tone, as they watched two members of the Argyll and Sutherland Highlanders turf the body of the terrorist over unceremoniously. Splaying his arms as they searched his corpse, his headscarf fell away, revealing the face of a teenager about the same age as Pimm. He realised some Jewish mothers would receive the news of his handy work that day, but could not muster any pity, as the boy's body was dragged by the heels over to the wagons and wrapped in tarpaulin with the others

Pimm looked at the soldier's hand as it hovered above his head "Staff?" he said, now noticing his arm badge and relaxed his grip on his weapon.

"I heard your CO. talking with our Rupert, he's going to cite you. Not bad for your first walkabout." The squaddie thrust down his hand again, grabbing Pimm by the forearm, almost pulling him up out of his boots.

"Staff Sergeant Bowman, Steve, I've seen you about at base, heard one of your blokes mention you being a Finchley lad, I'm from down the road, Camden Town both on the Northern Line, we're a long way from the Lyceum, let's make sure you get back there, c'mon." Bowman recognised Pimm was in shock and tried to set mental ground stakes to keep him in balance, he had read it in an NCO pamphlet, under the heading: **Not all Casualties are Bleeding.**

Pimm followed behind Bowman and was given a hand up into the truck, as he received nods of acknowledgement from the squad of men, he realised those inside were resting their feet on the wrapped bodies of some of those killed.

Sat in the back as the truck started up, he looked back at the telegraph poles, the bodies of the dead soldiers had been cut down now, but he wondered why they left the rope, as he smoked a cigarette handed him.

There was a loud bark in Pimm's ear by Bowman as he addressed one of his men who began quizzing Pimm on the action, and Pimm was thankful not having to speak up.

Travelling back the truck pulled to the side and there was a cheer from the group of soldiers in the back as they jostled into each other. Until they slowed to pass the wreckage of one of their own vehicles returning to base, caught by a mine, it had been a three-stage ambush that day. Now Sarafand had sent another troop to clear the wreck and remove the bodies, chaperoned by an ARV *(Armoured Recovery Vehicle)* and a Cromwell tank that sat at the side of the road, like some junkyard dog too fat and old to catch anyone, but mean enough to deter the most fanatical terrorist. Just one shell would rip through the entire line of traffic heading into the city.

Pimm noticed the usual swearing from the Jewish traders, and the horn taunting stopped as they slowed to pass the overturned Land Rover. It took him 2.4 seconds to realise it was James Tilley lying dead, pinned half under the passenger side. In that moment Pimm felt the eyes of the other squaddies he shared the truck with fall on him, he was the only survivor from that unit, sometimes this could be a curse, a sole survivor could easily be labelled as a Jonah, a bad luck omen,

The stigma of bad penny Pimm started with Amber squad, but fortunately, Lieutenant Tilley had vocalised Pimm's actions in taking out the chief gunner to those on-site including Bowman. So the squad of men he now sat with knew he was no lucky tourist that had watched his mates get cut down.

Tilly had also said enough that even though Pimm was convinced by the senior Officer in his debriefing, who introduced in himself as Major John Smith, to allow the main kill to go to Tilley, enabling the Lieutenant to earn a posthumous military cross, Pimm's record had been pulled from the main personnel files of Sarafand, by one that looked into all terrorist activity and clandestine operations within the Middle East, by the now established British secret service.

Smith's real name was Roger Thake, a Mi6 field operative working out of the Malta station, attached to Raleigh Division, over his shoulder a six-foot by four-foot mirror sat, making the room appear brighter and larger than it actually was. Behind its one-way glass Mi6 Berlin section Chief Albert "Bull" Gordon watched as Smith debriefed Pimm. Paying it little attention, Corporal Pimm had noticed the large mirror in the office as he straightened his hair, when removing his beret, at the start of the debrief, He had never heard of one-way glass of such a size and had no reason to think it, like the debriefing was anything other than ordinary.

"In your own words, if you please Corporal" instructed by Smith, Pimm began his report in a manner as advised by Staff Sergeant Bowman. Pimm had only just met the man, but his instincts told him Bowman was as solid as his two-foot broad shoulders and in the brief time he spent in Bowman squad he realised there was an earned respect by the squaddies under his command. The Sergeant had an almost paternal manner in the way he interacted with the squad, that said, when he said jump, they already knew how high and did it in a uniformed fashion.

So Pimm followed Bowman's advice and had spent time prior to his debrief with Major Smith breaking the day's events down, so that when the meeting came forward, he ran through the attack with straight forward accuracy of the timeline and spoke with little reference to his relationship with the other members of Amber troop and held back voicing his personal opinion that he believed Tilley had led an undisciplined squad of men into an ambush, like spring lambs to the slaughterhouse. There would have been nothing to gain in speaking up, slating the dead especially officers even when they had made a balls up, that had got men killed, never works out for the one that volunteers the information. Besides Tilley was beyond any form of reprimand, and regarding Amber, Pimm had only been with them as a replacement for less than a month. Apart from Ted Forrester, other than the usual new face stick, all newbie's expected, few civil words had passed between him and the rest of the squad members. If truth be told, apart from service details on the base, he had no point of reference to offer an opinion on the squad's efficiency, and like Tilley, they had learnt to their cost their last lesson.

Regardless of what had actually taken place, Pimm knew enough about the army that the fact they had all died in action made his testimony of significant importance for the regiment. So without being led, Pimm indicated all of the squad members engaged the terrorist simultaneously and exaggerated the numbers of the attackers, adding he had just been lucky that day to survive and mentioned for good measure the jerry water can that had taken a bullet meant for him. His suspicions that the debriefing officer was interested in creating a legend of the terrorist attack for the regiment, the grieving families of the fallen and the papers back home was confirmed when Smith began to refer specifically to the main gun and how Lieutenant Tilley had reacted, whilst referring to the dead Lieutenant's service history.

It was then Pimm spoke up with a final lie, with the hope it would bring an end to the proceedings

"I believe the Lieutenant was in error, Staff Sergeant Bowman informed me after the event what the Lieutenant had reported regarding his observations during contact with the main target on the hill, the H.A. With respect to the late officer, it is my recollection it was Lieutenant Tilly that responded first and neutralised the target." Pimm looked unblinking at Smith and waited as Smith looked down at the report, then glanced curiously to Pimm over his shoulder at the mirror behind.

"I see, well it would appear that puts a different light on the situation if you are sure that is what you observed Corporal." As Smith stared across at Pimm, the young Corporal sensed his disbelief in his version of the events.

"Yes, Sir, that is my recollection," Pimm replied.

Smith Strummed the document in front of him with his fingers then closed the folder and jotted some additional notes on Pimm's statement.

"Right then, I will have the report amended, we will, of course, mark the kill to the rear truck driver on your ticket, unless you have anything further to add." Smith could not help but turn his head back again, as if seeking affirmation from a senior officer, out of sight in the next room.

"No, Sir!" Pimm confirmed and this time studied the large timber-framed mirror, as Smith pushed forward his statement and set a Biro pen at its side.

"Good well that's that, just sign there and then off you trot, I may wish to speak further on this, but in the meantime, you understand, mum's the word." Smith gestured to Pimm that he could leave.

'Yes sir" Pimm signed his name and saluted, but before he left the room, he gave one last look at the mirror and remembering a black and white espionage film where they used a one-way mirror fitted on a small bathroom cabinet he wondered who was standing on the other side of the glass.

"This is bloody marvellous stuff, smoke and mirrors as they say?" Thake opened the rear door into the surveillance room having dismissed Pimm and handed Bull the report.

"Yes Rog, yanks invented it, so they claim, happen to know for a fact the new stuff like this was from a Nazi scientist working in Czechoslovakia, they pinched him from us during operation Paper-clip." Bull Gordon had worked with military intelligence at the end of the war targeting principal Nazi scientist to relocate to Great Britain. Since then running Mi6 Scott Division out of Berlin, it had become somewhat of an ongoing pet project, aware as were the American's and Russians there were still many German's involved in war crimes that had slipped the net, who could be turned to work for them and in exchange Bull could offer them an end their life on the run, with a new identity and house in suburbia. There was only one problem, the long arm of Mossad, not even a highly developed scientific skill set could save them from the hangman's noose.

"Bloody typical Yanks come to the dance late leave with the best looking dollies." Thake joked as he flicked through the photographs that had been taken of the dead terrorist's involved in the attack on Amber squad.

"Yes well Roger, same shit different war, back to the matter in hand CID had these two already pinned as Stern gang working out of Tel Aviv" Bull tapped two of the pictures of the dead Jewish terrorist, "my office gave your boys there headshots when they were caught in the act in Berlin last May, they carried out a hit on a newspaper vendor on Tiergartenstraße, turned out during the war he worked for Albert Speer's Armaments division an expert in demolition explosives, C4 or the Nazi's equivalent. We let them run home on the understanding they were under your watch. Listen, Rog, I haven't come over to point the finger, god knows how slippery these buggers can be, the top floor will grill you in their own time and good luck with that. They asked me on this just to take a look-see, as I was in the area.

Just put the thing to bed Rog, this kind of crap makes us all look bad to the bowler hat brigade at home." Bull shook his head.

"I know Bull, I saw your brief. They worked as porters at the old museum, we had a contact one of the curators, with eyes on them, he went missing three days before both men were reported killed in an explosion in their apartment in Tel Aviv-Yafo, there was little left, some kind of bomb-making factory. We assumed your paper-seller in Berlin sold them dodgy goods, an unstable formula. As you said, our boffin's reckon they were making some kind of C4 plastic explosive." Thake pushed forward a forensic report and a photograph of a bomb-damaged apartment that carried the blackened remains of human body parts. "Like I said, not much left."

"Well someone slipped up at your end, whoever it was that identified these matchsticks as the boys from Berlin was telling you porkies, my son. Take a look into the local Turks we have in play, see if any of them are flashing the cash around the bars, might be we have someone on Stern payroll. If we can trace him or her, you can try and turn them, if not I trust I can leave you to bury them where the sun never shines. Give me a greedy bugger any day, least you know they're thinking for themselves. Bloody fanatics are too much in a hurry to meet their maker for my liking, the Jews have certainly stepped up their game, a hat-trick to the home team, only this Lost Boy left out to bat." Bull looked at Pimm's file and studied his identity photograph.

"Well at least this Pimm chappie went for the PR of a Military cross for Tilley, Seems a decent sort, not that it will give Tilley's folks much peace of mind," Thake said, running a line through Tilley's original citation for Pimm.

"Yes he did, in fact, his whole report was unassuming, exaggerated just enough to give the other fellows some credit. succinct precise concise, and with not a jot of ego or excitement, very matter of fact as if he had taken a picnic hamper out and found the milk was off, I like that, perhaps something might come out of this mess" Bull was always on the lookout for another Lost Boy he could woo into his intelligence team, and Pimm fitted the bill.

"Might just be shock, not every day you see what's on your buddies mind from the inside." Thake's glib comment left no impression on his superior as he watched as Thake tried to place his hand on one side of the one-way glass and wave it so he could see it himself on the other,

"Yes could be but I think not." Bull shook his head in disbelief at Thake's antics.

"Yanks, clever stuff, I hear they are looking to beat the Ruskies to the moon, they'll probably do it as well I doubt any of the German's the soviets swiped are living as well as Von Brown and his team?" Smith said sarcastically.

"You're probably right, and that's part of the reason I'm here, Whitehall wants me to have a snoop around see how much cooperation the Jews over here are aiding the kill teams they have running amuck looking for Adolf's boys, they still seemed to think we have him. Apart from anything else it's screwing with the natives in Berlin, we have enough of a time keeping an eye out for the Reds. I'm only glad someone on the top floor at Century still thinks there's some mileage in picking up any of the loose ends. I don't expect anything like Von Brown will come my way, it would have been nice to have had a word with the paper man, you have to hand to him, hiding in plain sight, gives credence to the whispers we keep hearing of The Spider network lists coming to the open market, maybe somehow these boys got a hold of one, in which case we can expect more exotic and unexplained deaths, like that Otmar Von Verschuer, putting the RPA mentor of Doctor Mengele in charge of the world health organization was always going to raise eyes with the Jews, but I suspect while things like those working in NASA continue to reel in profits we will carry on with the hunt and there's always the missing gold, between you and me Rog I think they are hoping to get a lead, help us pay the Yanks back for pitching in. Funny enough amongst the paper man's effects, when they turned over his flat they found a stack of postcards from Brazil, between the lines it appears someone from his past was reaching out, you could almost think it was some kind of recruitment drive for ex-Nazi's. I've just sent another of our bods on a steamer to Rio. It would seem this Spiders web has strands catching flies down there, I reminded our man to keep an eye out for this new Israeli Intelligence crew while on ship. Just our luck to have a man overboard, one thing you can say for the Yid's they're a proactive lot. I'm having a word with our American cousin's see if they can talk some sense into the tribes. That said I'm not convinced myself their hands are clean. Trouble is 5 million dead everyone knows someone that suffered, and there's a river of cash coming into Jerusalem, hard for Mi6 to compete with that, I'm still getting fucking luncheon vouchers with my wedge at the end of the month from Aunt Bessy, makes me wonder if there's enough in the kitty for another Lost Boy, like this Pimm even if he makes the grade." Bull looked at Pimm's file.

"Well good luck with the Yanks Bull, like you I went to Auschwitz after the war, the Israelis won't be happy until every non-German Jew born before 45 is dead, one of them told me once, it's a calendar scratched as a celebration date, can you believe it."

Thake had worked with Bull in West Germany for two years before the wire had gone up between East and West.

"Oh yes, old fruit I can believe it like you say I was there a little earlier." Bull's eyes glazed over, as he remembered the scenes he had witnessed when being part of an advanced patrol group assigned to the U.S. 11th Armoured Division that discovered Mauthausen concentration camp, east of the city of Linz, Austria, in May 1945. Then his gaze settled on a folder on the desk, labelled Operation Agatha and his thoughts returned to that moment, and he turned to Roger Thake.

"I take it everything is set for Agatha? If the party goes to schedule, it should at least bring home the bacon for cock-ups like this." Bull tapped the Amber massacre incident report, what the attack on Lieutenant Tilley's squad had become commonly known as at Sarafand base.

Operation 'Agatha' 28th/29th June 1946 involved 100,000 troops and the Palestine police. 17,000 British troops descended into Jerusalem when lines

of communication to the Jewish Agency were cut, before simultaneous raids. Twenty-five Jewish settlements were cordoned with a forced occupation as hundreds of homes were violated, in a search and seizure exercise, approximately 2,650 men and 60 women taken into custody, incriminating documents were seized along with arms at the Agency, it was padlocked shut, a number of employees suspected of terrorism were arrested, including senior Haganah leaders.

"Yes all the senior officers were notified off-site, they will get their deployment routes and objectives at the designated rally points at 03:00, just in case anyone talks in their sleep should be a big show." Thake's confidence had an enthusiasm Bull took with a pinch of salt.
"Well let's hope so, we need a good win." Bull stared back through the mirror to the empty room.
"Do you think you'll still be around?" Thake considered the idea of having The Bull breathing down his neck for one of the most extensive and complicated intelligence operations they had mounted against the Israelis.
"If I am you won't know, it's your circus after all." Bull could see a multitude of reasons why the operation could fail, amongst everything else the Intel amongst the various Jewish terrorist groups was second to none and unlike the American's and British they shared. But even though he could envisage one of the senior troop officers letting something slip about Agatha, over pillow talk with a local prostitute, he figured it was such a massive trawling operation that they were bound to catch some big fishes amongst the minnows, and if not as he was keeping at arm's length, he would not get tarred with same brush as Thake and the GOC, *(General Officer Commanding)*

"So where are you staying, King David? I'm meeting a couple of the chaps there tomorrow for a bite they will all be doing their bit for Agatha, if you fancy it I'll do the intros, I know you like your slippers and pipe, not the type for stepping out into public for formal wear but it looks like you came prepared." Thake pointed towards Bull's tartan waistcoat. Bull thumbed his pocket watch and made as if reading the time, Thake got the hint,
"And what about this Pimm chap, we need to get him a new home, before Agatha kicks off, seems only fair to have him settled in." Thake went to place the reports including Pimm's service record into his leather case, but Bull stopped him and removed Pimm's file from his hand.
"Ah, you fancy him for one of yours? Why not, seems to have potential, but it could be it's a one-off, every dog has his day and that, my advice leave him as is, stick him with this Staff Sergeant Bowman, he's no fool, he'll spot if the Corporal gets the jitters, but my guess is he could be a natural." Thake watched a smile rise to Bulls lips as he cast an eye over Pimm's basic training stats and noticed his marksmanship assessment score was AA, *(Above Average)*

"Well we know he can shoot, why not give him some recon work move him to RCS *(Royal Corps of Signals)* get him involved with the cartography wallers, it would get him off the streets for a week or so. Let him settle his stomach, and you can find out if he knows his time's table and alphabet, keep me up to speed. Then he will be in the green for Agatha, whoever his unit is. In the meantime, I'll hang onto this." Bull pulled out his pipe and stoked it toying with the swan match, as Thake signed the fabricated confirmation of the action Pimm had taken in the exchange, substituting Pimm's name with Tilley and signed off the medal citation recommendation for bravery under fire and placed inside his bag.

"I get it Bull, you want to see if he's a one-trick pony, what about languages, we always need translators, we have this Turk in town been here since D day, never met him myself, but a helpful sort by all accounts with little titbits of information which made him some pocket money. He takes a class over at Kfar Vitkin for some of the officers and suits in the commission. French Italian, Turkish you name it he can teach it apparently, even Hebrew. I can offer it to your boy if he takes it up it shows he's got spunk to be more than in the PBI *(Poor bloody infantry)*."
Striking the match Bull lit his pipe and read Pimm personal section on the file, again tapping with his finger on the line recording next of kin and reading he had an English non-relative as a sponsor, no parents were listed.
"An orphan boy was he," he hummed, "why not, I'll spring the tab, I've got a desk full of luncheon vouchers I can trade in when I get back to Blighty. You say this Turks kosher, worked with some of our boys, papers all good?" Bull gave Thake a sideways glance over his glasses.
"Yes as I said he's been here since Jerry went home, goes by the name of Danis, Orran Danis" Thake gave a nod.
"That's settled Roger, keep me informed, and this is on the QT no need to tell any of you boys at Raleigh or let Century house know. As I said I'm off to Cyprus, have a chat with the Yanks. See what I can do about sorting this sham of the camps; sometimes I think some of our people have never heard of the world press, if we don't clean up our act, we'll be the Nazi's on the front page of the Mirror." Bull was a Telegraph man.
"You know if this boy turns out to be a smart fella, he will smell a rat, being singled out to move to signals'" Thake, mused as Bull was about to leave. "Perhaps I'll have the whole of Bowman's squad assigned as a security detail."
"Whatever you like Rog, as I said it's your circus over here, just keep me in the loop, cheers m' dears." Bull tapped his head with Pimm's folder and tucked it under his arm and left.

Pimm was relieved when he received his reassignment orders to Juno squad who had been attached to the RSC and spent two weeks to some extent settling in under the wing of Staff Sergeant Bowman. Steve Bowman was an original cockney, born on Wood Street, within the sound of Bow Bells, St-Mary-le-Bow Church. To back it up, he claimed to have grandparents that were Pearlies *(Kings and*

Queens). No one was going to question the Londoner's ancestry or mock his accent, not just because he was Staff Sergeant but because he stood 6'6 and weighed fifteen stone, in his boots with hands the size of casserole dish lids. That said Bowman rarely raised his voice except to pass down direct orders in the field and if he did you better listen. However, off duty, he was a mild, soft-spoken man, with only three loves in his life, the army, his wife, Lorraine and his nine-month-old son James. He had been there at his birth and counted the days to return for his christening, which would, of course, take place at St Mary-le-Bow, even though they had bought a flat in Woodside Park before his tour, they now they lived in the suburbs, and he loved it.

He and Pimm talked of the Finchley Lido open-air swimming pool as if they had spent time there together, before Palestine. Believing at some time it was quite possible they spent a summer's day laying on the large grassy knoll picnic green listening to the whistle of the lifeguard and watching children filling their buckets from the brass lion head water fountains, on days when the air was filled with chlorine, and the sun seemed to stay until the last bather stepped through the clanking turnstile to go home or cued for the Saturday matinee cinema at the Finchley Gaumont.

Their friendship was probably inevitable born from such a violent first meeting, Bowman was senior-only by three years but had seen far worse than Pimm had experienced in his first months when members of Amber troop were cut down on an ambushed beach patrol.

Like many Bowman saw the increasing numbers of arriving members of the Diplomatic Corp and his squad's assignment as security chaperones to survey teams, as a sign that hopefully, they would soon be withdrawing from the region.

At the end of the second world war the map and topographic divisions of the allied armies had swollen to excess, as new lines on maps were drawn and redrawn in executive boardrooms, then actually surveyed and committed into contracts of unions of the post-war peace, it was only bested by the increasing number of members of the Diplomatic and foreign Corp.

At the time Staff Sergeant Bowman saw no reason to question his CO's orders that his latest ward Pimm should remain on-base for additional training, with the hope the young Corporal would get a cushy number as a batman, fetching and carrying for a survey team officer and knew it was standard at the time that learning languages were encouraged amongst the lower ranks. A batman that could translate was an added bonus to an officer when hawking souvenirs. "Batman and Bootlickers" were how most were regarded by their privileged seniors, but Pimm was not destined to remain there long.

As for all of those that joined the base language classes, it meant the chance of more relaxed duties and possibly eventually an assignment to a consular office, plus anything that might help in Civvies Street when their conscription tenure ended

was a bonus. But when all was said and done, taking the twice-weekly, two-hour lesson in a classroom with overhead fans, however ineffectual against the heat, beat being out on patrol and above all made the days go faster.
So the ever-wise Bowman encouraged Pimm to accept, and although he wished he had got the chance himself, he figured it was the least the brass could do for Pimm in shafting him from a citation for his part in the attack at Hebron Pass.
Pimm never spoke of his action that day or the debrief, but Steve Bowman knew who really had taken down the Israeli terrorists as did the other members of the squad, who soon learnt Pimm could handle himself.

It didn't give the young Corporal a pass from getting ribbed as the newbie, but he had heard it all before and had a quippy comeback. In general Juno was a completely different squad of men to Amber, tighter, more alert, they each had a place and job to do on patrol and the most important was ensuring the man next to you had his back covered and would make it back to base, there were no jokes, no banter, no inane dribble, not until they were safely back at base after each operation.

Pimm thought possibly because they had witnessed other members of their team killed early on, but believed it was Bowman's guidance that had formed such an efficient squad and they recognised early his skills, he was looked to on patrol by others, glad to have him at their side if and when the shit hit the fan. He soon became accepted and was well-liked, playing his cards close to his chest, he was one of those that hovered on the edge of a group, but was never quite in it, when on R & R at the base. For the most part, he kept pretty much to himself, except with Bowman. That said he could never be accused of being the teacher's pet, not since they began sparring together and Pimm took the six foot six Londoner down, with his own pearler, a left uppercut that had now left him with a china chip cut smile to explain to Mrs Bowman for the christening photo album. When Bowman came round, his first words were, "Good hit, my son, I knew you were a dark horse, let's see what else you're holding back."
Pimm made no apology, sighting Father Eagen's after school boxing club at Finchley catholic and held out his hand, as he got a cheer from the other lads hanging on the ringside. However, Bowman made sure the next time he put Pimm firmly on his arse when he tried the set combination of blows again.
"I thought you couldn't teach an old dog," Pimm said spitting blood through his split lip. Sparring was part of camp life and like the open-air cinema and occasionally paired sightseeing, detracted from some of their monotonous duties like roadblocks, guard camp and port duties that each still held tension, in a heat that sapped the will of good men to concentrate on staying alive.

At this time increasing numbers of Jewish migrants were making the dangerous journey entering the country via the beaches. Many would fall foul of the undercurrents of the beautiful Mediterranean, travelling in small crafts

that were inadequate for the task and of such poor quality and age that often they capsized. To prevent this, sometimes passengers were forced overboard by unscrupulous smugglers, and there were some who had set-piece arrangements with British intelligence officers and would rendezvous out at sea or on predetermined landfalls, where the British soldiers would be waiting to capture the unfortunate migrants. Once processed many would be deported to British military camps located across the colonies including Cyprus where sometimes they had initially escaped from.

British conscripts like Pimm and those serving under non commissioned officers such as Staff Sergeant Bowman had a range of assignment during their tour and were involved in a variety of peacekeeping duties. Including the capture arrest and guarding of Jewish detainees, in smaller specific target operations, as well as the stop and search street sorties that often led to an exchange of fists and sometimes gunfire from an out of sight sniper, who would generally only let off a single round, more often than not, using old weapons they would miss their intended target.

Then there were the executive operations, generally instigated from the pressure of Whitehall, such as Operation Agatha, in which Pimm now a full member of Juno squad played his part and believed caught sight of the mysterious Major Smith/ Roger Thake amongst a group of other officers. Agatha was regarded as one of the successful highlights for the British in 1947 and included the capture of senior leaders, such as Moshe Shertok.

Apart from taking part in operation Agatha, Pimm now settled into a routine of sorts, working, split between Juno sorties and assigned to the Signal Corp. where he assisted in carrying out survey work plotting the routes and resources the new territories would take in as the division of Palestine and Israel became permanent markers on the new maps drawn by the British military survey teams. One thing that remained constant having accepted the offer of joining the diplomatic linguistic course was his Tuesday morning and Friday afternoon visits to Kfar Vitkin training base. There were a number of reasons why he chose to accept the Smiths recommendation, without needing Bowman to tell him, "You'd be a fool not to." not least because it gave him a lay-in till eight on Tuesday and Friday evening being cinema night he was finished early enough at Vitkin to bag seats for Juno squad members. Also on class days apart from some housekeeping for Signal Corp. he had free run of the camp all day, with no one counting his footsteps.

"No one barking orders and lessons in a fan-cooled classroom, what's not to like, you bloody fool" Bowman had added with a hint of jealousy.

Pimm soon discovered there was an additional novelty to the language course he joined in developing a new interest, people watching. Most of the other members of the class came from entirely different backgrounds to his own, and he found these characters, although sometimes obtuse and bizarre, interesting and at times perplexing. They were the type of individuals he would not usually be able to associate with on a one to one basis. Commissioned officers, some not much older than himself, many of whom were from wealthy parents, some of whom worked within the diplomatic corps. Inhabiting a world completely removed from his own. He began to emulate some of their more appealing traits, learning some of the tricks of the trade of their culture and etiquette.

In the Kfar Vitkin camp classroom predominately the commissioned officers sat at the front desks directly below the spinning fans, behind them civil servants and then Pimm who nested beside one of the windows at the back of the room, it caught the shade no matter the time of day and occasionally, when with a gentle breeze brought pleasant relief, with the sweet smell from the magnolia tree that clung to the wall outside.

In a past life as a young student, Pimm considered he would have probably have used the time staring out the window, but something was different about him, he sensed he had changed, and in addition, their tutor was by far the most interesting of the characters that he encountered in the classroom.

Their teacher was the thirty-two-year-old Turkish born, Orran Danis, to look at him you would think he was in his early twenties, a slender man who always wore the same black suit with a crisp starched sleeveless collared shirt. His tortoiseshell bifocal glasses carried tooth cuts on the ear tips.

"So who can tell me why we call French the diplomatic language, when now 65% of the western world speaks English, the Chinese even choose it as a mandatory study for their children's curriculum," Orran said removing his glasses from his mouth. This was another reason why Pimm liked coming to the lessons, Orran engaged the group adding general knowledge into the lessons, and his range of topics was as vast as it was varied. No subject was off-limits including religion and politics, which often had a few of the four commissioned officers arguing.

Sitting as the referee at such exchanges Orran would remain cool and calm, appearing to Pimm at times to be studying those taking part as he allowed them to vent their programmed British indoctrinated views, which could have come straight from the rear of Winston Churchill's "Y" fronts.

In the future, Pimm would look back and appreciate Orran Danis was probably assessing his potential and considering grooming him as an asset. But at the time he had no suspicions of any ulterior motive the friendly and interesting tutor may have had, after all, he had been cleared by base security. In fact, Orran Danis's interest had been peaked soon after Corporal Oliver Pimm's name was added to his student roster. As in the past the Turk had bribed a Turkish cleaner, employed at the Sarafand HQ, to check Pimm's service record, Being informed Pimm had no service record was like a fresh white cabbage to a slug and Danis called in a number of debts to discover all he could, which was very little, Pimm having always played his cards close to his chest, but he did discover he was an orphan. And being around the age of what Pimm's father would have been hoped to gain the young Corporals trust by playing the psychological card as a masculine seniority replacement, imparting worldly wisdom in contrast to the brute disciplines and skills he had received from his military service, seniors.

Pimm's acceptance of Orran Danis as a friend was a relationship that from its inception was totally calculated by the Turk who also played on the fact; Pimm was a social outsider to others in his lesson group.

Orran Danis read people like others read books and had been playing the great game, spying, almost as long as Bull Gordon. So when Pimm handed in his assignment papers at the end of the week, and Danis invited him to join him at the library the following day, at which time he would give Pimm additional study books in German, Pimm accepted with no concern, comforted by the fact that his teacher, although non-military, appeared to have the freedom of the base believing he must have been thoroughly vetted as a security risk. Besides as much to Pimm's surprise and others, Danis had by now managed to teach him French, to the point that he could carry out a general conversation with no fear of embarrassment and a near-perfect accent had now started him on German.

On one occasion Danis actually remarked to one of his British colleagues on the base, that Pimm was like a sponge and irrespective of any ulterior motive to his cultivating a relationship with Pimm, Orran genuinely found the young Corporal's thirst for knowledge refreshing.

At the same time, secretly, Pimm also questioned himself, why now, on the eve of his twentieth birthday, his intellect had suddenly switched a gear. At home, as a schoolboy, his aptitude for learning had been less than remarkable, even though he tried hard. Mostly from a sense of duty to the women who had sponsored him since leaving the orphanage at Nazareth House, Parsonage Street, Hendon.

Pimm's parents had been killed during a bombing raid in the Blitz while taking cover inside an Anderson shelter, Pimm miraculously survived having been placed beneath an upturned tin bath but received a significant head injury, he still could feel the scar through his crown. He became an orphan like so many thousands, one of the less visible tragedies of the war.

The trauma for some time left him as one less likely to be picked as a foster child when standing on display for prospective parents.

Something about the boy caught the attention of a genuine fostering couple, and he went to live with the McDonalds in the flat above their café in Eversholt Street, near Kings Cross, London. Pimm became sponsored, because shortly after he was taken in by the couple, Charlie McDonald died of a stroke, but Victoria, Vic McDonald was a strong, forthright woman, the salt of the earth type, with arms strong enough to cuddle a grown boy and keep him at her side, even when the authorities wished to take him back now her marital status had changed.

But Charlie McDonald had liked the boy the moment he set eyes on him, aged nine and that was it, they had paid over enough to take him there and then and the windowed Vic McDonald, later reminded the governor of that when they tried to remove Oliver from her care, now that her circumstances had changed. Pimm's adoption papers and records were subsequently lost, until he was of legal age, then it was up to him. When the time came Vic explained what had happened and of course, he chose to stay with Vic. Who also paid for him to be a part-time boarder at Finchley Catholic School just off the Great North Road, London. Now as the sole breadwinner she needed to focus on her business during the week, however come the weekends she devoted the two days entirely to her boy, "Ollie" and cried each time she left him, when she stepped back aboard the number 134 bus home and watched him shuffle back to the school, from the window.

In a London city council backed, compulsory purchase, Vic was forced to sell the wooden benched café on Eversholt Street, when they widened the road for new parking facilities at Euston station. She put the money she got into a pair of three-bedroom semi-detached Villas in Muswell Avenue, Muswell Hill, they lived on the ground floor of one while she let rooms in the rest of the house.

When home, weekend breakfast was Pimm's favourite time, he met people from different places and all walks of life, sitting in their front room parlour where he helped serve the plates.

He still sent Vic a third of his army payback, and she went down and put every penny into a national savings book in his name, which he would not find out about until her death in 1976.

But before then in the years after his time in Palestine, Vic was amazed when her "Ollie" demonstrated his linguistic skill, she especially became fond of him speaking in Russian. Doctor Zhivago being her all-time favourite, followed by Lawrence of Arabia,

"What I wouldn't do to have that Omar Sharif across the breakfast table," Vic said with no innuendo intended, in particular liking Sharif's eyes, Pimm always groaned with embarrassment at her innocent comment.

Oliver Pimm's skills for language may have started with Orran Danis in Palestine, but in later years he speculated if his violent brush with death on the Hebron pass, may have somehow acted as a catalyst, stimulating some part of the brain in an awakening. The boffin's he spoke with many years later at Mi6 HQ, Century house, London told him, "Some of us are late bloomers", and that was that.

When stationed In Palestine in 1946, Pimm liked the fact he now had an edge to some of his commanding officers and often when foreigners spoke he gave no inference he understood their language, learning precisely what they thought of the English soldiers, on a side note it assisted calming many of the inflammatory situations that occurred in the streets when they were on patrol. But for Pimm an unexpected bonus he soon found out, with each language he learnt, added to his mystery with the girls he would meet, who in the past he had noticed often looked at rank first.

His new XO Steve Bowman even got in on the act, getting Pimm to teach him specific sweetheart phrases, that he then incorporated into the letters he wrote to his wife, to impress her with his affections.

Meanwhile, Orran Danis charged nothing for this additional language tuitions, it should have been Pimm's first heads up that everything about the Turk was not kosher and those that were supposed to be keeping an eye on Pimm's progress Roger Thake should have smelt a rat.

"So, take this, you know the story of the man in the iron mask?" Orran Danis asked as he had the book stamped out on loan from the library. He had a unique way of teaching, by giving a pupil a book they may know or have read in their own language, that way as they read in the foreign words, phrases and images would connect and cross over.

"The French King?" Pimm said, trying to recollect the film Aunty Vic had taken him to at the Dominion in Tottenham Court Road, she would always be Aunty Vic to him.

"I have a copy at my home; my mother is making fresh honey Kanafeh tomorrow night, if you have never had it you should come. This is the address, above the back of the barbers in King George Avenue, it's perfectly safe, my brother has a taxi he will have you back before curfew."

Pimm knew the road and the area as being predominately Muslim, to date all attacks on British soldiers that had occurred in towns and cities had been confined to general or Jewish quarters. This was because the Israelis did not wish to antagonise further the Muslims who would have been roused to action if their homes and business had been raided and affected by the British because an attack had taken place in their territory.

"Good, so that is settled I will tell my mother. Unfortunately, she suffered an accident in a chemical fire, she is blind, not my student. She only speaks Turkish but loves to hear a different voice, accent." he corrected himself, and Pimm then noticed Orran Danis's reaction as he asked,

"Would it be alright if I bring my Sarg. Bows, I'm more likely to get the pass?" by now because of the increase in hostilities, it was rare if ever for a British soldier to move off base without at least one partner.

Orran Danis thought for a second and then nodded his agreement, "Sure, sure, maybe we have a friendly game of skittles?"

Pimm told Steve Bowman about the invite, and once he had spoken with base operations, they were given the green light. Major Thake was for once on Pimm's case and personally signed the unusual off base jaunt, reporting it along with Pimm's progress to Bull Gordon, advising he considered the ability to converse with the natives and build a network of contacts was a prerequisite to playing the game. Even if at that moment Pimm did not know he was being assessed by Thake, every experience that was outside the confines of the regimented base life would only assist Pimm, if he was to become a Mi6 spy in the future.

When Bowman received the word, they had been granted the leave of camp he was informed they must go armed and be back in camp by nine while it was still comparatively light, they set off from Sarafand at four-thirty on the afternoon of 15th July 1956.

Orran Danis's extended family lived in a two-storey apartment that was behind barbers. Approached by the side door the steps ran up onto an open terrace where the family had made a small plot to grow tomatoes and cucumbers, a few seats sat round a converted oil drum barbecue that could be lowered as a deck fire. There was even an extended sandy area where they played skittles, the deck had only a two-foot-high parapet edge wall that ran along the side and back and sitting on it, if you leaned back too far you would fall to the street below. Pimm noticed there was no guard rail as children played, sometimes dangerously close to the edge, but all knew the risk, and none ever fell, in fact, some of the teenagers would hang down as far as they could then drop the remaining distance, to avoid going via the room and stairs to reach the street.

The kitchen and lounge were open-plan, located on the terrace floor with the bedrooms on the second floor, which also had access to a smaller terrace roof above via a fire exit.

When Pimm and Bowman pulled up at the front, they looked up and could see the silhouettes of men sitting on the terrace parapet wall smoking, who watched them park next to a pair of old taxis. One of the men waved down at them, it was Orran, and he came down the stairs, in open-toe sandals and what looked like army regulation khaki shorts, a change from his pristine suit, but he still wore a starched white short-sleeved shirt as white as the bright smile on his expression, as his foot slipped off the last wooden step into a small open porch way which sat at street level.

"This is my XO Staff Sergeant Bowman, a friend." Pimm Introduced Bowman.

Bowman saluted "As Salām u ʻAlaykum." Orran smile appeared to widen if that was possible at Bowman's effort at a polite greeting.

"Wa Alaikum Assalam," he said, holding out his hand and bowing his head, both Pimm and Bowman knew most Muslims typically avoided shaking hands, shaking hands in a westerner's greeting style.

"I am pleased to meet you, perhaps with my family, we can forget tonight." and he held his hand up gesturing like a salute. "No disrespect intended Sir, but some are old, and they would not want to upset a guest by not standing" Orran's eyes flitted between the two soldiers looking for their understanding.

"No problem when in Rome, unfortunately, we must keep these with us, it was a condition of us coming" Bowman tapped the strap of his Lee-Enfield rifle slung over his shoulder. However, it wasn't, a sidearm was the only stipulation, but Bowman felt safer with a couple of rifles.

"As long as you put them down to eat, otherwise there will be no room on the table for the food." Orran joked and gestured to the door entrance and stairs.

"Of course," Bowman replied, and both soldiers slung their rifles upside down.

"Good, good, come we have lamb shish, I hope you are hungry, my mother may be blind and again with no offence intended, but she can still cook, better than an army chef, in my humble opinion." he kissed his fingers.

Pimm allowed Bowman to go first, and as they stepped off the pavement into the porch, before they placed a foot on the first tread of the stairs that led up to Orran's home each of them automatically checked the room beyond the glass door to their left, with its closed for business hanging sign, the entrance to the barbers salon.
Arriving on the terrace, Bowman gave a glance back down at their vehicle, and along the small street at the few cars parked either side of the shop and flat entrance of their building, the army Land Rover was hardly inconspicuous.
"I am Asil, Orran's brother-in-law welcome, your jeep, sorry Land Rover, I know how you fellows are about the vehicle, a Welsh soldier explained once, your Landy." Asil pointed back down to the street and his own taxi as he welcomed them, "It will be fine no one will touch it, or you here, you are our guests, you may relax." With that, he held out two cold bottles of Stella beer, Pimm looked to Bowman and noticed they had bottles of Efes on the table. Knowing they were Muslim the fact that they were drinking and had taken time to get a western beer to some extent immediately changed Bowman's threat concerns, as the pair had their expressions read by Asil as he handed them the bottles.
"Yes some Muslims drink, not all of us are the same. Personally, I believe we should each take from our religion what we can live with. When we meet Allah, praise be his name, or you meet your God, I am sure there will be greater sins he will ask us to explain that we have done, rather than why we shared some water mixed with herbs.....with friends and family and family is everything, in my humble opinion, aadab arz hai." Asil made the Aadab hand gesture, his smile was a comfort even though his teeth were stained gold by years of harsh tobacco.
"Tasleem" Pimm responded, and Orran then led the way and introduced the soldiers to the other men folk of the family first, before presenting them to Orran's mother.
"Thank you for welcoming us to your home." Bowman said,
"The lamb smells sweet." Pimm followed in Turkish, remembering what Orran had said regarding his mother enjoying accents and immediately the old ladies eyes began to flit back and forth excitably. She had less than three teeth in her gums, but her smile was as wide as the genuine hospitality of the family group of Turks, none of whom, apart from Asil were aware of the real motive for inviting Pimm.
"Fresh rosemary and garlic," she said as one of the older men basted a large leg joint on the half oil drum.

The air was filled with the smell of coffee, Pimm noticed that strategically set around the deck floor were small ashtray sized decorative dishes each held dried coffee, that smouldered in an effort to discourage the flies, and he was surprised to see how well it appeared to work. The flies in Palestine he remembered in later years as being like formula one racing cars, buzzing around a Grand Prix circuit.
The meal was a mixture of meze with lamb as the main dish, with fresh whole roasted peppers that dribbled melted goats cheese in oregano, the rice in itself was a meal, surrounded with a plethora of small bowls each containing an

accompanying dish or sauce, all served on a two low, intricately carved wide bleached timber planks, that Pimm realised must have once been ancient doors, in seeing the remains of rusted hinge ironwork on his side, he looked to the doorway down to the street and considered they were each too large to have been brought up the stairs and must have once belonged to an impressive sized building as both soldiers took their place opposite each other and sat cross-legged on the rugged floor and as bowls were passed back and forth sampling each dish they ate as their host did with fingers.

The men together at one end, some drank beer, while the women all drank water and wore low face veil's, except Orran's mother, who the other women sat around in a semicircle, as she drank from a bottle of Efes like the men.

Following the main course there was a short interlude of smoking and chatting, before the deserts that included the mothers homemade Kanafeh, a shredded dry pastry noodle dessert of layers of thick syrup and nabulsi cheese, complimented the strong Turkish coffee served in traditional small heavily enamelled cups, some set with gold leaf and semi-precious gems. The Danis family were bringing out their most beautiful wares for their guest, including the rugs they sat on that rarely came out to the deck.

Afterwards the soldiers were invited to play skittles, and of course, Pimm and Bowman gave the Danis men a run, but with a surreptitious glance from Bowman, Pimm allowed their host the final victory. They retired to share in the smoking of the two nargiles set on brass dishes, the bubbling infused tea hookah that was as strong as it was potent.

After the second time, Pimm had been passed the pipe he felt decidedly worse for wear, making his excuses, to the jeers of some of the Turkish men and Bowman, who continued to puff away like the caterpillar in Alice and Wonderland, he retired to wash his face and considered making himself sick.

On the way up to the third floor small shower room on the small corridor landing, he passed an open bedroom door and glancing through the door jamb, witnessed Orran Danis having what looked like a heated exchange with his brother-in-law Asil. Their voices were kept low, and he realised he had not noticed them leave the group. They did not see him, and he continued up the stairs. Having doused his head with water, he held his wrists under the running tap for some time to cool his blood, while listening out to hear for anyone else approaching, soon he felt decidedly better.

Coming back down the bedroom door where he had witnessed the exchange was now closed, but he got the distinct impression the men were still behind the door. Stealthily he took to the lower stair whereon, the lower floor opposite the kitchen he came across the mother sitting in the open lounge fronting the main street. The other younger women sat silently at her feet as she rocked back and forth, fondling the edges of what looked like a photograph album. Touching each image as she prayed, her bind eyes streamed tears which Pimm had always believed did not happen with the blind.

Pimm looked back up the stairs and then approached her slowly, "What is it mother, may I get your sons?" he said softly in Turkish, looking to the other female family members for inspiration, but their eyes focused forward avoiding contact with his, and they said nothing. Pimm took a step closer and he could see in detail the images captured in the selection of black and white photographs of varying sizes, some of which were old pre-war, cut with crinkled edges, each carefully pasted to a timeline page, some showing Orran Danis as a young boy with his mother, older brother-in-law and a girl, who Pimm took to be Orran's sister. Pimm looked at the women in the room and realised Asil had not introduced his wife.

As he watched the old lady, still sobbing quietly to herself, turn the pages, feeling the edge of each photograph as if remembering the image it contained. In some, the girl appeared between Orran and Asil, clearly, as teenagers, they were very close. Pimm smiled, seeing that Asil had far more teeth. Then and as the old women turned the pages back and forth, Pimm snatched a glimpse of a wedding photo. Orran's brother-in-law was with the same girl but older, perhaps in their early twenties. Pimm's first instinct again was to look at the women sitting, and he realised the girl in the photograph was absent from the group that night. He looked back at the book as a page turned, another picture captured, moments after the wedding with rice being thrown at the couple either side of another man who held their hands up as if presenting the couple to the family, It could have been Orran, but with his back to the Camera and hunched from ducking from the rice being thrown, it was hard to tell. But what Pimm did recognise was that on Asil's head he wore a kippah, the Jewish head cover and on his shoulders a shawl carrying the mark of the Star of David.

Pimm had only a moment to digest that quandary when the old lady turned the book pages back to the right and pages that were of earlier years. Four images on a double page made Pimm step back in disbelief, on either side it showed Orran Danis as a much younger man still in his late teens early twenties, standing with other soldiers some were Turks, others were German, and they were all wearing Wehrmacht uniforms. On a separate image, one showed proud parents, clearly, Orran's father, suited and his mother looking at her son with adoring eyes and not blind. The old lady turned the page to a single staged sweetheart photograph, typical of the era of the Second World War. Orran Danis stood next to a Roman urn with flowers in a portrait pose. He was dressed in some sort of Nazi SS uniform Pimm had not seen before, he did, however, notice the medal bar on his chest.

As he committed the image to memory, he heard the men coming down the stairs from above, still deep in conversation, Pimm reached over the old ladies lap and turned the page over to a picture of the family when the boys were children, just as the men arrived at the door.

"Sorry to intrude, something appears to be distressing your mother?" Pimm said, feeling his face flush the brother in law looked at Orran and scowled.

"Ask him!" Asil growled impatiently in Turkish.
Orran looked to Pimm he knew he would understand the words and he shook his head, then looked to his mother and the album.
"Ask him for Meriam?" Asil insisted and walked off back towards the outside terrace.

Pimm immediately began to feel they had overstepped their welcome and began to sense an ulterior motive to his invitation, which made him feel uneasy, he looked past Orran through to the terrace and could see their rifles still standing, leaning against a timber shelving unit. Although he had questions regarding the pictures of Orran in a Nazi uniform, he decided to hold back, considering a confrontation in front of the women may escalate, better to ask in the light of day, on-base ground, but he could not merely ignore Asil's words.
"What is it, Orran? What does your brother want?" he asked.
Orran Danis looked at his mother and taking the book from her hands, kissed her comfortingly on the forehead, placing the photo album on a side shelf he picked up a photo frame with the image of the young woman
"She is my sister, Meriam," Orran said, as he passed it to Pimm.
Pimm looked at the image of the women she had long jet black hair, oval eyes crowned with long lashes, she was quite stunning, probably in her early twenties, then Pimm noticed the photographer's date stamp 1940. Pimm considered she must be around thirty now. "She is very beautiful," Pimm said and went to hand the picture back.
"Yes, she is." Orran was about to elaborate when at that exact moment Steve Bowman stepped into to house looking for the way to the toilets.
"Ollie, I think it is time we thanked these people for their hospitality, time to get back to base." his tone was friendly, but Pimm recognised it was also a reference to the curfew and order, as he watched his friend disappear up the stairs, Pimm's eyes drifted outside to their weapons, that still stood untouched as they had left them.
Orran turned to Pimm and gestured to the photograph album "I know you saw the picture of me in uniform."
Pimm again checked their guns and was about to say "So you fought for the Germans?" in an off the cuff manner to diffuse the situation, but Orran held up his hands
"Not now, there is no time, I will explain when we meet after lessons on Tuesday, it is a complicated story; you need to hear it all before you judge, please say nothing,.....but don't worry I will understand if you do, it will cause a little upset, but will all work out, it was a long time ago, I leave it to you, do what is in your heart," he said.
Then he did something strange and unclipped the back of the frame and handed it to Pimm,
"Trust me, I will explain all, as I say I know you saw my uniform if it was such a secret would I leave it on display?" Orran Danis looked to the photograph album, this action and comment clouded Pimm's judgement and successfully deflected his

sense of duty to report what he had seen. He was hooked and realised he was going to get no answers that night, besides the Germans at least the West German's were no longer the enemy as far as he knew.

Pimm nodded his agreement, "Thank you for letting us into your home, I wish you and your family best wishes for the future," Pimm said in his best Turkish to the mother as he left the room.

Outside, Asil stepped forward from the other men folk and held out his hand, "Thank you, Mr Pimm, I hope my brother-in-law is right about you, I hope you can help, my family." But Orran came alongside and shook his head, signalling they had not spoken, at which point Asil moved away from the group clearly disturbed, Pimm let it slide as bounced out onto the terrace, his hair and top of his shirt wet having doused himself in water to shake off like Pimm had earlier some of the intoxications from the evening's lubrication. He was oblivious to Pimm's exchange with the brothers as he picked up his rifle and handed Pimm his. "Right let's be off before they send out the cavalry." Bowman joked, and they said their farewells, with many of the family leaning over the high terrace wall to watch them depart in their jeep.

With the afternoon sun beginning to drop into the horizon the journey back to base was fortunately uneventful, although both men were on edge watching for any vehicle lights ahead and behind for signs of an ambush.

As Pimm sat back allowing the warm evening air rush over his face, amongst other questions regarding his language tutors background spinning around Pimm's skull, he was considering if he should discuss the photographs he had seen with Steve Bowman, knowing his Sergeant would almost certainly report it to HQ.

His decision not to say anything that night would haunt Pimm in later years as a lack of judgement, not trusting a true friend. And the following day Pimm had still not mentioned it as he was ribbed about the girl in the photograph having left it on his pillow.

"She's old enough to be your mum, Tomo." Pimm pointed to the date, responding to one of his bunkmate's bawdy jeer, as Bowman also noticed the picture.

"What's this Ollie you never have family snaps, who's this lovely?" Bowman immediately recognised the age and the style of the girl and quickly put two and two together, with their evening meal.

"So it wasn't just a friendly invite, who is she? You know some of the cheeky Arabs are trying to set our boys up with their daughters, for a new life in Blighty?" Bowman looked at Pimm with a discerning eye.

"No idea Staff. the Turk teacher, Orran handed it to me before we left, said it was his sister, Asil's wife, the one with no teeth, could be she's trying to get in?" Pimm flipped it over and placed it back inside his bunk locker.

"Well don't get suckered in with family shit and don't make promises you can't keep. I knew they had us up there for a reason. Never mind, the meat was good, and the beer was free, just make sure it stays that way." Bowman then handed him another letter.

"What's this, Steve?" Pimm asked.

"It's yours, I want you to be the boys Godfather, I ran it by the Wassik, *(Which is how Bowman referred to Mrs Bowman)*, she agreed. Anyway, I had a word with the XO we've got three days leave in Blighty, managed to get us a couple of seats on a Shackleton going back to Cambridge for a refit. A week tomorrow, unless you have anything better on your dance card, might even introduce you to my cousin June." Bowman looked at Pimm's locker, where he had placed the photograph of Miriam, Pimm could see he was thinking of taking it further.
Pimm tapped the letter in his hand drawing Bowman attention back and was going to ask a question, but Bowman already knew the request forming on Pimm's lips and forgot about the picture of the girl.
"I'll make sure you get time to see your Aunt Vic, invite her to the christening if you like." Bowman slapped Pimm on the back.
Pimm also forgot all about Orran Danis's his sister and the German uniform that evening as he sat down and wrote to Vic McDonald, letting her know about the Bowman's christening and to go use some of that pay packed he had been sending home and buy herself a new hat, "The bigger, the better." he wrote.

Come Monday on standing at attention on parade Pimm along with the rest of Juno Squad were informed that over the next week they were to assist with surveying potential borderlines, in a particularly sensitive area. Some sort of truce had been arranged with the terrorist's, because of the religious Jewish festival of Shivah Asar B' Tammuz, in which the British had let it be known if they could carry out the survey task with a week without fear of attack, no stop and search sorties would be carried out during the festival period.
At this point, Pimm's new experience with previous assignments to the surveying teams came into its own, as the officer he was assigned too was taken sick with the Sarafand shits. The XO organising the survey having established Pimm could do the necessary asked if he knew anyone with the smarts to act as his staff carrier and pointer.
"It's just someone to hold the rod, I'm sure my Staff can sort that, and with a couple of lads from my squad, we won't need an additional security detail," Pimm winked at Bowman,
"Well if you're sure Pimm, would kill two birds, I'm stretched over the next week, they pulled a squad of your chaps down to Gaza a big wig flying in from Blighty apparently, this latest détente has opened up a doorway, let's just hope, Stern abides by the rules, keeping your eyes peeled out there, no matter what HQ says."
Pimm turned his head and raised his eyes at Bowman, as he looked towards a Turkish maintenance worker changing a fluorescent strip light in the next office, knowing it was unnecessary, talk like that got people killed, but the XO, bundled a dozen cardboard map tubes together and handed them to Pimm and allowed the Staff Sergeant and two others from Juno squad to assist him. "You know the drill Pimm, don't make a meal of it," he said, and Pimm and Bowman saluted and left.
Pimm had worked in the area they were assigned on a previous occasion and already knew the average reading tally for the other officer leading the other survey

teams and what score was required, so once he had ensured they had reached their target each day and generally superseded it, the four soldiers spent the next three days out of earshot of a command.

How they reached his daily goal was ingenious, they nabbed two additional reading staffs from the stores, so Pimm set up his Tripod in one central fixed point then had the other three set at equal distances behind in front and to the highest point on either side allowing Pimm to rotate taking three readings at a time. He just altered the times on each reading in the logbook, but was taking on average nine readings in the same time it took the other survey teams to take four, those that still had survey rods.

On returning to Sarafand, Pimm was informed, Orran Danis had been to camp to see why he had missed his language lesson on Tuesday. It was then Pimm remembered his sister Miriam and the photographs and again considered having a word with Bowman about seeing an image of Orran Danis in a German uniform. He had no idea why he decided to hold off talking with his friend, but he would regret it for the rest of his life.

Pimm went to his usual language lesson on Friday he was now just starting to learn Russian, having recently taken a written test in German. Danis said nothing during the morning, but at the end gestured Pimm to remain,

"To discuss the marking of your last test," he said loud enough for the other officers and students of the class to hear.

"I thought you had forgotten about me, my friend," Orran said, even though he knew the brigade had been pulled out by tactical, to carry out the land survey.

"Topo had us out in the field for a few days, army, you go when and where." Pimm began lightly, but began to feel somewhat aggrieved at clearly being used, "you would know something about that, being one of Adolf's boys" he added but felt the sarcasm did him no justice.

"Yes, I can see it looks bad, it was a different time, I was younger than you are now when they caught me, Turkey, Germany they were friends back then, Britain was the enemy, we didn't know what was going on in Europe with the Jews, if that is what concerns you, just like I am sure your people back home have no idea what happens here now, sometimes on the beaches."

"You can't compare the two, any way you working for the Germans, do you think it would have made a difference if you knew the shit they were giving our people or what they were doing with the Jews." Pimm snapped response was unlike him, but now as they spoke he began to feel more as if he had been played and above all upset that Danis had involved Bowman in something that could cause both of them as British soldier problems, Danis's response took Pimm by surprise.

"No I don't suppose it would, like you I was a soldier, you never really know what is in the mind of those that send you to try and kill another, I have nothing against any race, that is why I love to learn and teach language," he said with explicit knowledge of the acts of inhumanity perpetrated by the Nazi's, that still played in some newsreels.

"So you were a Nazi" Pimm watched Orran's eyes "and decorated!" he could see the word made him uncomfortable. "and SS, if the uniform was right, how does that work with the blonde, blue eyes thing they had going?" Orran Danis shook his head "I have no idea, my friend, they were in charge, their world, their rules" he whispered, "and before you ask, I never killed an Englishmen, I can tell you that. I never saw one till the end of the war."

"So you say." Pimm snapped, aware Orran had clearly been preparing for some time for their meeting and he sat in silence as the language teacher, whose friendship he now doubted as being truly genuine, explained that during World War II, his father, a strict disciplinarian, had been a senior chemist working for the I. G. Farben chemical company for the Reich. A company along with Schering AG and Degussa, responsible for development and production of the cyanide-based pesticide. Which was what Zyklon B. that was used in the Holocaust Death camps was originally developed from. Being the chemist only son, Orran had been recruited initially into the Wehrmacht, not because his father wanted it, according to Orran, although something in the way he spoke gave Pimm the distinct impression, his father had been a supporter of the Nazi's, irrespective that the Turk made the legitimate case that initially it was a way the Nazi's kept loyalty leverage over their essential non-German skilled workers, ensuring they remained committed to the cause. And because of his father high status, Orran was assigned to a security detail, so that the senior German intelligence officer was able to keep an eye on him, within the SS.

"I was good at the job they gave me, mostly I worked as a go-between, using my language skills again as I do now. Back then, the German's liked speaking German, like the British, English. Now, today, they have had to learn other languages. I was involved, as you do now security and looking for those aiding the Allies, yes the British and there were deaths, it was war. But I swear I never killed any English soldiers." Pimm listened without interrupting as Orran told his story as he chain-smoked, but noted he specifically said, English soldiers.

"I came into it late, they already knew they had lost the war planning their escapes long before it was over in Europe. One of the SS officers fled with a great deal of my father's research, he killed my father and all those involved in his work. My mother was a technician at the same plant, the officer destroyed the plant, the gas is what blinded her, I think chlorine, I am not sure, it was bad." Orran Danis's voice held true emotion and regret.

"I see but what of your sister how does she come into this, where is she?" Pimm pictured the time frame of images Orran was speaking of interjecting images he had seen at the cinema, to piece together a coherent visual record that would be plausible.

"It was the only good thing I was able to do at that time, my rank, and in the position, I held with the Nazi's, but I would do anything for Meriam." Pimm judged these words were honest and held a sense of pride, "Asil my brother-in-law, he is a Jew," he saw Pimm's questioning look, "I know right, Muslim and Jew, well it's what happened, and happens, more than you think, love knows nothing about religion or racial difference, especially when it happens far from a homeland."

Orran spoke of receiving word, that following an informant's disclosure Asil was caught in a Jewish trawling operation by the Nazi's and that Orran managed to use his position attached to the intelligence of the SS to get him out from the camp, as far as the Nazi's at that time were concerned he was shot in an interrogation. "I got them out and sent them here, they were safe for a while, until the British."

"So what is the problem he is Jewish, he is already in Palestine, don't tell me he is illegal, I don't want to know, this Orran, I'm in enough shit already, right now I can walk away, the schooling ends and we part...maybe not friends any more, but you go back to your life, I go back to mine." Pimm looked away, remembering Bowman's warning.

"No he's here, all his papers are now correct, your people have no problem with Asil, it's my sister Meriam." Orran Danis said, sitting back with his palms open.

Pimm thought for a moment "She converted; don't tell me she had it changed on her papers, her religion?"

Orran nodded his head "Yes and she crossed the border for the child, you met him on the terrace, maybe you don't know he was there watching you play skittles with your friend." Orran was clever, adding this to take Pimm back to a moment of friendship shared, between them.

"The boy was sick, needed some medicine an injection, they could not get from your people, Penicillin, he has asthma. Anyway, when she tried to cross the border on her return she was detained, now I think maybe she is on her way to Cyprus if she is not there already? I need to find her." Orran looked for a sign of compassion on Pimm's eyes, and Pimm gestured he understood even though he did not know why the Danis family had sent a woman in the first place, it seemed cowardly and against the nature of this man he once trusted.

"She managed to get the drugs to us, but because of her situation, there were complications." Orran looked at Pimm as if checking to see he was really taking all the information in.

"What complications?" Pimm really did not want to ask.

"She was pregnant, that is why she went, we thought it would be easier for her to cross over, it was stupid, my fault, now she is God knows where, with the child." Orran's eyes began to well. "So stupid, your people normally only stop the men, fighting age, they still are...as you say squeamish of searching our women."

"So what is it you want from me Orran, what do you think I can do, I'm just a bloody Corporal?" Pimm's neck began to burn, and he wanted to be anywhere but there, even on patrol, but it was time to cut to the chase.

"Maybe you know someone, maybe you can find what has happened to her, I have tried, my family have been to the commission." Orran went to speak, but Pimm interrupted.

"But because of the false papers, you had made for your brother-in-law you cannot prove she is of Turkish birth without exposing him as a Jew and you for working with the German's I understand." Pimm sighed and lit another cigarette as the pieces of the puzzle Orran had fed him all slotted together, he sensed there was more and that it was probably somewhat more complicated but he knew all he needed to know and want to know no more, believing the story held a solid ring of truth and made sense, But Orran had been playing the game a long time and knew he had Pimm as he watched him shake his head and offer him one of his own cigarettes.

"As I said, I'm just a squaddie, this is beyond me, you need Staff for this?" Pimm leaned forward and lit Orran's cigarette with his lighter.

"That's not true they sent you to me, with the other officers, they never do that No disrespect, but not for one that talks like you … with your accent, you're not the same as the other's in the class." Orran had been around enough British to know the class system that distinguished well-bred officers from the other ranks. "Someone is helping you, someone, you know." Orran insisted.

Pimm shook his head thinking of his Aunt and what she had done to aid him as a child and what she would expect from him, "No, no one knows me in the army just the Sergeant, and he has no money, I was told this language course was standard training when they put me on the Topo course, I'm just here to learn language, I still shovel shit at the latrines. I can have a word with Sergeant Bowman for you, if you like?" Pimm was unconvinced of Danis's motives and was becoming increasingly uncomfortable with the suggestion that he was something other than a squaddie, as he thought back to his debriefing following the attack below the Hebron pass incident and the loss of Amber, how he was first introduced to Orran and then had been assigned to the survey teams, but he said nothing as he realised now looking at it that two were probably connected.

"Maybe it is someone you have helped, someone you impressed, it is the sort of thing an intelligence officer would do, to see if you could be trained, it is the sort of thing I would have done." Orran pushed, but his suggestion was a little too casual for Pimm, "my reports on the progress of the students here including your own go to your headquarters, if you can find who reads them, then you will know who is watching you, and then maybe you can see if they can help Miriam." Orran had it already figured out a course of action, and that worried Pimm the most.

This man was no longer just a teacher, he was a calculating individual that had just admitted to working for German SS intelligence, all be it if he were to be believed as a junior advisor. Pimm now wished he had paid more attention to the pictures in the old woman's photograph album, but now something else began to bother him, regarding his own future and once again he thought back to his debriefing, with Major Smith.

Smith, Christ! Of course, it's Smith, he thought, but gave nothing away to Orran as he considered the motives behind Smith arranging his promotion and advancement. The only thing that made sense to Pimm was that it may have been some kind of behind the scenes trade-off, for his agreeing to allow the citation he had earned at Hebron pass to hot to Tilley.

Now as he sat opposite Danis he considered seriously that Smith was likely to be a phoney name, the fact he knew at least one real John Smith from Woodhouse Road, Finchley, had countered any previous speculation on his part, but now believed Orran was right, Smith could be Military Intelligence and perhaps it had something to do with Tilley's family back in Great Britain, if his father was some sort of bigwig back home the military might have been covering the bases, preventing some sort stink kicking off. That was all Pimm could come up with, he still did not realise it was all about him, and Bull Gordon's eye for spotting talent.

"I don't know what I can do, you will have to let me think on this, I'll let you know, if I come to the lessons, if I don't come, you know my answer." Pimm saw the disappointment in Orran eyes, but now he no longer trusted the man that sat across with him.
"You will at least try, yes?" Orran said, "I am worried my brother-in-law may be talking with others, to see if they can help find her. I am so desperate for news, he is a less patient man and loves her very much." Orran Danis spoke with sentiment but calmly and Pimm got a distinct feeling there was an underlining warning, almost a threat.
"I said! I'll see what I can do Orran, in the meantime, I think it better I stop coming to your lessons for now, if my enquires are picked up it could make trouble for you and me, my friend," Pimm deliberately added the latter and watched Orran's reaction
"If you think that is best of course, but please try." Orran gestured his understanding with a nod, but was clearly unsatisfied.

Over the following days, Pimm ran through the list of executive officers he had come into touch with since arriving in Palestine. None he considered were the type he would wish to approach with this matter. Furthermore, because he had already decided to entirely isolate Steve Bowman from the situation, he decided not to mention his discussion regarding the sister's whereabouts with the Staff Sergeant. Fortunately at that time Bowman was too preoccupied to notice Pimm was troubled, focusing on their forthcoming return to England and clawing back as much money as he could that he had loaned out at one time or other, whilst selling any souvenirs he had come across to the new boys on camp, to raise funds to pay for the after christening bash his wife had organized at the Bull and Butcher, pub.
Two days later Pimm had still done nothing regarding Orran's problem, and then without warning, he was promoted to Lance Corporal, on the day of parade standing in the Sarafand drill square, amongst the ranks of others that were to be honoured, he caught sight of Major Smith on the officer's platform and it hit him, he had been the one that instigated his meeting with Orran Danis, if he was military intelligence he would know what to do and if it came down to it, Pimm even considered retracting his statement that Tilley and set the record straight that Lieutenant Tilley had, through inexperience at least assisted the deaths of the Amber squad members.

There was an open tent refreshment service for all officers and the soldiers being honoured after the parade was passed out, but as Pimm approached the tent he was surprised that It was Smith that approached him first, appearing to catch Pimm's eye while in conversation with other senior officers including the base commander and stepped away to great Pimm as he was handed, a new drink that was becoming the rage.

"A Pimm's for Pimm, how apt," an insincere smile crept across the Majors lips as he studied Pimm, and then switched immediately to speaking in French, "how are you, I hear good things since we last spoke."

"Well Sir, and you" Pimm responded in German

"Very good, I said you smart cookie the first time we met." Thake looked at Pimm and knew instantly Bull had been right in choosing the Corporal, totally unaware of Pimm problem with Danis.

"And who was that too, if I may ask respectfully Sir." Pimm placed his glass on the table without drinking it.

"All in good time Pimm, all in good time," Thake smirked casually and drew Pimm out of earshot of any others as he informed him that he was from military intelligence and had been monitoring Pimm's progress.

"To be honest lad it was more what you didn't do, that what you did, that impressed us, you'll catch on I'm sure, but in our game, less is more sometimes." Smith teased. And as e spoke Pimm was surprised how informed he was of his progress and his activities since Hebron pass, he knew the stats and facts of the tests scores Danis had marked and details of the works he had carried out with the Signals Corp survey team and then dropped a bombshell to prove that he was serious by reverting to Russian, which Pimm only just understood

"I thought nicking the extra rods for your mates to play hook was inspiring" Thake said and handed Pimm a photograph that showed Pimm, Bowman and the two other members of Juno squad that he had used during the three day survey operation, laying back in the sun drinking with their shirts off, it what they had considered at the time was a remote sheltered and secluded hilltop.

Pimm went to defend and protect the others in the picture. "That was my idea, Sir," he said, trying to work out how the picture had been taken and why?

"I knew you'd say that , don't worry old fruit, bin it or keep it as a souvenir, if I'm right by the time you're done you'll not get caught napping like that again and call me Roger, Roger Thake, I'd rather start on a good footing." Thake held out his hand as he reverted to English. Pimm accepted it and then listened trying not to react as Thake boasted it was he that granted the joint pass for him and Bowman to travel home.

"Here's the thing before you leave for Blighty, I think we should have a chin wag, proper sit-down. Consider it a career opportunity assessment interview, a chance to get a glimpse of what's in store if you decide to take the plunge." Thake said, and then invited Pimm to meet with him at the officers club in the King David hotel in Jerusalem where he was staying.

Their actual meeting would be private, but understanding the ruling of pairing servicemen together during off base movements, Thake suggested he bring along Steve Bowman as a chaperone, Thake would arrange the paperwork.

"Think of it this way, what have you to lose, the least I can promise you, and your pal is a free lunch and some cool draft beer." Thake had a manner that was unlike most officers Pimm had met before, and he studied his uniform, noticing how it appeared tailored and new.

"Regardless of the outcome, Steve Bowman's going back home to see his family right, Roger," Pimm asked.

"Of course what do you think we are Indian givers?" Thake actually looked offended, and Pimm decided to agree to the meeting, considering regardless of what Thake had to say it would be the perfect opportunity to ask about Orran's sister and get the whole mess behind him.

On the morning of Monday, July 22, 1946, Bowman, Pimm and the rest of Juno squad left the base at 07.00 to assist in roadblocks for the market roads. Working in tandem with Delta they switched early morning for a routine sweep of the bustling side streets, Bowman and Pimm were excused by their CO and returned to shower and change into their formal uniforms.

"I hope this bloke is going to spring for booze otherwise all this grafting to take some wedge *(money)* home will have been wasted, I've only ever been in the Regence café once. It's ok bit posh, they have Heineken on draft." Bowman counted out some of the notes he had saved for home, taking a third he folded and pocketed them, then put the remainder back in his bed locker.

"Don't worry Bowsy I've got a bit stashed away at home no sprog's, no old lady, well apart from Vic and she lives off bubble and squeak and her nightly Horlicks, that and the odd bottle of Mackeson on race days." Pimm joked and grabbed some money from the bottom of his kit bag.

Meeting Major Smith/Roger Thake again had lightened Pimm's mood and to an extent he felt a rock had been lifted from his shoulders realising, whoever the officer was, he could clearly pull strings, the photograph of them playing hooky while carrying out the surveys proved that, if anyone could sort out the mess with Orran Danis, he could. Pimm should have destroyed it, but instead folded it nine times and buried it in a sock inside his kit bag and for a moment considered showing Bowman as he took out his money.

"The benefits of being young, how I remember that, make the most of it," Bowman said, replacing his army issue combination lock to his locker.

"Well, I look at it like this Staff. Without your sprog, we wouldn't be going on leave." Pimm winked and left the photograph in his bag.

Jerusalem was like a twenty-four-hour carnival of industry in 1946, with street vendors and stalls on every street corner, the noise and bustle of the city had a vibrant atmosphere that ignored the hidden tensions, a great many of its inhabitants had already survived far worse. At times it was like an over

wound watch spring, every backfire and every heavily closed car door raised eyes making many hunch their shoulders. But nothing would stop the industrious nature of a people that never felt as free than working for their own design and future. And while the sweat smells that drifted in the air from the fresh vegetable, and fruit stalls overpowered the unsanitary conditions of the time, the noise of traffic competed with a chorus of cottage rear shop industries that harmonized the sounds that seemed to come from every open shop doorway of a tailors foot-propelled Singer sewing machine or the tapping's of a leatherworker, jeweller or cobbler at a vice.

On the 22nd July 1946, Bowman drove Pimm through the city, passed the regular checkpoints and all seemed as normal as it could be, for a city, living on a pounder keg of rebellion, taxis lined up two streets away from the King David hotel as drivers dozed in their cars, then shuffled forward when prompted by a sharp toot of the horn from behind each time a vehicle was taken up by one of the hotels on the same street as the King David and as the traffic pulled to a halt again with Bowman focusing on the car in front, Pimm noticed Orran Danis brother Asil behind the wheel of the nearest taxi in the rank on his right and Orran Danis was reading a newspaper, sitting in the fare seats behind, which Pimm thought a little strange, Danis dropped the paper slightly as he turned the page and their eyes locked through his open car window. Pimm's initial thought was the wish to let him know he was going to meet with Roger Thake at The King David to ask about his sister. He saw Danis look forward to Asil and then the traffic ahead moved and Bowman sped away when prompted by the whistle of a British traffic officer. The moment was fleeting but left Pimm wondering about the coincidence of Orran being in the city at the same time as Bowman searched for a place to park. The Regence parking was full, so the Staff Sergeant parked in a military overflow compound off from the square.
"You never guess who I just saw?" Pimm said, about to tell Bowman as they walked back down King David Street, then stopped mid-sentence as ahead he saw Orran Danis waving and coming towards them.

At this point, the specific events that took place in Jerusalem at the King David Hotel are well documented but in the future looking back Oliver Pimm's recollections as someone who was caught up in the events of that day, like many participants, both the willing and unwilling from this point is stripped, like a shredded early black and white cine film, jumping from one scene to another, brief flash's of between four and ten-second bursts of memory and distorted time.
Pimm recalls stuffing some notes into Steve Bowman's hand, as his friend took to the first steps up to the hotel entrance and saying something like, "You go ahead get the first round, I'll just have a quick word with this chap, won't be a min." he then continued on past the hotel towards Danis and considered, he must have looked back briefly, because he has a faint impression in seeing Bowman's look of

suspicion change as he recognized Orran Danis and gave a wave, then proceeded up the steps disappearing inside the hotel foyer.

The last words Pimm later recounted as having total recollection of are Orran Danis asking "Where are you headed? From then on it is a jumble of half-memories," he later stated.
In Pimm's sealed debriefing report for Mi6 he wrote,

From this point, I cannot with one hundred percent accuracy confirm my observations are in correct chronological order and undistorted by the effects of the event and the head trauma I sustained.

Having drawn a line below this statement he then attempted to document the remaining events of that afternoon, referring to Orran Danis as TS 1 *(target suspect 1)* 1 and Asil as TS 2.

"Orran Danis, target suspect one, may have said something like, your friend stop him, he appeared agitated and I believe grabbed my arm, then said something like, no, it's too late." Pimm continued, repeating that he held a confused image as he remembered Danis's hand wave back to Bowman, but it was more like a gesture, as if he was signalling Bowman to join them, as he pulled Pimm towards a shop doorway to light a cigarette.
"I then heard what sounded like small arms exchange, seven shots I believe and looked back to where I had last observed Staff Sergeant Bowman, he was not visible, then there was a small explosion, like a mortar blast, to the left of my periphery vision and then nothing, at this point I lost consciousness as the main attack on the King David Hotel must have commenced."

In fact Pimm was knocked unconscious as he and Orran were simultaneously blown further into the double-sided, shop display entrance porch set back from the road, as the air was filled with the dust and debris of tons of concrete that erupted cascading down the street, from a massive explosion, somewhere close to the St David hotel, in seconds everything was covered with a thick layer of grey chalk. Pimm recalled his first memories in the aftermath that followed the second explosion were around two- three minutes later in him regaining consciousness.
He came round with a cut to the back of his head, where he must have caught the window display, behind. His eyes were encrusted with thick chalk and had already begun to stream from the lime as the dust drifted away, pulled up from ground level by the heat of the fires that were now taking hold all around the hotel building. Pimm caught the vision of the nearest taxi in the road, it had been shunted so that it was now halfway askew, across the pavement and the bonnet was dented, the driver was slumped over the wheel his face covered in blood.

There was no sound initially in his recollection, the air blast had temporarily deafened him, and as he pushed Orran's arm off his shoulder, as he watched a bowling ball-sized rock of concrete thunder pass, taking the wing mirror clean off the taxi. Pimm covered his face and realised his hands were cut from the glass from the shop front that lay in splinter on the floor. Looking up he saw some still hung dangerously in large guillotine sized shards from the window frames.
He tried to get to his feet and slipped on the glass at his feet, then as he watched Orran begin to raise himself, he sneezed, and a cascade of what looked like talcum powder showered both men.
"A bomb!" Pimm coughed blowing the guck from his nostrils then rubbed his nose across his sleeve and saw it was bleeding. Pimm noticed Orran's suit had the lining exposed in tears on the shoulder and what was a dark grey suit now appeared white. Orran appeared to Pimm less in shock than he would have expected, it possibly affected Pimm initially as he found it strange as a smile gripped his lips as he held his hand out to raise the Turk.
His memory of their moments in the doorway end there, as he recanted later in his official Mi6 report, which was never to see the light of day.

From the shelter of the shop entrance to arriving at the scene of the epicentre of the bombing in the hotel, he has no recollection, or of Orran Danis speaking or following him. Pimm's next complete memory of that awful day was standing outside looking up at steel girders and shredded concrete hanging down from ream bars and the hotel floor levels now exposed with corridors, bedrooms and bathrooms open to the outside, in some rooms furniture still sat in place. He noticed a wardrobe, door hanging by one hinge, flapping back and forth revealing its clothing contents that included a marine officer's whites, still on its hanger.
The whole of the Western half of the southern wing of the King David hotel looked like it had been cleaved away like someone taking a birthday cake slice.
At first, his mind had trouble realising some of what he was stepping over were people and parts of bodies, everything was covered in the white concrete dust and plaster, mixed with the occasional thick carpet pile fragment.
Smoke and fire in different degrees began to draw the air from the area, Pimm remembered with each step forward he found it increasingly hard to breathe, and looking back across the street he could not understand why so many people were faced looking in the opposite direction, only later he discovered that a smaller explosion had been set off across the street outside the cafe opposite the hotel.

It was reportedly said by Menarche Begin who at that time was head of the terrorist group the Irgun and claimed responsibility for the attack, that the first smaller explosion in the cafe was to draw people out and away from the King David Hotel, to limit casualties. Unfortunately, immediately after the first event, some bystanders were drawn in many coming to the front of the hotel reception, spectators who were then got caught in the main bombing target area.

Menarche Begin went on to become Israel sixth prime minister, amongst many other things he should be remembered for the signing of the peace treaty with Egypt in 79, for which both he and Anwar Sadat, shared the Nobel Prize for peace.

Oliver Pimm remembered taking out his handkerchief it was the only thing not ingrained in dust and he doused his head in the water cascading from a broken road pipe, he was thankful to find it was fresh water and soaked the handkerchief, then tied it so that it covered his mouth.

With ongoing threats to his own life still present, not just from the hazards of the partially demolished building but the fact there had been a first and a second explosion, why not a third, he fought against the natural instinct to hold back and pressed forward.

The first person he helped from the scene had a gaping wound to their arm. He could not tell if they were male or female, he stripped off his jacket and placed it on their shoulders. Having misplaced where he had seen the open water pipe previously, he led them across the street, where many injured now began to sit on the curbs and pavement propping against doorways and the remains of shop fronts. Someone had brought a short hose from within a café and was going along the line washing people's faces, some of those that queued, bickered about the time a woman was taking. Some of those not seriously injured stood silently in shock, some sobbed other's prayed in Hebrew and Arabic, while others helped with water from other sources and attended those with wounds at first with makeshift bandages, such as table cloths and shirts. Pimm remembered there was so much blood still flowing as the alarms filled the air from arriving rescue services and the water that spilled across the streets mixed with the blood and turned the grey dust to a pink slush at his feet that stuck to his boot soles.

Pimm remembered after he had brought out a second person, only a couple of steps down from the remains of the hotel foyer, that in returning he began to call for Staff Sergeant Bowman, and at this point, a conscious fear for his own life gripped him as without warning a large pieces of the buildings weakened section of floors and walls began to fall away. He braced himself as blocks of concrete weighing tens of tons, suddenly fractured and slid to the ground, and each time it happened the screaming stopped then started again from those still trapped further within the hotel.

Pimm followed the calls for help and sobbing, as he continued to help the injured, at one point removing his belt as a tourniquet for one, then helping assist others lift and lever heavy parts of the building structure off those that called for help, whilst all the time clearing debris, throwing anything that would burn away from the inside, broken chairs, fragments of doors.

It is a fact, many have reported in similar situations of such awful carnage that they soon came to know, almost instinctively, who could be saved and who had already moved on. Pimm was a quick learner, at first he checked for pulses, within minutes

of aiding the wounded he began to proceed with a defined purpose. Now working further inside the hotel's remnants, at risk from further damage, every third step he checked above. Sometimes he did not give some casualties a second glance moving straight to those he knew were alive, all the time now calling for his friend, "Bowman!"
As he came forward to what he presumed was the remains of the ground floor bar area, he could see a set of spirit optics still pinned to the last remnant of timber fitments and a long sliver of the mirror that had greeted guests behind the bar. The back wall was partially demolished, exposing the room beyond with the ceiling creased over, Pimm could see it had been part of the kitchens. Fire struck out from gas hoses that once fed the ovens and hobs, it fanned wide like a magnificent wave of pure golden-red heat, the flames devouring everything in its path. Upturned chair legs torched instantly like a match struck on a box and the groans of the dead and dying that moments earlier had been dipping into the bowls of complimentary olives and peanuts were as hard to distinguish as the limbs that were no longer attached to their owners.
Crouched low, frozen for the briefest moment in his own slice of reflection of what the exact moment prior to the explosion must have been like, it was then Pimm felt a hand on his shoulder, then in his ear a choked cough.
"Your friend, over there!" It was Orran Danis, he gestured through the debris, Pimm saw a broiled hand pointing in defiance, and called "Bowes!" Striking forward.

At the first grab of a steel ream bar that he went to use to steady himself getting over the rubble blocking his way, his hand sang like a sausage hitting a red hot pan, and he ripped his arm back in pain. He looked to the sides, and the jagged heaps were filled with razor-sharp blocks that would have been higher than the ceiling if it were still there. To reach Bowman he would need to get past a latticework of bent metal some of which fed back within the remaining structure and was now being torched by the flames lapping along the walls and open ceilings, the red hot bars appeared to move like fingers taunting, calling him in.
Pimm took a look at Orran who shook his head, gesturing it was impossible to get past the spider web of steel or over the mound of debris, Pimm felt the sting to his hand, looked at his swollen palm, then towards the hand in the distance that wavered, blackened and damaged, but still remained thrust up into the air and seeing the watch on the wrist, Pimm knew it was Bowman.
Without another thought, crossing his hands and arms forward, across his face and head Pimm barged through the steel rods that on the first contact sprang forward, then instantly back as he passed through as tree branches might do on an overgrown woodland trail. It took eight steps, each less than three feet apart to cross the short distance and reach his friend, By the time he had come to rest in the open area section in front of the disintegrated lounge bar where Steve Bowman laid amongst others that had been killed, Pimm's forearms were already blistering with welts. He went to pull the remains of a table that lay across Bowman, something he could have hurled away with ease before, but now his arms felt like he was carrying

two full jerry cans, and his head told him he was in trouble, he avoided looking at his wounds as he levered and rolled the table away. Looking down, he saw Bowman's body crumpled, his left leg was too far back not to be broken, foot up against his buttocks. But he appeared intact, although his shirt had been burnt through and the impressive mane of ginger chest hair, what remained, was singed and smouldering, while the upper part of the material of his trousers was smouldering down the entire right leg and the rubber of his boot was burning freely as if not attached to Bowman. Pimm dived on to the flames at first using the remains of Bowman's own uniform, and then tore the jacket off one of the dead officers that must have been standing near Bowman and smothered the flames at his foot. As he did, a bottle rolled along the floor, for a second, he thought of pouring the contents to douse the flames but realised it was scotch and kicked it away.

Pimm looked up and back briefly the way he came and saw a dark silhouette hovering beyond the bars now blocking his exit he assumed it was Orran, who appeared to be searching for others. Pimm knew he could die there unless he got out soon, taking one last look at his friend's trying to speak through broken teeth, he determined come what may he was getting him out, even if it meant using his body to barge through the hot steel.

"Oliver! Come now!" Danis called out, as behind Pimm fiery tins cans of oil took off like mortar rounds from the kitchen. Pimm leaned down and felt his wounds tear open as he thrust his right hand into Bowman's armpit and pulling his wrist with his left grabbed Bowman, hoisting him up and over his back in a fireman's lift. He rocked back for a second catching his balance, then locking him across his shoulders, he punched up with his back settling him into his neck then braced himself to dash forward.

"Come!" Pimm heard again and as Pimm felt his skin ripped from the flesh of his arms, looking through the glowing metal bars hanging across his path he saw Orran had wrapped his arms in what Pimm took to be tablecloths, he stood squatting forward, like a praying mantis with a chair leg ready to act as a buffer. Then with a gesture to Pimm with a nod of his head, he threw the whole of his body weight into his arms pushing the bars back, allowing Pimm to run the gauntlet. Within Pimm's first step, the chair leg Orran was clenching ignited and fell from the Turks hands. Their eyes locked, Pimm knew he was already committed, and both knew if Orran released Pimm and Bowman would be thrashed and cut down by the recoiling sprung steel, as the towelling cloth wrapped around Orran arms ignited burning instantly through four layers. "PIMMM!!!" Orran screamed, but retained his blockade, continuing to press forward, as his arm became like a firework Roman candle torch of flame.

As Orran shut his eyes and turned his head away from the flames, Pimm launched past, barging Orran out of his path, unfortunately, as Orran released the hair-triggered metal, it sprung back like an over wound Swiss watch spring, first away then within a fraction of a second back, it lashed at the Turk catching him across his chest catapulting him before Pimm's feet. Still, with Bowman across his back, Pimm

looked down and saw Orran had survived as was attempting to put out the flames to the top of his now branded shirt, discarding the rags from his arms, "Go!" Orran gestured.
Pimm ploughed forward out of the building, stumbling into the light, then felt Orran's hands pushing him from behind, helping with the weight of Bowman on his back.

As they hit the safety of the street and air, water coming in from the fire crews now attending the bomb site soaked them. Pimm felt his own wounds grip his body, through the pain he saw they were both steaming, as they were hit by a fountain of water from every angle. Pimm dropped to his knees as two stretcher-bearers stepped forward and as they removed Bowman off Pimm's back, they removed sections of Pimm's welted, branded arm skin. Pimm growled and felt his thighs buckle and as he closed his puss clogged eyes, falling forward into the dust, his last memories of that day were hearing someone ask,
"Are you all right, my friend?" Pimm thought it was Orran Danis, *(TS 1)* but wrote in his report he could not be sure.

Pimm was ready for questions two days later and was informed on the same day Staff Sergeant Steve Bowman died of his injuries on the first night following the bombing. Orran Danis apparently had walked out of the hospital having been treated for his burns and was not seen in Palestine again, neither was his brother, only the mother along with other female members of the Danis family and elder males were detained for questioning when the flat above the barbershop was raided.

"The Turk, he's gone, discharged, the doc said they wanted him to stay, but perhaps he had somewhere more important to be." Bull Gordon was standing at the end of Pimm's bed.
"I'm sorry about your Sergeant, I know you two were close." Bull felt for his pipe then read the No Smoking sign and picked up Pimm's chart as if he knew what he was doing.
Pimm looked at his coloured waistcoat and assumed he was a doctor until he spoke another sentence.
"Tactical thinks your man the linguist has fled the scene, but it could be the Israelis have him, they may even have decided to wipe his slate, I know it's nothing to do with you, we put you on him in the first place, someone else will be looked at regarding that, well John Smith to be specific, poor lad, he didn't make it." Bull tutted.
"You mean Roger Thake." Pimm found the words harsh to make in his throat.
"Ah, so Rog made contact, told you who he was, I see, that's why you were there, I did wonder." Bull smiled
"Well as I said, he bought it when the cards came down. You would have liked old Rog, and he liked you for our house, Six that is, Mi6 in case you didn't know. We are not sure how your Turk got caught up in this, something you may be able to

shine a light on, when you are ready. Of course we know the principals, the three Israelis that were killed, during the attack and who sent them. Your man Danis was more likely a dupe, possibly even blackmailed into it. Operation Shark is a knee jerk counter-intelligence operation I have helped orchestrate, while you have been resting, we have cordoned off the whole of Tel Aviv and Jaffa, our boys are going house to house, we also raided your Turks home just in case, found a blind old lady, his mother other members of his family unconnected with the attack, nothing else, the place was as clean as a whistle, not even a photograph frame. I considered having then sent to the Cyprus camp, what do you think?" Bull looked to Pimm, partially expecting some kind of vengeful reply.

But Pimm instead, shook his head gently, taking in the news that Roger Thake had invited him that day to the King David hotel to recruit him into Mi6, that was what it had all been about Orran Danis had been right. "No." Pimm croaked, considering responding to Bull's reference to a photograph frame.

"Probably right, I doubt they had any idea what these boys were up to, save the taxpayer shipping costs and as I said this is down to the Irgun they've staked their claim, proudly, I have to say." Bull looked at the other casualties from the bombing in adjoining beds, "I fought alongside many Jews in France, not that many bragged about it back then, I always found them a brave and honourable bunch, but then we were on the same side." Bull noticed Pimm's eyes shift to the others in the recovery ward.

"How many?" Pimm's question threw Bull, he had a knack of guessing what a person would say given any circumstance within three sentences. Pimm's question was selfless and direct. He had survived and had already moved on from his own experience, Bull knew in that exact moment, this was a Lost Boy he wished to cultivate. Pimm could kill he already knew that, but the fact he had the presence of mind to cut through all that distracted and request the most import question what did it cost, set him apart from the norm.

In this case, so far the casualties list was 91 dead (28 British, 41 Arabs, 17 Jews, 2 Armenians, 1 Russian, 1 Greek and 1 Egyptian) and 45 wounded. The Bombing was tacked to the Irgun terrorist splinter cell and was in retribution for the British Armies "Operation Agatha" It was a defining moment in Great Britain military involvement in Palestine, the power of the press, had by now begun to control the mass.

A week later Pimm was on a Hercules transport that landed scheduled for a refit at Cambridge's Marshal's airport where he was met by the first of many of those that would give him the best trade-craft British intelligence had to offer.

However, first, at Bull's discretion, he was allowed two breaks from deep cover both on the same day 1st August 1946, first to see his Aunt Vic in Muswell Hill. Pimm told her he liked the hat that she had bought for Steve Bowman's son's christening when he explained that he had died in the bombing attack that was across all the papers, she listened but was secret just glad it was him and not her Ollie. She told him she would take the hat back to Owen & Owen in North Finchley, where she bought it, but he told her no, and that she should go to the christening, if and when it took place, it never did, but Vic made a point of becoming involved in the child's early life. He informed her he was heading to work at an inaccessible research centre in the Falklands for Signal Corp. and was unsure when he would be able to call her or even write, he left one memento he had smuggled from Palestine and unfolded the black and white photograph Roger Thake had given him of Steve Bowman himself and the two members of Juno resting in the shade with some beer bottles in their hands, she smiled and set it in the gap between the wooden frame and the glass of the mirror that hung above the gas fire in her front room. Vic then handed him his post office savings book with all the money he had ever earned since his first paper round. Giving him a hug she knew it would be their last and then went to put the kettle on, with a tear in her eye, it was, and Pimm only ever saw her wearing the hat again when she was laid out in her coffin.

The second visit on the 1st September 1946, was to see Bowman's wife the "Wassik" and 10th-month old boy James Bowman. Pimm also met June, Bowman's sister-in-law and while she put the kettle on to make him tea, with the sound of the child's half cut mother, Lorraine, sobbing coming from another bedroom. Pimm leaned over the crib of the child sleeping and made a promise, then leaving half the contents of the savings book under the infants cream crochet shawl, he slipped away before June arrived with his mug tea.

Oliver Pimm ceased to exist for a time and BPP *(Bravo, Papa, Papa,)* took another step on the rung of British Intelligence infamy joining the ranks of the Special Air Service at Hereford. Then as with all of Bull's Lost Boy's he continued his training at a secret base on the island of Guernsey. Pimm emerged as an Assertive Field Operative, individually referred to as Sandmen, attached initially to Mi6 Drake Department, who were collectively known throughout the intelligence service as the No Noise Brigade. Oliver Pimm's name now became attached to a highly classified register of a member of the select group of eight individuals that worked, predominantly alone on assignment attached to their individual Mi6 global sector, to carry out acts of counter-intelligence and espionage within their assigned region, which included assassinations on behalf of the Her Majesties British government.

In 1959 off the coast of the Karpass Peninsula, Cyprus, onboard the minesweeper HMS Burmaston, now in the presence of his old language tutor from Palestine, Orran Danis, Oliver Pimm was reminded how naive he had once been, even though others may have thought otherwise.

Pimm imagined he could hear Bull in his ear, "You were never that innocent, that why we call you the Lost Boy's, lost souls that wash up on the shores of Mi6."

Orran Danis looked at Pimm's wrist "I take it by now you know who I am?" he said as he lit another cigarette and felt the ship turning back to Cyprus, Pimm did not turn to his question and said nothing as he let the water from the sink tap run over his wrist cooling his blood, "and still you came?" Orran watched as Pimm splashed water over his face then wiped it with the hand towel.

"You must know I was involved in the hotel bombing in Jerusalem in 45, maybe not me directly, but my family," Orran volunteered.

Pimm kept an eye on his captive in the mirror's reflection, watching him as he removed his broken glasses, repaired at the hinge with an old piece of tape.

Danis had aged beyond his years, he may have escaped Jerusalem, but something of the land had haunted him all this time, his eyes holding a yellow tinge were ringed with dark lines, like a man that rarely slept well.

Pimm rolled down his sleeves, hiding his scars as much as he could and picked up his lighter.

"So, what now? You are going to blame others again, come, come, we have moved past that, I know who you are now and what you are after here, I also know you lied back then about who and what exactly you did during the war for the Germans. I know it was your wife you were trying to trace in Jerusalem and that you helped your Jewish brother-in-law Asil, real name Benjamin Ousden move the explosives from his taxi to the milk floats, used in the bombing that killed 91 people at the King David hotel, 28 British military including Staff Sergeant Bowman a man you broke bread with, did you know 17 were Jewish and one Greek, no Turks." Pimm stubbed out his cigarette on the floor, "martyrs for the cause?" Pimm snarled sarcastically as he rested a foot on the chair and leaned forward studying Orran's glasses, remembering how his teacher would chew the ends while listening to the debates by his pupils, Pimm found it curious they appeared new but were broken and carried a dirty piece of tape as if made to look old, but there were no teeth cuts to the arms, he said nothing.

"And still you came, your friend the Sergeant who died, I know this and I am sorry." Orran was truthful about that if Pimm was any judge, he could see that.

"I came because when you helped me drag the poor fucker out along with the others you did not know he was dead and because I have one order, reclaim the list you have offered in this trade with my Government, for your relocation from this region. I understand the list holds amongst others, Nazi members of your father's scientific team and that you took it from him, before you killed him. However if it's all bullshit, I will tell you straight my orders are simple I'm to drop you over the side before we hit port, the guns we found with your friends help us with the Greeks today, so my presence here is covered by my people at six." Pimm's tone was resolute and unemotional as he watched Danis shuffle forward in his seat.

"My father was a pig. It was he that told the Nazi's where Miriam was when I would not give her up, even though he knew she was with child. He deserved to die!" Orran's voice still held venom from the betrayal by his father, but Pimm was not interested in any reason why Orran had done what he did, that was in the past, the only important thing was if what Orran was selling worth keeping him alive, he already knew he would lose no sleep in performing the task.

"That is maybe, but I'm not here as your priest. In the war for loyalty or love, you have had a hand in killing many. It is time to pay the piper." he said in perfect Turkish, and Pimm saw the capitulation of agreement in his eyes.
Danis sighed and unfolded his glasses on the table and without unwrapping the tape from the broken hinge pulled the arm back so that it snapped clean away from the eye lens frame
"Do you have a pin?" he asked, and Pimm removed his medal bar from his tunic and handed it over.
Using the safety pin fastener on the back of the bar Danis then prized from inside the hollowed glasses arm a thin piece of paper not much bigger than two cigarette papers rolled together.
"There are forty-three names on this list, some are important Nazis, some are international businessmen and bankers, not all are Germans, all important enough in 1945 to have access to the Spider network resources, maybe some dead, maybe some not. The lines of the web are still there for anyone who has the mind to trace them, and plenty across the water would pay for this list. You'll see Yasir Danis, my father is the third name." Orran licked his fingers and pushed the curling paper flat onto the metal table and watched as Pimm without moving from his seat tilted his head and within seconds had memorised the names even though from his perspective they were upside down.
A couple of the names rang familiar chimes from his past assignments, and he knew immediately Bull would want to get his hands on the list as would the American's and Mossad.
"If it is as you say, there are plenty in Jerusalem that would want to get their hands on this bauble, why not offer it to the American or even Mossad, you know if they find out we have this they will look for the source. You could be in for many sleepless nights if this sees the light and it still does not answer the question why call for me, now." Pimm took back his medal bar without touching the paper.
"I asked for you because I know you are a man of your word, even though I am sure your employment has changed your nature from the teenager I first met. I know you tried to keep your promise in Jerusalem. I found out on the morning of the King David bombing that you were taken off base before you could help me trace my wife. Unfortunately, it was too late, her brother had other ideas he spoke with people from Irgun. They traced her here in the camp at Caraolos, like everything there was a price, believe it or not if you wish, but I did not know the details of the King David, until that morning and then when I saw you, well." Orran opened his palms and pulled his shirt back over his head, the movement made the paper drift across the table towards Pimm, and he placed a finger on it before it drifted to the floor.
"You know, now I have seen this, there is nothing to stop me dropping you in the drink, why should you get to have a happy ending." Pimm didn't want Danis to beg, but he wanted him at least to realise if this thing were going to happen, it would be on his terms.

"I have cancer, maybe a year?" he tapped his chest, "This is for Meriam, my wife and my sons, I don't want them to be conscripted in another war over a patch of sand, the Khamsin winds, has blown outside our borders, and I think in spite of the years and your new skills. I hoped there is something of the young Corporal that is left, at least that is what I wished for."

Orran re-fixed his glasses and stared up at Pimm as he flipped over the paper, folding it neatly he tucked it into the breast pocket of his shirt.

"I will have our people make the arrangements; I will do this last thing for your family and hope your children live in the peaceful manner you wish for them, we will not meet again." Pimm thought deeply as one who rarely made threats, then said looking into Orran's yellow eyes, "If not the sins of the father will be paid for by the sons." in Turkish and putting his uniform back on stepped from the cabin, it was the last time they would speak.

On the 18th October 1959 by the time HMS Burmaston had pulled into the port at Famagusta, the detailed report documenting the capture of the crew of the Turkish motorboat Diniz listed only three Turkish nationals having been detained. They were charged and taken into custody for attempting to import munitions into Cyprus without a permit, intended for the TMT, Turkish Resistance Organization.

The three men were sentenced to one-year imprisonment, there was no mention of Orran Danis or a fourth man at the time of the trial and the British Governor, Sir Hugh Foot commuted their sentences at the end of the trial and the Turkish crew were allegedly deported.

Before the trial, Orran's wife and children were detained in a staged raid at their flat in Nicosia. Reunited the family were flown to Rome then relocated in Alghero on the island of Sardinia, where under the pseudonym of Simmeo, with modest financial support, the family opened a clothing factory and retail outlet. When Orran Danis AKA, Demitri Simmeo passed away two years later, his wife Sophia and eldest son Demitri took over running the business while the youngest boy Dominic was dispatched to be schooled in business studies as an apprentice notary in Olbia.

A week after operation "Seahorse" Lance Corporal Robert Gregory hitched a ride on a Hercules into RAF Lakenheath, from there was he was taken with no registration, no assignment papers and no passport control, in a blacked-out Ford transit to Hereford to begin his training with the SAS and career with Mi6. He was the first *"Lost Boy"*, Pimm had recruited.

Pimm rejoined Mi6's Cook Department *(South East Asia)* and the operation he had previously been involved with, before Bull requested his brief re-assignment for the Diniz Incident.

Oliver Pimm dropped off the radar soon after arriving in Hong Kong and arrived at Mi6's Hanoi station in January 1960, attached as a nameless Executive Officer to Robert Thompson's staff, who at that time was chief of the BRIAM, *(British Advisory Mission to South Vietnam)*.

BRIAM was a covert support group that was secretly offering counter-subversion and intelligence to assist the American security services and aid the South Vietnamese President Ngo Dinh Diem during the Vietnam War. At times over the past eight years Pimm was listed as an attached member of the American Special Forces, shadowing operations including the importation of munitions and chemical weapons such as napalm on board British flights from Hong Kong to Saigon, in contravention of UN agreements.

Oliver Pimm's abilities soon came to the attention of certain individuals belonging to the CIA as he began to develop his own robust network of important allies including many American business associates that aided the reinforcement of his own civilian legend through their collaboration, whilst he continued to act on behalf of Her Majesty's British government as an Mi6 Assertive Executive Field Officer, "Sandman" assassin.

Chapter 3: The Baitrunner

Travemunde, Lubec
The Baltic Sea, Germany
February 1961

Sebastian Westerberg stood up front watching with the other passengers as the seagulls flocked out from the Port of Travemunde to greet them. He smiled watching two boys with their mother as they threw small pieces of crust from sandwiches slipped from the ferry dining car, the birds swooped low into the bow snatching the morsels from the air, jostling and squabbling, their cackles sounded like calls of *thanks, thanks, thank you!* To the young feeders.
He looked down at the croissant in his own hand feeling no appetite, knowing it was not the movement of the boat that unsettled his stomach, a child to his side who had been watching the boys antics with the bird looked up gleefully at him.
"You need to break it small." Speaking Swedish she volunteered, pointing to a bird hovering only a few meters out from the side of the boat, it too had eagle-eyed the pastry in Sebastian's hand. He looked down at the child wrapped so carefully in her mother's choice of matching hat and scarf and handed her the pastry, the child's eyes widened, and she was about to thank him when she was pulled away by her mother towards the boys.
"Where did you get that?" he heard her enquire, raising his collar he sipped coffee from a flimsy plastic cup and turned his face away from them before the child pointed him out, avoiding the mother's instinctive glare of protective inquisition of an innocent gift from the stranger.

Sebastian focused forward oblivious to the mothers face flushing from thinking anything untoward as the child giggled, continuing to enjoy the attention the birds now showed her. His mind began picking at the images that pegged the strands of time since he was last in Travemunde as Stefan Robert Keplar, with Elizabet. "Elizabet", he said again in his mind and smiled, Elizabet, even the thought of her name was against the edict, a law they governed themselves by, "Streng verboten" *(Strictly forbidden)* like their mother tongue.
She was now Katrina Anna Westerberg married to Sebastian Westerberg, and that's how the world knew them, a Swedish family, pillars in the community of Uppsala, Sweden, not as an SS SD Colonel Keplar and Elizabet Kempe, Reich Chancellery liaison officer, Nazis on the run since before the war ended.
Sebastian's architectural eye looked as always to the skyline of Travemunde harbour, particularly the older buildings, which still carried the scars of the allied bombing of the port. It was an instinctive, natural interest when entering any city.
But this port held a more considerable significance and now, as on previous occasions when he travelled back to his homeland, he looked to see if anything would ignite a spark to complete a memory. Once again, he was disappointed with

receiving only waves of emotion that washed over his senses with each breath of cold sea air that hit his nostrils. Tainted with an infusion of fish and engine oil from the docks it combined with the taste of his cold coffee. A brief, tantalising bread crumb trail buried deep in his subconscious surfaced, and for a moment he felt his pulse race as he recalled sensations of excitement, panic and fear, from the last time he was there as Stefan. Suddenly he felt the coffee rise uncontrollably and retched, snorting he cleared his throat and turning from the wind, checking those nearest behind him could not see, he spat semi vomit. Removing his glove, he took a folded linen handkerchief from his pocket, wiped his mouth and blew his nose, the bitter taste burnt his sinus.

"Are you all right?" the little girl's mother mouthed with a look of concern as he turned back to steady himself gripping the rail, she noticed his small finger was missing as he raised a hand thanking her, embarrassed to think she may have seen his reaction in returning to the scene of their escape from Germany. He judged if she knew who he once was, she would have stuck with her original concerns for her child's safety.

Shutting his eyes he took in a full breath of the harbours aroma and for a fraction of a second began to slip back in time, then an ear-piercing feedback screech from the ships Tannoy system grounded all on deck to cover their ears while looking to the source. The Captain announced politely in various languages calling for the attention of the passengers,
"Monsieur et Madame would all drivers return to their vehicles we will be docking shortly." Taking a mouthful of coffee, he gargled then spat over the side before falling in line and queuing down to the car deck.

Below deck, isolated in a sea of cars, inside his little black VW Beetle, it smelt of home, her and the girls. It was a sensation he overlooked during his regular daily commute to the university where he worked. Placing his hat on the passenger seat, he noticed a fine long silver hair, one of hers. Then checking his own reflection in the rear-view mirror he pushed his thick blonde fringe back over his side parting and was caught in his own reflection, he stared back defiantly at the glacial melt pools, locking his gaze, challenging as if they belonged to someone else. At that moment while they waited for the ferry bow doors to open, his surroundings disappeared in a daydream of remembrance, as the jostling from the movement of the boat took him instantly to a time he believed held his first memories of waking and realising he was still alive, back in 1943, laying bound to a stretcher in the back of the ambulance with Günther Brahn.
In his jumbled memory, he pictured it as happening when they drove down from the facility in the hills above San Pantaleo to the beach dock at Baja Sardinia where Elizabet must have been waiting, out of sight in the boat.

He even believed Günther was saying something reassuring to him as he lay in darkness and pain. The truth was, at that time Stefan was still inside the experimental pressurised recovery cylinder, unconscious waiting to be released and revived by Doctor Dieter Myher. It was not until they got to the beach when Myher had de-pressurised the cylinder and injected Stefan with a concoction of adrenaline and then morphine that his senses began to reactivate to the real world. Stefan's mind had no accurate linear impressions of the boat journey, in which he had remained in an unconscious state throughout. In Genoa he lay like a corpse, at times left in the dark, whilst Günther and Elizabet manoeuvred him like a precious cargo, and after that for many days, he remained oblivious to the trials and tribulations experienced during the exchange of a succession of modes of transport that were required by Günther and Elizabet to get them across Germany. It took all their cunning to secure transport of another hospital wagon and passes to make their way across Europe betwixt an advancing allied force and a retreating German army, and it would only be in the back of the last vehicle they acquired that Stefan's mind would finally be released to its conscious state. The images that filled his mind were a patchwork of time and space that bore little resemblance to the truth, but it was how his mind coped with the extraordinary pressures that had been placed upon it in the Nazi experimental laboratory of Professor Oskar Heikkinen in San Pantaleo, Sardinia. For days after he lived in a semi-conscious state, drifting between worlds of substance and delusion, the morphine satisfying his body's need for pain relief, merging the two worlds on a schizophrenic roller coaster ride in his mind from the experimental drugs he had been subjected to while his body underwent a metamorphosis.

When the demons of his nightmares quietened, and the veils would occasionally lift, they allowed him a distorted glimpse of his world, which was itself on the brink of collapse. To Stefan, his recollections of that time and his awakening began with hearing the thunder of a storm that appeared relentless. At times it held such ferocity that he tried with all his will to raise himself from his bonds fearing for her safety, then exhausted slipped away again into the dreamlike state in which the storms gentle murmur invaded his thoughts and sometimes appeared comforting, until once more he would be pulled to his senses by an immense thunderclap or jolt of pain that felt at times as if he had been struck by lightning itself.
The sounds he heard coming from outside were often accompanied by the familiar tones of Günther's cursing as they journeyed through days and weeks that marked their escape from a Europe tearing itself apart and as time passed his series of correct mental recollection fragments of time and space increased in duration. The longer and extended periods of calm to his body's system was as if the storm itself was ending, as he returned to the world of the living and the drugs Professor Heikkinen and the Aktion T4 team had saturated him with seeped from every orifice and pore of his bandaged body.
Then her voice drifted like a partially forgotten rhyme from childhood, caught in the wind, words of comfort held in the melody of her tone were chorused by the occasional muffled sound of her sobbing at his side, while Günther forged ahead

judging every decision of the direction they should take, as if he was trying to path a way through a minefield.

At times Stefan's own security clearance documentation and identity cards assisted them with clearing passage past their own troops and for a time they were even able to hide him n a German military infirmary, where, with a stolen uniform Elizabet acted as his private nurse, this allowed them to change Stefan's bandages, and it was then that they saw for the first time the extent of the effects the Professor experiment had on Stefan's body, seeing that his whole body was now covered in a hard scab-like crust, Elizabet bathed him and applied oils to the dry skin, but with no knowledge of what they were dealing with, they once again bandaged him with the hope that Stefan, being young and physically fit, his system would compensate and stabilize with enough rest, while they continued to feed him using intravenous drips.

The hospital located in Kintzheim was a welcome respite, but with Elizabet's pregnancy developing, Günther became increasingly concerned that soon Elizabet would not be able to make the long sea crossing to Sweden and when Stefan's wounds began to draw too much attention they moved on, journeying north towards the Baltic Sea ports. While Günther continuously monitored the allied progress and with bluff and guile they continued towards their goal, Inevitably brute force would be their saving grace. Günther's hunting instincts, knowing when to go to cover and when to rise and attack was what eventually saw the trio safely to take rest in woods south of the town of Schwerin less than a hundred kilometres from the city of Lübeck and the port of Travemunde where they considered there may be a chance in securing passage across to neutral Sweden hiding amongst other refugees, fleeing mainland Europe.

They planned to abandon the ambulance wagon and their German identity documents, and they would need to secure papers if they were to make it through whatever security detail was guarding the docks. Relying on Elizabet's knowledge of the Swedish language would not be enough, so they began the gruesome job of trying to obtain any documentation that would assist their claim to be Swedish refugees, by searching every corpse they came across. There was no shortage of festering cadavers lying by roadside ditches, in half burnt-out houses and fields. At one point they came across a beautiful spinney set at the base of a hill rise in Holthusen, not unlike the wood Stefan and Leopold carved out to be the scene of interrogation and execution of the villagers of San Pantaleo, Sardinia when first they arrived in 1942 searching for saboteurs from Corsica.

At Holthusen another Waffen SS troop had completed their task of genocide killing 83 men, women and children, the wood was filled with the sound of over hundred thousand flies, feasting on their flesh.

Leaving Stefan in the wagon Günther and Elizabet searched the foul den, but all were from a nearby village. Except for two American captured soldiers, their mutilations indicating they had both endured horrific torture before being shot with the others. Günther speculated they possibly maybe advance American paratrooper fifth columnists, it may even have been their discovery in the village that had made the Germans exact such a heavy toll on the local population. Günther made Elizabet wait in the truck when she became violently sick, fearing that she may harm her pregnancy, but he found no papers that would aid them.

Stefan was by now beginning to raise himself up from his bed and when he attempted the task to make it to his feet, he had an exaggerated and painful limp to his leg. Still partially bandaged like a mummy, they had yet to unwrap his face entirely and see to what extent the doctor's work had aided or harmed him and each time they revealed another area of patchwork skin Günther would look for signs of the wounds he had witnessed Stefan sustain in the air attack at the Sardinian facility. Most peculiar, was what had been consider by the doctor's at the time the life threatening wound to his leg, it carried an unusual scar unlike what Günther, a man who had seen his fare share of battle injuries, would expect for such a deep wound and there was no evidence of additional bleeding or loss of tissue where it had been pierced.
As for the burns to his cheek, it was hard to distinguish his skin was encrusted with hard golden blisters that covered his face and exposed head he appeared like someone who had been lowered into a deep fat fryer. Although he complained at the irritation to his scalp as his hair began to pierce the scabs and caused him such horrific itching that they had to restrain him and force him to sit on his hands, surprisingly to Günther and Elizabet he spoke of little pain and his clarity of mind appeared progressively to become once again in tune with the world around him, although his speech was hampered by blistering to his mouth and lips. "Where is Leo?" These three words signalled his recovery, as she helped him dress in stolen clothes from a man three times his size so that the large ill-fitting trousers slipped over the bandages to his legs, she ignored the question and wiped her eyes as she saw him brace in agony as his leg cramped.
"If you ever need pants this big, you know I will leave you." The firelight caught the white of her teeth as she stuck her tongue out and bit it lightly. He tried hard not to smile at her as he noticed she wore not a trace of make-up, even in his poor health he caught the glance she gave Günther, as he tended a fresh rabbit kill, pulling the skin away to make a miniature rabbit onesie, before setting it on a stick spit across the fire. They sat for a while in silence watching the flames send embers into the air, while the night filled with the continuous crackle of distant battles, at times it sounded as if it was coming from all directions and it kept them on edge.
"He's gone, isn't he?" Stefan mumbled and then growled in pain as the crust to some of the blisters to his upper body were stretched as he forced his arm into the shirt Günther had pulled from a washing line.
Günther snapped a leg from the carcass and placed it in his mittened hands,
"Eat, you need to get strong you will need to be able to walk from these woods on your own, in case you have not noticed you are fighting for three now my boy," Günther said reassuringly and watched Stefan stumble back and forth, his legs

finding gravity for the first time in weeks, his muscles strained to take his balance, and he could see the pain in his eyes.

"Where are we? Something smells like death or is that me?" Stefan said, he had not caught Günther's reference to fighting for three and looking at the blisters to his hands, he made a grab to lift a bandage from his arm, and Elizabet stopped him.
"Not yet," she whispered, letting him lean on her as she guided him over to the fire as Günther stirred a knife in a pot and poured the contents into three mugs,
"It's not as good as Murtle's, but the chicken was fresh two days ago, that's how long we have been waiting here for you to be ready to move, we cannot stay here any longer." Günther handed him the clear soup, his eyes told Stefan Leo was dead and he turned back to Elizabet and offered her his cup as he placed his hand on her stomach and now saw clearly her womb held a roundness in the shadows, she dismissed the drink taking the smaller mug from Günther,
"Günther's right you need your strength, I'm good, the baby is good." The word made all around him, including his pain and the sorrows of losing his brother dissolve,
"Baby!" It was her joy in telling him, not his understanding of how his position in life had changed that he remembered affected him most from that time as he placed his mittened hand on her stomach. In all this darkness and uncertainty, she looked as happy as when they had first met as if she knew all was going to work out even though he could hear a barrage of guns and explosions coming from either side of their position.

In a distant future none of them could perceive at that moment, when fate had smothered them with fortune, fame and family, he would look back and consider this moment, as one of the jewels of his life experiences even though now, the perils in the darkness of the night prevented any relaxation or time to contemplate a future beyond surviving until the morning.
"They are Russian, Blankenberg, I think?" Günther pointed to the north eastern glow of light in the night sky, "And they are American and British, they are lighting up Hamburg tonight." he pointed south westward, where Ack Ack tracers filled the air, like a new years eve fireworks party, while searchlights scanned the auburn night sky in the distance Stefan judged to be a hundred kilometres away.
"Over there Hanover behind us, there is no going back, we are north of Schwerin in the middle, maybe fifty kilometres to the coast straight ahead north, but you must get across in a freighter, before the Russians take the main ports, Rostock or Lübeck, they are both in reach, I favour Lübeck it is further west and likely to be clear. We need to choose wisely if you get caught by them, it's over for you and them, better the Americans or British if any." Günther gestured, drawing a rough plan in the dirt at his side with a smouldering stick of wood.

Stefan's mind began to sense the urgency of the small window of opportunity they had in which to escape through and focused on the now, shutting from his mind the questions of the past and what had happened in Sardinia following the air attack when he had been injured, he reconciled himself to the hope, that his assorted fragments of memory would reconfigure to some extent as time passed.

"So we are back home, I thought these woods looked familiar, how far to Warren, can we holed up there?" then he stopped as his mind sifted back what Günther had said, "Of course not, what am I thinking, if the Russian's are in Blankenberg, they have overrun the castle already, my mind is slow, fuzzy I am sorry Gunt, you will have to bear with me." Stefan then looked over at Günther with his head down and knew exactly what he was thinking, realizing Günther's his concerns for his sister and nephews safety and Murtle Lansford,

"I'm sorry, Günther, thank you for staying." Stefan knew all back home could easily have suffered at the hands of the advancing Russians and yet he had remained with them. And Stefan knew right now, he needed Günther more than ever. He was too weak and must be governed by his teacher again, even though inside, he felt somehow more alert and alive with each passing moment of consciousness.

While Elizabet rested, Günther informed him in brief, sweeping statements, in his matter of fact manner how at times their journey from Genoa had appeared as farcical as it was dangerous. Finally, he handed him a Swedish identity card and travel papers.

"Sebastian Westerberg, did you?" Stefan said as he fingered the bloodstained paper.

"No, he was already dead, I came on a group of deserters, scouting ahead, a farm two fields over" he gestured north, "they had killed all of the refugees, maybe thirty or so hiding in a barn, baby's, women, children the lot. They wore Wehrmacht uniforms, but I think they were Latvians. One was sleeping, the other two were fucking two of the children."

"I'm glad she was spared that." Stefan looked at the ambulance where Elizabet was now sleeping, but Günther shook his head and raised his eyes.

"She has seen far worse on the way up here. We must have killed half of our own, there are no rules with this army as it runs away. A couple of times I thought sometimes it may be better for you if I ended it, but she has a good smile and you, well you're lucky, not that you haven't pushed it to the limit. I don't know what they did to you, but you have been snoring like a pig, I nearly had her gag you so that we were not caught back in a forest outside Hanover." he touched the scabbard of his Sawback forgetting it no longer carried his trusty weapon and now held an ordinary butchers blade, Stefan shook his head.

"I knew you would make it boy, now they have a real chance." Günther' eye glistened softly in the firelight.

Stefan raised his soup mug, "Well, you seem to have done all right so far Gunt, what had you planned next?"

Günther pointed toward the glow in the north-west, "Lübeck, twenty kilometres that way, you get on a boat, and that is it. She has family in Sweden, if our people still have it, we will use your papers to book passage. Tell them she is taking you back

to recover, I will stay in uniform, explain your injuries and that you are not a deserter, the way you look should work in our favour."
"What if we have lost the ports?" Stefan's eyes lifted to the glow in the sky, and Günther stood looking in the same direction and shrugged as Elizabet emerged from the back of the ambulance.
"Well, if they are not ours we still go that way and if we meet up with trouble, I will say you are my prisoners, as I said your wounds speak for themselves and Elizabet is quite the actress, you should be proud, also there is this, at least you three will be free." Günther tried to smile reassuringly, handing over the Westerberg's papers and his wife's ration card to Elizabet.
"That's all she had it may come in useful, it says she had two daughters, I am guessing those vultures had them, I think many of our boys have gone wild."
"Katrina, Anne... pretty name," she said, "do I look like a Katrina?" she looked at Stefan, seeing his concern in Günther words.
"Katrina, yes it is a nice name, you did well to find these Gunt," Stefan said.
"Sebastian, you know it could be you." Elizabet looked at the small creased photograph of Sebastian Westerberg held within the Reich factory workers identity card. The man wore a beard in the image and could easily be mistaken for a younger Stefan, especially with Stefan's face partially bandaged and still carrying the large burn like scabs to his cheeks.

"It will have to do, you wrap your neck, let Eliz...Katrina, speak for you, tell them his throat was damaged in a fire." Günther moved wood back from the flames concerned the fire was too bright and might attract attention.
He then explained that two kilometres further up the hill there was a train line with a rail exchange where the line was switched by hand, to north, west or northeast, and all the trains slowed, due to rock damage, possibly caused by resistance activity in the past. They would be able to jump aboard. He had waited and watched the trains heading north over the past two days in either direction laden initially with troops and arms, their routine altered, soon it became apparent they were filled with wealthy German refugees, looking to flee and the trains coming south especially from the northeast were laden with injured and troops recalled back into the heart of Germany for the final struggle.
"No one waits around, there is no checking of carriages any more. They want to get into the tunnel as soon as possible, there are signs from attacks by Resistance fighters, all along the rail, mostly I think anything going south. Once we are on board and make sure it is headed we should be ok if east you jump and we wait for the next one."

Stefan's mind began to work on their escape, "What about the gold?"
Günther smiled, "Now I know you are Ok." he gestured to Elizabet who in hearing the question got up and went to the back of the ambulance and returned brandishing a bar that glinted like the sun in her hands,

"There is something else." Günther said and went back inside the ambulance as she sat beside him cradling the bar of gold like it was her child as Stefan held her in the arms, "what shall we call this one?" she joked as she patted the precious metal. "Goldilocks, of course." Stefan groaned as he felt his lip scab split open again and tasted the ooze that touched his tongue, then reached up to scratch at his head and pulled back in frustration clenching his fist and touched his cheek.
"Don't pick!" she said as he bit his lip, then she watched as he pulled at a piece of scab, it ran further in a fine strip of skin across his cheek like peeling sunburn and lightly bled but revealed the first piece of smooth skin on his face that made him recognisable as human. Until then he resembled something more reptilian in origin, she tore a piece of cloth from her sleeve and licking it dabbing the welt, she noticed it tasted extremely bitter, not like blood normally did.

"I'm sorry I have to tell you, you look as sexy as when you wore that Japanese outfit, Katrina?" he laughed, then groaned as his facial scabs split open further, "don't make me laugh, it hurts too much, it's like having a mouth full of bee stings." He touched his mouth, feeling their roughness and swelling.
She saw tears of joy in his blue eyes that at one time she thought she would never see open again and letting the gold bar thud to the dirt she pulled him gently close and kissed the slither of cheek flesh he had unearthed.
"You taste better than that old rabbit a few days ago, you were lucky to be asleep." She made a sound of being sick as Günther appeared carrying Stefan's leather case and withdrew a black journal that Stefan immediately recognised and as he saw it, his mind flashed with images of moments from the day when he was injured in Sardinia, and he remembered his last exchange with Professor Heikkinen in his office, the tape recordings and the poor radio boy Jan Van Pope and assumed, as Günther had informed him of the poisoning of the troops, that Van Pope was killed at the same time. Stefan sighed and felt a helpless regret at failing to prevent their deaths at the hands of such an evil creature, knowing he had died at the same time as Leopold only gave him the slightest relief.

"I have no idea what is in here, but it has the last things they were working on, this Leo took from the Professor's safe, it is his own private book, it is similar to the one we made but, I think different, maybe in code, I don't know." he passed Stefan his copybook made from the original Vor Elle project journal and then a smaller book.
"They said they had done it, whatever it was, maybe it has something to do with you and the other one?" Günther shrugged.
Stefan flicked through the pages of equations, "The other one?" he said, looking up.
"Yes, when they brought you out from the laboratory there were two of you, two cylinders, you remember those, yes. I imagine the other one whoever it was, is dead. The Resistance nearly had us, they killed the young doctor, Myher, if it had not been for him, you would be dead too." Günther began to take the rest of the gold out of the back of the ambulance, as Stefan continued to examine the books he noticed that the Professor's book contained only his writings, whereas in the

copybook he had organized there was a change, from that of the Dutch boy Jan's very neat handwriting to Günther's, larger lettering.

"I did my best, you said it was important so there it is." Stefan smiled even though again the pain was excruciating.

"Also you should know in the back of your main book I wrote something Count Erichh told Walter and me before...." Günther saw Stefan was trying to grasp an understanding of what had taken place in Berlin, when he and Leopold had been forced to rescue Elizabet, from the Gestapo.

"Did they suffer?" Stefan suddenly asked.

Günther looked pensive as if remembering the actual events. "The Count saved her life and knowing your brother, I am sure he died fighting." Günther gave a half-hearted smile.

"For sure, he was brave." Stefan nodded in recognition.

"There's a lot to take in my boy, I know, we can talk about that later, I just thought you should know, in case something happens to me, or I forget, it was important, what Count Erichh told me to write, I think, for your future." he gestured to Elizabet.

"For now you rest, we leave early, I will watch and wake you before the sun's up. But first I need to bury these and those. From here on, we travel light." Günther said, pointing at the books.

Stefan stood propped beside a boulder holding a lantern, watching only until he had seen where Günther buried the gold and journals wrapped in blankets and thick waterproof hessian cut from the ambulance canopy for protection. The hole was then covered with broken slate tiles and earth, then they marked the site by pulling a small boulder over the top using the ambulance and took four visible reference points on the horizon marked by the time and stars.

Stefan had his first night of sleep inside the ambulance, sharing the cot with Elizabet, although for some time he lay awake, trying not to react to every low distant thud crackle of gunfire and the anti-aircraft pops that filled the night air.

In the morning they disabled the ambulance and began the trek north-west. It was as Günther said, as they made their way uphill towards the rail line they passed the barn that Günther had torched containing the murdered refugees including the real Westerberg family. Stefan required the aid of a makeshift crutch, Günther had fashioned in the night, Stefan found the cloth wrapped handle, which he assumed was an old broom head unusually hard, but he did not complain.

As before they slipped unnoticed, hiding amongst a procession of beleaguered refugee's with heads down focusing on each step, as they skirted between German and American troops. On more than one occasion they were forced to dive into the road ditches for cover, by now all recognized the sound of the Merlin engines of a British Spitfire and Hurricane, but they dived for cover regardless of if it was an enemy plane or one of their own, fortunately, they were all enemy fighters that buzzed low and none opened up on their convoy, that was clearly made up of civilians.

When directed by Günther they parted company with the refugee column and those travelling at their sides without a word and began to climb an old animal trail, still heading westward. Eventually coming up to a low ridge that lay on the steep side of the rail track, in long grass and heather where Günther had scouted ideal cover a couple of days before.

The first train that set their heads low held a line of ten or so tankers heading south, they watched it drop into the valley. About to stand the three ducked again to the cover of the scrub, within only a few feet above their heads the air was split from the sky in a deafening raw as a formation of five American Curtiss P-40 Kitty Hawks, distinctive by their shark nose decoration, swooped in low in pursuit of the train, strafing the track. In the distance they watched as erupting fireballs from the tanker fuel barraged in sequence and as they were hit carriages twisted with the engine tumbling from the track demolishing the rail line. The American fighters then continued on their way following the line south, hitting any target of interest.

"Well, that changes our plans somewhat," Stefan said and soon found staring into the view began to hurt his eyes and lay back with his hands over his forehead.

"Maybe not look." Günther pointed in the direction of the lower hills as smoke billowed out from the tunnel and a train emerged into the light, it had been hidden safely within the mountainside tunnel, on its way up towards them as the Kitty Hawks passed over. The only question was if it was going west or east.

"Come! We need to get in position, we have one chance at this." Günther said, holding his hand out first to Stefan and raised him up.

As the train carriages slowed on the incline bend it became clear it too had sustained damage with some trucks having their roofs blown off, many appeared empty, presumably returning, to pick up the retreating and injured troops.

As they climbed into the second from last stock carriage Elizabet went first, then Günther helped push Stefan through the open door, throwing his crutch aboard he scrambled aboard, the floor was covered with a thick layer of matted straw.

"Mind you don't get any of this shit in your wounds," Elizabet said, pointing out the cow dung as Stefan slouched against the timber wall, the light slipped through the timber slating of the carriage as Günther stood watching to see which way the signalman would turn the rail key.

"Remember if east we jump," he said aware of the fact it was likely now the rail in the valley was damaged no other train would be passing for some time. As they pulled away, Günther slumped back and sighed, "Fuck!" realising as their train carriage clattered when passing over the rail points and began to veer right it was heading towards the east, he went to stand.

"Come we need to get off before she picks up speed." Günther held out his hand but as he took Stefan's weight the train suddenly braked, Stefan's bandaged hand slipped in his and off-balance Günther pitched forward, falling into a particular urine and sodden dung patch of straw, as he lay there spitting the cow shit from his face the three looked at each other in silence and felt the train backing up. What they could not see but the engine driver could, was the east line rail ahead had also been attacked by the same American Kitty Hawk fighters. They heard the wheels

reverse passing back over the points again then stop, there was the clanking of steel and then the train began to move off this time to the left and now heading west.
Günther smiled even though he was covered in cow excrement and Elizabet started to laugh, holding her hand to her mouth, cover it from the smell.
"Don't make him laugh, it hurts him," she said, as Stefan tried desperately not to join in, groaning each time his scabs ruptured, and blood seeped from a fresh tear.
It was hard not to succumb to the movement and repetitive sound that closed their eyes. Each, in turn, stole a few moments of rest as the train trucked forward without stopping at the regular stations, winding its way towards the coast.

In the lowlands of Selmsdorf, when the train stopped to take on water, they climbed down from the carriage. They were surprised to see others emerge from the sides of the track, who had been hidden amongst the wagons once the train pulled away.
Each group scattered into the cover of the woods, while Günther led the way and they climbed up to a ridge overlooking the shoreline, from the vantage point they could see the towns dotted along the Priwall peninsula towards the port of Travemunde, it appeared to have suffered damage, but there was no sign of battle activity, whereas in the distance they could see a battle appeared to be raging further south towards Lübeck.
Ships sat outside the harbour wall like ballroom suitors awaiting a dance, while two cargo ships lay at the dock alongside what looked like a passenger's vessel.
"They are not ours down there. I think Yanks, maybe English, but not Russia." Günther could just about make out the design of the tanks and the tracked vehicles that were moving in convoy along the main South roads, towards Lübeck.
"How do you know?" Elizabet asked looking at Stefan who eyes were still too weak, but he knew the answer,
"Do you see civilians," he asked, she looked again and saw a steady stream of ragged people winding their way from the fields to join a single line procession towards the docks. "Yes, I see them," she said.
"If they are not running away from the docks, then the troops are not Russian," Stefan said, pulling back and resting below the cover, staring up at the sky.
"Soon time for me to change, I think, then we see how good your Swedish is and if we can get you over the water with the cripple here." Günther went to slap Stefan on the back then quickly halted remembering his injuries.
"From this point on, you keep your shut, one word they will know you are German, let her do all the talking, no matter what, keep your head down you are no longer proud, no longer a colonel, just refugees wishing to gain passage to Scandinavia, that it." Günther placed his hand gently on Stefan's shoulder.

It was a considerable gamble, but their hope was the soldiers would look at his wounds and with no bullet formed injuries would assume they were not of the type from battle. She would stick to a simple story and claim his throat was damaged in the fire that had caused his other wounds, he was caught in an allied incendiary bombing and they prayed the soldiers would feel sympathetic in seeing his wound so severe.

Once they had made their descent to the outskirts of Travemunde port, they began trawling through the open back gardens and small alleyways that backed onto the houses leading towards the docks they hid in an outhouse of a burned outbuilding. In the confined area, Stefan and Elizabet complained of the smell, until they realised it was coming from Günther's clothes. The sound of passing American troop trucks and tanks seemed to continue well into the night as wave upon wave of American G.I.'s ploughed past their position, onward to the main assault on the heartland of Germany. Günther braved the gauntlet just after dark, to scout the area for clean clothes and food, returning within two hours having scavenged a wheelbarrow with broken sides and some personal effects. Unfortunately, he was not able to find more trousers, so they suffered another night of his stench.

As they shared the meagre offering of some apples and carrots, he had sources form one garden they spent time going over their plan and decided they would approach the docks in the early hours and try and get passage.

Elizabet felt through her pockets and produced the lighter and cigarette case Leopold had given her in Sardinia, she struck the lighter and the open silver case that revealed the engraved Von Stieglitz coat of arms, shone like mirror lighting up the small outhouse, the case was empty, with only a few meagre flakes of tobacco.

"I could kill for a smoke." Elizabet perked, out of the blue and made the gesture as if puffing on a cigarette.

"Me to, I don't suppose." Stefan looked at Günther, and he made a play of checking his pocket

"Let me see, no and really I think maybe I should take that, if you are caught with it they will wonder how a peasant has something so fine and German." Günther sounded a little scornful and placed the cigarette case in his pocket, then feeling deeper inside produced a handkerchief "But I do have these." he said, opening it he revealed a ladies Swiss watch and two rings that appeared to be a male's and female's wedding ring.

"If you are to be married you need these, perhaps you can use them to buy your way on board, I took them off one of those animals at the farm. It could be they belonged to the man and woman, look, you can see one has an inscription inside." Günther handed over the jewellery to Elizabet. She took the ring and using the light from the lighter flame read the beautiful inscription inside the simple band of gold, slipping it on her finger. She then went to the place the man's ring on Stefan's hand, again checking his missing his finger and noticed how well the wound was healing but realised his other fingers were too swollen and injured.

"Well I can wear them, I will make some excuse if they ask, thank you Günther it is good thinking, paper money will be worthless for some time I think." Somehow she knew, even if Stefan had not realised, Günther was not going on with them.

As they stepped out onto the cobbled street that led down to the quayside American staging post, where the refugees appeared to be gathered waiting processing to be allowed to board the docked freighters, two Americans soldiers saw their approach and called them to the line.

"Hey! You two, where have you come from? Get over here with the others!" As the soldiers challenged them Stefan twisted back on his crutch and realised Günther was no longer at his side, then shuffled forward, as Elizabet pushed the broken barrel, she fumbled for the documents Günther had given her and began to speak Swedish. "

Yer, Yer, tell it to the officers, we don't speak kraut or whatever it is your talking lady, just get over there with hubby, come on we'll give you a hand, pups."

Although Elizabet was astounded and indignant at being handled and talked at as if she was an old woman by the young teenager, she was also pleased with their manner and to the couples amazement, the soldiers ignored the papers in her hands as they stepped in close and instead of cross-examining them, they grabbed either side of the barrow and carried it while she aided Stefan into the line with the other refugees.

Meanwhile, Günther hid out of sight, he had decided, they would stand a greater chance if they boarded on their own, but stood ready to attack or create a diversion if they did not get on board. As it was, the single charitable act by the two American soldiers cascaded, as they set Stefan and Elizabet before the duty desk Sergeant examining the documentation of refugees. It must have given him the impression Stefan and Elizabet had already been preliminarily searched and cleared.

"Name, where are you from, where are you going?" without looking up, he spoke first in English, his manner was curt and as he repeated himself, Elizabet, who understood what he was saying, shrugged her shoulders and began to push forward their papers as if she did not. The officer then looked up at Stefan and asked the same question in German, studying his bandages.

"We are from Stockholm we were workers in the factory, German factory, forced labour do you understand sir, forced we did not want to work. It was bombed, the Nazi guards left us, we have been trying to get back since, my husband was injured in the bombing, he cannot speak, the fire." Elizabet's Swedish was perfect, and the officer to the right of the one looking at their papers looked at them closely as he was passed the documentation.

"This say's you have children, where are they?" he asked

"They are with my Aunt in Uppsala, I need to be with them, we need to be with them sir, please." Günther had been right, she was a natural actor, with no overacting.

"Other's tell the same and hide things, we must search you, I'm sorry." The Officer gestured to a guard, and made her raise her arms, the soldier at the desk saw the anger in Sebastian's eyes and knew they were a couple and seeing the guard gestured she was clear waved him back and looked to Stefan, "You too, old man." he said.

Stefan stuffed his hand into hers and gestured to his pocket, where he knew she had placed Leopold's lighter, he grunted as the soldiers stood back and watched Elizabet put her hand inside and reveal it.

"I found it in the offices of the factory, I thought we could trade it, you can have it, we don't smoke, I'm pregnant again." Elizabet curtseyed as one of the guards passed the lighter to the officer, who could see it was silver as he examined the engraving of the swastika on its side, he flicked it open and lit it, then closed it and place it on the desk, again as he studied Stefan.

Then he asked Elizabet three questions regarding sights in Stockholm, where the medieval Storkyrkan cathedral clock tower stood, on what street was the Nobel museum and what was the name of the large lake in front of the Drottningholm Palace. As Stefan shuffled forward to be searched bearing down on his crutch, they did not challenge his need for support, his wounds were self-evident, and the officer gestured to let him be.

"We just wish to get back to our children Sir, so that they can be there for the birth of their new sister," Elizabet said, pushing out her stomach.

"She says she is pregnant." the officer told the other and they looked and gestured that they agreed the officer smiled and pulled two return tickets with boarding passes for the ship placing them into the identity cards she went to take them, but the officer who spoke Swedish held them firm, "One thing!" he said and paused and Stefan felt his grip tighten on the staff of the broom crutch, as he felt the two soldiers that had helped them move in close to their side,

"how do you know it is a girl?" the officer asked in Swedish

"After three, a mother knows." Elizabet chirped back in Swedish, and the Officer smiled and let go of the papers and the two soldiers on the side lifted the barrow out of the way so that the next refugees could be dealt with

"Have them take what they need off that thing, there is no room for all your shit, you two help him on board and here, call it a christening present from uncle Sam." The American officer ordered pointing at the wheelbarrow then threw the lighter to Elizabet who caught in both hands and curtseyed again. "Thank you, Sir, I will tell my daughter all about the kind American, when she is older."

"Be sure you do and when you're on board, ask the ship's surgeon to look at your fella's wounds, or you'll be looking for another father for your children," he said as the next family of refugees presented themselves at his table.

Günther Brahn saw Stefan and Elizabet come from under the canopy of the embarkation station with the soldiers and at first thought they had been captured. He crept forward to get a better view and lost them in the crowd. Then looking up to the ship he saw Elizabet turn back on the long stepped gangplank that led up the side of the ship behind her one of the American soldiers staying with Stefan until he got to the first deck at which time he came back down to the dock, they were free, Günther had managed to save one of his boys, his own son Stefan and his future grandchild, which as it happened, just as Elizabet foretold did turn out to be born a girl Grethe Beth Westerberg.

Günther did not wait for the ship to leave port for fear of getting caught himself, he had other family members to try and save and began the long, perilous journey back to their homeland of Mecklenburg, where the Russian army had already ransacked and looted the town of Warren. The spiral capped lakeside castle of Schloss Klink was plundered and torched, little was left of the Von Stieglitz legacy. Fortunately, the housekeeper Murtle Lansford had left long before the Russians arrived, Günther would never find out where she went or if she survived, his sister's family, unfortunately, like so many others were not so lucky.

As with all wars, toward the end of World War II across mainland Europe and in many regions including the Middle East, over the years that followed, there was an enormous logistical problem of dealing with refugees and displaced people, who once the Nazi had been broken, wished to return to their homeland. While others fearing the Soviets as being no better chose to head to find a new life in the west and to countries that had remained neutral, such as many parts of South America and Africa. At first the allied armies were on the lookout for any SS officers and individuals of particular interest, but in general, anyone that could establish a tentative connection with a foreign state was encouraged to get up and leave Europe and considered as one less mouth to feed.

Stefan and Elizabet slipped through the net and across to Scandinavia heading to the backwaters of the Swedish countryside to join her Aunt Krysia. Who made no issue that her niece had a new identity or the fact, Sebastian, as Stefan was introduced, was clearly not Swedish, she was merely overjoyed her Elizabet had survived the war, when so many of their family and friends were still missing and felt further blessed knowing that she would soon be a Great Aunt.

Initially, Aunt Krysia took advantage of her position in the community to secure documentation and confirm their identity with the local authorities by using her connections as one of the oldest midwives in the area.

Her medical experience although generally of a holistic quality, was based on a life of serving the community of Uppsala and using natures natural remedies her unique formulas of potions, poultices, and salves aided Stefan's recovery and although she did not understand what the scientist had done to him, she found it strange how well his body was healing. With no apparent scarring to some of the deepest wounds, including the one to his leg almost cost his life when the facility was attacked by the English bomber.

"It's unnatural, I'm good I know, but I'm not that good, if I was they would have burned me as a witch long ago." Aunt Krysia remarked in private to Elizabet, as she listened with an ear trumpet to the babies heartbeat inside her niece's womb.

"No point asking me, I know nothing of what they did?" Elizabet told her and Stefan later confirmed his memory of his involvement in the experiments conducted on Sardinia were hazy and patchwork at best.

When they lay in bed, Elizabet found herself examining in detail areas of his body she recollected as him having scarring from the wounds of previous battles that appeared now to be strangely much improved, even the shrapnel etching that covered his lower back and leg caused by the injury he sustained in Libya was less noticeable and looked no more than if he had once had a bad case of chickenpox.

"That tickles," he said as he felt her nails gliding over his skin, tracing the pattern of scars, her hand then slipped between and below the clef of his buttocks cheeks as she felt him rise in her hand and she began to massage his penis, back and forth pulling on it slowly. He groaned and went to rise and turn to face her, but she used all her weight to push him down, straddling across his back she continued to pull at his shaft, her nails occasionally tantalising his firm rump she grabbed the back of his neck and pressed her lips against his ear as breathed heavily feeling him gasp, trying to hold back the moment.

"You like that don't you," she snarled seductively and bit the tip of his ear, kneading her forehead into his hair, she gripped it between her fingers as, stopped brief feeling his juices in her hand she rolled her palm across the head of his penis, slipping back and forth she felt his muscles spasm and in her hand the warmth of his coming, she continued to at him jerking her hand back and forth as loins erupted, he felt her hand slip gently away, and she slapped her wet palm across his cheeks playfully wiping some of his seamen of her hand onto his buttocks.

She then sat back in bed and resting the book she was reading on her bump began to eat a sardine, and green pickle baguette, her taste buds like her moods had strange and exotic tendencies through the later stage of her pregnancy.

As Stefan's strength improved, so did his memory of the facility in San Pantaleo and the secret work the Aktion T4 team had been conducting for the Nazi's working on the Vor Elle project. Although he had no memory of how he had ended up inside Dieter Myher's experimental capsule or the attack by the British bomber on the site, he assumed Professor Heikkinen had used the injuries he had sustained as an excuse to silence his knowledge of what he had done to Jan Van Pope. Stefan further speculated that it was likely the Professor never intended to wake him and would have used the fact he had volunteered as a guinea pig in their experiments to place him eventually on an autopsy table. Stefan also considered that whatever the scientist had done it was clearly affecting his system, and for the first time he began to consider retrieving the books they had buried in the hills near Schwerin, whilst he conducted his own private experiments on himself to establish how his body had been altered.

In the autumn Elizabet gave birth to their daughter, named Grethe Beth after Elizabet's friend in Berlin, who along with Walter Thomas, the couple often remembered and wondered if they too had managed to escape. The birth was remarkably smooth, not least because of Aunt Krysia's experience, but also the baby, although she came three weeks early, was of a good size eight-pound nine and was extraordinarily calm and mother and baby were soon a welcome sight amongst their neighbours when they visited the local church.

During this time, there was an additional welcome surprise to their relatively meagre existence, on the day Stefan threw down for the last time the crutch Günther had made for him, by now it had become an unwelcome house guest by the girls, as its

arm stock material was threadbare and on more than one occasion Elizabet complained it smelt like festering cheese.
"Time I got rid of this," Stefan said, as he was about to snap it into firewood across his knee in celebration.
"Wait! we can still use the staff, you two have to learn we have no money for new things, everything on the farm is reused, that will make a butter churning pole or a rake, take the old head off and burn the material if you must, but outside." Elizabet's Aunt scolded lightly.
Stefan did as he was told and hacked at the thick wad of material Günther had wrapped over and over around the head of the broom, except when he came to the closest layers of material to the centre of the crutch he realized it was not a broom head and scratched the surface of what he took to be a solid block of metal, that had been roughly painted with white gloss.
Günther had drilled a hole in a gold bar that he had painted while watching for the trains one day. Keeping the filings in his pocket to be used in his own escape, he considered in not telling the couple it would release them from the burden to lie and just hoped one day they would discover it, as they did.
"We can buy a thousand new brooms now." Elizabet's Aunt joked,
"My God that old goat, I never considered it was anything other than an old bit of oak and to think I nearly threw it away a dozen times." Stefan's face was frozen in astonishment, but Elizabet could see even though he was pleased to see this unexpected windfall, in itself, it created problems, anyone turning up with a large chunk of gold would automatically have the suspicion of being involved with the Nazi cast upon them.

Stefan made them both swear not to mention it again and from then on it remained hidden, only brought out when needed and only once they all had agreed, he would cut pieces with a metal saw from the bar and smelt them into small matchbox-sized blocks. This was not an uncommon amount to have and trade on the black market or in the jeweller's quarter that now emerged again in Stockholm. However, Stefan still made a point of seeking out different traders across the country and would always trade a small piece the size of a coin first, only making a couple of trades with each dealer over an extended period.
The bar of gold did not aid them to live like kings, but it helped, and to their neighbours and the outside worked they still presented themselves as frugal people, who would go out of their way to help others, while Stefan and Elizabet continued to live in the converted hayloft on Ma Krysia Kempe's smallholding.
To begin with, Elizabet helped with the apothecary duties, rowing the small boat on home visits and assisting her Aunt's unorthodox medical practice across the remote water lands, while Stefan remained hidden from the world learning the language until fluent and continued his remarkable recovery.

Working the farm he grew stronger each day, by the third month with the continuous shedding of the outer scarred skin it was evident the experiments in the secret Nazi base in Sardinia had changed the physiological structure of his body significantly.

Professor Heikkinen had in his final days perfected the viral antibody serum and what now flowed through Stefan's veins bore little resemblance to the SS tattoo blood mark that he eventually branded off the inside of his arm. The problem he faced was now any wounds he sustained healed with remarkable ease, and although on each attempt the tattoo got lighter, it took nearly a dozen attempts and then, it resembled a smudged birthmark and was never complicity eradicated.

No longer healing as it once had, each time it was the same, the damaged tissue of his skins outer layer created a fine multi-segmented patchwork of hard crystal scabs, some not much bigger than a pinhead some the size of a nail head, but each would harden and eventually peel away leaving almost renewed skin beneath. If pricked before they became solid the scab's wept thick honey-coloured sticky sap that carried no smell, but Stefan tasted it and said it was like bitter lemon peel.

Initially, Stefan and Elizabet began their own trials to discover precisely how his body reacted to damage, without involving her Aunt. Simple fine cuts in varying depths each approximately five centimetres long on his chest and upper thigh, each healed remarkably quickly, unlike when Elizabet cut her finger while chopping onions, which took some four weeks to improve, the same cut with Stefan would take less than half as long and it was as if no cut existed.

The breakthrough came when Elizabet was attending to a particularly deep self-inflicted wound Stefan had scored on his leg. Elizabet hands that regularly held blisters from rowing came into contact with some of the honey-coloured sap and blood. Although she washed it from her hands, some must have remained within the pores of her own skin, and the couple realised that whatever was running through his blood system had in itself inherent healing properties.

Additionally, Elizabet noticed Stefan's skin had a softer texture to the touch in their lovemaking, which was often, Stefan appetite for sex was at time insatiable, and the barn doors were often locked from the inside as they rolled in the hay while Krysia took Grethe to the woods, looking for wild mushrooms and herbs.

"You know Aunt Krysia heard Mrs. Johansson talking to some of the ladies outside the church how lucky I am to have caught a youngster like you, actually the term I think she used was cradle snatcher, I had to stop her telling them you are older than me." Elizabet looked at his eyes and brushed back his blonde hair, it was thick with no sign of grey or balding.

"What the hell did they do to you, my love," she said as she lay on his back looking at the hay dust speckles drifting past the strips of light that broke through the timbers of the barn.

"They made me hungry." Pinning her down for the third time, they rolled back and forth in each other arms, nestled in the warmth of the straw, he was like an adolescent Trojan warrior, not an ounce of fat on his body and although he joked about how he looked as he stood in the makeshift bathroom they had created, staring at the whites of his eyes, which were as bright as a child's, with hardly a trace of a vein, he winked at his image and then parting his hair examined his scalp for signs of the red flecks of age he had once seen, but his hair held a golden lustre General Custer would have been proud to call his own.

With the realization his mind along with his body appeared sharper he knew that the Vor Elle serum had altered him beyond that which Himmler, Nestlar and Professor Heikkinen had envisaged and having the facts stare him in the face daily it did not take long for him to reach the assumption that appeared he was no longer ageing at the same rate as others. In fact he had reverted to a better physical specimen than when he was in his early twenties and it was now the whisper of his deepest fear began to drift into his thoughts as he perceived a problem, in that Elizabet would continue to age, unless he could in some way synthesize his own blood in a transfusion or rediscover what had been found in the laboratories, that still remained, buried deep underground in the watery grave of the Sardinian hills.

Stefan kept his worries to himself, but as in his previous life he began to formulate plans for their future and under the guise of needing to release some of this new energy and further improve their standing within the local population of Björklinge, he registered as a volunteer teacher in the local school where their daughter Grethe was enrolled. Björklinge was a small town with a population of less than a hundred after the war, located in the Uppsala County nestled beside Lake Långsjön some 90 kilometres from Stockholm.

Post-war Sweden was no different to so many of the countries affected by the war, those that assisted their communities were welcomed and embraced, with a solid sponsor in Elizabet's Aunt and having become members of the Björklinge kyrka *(church)* and Gävlevägen society, his post for full-time employment was unchallenged.

By now Sebastian had become fluent in Swedish to the point he could converse with the students proficiently, his given subjects were building and architecture, chemistry and of course sports. The Björklinge cross country running team became invincible under his leadership. As with other parts of his body the Vor Elle virus serum he now carried had restored the tendons and muscle damage to his legs from both the shelling in Tunisia and the wound sustained in the bombing of the Sardinian facility and he was able to enjoy morning runs once again, sometimes taking along Grethe strapped to his back, stopping to show her the animal tracks and watching her play with the ant hills just as he had done with Leopold.

Using the facilities of the school, Stefan began to experiment with samples of his own blood and using the school's basic scientific equipment he created small batches of a plasma cocktail that Elizabet would inject with some initial positive results. Her hair in particular regained colour and strength and in herself she felt an overwhelming sense of well being in the days after treatment. The couple began to believe they may have discovered a possible solution, even Aunt Krysia was eventually involved, and amongst her herbal remedies she would offer to the local people, she started to supply an ointment that included Stefan's plasma in its ingredients. Those women that took it found its healing properties to be remarkable and were soon requesting further supplies of the small lip balm sized tins she prepared.

Within the second year of his employment and with Elizabet expecting their second child, Stefan was offered a schoolhouse, closer to town and the school. They deliberated accepting the offer, in spite of their general acceptance within the community, they were still very cautious about being discovered.
He thanked the Dean for the offer of the schoolhouse and declined, citing they would remain in the lowland hills above lake Langsjon, as it enabled them to look after her ageing Aunt, this could not have been further from the truth, as Aunt Krysia, like Elizabet had begun taking a daily dose of Stefan's revitalizing serum as an added ingredient to her own health remedies, including adding it to her baking and handmade soaps. By now Stefan and Elizabet had told her Aunt the whole story, regarding Stefan's military service and all three of them knew If his true identity was discovered, without a doubt he would be arrested and possibly executed, depending who it was that captured him. By now the Israelis had already established the Caesarea elite assassination squad within Mossad and unlike the Russian's, American's and British, regardless of what information or knowledge an individual may have gained during their service within the Reich, even if you had cured cancer itself, if it was deemed you are a war criminal and participant in the holocaust, you would face the consequences, by trial if you were caught, while a great number of released ex-Nazi's met with unexplained and sometimes unimaginable deaths, that it was speculated was by the hand of the Caesarea.
Initially, Elizabet and Stefan made a pact of blood never to speak German in front of others and rarely to each other, including no longer using their real names in private, it was something they had already been loosely abiding by, but they made it official. At first, it was almost a joke, and they played at catching each other out. But then one day their daughter, Grethe came home from Kindergarten and asked the question all the boys at school were all talking about at that age,
"What did your father do in the war?" the uncomfortable silence between her parents at the innocent interrogator question was deflected by her great Aunt's call for help in baking more oatcakes.
Adults rarely asked or spoke of it, an unwritten law; so many had horrific tales of burden, and few wanted to unload as they knew most wanted to forget. But it was a graphic reminder if they needed one that the subject was never far from the thoughts of others.
After that Stefan Keplar and Elizabet Kempe ceased to exist for all time, she was the beautiful and sultry Katrina and he the strikingly handsome young husband and teacher Sebastian Westerberg and a year and eleven months after their arrival in Björklinge, Katrina gave birth to their second daughter.
Immediately they could tell there was something different about the child, her gestation was only seven months four days. She was born 9lb 4 ounces, and even

with Katrina's tall frame, it was a difficult birth. Fortunately, her Aunt was on hand, and six hours after going into labour, Lenora Anna Westerberg was born on the 4th January 1947, in the same converted barn as her sister.

Grethe had been conceived in the early stages of the experimentations Professor Heikkinen had subjected Stefan too, but Lenora, named with Leopold in mind was a pure Stefan Keplar hybrid, compounded by the plasma transfusions Elizabet had been accepting, what was in his veins flowed through their youngest daughter. However, what they would soon discover was, as with many drugs, Elizabet's own body was building up a resistance to the effects of the plasma infusions, for now, she enjoyed the new lease of life with her young family.
It was a stormy night when the subject once again came up between them in private, of cutting gold to cash-in off the block that remained. There was less than half a bar left and although they had been frugal themselves, they had helped other locals during the post-war period in an effort to seed good relationships with their neighbours.

Katrina looked around the draughty barn, which had been made the best home they could. Far more homely than it had been it now included a log burning stove, which meant they no longer had to abandon it on freezing nights to seek refuge, huddled together for warmth in her Aunt's house. But part of her longed for a little of the luxury they had enjoyed in Berlin as she looked at her babies sleeping and then at Sebastian, raising her eyes, as the April rains found the smallest cracks in the timber roof shingles and around the barn the plink and pop of droplets hitting strategically placed pots gave the room a more cosy feel, whilst reminding them how temporary their position was supposed to have been.
"We need a house, a proper house with no holes, can we not take the one the school has offered? No one is looking for us here, no one cares anymore Stef…Sebastian! Look at me, we made It." she shivered as a tiny rain droplet ran down her forehead, trying to smile and rise above their dilemma.
He raised his eyes to the roof but thought she looked tired and recalled the last time she had taken an infusion of his plasma, while feeling the angst of guilt he had not done enough to make their home more secure from the elements, even having repaired the roof on numerous occasions.

He had considered her request of moving before but was still worried about their past and how he was going to solve the problem of their continued future that stared back at him in his bathroom mirror each time he washed. He had even begun to rub brown wax die into his scalp and often wore a hat and glasses, though his eyesight was now twenty-twenty.
As he sat smoking at the rear window watching the draught take his smoke, a loud banging on the old single barn door made their eyes lock, Sebastian leaned over the rail of the bedroom level, where once hay had been stored and looked towards the door, "Maybe it was the wind?" Katrina said pulling the blankets over the girls

"Who is there?" Sebastian called and watched the doors, but there was nothing, he looked back to reassure Katrina then the banging came from the main double door and they heard the heavy timber cross beam latch raise. Sebastian looked for a weapon and saw the broom-staff he had once used as a crutch. He slid down the open stair and stood with the stick raised as if about to swing for the Yankees. As the latch lifted the door was caught by the force of the wind and rain railed into the barn catching his face, icy cold it prickled his sense of expectation further as a dark figure lunged in, almost toppling forward with the weight of what at first looked like a large sack across their back.

Sebastian held firm ready to strike out at the intruder as Katrina watched from the open balustrade deck lifting her oil torch, as the figure leaned down with a deep familiar groan releasing a small sleeping boy gently in front of the log stove fire, who uncurled before their eyes.
Günther Brahn lifted his frozen arms as if they had set solid and almost wrapped them around the stove without a word as steam blistered from his threadbare mittens and heavy wool coat stamping his snow-caked boots on the old rug floor as Sebastian pushed the door closed sensing there was no threat from their intruder.
"Günther!" Katrina saw his grey thatch first from above as Sebastian stepped back lowering the timber pole looking on spellbound.
"My God, Günther!" He said in German, all thought of their vow of pretence was lost in the moment as the pair greeted the old woodsman in their mother tongue "How, where? How did you get here?" Sebastian threw his arms around the old woodsman and immediately felt the dampness of his clothes and how cold his body temperature was.
"Tell me you found the gold set at the end of that?" Günther gestured to the broomstick with a smile, as he looked to Katrina coming down the stair.
Then Günther gave Sebastian a sideways glance as he tried to remove his coat as if at first he was not sure of him, seeing his face in the full light, then relaxed as he felt Katrina aid him, wrestling with the heavy, sodden wool.
"I have been travelling all night, I dare not speak, they would know I am German, I did not want to bring suspicion to your door." He coughed and began throwing small logs into the cast iron stove.
"We need to get him out of his wet things." Günther pointed to the child, as Sebastian thrust a bottle of schnapps into his hand and watched Günther pull the cork off and spat it across the floor, a low satisfying moan came from his lips as the pure spirit burned his throat.
Sebastian looked at Günther understanding this must be one of his sister's children, too young for Samuel Joseph he must be Vincent Henri, he thought.
"And you drop them where you stand, I'll get blankets." Katrina gestured to Günther's muddy, wet clothes.

As Günther sat back shivering beneath a blanket, he smiled as he watched Katrina wrap the child up and Sebastian then take the child up to the bedroom area.

Settling the child in their bed, he looked back to Günther and immediately envisaged the dark scenario of Günther's return home and as Sebastian threw an extra blanket over Vincent and watched the boy nestle into the pillow he saw a deep ribbon scar near his neck. He felt there was something strangely familiar about the child, as he checked the girls were both still asleep and smiled knowing Grethe would be beside herself having someone near her own age to play with.

"Wake my Aunt, get some more blankets from the house and ask her to put on some of her soup." Katrina placed the coffee pot on the stove as Sebastian wrapped his overcoat around his shoulders.

"Go! You can catch up later, go Sebastian!" she scolded him as he continued to stare at his old mentor, as Günther rocked beside the fire with his bare pale feet inches from the flame the white blisters slowly turning pink.

As Sebastian bounded with no limp out the door and into the storm, Katrina saw the look of curiosity in Günther face.

"I know, it is how he is now, try not to stare, I hide the mirrors after he shaves, it worries him, what can I say, he has a young heart." she understood the woodsman was immediately taken by how well Sebastian looked and how peculiarly youthful.

"It's like living with a teenager at times," she chuckled "don't tell him I said that and don't ask me how I have no idea with these things. He has tried to explain what he thinks the doctor's did to him in Sardinia, he even has me bring books from the library to study. It's not just the outside that has changed." Katrina touched her temple, "he's sharp, he was never dull, but now sometimes I think he has swallowed a dictionary and he has begun to find out for himself what they did. But in truth he is scratching in the dark, there is nothing like this, except in fairy stories. He mutters about it, frustrated. I am sure he will tell you, you have a lot to catch up, tonight you rest, it is so good to see you Gunt my heart needed a lift, my Aunt says it is like that after a baby sometimes." she watched his eyes raise towards the loft bedroom area and a smile come to his lips.

"Two" he whispered.

"Yes, as I said you have a lot to catch up with, we have two beautiful girls who will be so excited to meet their grandfather and young uncle, I take it the child is your sister's boy, I'm sorry for your loss, if he is all that you found in going back." Katrina rubbed Günther's feet and hands with a warm towel and watched the colour returning to his flesh, then pouring a cup of black coffee and having added three sugars, remembering his sweet tooth, she placed the cup into his hands.

Günther thanked her and felt the warmth of her hands over his, she looked into his eyes, "I have said nothing, now you are here and when you are ready, but you must tell him everything, he will understand his father taught him well, now if you can make the steps come to see your granddaughters at their best behaviour." she said pointing up to the sleeping girls and rested her arms on his shoulders he tapped her hand and signalled his understanding.

It was time to tell Sebastian everything about his mother a woman he had loved and about the doctor, as a child and as Stefan he had always been told was his father. But was in fact a despicable man, that Günther had eventually drowned, because he had been blackmailing Count Erichh, for falsifying the death certificate of Leopold's mother and because at the time Günther suspected Doctor Keplar had also killed Stefan's mother because she was pregnant with a child, the doctor knew could not possibly be his own.

When it came to it Sebastian listened to the man he had always trusted and had on more than one occasion saved his life, he admitted the idea of Günther being his biological father was a little strange but knew somewhere deep inside that there had always been a strong connection between them.
"If you think I'm going to start calling you Papa, you have another thing coming, you old gardener." Sebastian joked as they shared some of Aunt Krysia's homemade sloe gin.

A week after Günther's arrival, Sebastian was approached by the Uppsala municipal college and offered the position of faculty head of the science department and once again offered a schoolhouse, this time it was detached and only two street walking distance from the college, it came with the temptation of future promotion to deputy headmaster.
Having examined the laboratory facilities and with an energetic boost from Katrina he accepted, and they moved into a detached three-bedroom timber chalet on Krongatan, while Günther and Vincent Henri moved permanently into what had been their home in Aunt Krysia's barn.
Over the following months, Sebastian formulated plans to begin talking with the scientific community regarding carrying out research that would take in much of the natural herbal and homoeopathic medical practices that Katrina's Aunt had shown them. It was a pioneering development of alternative natural medicines when most general medicine of the day was produced using traditional methods. Although Sebastian had a genuine interest in the development of products for resale, it was under this guise that he began in earnest their quest to replicate the results of the Vor Elle project to do so would require the recovery of the journals. He would not know until he had them in his hands some months later but unfortunately, having the journal would prove to be only half of the equation.
It was decided that initially, Günther would return on his own to Neuendorfer Moor in the hills west of Schwerin, where they had buried their treasure in the woods at its crest. It took him three days to relocate the remains of the rusting hulk of what was left of last army ambulance they had used, in their escape from Germany in 1943. With its windscreen smashed and having been stripped of parts and heavily vandalised, vegetation now sprouted throughout its skeleton frame and collapsed roof. Climbing through the sharp decaying metal frame, he located the boulder, wedged as they had left it under the front bumper and appeared undisturbed.
Günther swore under his breath with excitement, realising it still held beneath it their future, however at the same time studying how machine and nature had fused together as one the woodsman realised even with Sebastian's assistance they would need an ingenious plan to retrieve the gold and journals and another concern

was raised with the sounds of mining explosions as he looked out from the wood, northeast, towards the next hillside less than five kilometres away and seeing the activity of an industrial aggregate mining complex he wondered how long it would be before the site would be discovered.

That afternoon he placed a call to Sebastian to come over and bring money.
"I will need to exchange some of the gold to take money for the journey and if we need to buy tools," Sebastian told Katrina as they lay in bed.
"Risky?" she said "it's not long since last you were in Stockholm, have you someone special you know for sure you can trust." she looked concerned.
"Well there is this old Jew, he is a bit of scoundrel, but he pays in cash, small notes and I think he has a shylock business on the side, so he will not be one for the authorities." Sebastian began to recall the address of the pawnbroker, he had dealt with previously, "you know me, I'll play safe." He tried to reassure her.
"No doubt, but be careful my love." she played with his hair, running her nails through his scalp as they lay listening to their daughters stirring in the next room getting ready for school.
"While you are away, during the school break, I was thinking of visiting with my Aunt, this is a nice house, but I don't like it without you, and it will give the girls some fresh air, they enjoy time with Vincent, especially Lenora, I watch them chatting, signing, sometimes till their hands are sore. That boy is growing, I see you in him, but I still worry about what those Russian bastards did to him, he still says nothing, not even to Gunt."
Sebastian closed his eyes and tried to focus on that moment of warmth in the bed with Katrina. Her words were well-meant, but they darkened his thoughts. He also worried about the boy's future, and it was clear to him, although many took his reserved distance as being down to Vincent being mute, something else was going on behind those blue eyes, something Sebastian once recognised in his own, when he wore a uniform, when he was an SS. Colonel and Commander of Einsatzgruppe 7339.
With the crash of their bedroom door opening, the girls bounded onto their bed and dived under their covers, Sebastian immersed himself in the love of his family, banishing all worries for the brief time of pure happiness, knowing he was one of the lucky ones, he had escaped the war and escaped himself, ensuring nothing threatened what they had become was his prime directive, nothing else mattered except solving the puzzle of his blood, for Katrina's sake.

The following day having used a fine hacksaw to cut a slice the depth of a matchbox from the gold bar, Sebastian drove to Stockholm, parking in a side street, he walked along the river then crossed the bridge by foot, over to the Hornstull, Södermalm district to visit a pawn-broker on the island he had used before.
The covered head that rose from beneath the counter was not the old man he had dealt with initially, and Sebastian took some time pretending to be inspecting the glass cabinets filled with artefacts for sale, watches, jewellery and old medals,

including some he recognised he had once worn. He heard the man explain to an elderly woman trading in two old silver photograph frames how he had taken over the running of the store from his father, he spoke with a Hungarian accent, and he listened as the pawn-broker beat the woman down, paying much less than the silver frames were worth.

"Can I help, Sir, looking to buy a watch or something for your good lady perhaps?" he asked as the woman passed Sebastian to leave muttering quietly about the pittance she had accepted as she placed the faded photographs of her loved ones in her bag. Stefan looked at the watches in the cabinet before him and felt the gold ingot in his pocket.

"I came to see the owner, I have dealt with before, perhaps I should come back?" he turned as if to go.

"No, no, please I can help, you must mean my father," he said, eagerly sensing a trade.

Sebastian stepped forward and then noticed another man in the backroom, wearing a jeweller's apron working at a bench and backed off. Sensing his hesitation, the man behind the counter shut the door between them.

"My brother, don't mind him, we have taken over my father's shop, bringing it into the modern-day, please how can I help you, buying or selling we offer the full service including lending with the appropriate guarantee" he smiled, his third front teeth top and bottom were gold, as if something had once happened to have knocked both out at the same time, he had a cocky, streetwise nature which Sebastian disliked instantly, he would later regret not listening to his instinct.

Sebastian took a deep breath and rechecked the shop door, then placed the gold on the glass counter, he watched the young man's eyes glow.

"May I?" he asked before touching it, his hands hovering expectantly.

Sebastian nodded, and the pawnbroker flipped down a jeweller magnifying glass disc attached to his glasses and scrutinised the gold. Instantly he realised with the jagged edge that it had been cut from a larger ingot. He hummed annoyingly as he placed it on a scale as if making out he was disinterested and shuffled weight until it balanced while occasionally looking up at Sebastian as if judging him.

"A good weight, twelve ounces, what currency are you wanting?" he asked, fingering the metal along what was once a fraction of the Reich stamp.

Sebastian had made sure when cutting pieces from the main ingot to avoid a large section of what remained of the wings of the Reich stamp that would allude to the origins of the gold.

"Krona, of course." Sebastian did not want to inform the man he intended to travel abroad.

"First I check, with respect, you say you dealt with my father, we are not my father." he gestured to the rear, and Sebastian agreed to allow him to take the gold into the workshop to confirm its metallurgy, within two minutes he returned from the rear workshop.

"500 Krona!" he said, placing the gold down on the counter glass, but closer to himself than Sebastian.

"That is less than half its worth, your father gave me more last time." Sebastian felt his hackles rise but remained calm, he knew the jeweller would come up it was a matter of how much, but he also knew he did not want to repeat the experience in other pawn-shops in the city.

"That is maybe, but this is the price today, gold is not what it was if this was a nice piece of jewellery a ring perhaps, maybe a broach for a young lady, I could sell it in the shop, this has to be worked." The pawnbroker sneered, almost dismissively.

"Yes, I am sure, and if it were a ring you would say you need to melt it down, I know this." Sebastian went to call his bluff and made a slight movement with his hand as if to take the gold back, the jeweller placed his hand cupping it over the gold

"650, I don't know where this comes from, you say you know my father, but I don't know you? I don't need trouble." His words were almost a threat Sebastian considered, but he pushed for more.

"900 or I walk," Sebastian said firmly and put his gloves back on.

"700 my final figure, look."

The man stepped back and pulled his apron to his side, revealing a leather money belt and began taking out notes counting them into hundreds.

"Alright, but you include those picture frames you took from the old lady, then we have a deal." Sebastian knew pawnbroker had only paid 50 Krona for the frames that were worth at least three times that.

The man examined the old frames again and seeing one of the strut backs was damaged which he would need to get his brother to repair, he nodded his agreement and held out his hand, and Sebastian shook it.

With the silver photograph frames tucked under his arm, Sebastian left the store, vowing not to go back. As he walked back through the street to his car, he noticed the woman from the store queuing at a greengrocer stall.

"Old mother, for you, I'll keep one," he said, handing her one of the silver frames, keeping the one with the broken back. He whistled contentedly feeling happy about his good deed. Unfortunately, his encounter with the jeweller's son's that day would lead to problems in the future.

"Viktor! Quickly follow him, find out who he is where he goes if you can."

The pawnbroker called to his brother in the back room and then went to the safe in the rear. Spinning the dials back and forth it opened. He pulled out an internal metal box opening it with a key on his chain he took out a small purple velvet bag, loosening the rope tie he removed two pieces of gold placing them down side by side, each was the same size roughly, like the one he had just taken in from Sebastian. He arranged all three together, the cuts appeared to align, and it was clear they were all once part of one piece. He turned them over and looked at the remains of the pattern on the back, and looked at the design through his magnifying glass as he heard the bell of the shop he covered the gold with the velvet and shut the safe about to go through to the shop as his brother appeared in the doorway.

"I followed him to his car Miklos, he didn't see me," Viktor told his brother.

"Come look at this, do you see, you know what it means?" Miklos opened the safe again.
"Yes, I know this." He said, and took a gold Reich pfennig from a stack inside the safe and held it against the design on the back of the gold slices, the design matched a tiny section of the eagle's wing.
"Yes it's Nazi gold, maybe he's a Nazi, there may be a reward?" Viktor looked at the design, but Miklos shook his head and slapped him on the shoulder.
"It means there is more," he said "What type of car was he driving?" he asked, as he wrapped each piece of gold individually, then placed them back in the bag.
"I wrote it down with the registration, a black Volkswagen," Viktor said, placing a strip of paper on the workbench with Sebastian's car registration number.
By that afternoon, using his contacts in the Swedish police, The older brother Miklos had Sebastian's address in Uppsala and decided to drive north with Viktor and investigate who Sebastian was, they did not speak on it, but he had blackmail in the back of his mind, and each carried a gun in their coat.

When Günther called from the outskirts of Schwerin, informing him that he had located where they had buried the journals and the gold, Sebastian instructed him to scout for possible sources of machinery that would aid their task of recovery, he would pay for whatever they needed when they met up. On the day he left Sebastian drove Katrina and the girls to her Aunts and as he watched the girls move their bags into what was once their home, he held his wife in his hands, admiring the alterations Günther and Vincent had made to their old home.
"He has made a nice job of it. Clearly, I don't take after his skills as a woodsman, I understand it even has a bathroom upstairs now, you should be very comfortable, part of me wishes I was staying," he said grabbing her close, as he gesture to the old barn where they had often made love, as they cuddled Vincent came out from the barn house.
"They are fighting over the beds?" Vincent signed, frowning and holding his hands up gesturing as if to say, "What do I do?"
"I'll deal with it." Katrina signed back and left Sebastian's side, their fingers lingering entwined to the last touch as they separated.
"You watch over Aunt Krysia while we are away, boy, make sure she has plenty of firewood, and the girls, don't let them bully you." He told Vincent as he roughly rubbed his hair.
Vincent signed "I'm not a dog." and smiled awkwardly.

Although Vincent lived with Günther at Aunt Krysia's smallholding in the hills, Sebastian treated him as he would a son, even though the boy was unaware of their true family connection. He sensed the boy felt a secure attachment to his family, especially the girls, they were growing up together in much the same way he had with Leopold, they were even referred to as brother and sisters by other school children, and teachers. And Sebastian considered it would be soon time to tell him who he really was and that the girls were in fact, although close in age, his nieces.

But Vincent held the memories of a terrifying episode of his youth, buried deep within his core, and it was not because the Russians had cut his tongue from his mouth and slashed his throat, leaving him for dead amongst the bodies of his family, that he never spoke of it, being proficient in signing and lip-reading.

"No? I thought you were a sheepdog with that long hair, are you one of these American hippies I keep hearing about?" Sebastian signed back.
"When I get back with your uncle we go hunting, maybe with the girls if you like yes?" Sebastian looked at the boy and realised how much he looked as he had at that age.
"Maybe, but no girls they chat-chat, spook the deer." Vincent over-exaggerated his hand movements of the girls talking back and forth.
Sebastian smiled "Ok no girls." he said.

In February 1961, as Sebastian started the seven-hour drive to the port of Malmo in the south to catch the ferry across the Baltic sea to Travemunde, his mind was filled with the apprehension off returning to Germany, he did not see, waiting further along the lane there was the dark maroon Citroen parked up. The brothers from the Stockholm pawnshop Miklos and Viktor had witnessed his parting. They considered Sebastian looked like he could handle himself and was probably an ex-German soldier and decided, having confirmed the remoteness of the location, confronting two women and three children would be an easier prospect, it was an assumption they would not live to regret.
In Travemunde's roll on roll of ferry dock, as the engines of their ship powered down, Sebastian received a tap on his VW Beetle windscreen from one of the ferry crew waving him off and his daydream of the past was blown away by the horn from the driver behind, who was irritated that Sebastian failed to respond quickly in joining the procession of cars dismounting by the hydraulics gangplank.
Looking into his rear-view mirror, Sebastian raised his hand apologetically to the driver behind and pushed the car into first gear.
His little air-cooled engine sounded like a tank inside the hull of the ship until it broke into the sunlit harbour, skidding off the ships smooth metal ramps with a squeal like a pig, the line of traffic moved quickly through the security check, and the gate was already raised at border control, without getting from his vehicle he handed his passport through the window, the guard gave it a single look while talking on the phone and Sebastian Westerberg, Occupation: teacher, had his Swedish passport stamped and was gestured to move on quickly.
At the main port roundabout, he took the exit for Hamburg, once he had cleared the suburbs he pulled over. Stepping from his car, he removed his coat and hat, placing them on the back seat then paused, leaning over the roof of the car and half-smoked a cigarette as he looked back to the harbour. It seemed so colourful and vibrant, cranes were moving back and forth with building materials as like the rest of Europe people continued to rebuild their cities to aid the baby boom of the 1960s.

His passport stated he was born on the 9th May 1921 in Stockholm making him 37 years old, Stephan Keplar was born in 1917 his real age was 45, even having lowered his age, when his official passport was produced Sebastian still looked over ten years younger than his Swedish passport stated without makeup, which he mostly wore when at home in Sweden. However, when travelling abroad, he had noticed people appeared to regard all the Nordic races as a group that generally had a naturally youthful complexion later in life.
"You made good time, how was the crossing?" Günther stood alongside his parked Land Rover SI with the wheel jack in place as if changing a tyre parked beneath a bridge on the 104 road towards Gadebusch, 22 kilometres from Schwerin.
"So what have you in mind?" Stefan asked then followed him to an engineering company. Two hours later Stefan settled the bill and then stood admiring their handy work.

"Nice, makes me wonder why you needed me?"" Sebastian gestured to Günther's front bumper winch they had fitted, "you could have done this on your own"
"It will come in handy, but you will see what I mean when we get there, you know, I see how they won the war with toys like this." Günther spent a while pressing the electric buttons back and forth, like a child with a new toy.
"The Land Rover may be British, but the winch is German," Sebastian said with a smirk, then Günther noticed his expression change as he stepped back and looked to the hills.
"Does any of it look familiar?" he asked, Sebastian took a while to answer scanning the horizon back in front and behind them, then shook his head, "no."
"Well I'm not surprised this was a dirt road when we used it back then, and there were bodies in the ditches, a lot has changed, that's really why I needed you to come to see for yourself we need to make a decision, come." Günther secured the winch cable and climbed aboard.

They took the minor roads south six kilometres passing an open caravan site on the way when Sebastian parked up and joined Günther in the Land Rover, and they began to use cross country tracks into Neuendorfer Moor.
"I don't remember the land being so sandy?" Sebastian looked to the hills.
"Yes well, unfortunately, that is the problem." Günther pointed towards the large cleared mining area, "Germany is being rebuilt, sand and cement are in short supply, we go this way." he punched the four-wheel-drive locating the gear and set up the steep hill into a wooded spinney.
Sebastian stepped from the Land Rover and stood for a while looking over towards the aggregate mine.
"So we must move it all and today," he whispered we are lucky they didn't start mining on this hill, turning back he followed Günther as he pulled the winch cable through the vegetation and between them they secured it around the wreck of the ambulance that sat embedded in the soft soil.

The Land Rover equipped itself well, even when most of the wreck of the ambulance disintegrated in the process, and within two hours they both stood before the boulder. Sebastian went back to the tree line and checked that their work had not been observed before they lassoed the rock and dragged it away.
"You know I did my best but, the books may be mush, it has been a while." Günther stood leaning on his shovel.
"Well there is only one way to find out, we take it in turns you keep watch first." Sebastian gestured at the ground, confirming where he should start digging, and Günther nodded his agreement. As it turned out, Günther had only just finished a cigarette when Sebastian felt the snap of the tiles Günther had laid over their treasure. "Gunt!" he called.
"Now, we see." Sebastian looked up from the small pit and began picking his way down to the canvas sacking that had once formed part of the ambulance canopy. Brushing away the sandy soil, he held his hand on the material "Damp, but not so much." Sebastian smiled up expectantly and then pulled the bulky wrapping from the earth.

As soon as it was released with the first shards of light hitting its surface, the hole he stood in was caught in a golden lustre as the top four bars of gold were hit by sunlight. Günther's smile widened and then as Sebastian handed him the first bar, he held it to his face "So smooth, even after all this time."
Sebastian raised his eyes remembering Günther had a similar reaction the first time he saw the gold the basement of the old courthouse in Olbia, Sardinia.
Having removed all the gold, Sebastian stepped away and laying the canvas bundles down on the lowered Land Rover tailgate he began to cut away at the rope holding it in place. Initially, he encountered a few bugs and sand, but in reaching the blanket material he immediately realised Günther had done well in safeguarding the journals, the cloth was completely dry and had no discolouration from the day it was placed in the hole.
"My God, you did it Gunt you old bugger, how could I have doubted you." Sebastian wiped his hand clean on his trousers and traced his fingers over the embossed lettering of Professor Heikkinen initials on his own private notebook, he began to turn the pages, and as his heart raced, memories of Sardinia came flooding back as he recognised the script and equations in the Professors handwriting then he turned to the copy journal he had ordered Jan Van Pope to record a copy of the original Vor Elle journal. Sebastian's scientific knowledge had moved on significantly since his days as the Colonel of the facility, and his mind translated some of the information and equations with ease.

Having replaced the boulder and to some extent covered their tracks, they returned to the road and Sebastian placed the journals in his Volkswagen.
"So now we have a problem, what to do with this?" Günther gestured to the Land Rover, meaning the gold "Here maybe you could trade slowly, but at home in Sweden, eyes would raise for sure."

Sebastian nodded his agreement, "I need time to think, somewhere quiet, the campsite on the way here we should check it out, we are just father and son camping yes." Sebastian smiled, and Günther acknowledged it was rare to hear him talk of him in that way, "One thing do you have a gun if there is trouble of any kind?" Sebastian asked

"But of course, under my seat in the truck, what do you think you are the only one that thinks, just in case, where do you think you get it from?" Günther placed his hand on his shoulder and gave him a playful tap.

They rented one of the wooden log chalets and parked the Beetle across the back of the Land Rover. Sebastian sat in the small porch flicking through his copy of the Vor Elle project notes and came to the page where Günther had written down the account details for the Banks initials and bank account Count Erichh had set up during the war in Geneva, Sebastian strummed the page, as the seeds of an idea began to formulate while he watched while Günther barbeque a chicken bought from the on-site farm store.

"I need to run, helps me think," he said, looking at his boots, wondering why he had not packed his running trainers.

"Go, it will be another half hour, the gold will be safe, I'm going nowhere," Günther said knowing Sebastian found running helped him think and held up a bottle of beer.

The caravan Park had a meandering dirt path where campers had set up tents or pulled in with caravans as he reached the furthest edge of the trail he came across a group of people sat around an open fire beside three VW camper vans, Sebastian noticed a for sale sign in one and the owner saw him looking, the man appeared to belong to a group Sebastian took to be hippies and was German.

"Are you interested, man? Come! Have a drink take a look." the man said.

Sebastian had noticed a number of the same type of VW camper vans on the ferry, and during his travels they were particularly popular, he had not been inside one but was impressed with the size and having enquired if the man would take a trade on the Land Rover, he considered the old camper would make a less conspicuous vehicle for transporting the gold and had ample places inside for concealment amongst the rear bench bedding and small kitchenette units. He finished his beer and arrange for the owner to come and look at the Land Rover in the morning, which would give him time to remove the gold and inform Günther he was selling his pride and joy.

However the owner would not do a deal on the Land Rover, but liked Sebastian car because it was air-cooled and newer and when it came down to it, It was Sebastian that had to remove the little black toy VW beetle, that he had made into a key ring some time ago from the gift Himmler had given him. It had been the one souvenir that Günther had retained when they escaping Germany, more by luck than judgement, but after a while, the woodsman came to look on it as a lucky talisman and handed it back to Sebastian when he first arrived in Sweden with Vincent.

Günther could not resist a smile as he watched Sebastian exchange the keys.

"I don't know what you're grinning at? You have to drive this thing to Geneva, the Land Rover comes with me." Sebastian said and sighed as he watched his car drive away.

"It's not so bad the guy left some beer in the fridge, come on, let me tell you what you have to do next, I think you may need to get some smarter clothes. Tell me again what Walter Thomas said, it was a long time ago you are sure of the bank name." Sebastian slid the side door back on the camper van and as they sat inside drinking he explained to Günther how he had decided they should proceed as Günther reiterated the details, word for word, of what Count Erichh's Adjutant, Walter Thomas had informed regarding the name and location of the bank that his accounts belonged to, before they parted outside Templehof airport in Berlin, Germany in 1943.

Chapter 4: The Float

Geneva, Switzerland
February 1961

Günther arrived in Geneva and having located the First National International Geneva Bank, *(FNIG)* parked two streets away. With six of the gold bars hidden in a padlocked tool cabinet beneath the seat of the rock and roll bed of the VW camper, he placed one ingot inside his soft canvas hunting knapsack along with the letter of introduction Sebastian had written while staying in the camping village. As Günther walked to the bank he repeatedly whispered the code instructions to himself, which he had initially written in the Vor Elle journal back in 1943. The words that had been passed to him by Count Erichh Von Stieglitz, shortly before his death, words that had been destined for Leopold's ear, but with his death, Günther believed only Stefan or Sebastian as he now also called his son was the Count's surviving ward and therefore had a legitimate claim to access the accounts and whatever they held.

The plan was to initially create a company based in Geneva that would allow them to conduct business outside and inside Sweden, at an arm's length association, so as not to create suspicion of their new found wealth, regardless of what was in the accounts set up by the Count they required a secure location for the gold they had recovered and Sebastian, considered if the bank the Count had been dealing with was already aware they held other funds that had originated from the Nazi regime, then it would be unlikely they would go to the authorities and having presented the correct account information Günther would be able to deposit there gold. There was a risk, they would turn him away, but they both agreed they could not continue to hide the gold and to carry on exchanging small pieces of the ingots was far more dangerous and would take too long for what Sebastian had in mind in Sweden.
Although he did not know it at the time, Günther was on his way to meet one of the principal orchestrator's who would assist them in creating an entity that would support them in the goal of the resurrection of the Vor Elle project and see Sebastian's ambitions exceed his greatest expectations.
A thirty-year-old Swiss banker named, Charles Merryman, one of the senior executive accounts director's of the FNIG bank. Who had under his umbrella of clients a selection of middle to high ranking Nazi escapees involved with the Spider network and apart from the Germans he also serviced the accounts of a number of arms dealers, dubious Arab and Pakistani entrepreneurs and North African statesmen, some of whom he was unaware were funded by the C.I.A. key in recent months he had also been assigned a set of accounts that originated with a client in the U.S.A that were linked to the IRA.
Merryman dealt with middle-level ranking accounts those holding 1-5 million US. Dollars, he reported to two senior executives, the Spanish born Managing Director

Plácido Zabala and Chairman and owner of the bank Peter Salter-Kingsley, each dealt with the higher echelon accounts, however, there was a distinction between the portfolios of the Senior Executives.

Plácido Zabala from Bilbao, whose family originated from the Basque region of Spain, operated entirely as the legitimate face of the First National Geneva Bank, to aid the bank's compliance with international banking regulations.

Peter Salter-Kingsley ensured Zabala remained at arm's length from the more dubious clientele's and although Zabala was aware their vaults held considerable wealth gained from nefarious activities both before and after the war and that many of their international clients were using the Swiss banking system of non-disclosure to avoid paying tax in their homelands and to conduct illegal trades with impunity. The Spanish twenty nine year old was unaware of the full extent, that a vast section of the bank's portfolio was funded by gold and diamond reserves deposited by senior Third Reich officers that Peter Salter-Kingsley's grandfather had worked with before and during world war two, even though Salter-Kingsley's grandfather's Nazi party membership certificate hung on the wall, behind Peter's desk in his private office.

The late John Morgan Kingsley was one of the banks founding partners, born in Munich in 1904, he relocated to Switzerland in 1930. An anti-Semitic, his Nazi party membership number was 222, which he was also proud to display whilst alive in his own private office.

Before the war John Morgan had worked with Count Erichh, initially to secure foreign investment for Hitler and the Nazi party, at a time when companies such as Ford and the Rockefeller foundation were providing assistance to Germany. During the war when General Count Erichh Von Stieglitz continued to represent the Nazi armament department of the Reich Chancellery, John Morgan Kingsley remained one of his most trusted commercial allies supporting the illegal trades through shell companies and later, when the war appeared to be turning against Germany, he assisted Count Erichh along with Lieutenant-General Reinhard Gehlen, Hitler's chief intelligence commander *(SS FHO 1942)* and Lieutenant Colonel Otto Skorzeny in setting up the Spider accounts and implementing the code words and information required to enable all Senior Statesmen of Germany to access their accounts, which was how the Nazi's became to be referred as. Kingsley senior held 42% of the bank stock, and when he died in 1951, it passed to his only son Morgan Peter Kingsley who was killed, allegedly, in a climbing accident in Salzburg. His son Peter John Kingsley inherited the family stock and married the only daughter of another founding father of the bank Peter Salter and in hyphenating his name and producing his own heir apparent was awarded by his father-in-law another 15% of the bank making him the principal shareholder.

As Executive Director, Chairman and owner Peter Salter-Kingsley now serviced a highly select group of elite clients including the principle accounts set up by the Spider network, which held the main bulk of the funds deposited by some of the

Reich hierarchy, including Herman Goering, Heinrich Himmler and Count Erichh Von Stieglitz. All of whom were deceased, but all having left details of the accounts to heirs and loyal servants to the cause, now had their ill-gotten fortune managed by the Spider network executive committee, all accept Count Erichh's private account, which although it was associated with the other Reich accounts and used to some extent as additional guarantee, the account remained dormant, with the assets accumulating interest over time, including a large share portfolio.

The original founders of these accounts and the executives that now managed them were known to the bank simply as the Senior Statesmen of Germany *(SSG)*, In general communications within the bank they were referred to, just as the Statesmen of Germany and this acronym persisted for all other accounts with similar high profile, anonymous clients, so the IRA would be the Statesmen of Ireland. PLO, the Palestinian Statesmen etc.

If Salter-Kingsley had been in the office and not on board the banks own super yacht in Monaco, entertaining a delegation from the Somalian Statesmen account, he would have quizzed Merryman, if he had witnessed him creating a new account using an old Statesmen of Germany code when Günther had first arrived at the bank and probably thereafter interceded and taken the meeting himself, he enjoyed embellishing the history of his grandfather with any of the old guard he came into contact with, also he was becoming far more conscious for the need to confirm the true identity of such individuals and their legitimacy in accessing such an account, by now tales of Mossad's endeavours in hunting down those suspected of war crimes against the Jews was tabloid news, those operations Tel Aviv wanted the world to know of.

As it was, on the day Günther Brahn arrived at the bank, with Plácido Zabala reputed to be on annual leave, Mr. Charles Merryman was destined that morning to be the first point of contact with the Westerberg's.

In his long new overcoat hiding his best jacket and trousers, the sight of which probably would have given the security guard Claude Dennee on the door less of a reason to immediately buzz him through the locked revolving doors of Salter-Kingsley House the headquarters premise of the bank.

Günther chose the younger receptionist, over the spinster as he rested his canvas knapsack on the counter. It made a thud that could only have come from a solid bar of gold.

"Morning, do you speak Swedish?" he asked Swedish and saw a blank look on their faces, "German?" he said politely.

The 24-year-old receptionist was well trained not to judge a book by its cover, unlike the security guard who kept an eye on Günther, she nodded and smiled "Yes good morning how can we be of service today Sir." Her German-held an Austrian, lilt but Günther considered she may be of Italian descent reading her name, Francesca. He took a breath and then spoke words Count Erichh had instructed him to pass onto his nephew, Leopold.

"Yes I hope so Miss Francesca, I was told that if I came to this establishment at any time and introduced myself as an acquaintance of Herr Wolff, informing you that I have travelled from Munich, there would be someone available that may assist me, that is Wolff spelt W O L F F." Günther's heart began to race as he repeated the sentence, precisely as he had been ordered. Then stepped back, half expecting she may call the guard to escort him off the premises.
But her welcoming expression remained, "But of course Sir." she said, and sitting back in her chair, span her fingers through a Rolodex, as her colleague on the phone, who up until that point had been avoiding eye contact with Günther, reached across and tapped at a section of the Rolodex, as if she already knew the position of the card for such an enquiry, then continued with her conversation, in what Günther took to be Arabic.
"Please take a seat someone will be down to look after you, may I get you some refreshments while you wait?" Francesca gestured to the low slung modern leather lounge seats behind, as she found a corresponding card with Herr Wolff's internal bank exchange account number 18, beside which attn. PSK was written and then in brackets extension 60.
"Some water would be nice, thank you." Günther said hesitantly, he had never been inside such an establishment, he had expected something far more formal and less clinical, there was something almost oriental in the design and layout.
"Still or sparkling?" Francesca's pleasant perky manner made the old woodsman blush "Why sparkling thank you."
He sat down, placing the bag at his feet, which again clunked on the marble floor as Francesca dialled 60 into her receiver and the blue telephone on Merryman's desk rang twice.
"I have a gentleman from Munich, a new client, he has informed me he is an acquaintance of Mr. Wolff. The exchange calls for accounts 18 and Mr. Salter-Kingsley, and in his absence, your extension is listed." Francesca said with no knowledge of anything untoward or the connotations to Hitler and the Reich.

Charles Merryman looked out of his window at the lake, the Geneva water spout feature had not started for the day, "One moment Francesca." he said and finished his double espresso while considering the name Wolff. He knew exactly who had once used the name as an alias and felt his pulse race, but considered it may be the coffee. He had met clients before on his own and in Salter-Kingsley's presence, individuals who undoubtedly had been members of Hitler's general staff. But unlike his boss he was not excited or intrigued by their history and saw them just as clients, whose business he hoped would increase his annual bonus commission, increase his standing within the bank and Salter-Kingsley and by insider trading, with prior knowledge of any significant investment they made, boost his own modest share portfolio.
He left the phone off the hook on his desk, then walked out into the glass-walled balcony hall that looked down on the bank reception and pinching the louvre blind

he peered down to the lobby at Günther for a moment, judged that he was of an age he would have fought in the war and then returned to his desk.
"That is fine, I will send Miss Bishop down, thank you, Francesca." Merryman hung up and pressed the button on his intercom box through to Alice Bishop, Salter-Kingsley personal assistant, who he would have to inform, regarding the meeting.
"Alice, I've been informed by the front desk, an unscheduled visitor from Germany has arrived, I will be taking the meeting in the absence of the boss, can you meet me in the vault please."
He met her in the outside hall, and they walked side by side onto the main trading floor of the bank, and towards the walk-in archive day safe, where a guard stood permanently on duty, while the door remained open during the day, it housed the details of all the bank's accounts. Inside at the back of the main safe Merryman and Bishop placed their own assigned key simultaneously into the access panel of a separate caged vault that held shelves filled back to back with the red account ledger journals of the priority clients. Merryman, looked at the numbers and identified a group of journals all with the prefix number 18, German statesman books, they took up a whole shelf, and at the front of the group, there was one book, that clearly because of the dust covering its binder and gold-edged pages, he knew had not been accessed for many years.
"I wonder," he whispered to himself and then took from the end of the group a new account ledger already stamped with 18 on its cover binding back and then the main SSG accounts ledger which held the details of each individual account set up and the additional account verification and activation codes.
"Did you say something, Sir?" Miss Bishop asked.
"No, nothing, It was just a thought, if books could talk," Merryman said as he closed the cage and they locked the vault.
"I think we might be out of the business." she smiled
"Yes you're probably right Miss Bishop, as always, can you pop down to reception, escort the gentleman to room four, thank you, and do the necessary for Mr. Salter-Kingsley, while I prepare the paperwork."

The entry name and location code words Günther had spoken at the reception would only get him an audience with the bank executive. If he wished to open an account, he would need another piece of information that would identify him as someone entitled to access the Spider network and if he wanted to obtain funds from one of the select Senior Statesmen of Germany accounts he would need the precise account number and Count Erichh's personal code word. Without such information, any funds that had already been deposited within his account would simply stay in the Banks vaults until doomsday.

There is no official estimate of the securities the Banks in Switzerland hold that remain unclaimed by the Nazi account holders, who were unable to survive the war, but it, is believed to be in the billions in securities such as gold and diamonds, and it will all remain unclaimed if no one has the correct

access codes. "Herr Wolf" was how Hitler was first introduced to Eva Braun by his official photographer in 1929, his actual code designation pertained to letters of the alphabet with "A" being the first and "H" being the eighth letter, in written form 1 and 8, eighteen.
In setting up the FNIG bank codeword's of initial introduction to the SSG accounts the spelling of the name Wolf was deliberately changed to Herr Wolff.

Günther had just time to take two sips and quickly wipe away the bubbles tickling his nose whiskers from his chilled San Pellegrino, refreshed by a slice of lemon when the sleek pinstripe suited Miss Bishop with stick-thin legs, and 4-inch black stilettos approached him.
"Good morning, please come this way, Sir." She asked in German, Günther stood with his glass in hand.
"You may leave that I will get you a fresh one, may I ask how you wish to be addressed while here in the bank." She asked and watched Claude Dennee, the security officer return to watching the passing pedestrians, outside the bank.
Günther picked up his bag, the bubbles had got trapped in his throat,
"Brah, Lansford!" he coughed, correcting himself with the pseudonym he and Sebastian had agreed on, something he should not forget.
"Mr. Lansford," he repeated.
"Good Morning Mr. Lansford I am Florence Bishop, Mr. Salter- Kingsley's personal assistant, he is the chairman and proprietor of this establishment. I also assist Mr. Merryman in his absence, he is the senior account executive that will be dealing with your enquiry today." she handed Günther Merryman's business card, along with her own as they walked towards the elevator.
"I do hope you are enjoying your stay in Geneva," she said, then took a brass key held on the long chain around her neck and slipped it into a hole by the elevator doors, instantly they opened.
The small elevator was not meant for such broad men as the woodsman, in the awkward silence Günther smelt Florence Bishop's perfume, it was peach blossom and for some peculiar reason reminded him for a moment of his little steam dory boat that he once used to cross Lake Müritz when travelling back and forth between Castle Klink and his home town of Warren in Mecklenburg. He began to feel out of sorts, almost claustrophobic compared with the large spartan lobby he had just left,
"Nearly there," Miss Bishop must have sensed his nerves "there we are."
There was a slight uplift, then the elevator settled arriving on the sixth floor.
Günther was shown through the glass corridor and along to the gust office suites that faced towards Lake Geneva. There were six identical soundproof self-contained small client conference rooms, they entered number four.
On entering Miss Bishop gestured to the first door on her right,
"This is the restroom should you wish to refresh yourself, I will get you another sparkling water unless you require another refreshment, coffee, tea?" 7
"No water is good, I mean thank you." He replied and bowed his head.

"Good, Mr. Merryman will be along to see you shortly, in the meantime, please, if you wish, adjust the climate control to your own personal preference," she said pointing to the air-conditioning controls and then she left.

Günther, went over to the aircon fan in the ceiling and let the cool air drift over his forehead, drying a couple of beads of perspiration, then placed the case on the table, the Spartan room held a cream coloured new style push-button phone, one wall held as single large white landscape oil canvas the size of a door, at its centre at an angle was a red trapezium no bigger than a table coaster, then in black the artist name took up a large area to the bottom right, Günther scratched his whiskers as he studied the image, but could not make out the artist name.
He sat down on one of the chrome and beige leather office chairs that matched the glass top table in design and positioned it back below the air conditioning fan in the ceiling. It was refreshing and comfortable, but he felt on edge and restless and having checked the startling views of the Le Jardin Anglais below and notice that the lake water jet feature had begun to cascade hundreds of gallons of water, he felt the urge and use the toilet.
Washing his hands and face, he calmed himself, and while checking his hair, outside he heard someone come in then leave. Returning into the room, he found a fresh glass of San Pellegrino on a coaster and checked his watch.
"They don't seem to be in a hurry for you old friend," He tapped the gold bar through the canvas of his bag, then picked up the drink and went over to the window watching the yellow taxi ferry's drift back and forth across the lake, carrying sightseers and shoppers and decided if he had the time he would take one.
There was a knock on the door, and Charles Merryman entered carrying a simple note pad, he smiled widely on entering and thrust out his hand showing no visible signs that he and Günther had not met before.
"Morning Mr. Lansford, I am Charles Merryman, how are you today? I hope our people have been looking after you, apologies there was a little proprietary paperwork, formalities before our meeting could be conducted, now that is out the way I am all yours, how may I assist you." Merryman was a confident executive that had seen all manner of clients walk into his cubicles.
As with the receptionist, he knew better than to judge a person on appearance and with the code Günther had given, speculating on his age, he may very well have one of the Senior Statesmen of Germany sat in front of him. He was going to play it by the book because even though he had given the right code for the Nazi network, for all Merryman knew Mr. Lansford might be a Mossad infiltrator.
Günther informed Merryman that he wished to open a new account with a deposit and gestured to the bag he had placed by the side of his chair.
"I see, I understand, so I just need one last piece of information to verify your status, and if you have an associated existing account number that corresponds to one held within the bank, I may also furnish you with that accounts details and allow access for any exchange transactions you may wish to organise today." Merryman

studied Günther closely and began to get the impression the man opposite him was most likely working for someone else, which he had experienced before.

Günther thought back to the last two things Count Erichh told him he would need at the bank. The word Arno, after his brother and the date he had married, this would allow access to the main account, but Sebastian had told Günther not to divulge the account number at this point. He was only to open an account and request assistance with a list of business requirements that Sebastian had included in a handwritten letter that was to be delivered only once the new account had been activated and the gold deposited.

"So that we may begin I understand you have a word or a phrase for the account holder?" Merryman asked.

"Arno! But I do not have the account number, the gentlemen I represent will be in touch with that at a later date, at this point, he wishes to set up a new account the details of which I have." Günther said, remembering the words exactly as Sebastian had primed him, Merryman's first reaction appeared puzzled to Günther, but in fact, the executive was pleased that he had been right, Günther was a go-between, for someone that possibly would turn out to be important, for the bank.

"I see, that is fine, please wait, I will just confirm these details, and then we may proceed. May I offer you anything else or are you fine with the water." Merryman asked on his best behaviour, Günther declined and breathed a sigh as Merryman let the room.

Sitting back in the chair, he took a drink then began to unbuckle his knapsack, satisfied with the way things were going. "No big deal?" he whispered to himself, but it sounded louder than he had intended and he checked Merryman had definitely left the room.

While in his office, Merryman opened the SSG code verification account book, and scanned down the pages of individual account information, each line holding unique code words and phrases that matched corresponded with names and associated account numbers. He did not have to try hard to find the name, Arno. It was the fourth listing on the first of three pages each page held only 33 titles.

This meant the individual that had set up the original Arno account, that Günther's new account would become associated with, had been one of the original senior statesmen of Germany and consequently a senior member of Hitler's Nazi party and if still alive would occupy a position within the hierarchy of the Nazi Spider network.

At this point, Merryman felt his pulse jump, and he knew it was not the coffee he had drunk earlier and considered contacting Peter Salter-Kingsley. He reached forward and picked up the telephone receiver and then looked towards the trading floor and Plácido Zabala's office and placed the receiver back down.

Mr. Lansford had confirmed he was some sort of go-between for the primary account holder, he would wait and see how this progressed, looking at the possibility of adding to his client portfolio a way to increase his standing with his employer and increase his ranking against Plácido, whose position he had his eye on.

"Thank you, Mr. Lansford, that all appears in order. So as I understand this is your first visit here to the FNBG. There is some housekeeping I must explain a brief formality." Merryman set his pen beside a blank note pad that significantly did not hold the bank's logo.

"While here in the bank, everything discussed is ruled under the Geneva International Banking regulations. As such, all conversations are of the strictest client confidentiality, in addition, any paperwork documentation other than that which represents a deposit of the account holder will be destroyed at the end of the meeting. Anything you wish to take with you is at your discretion, and the bank holds no responsibility if on such an occasion any affiliated material with the accounts should be acquired by a third party. In addition, the bank would deny any association or knowledge of such material, if requested to substantiate it providence. I must ask now if you understand and accept these terms."

Merryman looked over at Günther and smiled, knowing he would obviously say yes, which he did.

"Good, now that is out of the way, your account is from this moment active, so how may we at the FNBG be of service, Mr. Lansford?" The banker watched as Günther reached inside his knapsack, from the shape he had already assessed what Günther was about to produce before the overhead strip light was caught in the reflection of the gold.

Merryman had worked in the bank for four years and was accustomed to clients depositing all manner of valuables that arrived in an assortment of containers, such as diamonds hidden in the false bottom of a coffee flask, and he had visited the bank's vaults on numerous occasions, where considerable gold deposit sat neatly stacked, but like many, he was always impressed by the sight and touch of the precious metal.

"The parties I represent understand the information I have supplied is associated with a long term account, however as I explained, at this time they wish to open a new account and deposit this as means of security and they ask I give you this letter, I believe it explains their intentions." As Günther placed the gold bar neatly on the glass table surface between them, it made an uncomfortable sound, on top he set the sealed envelope.

Merryman looked at Günther then leaving the gold bar sat back opening the letter, while Günther took a drink from his glass, looking away as if he had no knowledge of the contents of Sebastian's requests, which he did.

Dear Sir,

We trust having received the correct information from our colleague Mr. Lansford, the bank will be in a position to provide a facility to service our international banking requirements and provide additional financial and legal assistance that would be associated with account holders of this nature.

Initially, we would be grateful if you would deposit the enclosed security and give Mr. Lansford the details required to access the new account in the future on our behalf.

Will you please arrange the contact information for the following discreet, professional services that may be used in conjunction with this account?

International commercial land and property Solicitor, Lawyer & Notary
Shipping Brokerage agent
International Maritime lawyer
International Patent lawyer
International Logistics operator of Commercial freight.

Thank you for your assistance in this matter,

Kind Regards, Mr. Westerberg

Merryman laid the letter on the table and looked at the gold.
"May I ask will there be more securities forthcoming once the account is established, Mr. Lansford?" he said, folding the letter and placing it back in its envelope.
Günther nodded "Yes, I believe so, dependent on our meeting, which brings me to an additional request of contact information that is not on your list. It is possible the Westerberg's may require the facility of a discrete security detail that will act solely on their behalf, to be available in the future when required to manage the solution of certain sensitive tasks, with a flexible and creative assertiveness when required to facilitate the removal of potential problems, while offering personal security services." Günther relaxed, having used the words exactly as commanded by Sebastian, and he watched to make sure Merryman understood exactly what he was being asked for.
He did but knew this was something he would have to discuss directly with Salter-Kingsley before putting in place, however, he saw no problem. The bank had arranged a meet and greet, bodyguard chaperones for clients previously that entered through Geneva's airport and escorted them safely back when they leave. However considering the link with the German statesman account and other information requested he considered the Westerberg's were looking for additional services and this would require looking at the military trained personnel that might consider a long term arrangement with a client, a far more personal arrangement.
"I see, presumably for business negotiations, security and such like," he said

"Precisely," Günther replied then raised a hand as Merryman folded the letter and placed it back in the envelope, Günther held out his hand indicating he required it back,
"I understand the Banks policy for discretion, but respectfully I have instruction to dispose of this letter myself if you no longer require the request information."
"But of course please, however, I refer to my original statement regarding material removed from these premises," Merryman said, handing it over.
"Ok, I believe I have an understanding of the Westerberg's requirements if you would allow me." he looked at his watch, "shall we say two hours? In the meantime, the bank would be pleased to offer you the facility of dining at Hotel de la Paix, where we hold reserved tables for visiting clients. I can recommend the sea bass and steak, surf and turf, it is quite superb. Then when you have eaten, I will have a car pick you up and have the contact information you require arranged for collection in reception, unless you require any additional service, in which case, I will be at my desk all day and at your service if you should so require."

Merryman then leaned forward and looked Günther directly in the eye, "Concerning your latter request, I must speak with a colleague to ensure we choose the right individuals that have the degree of flexibility I understand you require and who are available for a long term commitment. Such a request has an inherent client discretion privilege, and so we take the greatest care before recommending individuals for consideration. However as a matter of course, should anyone the bank introduces not perform to your expectations, the bank would feel obliged to offer reparation for the inconvenience and assume the responsibility to provide a solution to remove any potential embarrassment, under such unlikely circumstances. For information contact purpose this is my personal card, few clients use this manner of communication, but you may call to inform us that you will be visiting the bank. On the reverse you will see a number, it is a 24-hour contact for any emergency requests both lines are secure and checked for listening devices, but we would expect our account holders to limit the dialogue until meeting in person on these premises. I take it you have a contact number or drop box of your choice, if the bank should wish to contact you, again, I must stress this is unlikely, during the normal course of business with the majority of our clients, but has proved to be of assistance in the past, this information is retained on these premises and attached solely to your account." He said expecting a business card, but when Günther gestured no, Merryman called his assistant on the in house phone, "Miss Bishop, please bring in a new Metropolitan box key."

A few minutes later he handed a locker key with a brass disc tag stamped with the number 555.
"Take this to the concierge at the Metropolitan Geneva, and he will allow you access to the day vaults. You may leave letters, documents, instructions for the bank and we will accept correspondence this way, the bank has a duplicate access key, and the boxes are checked daily between the hours of seven and eight, any

correspondence thereafter remains until the following day. We do not believe it suitable for long term valuables and do not accept deposits through this service. Of course, we anticipate there may be time delays of your own access and are aware this may include months and sometimes years before your next visit to the city, however, we ask client to appreciate, that is not the banks responsibility, and we expect our clients to make their own arrangements regarding their access to the drop-box. That said it is a secure system of contact the bank has been operating for many years, if you wish to provide a contact number at some time in the future we will update your details and you will receive a single telephone message, one phrase with no reference or identity informing... You have post, do you understand this process."

Günther nodded yes, "you have post, that's it?" he confirmed.

"Yes that's it, one phrase, only if you wish to provide a contact number, of course," Merryman confirmed as he watched Günther slip the key into his pocket.

"In addition to the lockers, the FNIG bank retains rooms at the Hotel, and we would offer the Westerberg's and your good self a complementary suite whenever you should require. For example, you may if you wish to, rest there today when you have completed your business. If you wish I will have it arranged, so now if you will wait a moment, I will deposit this in your ledger and give you the information about your new account. Can I ask what name have you chosen, it can be a place, a name or a combination of the two as you wish, but something you must not forget."

Günther thought for a moment,

"Flint." he said, and Merryman wrote the name on his pad.

"Just so yes?" he said showing the name in block letters, Günther gestured yes.

"Perfect and lunch, would you like me to arrange a meal for you at the Hotel de la Paix." he said as he picked up the gold bar.

"No thank you, I think I will have a walk in the gardens, do you believe you will have the list ready by 3 o'clock?" Günther asked.

"Yes, no problems please just see Francesca at reception when you return."

Merryman then left Günther for a short while and returned with the new red SSG A4 ledger with the number 18 on its binder, opening the cover in the front under the name he wrote Flint and then in the number he wrote SSG/4452790 he then handed Günther another blank card with the number stamped in the right corner.

"This is your own ledger it is kept within our day vaults and will hold the details of any deposits trades or documentation such as deeds that we hold on your behalf which will be kept in our basement safe. There are no personal connections between the account holder and the account itself, and you will no longer need to use additional codes to be granted access to the bank in the future. But you will need both, the name Flint and the prefix SSG and the number 4452790 to access your account directly, this number you must remember I have written it down on this card, you may wish to destroy this, please understand we would allow access to this account from any individual that presented this identification information."

Merryman handed him a card with only the account number handwritten.

"I understand totally, thank you." Günther began repeating the numbers in his head.

"In telephone communications or telex we will request, to process an instruction such as a transfer or stock purchase, three of the original pass code words to verify the account holder and three of the account numerical digits in a correct sequence, such as the first four and sixth number of the account, there is only one verification opportunity, if the information is incorrect in some way then the account is considered compromised and only the physical representation and verification of the account holders details on these premises may reinstate, transactions of this nature. The designated telex number for account holders of the SSG is on my card. I will, of course, speak with my colleagues regarding your security requirements and inform you of their recommendations through the Metropolitan drop box and I will add an additional contact name of an estate immobilier here in Geneva, who offers a discreet service, for assistance in finding a suitable property for the Westerberg's, if they wish to arrange temporary personal accommodation."

"Very good, nicely done, Mr. Merryman." Merryman noticed Günther failed at restraining himself from clicking his heels as they shook hands,

"One last thing I noticed you have a car park under your building, are clients allowed to access these for parking?" Günther asked gesturing to the window.

"Yes, you will need to sign in at the desk, and one of our security officers will show you to a parking bay, if you think you will be using it on your return I will inform them to expect you."

Merryman then showed him to the lift where Florence Bishop was already waiting, and she took Günther down in the elevator to the reception.

Günther walked through the lake park, humming, it was a beautiful June afternoon the roses filled the air with a sweet fragrance as mothers picnicked with their children on the manicured grass lawns, office workers sat in small groups on the Victorian-style wrought iron benches scattered across the park, watching the birds dip and drink from the bejewelling fountains. In the background, there was the continuous whoosh from the magnificent column fountain in the lake which drew sightseers to the water's edge railings, while the occasional traffic horn and distant tram bell was overpowered by the chimes of the Mollard clock tower.

Günther sat with a Süddeutsche Zeitung newspaper drinking a cold Stella, satisfied with how he had handled his meeting with Merryman. He listened to those around him in the open-air café while occasionally throwing tiny crumbs from the crust remains of his chicken salad sandwich to the tiny sparrow that hopped between the feet of the chairs of a nearby empty table. With a final look around believing he was not being observed, he returned to the VW campervan. Content that the bank was legitimate and would act as Merryman had said he drove back and this time in recognising him the bank guard Claude Dennee gave him access to the lower basement car park.

Merryman was halfway through a club sandwich when Francesca informed him that she had handed over the envelope containing the information, but Mr. Lansford had requested an additional meeting with him.

"I don't know Sir? The security guard, Mr. Dennee, has been instructed to stand watch over a vehicle the client has parked in our basement?"
Merryman left his desk still chewing and again curious, lifted the louvre blinds of the glass wall balcony so that he could look down and see Günther sitting once again opposite the reception desk.
"What do you want now old fellow?" he said to himself.

An hour later, Merryman finished the remainder of his club sandwich satisfied with himself, having landed a new client that appeared to have access to considerable resources. He carefully went over all the documentation, concerned if he made the slightest error and it appeared he had not followed the bank's protocol to the letter, that on his return, Plácido or even possibly Salter-Kingsley would choose to take over the account.
Initially, Merryman had been surprised Günther asked to deposit another six bars of gold into the new account but accepted his explanation that he had wanted to see how he would be received, exactly how the bank worked and these were the precise instructions of his employers the Westerberg's.
For his part Günther was just as pleased with the way he had handled the meeting with Merryman and having witnessed the gold entry in the ledger left via the basement car park to begin the long journey back to Sweden, feeling that he had done well for his family. He whistled to himself as he watched the bank's security guard open the electric gate allowing him to exit and gave him a wave, which Claude Dennee acknowledged a little surprised, being used to most clients viewing him if at all as part of the bank's furnishings.

Unfortunately for Günther, each time he had entered and exited the FNIG bank on the Rue d'Italia, his image was captured in the lens of the Praktica camera, belonging to two Mossad agents stationed in a white municipal van across from the bank in a side street. They were part of an eight-man team staking out four separate banks suspected of having connections with the Spider network, and were photographing indiscriminately any individuals entering or leaving the building, following up information received that the wanted senior Nazi officer, Lieutenant Colonel Otto Adolf Eichmann would be visiting Geneva that weekend, organising financial arrangements for his exodus to South America, via Madrid in Spain..
The FNIG bank was targeted by Mossad because grandfather, John Morgan Kingsley's membership of the Nazi party was a matter of record, still held in West Berlin. Günther's image was just one of the hundreds of images captured over the three-day operation by the Mossad team.
The following Tuesday there was a confirmed lead from the Nazi hunter Simon Wiesenthal of a sighting of Eichmann in Buenos Aires. For the time being the Israelis pulled their surveillance teams from the banks in Geneva. However, Günther's image labelled Subject: FNIG/31 was stuck in a photograph album along with many others, which for now resided on the shelves in the back bedroom of a

small second-floor apartment in Rue René Jollien the Mossad Geneva safe house, where it would stay, for many years.

Chapter 5: The Downrigger
Uppsala, Sweden
October 1961

"What has happened, where are the girls?" Sebastian stood by the Land Rover for a moment scanning the area, looking past Katrina towards Günther's barn and then over to Aunt Krysia's wooden cottage, he had caught something in her eyes the minute she stepped out to greet him, a look of desperate relief.

"Elizabet! Where are the girls?" Instinctively he spoke in German, his fear for them breaking the chains of their dual existence. Then as she placed a hand on his chest and buried her head he saw over her shoulder her Aunt emerge with both his daughters clung to her side safe, he felt a weight lifted from his shoulders and relaxed a little letting out a breath as he felt her sob into his chest.

"What has happened, tell me, I am home now, it will be alright." he reverted to speaking in Swedish as he tried to make out the words in first muffled sobs.

"It was awful, these men..?" she wept.

As she drew closer, Sebastian could now see Aunt Krysia was brandishing a potato-sized dark bruise across her swollen cheek, and then Sebastian's eyes searched for Vincent "Vincent, what men! Where is Vincent? Tell me slowly, what has happened here." he held her hands and felt abrasions on her wrist, the kind he knew were made with force, by men, in seeing some of her fingernails were broken he felt his blood rise and tried to stay the anger rising inside and allow her to speak.

"He's in the woods…Vincent, he's ok we are ok thanks to him, come inside, we are all ok now you are back, but it was bad Stef, really bad." She fell under his arms, and he gathered his daughters up as he stared in disbelief at the injury Aunt Krysia had sustained, and his blood began to boil.

The only thing that kept him calm was what remained of his military programming, on entering the kitchen he poured a glass of water and took a deep gulp, as cool as it was, it burnt his throat as he allowed them to speak, staying silent, without reacting, as the girls were hushed away as Krysia led them to her bedroom, with promise of a bedtime story. Only when they were out of earshot did Katrina describe how on the day Sebastian had left for Germany they had been attacked by the pawnbroker brothers Miklos and Viktor.

"It was so quick, they knocked Krysia to the ground as soon as she opened the door, I thought she was dead, we thought at first it was you come back having forgotten something." Katrina's eyes began to weep again, as she relived the moment when the brothers herded them into the small kitchen of the cottage then threatened them to find out where they had hidden the gold.

"They were the ones you saw in Stockholm," she said, but Sebastian shook his head in disbelief, as Krysia joined them saying the girls were sleeping.

"It's true, what she said," Krysia added.

"But no one followed me on the road, I am sure? I stopped, I checked, how could they found us?" he sat at the table, his eyes flickering as he searched his memories of the day he had visited the pawnbrokers, sure that he had not left anything that may have given the brothers directions to their home, seeing his feelings of guilt and anguish, believing somehow he had caused this to happen, Katrina placed a hand on his.
"It does not matter now, my love, they won't hurt anyone again." Katrina filled the kettle and then placed it on the stove.
"I will need something stronger with that," Sebastian said.
"Hell has a special place for their type." Her Aunt said as she rubbed more of her own healing cream on her cheek.
Katrina then explained that when the brothers had forced their way into Aunt Krysia's cottage, they had been unaware Vincent had been asleep in the converted barn outside.
"One of them fired his gun to scare us, he threatened to kill Grethe, the other with the gold teeth kept smiling at Lenora, an evil smile, like a snake. Vincent must have heard the shot." Katrina's eyes showed something else now, pride in how the young man had come to their rescue.
"We weighted their bodies, they are in the lake, he is out there now hiding the car, until you came home, burning their things, this will change him I think.
Then a head appeared over the rail of the landing, and a small voice whispered.
"Vincent saved us, daddy." Lenora smiled down at him, and Sebastian looked up and tried to hide the tears to his eyes wiping them back, then looked to the window, considering the boy.

"Calm!" Sebastian held his palms up, as Vincent span from the fire where he had been burning the coats they had stripped from the brother's corpses, before wrapping them in stone weighted blankets and dropping them over the side of the boat into Lake Langsjon.
Sebastian joined him at the fireside as he propped his rifle against a rock, first checking the safety catch was on. On a small flat stone, he had laid the personal items he had stripped from their bodies. Two wallets, two watches, a fountain pen, a star of David necklace and a black ledger the sizes of a small diary and two matching gold initialled rings.
"I cut the rings from their hands." Vincent signed, and Sebastian noticed the blood on the two signet rings. Presents from their father for their Bar mitzvah, if found on the bodies of the brothers it would help identify them.
"Good thinking," Sebastian spoke as he signed back, his use of the language was limited, so he continued and gestured to his lips, knowing now was not the time for questions. Vincent's actions had saved his family, and although in his past Sebastian had seen far worse and performed more heinous acts of violence, a part of him felt revulsion and at that moment he knew he was no longer the man he had been made by the Nazi's and above this self-awareness he felt concern for the loss of innocence of the boy beside him, who had become a man in his absence.

Sebastian began to examine a small black ledger he assumed the older brother had used or inherited from his father. He had seen this type of book before, full of initials and names, each page holding a tally of loan repayments and interest applied, from a casual look it seemed the brothers were loan sharks, offering loans at exorbitant rates of interest and examining the side notes he took them to signify that they were not averse to applying physical pressure for those that failed to make their repayment on time or in full..

"These men were bad, you did well saving our family, I am sorry I was not here to help you thank you, Vincent." Sebastian watched as Vincent opened up the wallet and took out a small photograph that showed the two brothers as young men arm in arm, smiling, possibly only a year or two younger than he was.

"They were bad!" Vincent signed.

"They are gone now, they deserve no thoughts." Sebastian took the photo and placed it in the fire. "Sometimes bad men have to die, it is better that way, better they had never been born," he said, then removing any money, began to burn the remainder of the wallets. Placing the small ledger in his pocket he looked back towards the pawnbrokers maroon Citroen covered in branches and bushes cut by Vincent, and he began to consider what was the best way to get rid of it, suddenly he felt Vincent's touch on his knee.

"Have you killed good men?" he signed

Sebastian watched him repeat the question and then nodded gesturing "yes."

Sebastian stared into the flames as his mind conjured up images of just some of the faces of those he had slain.

"Sometimes, it is not always possible to tell the difference, and sometimes, unfortunately, you have no choice…or at least that is what you believe at the time, it is complicated when those you trust lie and all wars are built on lies, something I hope you will never learn, but this thing you did this was for family, it is not the same." Sebastian nodded, looking for acknowledgement from his young cousin.

Vincent smiled softly as Sebastian went to gather up the remaining items, but Vincent placed his hands on the Omega black strapped watch that Sebastian remembered as being the older brother's Viktor's watch and let him take it,

"Yes, but not until we get a new strap, burn the old one, do you understand?" He said.

Vincent signed "Yes." and using the same bone-handled hunting knife, he had once been given by Günther and used to cut off the fingers of the brothers, he cut the black strap from the watch and threw it into the fire.

That night they all slept in the old barn including Aunt Krysia, Sebastian and Katrina spent the night talking in whispers discussing what had happened and how something inside Vincent must have snapped, possibly reminding him of the attack on his own family to make him act so violently and so quickly.

Both he and Katrina were concerned about how the sudden disappearance of the Hungarian Jewellers would be received in Stockholm. Apart from their father

Sebastian knew nothing about them, except what was in their belongings. There were no photographs of family, and the ledger was the only item that connected them to other people, the gold signet rings he had already melted down. But he speculated those listed would not lose sleep if their loan sharks suddenly stopped coming round.

"I will go and make enquiries once we have got rid of the car, I am taking it north to the old mine and flooded pits. I will take Vincent, we will hunt, it will be good for him. I think no one else will come from the city here, these boys, I cannot be sure but believe were acting alone, but I think you should safer taking the girls and your Aunt to our house at least until Günther returns." he said, but held back what was still troubling him, how the brothers had found out where they lived.

Sebastian then explained how things had gone in Germany and the plan he had put into motion regarding the bank in Geneva.

In the morning Vincent loaded the Land Rover with their rifles and the camping equipment. While Sebastian explained all to Aunt Krysia, including, what he and Günther had done with the buried gold and in showing her the Vor Elle copy journal and Professor Heikkinen book, told her of his plans to develop her own herbal and homoeopathic remedies and potions, as base medicines for the backbone of products for a new pharmaceutical company, that would act as a legitimate business front for their primary task of solving the puzzle of the ageing process, their ultimate goal being to successfully reproduce the results the Professor had discovered in Sardinia with him.

As Sebastian spoke of his past life, it was as if he was talking of someone else, and Katrina's Aunt already knew of the healing properties of his blood. Even the bruising to her face was healing faster than it would normally, having used her own aloe vera and arnica cream that Sebastian had incorporated his plasma extract into the ingredients.

As a healer by nature, Krysia considered pragmatically that something good should be made to come from something so wicked. With Katrina at her side, she spoke thoughtfully, and with an earthly wisdom of how she had come to know Sebastian, as a caring father and husband, a man she could not think was possible of the crimes of his past, whoever Stefan was, he was not the man in front of her and she told him that.

Vincent drove the Land Rover, and with the use of the new electric winch, they were able to take the Citroen saloon further than a car of that nature would typically go. They headed just over 150 kilometres northeast to Dalarna County and the Östra Silvberg mine at Borlänge, where they pushed the Citroen of a cliff into a flooded mine pit, having made sure the windows were open, it sank almost immediately, without a trace, bar a few ripples which they stood and watched settle. Then they head back slowly, camping in the woods and hunting deer, with two hides on the Land Rovers roof rack they approached a wooded clearing they had used before, approximately thirty-five kilometres above Lake Taamaren, where a figure sat alone on familiar logs, with a fire at the centre, with the window down

Sebastian smelt the sweet aroma of roast wild boar piglet before he applied the handbrake.

"If you have burnt the clutch you pay for it." the voice brought a smile to both Sebastian and Vincent's face.

"I have been waiting two days, for a moment I thought you would go straight back without stopping, but then something told me you would, I see you have been lucky." Günther gestured to the hides on the roof rack.

"Him, not me," Sebastian said with a smile.

Günther gave him a sideways look "Ah, ha." he grunted churlishly, as if he knew Sebastian would have let Vincent take the shot, and cut a strip of flesh from the small hog he had been basting in its own fat, tasting it with a bite he handed the remainder in his hand to his son.

"So we have much to speak of before we return, least of all now we know this young man can shoot, time to get him an upgrade, thank you, I'll take that," Günther said, taking his own rifle back from Vincent, which he had been using in Günther's absence.

"Go get your stuff pitch over there, before you eat, for the kills you made tonight you get the best meat." Günther tapped at his chin as he went to speak to Vincent and the young man read his lips. Apart from a few simple gestures, Günther's signing was far too confusing for Vincent, and strangely, in general, the boy always knew what Günther wanted before he spoke. This time he was not sure if the old hunter was referring to the pawnbroker brothers or the dear he had shot until he gestured to the Land Rover.

As Sebastian and Günther drank coffee and watched Vincent erect the tent, caught up with each other.

"Katrina, told you all?" Sebastian asked

Günther nodded "yes, a bad business."

"Yes, we will talk on that, but first tell me of Geneva." Sebastian's, mind was once again automatically prioritising, what was in the past and what was important for the future and Günther began to speak of how things had gone with the bank and his first impressions of Charles Merryman. He handed Sebastian the letter containing the contact information he had requested. Sebastian sat in silence as Günther prepared their food carving off the largest portion of crackling for Vincent and then as the young man joined them, Sebastian spoke again,

"Good work Gunt, very well, now we can begin," he said and handed Vincent his plate.

They ate as friends and family, Vincent described where they had been hunting the wildlife they had seen including bear and how he took down both of the bucks he had killed. Then they turned their attention back to concerns nearer to home, the older men speaking openly in front of Vincent.

It was decided that once they had settled Vincent back at the barn house where Aunt Krysia, Katrina and the girls had now returned, they would go together to Stockholm and investigate if anyone was looking for the pawnbrokers and if possible discover how they had found where Sebastian lived.

By now he had, had the time to study the ledger and one name of the many that the two loan sharks had under their screw stuck out as having used their extortionate loan facility repeatedly, possibly because of some addiction, gambling being the main suspect. The name of the borrower was a policeman, called Nilsson, Polisintendent, *(Chief Superintendent),* Dirk Nilsson.

According to the ledger he still had an outstanding balance of just over two thousand Krona, but at times had owed over three thousand and appeared to be a regular client that had defaulted on his loan repayment.

"Perhaps he helped them trace me? I know I was not followed and I left no details, I can only think they must have got hold of the car registration? That is the only link that could lead them to home, it must be that." Sebastian theorised correctly.

"So what you think we pay this guy a visit, find out what he knows, risky a police chief?" Günther advised caution.

"Perhaps, it depends, if there is a Mrs Nilsson, he is a chief yes? But I think he must have a boss, family, they would not consider it good that he has money problems or owes a debt like this. It could be used against him, maybe this is not the only thing he has a weakness for, it could just be this may help us in the future, I need people in power." Sebastian tapped the page of the book.

Günther realised Sebastian's mind still span with ideas at a rate of knots that he, himself found giddy, but he understood. There were possibilities in having the information in the ledger.

Sebastian looked at Vincent and then at the ledger and to Günther's rifle.

"It is time, woodsman, tell him who I am, who he is and who you are, he is a man now, and I want him to know he has a future as well as a past."

Sebastian took from his pocket the last remnants of his previous life that he held close to his heart and opening it revealed the Von Stieglitz crest, Leopold's silver engraved cigarette case, he lit a cigarette and offered one to Günther then to Vincent.

"I found the butts behind the barn, we know you smoke." Sebastian signed and said, with a smile.

"Well if it's going to be one of those nights?" Günther took from his jacket a bottle of Stolichnaya Vodka,

"First you must learn to appreciate sometimes your enemy has things you like, not to enjoy them out of spite, would not harm them only deprive you," he said, noticing Vincent's eyes fixed on the Russian writing as he poured some into his mug.

Günther then told their story as if it was an ancient history of a dynasty that had once ruled an empire. He started at the beginning, with facts Sebastian still was coming to terms with himself, and when he finished the three would be as close to each other as any family could be, with no secrets.

Günther informed Vincent of Sebastian's true lineage how he, not Doctor Keplar was his true father and as Sebastian listened to the gravel, guttural tone of his father as he occasionally slipped in and out of German, it was as if hearing it for the first time.

"All those years and Count Erichh knew?" Sebastian thought, his mind replaying every moment of his childhood as Stefan Keplar the ward of Count Erichh Von Stieglitz and the hundreds of memories he shared with the old woodsman, searching to find a hint that he may have received some kind of an inclination that Günther Brahn was his father, but there was nothing.

Over thirty years later, now as Sebastian, he had no allegiance or resentment as Günther described again how he killed the man he had always been told was his father. The doctor had been emotionally detached since his wife's death, increasingly prone to aggressive mood swings, although he had not been physically violent to Stefan.
If what Günther informed him was correct and he had always trusted the man implicitly, the doctor was most likely abusive to Sebastian's mother and directly responsible for her death in a botched abortion, soon after returning from the mines in Swaziland. Having found after fourteen months working away that she was once again pregnant, this alone would have sealed his fate by Günther's hand, but it was not this that led to his death.
The doctor had been treating the melancholy widowed sister-in-law of Count Erichh, Leopold's mother, who was the Count's, only true love.
Following her suicide from an overdose of laudanum, Doctor Keplar had begun to blackmail the Count, over falsifying the death certificate to save the family from scandal.
In reality, Günther had sworn a graveside oath and always planned to exact retribution on the doctor for the killing of his love Karen Keplar. Until the blackmailing, it had been the Count who had stayed his hand and cautioned a delayed response, impressing upon him to consider Stefan's welfare, in having lost his mother and then to lose the man he believed to be his father would be a travesty for the child.
However, Stefan safety in the hands of such a man always concerned Günther, and when the situation with the gambling-addicted doctor became untenable, Günther confronted him. Doctor Keplar had always suspected Günther as the other man in his wife's life, through the location of Günther sister's house to his own, but had dismissed the notion because of their age difference and the difference in their social standing, he was after all just gamekeeper, a woodsman.
The truth being, they had loved, and Stefan was his son, she had not told Günther she was pregnant again, but intended to leave with Stefan soon after the doctor came home if she found he was not returning to Africa. During Günther's confrontation with him, the doctor made the mistake of casting one too many aspersions against Karen's nature and Günther reacted in one explicit, decisive action, no threat was given he drowned him at the quayside, then towed his boat to the centre of Lake Müritz and dropped the body over the side setting his boat adrift.
Günther then returned to the castle to inform Count Erichh his oldest friend and master, what he had done, it was then that it was decided Stefan would become the Count's ward alongside Leopold, and Günther would be their watcher.

Even knowing and accepting the change in the circumstances of their relationship, the two men felt more comfortable continuing as they had. Günther was Gunt to Stefan, the most reliable and loyal man he had ever known. Nothing could change that and Stefan may have changed his name to Sebastian, but he was still the one person that filled some of the void left by Karen Keplar's death in Günther's soul, the only other being that of Vincent, his sister's child.
"So there you have it, that is our story so far." Sebastian raised his glass "Scholl", and the others joined him, "Now our future is a little more complicated, but that can wait for another day, go get to bed we will keep watch." Sebastian smiled, seeing Vincent was struggling to stay awake and feeling the hand of his father on his shoulder as the sparks from their fire drifted up into the night.
"Fuck that, I can sleep long enough in my box when I'm done, your blood makes me burn boy, now we swim." Günther stood in front of the fire and then to Vincent and Stefan's astonishment, with no modesty, tore his shirt over his shoulders then ran down towards the lake, his trousers palling from his ankles as he dived into the cold water naked.
"Come on you pair of Bokkelul's." Günther's voice echoed into the hills, Sebastian tilted his head, remembering he had heard the expression somewhere in his past and saw the smile on Vincent's face.
"Well, what are you waiting for?" Sebastian signed, then raced Vincent down to the water, as they stripped. While Günther, watched from the water and was struck how his son's body was not only far more athletic than it should be for his age but looking at his leg, where he had once witnessed many years before, the sight of a significant injury the scarring was far less visible than he remembered, but as they frolicked in the ice-cold water, he soon forgot his curiosity and enjoyed the moment with his family a grandfather that felt unusually younger than he should. Like Katrina and Krysia, he too had been receiving an infusion of Sebastian's serum, held within the balm that Krysia often massaged into his back.

When they returned to Aunt Krysia's the following morning, Katrina moaned a little that they had stayed away one more night, when they could have come straight to Björklinge, but when he explained the fireside chat with Vincent, she understood.
"Well, no more secrets, that is refreshing, it's bad enough keeping it from the world, you don't want to have to lie under your own roof." she smiled.
The following day Sebastian and Günther drove to Stockholm in the VW camper van. Stefan decided, he would also use the time to find a replacement VW beetle. The girls had asked him to look for a red one before they left. Disappointed about being ousted from their new playhouse, having already claimed the camper van.
"What is that for, the car?" Günther asked when he saw Sebastian place a small ingot of gold cut from the remains of the first gold bar.
"No I have cash still left for that, this is just in case the police chief needs a further incentive. Hopefully when we return to Geneva, now you have set up the account, fucking about cashing this stuff up will end." With Sebastian smuggling in one of the gold bars they had buried, their financial circumstance once again was not a major

issue although the experience with the pawnbrokers in Stockholm made them consider going wider afield and he decided to smelt the gold into smaller ingots before trading.

In Stockholm, while they staked out the pawnbroker shop for two days, sleeping in the camper van overnight, Sebastian took the time to search for a new car for himself, he did, in fact, settle on the purchase of a red VW Beetle from a garage, although he preferred the black older one they had in stock. In 1961 you could generally find at least two VW beetles sitting for sale on a car forecourt.
The pawnshop metal grilled shutter remained padlocked closed, and no-one came by except a few customers, some with an assortment of items they intended to trade. Using a nearby café, they learnt that the brothers had no other family apart from their father who was hospitalised, stuck in a bed on a ventilator waiting for his last gasp.
What was understood amongst the few locals they overheard talking was the absence of the brothers from the community was seen as somewhat of a holiday from their payment plans. One bulky looking Swede, who appeared like he may sleep rough, appeared to know more than others and from what they could gather had been used by the brothers as an enforcer when payments were not made, but even he appeared disinterested in his part-time employer's disappearance.

Sebastian considered breaking into the shop but decided it would be too risky until they had found out if it was wise to approach the Chief Inspector, and they switched their attention to Nilsson and began to watch his house.
It was not long before they discovered his nocturnal activities included, as Sebastian had suspected, gambling. Not only with the regular card school made up of other police officers but also within criminally organised gambling houses. Although he used his authority to avoid the penalties of failing to pay his debt on time, they found out his outstanding gambling debts were beginning to test the patience of some of the criminal fraternity and action may soon follow.
It was after this Sebastian decided to act and he approached the chief Inspectors house on the following Saturday, while his wife and son were still at home. When Nilsson came to the door, he looked quizzically at the suited man on his doorstep as if he expected him to announce he was a colleague, then looked past Sebastian to Günther, loitering, beside the red beetle. Sebastian removed his wallet, which showed his identity and on the opposite side were pictures of his daughters with Katrina.
"Chief Inspector Nilsson, my apologies for disturbing your weekend, but I required to meet in-person to introduce myself. I am Sebastian Westerberg from Uppsala, I am a teacher and a father amongst other things."
Nilsson was taking in his name and the photograph as Sebastian then removed the pawnbrokers ledger from his pocket, which the Chief Inspector immediately recognised, he looked over Sebastian's shoulder again at Günther then up and

down the street for other vehicles, as Sebastian opened the ledger at the page documenting the details of his loan that carried his signature.

"What do want Mr Westerberg, why do you bring this to me here?" the Inspectors face flushed, and Sebastian sensed there was a tinge of anger mixed with the fear in his eyes as he pulled the door behind him shielding himself from his wife who could be heard in the rear kitchen of the house.

"The men that owned this will not miss it, which is all you need to know." Sebastian felt awkward talking on the step but needed the Inspector to volunteer inviting him.

"So blackmail?" the Inspector made a half-hearted bluff of a laugh.

"If this were blackmail I would not have shown you, my family, looking from the dates, I suspected you had wondered why they had not contacted you for their regular payment, they won't."

With that Sebastian tore the page from the book and handed it to the Chief Inspector, who took it and appeared physically shocked, rocking back and letting go of the door so that it opened wider, again his wife looked to see who was outside.

"But I have not come to talk of this," Sebastian said as he saw the wife approach from behind. The Inspector stuffed the paper into his pocket, and Sebastian closed the ledger.

"This is Mr Westerberg darling, from Uppsala, please make him a coffee?" he gestured for Sebastian to enter and took him through to his study and it was only as he repeated Sebastian's name that he realised this must be the man that the pawnbroker Viktor requested he trace through his car registration. As he closed the door to his study, he said nothing and then listened as Sebastian explained that he understood that the brothers had left Stockholm indefinitely and that he had come into the possession of the ledger.

However, the book was not a significant issue, other than it aided his introduction to Nilsson. Sebastian then explained that he was in the process of setting up an international pharmaceutical company based in Geneva that would carry out business in Sweden and that he had need of individuals that held positions of authority that may on occasion be requested to offer assistance, in his future business venture.

"If it involves drugs I am not interested, I have a child of my own, junkies cannot be trusted, all those I have met that deal eventually take!" Nilsson, moral stance took Sebastian by surprise.

"I understand, as I said I am a father myself, rest assured it does not involve drugs, at least not of the recreational kind. That is all I am prepared to say of my business at this point, you need only be content that it is nothing to do with any criminal activities or criminals that you may have previously been associated with, who from this moment on, if you agree to my proposal you will terminate your association with, and how you deal with that is your business, think of it as a second chance, a new life for you and your family."

With that, Sebastian placed the gold ingot on Nilsson's desk and then picked up his coffee and drank while the Inspector examined it.

"A sign of good faith like the page from the book, to show you I am a determined, resourceful individual, I have a goal which if you are willing to assist in, you will become a very wealthy man and I assure your gambling debt will be a thing of the past." Sebastian studied Nilsson and could see he understood the implications of what he was saying.

Nilsson was a career police officer that had reached his highest rung, those above him already knew his character was flawed. To find he was released from an enormous debt with the pawnbrokers, the gold was a carrot he could not resist, Sebastian knew he had him.

"I am returning home today with my companion. But before I go, I think it would be remiss of me if I were not to mention, the pawnshop is unattended. You may consider that the page from the ledger is not the only evidence that was kept against you. Also, I am sure that certain individuals, people you may be acquainted with, might consider it an attractive proposition. If those individuals were to act on this knowledge, it would deflect suspicion for the disappearance of the owners in their direction."

"And you are sure they are not coming back?" Nilsson looked to Sebastian as he placed the gold into the top drawer of his desk and understood he was dealing with a man who skilfully calculated every eventuality.

"It is something I have never done before, but I swear it on my daughter's lives, you will not see those men again." Sebastian got ready to leave.

"We will create an account in Switzerland for you that will facilitate any future payments. I believe a formal letter of representation as an advisor to the Geneva-based company may assist with any awkward questions, I will arrange this with contact information. There is one last thing, I assumed that the brothers traced my details through my car registration, do you have it?"

Sebastian could see that the Chief Inspector was now recollecting the telephone call he received from Viktor and he began to flick through the pages of his desk diary and tore the bottom of the day notation that carried Sebastian's details.

"A sign of good faith Mr Westerberg, I look forward to working for you," he said, and they shook hands, in no doubt of his position within this new business relationship.

"And I, you Mr Nilsson and a last word on that, loyalty is a value I treasure above all other attributes in those I call friend and ally if you appreciate this I see no reason for us not to have a very long and mutually beneficial relationship." Sebastian held out his hand, and they parted.

Sebastian could not know it, but the Chief had for some time been attempting to make a break from his wayward lifestyle, which had begun to spiral to depths that would have seen an end to his career and marriage. His efforts had been hampered by those that he had fallen in with and like many gamblers the wish to win back enough to clear his debts. Sebastian's offer was to set him on a new path, for himself and his family, and he would never forget that debt.

The following night the pawnshop in Hornstull was burgled and set on fire. There were no arrest, a selection of known felons were brought in for questioning, no arrest followed, it was suspected that the brothers had been killed and their bodies disposed of in the river, the case remains open, all outstanding debt's that the police chief Nilsson had were cancelled that night.

In the future with his many contacts, the Chief Inspector would prove to become an essential asset in the meteoric rise of the Westerberg Pharmaceutical Company and of the acceptance of Stefan and Katrina Westerberg in Stockholm's elite society.

Chapter 6: The Hook Shank
Geneva, Switzerland
November 1961

On the day he returned to his office, Peter Salter-Kingsley held a meeting with his account executives. His mood was irritated having learnt Plácido Zabala had notified the bank, following a visit to his homeland, he was having a forced extension of leave, for an indefinite period due to a family illness.
"I thought Zabala was an orphan?" Salter-Kingsley looked to Florence Bishop.
"I'm not sure, Sir." Florence Bishop shrugged lightly, as she handed around separate folders, having divided up his workload in his absence, amongst the other accounts executives including Charles Merryman.
When all standard banking business was completed, Salter-Kingsley held back Merryman, to further discuss the visit by the German, Mr Lansford, Günther, and the account information he had provided to open the new account for the Westerberg's.
Salter-Kingsley opened his top right draw and flipping a switch on a sunken control board the timber panel behind his desk slid to one side revealing four black and white screens hidden behind. He hit the videotape rewind on room four then pressed play, and they watched the black and white image of Günther's visit.
It was the first time Salter-Kingsley had allowed Merryman access to the internal surveillance equipment that all executives knew their boss used to keep watch on internal bank proceedings. Merryman took the time to note how the system worked and where he kept the key in the centre drawer of his large antique yew panelled leather-topped partnership desk.
"I from Francesca understand he spoke Swedish when he first arrived in reception, you sure he was German?" he asked as he watched the tape play, then paused on the image of Günther as he was seen emerging from the bathroom in conference room four.
"Yes Sir, he was definitely German," Merryman said and watched his own image appear on the screen as Salter-Kingsley allowed the tape to continue.
"Ok, well let me know if this gentleman visits again or if this Westerberg character, presumably his employer, contacts the bank. In the meantime, use the Metropolitan drop box you gave him, send him a letter of welcome as a new client, with my details and Merryman, good work. With Plácido away, I am going to be looking especially to you to take up some of the slack with some of special client's, I'm going to have my hands full dealing with the Ferranti merger and have to brush up on my Spanish, to be honest, Plácido could not have picked a worse time to go AWOL. I hope I can count on you to step up to the plate." Salter-Kingsley said.
"Of course, Sir, whatever it takes. I should just mention, when I was informed of Mr Zabala's absence, I decided it may be appropriate to reschedule my own break and

cancelled my skiing trip to Mayrhofen." Merryman played down his munificence brown-nosing.
"Very good, if you are out of pocket in some way Charles, then see Miss Bishop, she will bill it to expenses, in the meantime let's have a morning brunch just the two of us at the end of the week, catch up, my treat."
Merryman noticed his boss responded with his first name and held back a smile, while praying inside that whatever was wrong Plácido Zabala's family, long may it continue.

Two weeks later, during a first-quarter audit of the German Senior Statesman accounts, Salter-Kingsley played the same videotape showing Günther's visit to the bank to Friedrich Fischer, a financial executive who was a member of the Spider organization and acted as their in house accountant.
"As you are aware, I cannot access the funds on your client's behalf. Mr Lansford and the Westerberg's are separate clients to the bank in their own right. Strictly speaking, I should not even speak of them, however as they provided the correct security access codes that are associated with one of the original investment accounts and because of our long association with the GSS, I thought your clients should be made aware of their contact."
Salter-Kingsley gestured to his grandfather's Nazi party membership certificate. "I considered possibly there will be some connection that your Executive Directors may be aware of, that may benefit both parties, possibly in the future." Salter-Kingsley pressed the pause button freezing the image of Günther on the screen.
"I don't know this person myself and have no recollection of the name Westerberg as being associated with my client, but they will require immediate notification. An associate of the Chief Executive Director or I will contact you directly regarding any action that is required." Fischer studied the image as it juddered back and forth, caught in a fraction of a second.

Twenty-eight year old, Friedrich Fischer was the only surviving son of SS Colonel Hans Fischer. He had been indoctrinated into the Spider network organization, in much the same way most of the younger serving members had.
With his father killed in defence of Berlin in 1945 and having been recognized by the Executive Directors of the Spider organization as a loyal hero of the Reich. Friedrich and his mother were supported in the years immediately after the defeat of the Nazi's and he was groomed and educated, with a clear path to serve their purpose in the future, he finished his education top of his class in Edinburgh, Scotland and became a member of the Association of Certified and Corporate Accountants with international credentials. A loyal and officious representative that had one purpose, to serve a cause that had effectively saved his mothers and his own life and to continue his father's legacy, in the service of only one client, Spider.
"Please take the tape." Salter-Kingsley pressed eject and then waited for an age for it to rise from the player before handing over the large videocassette along with the

latest reports of the Spider Networks account statements of banking transactions and the details of the gold ingots Günther had deposited.
"Please secure their gold in our reserves, replace it with unmarked examples *(with no Swastika)*. Also, I will require one bar as a sample for examination, to withdraw today." Fischer requested, then smiled as Salter-Kingsley opened his personal safe and removed a single bar of gold, having already perceived Friedrich's request.
"Very good." Fischer gestured with a gesture of satisfaction.

That night having discussed the matter with the Chief Executive Director *(CED)* in Rome, Fischer was instructed to call the Senior Director of the Spider organization responsible for finance and international funding.
"I am sorry to disturb you so late Herr Director, there has been a development at the FNIG bank in Geneva, and we thought you should be made aware of before you leave for New York." Fischer was respectful in his tone.
"I will be sending you a facsimile through to your machine at the end of this telephone conversation. It concerns the arrangements of a new client to the bank, which may prove to have legitimate access to a senior Statesman account, however considering the account the identity of the individual is of concern to the CED."

In his small study with its walls plastered with family photographs that chartered their lives and his children's growth from ski school to both his daughter Stefani and son Erichh's proficiency in having won numerous cups and medals which he proudly displayed in a wall cabinet, Walter Thomas stared out of the window over the mountain views towards the speckled lights in the distance of Geneva.
"The committee is aware and respects your wish for a detachment from this specific location in Geneva. However, the CED considered on this occasion because of the historical connection, you may wish to take an active role. The account access information in question relates to one of those from the early days. I have the committee's authorization and can, of course, make arrangements to have our operatives in the region deal with this if you wish." Fischer paused, awaiting instructions.
Walter looked at the bank account numbers he had been given of the SGS associated accounts and the account code word used by Günther,
"Flint," he whispered, something stirred in his subconscious, but it was deep belonging to a distant time, memories that held vague recollections of his youth.
Like a summer's day with his family at a beach, when as a child playing with his elder brothers, none of whom survived the war, the warmth of the sun and the smell of the sea he could remember well, but the face of his parents and brothers were blurred. He made no connection to his own past from the words and names Fischer had given him. Tired he traced a ring around the names, Lansford and Westerberg then looked up at a picture of his wife and children.
"The names mean nothing to me, there was a General Ralph Westring a member of the armaments division, I knew once, but he never made it out of Berlin. Have they

made a withdrawal, these people?" he asked, writing the account number in the margin of his private diary, then placed it in his briefcase that held his passport and a flight ticket.
"No, the opposite the banker Salter-Kingsley, you will remember his grandfather, he has informed us an initial separate account was opened, and a deposit was made in gold, along with a detailed request for information and personnel to assist in what appears an international commercial venture. The Chief Executive believes that it is likely a younger relative of an old acquaintance of Mr Wolff or member of the original Senior Executive that has inherited the information. Interestingly, whoever it is they have not requested contact at this time with the organization. At this juncture until their identity, original link to the accounts and their intentions are verified by an executive member, such as your good self, it has been decided by the Chief Executive Director to withhold contact information to our organization if it is requested at some future date. The bank has no specific contact information at this point, the individual that made the deposit used the pseudonym Lansford and initially they are only using the secure hotel drop box for occasional communication with the bank in the Metropolitan."

Walter opened the Pan Air flight wallet removing his ticket and considered the timing of the call, bearing in mind his plans for the forthcoming week or so.
"No, quite right, it is unlikely but possible there is an error on the bank's behalf, but it should be examined. We cannot rule out the possibility this is an attempt of infiltration by the Israelis. What are the C.E.D.'s action recommendations?" Walter asked as he tried to recollect the significance of the account information.
"He believes we should make initial enquiries if possible, locate the individuals. The banker has been instructed to inform us if there is any significant increase in the account's activity and to inform us if any representative for these people comes forward, in the interim we have placed a watch on the hotel drop box our man is on the reception Bennick."
"Yes, Yes, I know Noah Bennick assistant concierge, a good man, discreet," Walter said, remembering a breakfast meeting he had at the Metropolitan.
"Exactly, well he is well placed to pre-empt any unnecessary exposure. Respectfully the Chief Executive Director, is well aware of your wish that our organization should remain discreet at all times within Geneva." Fischer added, aware of the close proximity of Walter Thomas's private residence to the city.
"It is a little hard when he insists on dealing with the dogs of war, butchering the African states, inviting such creatures to our table we must expect to get our fingers bitten," Walter whispered under his breath.
"Pardon Herr Director, I didn't catch that?" Fischer asked aware Spider was negotiating with a Somalian group at that time.
"Nothing, nothing!" Walter said, realizing he had spoken aloud.
"Good very wise, It would appear you have things covered, for now, I see no urgency, inform the Chief Executive Director I will look into this when I return next week." Walter straightened one of the photo frames hanging on his study and

smiled at the image of Grethe, who in the picture was holding the bump in her stomach, during the pregnancy of his son. "One thing, you say they deposited gold, I take it you retained a sample, was it ours?"

"Yes Director, it carried the eagle." The gold sample Fischer had taken from the bank from those Günther had deposited had been identified as Reich gold, Salter-Kingsley had also supplied the individual bar identification numbers of the others. They were all confirmed as being part of an inventory issued from the Reich Chancellery in a shipment destined for the to the RPA department *(Office of Racial Policy)* in Kaiser Wilhelm University in 1942.

"So to be precise, I can inform the committee you will speak with the bank on your return, and you approve of their action," Friedrich asked.

"Yes, yes! I will look into it. You say you have a photograph, please send it and inform the other members of the Executive committee I will call an extraordinary general meeting on my return, at which time I will advise regarding our interest in Texas and will report if there is anything that concerns me regarding the new account, as I said the name Westerberg means nothing to me." Walter threw his pen inside and closed his briefcase.

"Very good Herr Director, good evening." The line went dead, and Walter switched the lever on his facsimile machine, within a minute his study phone rang again and then began playing the high pitched musical notes signifying a fax document was coming through.

There was a soft knock at his study door, "Come." Walter announced, and his personal assistant Max Binder entered.

"I saw your light on Sir, can I be of assistance?" Binder was the only other resident of the large traditional brick and timber chalet Walter had purchased after the war, set in the most scenic ten acres of the mountainside of Parc Jura Vaudois, just 50 kilometres northeast of Geneva. Occupying a modest annexed staff suite Binder's duties were much like a gentleman's butler, but he also acted as cook, chauffeur and of course, befitting an Executive Director of the Spider network, armed bodyguard. He had been with Walter for seven years and twelve years his junior, Walter treated him more like a companion, especially since the death of his wife and now that his children only visited during their holidays, each having their own homes in France.

"No thank you, Max, the committee has a flap on, it's nothing, we have an early start tomorrow get some rest, I'm just finishing up," Walter said and then swore as he struggled to tear the fax paper away and pulled more clean paper from the roll of the machine than was required. "Piece of shit!" exasperated at his clumsiness Walter cursed the machine.

"Please let me, Sir." Max stepped forward and pulled the paper from the roll then folding it back in a line, used a six-inch pocket knife, as sharp as a razor that he removed from his pocket and in one action cut the page clean and handed it to Walter.

"Thank you, I'm tired, perhaps Max, some green tea would be calming, before you turn in," Walter said as he put on his glasses to examine the image.

"But of course, right away, Sir." Max bowed and left.
The fax contained a still photo, taken from the bank videotape of Günther's meeting with Merryman in the bank. It was very blurred, and where he had caught the paper, the crease had smudged the image, but as he held it up away from the light, adjusting his spectacles something again stirred within him.
Rubbing the back of his neck, he swore under his breath again, "Piece of shit." Squinting at the image he felt there was something familiar about the old man in the image sat at the glass desk in the bank office suite, but his face was obscured by the distortion of the crease in the print. Walter sighed and turned off his desk table lamp, as Max arrived with a mug of tea, then retired to his quarters, leaving Walter debating whether to call Friedrich Fischer and request another fax, he looked at his cuckoo clock, his children had bought him one Christmas and decided to leave investigating the true identity of Lansford and the Westerberg's until he returned from New York, considering there was no immediate issue, bearing in mind the individual in the photograph had deposited and not attempted to access any existing accounts.

Outside his window, the lights in the lower valley now intensified so that they formed familiar fine trails of orange street lights that wound in the hills, before joining the motorways, mingling in straight lines they reminded him, yet again of a spiders web. Folding the image of the man on the fax paper he placed his letter opener on it setting it in his draw. He considered going back to bed, for the last few hours before the sun rose, but the telephone call had stirred memories of another time and as he sat back in his old leather desk armchair, in one of the only rooms he now occupied of the large chalet he had shared with his late wife Grethe and family, images of a time before they had children made him smile and he drifted to sleep to the sound of the cuckoo clocks gentle ticking.
With an ache in his neck, Walter cursed himself for falling asleep in his study chair as he ducked to climb into the back seat while Max held the door to the car open, and then cursed once again during the long flight to Dallas, as he arched his back, stretching his spine. Ever attentive at his side in first-class Max ordered from the stewardess some aspirin and water. He then ensured his master was not disturbed during the remainder of the flight as he watched him sleep, aware that he had a busy schedule ahead as a senior representative of the Spider organization.
Walter was travelling to America to carry out talks to strengthen ties with a selection of Neo-Nazi businessmen. Most he was scheduled to meet were originally of German descent, some still harbouring ex-SS officers within their corporations or out of the public eye, on their vast ranch estates.

He was still carrying on the work that Count Erichh Von Stieglitz had started prior to the Second World War, building relationships with individuals that supported Hitler's original ideology of National Socialism. However Walter was no longer an SS Adjutant assigned to the Armaments Department of the Reich Chancellery, and on many occasions, he now dealt with the sons of the

men his master knew and on behalf of the Spider organization he represented as one of its Senior Executive Directors.

There were always the discussions amongst themselves that Walter was often party to in secret, which debated in hindsight and with the certain knowledge that the Reich had united individuals that would never have fought alongside each other if it had not been for the opposition to some of Hitler's more extreme dictations.

Many of his colleagues considered and expressed wistfully, "If only they had prevented the American's entering the war, if only they had not sided with the Japanese." A regret he confirmed to those he trusted, that his superior Count Erichh believed and advocated was possible, before and during the early period of the war, including and up until the Japanese were cultivated as allies to offer assistance in vanquishing the Russians.

When he like Hitler and many of the Reich hierarchy wrongly believed German forces would be relieved by encompassing the Russians in a pincer movement with the Japanese attacking westward.

The Japanese didn't, and continued to focus their forces in the South Pacific and in the same event, Russia in spite of being allies with Great Britain and America bought itself valuable resources and time by not declaring war on Japan, until two days after the "A" bomb was dropped on Hiroshima and America announced they were planned to use the weapon again to force the unconditional surrender of Japan.

Walter would give lip service to honour his late master Count Erichh during discussions, but, the what if's, and blame for the fall of the Reich was, like it's rise, not just because of one man, their Führer, although like his superior at the time, he personally believed in 1940, it was the original exponent of the principles of Germany governed under a National socialist rule, Hitler himself that had warped the direction of Nazi Germany towards a flawed ideology.

However Walter and those closest to him believed irrespective of Hitler's failings, they could have so easily have won and dominated as their Führer had promised. The 1000 years Reich was lost in a photo finish and even in its now broken state, there was a sense that so deep had the youth camp indoctrination seeped into the spirit and soul of the German psyche, the people of Germany even though they were now lived in a divided Fatherland, would never consider themselves as the other races, they now shared the continent of Europe with.

Walter now saw the task of the Spider organization as like so many of the remnants of the old guard, to ensure those that those had risked all and served loyally should not be forgotten and with a divided Germany, the challenge was to ride out the storm. To not lose all in reparations to the victors, to recoup, reassess and with more subversive tactful diplomacy *influence the direction of their country and its future and eventually set it back on the path of true National Socialism.*

His specialty was by changing opinions subtly through the use of their vast business network, in which like-minded individuals were being cultivated, whilst serenading, sponsors by capitalizing on their aspirations and fears of identity loss and the dilution of the Aryan race through racial integration.

The Spider Senior Executive committee consisted of one Chief Executive Director and eight Senior Executive Directors. There were nine Executives because it signified Hitler's own code number during the war of 18 when the 1 and 8 were added together. In addition, each Senior Executive Director was referred to in sensitive documentation by the combination of their own first and second initials as pertaining to their position in the alphabet, so Walter Thomas was referred to with W =23 and T =20 as SED 43.

Walter occupied the place of financial co-coordinator effectively Chancellor of the Exchequer, in charge of the purse strings whilst also being the organization's ambassador to America. His less radical proposals were largely supported by the nine Senior Executive Directors within the Executive committee, however at times his strategies brought him into contention with those of a more single minded approach that he sat next to on the Executive committee, in particular, regarding the methods of the Chief Executive Director, who Walter considered, often sailed too close in their association with other extremist and criminal groups, that ultimately followed ideologies at odds with their own.

This was an opinion that was secretly harboured by many of the other original members who like him, were older men, in their reflective age of life. And although they hankered for their youth and days of the Reich, many were realists, that if such a time came again for a new Reich, it would be through global social and economic change. Through battles fought in boardrooms, and a war won with mergers and takeovers.

Ultimately although it may not be admitted many of the old guard favoured the status quo of Walters long term designs and were happy to collect their Spider pension and living out their existence without going to jail or at the end of the hangman's noose in Israel. But all in the Senior Executive were aware while Mossad and to some extent Britain and American continued to seek their capture, the employment and enlistment of fanatics was to some extent necessary for the enforcement of the will of the Spider organization and protection of those that had created it.

Day to day, for his part Walter had little connection with these people and was seen as a moderate, a calm family man, and safe hands for their investments. He held the keys to the vast sum of money that he and Count Erichh had siphoned from the Reich on behalf of some of the hierarchy who would never claim their treasures, but as the key holder, he had been given all the bank access codes. To some within the Executive committee in private, they considered Walter as paymaster, to be more important than the Chief Executive Director, something the CED negated when possible.

By the time Walter had returned from Dallas, the facsimile page, Friedrich Fischer had sent that depicting Günther in the FNIG bank being in those days printed on heat-sensitive paper, had turned totally black and finding the page still in his desk drawer he screwed it up and threw in the bin. Walter then had Max deliver a meeting request to Peter Salter-Kingsley through the mail drop-box system at the Metropolitan and while in the Geneva, Max made a call from a payphone advising the banker on his private line with the single phrase "You have post." Which sent the banker scurrying along to access his own personal safe-box in the side lobby of the Metropolitan hotel.

With no contact information and no way of establishing his true identity at this time and with no funds having been withdrawn, Walter decided to advise the Executive committee of Spider, that he had instructed the bank to notify them immediately Mr Lansford or any representative of the Westerberg's approached the bank again and to notify them in advance of any meeting. In addition, he requested that along with the operative they had placed on the reception of the Metropolitan hotel, who would inform them if the Westerberg safe box was accessed, they should place the names of Westerberg and Lansford within the list of persons of interest in relation to their global assets.

The Executive committee accepted Walters's judgment, partly because it was considered a distraction from an important opportunity that was being negotiated between individuals within their organization based in Brazil and a Somalian warlord that would involve the FNIG bank in Geneva.

The chief executive Director had agreed Spider would provide weapons and training that would assist the Somalian's military coup. This was an arrangement Walter had personally guarded against and completely in conflict to the one that Walter had brokered with members of Interpol and the CIA including General Carter-Wallis, who were assisting with the international logistics required by the Neo-Nazi group for personnel and resources in the development of biological warfare weapons off U.S. soil, such as deadly nerve agents, by a team of scientist led by ex-members of the Third Reich.

Nazi members of the Third Reich that were obtained in such operations as Paperclip, during and after the war and resettled in the United States, such of Von Brown, who went on to lead NASA's space propulsion program, were not the only Nazi's that worked with the American's after the war, it is believed many were employed in black operation by the various developing spy networks operating around the world.
No one has been able to fully explain how Doctor Josef Mengele was able, after 1945 to move back and forth between South America, Spain and Germany, sometimes under his real name several times without being detained by the for runner to Interpol the ICPO that has amongst the listed

Presidents of its foundation organization the ICPC, Otto Steinhäusl, Reinhard Heydrich, Arthur Nebe, and Ernst Kaltenbrunner, all of whom were once generals in the Reich SS.
Paul Dickopf, who had been President of Interpol since 1968 during the war, was himself an SS SD Untersturmführer (Lieutenant) his SS number was 337259. Washington documents would be released in 2007 showing the CIA made payments through the 1960s into the 1970s, he was officially listed as having a relationship of a secret nature with the CIA as a unilateral agent, as president of the BKA, German Federal Criminal Police Office, there were many that he recruited that came from the same background and had affiliations with the Nazi party, during and after the war.
Interpol did not begin prosecuting Nazi war criminals until the 1980s.

In the agreement brokered with the head of the Spider Organization, for his part the Somalian warlord, General Mubarak Ali Hassan had agreed a substantial payment in gold and in aiding to overthrow the existing military dictator he further agreed to set aside a vast area of land from which Spider would be able to operate indefinitely, outside international law.

Some within the Spider organization considered it would give them the opportunity to create a modern-day youth camp and an advance training camp for their field operatives as well as a base to carry out their own military developments, including further development of biological weaponry.

The Chief Executive Director, in particular, believed the day would come when Germany would reunite again and then if they had the right people in place and the muscle and funds behind them a National Socialist Party *(Nazi)* would once again rule the Fatherland, if not under another acronym.

As for the man that had once been SS. SD. Colonel Stefan Keplar, Sebastian Westerberg, having returned to Sweden and set up a line of credit that eventually filtered back to the FNIG bank and Peter Salter-Kingsley, through assorted offshore shell companies that retained their personal anonymity and dispensed initially with the need to visit the bank, Sebastian continued working for the moment in isolation, with no assistance from an organization that would have welcomed him in, with open arms once they accepted his true identity.

For now, at first, through his connections working with the University, Sebastian identified specialist within the Scandinavian scientific community and began to employ a number technicians and scientists to aid his work, in both the development of products and analysis and synthesizing of his own blood. For now, he carried out much of the investigative work concerned with the Vor Elle project on his own and occasionally with Katrina.

The gold Günther had deposited at the bank helped accelerate the creation of the Westerberg Pharmaceutical Company in Sweden, and initial demands for the homoeopathic products allowed the expansion from a warehouse built on Aunt Krysia's smallholding in the first year to a purpose-built self-contained site set on five hundred acres adjoining her land. The production plant produced what was marketed as herbal based natural Scandinavian health products that were produced using local materials, however each in some way incorporating in their ingredients, synthesized elements of Stefan's blood. Initially, they sold through a mail ordering system to specific high-end retail health and fitness outlets.

At first, the whole family was included in the production and packaging process, including the girls sticking the labels on the assorted pots and cream balm lids. It was their first daughter, Grethe Beth, being the most creative that came up with the logo of the combination of the W and P.
"It looks like someone asking for help with their hands up."
Is how she described it, and the rest of them agreed, a vote was called, and it was adopted for all the companies' stationery and labelling.

It was truly initially a family business, although neither of the girls were aware for many years of the source of the secret ingredients, even though their younger daughter Lenora Anna by now was quite use to giving blood, clearly aware something was different about herself, compared to other children of her age, being as tall as her two years older sister and almost albino in completion. It was this, for this reason, Sebastian described the necessity for her blood samples being taken, and as with him there was no bruising or sign of the piercing of the syringe needle within days of the samples being taken, and no teachers at the girl's school were alerted, to her participation in the tests. However, eventually within a few years, her own interest in science would lead to her work directly with Sebastian and with full knowledge of what their ultimate goal would be.

These first years of the creation of the company, when they were all working together, with no pressure from the outside world, Sebastian and Katrina would later consider as some of the happiest times for their family. As their own name and reputation grew amongst the people of Uppsala County, Sweden, it acted as a double-edged sword aware of their heightened profile even though they had made the transition of total relocation to their new identities. Some local family members of Björklinge and the Gävlevägen society even claimed they had known Sebastian when he was a child at school.
Their social standing was reinforced by a commercial, financial and political network of individuals with power, such as the police Chief Dirk Nilsson, a network of loyal allies cultivated by Sebastian that ensured the family's status as being of Swedish origin was secure and unchallenged.
Meanwhile shrewd investments by Katrina who was without doubt the more financial astute of the couple would see their company go from strength to strength, diversifying into other health-based products, including kelp farming and processing, used throughout the world, as a natural emulsifying agent and

thickening ingredient, in the manufacture of many products including ice cream, paint and many cosmetic products.

But before all of that when Günther eventually contacted the FNIG bank through the Metropolitan drop box, the name Westerberg would once again be drawn to the attention of Friedrich Fischer and the Chief Executive Director of Spider.

Chapter 7: Deadbait

Mi6 Headquarters, Century House
100 Westminster Bridge Road,
London, Great Britain
October 1968

Oliver Pimm arrived back in London Heathrow on the 20th October 1968, for permanent reassignment to Mi6's Raleigh Department, Global Logistic Corp. The long-haul BOAC flight from Hong Kong had taken twenty- eight hours, with stops in Calcutta, Tehran, Rome and Paris, It had brought an end to Pimm's assignment with Cook Department in Hanoi with Robert Thompson and the BRIAM. It was raining as Pimm stepped off the 707. Umbrella wielding escorts from Department Drake of Mi6 were waiting at the bottom of the steps. He breezed through the diplomatic channel with no search and was driven direct to Mi6 headquarters, which at that time was the 22 storey office building, Century House, 100 Westminster Bridge Road, Lambeth, London.

On arrival, Pimm rode the elevator straight to the top floor and the Mi6 boardroom that was known as the "Wheelhouse" he stood before a large nautical stylized desk the "Captains chair" similar to that of a court room Judges desk, that sat above a large circular boardroom table known as the "Compass" to receive his promotion and new orders.

Mi6 by now was firmly established with an inner circle of eight international departments operating within their own specific sectors of the globe and each department head occupied one of the seats that was set at the Compass boardroom table and which represented one of the positions of a compass point. Each Mi6 department head was responsible for its own regional sector's intelligence gathering and asset protection. The Departments were named after venerated British explorer, reputably to be amongst the first spies in history.

Department Cook: *South East Asia and China sector, operating from Hong Kong.*
Department Drake: *Great Britain and European sector, operating from Mi6 GCHQ London.*
Department Hudson: *North America and Canadian sector, operating from New York.*
Department Malory: *Middle East sector and Central Asia sector, operating from Calcutta.*
Department Shackleton: *South American sector, operating from Road Town on the British Virgin Island of Tortola.*
Department Speke: *Africa sector, operating from Cape Town.*
Department Scott: *Scandinavia and Polar sectors, operating from Oslo.*

Department Jenkinson: Russian Sector and Eastern bloc, operating from West Berlin.

The Compass seat of North was occupied by the head of Drake Department and the Captains chair was set higher and directly behind this position within the Wheelhouse room. This Chair was reserved for the head of Mi6, who was referred to In general communications as "Control" However In transcripts signed his name "C" after the first Director of the SIS, Captain Sir Mansfield George Smith-Cumming, KCMG, CB.
Control in 1968 was Sir Dick Goldsmith White, "Dickie" to the very few he felt comfortable with, including Bull Gordon.
Along with their seat at the Compass table, each department head held an operational office within GCHQ London and would return to sit on the top floor boardroom table alongside Control at regular intervals throughout the year, while their field teams remained based for the most part within British consulate embassy buildings and the safe houses they acquired within their regional sector.

And then there was Department Raleigh, the Global logistic Corp. Mi6's own head hunters that filled in the gaps across the main eight departments and seconded under generally extraordinary and extreme circumstances to assist all regional sectors by the department heads.
Although all regional sectors had their own assigned Sandman, Department Raleigh consisted solely of Sandmen, they generally had no permanent assignments and were referred to within the organization as "Scalphunters" a request by a department head for the support of a member of Raleigh could not be refused.
Considered the elite of their profession and above reproach, they could be called upon to ensure the continuation of Mi6's global operations, including the temporarily assignment of command of a department during the transitional period of the appointment of a new sector head. However as Sandmen at a moment's notice they were often required to assist in high profile operations such as asset recovery, deep cover agent retrieval, investigations when a regional Sandman was MIA or KIA and the termination of Mi6 agents that had gone rogue.

Oliver Pimm had become a Scalphunter and like the other three members of Raleigh team he was recalled to London on the 20th October to accept his promotion direct from Control and receive his first assignment. But before commencing his first tour of service, he was granted a two week R and R, which he was to spend with his wife June.

"So you made the grade, a Raleigh boy, always knew you'd make Scalphunter good for you. I'm sure by now you know they'll leave you hanging out there, it goes with the turf, but don't let the bastards burn you out and my advice from here on in consider all the other sectors as having a mole, regardless of your past history with them, you are like internal affairs, no one wants to be one, but every agent in the field is happier knowing they are there." Bull Gordon had once been a Scalphunter himself and studied Pimm, who as expected appeared unphazed at his recent promotion, he wondered if Pimm had told his wife of the near nomadic nature of his new posting and looking to Pimm case smiled knowing exactly what the first assignment Dickie White had just handed him.

"That it, that's my speech. Now moving on, still got you attached to the FCO I see." Bull raised an eye at Pimm's battered leather Foreign Office diplomatic case sporting the embossed HBM gold lettering.

"I swear Bull, if I have to listen to another Lloyd's broker, I'll book a flight to Moscow, those guys must get paid by the word, each contract takes up a rainforest. I hear Toby Morris has a legend attached to a Skye scotch distillery, have a word in someone's shell-like, would you old pal." Pimm laid his briefcase on the floor, opening it he removed some manila folders, one of which Bull knew held Pimm's first assignment brief. Hiding beneath was his revolver, a silencer, spare magazine and a bottle of duty-free Gordon's gin he handed it over to Bull along with two pouches of Golden Virginia tobacco.

"Glad to see FCO resources being used to their full potential, now all we need is my drinks cabinet to arrive." Bull smiled.

Like many Mi6 field agents, along with his regular daily cover story as an International loss adjuster for Lloyds registered, Newmarket Insurance Company, Pimm used a number of pseudonyms when travelling on domestic flights, including occasionally a legitimate Foreign Office position, it secured him the rites of passage with the benefits of diplomatic immunity and allowed him to be in possession of one of Her Britannic Majesty's diplomatic cases. In certain countries, it still aided unrestricted clandestine material including weapons smuggling and the odd duty-free, when re-entering the UK.

"It's been a while since Cyprus, I spoke with our American cousin's, it appears you made an impression in Saigon, probably why they mentioned you by name in Akrotiri and on that note of working with the Yanks, that was clean work clearing up that mess with the Finn Tuomioja, he was well liked, impressive dodging back and forth from Hanoi like that, your feet must not have touch the ground." Bull watched Pimm give an effacing shrug of his shoulders at the compliment, "I suspect that will be the way of it in our future, caught in the middle of a chess game between the CIA and KGB each chipping away at the others pieces. to gain leverage and a receptive ears in the global arena, it's a shame, he was good man by all accounts."

The unusual death in Helsinki of the fifty-eight year-old Finnish UN mediator in the Cyprus conflict Sakari Tuomioja, was considered more than suspicious by many of his colleagues in the United Nations, Bull knew Pimm had all the answers.

"I understand you know some of the American security detail they have generously supplied as personal guard for his replacement, Vietnam boys?" Bull began to pace back and forth as if which of the three main offices offered the best London skyline, while listening for an answer and Pimm indulged Bulls discreet fishing expedition for him to fill in exactly what had happened in Cyprus, even though he was tired after his long flight and somewhat put out to discover once again, what Mi6 gave with one hand it clawed back with the other, his two week holiday being one, which was now looking like it was just another convenient coincidence for the service to carry out their work while abroad.

Bull was one of the few aware of the operations Pimm had recently been involved in over the last eight years, along with being assigned to Robert Thompson's staff and working with them from Hanoi, because of his time in Cyprus he assisted the Americans round up and eliminate Soviet agents suspect to have been involved in Tuomioja death. It was cited by the CIA that the Soviets aim had been to influence UN mediation talks in the region by arranging the succession of their own Russian, Turkish sponsored candidate, who would have affirmed the call for the removal of the British military bases from Cyprus, which neither the American's or British could let happen.

"Yep, Cook had me running with a tight seal pack for a while in the jungle, made some interesting friends. It was an easy fix assisting them with the Finn, they have all the toys, sometimes I was knee deep in leaches before the sun came up, only to shit shave shower and suit up to ride a jet and be in the Manila club before they called last orders." Pimm said remembering the expression on the Soviet agent's face, a member of a Moscow trade delegation, that had been implicated in Cyprus a targeted that the American had requested he remove, as well he did.
"Well, at least the Americans are satisfied with his UN replacement Galo Plaza, more brownie points for the P.M." Bull raised his eyes to the ceiling.
"Might have something to do with him, being born in New York and going to Berkeley." Pimm smiled, "But I never met the guy or the Finn for that matter."
"I read the Thompsons report of your work with BRIAM, you're not in there per se, but those that are important know it was you. It didn't go unnoticed up stairs, hence Raleigh, don't be surprised if they don't offer you a section head with three tours as a Scalphunter, I hear Green's retiring next year, fancy running Malory?"
"Maybe one day, I'm not ready to get strapped to a desk, and June's not keen on curry, then there's the paperwork, all that red tape, it's not me. I know it's coming with all the new compliance records, but if I had known there was this much involved, I'd have chosen a job in journalism, you can thank god you have Monty." Pimm replaced the files back into his case labelled top secret, some of which held his expenditure details for the last three months.

"I know you have been back and forth like Yoyo, but I take it you've read the reports from Drake, your Turks goods were original, apart from the handlers for a few obvious big hitters, Von Brown and Mengele, but significantly most on his list were foreign nationals all worked within the DWB *(German Businesses Ltd)* for the

Nazi's, accountants and lawyers, two bankers we believe still operate from Geneva. More important only ten of the scientists that appeared on the list were named on the list the Yanks found, stuffed in that bog in Cologne University in 1945, that still beggar's belief." Bull was referring to a list of 1500 Nazi scientists found when Cologne was liberated at the end of the war hidden in a toilet within the University.
"That makes three that we've taken in so far including the one Drake bagged last week, a fuel engineer that worked on the propulsion system at Peenemünde V1 & 2's, held up in a safe house in Cartagena, had a one-way ticket and cases packed, was on his way to Brazil. Interesting chap, Austrian, originally from Kitzbuhel. I flew out had a three hour sit down with him, same old same old, made a convincing case, confirming what we always suspected, like a great many scientists like himself that went to ground after the war, he had no idea he'd already been cherry-picked by a pre-assigned Spider network handler. But confirmed he had been segregated for interviews with officers belonging to the SS Allgemeine two months before Berlin was taken, he understood at the time they were assigned to the DWB. Irrespective of what both sides of the wall are saying the consensus is they intend to orchestrate a revival of the Nazi's party within post-war Germany when all the shit settles, they'll have the money, knowledge and power. The yanks are convinced they have only recovered enough ice to add to a glass of scotch compared to the iceberg of Nazi bounty still out there. Personally I doubt we will ever unscramble them all from the system without taking out companies like Mercedes, unfortunately too many they are seen to be needed, by the powers that be and to those that still rely on them for their daily bread, like Josef Mengele's own tractor factory, news is they are expanding. The Israelis are livid it's not been confiscated. Anyway we'll keep plugging away, what is clear is those that remain off radar have a propensity to create alliances is relentless, with others with similar criminal intent is relentless, such as our Irish friends. So while they continue to muddy the waters, there is still a place for old dogs like me and of course, Mossad." Bull arranged two chairs in front of his desk and Pimm sat down in one.

"Well, I'm glad it was worth the trip and I hear good things of Bob Gregory in Hereford, I would think the boys in the wheelhouse would consider the Diniz incident as a win, win. But that said, somehow doesn't look like you got a victory parade? What did you do with him, the Austrian?" Pimm looked around the vacant office, so different to Gordon's previous office four floors up, waiting for an explanation, to what appeared a demotion.
"We made an exchange with a Langley lad, a colleague of Tom Quinn's, like the Austrian worked with Von Brown's lot and the Yanks want him for NASA. Don't ask me what we got back, above my pay grade now. Knowing Dickie, it will involve a chemistry set and Porton Down, funny that the Yanks are happy for us to deal with the really shitty stuff like nerve agents. I often wonder what would happen out there now if the plague hit the streets." Bull looked down towards the Thames "unfortunately from what I hear from Jenkins and the East Berlin sector, Brezhnev is wondering the same thing."

Bull Gordon looked at the typed names on the list Orran Danis had given Pimm in Cyprus, he knew to many, somehow chasing down aging individuals that had been involved with some of the most heinous crimes of world war II seemed less important, but he also knew their story was not over. He raised he eye to the skyline view of London, if he tried real hard he could picture it as he had once seen, with barrage balloons drifting back and forth on their steal line tethers as search lights scanned the skies of Luftwaffe bombers.

His thoughts returned to the day as behind him he heard Pimm move through the abandoned office, where the occasional carpet tile was set askew no longer in place, sockets hanging mid-air no longer supported by the desks that the previous Mi6 team had moved to the walls when they vacated. On the walls and half glass partitions the remnants of tape and pins that once held significant information to the project, they had been working on.

Pimm picked up one of the dusty green phones, "Switchboard, Operator four." the building exchange operator snapped.

"Well, the phones work which is something, but really Bull who have you pissed off, upstairs?" Pimm replaced the receiver.

Bull did not turn back, smiling to himself, thinking, where do I begin? As he watched the sunlight dapple on the muddy waters and in hearing Big Ben chime, ten o'clock, he felt the glass of the window. "Yes well, the mid floors may be known as limbo land, but they still want you back top when they need you."

The silence between them was broken by the ping of the lift bell in the outer hall, as Pimm read a stuck on caption on a desk glass, partition panel where some previous occupier had left a smiley face that turned from yellow to red and switched to an angry face "If you are reading this, you are too close!" he presumed the owner considered the Russian connection.

The office doors opened, and two stores men wearing identical brown cloth overalls entered carrying a wooden tea chest

"Where to Governor?" the older man asked with a rasping cockney accent, clearly ex-military he made a light stamp of his foot an old habit.

"Anywhere will do lads, same goes for the rest you bring down, except my medicine cabinet, you'll know the one when you find it, it jingles, that's in here." Bull said.

The two men looked at each other as if they had been asked to solve ten down, in the Times crossword and then marched up to within six feet of Bull and set the chest neatly against the far window wall.

"Look enough of me, so you have two week leave. I understand you are taking June on the Queen, over the pond. a Jamaican cruise, very nice." Bull began to move some of the chairs that had been stacked around the room and seeing what he was doing Pimm walked into the main open-plan office and did the same.

"Her idea, I think she thinks it's the only way to have my undivided attention and no way six can call me up, I haven't told her about Raleigh yet, I'll do it on the voyage home, if we are still speaking. Unfortunately, Bernie Martin over at Hudson got wind I'm in his neighbourhood and now I'm Scalphunter, well I'm already getting the feeling my dance card is full for the next five years. As you said it goes with the territory, I cannot refuse a section head request. He wants me to take a run through something the Yanks are putting together in Cuba, I know some of the guys they have on the old naval base at Guantanamo. Not sure what the Ruskies are going to make of it, they're very pally, pally with Castro these days." Pimm scratched his chin as he looked towards the Thames and in the direction of Parliament and to those they served, "You know if Eisenhower had met with El Caballo *(the Horse was Fidel Castro's nickname)*, back in 1960 they wouldn't have this problem now."

"Politicians are just people, so I have been told" Bull nodded his head in agreement. "Well Anyway, it's eyes and ears set up, since the mafia were thrown out there playing catch up, like us in Ceylon." Pimm smiled across at Bull as he took the weight of the corners of the desk in his hands, and they moved the first table away from the wall.

"Yes I know, Control grabbed my ear, told me about you and Raleigh and this thing, we were sharing a bottle at the club, I spoke with Tom Quinn, if it was anyone else I would say they were carpetbaggers, but he showed me his budget for the CIA Miami branch. It's almost the same as Six's annual allowance, all the toys, like you said. Just make sure you book the hours with them while you're out there. June does know we have things called submarines, I hope you let her know, it's going to take more than a couple of rounds of bridge. She's bound to notice you've jumped ship." Bull squatted behind the desk to see what the view would be through the facing window and had Pimm nudge it back and forth until he was satisfied.

"I'm joking old fruit, I co-signed the papers one of the last loose ends while up top, sea kings going to scoop you from the deck along with the Pye tech boffin you'll be chaperoning. Get her a bucket of dimes for the fruity machines, she won't know you're gone. While we're on the subject of confessions, I 'didn't know they would pull you on it, but it was also me that dropped the casino and hotel expansion papers in Cuba on Martin's lap, a nervous friend of Tom's in Miami. All they're asking is a look-see, what the mafia is up to and just how cosy they are with Langley, while you're helping them out. Truth be known, I'm buying some love, god knows the yanks don' need it, but as it says in the bible, you reap what you sew, and Tom's always been as straight as wicket at Lords. Six has even sprung for some playing buckshee, just don't forget the chit, anyway I wanted you to hear it from me, call it a busman's holiday and for old times' sake." Bull looked to Pimm to help him lift one of the tea chests to his desktop.

"I might have guessed you had a hand in it, you're the one who convinced me to stick out that technical surveillance course, don't tell me the Yanks have swaged another invention from us, holding this Boffins hand was sold to me as a walk in the park by Martin, sounds like I should take my full kit, if anyone looks cross eyed June on the Queen, I telling you Bull, there over the side, I'm not going wait and see if they are wearing red shoes." *(Red shoes was regular reference within Mi6 to Dorothy in the wizard of OZ as being CIA)*

"Christ knows I could do with a stress break and June was looking tired before I left, so I'm not that impressed, at least she'll like the cruise. Busman holiday my arse, so come on lets have it. Is this what this is Bull? down here a busman's holiday for you, time out from dodging shells or something else, old history catching up, I hear things?" Pimm unravelled the coiled telephone cable and set it on Bull's desk.

"Ah? You heard about my Irish lad, the number of souls I've collected, it was bound to happen, no, I've earned enough brownie points, to survive having one turn on the hand that fed him. But it's a pity, Harry Mac had great talent, but there it is at least he didn't go with Philby and Maclean." Bull began to carefully take out from the first tea chest, one at a time, miniature cacti plants each in its own individual bowl, he brushed their spines and flesh with a dry four inch soft paintbrush removing any dust before setting them on the long window shelf, taking time to turn them to the best angle he would view from the position of his desk.

"I never met McLoughlin, is that why you have called for this, if it is cleaning the slate for you, unfortunately, you are talking to the wrong guy, even if I had time, Bernie Martins got me on a tight leash they even keep my spent casings on the range these days, soon you'll need an expense chit for bog roll, just wait and see"

Pimm knew about the rogue Mi6 agent that had been in play undercover in Southern Ireland infiltrating the IRA, who allegedly had gone native and was probably already on a hit list with Mi6, Harry McLoughlin, first recruited by Bull, like Pimm.

"No, no, he's not for your dance card. I don't think I ever told you, I picked up Mac in Burma, three weeks after the Japanese surrendered. One of the few nineteen-year-olds the railway didn't break. A true survivalist, king rat, a real talent, ten years before you cut across my bow. I wouldn't ask you to take out one of our own, well not one that I'd recruited, though I understand you might think so. He's in the States now, rattling the tin, raising funds for the Boyo's back home. No! God forbid, two wild child's like your selves, tearing up the windy city, would definitely muddy the waters with our American cousins. They know he's there when they have seen enough it will probably be less OK Corral and more Samson and Delilah. I have something in mind, the bloody fool left two home-growns in Cork. Unfortunately, the mother in his legend was killed by one of ours. Mac had bitten into the lie deep gone soft on her, blames us. Japs could not turn him, but how could we compete with some pretty Limerick lace, love weakness men love to exploit, strength only women understand."

Then Bull sighed and turned with his head bowed in embarrassment back to Pimm, "Sorry Pimm, I'm getting on, half the reason what this is all about, I'm feeling it these days, especially when I make cock-ups like that with a friend, apologies old fruit."

"Forget it, carry on what are after?" Pimm gestured his acceptance of his apology.

Bull had realised the mention of children may strike a chord with Pimm. June had the previous year undergone a hysterectomy during a six-month pregnancy, she lost the child, and there was no chance of trying again.

Pimm at the time, as always kept his cards close to his chest, even from his wife how he felt. But while she was still in the Royal Free Hospital, he took the time to trawl the Irish pubs in Kentish town, finally ending up in the Archway Tavern Holloway Road, where priming the largest labourer he could find, they went at it, the poor man who was genuinely a decent sort, just out for the crack with his mates, stopped pounding on Pimm once he had knocked him firmly on his arse for the fourth time and in spite of the fact Pimm's uppercut had once again claimed another front tooth, his bemused opponent then stepped in, pulling others off trying to put the boot in to the totally wasted Englishman. The Irish gentleman took from Pimm's wallet enough to pay for what he hoped a dentist would charge and threw Pimm in the back of a black cab.

"Do I look like I give a fick where he lives drop him on the common let him sleep it off there, just get him off before my boys lynch the sad bastard."

Pimm was back in service within a week, June returned home, to the house he had inherited from Vic McDonald in Muswell Hill. Unfortunately unbeknownst to Pimm, while he was out in Cyprus for the second time, dealing with the fallout from the death of the Finnish UN mediator, during a routine check-up on her recovery the doctor had discovered June had cancer of the cervix that had spread.

That's was why she had insisted they take the cruise knowing it would be their last together and give her the opportunity to say her goodbyes to a man she knew never shared his affections with anyone other than herself and his Aunt. June was scared, not for herself, but for Pimm, and what kind of Lost Boy he would become, finally she confided in the only person she could trust to watch over him, Bull Gordon and Bull being Bull pulled some strings.

"Like you, this is a break, just a longer sabbatical, never understood the appeal of a world cruise having already done it in service, courtesy of HRH and I'm not ready to put on the slippers in spite of the house Doc telling me to cut down on the pipe, thanks for the baccy by the way. I called a few favours they've given me this spot, a few filing bods and I get to keep Mrs Thompkin, bless her hairy knees, I swear sometimes I think she wears that kilt to make it look like we are joined at the hip." Bull said referring to his long-suffering personal secretary, a four-foot-six war spinster from the Worms Head, Gower, as stocky and as broad as a Welsh fullback, akin in character to General Montgomery, hence her nickname in the section "Monty" although not to her face she was "Mrs T" to all but Bull.

"So what is it, if not something with Ireland?" Pimm moved the empty tea chest back over to the front door for collection.

"Well, like I said I wanted you to know I stuck my oar in, regarding your diversion to Guantanamo Bay. As for this here," Bull waved a hand gesturing the offices, "this is your man's doing, the Turk Danis, fallen on my lap as it were, the remains of the day. You know I had history with this sort of thing, long before your time, after the war, call it a hobby. C's given me just enough rope to keep me in house and entertain myself and who knows if in getting some of these old Germans on the Turks list we turn over some loose stones, connections with Spider they'll be happy upstairs. These terrorist groups all use the same banks, solicitors, judges, arms dealers, training camps. With the Russians safeguarding some of the African and Arab states, what I wouldn't give to get a peak of Brezhnev's Rolodex, PLO in Palestine or FLN in Algeria. They're setting up a global network of arms dealers, soon it will be like Woolworth's, one in every town. There are many mouths to feed with the *Reds* stirring the water globally and making hay every time the US balls up their foreign policy. As for the French if I had my way I'd repatriate every one of our boys from both wars before they all start turning in their graves, Jeux Sans Frontières, my arse. You know how it is people get greedy sloppy and dead, then its chaps like us that have to charge in and save the bacon, well you."

Bull took a deep breath as he set his pipe on the timber pipe tree with a well-worn leather tobacco pouch on one side and a packet of Swan matches on the other, then he set the list of names Pimm had retrieved from Orran down in the centre of his blotting pad and began to place his office supplies around the table in military fashion, as Pimm looked over the parapet of spikes from all the cacti plants like some castle, down towards Waterloo towards and the Thames.
"No, I'm going to bring up a Christmas hamper from Fortnum and Mason's full of Gordon's, pull up a chair and take my time going through this lot, any tickles I get that may have appeal to the other floors I'll drop in the pipe." Bull pointed to the internal air pipe memo system that shuttled small glass, and brass torpedo cylinders between the floors along a *"Heath Robinson"* styled vacuum pump air communication system.
"Good luck with that, I heard they are fitting some key lamp system over the next few months, IBM, it will take them a year to sweep them for bugs." Pimm knew that would ruffle Bull's feathers, he hated technology, he tore a sheet from the small memo pass and without filling in the designated machine or a destination scratched the word, Hello! Then stuck it inside a cylinder cartridge to see if the system still worked. Once loaded, he pulled the lever and with reliable precision, there was a whoosh of air, and the cylinder was shot like a bullet downwards.
"Why do they always need to screw around with something that works perfectly, call it progress, more like digress? I think that is why I have a fondness these pretty ladies, they never change, the one you and June gave me must be five years old, it's still the same size has never flowered, anyway like that machine, that's it I'm winding down, call it a prelude to retirement." Pimm took out a packet of Benson and Hedges gold and lit a cigarette giving Bull a look of, *whom you trying to kid, The Bull, retirement, I think not.*
Pimm flipped the air breather above the window, and his smoke began to escape through the fresh air vent into the London skyline.

"No truly between you and me, and I'm mean to a reasonable man!" Bull was making a side reference code between the two men eluding to the fact they were both Master Masons from Lodge 17 Kentish town Freemason's society and indicated the next words spoken were in strictest confidence.

"I am getting a bad taste in my mouth every time I sit in the room with some of the Eaton mob, Dickie White has at his dining table, now he's getting on a few are becoming a little excitable to sit in the Captains chair. I'm too old to play when the music stops, finding a quiet place on the lower decks like this, suit me fine. There's no chance of getting trampled in the stampede for the free chairs." Bull watched Pimm's hand slip to his Braille Sea master Rotary wristwatch and knew he had checked the time.

"Never fancied the top slot, you'd get my vote" Pimm asked, having always considered Bull as being an ideal replacement Control for Mi6.

Bull chortled, "No! God no, saw Dickie in the gents once, hung like a mule, goes with the territory, leave that to the ones with big balls. Besides sorry to say when all said and done, even in this place old fruit, there are few I would regard as true friends and only one I would trust, and he's standing before me. Out on the side-lines suits me to a T. The Turks list still shows promise to reel in some old dogs with new leads and masters, but who knows we may strike lucky get a nibble of some of the loot. Thing is old fruit, I'm on a shoestring here, other than what Mrs T can beg, borrow and steal for me, once she returns from her annual yomp along Hadrian's wall with that hound of hers."

There was another ping of the hall elevator, and the same two store orderlies rolled in a dolly trolley that held a large walnut HMV *(His Masters Voice)* gramophone cabinet the size of a chest of draws.

"Ah just in time, I've no ice, but stay, wet your whistle," he said as they pushed the jingling dolly towards his office, then lifted it carefully setting it where Bull had cleared a space. Having checked it was undamaged externally, he lifted the top exposing the area that had once housed the record player this had been removed and in its place was a selection of alcoholic beverages and glass tumblers. Seeing none were broken, he handed each of the store men a single pound note.

"For your trouble today and for the rest, you will need to bring up just set the office supplies my bods will do the rest." Bull blew the dust from two tumblers and found the jar with some cut lemon slices.

"Thank you, Sir, gentlemen." the older man coughed, and he and his apprentices saluted Pimm and Bull to which the pair raised their hands in formal acceptance.

"Come on old sport it's past the yardarm somewhere, call it congrats for all the work you did for me when I was upstairs, they may not appreciate it, but I do." Bull said seeing Pimm recheck his watch.

"Just one, I promised June I'd spend the afternoon helping her brother strip the wallpaper, just got a place off Swiss cottage handy for the ponds." Pimm pulled up a chair.

"Never took you for a DIY man Pimm, wonders never cease?" he said handing Pimm a large double gin and tonic, with lemon

"No I make the tea mostly and watch, she has a good family, I like to see them together they have been a great help, solid people with no complications except if they have the money for the man from the Pru. Reminds me there are still some out there that can close their eyes at night without a Browning three inches away." Pimm took the glass.
"Still think you're in insurance, June's never let slip in all these years, marvellous women." Bull raised his glass in cheers to Pimm's wife.
"So are you going to ask me, Bull?" Pimm stubbed his cigarette out in the empty Marmite pot. "I know you didn't just get me up here to help you move house and wish me bon voyage." he took a half measure of his drink.
"Well it's as I said I'm on a shoestring, I know you are off to cover Jem Stapleton's old patch in Paris with Raleigh Department when you get back a fill in. It will be a light duty for your first Scalp and they have extended it for a year term, so you will have time to put your feet up with June at night, my way of apologising for fucking up your cruise. Bumping Jem upstairs was a smart move by Control, he'll be a good head for Drake, London needs calm hands at the moment and you'll like Paris at least you know you're not inheriting a warm seat, he's kept things tidy over there, they are a good lot, I understand you were expecting a short tour being a Scalphunter now, but perhaps things happen for a reason, you have been running on the rat wheel of Six for while. I know you will find it hard not being in the field, I'd tell you, you get over it, but the truth is, I still miss it and I was not half as good as you. What I know for sure is June should enjoy the social life and sleep better. Plus the apartment they have, it's a good spot, the Yank embassy is around the corner, she'll be as safe as in number 10. That said while there it's possible I may require extra eyes and maybe a shoulder for any youngster I send over to cry on. I don't expect any firework unless Mossad gets the scent of the same quarry, but just in case it would be handy have an old sort I could trust not to tell tales to whoever is whispering in Control's ear that day, every time I ask for a snap of the Eiffel tower and after Paris, really the same, I'm not a section head anymore so you can say no anytime" Bull took out his Swiss army knife and began cleaning his pipe occasionally blowing through the mouthpiece and tapping the debris into his crystal glass ashtray.
"Now that was TFM talk about a sob story, have I ever hung up on you, Christ sake Bull, date and time that's it, unless I'm on the job," Pimm shook his head.

"Well you know me, I like to know where I stand, Maybe this McLoughlin thing has got me turned around a bit and I want you to know as always one hand washes another, I'll play fair if I get anything that is remotely in your arena, and we'll talk on the square as reasonable men." Bull finished his drink and held out his hand.
"Bull you hear anything I am always happy to listen, but there is no trade with us, whatever you need, you ask, I'll make sure Mrs T has all my details before I settle when I get back, establish a private drop box, just for your people in Paris and one near the Knightsbridge underground, so you can use it on the way to the Service club, but knowing Monty she probably already has one in play." Pimm smiled.

"In the meantime enjoy the view and get some ice for next time I visit, let the young ones do the running. As for good advice, stay away from the top floor, I know I will. You know me I'm polite, but I felt I had a touch of shingles coming on as I stood before the Compass." With that Pimm turned to leave considering his last debrief on the 22nd floor of Century House with Control and five of the eight Mi6 Department heads present at his promotion, some of whom made his skin crawl.

"Talking of settling down, I never asked you, did you tuck your Turkish friend to bed in the end?" Bull folded Omar Danis's list tucking it into the leather corner of his blotter.

Pimm nodded, "Yes, but don't expect any more, I thought you'd have heard, he was he was telling the truth in Cyprus, six months after we dropped him Alghero, Sardinia he died, throat and lung cancer." Pimm waved a hand and disappeared out the doors towards the elevator.

"No I didn't" Bull shook his head, "Bon voyage give my love to Mrs Pimm," he called after him as Pimm passed two of Bull's new team members in the corridor as Bull considered there was not a fleck of emotion in Pimm's statement regarding his old language teacher. But as Pimm rode the elevator down he realized he had and irresistible urge to scratch at his arm scars as if just thinking of those around the Compass table or the mention of Orran Danis rejuvenated them.

"Well, at least you put that chapter to bed." Bull whispered as he poured himself another drink and raised his glass again,

Leaving Southampton dock on the start of their cruise, Mr and Mrs Oliver Pimm were delighted to find that their cabin berth had been upgraded to an exterior port side berth with a small balcony, courtesy of the Newmarket Insurance Company. In true style Bull even had a small bouquet of yellow roses placed on the nightstand for June, the message read "Good Luck." AG.

Bull already knew that June Pimm intended to tell her husband she was dying, She could not be sure how Pimm was going to take the bad news, there was little in his life that bore a resemblance to normality nor in some respects to their marriage. She knew her husband had killed people during his national service in Palestine and although he did not speak of his work, there was an understanding between them to overlook each time he returned home covered in bruises and on more than one occasion having received a bullet wound.

June devoted herself to Oliver and when home, with no expectation of a child of their own helped raise Bowman's son, James. While comforting his mother, her cousin, Lorraine who had succumbed to post-natal depression, seeking refuge in more than one bottle of Pernod. In fact, invariably it was June that the school called when James had been involved in some kind of childish skulduggery.

However now June's own illness had begun to take effect, she was becoming increasingly tired, although she would not admit it in front of Pimm she felt her own end game was nearing and as much as she wished to help with watching out for young Jimmy, she needed to focus on her husband, this included confiding in his oldest and only real friend, Bull Gordon, who other than herself, knew something of his true nature. She also hoped he would be in a position to give Pimm some latitude with his employers and after her death make allowances if he did something entirely against Mi6 policy like going walkabout.

In the 1960's Mi6 Assertive Field Operatives, Sandmen, were kept on a firm leash by London and not simply allowed to walk away, except by Controls executive approval, unless it was a forced retirement due to injury. If one tried to remove their collar without an approved retirement package in place, it was likely they would be terminated by the very country they had served faithfully for years.
Now Oliver Pimm was with Raleigh his leash to London would be a great deal firmer and although June knew nothing of the extreme disciplinary measures his employers might take, she considered if anyone would be able to safeguard Pimm, if he became emotionally compromised and fell by the wayside, Bull Gordon would.
Bull may have been relocated to the periphery of Control's inner circle, now occupying the west quadrant of the 10th floor of Century house with only four offices, when once he had his own floor seven levels higher, but he had enough history with the service, that those that sat at the Compass table in the Wheelhouse on the 22nd floor, all knew him and respected him publicly, those that did not knew his service record and the allegiances he had forged across all the intelligence communities over a lifetime of service and recognised even those that were his enemies respected his abilities and achievements.
His network of Lost Boy's helped win the peace in the latter half of the twentieth century. Only one ever turned on him. Harry McLoughlin and like all betrayers, he would eventually be betrayed by those that had tempted him away from the side of Bull.
It was a loose end Bull Gordon had already begun to conspire to have cut away. For now, he was satisfied in the knowledge from his most trusted CIA ally Tom Quinn, that the American's had McLoughlin under surveillance. Bull settled back to watch how the infighting between those vying for the throne of Mi6 would pan out. Whoever they were, they would keep him for a time near, until they were comfortable and confident enough to remove him completely, that was unless they were a "Reasonable man of good standing" as for Pimm, he waited for his return from the cruise and to hear how he had taken the serious news regarding Junes Illness, for now he had done all he could pulled in every favour, especially with Raleigh Department to ensure in taking up the slack by acting as the temporary operations head in Paris for Drake department the Pimm's would have a relative stable existence of a year, effectively postponing his full membership to his new Department and assignment to the type of operations they would generally perform, which necessitated an almost nomadic existence, during their service.
"Honestly Dickie, he's one you'd hate to lose and after all he's done," Bull had said in making his case to bend the rules of Scalphunters assignment in Pimm's case to Control, while they shared a drink at the Knightsbridge service club, "If the Bad

Penny takes leave to help his wife and Six falls apart, then maybe we should all consider brushing up on our Russian."

Bull raised an eye from postcard that carried a night time view of the Arc de Triomphe from June Pimm and placed it on the windowsill, alongside others he had received from the Pimm's during the cruise that he had received, resting long side his cactus collection.
With the ping of the elevator and the arrival of the latest office equipment including six new IBM telex machines. Bull settled back behind his desk content in his world that for now, his position was secure. Those that sat around the Compass on 22nd floor clearly considered him worthy of respect even if they all knew he was a complete technophobe.

Over the next week or so, a small team was established. Consisting of two midterm operator and four trainees, "Bulls runners." as they became known.
Bull began to build profiles and a program of priority of acquisition the names on Orran Danis's list of Nazi's and the resurrection of operation "Paper clip" began in earnest, all be it with a fraction of its original resources. Its retrieval and assessment assignment code was designation "Delight" named after the Turkish sweet.
Bull addressed his new team on the first morning brief with the operation room now set with no appeal as a sweet,
"A little Random scenario for the off, imagine you are starving on a desert island unexpectedly the surf washes up a can, no label opening it you discover its bait worms, you must decide which are the juiciest to eat to survive. The question is what to do with the rest some may grow to be big juicy worms, some will always be grubs the choice you have to make as they wriggle out of the can is which worms you keep and which you feed to the others. We need to keep all the juicy worms to make this operation a success, to survive, any questions?" Bull was not surprised to see a mischievous twinkle in Nicola Cartwright's eyes as she lifted her hand slowly, an intelligent young woman, Bull had recruited from the back rooms of special branch, where she was overlooked by her misogynist colleagues, well-liked by the rest of the team, even Mrs T had taken a shine to her, you need some loyal anchors the others can focus on, Bull gestured for her to speak, "What if you're a vegetarian Sir?" she asked with a mischievous grin.
"Well, Miss Cartwright with your size 27-inch waist, I am sure the rest of the team will thank you for your sacrifice, your bloated corpse no doubt will attract more flies, and we won't need to worry about looking for worms, they'll all be juicy. In six there are no vegetarians, only carnivores." Mrs T said sternly and then smiled.
"As it happens and as I'm sure you are aware Cartwright we start with the mother of all vegetarians Mr one bollock himself! Adolf until we have the next confirmed living principle to replace him of the Die Spinne *(The Spider)*."
With that Mrs Thompkin pinned a black and white image of the last photograph of a frail-looking Adolf Hitler, fixed dead centre in the Atlantic ocean on a world map from which other pins held strips of ribbon stretched to various global locations and

images of Nazi's such as Eichmann and Mengele along with individuals belonging to known terrorist organization.

"Right this won't buy baby a pram, let's get on with it you all have your assigned heads let's start a string list." She tapped on the photograph with a ruler then slapped it across her palm with a crack, and each of the young analysts scurried to their designated team desk pods.

"Good Mrs T, see if we can't bring some bacon home to daddy before Christmas show Control there's life in this old dog yet." Bull primed his pipe with tobacco.

"I see we were offered the olive branch from Tel Aviv." she said, picking up a postcard leaning up against a new addition to his cactus collection on Bull's desk, it showed the image of a Japanese whaling ship running down a great whale, it had arrived at Gordon's home address.

"Happy hunting, I'll keep an eye for your sail." it was signed Little Isser.

Isser Harel was the head of Mossad his work with Meir Dagan had instigated a global Mossad operation codename "Harpoon" that effectively Bull's team would be competing alongside.

"I assume it's been swept for bugs," she asked, and he nodded his head gesturing it had. Picking it up, she looked for space amongst the collection of others set in a line on his window sill. She recognised one and pulled it from the collection replacing it with the new one and turned back to Bull and he also recognised the cactus she had removed as being a gift from Harry McLoughlin.

"And the Mac situation, Sir?" she asked "I was remembering how the papers made a field day of George when they found out we had trained him as a paratrooper." she held the cactus hovering over his waste bin.

Gordon strummed at the dry pipe in his mouth, "Ah! Cut away loose ends, as always Mrs T, quite right, no point tying them, they always come undone, time to clean the deck. Put a call in with Tom Quinn will you duck, set up a meet at their place, Highgate Hill, tell him it's about the shamrock they picked, that will get his attention."

There was a tap at the door, and Mrs T was handed a cup of tea which she placed squarely on the Double Diamond beer mat on Bull's desk and a small chipped tea plate with three Mcvities jaffa cakes, as he sat down.

"Time to take out the rubbish," he said, raising a finger to the cactus in her hand and Mrs T promptly obliged by dropping it into the waste bin, then removed it from his office and emptied the entire contents into the daily burn bin. She looked at the group of young analyst and was pleased to see their heads were down working well together, while Gordon sipped his tea and stared over the brim of his cup at the new addition to his collection, considering what he had planned for his rogue agent in America.

Four days later Bull met with his oldest acquaintance from Langley, Tom Quinn, Senior European Operations Executive. "Collingwood" the CIA regency styled safe house on Highgate Hill, Hampstead, had battleship blue double traditional double, timber panel front doors that could stop a direct hit from an RPG *(Rocket-propelled grenade).* The well-tended flower tubs were made from reinforced concrete and set deep into the ground at precise angles acting as tank traps, with an extra-wide and deep integrated brass post, that was actually a machine gun slot, the eight-bedroom detached house looked like so many along the same street, its open red block paved drive offering a clear line of sight to the electric ten-foot-high steel gates. Security cameras on the entry porch and walls were already no longer a novelty in the area, but at number Twenty-four they continued around the back of the house and internally in every walkway and stairwell and were monitored twenty-four seven.

Upstairs the back room was well lit from a large balcony patio door and a guard sat relaxed with a Stoner 63 light machine gun, resting on his lap, covered by a copy of the American Herald, so as not to upset the neighbours, not that they could see over the high rear brick wall, coated with bottle shards.

"Collingwood" was ten doors from number thirty-three, the Russian KGB safe house at the time.

Inside Tom Quinn, a tall, heavyset, African American, with a crisp grey cropped head of thick wiry hair, wearing Clarks' suede Hush puppies, buzzed on the radio microphone alerting his men in the reception,

"Forget the tackle gentlemen, send Mr Gordon straight up, he's an old friend of old McDonald," he said, seeing his team about to frisk Bull and knowing he would hear his reference to the farm and recognize his pitiful attempt at the English accent and humour. They were as close as friends could be at the level of seniority they had risen to in the career that chose them.

Quinn like Gordon had begun his journey into the security service, crouched inside a vomit sloshing amphibious landing craft at 6.30 on the sixth of June 1944. His hands landed on Omagh beach on D Day aged twenty, his belt size was 32 inches, sixteen inches less than it was now.

As Bull entered his room, he was already at the nightstand table where a single bottle of Malt and a bottle of Gordon's sat, he poured Bull's first, remembering the ice and lemon and offered it before pouring himself a good measure with a single cube.

"The brave, the dumb and the dead," he said with smiled handing him the glass.

"The brave," Bull repeated and joined in the toast to their fallen comrades from the sixth of June.

Bull and Quinn had evolved a close working relationship over many years, serving their own governments and a carousel of individual superiors, which they both on occasion had at times not informed when they had corresponded or shared Intel and resources between themselves, in the interest of global security. Choosing to by-pass the red-tape and internal paranoia and politics that both the American and British secret service were subjected to by some members of their senior staff. On many occasions, their informal arrangement had saved the lives of field operatives and assets, not that it would ever be recognized.

"Thanks for the intro with Antonio," Quinn said, raising his glass.

Both men had been present in Barcelona four months earlier, at an Anglo American security meeting promoting an environment of trust amongst the American and European security services, effectively what the two men had been doing for years. Discussions focused on increasing the co-ordination of information regarding the cross-contamination of paramilitary groups within the European arena and the assistance they were receiving from North African states. In particular, the Libyans were blatantly offering sanctuary, arms and training facilities which saw all manner of terrorist groups training alongside each other, in a haven that created dangerous liaisons threatening the free world.

Bull was there to support the British service, who voiced the key concerns regarding the cooperation the IRA were receiving from other groups including the Basque separatist movement ETA and had introduced Quinn at one time during the conference as a friend Antonio Joseph.

However both Quinn and Bull were aware their attendance had been orchestrated by their superiors to decrease tensions regarding

American sympathisers for the IRA, as the pressure cooker of the troubles by now, had reached an apocalyptic level.

Bull, with Quinn's assistance, was providing Intel that funds being raised in America by IRA supporters could conceivably be falling into the hands of other right-wing terrorist cells to be used against Americans.

"No problem, he's a solid sort, like all of us his hands are sometimes bound and happy to shake the hands of those that can loosen them. Personally, I have found him useful with the French, they won't talk to me, per se, but they will talk to me through him, well they pick up his call, a bit like you and I with the Israelis and Zavi." Bull's smile echoed the notion that the two men had often shared the price of the British Empire.

Today Bull had called a meeting with Quinn to assist him with McLoughlin once and for all, and he would not involve the top floor of Mi6.

Quinn knew without Bull informing him of the specific's Mi6 had operatives working in deep cover within Northern Ireland and suspected held unofficial assets placed in the United States at least monitoring those raising funds and supporting the campaign in Ireland. Although there was a great deal of talk of an agreed sharing of information and disclosure of assets in play, neither the senior American's nor the British heads of security were totally transparent about their operations. However, as in all games of chess, when it came to sacrificing a piece, like a rogue agent, it was common sense to at least Quinn and Bull that as much gain as possible should be made from removing the problem.

They were not Mossad, the British couldn't just send another Mi6 agent over to the States with a kill order, even if it was one of their own and Bull's frugal brain saw an advantage in boosting Mi6/CIA détente in having the American's assist him in removing Harry McLoughlin. Hopefully, Quinn would be able to fill in the missing pieces, although he knew he would owe him in their own private game of chess.

"So your man is moving along nicely, and this will see him advance in good stead, We cannot be absolutely sure who they will use to set up the first devices, but once the detonators arrive back in Ireland we will have a timeline, then it is all down to when the first touch paper is lit, or battery is attached in this case," Quinn said, and Bull raised his glass of gin and tonic.

"I will make sure our boys in play from next week. Bull you understand once he hears the raid on our supply store is confirmed, there is nothing that can stop him we have no wish to compromise his position. This is purely a courtesy from me to you. Call it my appreciation, watching my back when you sat in the higher stalls of Century House. I have to ask, are you sure there is no retrieval of this McLoughlin guy? Nothing we might salvage taking him back in, perhaps on our side?"

Bull raised his eye, "Unfortunately no, we trained him too well. Your boys could practice their dark arts, but not even sodium thiopental or scopolamine, will get his name, and anything he did tell you could turn out to be a death pit, for whoever follows it up. No this is the only way, your man takes him out, and he gets to move up the rung and buries deeper in the belly of the beast." Bull Gordon's plan if executed, could potentially harvest three crops, the death of McLoughlin, the advance of an American deep-cover agent within the IRA community in America and the end to a bomb-making team.

Bull was aware McLoughlin was still receiving Intel from an asset he had cultivated working within the BSA manufacturing company. The plan was a mousetrap allowing the mouse to escape with the cheese, McLoughlin would learn of a shipment of arms being transported for disposal along with Semtex explosives and detonators that may be acquired with little risk, it would be too attractive an opportunity for the IRA not to consider taking a punt at, but the detonators and explosives would be designed to prematurely detonate whilst being assembled.

Once the IRA had taken possession, and the weapons were in play, through a trail of covert drop boxes known to be compromised, leaking transmissions, both in the U.S. and G.B. evidence was planted indicating McLoughlin was still working with Mi6. So when it was reported an Irish bomb-making factory was destroyed. Tom Quinn's man would be in a position to cast suspicion and execute McLoughlin as a Mi6 spy, who could question his loyalty in eliminating a Mi6 agent.

"Any fall-out at this end, does he have any stones he can turn over, anything left to trade to buy his way back into the game?" Quinn studied Bull carefully, he was one of the few English men he felt comfortable talking openly with and who he knew he could work alongside with the minimum of red tape and not run for cover if something was not to go as planned.

"No, we pulled all the people from the field on our side he knew, except the few like this girl at BSA so we could at least know he was out there nibbling for titbits. No, he's totally burned his bridges with me old sport, nothing personal, except?" Bull looked to the patio window and the tall willow strands swaying back and forth the wind caught the paper of the guard, and he readjusted his Ray-Ban sunglasses Tom Quinn leaned in, "except?" he questioned.

"Well it's the old sons of the father thing, he has a couple, if they grow up anything like their old man they could be a handful, but that's something for another day, a bit like asking would you have killed Hitler in his crib."

Then Bull smiled, knowing Quinn's response would be like his,
"In a heartbeat." they both said at the same time.

On the 26 June 1970, two Provisional IRA volunteers, Joseph Coyle and Thomas McCool were killed in an explosion; it is believed during the assembly of an incendiary device the detonator activated prematurely at the McCool home at Dunree Gardens, Creggan, Derry. It would have been covered up as a house fire, if it were not for the presence of McCool's two daughters, Carol Ann, 4 and Bernadette, 9 both also killed. A third IRA volunteer believed present, Thomas Carlin, died a few days later of his injuries.

An investigation was launched on both sides of the Atlantic by the IRA hierarchy, at this point Tom Quinn's deep cover agent Cromwell just began to make suggestions about the source and quality of the ingredients used. Suspicion of foul play was rife as the individuals that had been killed in preparation, were known to have been experienced in explosives. There was an immediate suspension of activity for three weeks, then when another two members of the IRA were killed under similar circumstances taking out the public bar of the Prince Regent, Belfast road. The CIA's man, Cromwell began to press the executive for a closer look at the products involved, while citing the fact that at the time they were acquired, McLoughlin had reported they would be accompanied by a significant arms cache. As it turned out most of the modern weapons were already decommissioned, or of little use except as spare parts, the only operational rifles, were Browning 303's not the most tactically efficient weapon for urban street warfare.

Having set information bait trails for others to find, which indicated McLoughlin was still working with Mi6, he was picked up. Few needed convincing he was a double agent and Cromwell was on hand when requested as he had to some extent instigated the accusations to put up or shut up and was took an active role in the questioning. Fortunately for Cromwell and Mi6, McLoughlin reverted to his own tradecraft during the violent beating and during the several hours of questioning that followed and this in some respects worked against him.

Cromwell was one of the four that cast the unanimous vote McLoughlin could not be trusted and with no hesitation, knowing it would assist his own legend with the IRA, executed Harry McLoughlin and dumped his body in the Chicago Bay area. The CIA now had a man firmly entrenched in the IRA executive in America.

Meanwhile, Harry McLoughlin sons in Ireland, Sean and Connor were informed their father was killed by the British, soon after they went to live with their Mothers half-brother, so-called half brother, Brian O'Connell in Mitchelstown, Cork, who was an active IRA elder member of the council.

Their indoctrination was fuelled by their passion for vengeance on the lie of their parent's death. When the opportunity arose in North Africa, they joined a new group of terrorists emerging across the globe, each, in turn, fighting for their own cause, but now highly trained alongside brothers of blood in specialized camps operating within countries that offered them sanctuary, such as Libya and Somalia, effectively

Sean and Connor were programmed and trained very much in a similar way to the Hitler Youth and held the same conviction and dedication.

Chapter 8: The Steelhead Runners
Kentish Town, London
October 1972

"Your boys are out of control, the action was not sanctioned, we can't have two gunslingers like this think their running the show, making deals with a bunch of hippies, ficking Angry Mob, I've shat harder things, bunch of sandal-footed shirt lifters!" there was a long pause on the line.
"I'll have words, tell 'em to pull in the reins, they're good lads Danny eager as fick to get stuck in, you know these boys." O'Connell already knew what was coming a whisper had come down the wire the McLoughlin boys had gone too far involving the Angry mob in the blowing up of the Post Office Tower on 31st October: "I'm sorry Pal, it's too late for that, they're out, they were warned before, you said you could handle them over there, this is on you Bri." Danny Docherty's tone was resolute.
"Surely not Danny they can't mean that these are loyal lads, they'd do anything for the cause, I know they're a pair of hotheads, but you said it yourself it's time we took the blood to the streets of London."

Brian O'Connell had spent the last five months living with the McLoughlin brothers in the second floor two bedroom bedsit at 109 Kentish Town Road, following their expulsion from Belfast for carrying out a number of unauthorised attacks on Loyalist. The executive heads of the Provisional Irish Republican Army were strict disciplinarians, punishing with beatings and kneecapping's individuals that disobeyed their orders or carried out attacks of any kind without prior consent, keen to be seen by the Irish Catholic community as an effective, coherent paramilitary force with a command structure with as much control, if not more than those they were pitted against.

"Are you not listening to me Bri O'Connell? They've had enough at home, they want a full stop on this one. Don't forget we know where these two blueberries came from originally, some of the old boys wanted to take it further before, but I stood up like a twat and told them Bri O'Connell's your man he'll bang their heads together set them straight, you've made me look a right eejit, you cunt you." Docherty's voice sneered down the telephone line with contempt for the McLoughlin boys knowing that their father had been a British agent.
"You know as well as I, when we did their pappy in the windy city some of the old boys wanted the bairn's done back home, so twice now they have been given a pass, it not on Bri!"
Docherty's own authority and command of the members of the terrorist cells under his control based in England was being scrutinized by his superiors if he failed to deliver a suitable punishment to the McLoughlin brothers he knew he would find

himself relocated back to Belfast, which was a far less attractive location compared to London in the early '70s where he would not hold the same kudos as the head of the Kilburn Brigade of the IRA.

"So what are you after me do'in with them." O'Connell relented with a sigh and heard a deep growl come from the other end of the telephone line. "Get rid I don't give a fick how you do it, get them off the streets of London by morning or the Brits will get a nice present with their heads, the same goes if they show their face's back home, I'd deal with it myself if I wasn't sitting on this scratch *(money)* for the boys, but you mark me Bri O'Connell, you had better have sorted this shit out by the time I'm back from Switzerland." Docherty was effectively banishing the McLoughlin's for all time from their homeland.

"Jees Dan, that's a bit drastic, what if they won't go?" O'Connell knew it was a stupid question, but the idea of trying to order Sean McLoughlin to leave was a daunting challenge.

"Can you listen to it? A bit drastic says he, can you hear yer 'self man!" Docherty could then be heard swearing at someone in his company the other end of the line. There was silence then he spoke calmly but with a precise threatening tone that focused O'Connell's attention. "Listen Bri we all know you did your best lad, taking them in as you did, fair play, we get it, you blame yer self for their Ma's death, you were not to know the old fella had skipped across to make a deal with the American fathers, I know that one needed a muzzle on a good day, it would have been you or her, O'Shea told the council all about it, but her wild dogs are ficking Rabid and we can't be hav'in that now. Take my advice let them out on the crack to the Archway say it's to celebrate the win and then tuck them up in a warm blanket with a wee fire like we did Freddie Malloy's boy, if you've no stomach for it, I tell you what, I'll do and you'll owe me this, I'll send one of my fella's over later with the juice."

Docherty was referring to the killing of John Malloy confirmed as an informer he was found dead in his bed, following a fire in his flat, allegedly started by a dropped cigarette following a heavy drinking session, but Malloy never smoked.

"No! No, if it comes to it, I'll do it, I'll have words with Sean, explain it, suggest they look maybe to the African's they seemed to get on well over there, who knows they may even come in handy again." O'Connell had considered lying to the boys to get them out of the country by sending them over to one of the new training camps they had established in Libya.

"Fuck no I'm not having them poison the well there, we've only just got in with that black fella, I'm over with the bank next week make sure a gravy train he's putting in place finds the right station. For Christ sake you keep these lads away from any of ours, I mean it Bri put them on a slow boat to China, If I hear of the McLoughlin boys again, I'll be sending your Aunt pat a sympathy card with your name, now this conversation's over!" Again, O'Connell heard swearing on the other end of the line and then it went dead as Docherty hung up and just before O'Connell placed the phone receiver down he heard three unnerving clicks on the line, he held his breath.

"Hello?" he spoke softly, as his hand pushed the filthy net curtains back from the window and he scanned outside, up and down the street, looking specifically at the work vans and noticed a new looking dark green Bedford CF220 parked on the same side as their flats four car spaces from their window beside the main telephone pole. As he was considering the possibility of it being a surveillance vehicle Sean McLoughlin entered the flat carrying the fish and chips closely followed by his brother with a bottle of Johnny Walker.
"What you do'in Unc?" Sean said, seeing Brian at the window as he placed the rolled up newspaper parcels on the kitchen table, Brian let the curtain drop, to say he heard a suspicious click on the line would provoke questions of the call,
"Just checking the street, as you do." he said, as he watched Connor flip through the kitchen cabinets for the Heinz tomato sauce, vinegar and salt.
"Did you get me haddock, as I asked?" Brian acted cool dismissing his suspicions of the green van, his mind was too tied up with his situation with the brothers to consider there may be a Mi6 team listening on their telephone line, but Sean was always alert, he pinched a chip.
"Got a wee touch of flat skittles *(paranoia)*, Unc there's 50,000 Irish in Camden alone, why'd they knock on our door?" he joked but looked to the window.
"O fick, I knew we had it wrong Sean, I thought you said plaice." Connor cut in with a cheeky grin as he turned his chair around and opened his own dinner and watched O'Connell's face drop in disappointment.
"Go away with yer! Course we did it right, even got you a pickled egg you old bastard, sit yer self." Connor said smothering his food with ketchup, he was nineteen younger by two years to Sean and had a juvenile taunting sense of humour that often annoyed Brian, but he knew the Hyde side to his character had a darkness matched only by his brothers ruthless aggression, they were both pure breed psychopaths who fed off each other's wish to destroy the British.
As Brian got the whisky tumblers from the cupboard Sean went to the window it had begun to rain, and he watched the evening traffic heading home there were now four vans parked in the street and he marked the position of each, then slipped the Browning from the back of his jeans and placed it on the table and opened his own cod and chips.
"Save some for me you greedy fuck." Brian said seeing the last few drops drain from the Sarsons vinegar bottle over Connors chips, to which Sean slapped him lightly across the head in punishment.
"What're you like," Sean said, as his brother sniggered.
"I fucking hate chips without vinegar." Brian scolded unimpressed with the pair of boys.
"Fuck it." Sean swallowed a double measure of Teachers and wrapped his food up, "I'll get some from the corner, I'll be a minute, stick mine in the oven Bro." he said stuffing his pistol back under his waistband.
"Don't bother Sean, I'll be fine, eat up boy." Brian smiled.
"No bother Uncle, we need some shit paper anyway, this little fuck used up the last." he winked at Connor.

"You're a good lad, see that Con, that's respect of your elders, you do well learn the lesson." he said, getting a mocking smirk from Connor. With Sean from the room, Brian picked at his chips and decided to begin to seed the field of getting the boys out of London "I had a word with the Doc, could be he wants someone to take another look at how those lads do things abroad."
Connor carried on eating occasionally flicking an eye in O'Connell's direction.
"Well Sean reckons we need to hit them again here, what Doc say about the mess we made of the tower, Sean reckons it's going to take years to make it right, said they may even have to pull it down, have they claimed it for us yet, they should be setting a ficking statue for the McLoughlin boys in Derry, Sean says"
Brian winced "Well these things take a while to sort, not everything Sean says happens the way Sean says, turns out some of the American's had an interest in the machines in the building."
Connor stopped eating and looked closely at the man he had always known as Uncle, then snarled lightly, "Sometimes Uncle you talk such bollocks."
O'Connell knew better than to press any further, explaining that the Post Office Tower housed IBM's machines that had been owned by an unofficial financial supporter of their cause based in the U.S. would be a leap for Connor to understand. It was this fall out from the brothers attack that was principally why Belfast was so angry at the bombing, jeopardising relations with those that would come to be exceptionally important to the cause within the legitimate political and commercial elitist society of wealthy Irish Americans and because Belfast were made to look as if they had no control of their own people.

Sean stood on the steps of the Greenland flats sheltered from the mild rain by the small canopy, he looked to the street and judging the traffic before stepping onto the pavement to cross the road for the corner shop on the other side he whistled checking the cars and vans parked in the street. Seeing the number 14 bus pull in holding the traffic on his side up he hopped out and dashed across getting a toot from a gas van that came inches from catching him, he span and stuck his fingers "póg mo thóinr!" he swore in Gaelic, drawing attention to himself in the street he got a cat call whistle, then a wave from a tall older women whose dark roots had begun to show through, dressed in clothes that showed off her assets and would suit a younger girl. She was a local prostitute that worked the pub drunks in the area that had come on to Uncle one night.
"Fuck you look rough girl just finished." he called as he waved back with a cheeky kiss to his hand, she gave him two fingers as she searched her bag for a lighter and as he twisted back to the pavement he caught sight of a dark haired man wearing a similar Levis jean jacket to his own except in black, he had considered black when getting his and it was that which caught his eye first, but then something else stuck in his mind, the man's hair, he looked like he had just visited a barber, short back and sides, it was the first tell and the second was that he wore "army issue" shiny, black Doctor Martins boots.

Sean smiled himself thinking, knowing all the years of polishing up for parade had formed a habit many soldiers continued long after they had left service. Sean's gaze drifted briefly to the dark green Bedford van the man had stepped from as he caught himself stepping awkwardly on the curb edge. Then in the bakers shop window in front of him, he watched the man in the black jacket cross the road coming in his direction. Sean continued along the street whistling, "Sweet Molly Malone", sensing the man following behind him, then in hearing the bell of the bakers go he glanced back "You're the one getting skitty Sean boy." He sighed and felt his shoulders relax seeing the man disappear inside the bakers.

"Evening! Luv do you have any vinegar?" Sean got a smile off the woman behind the counter as he entered the store and he winked at her in thanks as she pointed to the far side of the two long aisles of goods and he drifted down towards the back of the shop. Finding the vinegar, he moved along the aisle leaning down to look at the different types of toilet paper, as he did he dropped from the sight of the Mi6 surveillance officer in the black Levi jacket, who had now returned to follow him and was watching through the window as he pretended to read the small private advertising post cards in a shop display.
In not seeing Sean in the shop aisle the Officer made the mistake of entering, just as Sean stood up from the back and as Sean raised his eyes from looking at the packaging of Soft toilet tissue, he saw the image of the man illuminated as the lady behind the counter turned on the store lights for the evening, their eyes locked for a moment and the man moved down the aisle on the opposite side to Sean and began looking through the chocolate bar display. Sean reached around his back and placed a hand on his Browning he then grabbed a newspaper from the rack and slipped the gun between its folds. Then he took the paper with the toilet roll on top and the vinegar to the counter. He glanced at the Mi6 operative as he stepped around and knew in an instant what he was and that his initial instinct of the man, had been right.
Sean smiled at the women as he paid and left, but he could not resist another glance through the window at the man, still making out he was looking for a chocolate bar.

The Mi6 Officer did buy two "Picnic" bars of chocolate and hovered in the doorway of the store as it began to rain and watched Sean dodge the traffic, then disappear into the apartment lobby, before the Officer returned to his surveillance van, climbing into the passenger front seat.
"We're good, I'll be happier when we get in the flat above, all this jumping in and out is a pain in the arse, don't understand why we don't just pull these Bog boys, there's something itchy about this one." He said placing the chocolate on the dash and turned in the front seat to his partner in the rear of the van, listening on the tape equipment linked to the telephone line outside.
"Well once they hear this maybe they will." His partner said, handing him his headphones. The officer up front in the van cab caught the briefest flash of fear in

his partner's eyes at his realization they were in trouble, as there was a click of the door handle, "I told you to keep the fucking door locked" his partner screamed, and turned back seeing one of the rear doors wrench open. Seeing the toilet roll attached to Sean's gun threw him for a fatal second as he reached for his weapon in the holster set on his work station, then felt the first slug from Sean's Browning rip through his side and he was slammed against the back plate of the driving cab. "Bastard." The Officer up front in the black Levi jacket ranted, dropping the headset he went to pull his own Smith and Wesson revolver from his shoulder holster, but Sean raised the toilet tissue packet, now set with a flame and pointing in his direction fired three shots through the cab back plate, the man let out a violent cry and slumped down in the foot well and across the internal engine canopy, below the dash board.

Sean stepped fully into the van and stamped out the flames of the toilet tissue paper, using the blankets the men had kept themselves warm with during night surveillance. Coughing from the smoke he threw one of the blankets over the cab back plate and seat covering the Officers body in the front. Fortunately for Sean, the rain obscured the glass and his shots had been muffled by his improvised toilet roll silencer.
Sean stuffed a cigarette in his mouth and opened the back door allowing some of the smoke to escape, stepping from the van he raised his collar and stood smoking in the light rain, occasionally wafting the door open and then shut, allowing more smoke to escape, concerned someone might have witnessed his attack, but no one was in the street on that side, and the cars on the road slushed along the tarmac their owners too eager to get home after a hard day.

He threw his cigarette to the gutter as he stepped back inside and closed the door lightly, then heard the faint sound of talking and peeked inside; again seeing the carnage he had created he realized the radio operator was still alive. As the man laid wheezing, Sean instinctively withdrew his gun and grabbing the barrel this time smashed it three times into the base of the man's neck until he heard a crack. He then flinched as again he heard the faint sound of talking then noticed the reels of the tape recorder were turning. His heart was racing, and he held his breath as he pulled the headphones out from under the dead operative in the front seat and placed one half of the headset against his ear. His first reaction on hearing Uncle's voice was to smile, then he looked at the dead agent and considered how long they had been listening in on their conversations, he slumped down in the van, then he heard what Danny Docherty was saying and he looked at the machine, working out how it operated he span the tape back until it stopped squealing to hear the beginning as he searched the nearest dead man, he took his sidearm first then his wallet which included his warrant card.
Sean stopped listening when he heard Docherty admit to Brian O'Connell they killed his father and his first thought were for Connor's safety, finding the keys he locked the van and cut the wire from the telephone pole that fed into the van, he

considered it was only a matter of time before another surveillance team would be on the scene. "Where d'you go for that Egypt?" Uncle said showing Sean he could not wait and had finished his fish and chips, while Connor laid on the couch reading the racing times. Sean placed the Sarson's bottle on the table, "Sorry Unc got talking with that blonde brass from the Anchor, Shelia." Sean said mixing in a half-truth while considering how he was going to play the next ten minutes. "Stella, lovely girl, she has a peach of a pair I could lose a weekend in there." Uncle corrected the name remembering having his head placed firmly in her deep cleavage last time he saw her.

"Stella, of course, more mutton than lamb but a polite woman, you'll be in there for sure Unc sorry about the time, she's a talker as you know." Connor let out the sound of a sheep barring in the background as Sean watched Uncle pour him another drink.

"Well, they say it's the thought that counts." O'Connell raised his glass.

Sean looked to the telephone and then to his brother as he grabbed his food from the oven then sat down and began to eat.

"Tell you what Unc, eejit I am, I forgot the bog roll, I'll get the kid to run back down and he can get you some raspberry ripple, yer favourite, Con, go get Unc some ice cream!" he ordered, but Connor carried on reading.

"Con now!" he shouted, Connor looked at his brother then at Uncle and slid off the couch curious at why his brother would be acting strange, but he knew that tone as the latch of the door flat door closed behind him.

Sean dropped the chip he had in his hand and opened his packet of cigarettes "Fuck I'm out."

"I'll roll you one, here?" O'Connell said, taking his tin of Golden Virginia out of his pocket.

"Narrrr fick it, I'll get the boy to pick me up a pack." Sean said, getting up and before Uncle had licked the paper of a rolled cigarette, Sean was out the door.

Sean caught Connor with a whistle before he got to the corner shop, and he waved gesturing him back over the street, as he checked the other pedestrians nearby then climbed into the driver's side of the Bedford Mi6 surveillance van. Connor kept watch and waited to be allowed in the passenger side, as the door opened he caught sight of the shoes of the dead Mi6 operative laying in the front under the blanket.

"Get the fick in." Sean growled, Connor squashed his legs up against the dead agent and looked into the back of the truck at the surveillance equipment and then down at the other dead agent as Sean showed him the Mi6 warrant card of the dead Officer.

"So they're on to us, we need to get Uncle and piss off out, he was saying Doc has a job abroad." Connor pulled the Smith and Wesson out from the front agent's hand "Shut up for a minute Con, let me think." Sean knew he was right they needed to get out of there, but who could they now trust.

"Drive this down to the Edmonton lock up and wait for me there, bag these fella's and give this heap of shit a coat of paint see if you can get some plates off a similar van, if not any van will do, I'll be over there before morning." Sean checked the wing mirrors and stepped out of the van allowing Connor to slide along to the driver's seat "What colour?" Connor asked with a mouthful of the warm chocolate he had found on the dash, left by the Mi6 Officer.

"What?" Sean looked at him bewildered and shook his head gesturing no when offered the other Picnic bar.

"The van what colour?" Connor shrugged his shoulders and proceeded to open the second bar of Chocolate.

"Anything ficking colour but Green and Con watch your speed, get off with you now!" Sean banged on the door, "and don't leave your sticky prints all over the wheel."

"So what now?" Brian O'Connell stared at the Smith and Wesson resting on the armrest inches from Sean's fingers.

"Now we finish this bottle, and you tell me everything you know, just like we were family," Sean said raising his glass, then sat back and listened without saying a word as Brian told him the truth regarding his father. How his mother a loyal supporter of the cause, had died without knowing she had fallen for a British undercover intelligence officer.

"So what you're saying is me and the kid are fucked, not just half Brit, we're army brats and one better you think maybe our Da was some sort of spy." Sean now no longer looked at the man before him with anything less than contempt, as he asked about Docherty's involvement in his father's death, O'Connell told him everything he knew and saw no reason in not to telling him Docherty was holed up with three of his own security detail in a Finsbury Park flat and was on his way to a bank in Switzerland with cash raised in the UK mainland. Brian O'Connell did not know the details, but slurred something about him heading off on a ferry and that he believed it concerned their Libyan connection as Sean refilled his glass.

Sean knew of the safe house, having spent time there before and already was aware of entry and escape routes from the third floor flat.

"Yep, that's about it Sean me, boy, double fucked." the whisky had taken effect, and Brian was now talking far more relaxed, and confidently than he should.

Sean took a deep breath and lifted his hands behind his head as he stared into the eyes of the man that had cared for him most of his life, he felt a tear in his eye and plucked from his cheek with his finger then licked it tasting the salt.

"Well, I tell you, two things Unc." he said reaching behind his head and pulling out the cushion he was resting on.

"What's that?" Unc said his eyes barely open, smiling in his stupor, believing he had convinced Sean to leave the UK.

"One I'm not yer boy and two I may be fucked, but I'm not as fucked as you old man." with that Sean pushed the Smith and Wesson revolver into the pillow and let off two rounds into Uncles face soft white feathers some singed with the heat

covered Uncles body as the cushion disintegrated and matted red feathers fell to the floor.
Sean arrived at the Edmonton railway arches, with a single black Adidas kit bag containing a change of clothes for them both. Including Connor's favourite Liverpool shirt and the Smith and Wesson he had used on Brian O'Connell.
He had staged the scene at the flat to appear as if Uncle had been disturbed by the Mi6 officers and left O'Connell's old faithful Enfield revolver on the floor, a short way from his hand, but not before placing a shell into the front door frame. Making it appear as if Uncle had got at least one round off before being gunned down.
Connor was already sticking the second coat of pineapple orange on the Bedford and pulled his mask off as Sean came through the wooden side door.
"Did you bring some smokes?" he called over as he stepped back to admire his handy work.
"They say the luck of the Irish, pulled on to the north circular and one of these sat at the lights with me that's the plate," he said pointing to a registration scribbled on the back of an empty packet of Embassy number one cigarettes, as Sean placed the kit bag on the tool bench.
"Where's Uncle, did you bring my football shirt?" he began to rummage into the bag placing the handgun on the bench beside a case of coke cans and nail bundles prepared for use in a bomb, as Sean went over to two rolled half carpet rugs roped up with old cable, containing the bodies of the two Mi6 agents. Connor looked to the door and saw Sean had pulled down the main cross lever of garage door, locking it.
"I didn't know what you had planned for these two, so I kept them as is, emptied the shit they had on them over there, where's Unc Sean?" he said, realising he was not coming.
"How long do you think they were on us?" Sean ignored the questions crouched down and pulled at the cable making sure the bundles were secure he took out his cigarette and handed them up to his brother.
"Does that thing start?" Sean pointed to an old Austin A4 half covered with a dust sheet.
Connor went over and pulled the sheet off "Did the last time we were here, don't be thinking we'll be making a quick getaway, gutless piece of shit, are you going to fill me in what we're about, with these boys and where's the old man?"
Sean leaned in and grabbing the keys from the dash pumped the accelerator then smiled as the Austin turned over once before starting.
"Good half a tank that'll get us there and back." he whispered to himself then looked at his brother adjusting the carburettor of the Austin through the fine slit in the raised bonnet.
"It's just you and me now Con, Uncle turned out to be a wrong'en, see that there, have a listen to the tape on the reel in the back, then you'll know all I do, I need you focused if we are going to take down the chicken man today." he said turning off the engine and stepping out.
Connor rubbed the oil from his hands on a rag taking in what Sean was saying and looked towards the back of the Bedford van that still contained the surveillance

equipment, "What the fuck are you on, taking down Docherty, have you and Unc been at the lightning again?" Connor shook his head as he lowered the bonnet of the Austin.

"Just listen to the tape in there, then put anything useful you have on the table, while I check out if we left anything in here we could use." Sean then went through to the back room to check a hiding hole beneath the rear toilet block they had used to stash weapons and explosives before, the floor was sticky all were encouraged to miss the pan, to throw off the scent if they were ever raided with a Police dog searching team.

Connor took out the Smith and Wesson he had removed from the agent and the extra shells and placed them along with his own Browning on the workbench.

Then checking he did not touch the tacky orange paint, he opened the rear doors of the van and rewound the tape spool to begin listening to the tape. Like Sean when first he had heard his own voice he smiled as he listened to a call he had made from the Archway pub call box telling Uncle they were both stopping out there watching the game on the pub colour TV. Then he heard Docherty's voice.

Doc was also known as the "chicken man" because wherever he stayed he kept a live hen in a cage to have a fresh egg, the bird was an Irish flurry hen,

"If I'm going to have anything that comes out of an arse it's going to be out of an Irish arse hole." is how Doc put it, but Connor had been there when Doc had told Sean he heard from a "reliable source" that the CIA tried once to kill off Stalin by injecting hens eggs with cyanide, all Connor knew was the birds name was Monroe after the actress

"Fick the egg I'd use her shit as toothpaste." Doc once bragged about the real Marilyn.

As his brother listened to the tape, Sean placed two sticks of dynamite and one fuse detonator on the bench next to the guns and looking at the tools around found a small hand axe. Grabbing a pencil, he turned over a receipt for tyres and began to scratch out the layout of the flat in Finsbury Park. Remembering where the external watchers had been stationed, which he marked with X's occasionally, he looked at the van to see Connor flipping the tape back and forth, as he re-listened to the same part where Docherty spoke of their father, Harry McLoughlin.

They had always been told he was killed by a black and tan kill squad it was what fuelled their desire to join the cause at an early age. He knew he felt like his brother, betrayed, all they had known all they were was a lie, but he had come to terms with what they should do next, how Connor would react was his only concern, he sat touched the orange paint and found it was dry and sat in the back of the van and lit a cigarette then passed it up to his brother.

"So they killed Da and Ma, the boys back home, the boys we have been fighting for all this fickin time!" Connor said switching the tape off.

"Looks that way kid." Sean took the cigarette back off his brother; he knew anything he said would just aggravate his brother further, so he waited.

"And Uncle knew, all this time too?" Connor's mind was still working out the depth of the betrayal he and his brother had been subjected to, and Sean nodded in agreement to each of his epiphanies.

"Don't you worry nothing about Uncle now, old Nicks probably ripping him another arse hole by now." Sean spat and handed his brother back his Browning.

"I'm off to face Doc, he's at the Finsbury flat, he may know some more on this, are you with me Kid?" Sean went back to the table and began to tape the two sticks of dynamite together with nine-inch nails set in the tape around the explosive and looked to the small propane gas bottle.

"About Da, being a spook an all, you think it's true then?" Connor joined his brother, checking the chamber on one of the Mi6 operatives Smith & Wesson revolver was full, he closed it and tucked it alongside his browning in his waistband.

"Well there's that and Uncle mentioned Doc was going overseas, it may be a way out for us. Sure as shit after tonight we won't be welcome here or back home. But if they know what's best for them, they'll give us a wide birth." Sean looked at the bodies of the two Mi6 agents wrapped in carpet.

"But Seany we're going to kill 'em?" Connor's eyes burned as brightly as the orange flecks in his hair.

"Behave yer self, course we are, we'll kill the fickin lot." Sean handed him the dynamite bomb and pointed to the gas bottle, and he began to tape the two together.

The boys placed the corpses of the two Mi6 operatives into the back of the van along with the homemade bomb and with Sean in the Austin A4 and Sean driving the Bedford van they drove to Portland Rise, Finsbury Park.

Parking up a street away from the front of the flats Connor joined his brother in the Austin and they moved in closer.

"If we can get'em all inside, it'll save all the fucking about." Sean told his brother as they watched a shadowy figure leaning over the concrete balcony blowing smoke into the night air and then Sean pointed further along the same landing to another one of Docherty's sentry's that came into view.

"I have an idea Con, you're going to need some nerve for this though kid." he said, looking at a nearby phone booth.

Leaving Connor in the car Sean went to the rear of the apartment block and began climbing up the outside of the building, balcony by balcony until he came to the floor below the one he knew contained Docherty. He rested crouched low and peaked through the windows at the owners, they were watching, it's a knock out on the television, the voice and laughter of the presenter, Eddie Waring of "Jeux Sans Frontières" made him smile.

Hearing voices above talking in Docherty's room he tucked his head in as he heard the sound of the telephone ring, knowing it was as he had arranged with Connor. He was calling Docherty from the phone box to tell him they had caught two Mi6 officers and killed them. He heard Doc call his man inside and Sean began to slip to the outside of the balcony and climb up.

"Jesus those wild boy's you have to love'em the young pup, Con says they've only bagged a couple of Brits. He was crying like a bairn says his brothers been hit, he's on his way over, reckons Uncle has them trussed up like a couple of turkeys for Christmas." Sean heard Docherty explaining what Connor had told him to one of his security team and then recognised the voice of his enforcer Tom Gormally, who had been at the same Libyan training camp with Connor and him eighteen months earlier. Sean looked back out towards the road and hoped his brother would hold back as he had told him, to make out having driven over from Kentish town.

"It's a Fickin shame; you have to credit that eejit brother of his, Sean, going for the big game. I always liked the boy myself." Gormally joked, clearly impressed.

"Yar, yar, yar, we all like the boys, don't you go soft on me now Jon, Jon, if Sean's out of the picture, that suits me fine. Connor McLoughlin's on his way waits down there and get the other lads to check they haven't taken out some fickin TV licence detector van, then bring the McLoughlin pup up here, I'll be having a word before you take him on the long drive, now go in the back and get me a tarpaulin sheet." Docherty ordered.

Sean then watched him go to a draw and take out a revolver.

"No chances Jon, Jon, if he so much as winks at you wrong, put him down. In the meantime I'll get Uncle's side of things." Docherty said as Gormally began to unfold the plastic sheet on the carpet.

When Gormally left the room, Docherty went to the kitchen leaving his gun on the dining table beside a copy of the Irish Times, he poured himself a good measure of scotch and did a little jig as he fed crumbs from the open biscuit tin to his caged bird. When he walked back into the lounge he froze at the sight of Sean standing in the hallway. Sean had already slipped the latch on the front door, so they would not be disturbed.

"Sean boy? I was just going to call Uncle, see what the craic is, yer brother said you were caught up in it, must have heard wrong, showing me age" Docherty looked to the table and saw his revolver was no longer where he left it and set the bottle down.

Sean tapped his jean belt and wagged a finger and Docherty then noticed the grip of his own gun poking out from Sean's jeans.

"You can call Uncle till doomsday Doc, but he'll not be answering." Sean pointed to the armchair Docherty clearly had set as his throne as he stepped around the plastic sheet laid out on the carpet and shook his head tutting, "Expecting someone else, were yer." he said, knowing full well it was meant for Connor and that Docherty intended to kill his brother on his arrival at the flat.

"Other business, nothing to concern you, I was just about to clean out me birds cage, didn't want a mess on the carpet." Docherty bluffed.

"Is that it, for sure don't want a mess now do we." Sean watched Docherty take to his seat.

"So what are you about lad? You must have hit every light to make it here, hope you have not brought the door knockers with you." Docherty glanced towards the hallway door and began judging his options, knowing he would be dead before he had a chance to cry out to Gormally who was still waiting outside for Connor's arrival.

"Don't you worry about yer boys for now, I need a few wee words, just the two of us, like." Sean moved over to the sideboard where two tartan duffel bag sat open both stuffed full with wads of cash bound with elastic bands, on top were their passports and ferry tickets and a black diary.

"Uncle said you were off on a trip before he took his...nap." Sean watched Docherty's expression in the sideboard mirror, "I take it this is the tut for the bank in Switzerland."

Without turning, Sean held the black diary up.

"There's nothin for you there Sean my son, best you close that now before stick your nose where it's not to be." Docherty tried again to bluff by expressing his past authority.

"You know, I'm getting a little sick people claiming me as their boy, as you know, I'm a bastard, a black and tan's bastard." with that Sean swept round and fired a single shot into Docherty's knee, it splintered like a boiled egg shell as Docherty screamed dropping his drink and grabbing at the wound with both hands. "You fickin eejit what the fick are you do'in, fuck boy you're in some shit now boyo." Docherty's eyes glared in defiance, "You know the men that stand behind me, they'll hunt you till the end of time, so they will, you and your kid brother will be sausage meat, before their done with you."

"Fuck off old man, those two Brits I killed today, Con told you about had you and Bri wired. Who's the eejit it now, we heard you brag about killing our old fella, what you recon Belfast would say if they found out you'd been spilling your guts to the Brits, because yer to fucking fat and to fucking tik, you old bag of shite" Sean sat with one eye on the half glass front door and checked his watch, his fingers slipped to his wrist and he felt his pulse, then taking a breath calmed himself as he had been trained, by tightening his watch strap.

"Listen, Sean that was years ago, you two boys were nothing but babes." Docherty's face began to strain with the pain as perspiration dripped from his face as he whipped his own belt off and started to tie it on his leg, he had been involved with enough knee caping's to know how to stem the blood loss.

Sean watched him carefully ignoring his statement as he grabbed Docherty's trilby hat and placed it side on resting the silencer of his gun on its bridge.

"When you sent us boys over to see that mad fucker in Africa, you know they showed us all sort of shit. They play no rules hard ball, not like here they even use live ammunition, fick a few times they made me wonder if you hadn't already sent the kid and me off for the "Long Walk".

Docherty realised Sean had obviously listened to his earlier conversation with Gormally, there was no point pretending.

"They even had us practice on live fella's, showed us how to make a man such as yourself wish he had been shot in the head." Sean gave a glib smile, then with a snatch of his gun set another slug into Docherty's arm pinning it back against the armrest of the chair, his armed felt like it had been pierced with a red hot poker and he dropped his belt, "Fuck Sean, Fuck, there no need for this. What do you want boyo?" He gasped, now his eyes began to water.

Sean held up the black book, "The name and the account number, is that all you need to get the money from in here in and out?" he said, standing up he placed Docherty's gun back on the dining table.

"Yes that's it just the account number and the words, your fucking crazy if you think you'll get away with this, you should it's not the man in front of you it's the hundreds behind that will come, you should know that laddie they'll hunt you to the end of time for this one." In repeating himself Sean knew Docherty was going into shock as his lips now began to grey with blood loss.

Sean held up his gun threatening to shoot again and even in his pain Docherty knew what he wanted. "November the 5th and April 24th, what you think you and the kid are off on the jollies, yer dreaming." The significance of the dates were the gunpowder plot and Éirí Amach na Cásca *(The Easter uprising)*."

Sean flicked through the pages and saw a telephone number under the name Mr Dave Cathill scribbled on the day of November the 5th and on 24th April he saw the words two-horse race on the opposite side and there were what appeared to be the names of four horses running at Tipperary and the words,

Recommended by Mr Patrick O'Connor, from Rathmore, a name every Irishman knew.

Sean closed the book and placed it in his top pocket as Docherty's breathing slowed.

"You know it was nothing personal, we all knew yer Da was trained by the Brits, that wasn't the problem, enough of our lads have taken the Queen's shilling to learn the trade, know your enemy to kill him, you know that, but the word came down, some weren't convinced he wasn't still undercover, nothing personal, you know how it is, my son." Docherty leaned back as Sean drifted thru to the front door and slipped the latch off, peaking along the outside corridor balcony.

Behind him Docherty looked at his gun on the table, he went to lift himself then slumped back in the chair and knew he was done, too weak to muster even the strength to raise his arm and grab a drink from the bottle in front of him.

Sean looked at his image in the hall mirror and slipped on a coat with a fur collar he had once seen Docherty once wearing in a Falls Road parade, he laughed seeing his arms were longer than Docherty's.

Turning off the light in the hall he opened the door and stepped into the half-light of the balcony walkway of the building, still wearing Docherty's hat.

On the next landing stairs John Gormally stood watching the other two sentry's moving into position to greet Connor as he drove the orange Bedford van into the flats car park.

Sean tried to make himself appear a wider man, somewhat like the shape of Docherty and sagged his knees, dropping his height then whistled at Gormally from the shadows and beckoned to him to come back to the flat.

"Well, I tell you what chicken man that's no TV detector van," Gormally whispered to himself as he took to the stair two treads at a time heading back to the flat.

As Gormally stepped into the doorway he could see through to the back room and heard the television on and hit the light switch, immediately Sean appeared in the kitchen doorway with his gun pointed at his chest.

"All right Jon, Jon," Sean winked, "No! We'll be having none of that." he shook his head and cocked his gun as Gormally appeared to make a move to the gun holster beneath his jacket.

"I'm not after you boyo, do as we were shown in Africa and it'll be fine." Sean pointed to the ground, Gormally looked through again to the rear room and now saw the side of Docherty's foot.

"What's this all about Seany, we heard you took out two Brits." Gormally said, as he knelt down slowly with his arms forward and then placed his hand under his knees. "Leave it out Jon, Jon, the old man's dead, Unc's dead, carry on like that, treating me like some ficking eejit if you wanna make it a hat-trick, I've got bullets to spare and place to be." Sean stepped forward and placed the muzzle of his gun on the top of Gormally's head, while he felt inside his jacket and removed his sidearm with his other hand.

"Yes I killed to Brits, Mi6, smart fella's, now dead smart fella's. Listen on now Jon, Jon, I have no beef with you or the boys down there, me and the kid are just settling old scores and will be on our way, no fuss, no bother. The couple of Bizzies, were sitting in a Divvy van, can you believe it? Set up shop outside Uncles, pad they were, bold as brass. You'll trust me on this now, they had been listening to everything from the sounds, they won't like that back home. So play your cards right, it's could be your feather in your cap for the Father's, take the credit, and we'll be on our way. Fuck Jon, Jon they may even make you the new Capo for the Kilburn brigade." Sean stepped back and gestured that Gormally get back to his feet and then to Gormally's surprise Sean turned his back on him and signalled with his gun that he follow him inside to the lounge. Gormally looked to the outside and for a moment considered making a run for it, but he had seen Sean shoot in the North African camp, he judged he'd make it to the top of the stair and then there was always his brother Connor to consider, God knows what these boys had been brewing up.

"No bullshit, so how are you play 'in this thing of yours." Gormally looked at Docherty's corpse and scratched his chin, as Sean grabbed the duffel bag.

"Do I know the fella's outside?" Sean asked.

Gormally looked back to the hall and shook his head, "No, I don't think so Sean, they came across from Westport, I only met them me self when I got the call from the chicken man" Gormally looked back to Docherty.

"Well that's something now, get those boys of yours to bring those two Brits up here, we can do the intro and Connors got something that will take care of all this." Sean nodded to the door "Go on, I'll be here."
Gormally looked to the bottle of scotch and Sean gestured he could help himself and he took a drink straight from the bottle of whisky and looked at Sean trying to work out what he had planned, and if it was worth jumping Connor,
"Jon, Jon, don't make me regret letting you go now, I love my brother, but I'll walk this night if you make a play and then you'll never sleep tight again, nor will any of your kin." Sean's threatening words were still fresh in Gormally's ears as he went down to the Van.
"Alright Jon, Jon how yer do'in" Connor said opening the back, while one of Docherty's guards kept watch.
"Just fine, I hear you and your bro had some trouble tonight." Jon, Jon looked at his armed colleagues, but thought better of making a play to take down Connor.
"Nothin, we couldn't handle, you know Sean, slippery as ficking page three girls bar of soap and twice as lucky." Sean watched Gormally for the slightest sign that he was going to betray Sean's plan, as they carried the first body up to the flat
"Where's Doc?" One of the sentries asked seeing the lounge door shut as Gormally lowered his end of the rolled up carpet parcel on to the hall floor,.
"Never mind that, he was taking a nap, just get the other one in here before the milkman comes knocking, we have to be out of here early for the ferry in the morning." Gormally barked.
Gormally watched as Connor went to the back of the van and through a potato sack over his back before he followed behind the two carrying other bundled corpse of the other Mi6 Officer.
Having dumped the body on the floor, they walked into the lounge where Sean stood with his back against the balcony window, before either man could raise their hands to their own weapons in defence he had dropped the pair, leaving Gormally standing in the hallway, Gormally saw the handle of the revolver of one of his colleagues poking out from the rear of his waistband and flinched back choosing not to grab for it as Sean shook his head and he heard Connor step through the entrance behind him.
"I told you, Jon, Jon, my beef is not with you, but they were just too loose ends, now it's just yews and us," Sean said, as Connor barged past Gormally and removed the homemade bomb from the potato sack and placed it on the dining table along with a the surveillance tape real he had taken from the Bedford van recording their conversations.
"Don't just sit there set them two in the chairs before they go stiff, when this thing goes off there'll be nought, left of them," Sean said and lit a cigarette and offered Gormally one.
"Take this down and wait for me in the van kid." Sean told Connor and caught a look of concern towards Gormally from his brother, "I'll be fine Jon, Jon's about to make himself a popular man back home, aren't you Jon, Jon" Connor's eyes

widened as Sean opened one of the duffle bags and removed three bound wads of notes and then handed the bags to his brother.

With Connor gone, Sean took a bread knife from the kitchen and first cut the elastic bands from the money and began throwing it around the flat and the cut the rope on rolls of carpet rug that covered the two Mi6 Officers.

"As I see it, the chicken man here decided he didn't wanna be outdone by a couple of "Gunslingers" decided to make himself a name back home." Sean began to set the fuse into the dynamite, as Gormally looked on.

"Bring one of them bastards in here." Sean gestured to the hall.

"Best you get what you need and take these," Sean said, handing him the two Mi6 warrant cards. "You'll need it as proof you did them in. If the old man was soft enough to lead the Brits to your door, then he wasn't worth shit, ten will get you twenty the old fathers feel the same in Belfast."

Gormally opened both and read the details of the officers, then watched as Sean leaned over and passed him back his own revolver, he held it for a second and then holstered it and grabbed his passport and wallet from the bedside table. "If I take much more they'll be asking why, and you boys what do I say of you."

"Nothin, give this tape to the old boys," he said handing him the surveillance tape, "tell them Doc told you Unc had got rid of us, before these two saw him out." Sean said pointing to the bodies in the hallway. "As far as your concerned, you found that tape in the van, we'll be leaving that in the car park, say shit went to shovel why you were having a drop of the black stuff, came back found the tape don't make it complicated, everyone knows the chicken man wanted to be a rooster back home, trust me they'll be a few glad he's gone, I'll give you a head start to get down the Archway, rattle the tins for the boys back home, show yer face before this goes up, just make sure you get back here before the real Bizzies turn up and find their van." Sean winked, and Gormally looked at the small camping gas canister on the table and the room, there was scratching in the kitchen, "What about the bird?" Gormally looked to the Kitchen and caught a look off Sean.

"Take the fucker, have it for yer supper, what happened to the hard man I knew in Africa." Sean sounded bemused and watched as Gormally walk into the kitchen. Gormally opened the cage door and looked at the Irish hen and saw a single egg lying in the cage nest, sticking his hand inside he removed the egg leaving the bird and its cage door open and shrugged.

"Never above yer." Gormally said, brandishing the egg to Sean as he emerged and then took flight down the hallway almost tripping over the other Mi6 Officer's corpse. With the timer running as Sean went to follow him out the door, he saw the chicken standing in the Kitchen doorway, it tilted its head and Sean sniggered.

Gormally acknowledged Connor as he left the car park and as he drove past the front of the buildings roadside gardens he caught sight of the clipped hen being thrown from the balcony. "Fickin hard man my arse." Gormally said, and then before he had got to the end of the street with the flats still visible in the rear-view mirror of his Cortina there was an almighty explosion, his rear view window shattered and a fireball erupted from the balcony the bird had just been tossed from.

"McLoughlin! You fickin eejit." Gormally swore and throwing the raw egg out the window throttled back, heading towards Holloway road, as the lights in the nearby houses and flats of the neighbourhood sprung to life with the inquisitive and frightened.

Chapter 9: The Pennel Rig Spinner

Geneva, Switzerland
November 1972

The receptionist Francesca announced two gentlemen named Byrne had presented themselves at the front desk as associates of Mr. Patrick Collins from Rathmore. The name Sean and Connor were travelling under and this phrase, which Sean got from Docherty's black notebook, identified the McLoughlin brothers as having a connection with the Irish statesmen accounts. Hanging up the receiver, Salter-Kingsley thought for a moment remembering what accounts they held and the significance of who the individuals might be as he stared up the boardroom table at his executives.
"Would you like me to take that SK.?" Plácido Zabala began to tidy his papers and place them in a folder.
"No, I want to talk further on where we are with the Argentinean's and the transfer to the French, Merryman, you go see to it, and Charles come see me when the gentlemen have left, have Miss Bishop place them in room one, would you please," Salter-Kingsley ordered, and Merryman felt elated hearing his boss use his first name in front of the other executives especially Zabala.
Charles Merryman then instructed Miss Bishop to place them in conference room one and to notify Salter-Kingsley.
Then Merryman went into the corridor outside his office and from the vantage point of the glass-walled third floor balcony, twisted the cable on the Louvre blind and looked down at the two dark-suited stocky young men sitting on the designer cream leather chairs in reception, seeing Sean's eyes drift up in his direction he closed the blind.
"Excuse me for a moment, people, talk amongst yourselves, fix yourselves a coffee." Salter-Kingsley got up from the head of the boardroom table and used his direct door through to his private office suite from the boardroom.
At his desk, he opened the surveillance control draw in his desk drawer, flipping the switch the timber panelling behind his chair slid to one side, revealing the four black and white screens. Turning dial number one on the control panel, the display began to glow. As slowly the image of the small conference room came into vision, he watched Sean and Connor enter, and he pressed the record button on the videotape recorder.
Connor sat down first, while Sean paced around clearly checking the ceiling and walls for signs of surveillance equipment, he disappeared into the bathroom, and

Salter-Kingsley flipped the toggle switch to camera B, and the screen image shifted to Sean in the toilet again appearing to check the room.
"Nothin' to worry about here, if you can't trust a Swiss banker who can you trust?" Sean answered to Connors mutter of "What's up?"
Then winked gesturing up, having seen the dark lens of what he had decided was a camera planted behind the air conditioning vent grill in the wall panel.
"Good Morning, I am Charles Merryman, how are you today, gentleman?" As Merryman fell back on his well-rehearsed professional patter, Salter-Kingsley, leaving the tape recording running, closed the false partition and returned to the boardroom.
"I understand you have come to us from the Emerald Isle, you have the account number for access today?" He asked, and Sean wrote the numbers he'd received from Danny Docherty before he'd killed him, on a corner of a fresh note pad on the desk, tore it free and handed the triangle to Merryman.
"Good, I just need one last piece of information to verify your status, and if you have an associated existing account number held within the bank? I may also furnish you with that account details and allow access for any exchange transactions you may wish to organise today." Merryman held his confident business persona, while all the time considering it was likely he was in the presence of two trained terrorists. However the meeting went surprisingly smoothly Merryman thought, noticing Sean did all the talking, while Connor stared at him occasionally blinking, in an unnerving way.
An hour later Merryman joined Salter-Kingsley's outside his office door, behind the Louvre blinds of the glass landing gallery as they watched Miss Bishop escort the Byrne brothers to the reception to leave, both bankers noticed the way Connor appeared to measure himself up against the bank front door security guard Claude Dennee just before they left the building.
"Can I help you, Sir?" Claude asked Connor
"No, just admiring the cut of your suit, that's fin suit, how much would a suit like that cost?" Connor asked as Sean raised his eyes
"I wouldn't know Sir, the bank supplies our uniform, from a tailor here in Geneva, I can get the address if you wish," Claude said with a look to the reception.
"Don't mind him, he's not used to the mountain air." Sean said with a smile, "Away with your Connor leave the poor man be." He ordered his brother, and they left the building.
"So they withdrew two thousand Swiss Francs that's it, no mention of the associated accounts?" Salter-Kingsley flicked through the account book and noticed the inception date was two years earlier and funds having been transferred from an

existing American Statesmen account, not the Irish Statesmen account as he had thought, with the withdrawal Sean and Connor had made there was $150,000 balance left in the account.

"Not the social types were they." Salter-Kingsley remarked, "I take it you've not seen them before a long way to come for what you spend on a good night out, with our Japanese clients?"

Merryman felt his face flush but breezed over the comment about a previous expense chit he had submitted when entertaining clients from Tokyo in a Karaoke bar, which he had been, pulled up on sixth months earlier.

"No, and there was no chit chat, the older one did the talking, I'd say they are ex-military, no mention of any parental account, probably bag men, you had no prior knowledge of their visit to the bank, Sir?" Merryman said, scratching his initials on the withdrawal note on the file.

"No… which is unorthodox, but it's not the first time, never mind." Salter-Kingsley mused as they went through to Merryman's office.

"The account details were correct, do you see a problem? Do you intend to contact the senior statesmen account holders in Ireland." Merryman asked then thanked his secretary for serving them coffee as he watched Salter-Kingsley settling behind his desk and began to go through a batch of account folders Merryman had been studying before the board meeting had been called and the Byrne brothers arrived.

"No, these people are not the kind you call, as you say they had the right to access the account, if there is some confusion on this matter we are covered, but let me know if they revisit the bank, take a look at the other related Irish account holdings and give me brief summary, by the end of the day, if you would Merryman, please" as Merryman acknowledged his bosses request his telephone rang from the reception, still seated behind in his employees desk, Salter-Kingsley gestured he should answer it, as it was Merryman's phone.

"Yes, Francesca?" Merryman said, as he watched Salter-Kingsley leave his office then hover outside his door and a curious expression grow on his superiors face as he peered down to the reception.

"Well I didn't expect them back so soon, what do you think that's about." Salter-Kingsley looked down at the image of Sean McLoughlin alone in the reception with the two tartan duffel bag in his hands.

"Have Miss Bishop put him in room one again." Merryman told the receptionist, "Odd, you want to sit in on this, Sir?" Merryman looked to his boss, as he grabbed Sean's account file, then his telephone rang again.

"The gentleman from Ireland has requested he be shown to a different conference room than the one from his last visit." Francesca conveyed Sean's instructions as she smiled at him.

"He wants a different room?" Merryman relayed the message to Salter-Kingsley.

"I think I'll take it, Charles, have Florence show him to my private office, whenever I meet one of their kind, it surprises me. The English joke that they are dim-witted, personally I have found its best not to underestimate them." Salter-Kingsley took the account ledger from Merryman's grasp, "Could just be the joke is on the English." he said, "Come on, you can sit in."

Merryman slipped in behind his boss and settled in a seat at the rear of the office, he noticed Sean tilt his head back, checking his position, as Salter-Kingsley sat behind his desk.

"That your grandpa's, refreshing?" Sean nodded towards the Nazi membership certificate hanging on the wall, lost in other financial awards, he could not read the words, but he recognized the symbols.

Salter-Kingsley looked at the certificate, "Refreshing?" he repeated it was a word that had never come to mind.

"Yer most people hide their skeletons in a closet." Sean winked.

"Mr. Byrne, I am Peter Salter-Kingsley this is….my bank. I understand you visited with us this morning, my colleague Mr. Merryman dealt with your request. I hope, to your satisfaction." he smiled politely and looked at the bags either side of Sean's seat.

"The owner, excellent! Saves time going to the source." Sean said, unzipping the first bag and removed all the cash and placed it on the desk and then did the same with the other bag, Salter-Kingsley looked to the back of the room at Merryman.

"I see, you wish to make a deposit, Mr. Merryman can assist you with that." Salter-Kingsley held back what he was thinking having estimated that the total in used mixed notes that now lay sprawled over his desk was probably no more than two hundred thousand pounds, not of an adequate size that he would normally be involved with unless the client was one of his own special clients.

"There has been a change of plan, I would appreciate you depositing this back into a new account in my name. The Swiss franc's I withdrew today I need for expenses. You see my brother, and I have decided to stop a while in your lovely city."

Sean heard Merryman's Spanish made Carmina shoes squeak on the oak floor, as he poked his head to the side to see the stack of Great British pounds placed on the desk as Salter-Kingsley sat back in his leather chair looking pensive then raised his eyes to his grandfather's certificate.

"In answer to your question, yes, my grandfather lived in a different time, he believed in a cause. Not I think, unlike something in your own way, you may be aware of today, in your own country." he watched as Sean smiled and gestured his understanding.
"So as I understand you wish to open your own separate account with these funds with no future connection to the associated accounts. Perhaps first I might share some of the banking policy we here at the FNIG strictly adhere to, information my colleague may not have conveyed that may allay any unnecessary concerns that you possibly are harbouring, cut to the chase as they say," Sean gestured his agreement allowing the banker to continue.
"All accounts held within the bank operate as separate entities, even when they have been conceived by an existing parental account. The bank is obliged to be aware of the activity of all its accounts to service the individual account holder's needs, but it is strictly against our practice and against the international financial conduct agreement here in Switzerland for the bank to enlighten any individual or organization, including governments of the activities of the accounts held within these walls, that have not fulfilled the required access information." Salter-Kingsley's smile widened "Simply put and with no disrespect intended, we are much like a Catholic priest in a confessional."
Sean shook his head in agreement and turned back, catching a smile off Merryman. "Well, that's just fine to know Mr. Salter-Kingsley, is it?"
Sean then removed from the bag to his right a Browning revolver, and Salter-Kingsley eyes widened, as he watched Sean place the gun with a wink on the top of the pile of banknotes, again he heard Merryman's shoes squeak, shuffling back in his seat. "Alright, Mr. Merryman," he said calmly as Salter-Kingsley hand hovered at the end of his chair arm, less than six inches from the hidden alarm panic button hidden under his desk. Sean conceived such as device may be in place and shook his head once.
"No, don't you worry, calm your selves fella's, I'm not here to play up," Sean said, wagging his finger gesturing to Salter-Kingsley and the banker slowly inched his hand back.
"No, this with respect, this is a sign of good faith, you see, my brother and I sat for a while across the street in that lovely little café in the park Schmooze is it?"
"Schmutz, I know the café Mr. Byrne" Salter-Kingsley corrected him on the name. Merryman interjected, from behind "They use Lavazza coffee, Italiano, its good." he added, and Salter-Kingsley gave Merryman an indignant but nervous look for interrupting.

"Schmutz yes that's the one? Yes well, they did make good coffee Mr. Merryman anyways here's the thing, I was watching for a while how you have clients, many like myself... to be honest, and we should start honest, we've been watching your bank for a few days now, call it market research." Sean could see in sitting back Salter-Kingsley was beginning to relax, fear had turned to intrigue.

"As an interested party with some security experience. I noticed how some come with bags full and leave with bags empty and vice-versa. As I watched these gentlemen your clients, some of them, again with no disrespect for their athletic abilities, let's just say there's a bonny boy back home, eight years old, got caught in the troubles lost his foot, poor lad, but I'd wager he could outrun some of your people." Sean looked at the gun but saw no flash of understanding from the Swiss banker.

"I'll cut to the chase, I'm not after robbing them, your clients that is, watching them it occurred to me of all the services you offer from your establishment, I wondered if discreet but effective security is required, to and from, say the airport or while "Special" account holders are visiting like ourselves. Call it, for me and the kid, that's my brother Connor by the way, call it a bus man's holiday if you will, in the meantime you have our money at your bank as security." Sean picked up the gun and placed it back in the duffel bag.

"This was just my CV as it were, show we are the serious type." Sean sat back and strummed his fingers on the chair, armrest, "that's it, in a nutshell."

"I see a business proposition, well I assure you my colleague, and I never consider it would be anything but a legitimate enquiry" Salter-Kingsley, felt himself swallow deeply.

"As for your offer, I will have to think about it, but it has possibilities, the bank is all about providing service and for your information, you are quite correct, we have on occasion provided security escorts of formal discipline, including the use of the city police. But as you say, there are those that wish to conduct business in a low profile manner, with less documentation, etcetera. I cannot see why we should not add your contact details to our registered security contractor's information, we do after all hold, including funds on your behalf." Salter-Kingsley, felt the unorthodox job interview, was a story he would dine out on with his closest friends for the months to come, but of course, would mention no names, he had no doubt Sean was as he put it "the serious type."

Sean leaned forward, "For your special clients, so to speak, though I would only want to speak if this proposition is accepted, with your good self or Mr. Merryman on such occasions."

"I would assume you and your brother would not object to the bank receiving a finder's fee for arranging these assignments." Merryman interjected from the rear, and Sean leaned back in his chair and spoke without turning back "Naturally, in cash, of course, I am sure you boys have enough paperwork to deal with here." "Naturally," Salter-Kingsley replied.

"Good, so we have an understanding, and I can expect a call, no hurry as you like, as I said the kid and I are going to spend a little time exploring your wonderful city, get to know what's what, who is who, so to speak. We intend to purchase a small vessel for the lake. It's in our blood the water, our people, I'll drop the details to Mr. Merryman when we have secured a berth, along with a contact number. In the meantime, as I said if you could do the honours pop this back in your safe and give me a new account number, I'd be obliged" Sean stood and held his hand across the table, and Salter-Kingsley shook it and then walked out of his office.

"Use my desk to Charles to assist Mr. Byrne's request, I have a previous engagement a luncheon, I must attend, I will say good day Mr. Byrne, I hope you enjoy your stay in Geneva," he said, and as he left Merryman could hardly contain his feelings as he moved forward to sit behind his boss's desk.

"Look at you now, tis himself, the big man, who'd know you're not the boss, Charlie boy," Sean smirked and gave him a cheeky wink as Merryman settled into the leather chair.

"Has he gone," Salter-Kingsley, had no luncheon appointment and had been hiding in his own private bathroom having a cigarette, waiting for the Irishman to leave, guns on his desk had tested his IBS *(irritable bowel syndrome)* to its limits.

"Yes he has gone, interesting chap, seems to have it all worked out, do you think they can be trusted." Merryman was filling in the details of the cash deposit in the new registry account book he had issued to Sean, along with a key to the Metropolitan hotel day safes, Salter-Kingsley gestured him to get out of his chair.

"Well it's as I said, they're an interesting breed, but if they were to become troublesome, I am sure our German Statesmen account holder connections can remove the problem. For now, offer their service to anyone up to your midterm accounts nothing above five million and Charles no Irish clients or those associated with the senior Irish statesmen, keep them completely separate as far as the bank is concerned the Byrne brothers are nomads, my wife would never forgive me if they bombed Globus in trying to clean house." Salter-Kingsley slipped his initials under Merryman's in the account book and closed it.

"But Merryman, while you are at it, just double-check the note count before you place it in the vault."

Over the coming weeks, Sean and Connor purchased "The Helena" a 1960's twin-berth timber cruiser and rented a mooring on the East bank of Lake Geneva in the small timber harbour of La Bellotte with access to the landline in the nearby family-run guest house, the White Swan, where they often drank and dined.

So began a business relationship of sorts between the McLoughlin, nee Byrne's brothers and the FNIG bank. They were called upon to safeguard and chaperone visiting clients during their stay in Geneva and on many occasions to escort the client to their final destination, often acting as a long haul taxi service, in a smart new silver BMW series 3 Sean purchased. In which they included modifications they had devised from their days smuggling guns in Ireland, including fitting a smuggling hold for the client's money and gold, hidden behind the fuel tank and accessed with the removal of the rear bench seat.

Their service fees were assessed by the bank, through Merryman, were negotiable according to the client and the value of the commodities they may be depositing or withdrawing from the bank, this was paid via transfer straight into their new bank account immediately an assignment had been completed. While the under the table commission to Salter-Kingsley was paid on the first Tuesday of each month and consisted of a deduction of 25% paid in cash.

Merryman alone handled the assignment details and acted as bagman meeting Sean or Connor, but never the two together the handover was always the same, on board one of the yellow taxi's steamboats that drifted back and forth across the lake and each time the brown envelope was passed to Merryman within the folds of a newspaper, the exchange was caught in the crosshairs of a sniper rifle held in the hands of whichever brother was not present at the handover, laying beneath sails laid on the deck of the Helena. Sometimes Salter-Kingsley's personal commission was as much as $10,000. It took some time for the brothers to realise the bank had no intention of contacting the IRA and informing them that two of their members had taken up residence in Switzerland.

The assignments were low key assignments, in comparison to their time in London and initially it took them a few runs to get to grips with not dropping their clients to the floor each time a car backfired, or not considering taking out an approaching traffic warden about to write a ticket, while waiting for clients at the airport.

For the most part, the clients were foreign businessmen, tax evaders, English politicians; Salter-Kingsley had given Merryman initial instructions, nothing above $5 million. However, the clients they were introduced to sometimes requested they travelled further afield. In particular the African clients they dealt with appreciated their level of paramilitary skill when escorting them home, it did mean both boys having to take their vaccination jabs and keep up on their Lariam malaria tablets,

Connor in particular initially suffered from the side effects of depression, following a heavy drinking bout, but eventually his system appeared to settle.

Within a month of their new employment, Sean began to get the sense that Owen Merryman had additional interests outside of banking. He was first alerted by the change in his attire, it was nothing initially an extravagant designer shirt, then a few weeks later he noticed a new Submariner Rolex watch on his wrist and he soon began to be concerned that the senior management agreement the boys had undertaken with Salter-Kingsley was not being honoured, by the middleman Merryman. Finally, it was a chance encounter that confirmed his suspicions. He had just made an envelope exchange, and the boat taxi was turning into the pier when a young Japanese girl, 22-25 not someone he would expect a Swiss banker to be associated with and whose presence clearly unnerved Merryman when she bounded over from the other side of the boat taxi, gushing over him,

"Merry-Merry!" she said as if they were more than just friends and forced him to introduce Sean. He appeared even more upset when the girl pressed a black night club card "The Senkin gentleman's club" into Sean's hand expressing the desire that Merryman should bring him along, introduce him to her "Posse" Merryman, was standoffish almost dismissive.

But Sean thanked her, "It's a date," Sean said, placing the card in his wallet, her large Japanese minder who had been watching the exchange gave Sean a predatory and challenging glare, Sean blew him a kiss as dutifully she returned to his side when he grunted.

"She is no one, a girl from a club, we have taken some clients to, in the past, very loud, very hot." Merryman smiled uneasily as Sean watched the girl get into a black Mercedes with another waiting Japanese man waiting on the dockside. Sean parted company with Merryman and headed towards the pickup point with Connor as he walked along the bank he twisted the nightclub card through his fingers his curiosity raised.

Two weeks later Sean was walking through the city having already had a coffee at Café La Clémence he skipped off and on the tram and headed towards the morning market, the fruit stalls reminded Sean of the Tipperary food fare that he and Connor would steal oranges from when they were kids, but it was never displayed with such artistic talent or with such a range of products as the market stalls off the Rue Due Rhone. He picked an apple and saw the elderly greengrocer was engaged with another customer and was about to turn away, it would have been so easy to steal it, but he chose to turn back and handed the grocer a two Swiss Franc coin, adding he could, "Garde Le", *(Keep the change).*

"I saw that you could have walked." The eastern accent in English cut through the busy side street, and he turned, immediately recognising the Japanese girl from the water taxi that had handed him the nightclub card, he tried to remember her name as he smiled and finished chewing the bite he had taken, and then remembered Merryman had failed to introduce her.

"Well they say you always pay in the end, I figure the almighty already has plenty on me." He offered her a bite, jokingly and was surprised when she took it holding his hand close to her mouth as she cut into the fruit with her pristine white teeth. Sean looked intensely at her face, she was younger than he remembered and wearing little make-up, to him she appeared far more appealing, less brassy, even her clothes were a simple design, a single red dress with a long, tempting zip from the pleat to her low neckline, she stood around five two, but Sean set her black thigh boot as having a three-inch heels.

"I'm sorry I don't remember" he began to apologise.

"Suzy Bell" she offered her name

"My father was American, I'm Vietnamese, named after the helicopter he flew," she said recognising the surprise at her surname.

"Sean" he found himself pointing to his chest like he would if someone could not speak English and felt stupid.

"Look I'm just off for a coffee, do you fancy joining me?" he asked and looking at her shopping bags he looked around to see if her minder was with her then offered his hand.

"No he's not with me at the moment, no doubt he will find me when he wants, I must be back soon, but that would be fun yes, I know somewhere close," she said handing him one of her bags.

They walked down to the Globus food hall and sat on the front window bench facing out to the street, she waited, checking for her chaperone, while he got them each a coffee and croissant.

Sean displayed his skill of deflecting questions aimed in his direction by asking about her. With the girls he had talked with in the past he had found they appreciated the interest, but although he felt an attraction to Suzy, at the back of his mind her relationship with Merryman kept taunting him. Sean considered she must work as some sort of high-class escort, she spoke at least four languages during their conversation, not the norm for the girls of the night he had met on Argyle square, in Kings Cross, London.

Although under normal circumstances, it did not bother him if she was a prostitute if it was just going to be sex. However, on this occasion, he hoped she was not for a change.

"So how long have you lived in Geneva, your English is good, sorry I forgot you said your dad was a Yank, I mean American?" Sean started gently, but soon found the question of how she knew Merryman became less important, as they chatted and joked, comfortable in each other's company while making light fun of some of the other patrons in the café and passers-by in the street outside. Sean could not remember the last time he relaxed with a beautiful woman during the day, while Suzy could not remember the last time a man looked at her and talked with interest that did not involve trying to remove her clothes and stinking of alcohol. Even though she had a problem saying the words to herself, she knew she wanted this Irishman, and again that was something she had not felt for some time about a man.

As the couple continue to flirt with each other, there was suddenly an impatient rattle on the opposite side the window glass, which brought their conversation abruptly to a halt, standing outside, eyes shaded by dark glasses, her bodyguard gestured for her to come with him and turned back to the curb where a black Mercedes had pulled up,

"I have to go, it was nice to have seen you again, thank you." Suzy tapped his hand as he began to rise from his seat to help her with her bags.

"For what? I had just as much fun as you," he said, standing.

"For not asking about your friend Merry-Merry, I am sure you wanted too." She smiled as he held the door open for her, he had gathered she was bright from their conversation, but now he knew she was smart.

"If the offer is still open, maybe I will call into your club one night," he said, unsure if she would wish him to see her at work.

"The Senkin, of course, I will make sure you have a good table." her voice said one thing, but her eyes held a sadness that Sean took to mean something else and he nodded.

"Well, I hope we meet again." He said and watched her disappear inside the car, receiving the same challenging glare from her guard as he took his sunglasses off. Sean watched as he slid into the front passenger seat and before the door was closed, he was across the street and thrust a fifty Franc note in the ear of the driver "Stay with that black Mercedes without being seen and there's another one of these for you." Sean pointed over the front seat.

The driver followed a discrete distance behind amongst traffic that contained enough other taxis for camouflage, as they left the city they drove northeast following the lake road along the Route Suisse heading towards Lausanne.

"Hang back." he tapped the driver on the shoulder, seeing the road opened up with fewer cars and clear sight of her vehicle. Sean noticed how the sizes of the

residential house changed in grandeur as they passed field after field of vineyards and well-kept medieval stone walls. With little warning, ahead of three cars, the Mercedes turned off right down a hedged and tree-lined private gravel road toward the lake near Saint-Prex.
"Keep going!" Sean ordered and then gestured for the driver to pull over thirty meters or so past the tall pink and white stoned châteaux that was nestled just visible behind a dense tree line at the lakeside.
"Wait here." Sean took two-fifty Franc notes from his wallet and tearing them in two, handed half of both notes to the driver.
"You'll get the rest when I'm back two minutes tops." Sean then darted from the car and dropped down from the road, disappearing into the private wood, he could see the Mercedes still winding its way along the main drive to the front of the châteaux. Sean hid beside a beech tree and watched the double doors of the house open before the car had come to rest a suited oriental servant stood on the stepped balcony of the entrance checking his field of vision as his master, clearly a westerner, wearing sunglasses a garish Hawaiian shirt, flannel pants and flip-flops came dancing down the stairs.
Sean tucked himself low, Suzy's chief bodyguard was the first to exit the car, he scanned the perimeter once, before opening her door then stood to the side as she stepped out, as the driver removed her bags.
Sean felt hollowness as he watched the warmth of their greeting and the old man threw his arms around her to lead her inside, although not close enough to hear exactly what was said, from the tones Sean heard the man barked his order to his servants in their common tongue, which became drowned by the barking of a small Sheltie dog that dashed down the stairs to greet their visitor.
Suzy obviously was well known to the animal as it pawed at her and rolled on its back for her to stoop down and rub it before they continued on their way up to go back inside the building.
Sean had seen enough, and he felt a strange disappointment about to withdraw, his eyes caught the stationary image of the dog looking directly in his direction; Suzy's bodyguard noticed the Shelties curiosity and turned his head.
"Shit" Sean froze as the dog let out a single bark, and the bodyguard turned his body to see what the dog had sensed as did the guard on the balcony platform set before the main entrance door, both appeared to be scanning the wood in the direction the dog's attention had been drawn.
"Come Binki!" Suzy called, and the dog gave a sniff and dashed to be at her feet as the couple climbed the stairs.

The bodyguard stood his ground his eyes delving into every shadow of the wood. Fortunately, the sun was behind Sean, the guard looked to his colleague on the balcony and received a shake of his head gesturing he saw nothing.

Sean held his breath as the man now arm in arm with Suzy turned back and called the bodyguard to bring her shopping bags inside. For a brief moment, Sean thought the master of the house also turned in his direction before ushering the Suzy inside. The bodyguard turned to go, and Sean stealthily stepped backwards six steps before turning and retracing his path back to the taxi.

He was within breaking cover of the road when the impatience of the driver got the better of him, he honked his horn. Still, on the stairs, the Japanese bodyguard heard the sound and twisted back to the trees now from his vantage point of the balcony he could see the distant yellow shadow of the parked taxi and grunted his dissatisfaction at the door guard at his side for missing it, as he watched it pull away and "U" turns back towards Geneva. The driver looked at Sean as he sat slumped in the back and feeling his eyes on him, Sean handed over the other half of the Franc notes.

"Do you know this club?" His surly tone received a quick response, and the driver told him it was a night club run by Japanese he even went as far to insinuate that it was a Yakuza club after he had praised it as being one of the more exclusive and expensive clubs,

"Nice girls, real models, I drove Mick Jagger their once, and that mad Englishman Richard Harris, very expensive, many famous go there, you need a suit, tie, but it still does not mean you get in." The driver could see his passenger was improperly dressed for such a place.

"Irishman!" Sean said, correcting the driver who looked confused at him through the reflection in his rear-view mirror.

"Harris is Irish," Sean said, reading the red and white thank you for not smoking sign on the back of the driver seat.

"He's a Limerick boy." Sean sighed, looking to the hills of the lake and remembering the green of his home and lit a cigarette, but the driver made no objection and opened his window slightly.

"Are you Irish, a Limerick?" The driver smiled but saw no change in Sean's mood "Mitchelstown, not far." Sean brooded, volunteering something he would usually have kept to himself.

"So where to now boss." The taxi driver asked as Sean scanned the lake looking to the far side where he knew somewhere their boat the Helena was moored and where Connor would be waiting.

"Take me to a bar, somewhere the mad Irishman would go." Sean snarled and snapped his fingers to get back the Senkin card, he looked at it and went to toss it from the window, deciding it was likely Suzy was a prostitute and the man he had seen her with was a client, then at the last moment stopped and placed it in his wallet.

"Well, well, maybe you have some of our Da's bad blood in you." Sean slurred at his brother, referring to him being a British agent. By now it was six in the afternoon, from the empty pint glasses in front of him, Connor could see his brother was on a bit of a session, and he judged his first words to gauge his mood, it had taken him six pubs and three Cafes to locate his brother, but he wasn't going to let on.

"It wasn't hard, there's a ficking great shamrock and Guinness sign hanging out front." Connor whistled over to the bar, sticking two fingers up and pointing to the empty glasses on the table and received a nod from the barman who began to pour two pints.

"You're a good kid, Con." Sean slurred as the Guinness arrived and the bartender cleared some of the empties.

"Keep 'em coming, until one of us falls off the stall and then get a bucket of water." Connor laid 100 francs down on the table and gave ten to the bartender, who was well aware of the immense capacity Irishmen had for the "Black stuff." But judged, these boys were a "handful and cartwheel away from hell." A phrase the bartender had picked up from another Irish regular.

"Not a bad pint, Connor said draining the dregs from his glass." before the barman had set the glasses in his new dishwasher.

"You'll need to be quicker than that!" Sean joked loudly raising his glass towards the bar.

"What happened to keeping a low profile, not that I'm complaining an all, just wished I'd had a heads up we were on the craic, I'll bet you the night I catch your back before closing," he said having counted how many beers his brother had already sunk and handed him a cigarette as another two pints arrived.

Connor looked at his brother nursing half of the first one he had bought and wondered if he was already done on drinking and ready for something a little more livelily, like fighting.

"Are you gentlemen wanting any food our kitchen closes shortly?" Connor looked at the barman, a tall Swiss, German with what looked like naval tattoos a mild man with a wife, two under ten daughters and a husky dog, all of whom were in the flat above the pub. Connor smiled, considering his remark, the man was obviously becoming a little concerned with the amount Sean had been drinking. However,

Connor was unaware the barman had also noticed the gun-shaped bulge tucked in the back of his jeans under his short lumberjack jacket.

"Bless your heart, what a gentleman, some French fries, two portions, soak some of this up, thanks and another couple of pints, in yer own time, no hurry like" Connor ordered.

"So brother of mine, what are we drinking too?" Connor raised his glass and looked around the relatively empty cavern bar. His brother slumped back against the timber bench booth wall and tilted his head his eyes bleary and winced,

"When did we need a reason?" Sean emptied his glass, "We're McLoughlin's, gunslingers and girl heartbreakers."

"So that's it you found a bit of skirt, who is she?" Connor caught his words as Sean gave him a glare and realised the subject was off the table, at least until he was sober and changed the subject.

"These people here, French, German, Swiss and especially the Italians you ever notice how they seem to take their time, meals, drinks, enjoy it, back home if your plates empty in the café, you give the table up, like we are on the hop, like them two over there." Connor gestured to a couple "here's us in double figures, they've been nursing the same glass of wine since I got in here, in the old country you'd have marked them as Bizzies, probably even clipped them by now."

Sean looked over at the young couple, who were obviously just two young tourists and in seeing that they were holding hands, shrugged feeling a melancholy dissatisfaction with his own love life.

"Well, I enjoy my drink just fine, and we left the door-knockers *(Garde)* back in the old country." He raised the fresh pint then sat back again.

"Do you ever think we'll get back?" Connor looked again at the bar and all the various maps and flags including some from Ireland, it's flashy commercial advertising so different and continental to the bars of home.

"One day when they no longer have a need of fella's like us, maybe, when the Brits are out." Connor could see Sean's tone had turned maudlin, "Maybe I'll get me one of those old mansions at Waterford a stone away from the Tramore, so I can go racing and walk a dog on the beach on Sundays." Sean remembered a fleeting image of a sunny day out when he and his baby brother fought against the surf to make sandcastles, while his mother sat in a deck chair alongside a man he took to be his father, listening to a red plastic handheld radio playing Billy Fury singing Halfway to Paradise, Sean tapped his head against the back of his seat and the image was gone, without mentioning the memory he reached forward and swallowed a mouthful and looked at his brother and smiled.

"Well until then Seany boy, the banker sent word he wants a meet, there's a week-long gig if we want it's at the end of the month, Genoa and back, it's a rich prize he said!" Connor gestured his thanks as the waiter deposited the bowls of thin French fries and then sat a basket full of sachets of sauces at its side, which the boys began to demolish.

"I never understand these little things, anyone would think ketchup was on the ration, must cost them a shit load just for the packaging." Frustrated that he could not open a sachet of mayonnaise, Connor bit into the plastic and squeezed it like toothpaste over his chips, then looked disappointed at the meagre amount that appeared and grabbed another two of the same.

Sean looked up from his pint considering Connors talk of a work assignment with the bank, trying to forget his disappointment at finding out Suzy was a prostitute. "A rich prize, you say?" waiting for Connor to explain but he kept stuffing his face with chips. "Don't want those." Connor eyed Sean's basket.

"Go ahead kid, fill yer boots, you know me, drink or grub, not both." Sean loved his brother and for the most part, enjoyed his company Connor was not a great talker which was a plus. But perhaps on this occasion that's what he had enjoyed about Suzy Bell, an adult conversation. That said he would not have said no to a bit of sex. Sean brooded to himself on the thought, if she was a prostitute, the sex was a given, so why was he so pissed. He looked at the couple in the bar still enjoying the same drink, sitting even closer together, the girl's hand was on her sweetheart's knee. Maybe he had just liked Suzy's company, maybe he wanted a change, love? "Please!" he voiced his thoughts and burped dismissing the notion as his brother ignored his outburst.

"So how rich kid? Don't make me ask again, or you'll be wearing the rest of them chips, and I'll make dammed sure they're covered in enough sauce." Sean asked with a slur.

"Strong man is it, come on then big man." Connor smiled and stuck out his arm for a friendly arm wrestle, thinking with the amount Sean had drunk maybe this time he could take him. Sean shrugged with a grin and pulled back his sleeve, placing his elbow on the table. "In yer own time."

Two days later the brothers met with Merryman, who informed them the client of their latest assignment was a Somalian warlord, Mubarak Ali Hassan. The pickup was a 20ft half container travelling from Tripoli to Istanbul then Genoa, their assignment was the logistics and security from Genoa by road to the bank in Geneva.

"You've not asked what's in the container." Merryman looked at Sean.

Sean scratched his cheek "Do you know?" And looked to Connor.

Merryman shook his head no "I think."

"So you don't know." Connor smarted,

"Will the package be accompanied?" Sean asked, looking over the balcony of the Tse Yang restaurant, where the three men would meet for lunch to discuss future work. It was the brother's choice of venue, both enjoined Chinese food and Sean counted five exits from the restaurant, including the long balcony, which sat above exclusive designer clothes shops on the north bank. Sean checked the cars parked in the street below out of habit and stared out noticing swans resting with singlet's on the park that sat above the lake bank, he flicked the cigarette in his hand into the road.

"I would expect perhaps some in house security, but the bank has assured the client our personal security offers additional experience, essential for safe deliveries on the continent." Merryman smiled gesturing at the brothers.

"Well just make sure they know we run lead over here, and we won't wait if they get held up at passport control." Sean was never keen working alongside the personal security teams some clients employed, it was normally just one individual, but there was always the chance they would run into an ex-British military type or even an ex-British policeman, that may take an interest in their accents.

Merryman signed for the meal and Sean noticed the black bezel again on his Rolex, as he passed the envelope containing the shipping manifest across the table before leaving.

"I don't trust that fuck, maybe after this one, I'll talk with his boss, see the watch something tells me he's picked up expensive tastes." Sean sniffed running his finger under his nose, for some time he had considered Merryman may be supplementing his lifestyle and a coke habit with money they paid him destined for his boss Salter-Kingsley.

"So, you think he's a crook?" Connor stuck up two fingers ordering two more bottles of Tsingtao.

"We know he's a crook, but if he's fucking a boss, he has known for years, how long before he fucks us." Sean stood up, looking across the lake to where he knew out of sight, their boat lay moored.

"Find out how much it is to get a forty-footer over from Tripoli." He said noticing the swan's that were on the bank were now in the water leading their offspring towards the city bridges, in the majestic way that swans do, but regardless of the tranquil scene, something in Merryman's manner had triggered Sean's survival instincts that this assignment was different. The fact they were dealing with Somalian Shifta only added to the edge.

"What's your thinking?" Connor could see his brother was scheming.

"That kid you got on with, over there in the camp, what was his name?" Sean asked, thinking back to their eight weeks training, sponsored by the IRA, at Bani Walid, one of Muammar Al Gathafi's, international terrorist training camps.
"Who that cheeky Arab Bill? Benghazi Bill" Connor remembered one of the few other conscripts that spoke English stationed at the camp that he had come to know, purely because he also happened to support Liverpool F.C.
"Yer Bill, he mentioned about giving his brother a tug if you were over there and needed a friend, something about his sister, her name?" Sean's attention turned back to the inside of the restaurant, as he saw a large party of diners had arrive.
"Sharon, he told me to say her name, never explained the details, she was killed, you know that's not his name."
On arrival at the camp in Libya, you were given a number, discussing personal details was forbidden. However, they were often grouped with other members from other terror cells and sharing such extreme conditions with other young individuals, curiosity often led to friendships. It starts with a nickname Irish one for Sean, Irish two for Connor and Benghazi Bill, a twenty-year-old Algerian who if it were not for Connor would have not survived the training camp, very nearly making a fatal error in the creation of a coke can nail bomb. With live ammo being used in desert exercises and munitions deployment, fatalities were frequent, graves were unmarked.
In Geneva Sean noticed the waiter of the Tse Yang restaurant was about to show another party to the balcony tables that had been empty behind them, he raised a finger to his mouth, gesturing to Connor "Come we'll talk in the car."
On the way back over to their boat Sean laid out his plan, it was an adaptation of the shell game, they would book a container of the same size on board the Swiftness container ship.
He would break into the port in Tripoli swap the containers identification markings using spray cans and stencils. Then when the ship arrived in Genoa, and the containers were unloaded in the dock, they would pick up the empty container first, and Connor would then rendezvous as arranged with Somalian's own security detail, who had no access to the main dock itself and then continue to the bank. While he would return to the port and pick up the real consignment belonging to the warlord, Mubarak Ali Hassan.
There was always a risk the first container may be opened, but it was unlikely that it would be by the Somalian's and Connor was under strict instructions from his brother if there were any problems he should walk away and Sean would meet up with him as he travelled north to Geneva.

One thing Sean was sure off, whatever was in the container was extremely valuable and regardless of the fact the warlord Mubarak had his own team in play, if the consignment was lost, it would be their necks in rubber tyres. Necklacing was something the brothers had witnessed first-hand when the camp klaxon in Bani Walid sounded in the early hours one night. The assembled was told the individual that resembled a clubbed seal, having been tortured and beaten senseless, was a spy for the French DGSE. But the man Sean believed was Moroccan and could have been any one of them was being used as a shock tactic. The lesson he had no doubt burned in the memories of all he stood alongside that night including his brother as two of the poor soul's assailants thrust an old car tyre over his shoulders and then poured half a can of petrol over the tyre and it was set alight.

"They don't fuck about these boys," Connor whispered to him.

Victims of "Necklacing" can take up to twenty minutes to die. It wasn't until two days later with a strong southern gust of the Ghibli desert wind that the smell lifted from the camp.

Staring to the lights in the distance of Geneva flickering across the lake, the idea of returning to such an uncivilized regime as Libya made Sean consider, had he become soft since leaving London and for the briefest moment he felt like backing out of the assignment with the Somalian's, but he knew if he cancelled now and something did go wrong, then Mubarak would hurt them down, thinking they were involved, he snatched a sip from a glass of J&B he had poured himself.

"Fick'em," he said, putting such thought out of his mind, as Connor came into his bedroom.

"Where you going in your glad rags?" Connor asked as he watched his brother swap ties,

"I think it's about time we found out a little more about our banking friend" Sean placed the Senkin club business card down.

"No trainers," Sean looked as Connor's feet as he sat on Sean's chest of draws, "I'm taking my motor," he said referring to his latest pride and joy a white VW GTi golf. "Don't wait up and for Christ sake don't put the latch on" Sean snatched up the keys ad left. The "latch" was the brother's code for attaching the wires on the booby trap explosives they had installed in on the Helena, just in case someone from the old country ever came nosing around.

Sean did a couple of circuits past the club without the Japanese doormen noticing him park up two streets away, just off the embankment. He stood the other side of his car smoking as he rested against the embankment low concrete wall and watched the exclusive type of clients, that were allowed past the rope pole and up the steps to the double lacquered crimson doors of the club, while a small queue gathered of expectant patrons deemed not worthy, to enter immediately.

Having established which doorman held seniority and witnessed his handshake bribes, Sean crossed the road. As he ignored the line, both doormen gave him a glance, judging him as he took his hand from his pocket. The larger of the two bouncers had already spotted the colour of the note in his hand and gestured for his companion to unhook the rope allowing him to pass before he took Sean's hand, Sean noticed a small red ring tattoo between his thumb and forefinger.

Inside Lindisfarne's Lady Eleanor played in the background, the air held a pleasant eastern musk scent, and although many of the guests were smoking, unlike the stuffy seedy clubs he had once visited in London and Liverpool, the air-conditioning kept the air cool and clean.

"I'm expecting company." he gestured to one of the cup-shaped wall booths, again Sean discreetly handed a banknote to the maître d and was led past the low tables, laid out on the main floor, most of which were occupied by mainly male revellers, some being serviced and entertained by their own scantily clad oriental escorts.

As Sean climbed the step to the wall booths, he noticed some along the same wall had fine curtain veils that were drawn and in each exotic dancers were visible within carrying out suggestive, personal dances, for the patron inside.

The booths were far more personal than the open stalls around six, circular dining table-sized dancing stages. Raised above the chair height, each was bejewelled top and bottom with rope lights pulsating to the music, while dancers raised the pulses of the onlookers with erotic gymnastic performances of strength and balance clinging to the chrome poles.

"My name is Dominic, I am the Maître d, here at the Senkin, if you have any particular requirements, please inform me. As it is your first visit to the Senkin, there is a membership formality, if you would please Sir." The young black Maître d spoke in a thick New Orleans accent as he opened up the membership ledger for Sean to sign as he sat down. "The name you choose to use here at the Senkin is discretionary. However, it is how you will be addressed while on these premises."

"My names Byrne, Sean Byrne," he said, signing the book and Geneva in the column city of residence.

"Very good Sir, welcome Mr Byrne, may I get you something to drink?" Dominic appeared to be the only westerner employed in the club, from the look of the doorman and the security dotted around the room Sean took the others to be Yakuza, from what he could see each, including Maître d, carried the same small ring tattoo on their right hand, clearly a clan tattoo and what would have been in the past their sword hand.

Sean dismissed the menu looking over to the well-stocked bar,
"I notice you have Jameson's Midleton, if you have one sealed, I'll take the bottle two glasses and a bucket of ice, please Dominic."
As the Maître d took his order to the bar, Sean scanned the room, there were the odd couple, but most tables appeared occupied by suited executives. He was not the only man sitting alone, then there were the VIP groups set in raised sections branching off from a scaffold stair system where a bouncer he recognized as the one that had escorted Suzy Bell stood barring the way.
On a small sunken dance floor set below the scaffolding, lights danced across those executives who had dropped their reserve.
As Sean's eyes drifted past the shielded VIP lounges noticing at least two camera balls set into the ceiling, a voice chirped brightly in his ear drawing his attention back to his own table
"So, you decided to come visit." Suzy's voice sent a ripple of electricity down his spine just as he caught sight of the reflective flash from a wristwatch, the style of which he thought he recognized, that hung over the back of one of the VIP sofa's above, it could be anyone, but she confirmed it, "Merry-Merry." she gestured up.
"Dom said you have company joining you?" Suzy looked to the Maître d and placed the tray down she was carrying and then set the glasses down on coasters carrying the design of the club's insignia.
"Expensive taste, you and your friend," she said, showing him the bottle of Midleton's in her hand was unopened before breaking the seal with her sharp black nails. It was at this point he noticed she also carried the same red ring tattoo, close up he now saw inside the image of the ring a Koi fish.
"I just said that hoping you may." he smiled gesturing across to the bench seat opposite him, he poured himself a glass and was about to pour another, then watched her walk away still carrying the tray. He held back his frown of disappointment and noticed the bouncer at the stairs had been watching their exchange. Sean lit a cigarette, took a sip of his drink and looked up to Merryman's lounge group that was made up of three female hostesses as they came down the stairs to join those on the dance floor, Merryman appeared to be partying hard, Sean turned away to avoid being seen.
Looking back to the bar he watched Suzy Bell pick up the house phone, she glanced in his direction, then hanging up spoke with the barman, pointing towards Sean, and then she grabbed a small ice bucket and walked back across to Sean.
"Did you need permission?" Sean asked when she slipped into his booth and dropped ice into their spare glasses

"You're funny, I just called my dad, when we can, we meet up to eat. I told him to go ahead without me. He worries about me, even now." she smiled, taking one of his cigarettes and rattled the ice around the whisky in her glass, then downed the drink in one.

"Looks like he's not the only one that worries about you, your boss seems to keep tight reins." He nodded towards the bouncer at the bottom of the stairs that was now clearly focusing his attention in their direction, she looked over her shoulders. "Hong, ha!" she laughed wide-mouthed and took a deep sip then slipped round to be closer to him.

"Something I said?" he felt as if he had missed something, as he replayed the scene he had witnessed of her meeting with the older man at the château by the lake. He could hardly contain questioning her about it, but his eyes turned again to the VIP lounge seats as he watched Merryman return to his table and he remembered the main purpose for his visit to the club.

"He seems to be having a good time, your man Merry-Merry, does he come here often, must pay well being a banker." Sean didn't need to check the menu to know the bottle he had bought was going to cost an arm and a leg, but Suzy was evasive. "You mean your man Merry-Merry, I think. The other day, you never told me how you know him, you're not a banker, not a lawyer, not a businessman, well not like the ones that come here with Merry-Merry." Suzy studied Sean, she knew enough to know he was not going to enlighten her and allowed him to change the subject. "Some club this, have you worked here long?" Sean also sensed a resistance for her part in talking to him about her work, as she refilled their glasses for the third time.

"Well if we are not going to talk, how about a dance." She said, getting to her feet holding her hand out, Sean sunk his drink and got to his feet allowing her to lead him past Hong, the bouncer scowled, but stayed at his post as they dropped down to the sunken dance floor, just as "Alright now" by the band Free began to play. Suzy danced like one of the professional exotic dancers on the small stages, she appeared to know all the other girls who twirled around her. During the third song, Sean glanced up and noticed Merryman was leaning over his Sofa back, looking down at the dancers, with a girl on either shoulder laughing. Bedazzled with flashing light bubbles in the dimly lit dance floor Merryman did not appear to see Sean amongst the group of dancers, but Sean felt unease at being overlooked turning back towards his table he saw someone was sitting in his booth. Suzy noticed he was distracted from dancing she caught a look in his eye and let him lead her off the dance floor. As they approached the booth, he felt her hand stiffen in his, and she drew up close beside him and then let go.

"You have good taste." The old man from the château sat cross-legged in open-toed sandals with his arm stretched out, resting across the backs of the loungers, with his bright Hawaiian shirt open to the top of his white chest hair it revealed extensive tattooing, and he carried the same distinctive Koi fish ringed tattoo on his hand, but Sean's eyes went straight to the gold jewel-encrusted Patek Phillip chronograph watch on his wrist, similar to one he had seen in a watch shop in the city he knew its value was around twenty thousand dollars. Sean saw his own reflection in his blue circular sunglasses as the man spoke,

"Do you mind?" he asked gesturing to the bottle of whisky, Sean noticed there was already another empty glass on the table alongside theirs.

As he felt Suzy come forward from behind him, Sean gestured with a nod allowing the man to help himself to the bottle and he poured three glasses adding ice to Suzy glass as she sat down. Sean stood for a moment judging the situation, but could not work out his next move, so he sat.

"Do you know what today is Mr Byrne?" The man took out a tin of Panther Sprint small cigars, lit one and without offering them, placed his 22-carat gold DuPont lighter on top of the tin.

"Sean this is Mr Copeland, he's the owner of the club.... my daddy." Suzy said with no concern the term might raise, then added "My real daddy, daddy this Sean."

Sean clearly could not hide his surprise as Copeland winked, "True."

"I'm pleased to make your acquaintance Mr Copeland, fine club you have here." Sean focused on Copeland's glasses as he could not see his eyes, at that, began to annoy him a little.

"Yes it is thank you, I may be the owner but strictly speaking Suzy runs the club, Mr Byrne. I understand from Dom, you signed in under the name Byrne, so I shall call you Mr Byrne until I know you a little better. Anyway, welcome to the Senkin Mr Byrne, I hope you enjoy your visit. We have many traditions here at the Senkin club, some we enforce for our member's benefits and some for the sake of....let's say the management, for example, today is lucky Tuesday. So-called because it was on a Tuesday young Suzy came to me and as with all my darling daughters, of which I am blessed with four, on the first day of each month, religiously without fail I dine with each of them on their own, on their own special day.....to have a heart to heart, so to speak. So when I received a call cancelling our dinner date I just had to leave my chateaubriand, and come find out who I had been dumped for." Copeland's tone was playful, but Sean sensed menace laid less than a gap-tooth smile away.

"Well, as I said, it's a pleasure to meet you, Sir, my apologies if I have interrupted a previous engagement, I was unaware of the arrangement." Sean smiled at Suzy, giving her a look as if to say "Thanks for dropping me in it."

Copeland nodded his understanding and went to speak but was interrupted, by the distinctive voice of an approaching inebriated patron.

"I thought that was you?" Merryman said as he crashed their table with two of the club girls slouched over his shoulders. Sean assumed the others noticed the white dust around the banker's nostrils, but felt his own hand reach up and rub his nose, as if to warn Merryman and although Merryman did not catch the meaning behind Sean's gesture, he too wiped his nose, in the way people sometimes mimic another individual's action by a subconscious impulse, as when caught in a waiting room and someone yawns. Unfortunately, on this occasion, it made the residue cocaine under Merryman's nose more conspicuous.

Seeing the company Sean was in the escort girls stepped back respectfully and Merryman being no longer supported, staggered forward, un-aided, he was forced to rest his hand on the booth table to remain upright, their glasses chinked on the black marble table, and Sean caught the bottle of Midleton's as it wobbled. Before Sean could say something, Hong the bouncer was at the banker's side.

"Girls, your guest wants to dance." Suzy snapped, with unquestioning authority and Merryman's two escorts tugged on his arms, directing him away towards the dance floor.

"Yes, yes must party on, catch you later boyo." Merryman slurred, and as he stumbled away, Copeland received a reverent apologetic gesture from Hong for the intrusion.

Sean was still smarting at the casual term Merryman used to address him, as Copeland gave him a look of intrigue in the same way Suzy did on their first meeting on the boat, as if why does Irishman like himself know a Swiss banker. Sean was tempted to say *"Yes, it's true we have banks in Ireland too."* But he held his tongue as Copeland opened his cigarette tin and seeing it empty Suzy went to stand and get him another one, but Copeland gestured that she remained seated and tapped the tabletop lightly with his lighter.

"Well, unlike our friend, I know when I am intruding." With that Copeland finished his drink and was escorted by Hong back across to the bar, Sean watched as he spoke with Dom the Maître d and then left.

"So that's your father, and this is his… your club, interesting man." Sean examined the empty Panther tin.

"It's too long a story for one night, listen I'm sure you have family ties, he'll sulk for a week if I let him leave alone and my sisters will give me hell for a month." Suzy touched his hand, and he knew she would rather stay with him.

"No, of course, please go, to be honest, I was going to call it a night, I'm leaving town for a few days but maybe when I get back we can catch up, have a coffee, maybe be the same place as last time?" Sean saw the look of relief in her expression at his understanding of her predicament.

"Yes, that would be nice, call the club when you get back, I'm normally here, paperwork and if I'm not let Dom know, but only Dom." She leaned in, kissing him on the lips then left the table. Passing by the Maître d, she also whispered in his ear.

"Miss Suzy asked me to give you this." Dom laid down a club business card on the booth table, on which he had written Suzy's private club number on the back.

"Also you should know Mr Copeland has settled your account this evening, and this is your new membership card. Show it at the door they will let you straight in, and there will be no need for this next time." Dom then placed the bribe money Sean had given him and the doorman on entering the club. Sean sensed the Maître D's smile was genuine and that there was some kind of special relationship between Suzy and him, but he looked more surprised than Sean felt.

Cleary It was a show of control by Copeland, Sean thought as he sat for a while looking at the plastic credit card style gold card inset with a small image matching the tattoos all the employees carried. As he finished his drink, he watched Merryman still gyrating on the dance floor clearly the worst for wear, being partly held up by his escorts, a couple of other patrons objected to his exaggerated arms movements, which Sean to be as the bankers impersonation of Mick Jagger, Brown Sugar, was being played by the DJ.

Considering that now he was alone and that that he may get captured by the banker and his posse, Sean got up to go, but first, he went to use the toilets.

Again he was impressed by the stylish, sleek interior of the restroom, it even had an assortment of hand balms, and expensive aftershaves, a tray of mints sat in a bowl, and he had never seen condom vending machines before, this was nothing like the strip clubs back home.

On his return to the main room, in the corridor, he was surprised as much as they were to witness a furtive exchange between Merryman and Hong. Sean took it to be a drugs buy. And in that brief moment, Sean took there to be some kind of problem with the banker's line of credit. Seeing Sean approach Hong shielded the exchange, nudging Merryman from Sean's sight and the banker danced away back towards the club. Hong then turned back and eyed Sean as he passed by, then looking over his shoulder Sean realised another bouncer was at the end of the hall and a third appeared in the doorway barring his way back onto the main club floor. Sean turned back facing Hong who gestured Sean towards a side corridor and the clubs rear fire door exit.

With nowhere to go apart from where they wished him, Sean tensed preparing for the ambush assault. Feeling them bear down behind him in the tight corridor, suddenly the two escort girls that were in Merryman's company appeared laughing and joking from the ladies toilet. The three bouncers froze, it bought Sean enough time to weaponise his environment, and as he passed the ladies he grabbed a fire extinguisher from the wall, yanking the safety pin he span back pressing down on the handle while flaying the hose, shouting "Fire! Fire!" within seconds the corridor was full of a choking thick cloud, the girls ran screaming past the bouncers, Sean hurled the extinguisher forward, there was a heavy thud and groan as it hit one of the bouncers, obscured in the dust cloud. Sean smashed the fire alarm button and feeling his hand on the door bar, yanked it down and was outside in the next second. Before his pursuers could follow him, he tore down a stack of plastic crates, full of bottles, ramming one of the bottles to jam the doors outer lift bar down.

"Been having fun?" An unexpected but welcome voice in the dark yelled over the siren, Connor stepped out in the alley as Sean brushed some of the white powder from his shoulders.

He was about to answer Connor and ask him why he was waiting behind the club when a bouncer appeared from the street blocking their exit. At first, Connor smiled, relishing the idea of a brawl, then Hong, sporting a bloody gash to his forehead and two more of his colleagues arrived on the scene. Out of breath, covered in fire extinguisher powder, they split into pairs and began marching towards the brothers.

"Fick this!" Sean said as two of the bouncers reached into their coats and pulled out meat cleavers, Sean grabbed the nearest empty bottle and smashed the end off and thrust it forward. While his brother immediately slipped his hand to his back pulling free the revolver he had tucked into his waistband, and as one of Hongs colleagues lunged forward toward Sean, he fired the man span through the air like a badly thrown Frisbee as he was caught in the arm by Connor's bullet.

"Any more for any more!" Connor crowed, and the Japanese heavies backed away, Hong looked towards the street and the sound of an approaching police and fire brigade, then glared back at Sean, brushing the dust from his shoulders he gestured to his men to stand down, and they concealed their weapons.

"Nice company you keep, friends of that wanker the banker, I take it," Connor, waited until Sean was behind him and then covered their exit from the alley.

An hour later Sean was still trying to make sense of the evening and why Copeland would make a display of offering him a membership to the club only to have him beaten up.

"A protective father is one thing, a protective father that's Yakuza something else, you certainly know how to pick 'em boyo and theirs me think'in this city is all suits and toffs." Connor jested as he handed Sean a beer, and they sat with their legs dangling over the side of the deck of the Helena as they watched the flashing blue lights outside the club on the opposite side of the lake drift off from the false alarm. "I'll sort it when I get back from Tripoli, meanwhile did you get that information about the crate, I asked for?"

Connor passed him the details, "The ship's name is Swiftness Merryman said, it's all there, times, Tripoli to Tunis, then on to Genoa I got an empty container booked, and that's all the stuff I can remember about Bill. His Uncle owned a barbers, but that was four years ago, I'd be happier going with you, if he's not there get your arse back pronto, they don't fuck about over there, not like those eejit's tonight." Like Sean, Connor remembered the necklacing vividly at Bani Walid.

Chapter 10: The Pulley Rig

Tripoli, Libya
December 1973

Two nights following Sean's visit to the Senkin Gentleman's club, in an impoverished district of Tripoli, a Libyan dockhand sat opposite his wife while she held their four-year-old daughter, a single tabletop candlestick held a flame that flickered in their wide eyes as they stared at a wad of Dinar banknotes, more than they had ever owned or seen.
"Tell him to think of his daughter, a year's money for one night." Sean ordered and the twenty-two-year-old Algerian standing armed at his side that he and Connor had come to know as Benghazi Bill at the terrorist camp in Libya, whose real name was Sami Arith translated.
Sami had made good on his promise to Connor, when Sean arrived a day earlier and introduced himself at his Uncle's barbers and now as agreed assisted his brother in arms, with no questions of their purpose.
"Tell him we are not stealing, no one will know, he only has to get me in, I will make my own way out, if I am caught, I will say I am a stowaway, you know nothing about me." Sean saw a look of apprehension in the Dockhands' eyes at their guns, "Tell him it's his choice, he will not see us again if he decides to say no." Sami looked to Sean for confirmation as he watched the Irishman lay his revolver on the table. "Tell him," Sean ordered.
The docker looked with questioning disbelief at Sami as he spoke Sean's words and Sean nodded when he finished speaking "yes" looking to his wife and watched as she placed a hand on the money and pulled it back off the table and out of sight.
"Next time bring that crazy fool brother of yours," Sami as he handed Sean the knapsack of supplies for the two-day crossing, as the docker waited in the cab of his three-wheel Piaggio truck, with the engine running. As he arranged the toolbox and blankets in the back of the truck to conceal Sean, he leaned in and whispered in English. "This man who takes you, I know your promise, but if you are caught, you should know I will kill him, his wife and child I will have taken from the city, it was not my word that was given, my friend."
In the street light, Sean could just make out Sami's chipped tooth smile through the rough hessian blanket as he banged on the side of the van and Sean felt a jolt as they pulled away.

Moments later Arith stood watch, with an Ak47 Kalashnikov, resting on his passenger seat, ready to cause a diversion as the docker drove through the dock security gate at Tripoli. "altawfiq al' iirlandiu" *(Irish Godspeed)* he whispered in seeing the lights of the little three-wheeler as it moved around on the other side of the dock gates, between the rows of high stacked containers.

Then as he drove away, he noticed three black men in a buff-coloured Sedan parked along a side street overlooking the dock. The Somalian warlord Mubarak had three of his men stake out the Panamanian Swiftness container ship lying at berth until its departure.

That night using spray cans and stencils Sean successfully swapped the identification markings of the warlord's container with the one Connor had leased for the same journey in which the docker locked Sean inside, along with some rough bedding the nap sack and a copy of George Orwell's 1984 that Sean had picked up at the airport.

As he heard the docker snap the replacement security door seals on the outside of the container doors, Sean checked his torch, "Not so bad." he whispered to himself unconvincingly. The air was warm and still and held an odour of machine oil, but the inside of the container was cooler than Sean had expected as he settled down, making himself as comfortable as he could.

He woke the next morning with the grinding of metal and the movement of the straddle carrier stacking his container with the others on the deck, shortly before the vessel started the first leg of its seventy-two-hour journey.

He was relieved to see the ventilation holes allowed a modicum of daylight, banging his head, yet again on the metal container wall as he sat down, he checked the meagre supplies Sami Arith had loaded into the knapsack, a small round loaf of what appeared to be some sort of unleavened bread, two cans of peaches and one can of Heinz beans, with two large plastic Coke Cola bottles filled with water, he took a sip from one and gargled, before swallowing.

Lighting one, he checked how many cigarettes in his packet and cursed, realising he would have to ration himself. Then hearing members of the Greek crew talking outside he noticed the smoke drift to the ventilation holes and cursed himself again at his stupidity, then raised his eyes to the heavens looking at the crushed remains of almost a full cigarette that he had just stubbed out. He would have to wait until dark to smoke, just in case. Taking out his new Swiss army knife he began to open up all the blades and appendages working out their intended functions and which would be the best to open the food cans, that, he would later realise was one of the highlights of his day.

However once they cleared Tunis where they picked up more freight, although by now stripped to his underwear because of the heat of the day, he was calm in the non-eventful routine of the journey as minutes drifted by at a snail's pace and the ships sounds became familiar to his ear, along with the different accents and tones of the crew members, that he occasionally heard doing their rounds, who he began to name.

Sleep was Sean's main salvation from the tedium of the journey, during the day. However, he woke shivering having slept into the evening on two occasions and before reaching their destination resorted to attempt and straighten the cigarette he had first stubbed out when finding he had none left in his packet.

Seventy-five hours later, Sean felt the boat nudge into its berth at Genoa. Soon after, the alarm and screeching of high tensile cables could be heard from the crane removing the containers from the ship. He lay flat as he listened to the clamps lock onto two sides of his and was bounced slightly as it was set on the ground inside the ports container storage and collection park. The last couple of hours were the most pensive, then he held his breath biting his lip from speaking out as he heard the familiar Irish voice of his brother talking with the security control in Genoa and Sean checked his revolver that he had stripped and cleaned three times during the crossing.

The shudder and sound of air breaks signalled they had stopped and he stood ready. In his planning, Sean had judged they had a small window of opportunity in the lorry park for him to be set free before the road from the dock in Genoa turned onto the main exit road leading out of the port, where before the first roundabout on a lorry slip road rest area, they had been informed a contingent of Ali Hassan's security staff would be waiting to greet them and then escort the container to Geneva.

"Brother of mine.... Jeese that's ripe!" Connor covered his mouth and nose as he opened the door, then held his head away from the foul smell taking a deep breath of clean air.

"That dozy Arab Bill gave me beans and peaches, what do you expect and I think the water gave me the shits." Sean said, shielding his eyes holding up the 1984 paperback, which by now had a number of pages missing, having been used to wipe his backside.

"It's the blue Volvo, paper works under the seat, including a map your wallet with licence and money. I also bung in a bag with a fresh top, not that it will get rid of the smell" Connor said, handing Sean a set of lorry keys and backed away quickly.

"Fuck' you very much. Just remember kid any trouble walk away, no point fighting over a bag of my shit, I'll keep an eye on the route for you." With a waft of fresh air

The Sardinia Prinz: The Rising

to his nostrils, Sean began to appreciate what his brother was talking about, he smelt like a camel's arse.

With that Connor set off as Sean located the second truck they had hired and returned to the container port to retrieve the genuine container belonging to the Somalian warlord.

Approximately 400 kilometres seven hours to Geneva, Sean considered there were far too many opportunities for an ambush, regardless of Mubarak Ali Hassan having sent over a team of his own personal security force, who as arranged met and fell in convoy in front and behind Connor's lorry in two cars on the slip road.

Connor could see immediately the five men were armed and shrugged when told he was to follow,

"Whatever you say, fella, I'm just the driver." he told their surly leader as he barked orders checking the containers identification markings and door seals, but as he climbed in the passenger seat, Connor slipped his revolver to the side pocket of his cab door. The man grunted aggressively as his colleagues in the car in front moved off, and Sean flicked his cigarette from the window.

The journey back to the bank should take 7-8 hours and would involve at least three stops. Sean having picked up the real container, was now following an hour behind and checked the marks on his map for fuel stations that he had prearranged with Connor they would meet up at, if something should happen to Connor's convoy, what neither of them counted on was Ali Hassan's men had their own ideas and separate orders from the warlord.

For Connor, all went according to plan for the first 3 hours, "Think your boys need fuel or a piss," he said, seeing the car in front indicating to turn off as they approached the first fuel station after they crossed the border into France just before heading into the Mont Blanc tunnel.

There was a grunt from the seat to his right, "Follow him." It was the first words his passenger had said since climbing aboard although he had helped himself to two of Connor's Marlborough cigarettes.

Connor watched the two cars at the pumps, three of the men stood guard around his lorry.

His passenger tapped the dash with the barrel of his revolver, drawing Connors attention back to the cab, "You go use the…. toilet." The Somalian struggled for the right words.

"No, you're alright pal I'm fine, my orders are to stay with the cab, we have a schedule to keep, I have a plastic bottle if I wanna piss." Connor reached down showing he had an empty Whites lemonade bottle, as he placed it back in the door shelf he caught sight of one of the men at the rear in his wing mirror, and it occurred to him they may choose to open the back, he went to question what was taking so and turning back in his seat he saw his passenger now had his revolver pointing at his side. "You go now, hands up" The man snarled and placed his hands on Connor's cigarettes.

Connor raised his hands off the wheel "Whatever you say, fella, fuck it I'm out' o' here." He looked to his gun and remembered Sean's words and left it.

As Connor stepped down from the cab the Somalian moved over to his side and winding down his window shouted to his men to get back in their cars, then seeing Connors gun in the door pocket shelled the bullet clear, sprang out the cartridge then tossed it to Connor "Just a driver." he said smugly as the air brakes hissed, and then he pulled away.

Connor watched them for a moment as they disappeared up the motorway, "Seany, Seany, remind me to have you pick the next national winner." he said, looking up at the petrol station sign recognising he was at a stop he knew Sean would pull into and as arranged Sean found Connor sheltering from the rain under the bridge before the station siding, eating the remains of his second cheese and onion baguette just over an hour later.

"They told me to fuck off, our services it seems are not required" Connor spoke with a mouthful and showed Sean he still had his gun, then opened his window, but refrained from telling his brother he still smelt of BO and shit.

"Fick off and give me a bite of that, I'm starving." Sean held out his hand, and Connor gave him possibly the last two bites of the baguette, he didn't have the heart to tell him, in fact, he had bought it for Sean and then got tempted into eating it himself while waiting for him to arrive.

"There could be anything back there, tell me you're not tempted to take a look." Connor asked when they were about to emerge from the 11.6 kilometre Alps tunnel. "Only thing I'll be interested in is a hot shower, and the look on the face of those eegit's when they open that container." Sean smirked, then eased off the gas as he saw flashing police lights ahead and both boys braced themselves, pulling their guns free out of sight as the traffic slowed.

"Is that them?" Sean whispered nodding forwards threw the cab window screen, as they were directed to a coned offside lane, then watching a gendarme approach their wagon, Sean wound down his window.

"Papers." the Policeman held his hand up demandingly, and while Sean waited as the French Policeman on the other side of his door checked their passports and cargo manifest, Sean and Connor watched the scene unfold to their right. It looked from the wreckage of the cars and bodies strewn with bullet holes that the Somalian's lead car had been forced into the inside barrier shortly after exiting the tunnel. Presumably, the container lorry Connor had previously been driving stopped to sharply and had jack-knifed across two lanes of the carriageway, at least six cars remained crumpled having been caught in pile up.

Sean could see to his right from the number of spent brass shells covering the paving and around the central barrier dividing the north and south carriageways, where one of the attackers had been stationed, shielded by a metal services cabinet. The attackers appeared to have cut down the Somalian security team in the front and rear cars before the men had time to open their doors, there was no sign of Connor's container lorry.

"Move on." Sean was ordered by the gendarme and reached down to get his documents, and as he went to pull away he heard on the Policeman's radio, in French "We have another one!" there was a scramble of activity by the Police officers as he pulled into the left-hand lane past ambulances treating the wounded. A short distance out of the tunnel further along the road they could see a scene of activity, and they were slowed again as they passed a group of gendarmerie examining and standing over the twisted body of a black male.

"Fuck off, that's the fella that hitched a ride with me," Connor said.

"Keep your eye's keen lad, I'll not stop now till we park this shit outside the bank."

Seventy-six kilometres northeast of Geneva, in the hills above Laussane, although the wind was whipping hard around the disused quarry above Savigny. Copeland's excitement held back the cold from his Hawaiian shirt as he gestured to Hong.

"Open it" he smiled signalling the forklift to come forward to remove their bounty.

As the hand carrying the red Yakuza tattoo snipped the seals of the container before the door had swung open, the western words "Shit" reached Hong's lips, and he raised a hand to his mouth while peering inside at the remains of Sean's foul-smelling den. Copeland dropped his blue sunglasses down to the bridge of his nose as he looked on then a gust of wind caught hold of the 1984 paperback on the floor of the container and tossed it out into the quarry.

Copeland looked heavens and then to the paperback as the wind caught its pages, back and forth, "Pick up the banker, burn It." he ordered with a smile, then in seeing that some of the book's pages were missing his smile widened. He could not be sure if his daughter's Irish friend Mr Byrne was involved in the deception but what he did know was whoever it was, they spoke English, and they had no respect for good literature, he reached down and pick up the book and dusted it off against his designer khaki cargo pants.

His tone turned stern as he addressed Hong separately "I want that fuck hanging by his balls in my office by the time I have finished my T bone. This is going to make me look like a right prick with your people in Tokyo and mine back home. There were a lot of fingers wanting a slice of this pie, and Hong, get that dozy tart that gave you the heads up on this deal first, Katie, before she starts her shift. I want to make sure she didn't sell her song to another punter before I start pulling teeth, Hong, no need to involve Suzy, she'll find out soon enough."

Just shy of six hours from Genoa Sean woke Connor, only pulling on the air brakes when they parked in the street in front of the gated underground car park to the FNIG bank in Geneva. Within minutes the street was cordoned off by security guards and they were joined first by first Charles Merryman and then by Salter-Kingsley, accompanied by a well suited middle-aged African man, wearing a red waistcoat and dark green tartan suit, dressed as if about to go grouse shooting, except attached to his wrist was a gold and ivory zebra tail fly swat, which he occasionally flicked at the two members of his personal guard that flanked him and each raised their hands to their hip guns as Sean dropped down from the cab and approached the quizzical Salter-Kingsley as Merryman

checked the markings on the container against those on his documentation.

"This is not my container!" Sean immediately realised this was the Somalian warlord Mubarak Ali Hassan, as he walked up to Merryman and Salter-Kingsley Connor came round from the passenger's side.

"As promised, your client's property delivered." Sean said throwing the bank security guard Claude Dennee the keys, then both he and Connor turned in surprise, as the doors of the container were opened and out fell a young Somalian man, clearly suffering from dehydration. The gun in his hand was removed, by one of Ali Hassan's men, as the warlord went round and examined the contents of the container, with a grunt and flick of his fly swat one of his men climbed inside and pulled clear the loose tarpaulin covering two timber pallets.

"They are here Papa" the man confirmed as he revealed each pallet was stacked ten high and ten deep with gold bars wrapped in cellophane.

Satisfied Ali Hassan's attention turned to the man that had emerged from the back of the container. Sean noticed the affectionate way he placed his hand on the young Somalian's shoulders and spoke something to him in their native tongue with a smile. The Irishman could not be sure, but from the young man's reaction, he considered it was likely that as when Connor had opened the container to let him out, Ali Hassan was commenting on the smell and he barked at his guards to aid the young man inside the bank.

"Yes let's take this inside please gentleman, please," Salter-Kingsley said catching a whiff of excrement, as a forklift came up from the banks lower car parking area which accessed corridors to the vault and began unloading the gold.

"Wait! Ali Hassan shouted halting the forklift driver, "what is your name?" he asked, looking at Sean.

"Byrne Sir, Sean Byrne, my brother Connor, your other men forcibly removed him from the other wagon." he pointed to his brother then watched as Ali Hassan tore open the cellophane and pulled free one of the gold bars.

"I take it you have heard about your men." Sean asked as Ali Hassan inspected the gold in his hand.

"Gentlemen please, we really must discuss this inside, the street needs to be opened." Salter-Kingsley's tone was abrupt as he looked up and down the street past the armed guards towards other pedestrians, curiously looking on.

Inside Salter-Kingsley's office, Sean explained what had been done as a call came into the office that a client had arrived for Merryman, Sean watched him leave, he was a prime suspect in his mind but felt now was not the time to voice his opinion.

"So you didn't think to inform us of your arrangements, what if there had been a second attack." Salter-Kingsley sounded irritated.

"Then possibly we would also be dead as would my brother if you men had not changed the arrangements." Sean was tired, he had delivered the package as agreed and felt no need to further explain his actions, he had not ruled out Salter-Kingsley being involved.

Ali Hassan smiled and looked at the gold bar he had placed on Salter-Kingsley's desk and tapped his teeth gently with the ornate gold cap on his fly swat handle.

"It would seem there is a lesson to be learned. I will send a man for the papers before I leave Geneva Peter regarding our acquisition." he said as he stood to leave, shaking Salter-Kingsley's hand, then as he turned he stopped the banker with a flick of his fly swat as Salter-Kingsley leant over to take up the gold bar. "The boy in the back, he is my nephew Cawil, so-called because of the death of my own son." Ali Hassan said and passed the gold bar to Sean, "One day he may wish to thank you personally, for now, you have my thanks in not having to explain his death to my sister." He turned to go.

"And what about the men that carried out this attack?" Salter-Kingsley's eyes continued to look at the gold bar in Sean's hands as did Connor's, Sean was focused on Ali Hassan, he was considering how the warlord would have reacted if on opening the back of the container, he had found his nephew dead.

"They failed, thanks to these gentlemen, my gold is safe in your bank, in my country failure rarely is accepted, whoever organised this I assure you is unhappy and let us hope they vent their frustrations on those they trusted, unwisely, to deliver...gentlemen." he nodded.

As he left Sean placed the gold bar back on the desk, "Place it in our vault please, considering the challenges and additional expenses set with this assignment we would not expect to pay a commission on this bonus." Sean considered if now was the time to talk about Merryman and the arrangements they had in place and his suspicions, but he needed a drink, and above all, he needed a shower.

"Of course, I will have Mr Merryman make the arrangements and considering the subtle manner in which you have handled this assignment, I have decided to raise your access to certain members of my own client portfolio if you wish the assignments? But first please understand these clients are most important to me personally, some have had a history with the bank for many years." Salter-Kingsley saw Sean's eyes go to the Nazi membership document on the wall, and his eyes appeared to flicker in recognition.

Before Salter-Kingsley left for the evening he called into Charles Merryman's office, "That was pretty intense today, you did well Charles, handling the Irishmen, it's good to keep them in check, but I was impressed, with the way Steve handled it"

"Sean Sir, the Irishman's name, Sean Byrne and his brother is Connor." Merryman corrected him.

"Yes Sean, look Charles I was remembering, you were good enough to cancel your skiing vacation to cover for Plácido while he was off. I have booked five days at the Chemin de Plan Pra Chalet, you have not been before have you, it's just myself, I need a break from all this including Martha and the kids, clear the cobwebs so to speak, why don't come along, we'll book it on my expense account, tell accounts we are courting a new client." he smiled.

"Yes, very much, I hear the snow is excellent this year." Merryman held back the need to gush forward.

"Good, good, I'll have Miss Bishop pass you the details, I'll take the Porsche, we'll pack light, yes, I am aiming for the end of next week see if you can clear your desk by then."

As Merryman turned off his desk light to leave, he had almost forgotten about the meeting he knew was coming with Copeland regarding his recent extreme partying from three nights earlier at the Senkin club and his outstanding cocaine bill. That was until he stepped out the door of the bank and noticed one of his men waiting across the street, Hong gestured to the back seat of the Mercedes.

Meanwhile, Sean and Connor were already on their fifth pint of Guinness.

"You could have least allowed me to hold the ficking thing for a minute, I've never owned a gold bar before." Connor shrugged, as they sat at the bar of the Metropolitan hotel, occasionally Sean would get a whiff of himself as two fresh pints arrive.

"Half a gold bar, you own half a gold bar, phone the bloody man up if you like in the morning, he'll let you down the vault for sure. In the meantime grab a taxi bring some of my gear back, I'm stopping here for a bit use the spa, I still stink, likely as much I'll stop for the night, I'll buy you a steak later and leave word at the desk with my spare room key. Don't forget I' left a moonlight surprise on the step, don't go give the people some free fireworks tonight" he told Connor reminding him of one of the booby traps they had left in place as usual onboard their boat the Helena when they went away.

Sean needed time to think, alone with no distractions, he kept playing over the events of the day, looking for signs of who had been behind the raid. Merryman was still chief suspect for him, as the man inside, but the muscle, whoever was in charge of them and planned it, irrespective that they had failed they were armed organised killers, there was a military feel to their engagement, they knew who they were stealing from and that did not concern them and one thing stuck in Sean's mind that the Mubarak Ali Hassan had said, "They won't be happy."

Chapter 11: The Handling

Geneva, Switzerland
December 1973

From the gnawing on the last fleck of flesh on his T bone steak and then washing his fingers in the fragrant bowl provided by the waiter at the Relais de l'Entrecôte Restaurant, to arriving back at his chateau it took Copeland only twenty minutes, the half bottle of Malbec he had shared with Suzy mellowed his mood, somewhat as did her company, as always, possibly because he did not speaker of the failed container heist.
"Thank you for a wonderful meal daddy, come Binki lets do your shit." she said kissing Copeland on the lips, as she disappeared towards the edge of their private spruce wood that lay before the open gravel car park and hovered in her two-inch stilettos and fishnets smoking, waiting for Binki, oblivious to the fact her "Daddy's" men in their attempt to steal a container belonging to one of the most dangerous men in the world had not only failed but left six Somalian's dead on the roadside of France, or that Charles Merryman had been waiting nervously inside "Daddy's" office for the last hour.
"Watch her," Copeland told one of his guards as he skipped up the last steps to and then disappeared inside.
"Thank you for coming to see me at such short notice, Mr Merryman" Copeland announced as he breezed into his study and gave Merryman a light rub on his shoulders as he passed and felt the banker flinch. Taking a bone-handled pen knife from his pocket, he began to peel a peach he had plucked from the fruit bowl of the restaurant, as he sat down behind his cherry wood leather top partners desk, some of his associates had shipped as a gift to him from Tokyo.
Copeland adopted his most deadly serious, stern expression, a posture he sometimes practised on in the privacy, in front of the wall mirror of his marble-tiled en' suite. Normally it worked with those he detained and was effectively intimidating, that evening, however, Copeland was unaware he still had a thick smudged imprint of Suzy's L'Oréal Paris cherry lipstick across his mouth.
Hearing the tap of Suzy's stilettos in the hall and the irritating yap from Binki, he gestured to Hong to close the doors to his study, before she passed by the door.
"You must be wondering why you are here?" Copeland smiled, placing a piece of the fruit in his mouth, dancing the blade lightly in the air, he handed Merryman a slice of peach.

Merryman took it and was surprised he noticed how sweet its flavour was, considering his predicament, his heightened sense of angst made it seem the most delicious peach he had ever tasted. Then his eyes once again drifted to the girl sat at his right, with her back against the wall, and he swallowed hard. Although Merryman recognized her as one of the escorts he had enjoyed during his hedonistic partying in the Senkin executive rooms last. With the bruises to her face, she was a shadow of the sexy party girl that had snorted his cocaine supplied by Hong, from the tabletop, and later off his erect penis.

The girl had held back her sobbing and said nothing to him since he had arrived and been forced into the seat, only occasionally sniffing while clutching a stained damp paper towel to her bloody nose, painfully breaking the silence.

"God where are your manners Hong get Mr Merryman a scotch, you'd like a scotch wouldn't you, I'd like one too, fix it, Hong." Copeland theatrical magnanimity was unnerving under the circumstances.

Hong smiled awkwardly not knowing if he should tell his boss and surrogate father about the lipstick, he decided to keep quiet and then got a glare from Copeland when in taking his first sip of his drink Copeland saw the rouge smear on his glass and then wiped his lips clean on a napkin, "Where were we?" he said raising his eyes to Merryman.

"I assume it concerns my outstanding account at the club, I have a bonus at the end of the month which should clear most of it, I assure you." Merryman felt tense but knew he was a big spender. He looked to Hong for some confirmation to reassure him, as he considered that Copeland must know he worked for the FNIG bank and was good for the 22,000 Swiss Francs he had racked up, in booze drugs and girls. To some extent, Merryman felt a little relieved believing that was all it was, an unfortunate misunderstanding, as Hong reached into his pocket and handed Copeland what looked like an itemized bill. But then as the girl, whose name he was still having trouble remembering, sniffed again his eyes drifted to her, and he could not understand her presence.

Copeland raised an eyebrow at the total on the bill and tapped it with his knife as rolled the peach pip around his mouth, sucking the last ounce of juice from the fruit, it made an unpleasant sound as if someone was tap dancing inside Copeland's mouth, until he stopped and pushed it to the side of his jaw to speak, making him look like he had some kind of tooth problem.

"It would seem you have been partying hard, but far be it for me to criticise a patron for enjoying our hospitalities, that after all is why we are in business. However I must confess, some of my associates would view such an outstanding amount as disrespectful and would insist its late payment incurs penalties of, some description.

In the same way, I am sure your own bank expects interest on those who default on loans." Setting the bill paper on his desk, he removed the peach pip from his mouth and placed it squarely at its centre.

"However no, it's not your bill that concerns me. How's the scotch, good? Let's have another." Copeland said, as he closed the blade on his knife and set it to the side next to the bill, then got up and poured himself another scotch from his decanter, gesturing to Merryman who nodded, "Thank you, as I am glad as I Have explained to Hong I have a bonus due, which will clear this matter up, immediately, thank you again for your patience."

"Yes of coarse your bonus, so that brings us to young Katie here, you remember Katie." The girl also flinched as her boss passed by and placed a hand on her shoulder as he handed Merryman his refill.

"Yes, of course, Katie." Merryman smiled awkwardly at the poor girl, who raised her tear-filled eyes towards Copeland and gave a meagre smiled of recognition.

"She was very entertaining, if it is a case I was remiss in some way in showing my appreciation, I am sure it is something that can be rectified," Merryman said trying to remember the girl's part in the entertainment, but caught only fleeting images of his drug-fuelled orgy.

"No I understand you were a perfect gentleman, tipped well, but Kelly informed me apparently you were somewhat unreserved with regards to this bonus of your that you are expecting and the banking assignment it was associated with. A new client of the bank where you work, depositing quite substantial funds, I understand something or other about a container." Copeland pretended to have a vague interest as he coaxed Merryman to volunteer a confirmation of the Somalian's gold deposit.

"Unfortunately this information was passed to some focused individuals, associates of mine that considered it rightly or wrongly, a business opportunity and because this indiscretion took place on my establishment's premises I was required to become somewhat involved." Copeland began to lightly spin the well-balanced penknife on his desk as Merryman looked to Hong and then back to Copeland and then the penny dropped as he realised Copeland had been behind the heist of the container.

The banker looked back to Katie, desperately trying to recollect what he had boasted, but there was nothing. Then his mind turned to concerns of his own welfare as he remembered all of Mubarak Ali Hassan's men had been killed by their attackers, by Copeland.

"I don't understand Mr Copeland, what has this got to do with me, I got drunk, maybe I said too much, but I never expected?" Merryman felt a sudden hollowness in the pit of his stomach, and he took another sip of the scotch, this time it burnt his throat, as he finished speaking he regretted asking the question and wished he had said nothing. Copeland stopped spinning his penknife and gestured to one of his men to take Katie away.

"I don't blame her, unfortunately, she was ill-advised, it happens with the young sometimes." Copeland looked at Hong, "you would think at my age I would have learned. If I had spoken with you direct, got the precise details, then the enterprise would have been successful for my associates, there would be no problem, but we can never go back." Copeland looked at Merryman's bill from the club, "You see Chas, alright if I call you Chas." Merryman hated the abbreviation of his name but smiled and nodded yes as Copeland tapped at the bill paper.

"Good, you see Chas, the dilemma I face is that like in the case of poor young Katie, who unfortunately will not be able to earn her keep as bruised goods if my associates decide to widen their attention to the source of the bad information to vent their frustrations. I am somewhat concerned you will be unable to work and therefore be unable to fulfil your obligation to my club. So I have been forced to intercede with individuals I have had a long-standing relationship with, in an effort to…how shall I put it save your face." Copeland paused, staring at Merryman with a menacing expectation.

Merryman smiled nervously thanking him, but knew this was not the end of the matter, the hollowness he felt inside began to bottom below his chest and he felt his bowels grumble and wondered if Copeland heard.

"Of course my employees discretion regarding your part in divulging the details concerning the recent African bank consignment, will require a degree of intervention on my part and as you can appreciate, those that took part in the failed acquisition will be very disappointed, some particularly vexed considering that members of the French gendarmerie and Swiss Cantonal police are investigating the incident, which no doubt will require some kind of deflection by financial intervention, this bill of yours is beginning to add up." Copeland raised an eye shaking his head.

"Yes, yes your associates, I can see that, but I really had nothing to do with it. You have my word I won't speak of this. These clients' arrangements were made by my boss, and he is totally satisfied, very satisfied the container arrived safely at the bank and not concerned with any problems that may have occurred in transit. And the Client the African gentleman, as for the police, he has expressed no wish to investigate the unfortunate loss of his people, in fact, I think he would rather, not be associated with them, you ….you do know who he is?" Merryman asked his hand shook as he finished his drink and placed the cut crystal glass on a desk coaster that held the slogan, "Surfer's do it standing up!"

"The Somalian, yes, my associates are aware of Mubarak Ali Hassan's reputation. However, I assure the notoriety of my associates is somewhat more infamous and unyielding and my intervention on your behalf…. well let's call it an act of goodwill, to show my wish that we start a new relationship afresh, so to speak, one were there can be no confusion, so another drink to seal that I think."

Copeland gestured to Hong who then leaned in close over Merryman, in an almost threatening manner as he refilled his glass.

"So to business, your boss Peter Salter-Kingsley, certainly appears to have some interesting clients, with dubious transaction requirements, don't you think, not quite kosher?" Copeland gave Merryman a knowing look, fully aware it was unlikely any individuals depositing illegal funds in such a way to the bank would report them as being stolen and neither would the bank, in some respects if you could succeed it was a perfect crime.

With the scotch running in his veins, the bankers confidence grew, and with it a sense of self-preservation kicked in, and Merryman decided to promote his usefulness to Copeland by emphasizing his position within the bank and exaggerating his relationship with Salter-Kingsley, at this point he would have said anything to get out of the room, and he decided to play the salesman.

"Yes, as I said my boss Peter Salter-Kingsley, he was so impressed that it was sorted out by security personnel I had introduced to the bank, he has invited me skiing next week." his light-hearted tone was a total bluff, and although it was aided by the alcohol now in his blood system Copeland liked the fact he sounded confident for someone that moments before he had considered dumping in the lake.

"Really that is good to hear, for you, but as I said there are associates that feel again rightly or wrongly that they wish to chastise the individual that instigated the venture, and again I will be called upon and required to dissuade them on your behalf. They may even contemplate contacting the bank and Mr Salter-Kingsley directly, which I would assume would have unfortunate repercussions for your employment and possibly involve a criminal investigation." Copeland licked his lips savouring the way Merryman squirmed, knowing he would say anything to get out of that seat. "As I said, these are very much focused individuals committed into achieving a positive outcome with all endeavours they invest in. However, this problem may possibly be alleviated if I can assure them that should a similar opportunity emerge sometime in the future, the precise details regarding any transaction would be made available… by your good self." Copeland watched Merryman fidget uncomfortably to the front of his chair as if he sensed the meeting was drawing to a close, but he knew he was now cornered by Copeland's bribe and threat of informing on him to the bank.

"To be clear, I need you to say you understand." Copeland's face was stern as he sat forward, peering into Merryman's eyes, and he wiped his lips again.

"I understand, you wish me to inform you of an incognito bank transaction, but I have to say they are not as common as you might think, at least not a significant sum of this nature and size, possibly two or three times a year." Merryman shook his head.

"Well, I am told I have patience, and I will prevail upon my associates to refrain from taking action. However that said, if it should come to the attention of my associates that a significant deposit or withdrawal at the bank had been made without them being informed, then I believe our relationship will need reassessment and termination is most certainly the outcome, is that precise enough for you?" Merryman nodded, "I understand completely."

"And as for this" Copeland pointed to the bill Merryman had run-up in his club, "Let us say, as an act of goodwill, the balance remains as is, on hold unaffected on this occasion by any penalty and for good measure, to prove to you I am a man of foresight," Copeland wrapped the peach pip in the bill paper and then tossed it into his waste paper bin, it chimed like a bell, "you pay it when you can, but please not too long. In the meantime, give Hong the information of this skiing trip of yours, and now we have an agreement, please feel free to enjoy the facilities of the Senkin club, Hong will take you back there now if you wish and extend your credit accordingly." Copeland pointed to the door as he took from his drawer a new tin of Panther Sprint cigars and broke the seal with his fingernail.

"One other thing Mr Merryman..... the Irishmen, what can you tell me?" Merryman looked at Hong who was still sporting the damage to his face from the fire extinguisher, Sean had lobbed at him.

"Very little they turned up a few months ago, activating an account now they freelance for the bank, As for the men I used they know nothing about what happened, they were travelling in a separate lorry, they had made the arrangements themselves, they were the ones that delivered the Somalian container, my... my boss Salter-Kingsley believes they are IRA, concessionally they act as security couriers, that's it, the older one Sean is the brains, they are brothers, so they say,, but I doubt it is their real name." Merryman felt no allegiance to Sean and Connor, but it suddenly occurred to him, what they would do if they found it had been him that had almost got them killed.

"Are they? Interesting, I wonder why a couple of boys from the bog would decide to settle down here, thank you, please don't forget our talk, I shan't."

Merryman looked again to the cub girl Kelly, now sat in the hall, as he passed through and wondered what would happen to her as he left.

There were the echoes of the splashing of water and Copeland glanced through the double glass beaded doors that led off the study and towards the internal courtyard and poolside, seeing Suzy in the external steaming Jacuzzi, he raised a hand, and she raised a glass. He picked up the receiver of one of the three telephones on his desk, looking at the time in New York on one of the world clocks on the back wall of his room and having dialled the number he opened his top drawer and placed the receiver into a phone scrambler holder, taking out a small triangular speaker connected by a cable belonging to the machine in his draw.

"Operator 4452790, please hold." the woman on the other end of the line had a distinctive southern American accent, she paused then asked,

"Operator 4452790 line secure, confirm."

Copeland looked at the three lights on the scrambler and waited for them to change from red through orange and then to green.

"Operator 4452790 line secure confirmed," he said towards the speaker on his desk.

"Operator 4452790 please state your designation?" The operators' voice was almost monotone.

"Operator, Charlie Oscar Lola Alpha designation Craftwork." Copeland waited for the operator's confirmation of his call sign and to patch his call through, as the line rang on the other end he looked at the clock again and raised his eyes as he heard a male voice groan at answering the call at the other end obviously having been woken.

Copeland then heard the operator address his caller,

"Operator 4452790 Craftwork line secure contact, Charlie Oscar Lola Alpha, designation accept?"

The man at the other end of the line switched his bedside light on and got a slap on his back from his wife, lying beside him.

"Operator 4452790 this is Craftwork accept. Frank hold while I get up before Meg sticks me with one of her hair roller pins," he said as Meg shooed him off the bed with a kick of her heel.

He went through to his study and immediately lit a cigarette, then picking up the extension called for her to hang up, Copeland heard her fumble with the receiver then click on the line before speaking,

"Benj give my apologies to Meg will you, tell her I'll bring her some Swiss chocolate next time we have a face to face."

"Leave it out Frank, she's already cost me a fortune in slimming aids that are hiding in the garage, so what up Cola?"

Benjamin Carter-Wallis looked across his desk at the regimented display of his service memorabilia, and photo's chronicling his military career that hung on his wall, and specifically at a small colour photo, with dense jungle pictured in the foreground, of a squad of eight camouflaged U.S. Rangers posing hanging off a tank sporting various weapons, taken prior to their mission, from which three of his team did not return from.

"Thought you'd want to get on point before you get to the farm, the funds are still in play with your African boy, you'll have to go to the sweet shop if you don't want him to get that candy he's after." Copeland looked at the scrambler hearing Carter-Wallis groan.

"Well that's a shame, just once I'd like to get woken with some good news, thanks for the heads up." Carter-Wallis walked over to a world map and turned his attention to South America and Brazil and looked to the clock marked Cuba.

"Yer well it's not too late, he's still in town it will be messy, but it's doable, if you don't want him back home, save all that shit with the Jews. I take it your boys still have them spinning their heels in Rio with the carrots you gave them."

Copeland would have no issue killing Ali Hassan, the warlord had plenty of enemies in his homeland capable of mounting an overseas assassination, but it would probably mean to avoid suspicion falling in his direction he would need to tie up all loose ends, including Merryman and the Byrne brothers.

"No, you had your chance, Frank, we need Ali Hassan in play, we just don't want him spending his pocket money with our competitors, fuck!" Carter-Wallis looked back towards his bedroom, "forgetting Uncle Sam's farm business, the kickback would have been nice for Meg, she's got it into her head to visit London, apparently one of Queen Liz's brats is getting married next year, the daughter I think, I managed a foursome with our ambassador at Buck house, you should see Meg at the table, practising with her pinkie in the air, every time she drinks."

"I'm sorry Benj, if it's any consolation, this has cost me big time, too." Copeland sighed, knowing Meg may be married to a CIA chief and an ex-member of the LRRP's kill squad he once belonged to, but she wore the trousers in their house.

LRRP pronounced Lurps were members of Long Range Reconnaissance Patrols (often many were involved with covert security operations, including assassinations and on many occasions their work brought them into close contact with criminals often working both sides of the war, gun smugglers, people traffickers and the south eastern drug cartels of the Yakuza.)

It was towards the end of the Vietnam War, while serving in the US 75th Airborne Rangers as a LRRP Frank Copeland was recruited to the CIA, In particularly he was part of a team that went deep into enemy territory and created alliances with the opium dealers.

"Shit Frank, it is what is, I'll make some calls had hoped to keep the gas factory in South American in play for a rainy day. I suppose I'll have to settle for the German chefs in charge, that'll be something, don't fancy bringing them stateside, but what will be, as they say, there's always the bay for storage of this shit they've been brewing. I'll send in the teamsters to pick up any scrap and burn the shop. Tel Aviv will play a part, stirring the shit down there, no point keeping a dog like Mossad on the leash if you don't let them loose now and again" Carter-Wallis paused as he began to envisage the fallout from Copeland's failure. "Of course the Brazilian's will have to be brought on board now, and the Brits won't like not being invited to the party. Can't hold it back Cola you've thrown me a doozy of a curveball." Carter-Wallis snarled as he began to consider how many favours he would have to call in and looked along the wall of other framed photographs, in which he was pictured amongst high ranking military officers, government senators and past and present American Presidents.

There was a groan and loud curse that came from the direction of his bedroom and wife and his thoughts turned closer to home as he contemplated the loss of his back-hand commission he would have personally received from Copeland for his involvement in acquiring Ali Hassan's gold but that was the least of his concerns. The gold was destined to be used in the transaction by the Somalian warlord to purchase chemical weapons from a laboratory-based in Brazil set up by the Neo-Nazi group Spider and created by Doctor Josef Mengele and Doctor Merill Nestlar, overseen by Philipp Bouhler all Nazi's that served within the RPA and Aktion T4. The nerve agent weapons were intended to used by the warlord in staging a coup d'état in Somalia, that could see thousands dead. It was not that the CIA didn't want the wannabe dictator to have weapons and succeed, but they wanted him to buy American, thereby controlling the manner in which Ali Hassan usurped the crown of the existing dictator.

If Copeland's heist had been successful it would have placed Ali Hassan in a positive position to be receptive for cultivation as a CIA head-of-state asset and have boosted Carter-Wallis's place within the CIA, he had his eyes on the Chief Director's seat. Now Copeland's failure to remove the payment gold from, the equation and thereby prevent the weapons being purchase, would mean Carter-

Wallis, would have to intervene and stage an American based operation using CIA assets and US Seals, to acquire the chemical weapons and the scientist involved in making them before they are delivered to Somalia.

Carter-Wallis considered the US naval base at Guantanamo Bay, Cuba would be a possible storage site, but if the retrieval of the nerve agents was not an option, full termination would be necessary. Primarily because in obtaining the delivery of the weapons to his homeland Ali Hassan had negotiated a rite of passage from the east coast of Africa across the land to the west via the bordering African states of Zaire and Uganda, an alliance of sorts, something the CIA wished to discourage in the region. Divide and conqueror was still ever the motto, especially as the Russians were adding fuel to the fire with many African countries leaning towards Marxist-Leninist state rule.

What Carter-Wallis failed to tell Copeland and some of his superiors, running the whole South American operation as a private Black rogue operation, was that his section of the CIA had known for years of the whereabouts of Doctor Josef Mengele and his co-Nazi scientist and indirectly supported them in various facilities in developing a range of weapons. It was only when Carter-Wallis had discovered the German's had begun to export their wares, without consulting their main sponsor that the American decided it was time to rail them in fearing his rogue operation may go global, unaware that the CIA itself was already compromised by Spider Organization mole operatives.

In the meantime, Carter-Wallis had been leading Mossad a dance with false trails to prevent their capture of Mengele and his cohorts, even, with the assistance of members of INTERPOL allowing Mengele, *"The Angel of Death"* to return to his home in Günzburg, Bavaria on more than one occasion using CIA facilities.

Worst case scenario Frank Copeland's failure in Geneva could see weapons sponsored by the CIA used in a Somalian genocide. However in preventing this by destroying the evidence, it may just bring about a major international incident between the American's, Brazilian's and Israelis and may cost Copeland his position.

As Carter-Wallis listened to Copeland's explanation of what had gone wrong with the bank in Geneva he considered a plan of action and immediately realised it would have to involve an operation that would include the sacrifice of some of the German participants to appease the involvement of Mossad in the destruction of the chemical weapons facilities in Brazil, whilst preventing the discovery by the Brazilian government that the U.S had been involved in the production of the deadly

nerve agents in their country. Mossad's involvement on the guise of hunting down Nazi's, would act as a smokescreen to cover up the destruction of the site and would actually be a positive aspect in the removal of any products and personnel that could prove useful in future weapons developments for the American's.
He began to pencil one name Zavi, on his not pad that held the logo of the Oval Office Presidential seal.

"Well you know where I am, in the meantime, I'll spring for the tickets for Meg, as Dalton use to say there's another war over the next horizon. I'll fill the gap you know me, and I'll keep an eye for the German cooks if they turn up here. It's the least I can do." As Copeland spoke, Carter-Wallis's eyes turned back to the photograph of the US Ranger squad and the man they were centred around, the leader of their original LRRPS squad, Captain Dalton Brooks, one of those that were killed, shortly after the picture had been taken, in one of their last missions in Vietnam.
"Pretty big gap, your friends in the east won't be so easy to smooze, I take it you have that end covered, all that cutting fingers off, shit, disturbs my digestion when I sit and eat with them, which thankfully is not that often. Anyway I'm glad we kept this between us, look after yourself Frank, say hello to the girls and Frank if they do come knocking at your door with the bolt cutters, be sure to burn my number and torch the set you're on now. I have enough trouble holding my chipper and I'm not talking about golf." With that Carter-Wallis hung up and poured himself a bourbon, knowing his wife Meg would scold him if she smelt it on his breath when he got back to bed, but that was going to be the least of his concerns that day, he was going to have to call in some big markers to wipe the slate clean in Brazil.

In Geneva, Copeland smiled at his joke as he topped up his own drink and poured a second into a glass with ice as he considered the need to fulfil his promise not just to Carter-Wallis but also the Yakuza crime syndicate who had been expecting a share of the bounty, then he walked out to the courtyard pool area where Suzy was still listening to her eight-track in the Jacuzzi. Watching her, he began to consider the Byrne brothers and the part they had played in the fiasco of the hijacking of the container if he was going to avoid a similar occurrence he would need to know more about them.
"So you were entertaining Merry-Merry, I thought you were quiet at dinner, come on daddy, tell Suzy all about it, I promise I won't be cross." she said with a questioning smirk as Copeland shrugged and then stepped into the Jacuzzi fully clothed.

The next morning in the Metropolitan hotel in Geneva, Sean sat in the steam room and sighed with relief as two Swiss ladies got up to leave, having spent the last fifteen minutes listening to their sniggering, backstabbing of one of what Sean took to be their closest friends, whose daughter he understood had run away to join some sort of cult called the rainbow family in Guyana, taking their friend jewels. Sean poured water on the stones and lay back inhaling the eucalyptus scent, he sniffed his nails, and was happy that he had completely eradicated the slightest scent of the smell from his time in the container he mulled over the timber pine-clad box he now sat in, comparing it to the similar-sized space of his ordeal on board the ship, then he raised his head, turning an ear sensing something wrong there was no noise of other guest using the spa, raising his eyes to the glass door covered in condensation, he sat back as Hong appeared on the other side. Cornered, naked apart from his towel Sean stared in expectation of an attack as the cool air rushed into the room, but Hong stood back allowing Copeland to enter who was also stripped with a towel around his midriff and sat opposite Sean.

"I believe Hong has something to say to you, Mr Byrne." Copeland splashed water over his head as Sean looked at the suited Hong sweating profusely.

"Please accept my apologies, Mr Byrne." Hong avoided Sean's stare his tone as abrupt as if he had been asked to eat glass, he then got a raised eye from Copeland, and reluctantly Hong added, "Sean."

"Hong here has known my daughter since they were children, I think he considers her more than family, unfortunately, he has been known to be somewhat protective, I would like to assure you I was unaware of his actions, but I think it is likely you will need some convincing of the fact," Copeland added more water to the coals the heat swept over Sean's face, and he had to hold back a smile, looking at the suffering Hong.

"Well, you are not the first overzealous father I have had to deal with." Sean smiled, relaxing in the knowledge this was a social call by Copeland.

"Give it to him," Copeland ordered his most trusted bodyguard, and as Hong reached into his inside pocket Sean saw his white shirt was saturated as he pulled out two silver credit cards and handed them to Sean, then Copeland gestured with a nod allowing Hong to leave.

"My associates and I have a number of worldwide organisations dedicated to the fulfilment of hospitality, for you and your brother, platinum cards, giving entrance and ensuring exclusive benefits, ...free of charge." Copeland watched as Sean flicked the cards back and forth in his fingers then placed them on the side.

"That really is not necessary; I accept the apology, Mr Copeland." Sean knew no gift from this man would ever come without strings of barbed wire.

Copeland got to his feet, "Well keep it anyway, as a sign of good faith."
Sean was now convinced Copeland was involved with the container heist, this was too much of a coincidence, but why was he sociable, he had just lost millions? But he would love to have seen a look on Copeland's face when he opened that container and held back a smiled as he studied the cards.
"You know Mr Byrne, like many of your countrymen I have had little time for rules, especially those imposed by others, that said there is one I have never broken, concerning the fairer sex."
Sean looked up, quizzically.
"I have always made it my business never to keep them waiting, even when the meeting may be acrimonious, again a sign of good faith by a….overzealous father."
Copeland strummed his naked knee caps and then got up slowly and left.
Sean for a moment looking at the platinum card, nagged by his curiosity of Copeland's statement he showered and by the time he had dressed Copeland was already heading down the steps of the reception to his waiting white 1950's vintage Mercedes limousine, passing Connor in the corridor, who received a defiant glare from the still very hot and sweaty Hong and two of the men Connor and Sean had fought within the alley behind the club, including the one that still sported a sling to his arm. Nervously, expecting the worse, Connor picked up his step then slowed seeing Sean coming down the corridor from the spa and gym.
"I expected to find you face down in the pool," Connor said as the pair looked through the open dining room catching a wave from Suzy sitting by one of the tall windows that faced towards the lake.
"I don't know what game this yank is playing at, but it seems he just gave me his blessing with his daughter and an unexpected bonus for you." Sean showed him the platinum membership cards then handed him one.
"Do they serve the black stuff?" Connor said with a wink, "You have a good day with the girlie, I'm going to take a closer look at that gold bar of ours, I'll see you back at the boat sometime and maybe I'll get me some new threads seeing how they have worked for you." As Connor spoke of the bank, Sean's thoughts turned to Merryman again.
"Why not take a look at Merryman, spend a couple of days in his shoes and get the boat ready for fishing, I think maybe it's time we cleared the air, that could easily have been you on the other side of the tunnel Con, from now on I want the latch key on every time you leave the boat," Sean said referring to the booby trap explosive device designed to kill anyone that came snooping on board their boat.
"No problem, catch you later." Connor caught a smile from Suzy as he left.

"I take it that is your brother, he can join us if you wish, or with a call, I can find him a friend if you like?" As she spoke, Sean realised Copeland had taken the time to find out Connor was, in fact, his brother and that she knew about the altercation in the alley behind the club, but of course, she would, he thought

"Another time, perhaps, he has some errand, besides his table manners are terrible, that said I'm not sure where to start." Sean gestured to the number of cutlery before him.

They both ordered smoked salmon with scrambled eggs and coffee when the waiter approached and sat making small talk eating their breakfast, as the tone s of Vivaldi's four seasons played softly in the background from hidden speakers as outside the window the city of Geneva began another industrious day.

She waited for him to bring up the topic of her father, while he wondered if she knew about the container heist.

Suzy broke the ice. "He told me what Hong did, the other night, he has always been like that, including with my sisters, my real brother was killed, Hong has no family except my father." the way she talked it was as if it was an unnatural thing to have normal biological parents.

Sean must have looked confused because she then went on to explain that Copeland, Frank Theodore Copeland, had adopted her and her sisters while still a Colonel serving of the US 75th Airborne Rangers towards the end of the Vietnam. War. Suzy then detailed how Copeland who had been designated with the CIA codename COLA, had become connected with the Yakuza during his time serving Uncle Sam and that on leaving one of the establishments he had been using as a front, catering for the hospitality of the troops, before it was overrun he secured the release of five children, including Hong that he adopted and also what Suzy did not know at the time, was on board the Bell "Huey" helicopter she was crammed into on leaving Saigon, there was a significant amount of Cocaine.

Although he still held connections within the CIA as a freelance operator, Copeland's association with the Yakuza became a point of concern whist still holding a visible rank, so he retired permanently to a life of crime one of the few westerners to have achieved the rank of Oyabun *(Boss)*, now he acted more as an advisor to the crime syndicate and assisting with overseas money laundering, through Switzerland, semi-retired, or so that is what he led his daughters to believe.

"Well, that's the story he tells everyone, most of its BS" she looked deep into his eyes as if looking for some judgement from him on her tale.

"What so you didn't come stateside on a bag of china white?" Sean didn't blink.

"No that parts true, the rest who knows, the boys are certainly clan, they wouldn't be up to scratch back home, mmm perhaps Hong would, but like I say Daddy is supposed to be retired." She had a way of describing something as sinister as the Yakuza as if she was ordering from a dessert menu a sorbet.

"Is that why you have that." he gestured to her the red tattoo on her hand.

"Daddies idea, makes it easy dealing with the occasional idiot, he's covered in them, head to toe, you must have noticed...in the sauna, he's addicted to it, personally I think he is going through what they call a mid-life crisis, I noticed yours the other day, army?" she said sipped her black tea.

"What makes you think that?" Sean choked, he had met Copeland only twice but he reminded him more and more of some of the serious old men from back home and now he knew he was a retired US Ranger, bearing in mind the company he now kept, retirement seemed unlikely for someone like him, that much he knew was BS.

"We have clubs in Paris and Monaco, for years he has been winding down, happy to let me and the girls with Hong watch over things lately he seems restless, I have a feeling he is getting involved with his old friends." She flashed her long eyelashes at him as if trying to convince him.

"No, sorry you misunderstand, I meant my tattoo's what makes you think they are army," he said, pouring himself another coffee and offering her a cigarette.

"Dates, most of the men I know who carry that type of thing it's normally a child's birthday, with no children no wife, it's normally something else, the first kill, a battle and they looked like army ink, that or prison?" she winked.

"Sorry, nothing as interesting, I got pissed up we got pissed up when we were kids, me and Con we support the greatest club in the world, Liverpool, you know, football." he made the action of heading a ball.

"The dates are the F.A. finals 63-64 and 65-66 and the final scores, as I said nothing as interesting as your pops, on both occasions me and the kid had, had a few too many bevies, drinks, daft now I come to think of it." Sean's smile was disarming, and his accent and language made her laugh as he deliberately deflected the attention away from himself. Like an itch from an old mosquito bite he wanted to scratch again, he began to feel Suzy was digging too deep, allowing someone to get close would mean lies, Uncle, Brian O'Connell, had taught them you have to have a great memory to lie, "You may be smart boyo, Seany, but smarts count for shit between the sheets, when the little fella's doing all the think'in." He would tell them, and even though he now knew Uncle had lied to them all their lives, he still found himself, living by his lessons. Even noticing how his heart raced when he saw a British flag, but now he no longer felt the need to spit.

He looked at Suzy's tattoo as he poured cream in his coffee and wondered what lies her adopted father had told her and what she would do for him.

"As for your ...Daddy, perhaps he needs a hobby." Sean smiled, now totally convinced it was Copeland that had made the hit on the container, she did not know was the only question and then she confirmed it.

"Seriously, Sean, I don't know what you do with the banker Merryman, but I would be careful, Hong is not as bad as some of the company my father keeps, sure he breaks a few heads, but that's it." she placed her hand across the table on his, and he could see she was sincere, "they still send the hired help from home, when things get serious."

"Well I doubt our paths will cross in business, let's hope he takes up golf, or fishing, that reminds me I have a small boat if you ever wish to go out on the lake, it's nothing fancy, you will have to give me notice so I can get Con to clean up his stuff." He smiled.

"So you don't live here?" he caught the disappointment in her tone, "I meant I thought you stayed here had a room?"

"No ... well yes, I've got a room, I just come here to relax, use the gym, but I have a small suite actually it's on the third floor great views, would you like to see." her smile cut straight to the answer he wanted.

Thirty-five minutes and 23 seconds later, he had her pinned beneath his chest as they climaxed together, her thighs clamping his hips to hers with her legs crossed over his rump as he erupted inside her, she was still wearing her stilettos.

They spent most of that morning discovering the individuality of each other's body and by the time they showered together her teeth marks etched the fine ribbon scar to his left shoulder caused by a ricochet bullet in the Libyan training camp and he realised how turned on he was by her nipple piercings, which were now sore from his teeth teasing. They had two attempts at trying to get dressed again that failed and ended with them taking another shower together.

Sex with her was like a triathlon and they used every piece of furniture to prop rest and balance on, breaking one of the legs off a low foot stall as she balanced on her back while he held her legs high with one arm, around ten o'clock she called the club and told Dom she was taking the night off, then Sean allowed her to order a selection of Thai curries as take-in, in revealing he had never had a jungle curry before she was surprised, at Sean's appetite for the hottest dishes.

Unfortunately the last few days caught up with Sean around eleven-thirty and with dishes still between them on the bed, unusual for him, with someone he hardly knew at his side, he drifted asleep. Suzy looked to his clothes, his jacket hung over a chair where she knew he kept his wallet and then to the holdall Connor had brought him. She watched him sleep and turned on the TV a dubbed episode of Kojak was playing and for a change the producer of the show had chosen a voice-over that held almost the same husky velvet tones of Telly Savalas, but she switched the sound off, so as not to disturbed Sean and by morning she would know three more things about Sean Byrne apart from the fact he was a good fuck, that he carried a Glock revolver, had a trucker's license and had recently been to Libya.

When Connor had left his brother at breakfast earlier that day, he had stood for a while on the steps of the Metropolitan as he smoked and examined the platinum Senkin membership card Sean had given him, he noticed how the doorman gave him a look each time he stepped out to welcome other well-dressed visitors to the hotel. Connor wore an off the peg black suit most of the time they were on bank assignments, but standing in his jeans and Harrington green jacket, he considered an upgrade and tucked the Senkin card wallet.

Merryman saw Connor arrive in the bank and although he was still rattled by his meeting with Copeland, as Sean was not with him, he decided he might use the opportunity to see if there was any indication the brothers considered he or Copeland had been involved with the container hijacking.

Once he discovered the reason for Connors visit to the bank, to pick up cash from their account 10,000 US dollars and to visit the vault to see the gold deposit, Merryman chose to give him the grand tour himself and then invited him to lunch.

"So you and your brother, you enjoy living in Geneva?" Copeland watched as Connor tore a chunk out of the largest American style burger on the menu of the Spring Brother Irish Bar on Rue de Coeval then washed it down with a gulp of his pint of Guinness

"Yes and I like this place I've never been here, you know all this stuff on the wall the bling-bling, flags pictures and stuff from Ireland, its different to back home most pubs are dark shit holes you're lucky if you get a jukebox, but the black stuff makes up for it and our girls." He raised his glass then downed the remains of his pint.

"I thought you might like it, another of your countrymen a shipbroker who banks with us, he told me about this place, but this is the first time I have had … the black stuff here, I am more a lager man. Skol!" Merryman looked at his glass still half full and then at Connor's two empty pint glasses as he ordered a third, amazed at the Irishman's capacity and the fact he seemed to be speeding up. "So I understand that was a close thing your trip from Genoa, the bank has used a contact apparently the Italian police have no leads, but they think it was organized crime." Merryman did not catch the look through the froth at the bottom of his glass, Connor gave him, he turned away, raising his glass to the waitress signalling another pint.

"Yer well shit happens, that why your banks paying us, I guess." He thanked the girl that arrived with his drink.
"I understand you saw the men that were attacked but not the attack itself?" Merryman's approach was ham-fisted as Connor finished his meal.
"Yep, it was all over by the time we came by, no one about except the police, whoever it was they were well trained, probably ex-army." Connor smiled, seeing Merryman click his fingers for the bill.
"Why do you say that?" Merryman looked at Connor's tattoo and wondered if they had any army significance.
"Well it didn't look like the black fella's had a chance to grab their guns, as I said shit happens but this shit was well planned." Connor raised his eyebrow.
"You can take care of that sort of thing can't you?" he stared accusingly into Merryman's eyes, there was an uncomfortable pause as he waited for him to squirm and blink away, "the bill, you can take care of the bill, put it on the bank's expense account, eh" Connor smiled and slapped the relieved banker on the arm.
"Yes, of course."
Merryman gushed a smile, taking a gulp of his beer.
"Excellent, a wee chaser for the road then, that was some good scrum filled the spot, must bring the bro here." Connor gave a cheeky grin as he ordered them each a Jameson's, but when they arrived fearing the alcohol might take hold of his wits, Merryman refused his, announcing he had to get back to work from his extended lunch break and Connor happily downed both in quick succession.
Irrespective of having consumed twice as much drink as the banker, Connor faculties were completely intact, and by the time they parted on the main shopping parade, Connor was convinced Merryman had been involved in the attempted heist. He watched the banker for a moment as he disappeared in the crowded street full of busy shoppers and tourist, then looked up at the shop window display in front of him and staggered a little as he examined the suited mannequins in a gentleman's tailor shop window, he felt for cigarettes and found his wallet opening it he looked at the platinum Senkin card.
"Have you fella's ever seen the film Goldfinger?" he said, ignoring the tailor's disdainful glance as he raised his eyes at the old fashioned doorbell.
"Yes Sir," the tailor called his colleague from the back room, possibly for support Connor smelt like a distillery, at first he blinked seeing the two tailors standing side by side he thought he was seeing double.
"Are you two brothers?" Connor realized the men were twins and they confirmed it with a nod introducing themselves as David and Elias Coe.

"I have a brother, he always looks smarter than me, I said today I'll be changing that, so here I am" Connor looked around at the manikins and cloth samples.
"So Sir's after a suit, we only make handmade suits here Sir," one tailor said and was echoed by his brother
"Handmade suits Sir."
"Well, that good, because I want the suit you're man Connery wears, light grey." Connor went over to the cloth samples and as he bent over his jacket rose up just enough to reveal the distinct bulge of the revolver tucked into the back of his jeans waistband
"Do you mean and Anthony Sinclair conduit cut two-piece suit Sir?" he gestured his brother to the gun as Connor turned his head.
"Is that the one he wears when he's driving that car of his, the one with the guns in the lights?" Connor sensed their nervousness and turned back to the glass cabinet display counter.
"Yes sir, I believe so, we like the cinema, don't we Elias." the tailor looked to the busy street.
"Well, I want one made the same cut." with that Connor took out one of the wads of dollars from his pocket and placed it on the counter, and both men's spectacles dropped down to their noses as they looked over their glasses with an eager glint in their eyes.
"Yes we like the cinema especially James Bond, David." their manner immediately changed as Elias went to the front door and changed the open sign to closed as David came round to Sean and began sizing him up with his measuring tape, and with a flick of his wrist jotted measurements into a tiny black pad.
"Can I ask would Sir require additional support for ones instruments?" one brother looked at Connor's waist and Connor turned back, at first not understanding, then smiled as he pulled his revolver free from his back, "Yer, I suppose that makes sense 007 carries a gun, doesn't he." he looked at it and placed it on the counter. The tailors chuckled together and then set about their work that afternoon, while Connor accepted their advice and allowed them to bring into their shop a select group of highly skilled craftsman to preen him with a full gentleman's makeover, which included a replacement, pigskin revolver shoulder holster with spare magazine holders.
"And to complete your ensemble" Elias offered forward a mahogany box with green velvet lining that held a black .38 Walther PPK revolver.
"We thought Sir would appreciate how complimentary the original instrument sits as per Mr Connery's character, in comparison to." David looked at Connor's Colt revolver.

"You guys, you shouldn't have" David and Elias looked at each other considering for a spit second were they about to be robbed, then Connor's lips broke to a smile, "I'm joking boys, I'll wear it to go." Connor hit the safety slide lock on the revolver and chambered a round. "Bag my shit up gentleman and no receipts." he winked. "Glad to be of service, Sir." the tailors both bowed as Connor began to count out his money.

Chapter 12: The Rod

Muswell Hill, London
July 1974

Albert Gordon sighed as he sat for a moment in his Austin Wolseley Six looking at the overgrown front garden at 72 Muswell Avenue, where Pimm's gold and black vinyl roof 3 litre mark1 Ford Granada Ghia coupe sat festooned with bird droppings on the drive, alongside the rose borders that he knew were once so well-tended and now were being strangled by nettles and weeds, what few yellow petals there were lay bleached and browning.
June had taken great exception ensuring the garden was looked after during their time in Paris. It was suppose to have been a twelve month assignment for Pimm as a Raleigh department Scalphunter running Mi6 Paris, but the man who was due to replace him was shuffled up to sit on the Compass table and became head of Cook Department in Hong Kong, when there was a change in the head of Mi6, and John Rennie became Control. Pimm, remained assigned to Raleigh and during this time, worked on various operations for Department Drake from their Paris base but also assisted other Mi6 departments with regards their own personal requirements when their operators were involved in activities in the region, on occasion when asked he assisted with Bull's operations, off radar from his main Mi6 duties.
Regardless of June Pimm's illness it was one of the happier times for the couple and Pimm would have been happy for it to continue, until June had to return to London to begin chemo therapy at the Royal Free hospital in Hampstead. During this time Pimm was fortunate, Jem Stapleton was still head of Drake and because of the way Pimm had handled Paris, when Pimm requested to stand down as a member of Raleigh, because of compassionate issues of caring for his wife Stapleton supported his request along with Bull Gordon and Rennie agreed to allow Pimm to be assigned to Drake in London, where he continued to work until February 1973, when there was a behind the scenes a gentleman's agreement made between Rennie and Pimm in the Wheelhouse, which allowed Pimm to take extended leave with June illness having progressed to its terminal state.
John Rennie's son, Charles and his daughter-in-law were arrested for allegedly importing a large quantities of heroin from Hong Kong, it was a set up by a foreign agency believed to be the Chinese although Rennie considered rogue elements of the CIA may have had a hand in it, however it made the New York Times and Rennie was forced to resign shortly afterwards, but not before he had agreed with

Pimm, Because Pimm had many contacts in the region and was not strictly assigned to Mi6 Cook Department, that he would fly to Hong Kong and bring back his son and daughter-in law, so that they could be remanded safely in custody at the Old Bailey, which they were in February 1973.

Pimm was allowed to stand down as a Sandman from Drake, although he continued to show his face within Century house working with Drake he was effectively decommissioned as an Assertive Field Operative, during Junes illness until her death in May 1974, as yet he had not returned to his office, fortunately a network of his most ardent supporters within the service had been covering his absence, including Jeremy Stapleton of Drake, Bernie Martin of Hudson and of course Bull, but time was now up, something close to home needed his attention.

"June, June...." Bull grizzled with despair, "Sorry old love, forgive me, I took my eye off the ball," he whispered, "BP old boy, you've let yourself go."

As he rang the doorbell looking down at the pile of junk mail and unread free Weekly Advertiser papers on the floor and heard movement inside a shadow lifted the edge of the dusty net curtains in the bay window. Pimm looked out as Bull withdrew a bottle of Gordon's gin and a brown paper bag containing two lemons from his battered old alligator skin briefcase that in a previous life held some of the country's most sensitive state secrets, before that it was Louisiana alligator one of the first harvested from the Rockefeller alligator refuge centre. Bull listened and waited while the front door latches were unlocked.

"I was in the neighbourhood, so to speak." Bull followed Pimm through to the rear parlour and passed a made-up bed, the room in which his wife June had spent her last months at home, no longer well enough to climb the stairs. It had remained as it was the day they took her out in a body bag, an oxygen bottle beside the nightstand the Daily Mail open on a half-finished crossword they were sharing the night before she passed and a china cup with the dried remnants of the last roses Pimm picked for her from their garden.

Pimm pointed to the patio doors "I'll get some ice, I was out back."

Bull bit his lip and said nothing, slowly moving past the end of the bed and placed the bottle on a small table between two beach deck chairs on the small terrace at the back of the house, he could see from the blanket Pimm had most likely been sleeping there. Pimm handed him a glass with ice and tonic, as he sliced the lemon Bull had brought with him.

"So just passing?" Pimm said raising his glass as Bull topped it up with gin, Pimm stirred it with a teaspoon, handing it to Bull he gestured to the newspaper, Bull moved to sit.

"That was bad business in Aldershot, is this, what this is? I thought you were off the heavy list, retired to your pet project." Pimm appeared to have a whole rain forest of Sunday newspapers each detailing the IRA bombing at the Aldershot barracks on the 22nd February. Seven died when a car-bomb parked outside the officers' mess detonated. 6 women civilian cleaners and 1 army Chaplain were killed, 18 were injured.

"Someone screwed up, not jumping on Jenkinson sooner, he was mentioned in three files, Special Branch had a sniff at him when one of their operations tagged all the members at a CDRCU meeting." *(Committee to Defeat Revisionism, for Communist Unity)*

The original Irish Republican Army member was captured after the car used was traced to two members who implicated Noel Jenkinson as the bomber of the barracks. A former Protestant, he had already drawn the attention of Mi6 as a member of both the Marxist-Leninist group CDRCU and the Communist Party of Great Britain, two more bombs were discovered in his garage he was sentenced to life but died in prison of an alleged heart attack having served 4 years.

"But no Pimm, in answer to your question Control keeps me about as an old friendly face gives me a bell whenever there's a pre 60's enquiry and the other boys on the top floor call me up when they want to pick my brains, but only when their computers have crashed, other than that I'm still looking for Hitler's treasures, dodging Mossad. Truth is as you know it's more about the legacy the Nazi's left behind, just like the top floor and any boardroom director knows, it's all about the networking, now terrorist groups from our emerald cousins break bread with Arabs in training camps on the banks of the Indus in Pakistan while Russian Spetsnaz train Cuban's in Argentina how to use weapons, supplied by French arms dealers and the web of Spider has strands running all the way back to Langley. At most my little team help fill the gaps with the other departments if they have something on and they need eyes or a hand, but they still let me just do my thing, quite a low key affair really and we don't exactly break the piggy bank?" Bull looked over, studying Pimm's face, judging he would soon pick up that he was not there just to talk about old times and offer sympathy. But for a few seconds Bull considered he was on a fool's errand, Pimm looked out of shape, he had clearly lost weight since last he saw him and his stubble face aged him, drawing you into his bleak eyes, making his direct stare furtive and edgy, hardly someone that could blend anonymously into a crowd.

"That said, you know me, being old guard I tend to poke my nose where it's not wanted now and then ruffle a few feathers, gets my blood stirring." Bull looked for a spark of curiosity, but Pimm stared ahead, watching the strands of the large willow at the end of his garden drift back and forth.

"So that what this is." finally he said wistfully, taking a cigarette from his packet and lighting it, "I knew they'd send someone, can't have British taxpayers money wasted. Sitting around, there's a war somewhere we have to start, stop or fuel?" he said with a churlish grin.

Pimm had taken a four-week compassionate leave of absence following June's death, and it had now been four months. In that time he had shaved and dressed to report back three times, and the furthest he'd got was to place his key in the front door to double lock it and leave, only to pause and go back inside.

"Well you know they like to get their money's worth, besides forgetting the bog, we're kind of up to our neck in it at the moment. Russians, East German's even the French are being an arse selling their wares to the wrong sorts as I said, Africa and South American's it's like giving a baby a grenade expecting them not to pull the pin, as for the Yanks they just want to bomb the hell out of anything red." Bull registered a trace of a smile on Pimm's lips.

"Look why not let me take you for a jolly good fry up, and I'll fill you in, it's nothing major, something I need a hand with maybe just the thing to get you back in the driving seat." Bull watched as Pimm refilled his glass and then offered him the bottle.

"Go on, I know I'll regret it, get it over with Bull, then I'll decide if I can face a breakfast." Pimm got up and began to walk down the garden path slowly, and Bull followed him.

"It's probably nothing, but I had two of my youngsters, check out a lead, their on Daily Express press pass legends, investigating a report that came in from Rio, three elderly German's seen in a bar along with a third younger man black, possibly Ugandan, Somali. Thing is one of the German's was reported by this ex-pat RAF Captain as being a ringer for Josef Mengele." Bull handed him two black and white holidays snap taken by the airman that pictured his wife and child, caught over their right shoulders, on a table behind were the four men. Pimm studied the image as Bull handed him a magnified blow-up of the men in the background.

"It's not the best, but we had a fellow do an age construction on the last images we have on him,"

"Could be." Pimm agreed, "Did the RAF chap follow it up in any way?"

"No apparently the Captain was keen as mustard, but they were on a cruise excursion. Probably just as well, these old kraut's still value their privacy, the idea a Brit family was caught up in this sort of thing would have been a shit storm, so I sent two of mine to take a look-see." Bull took from his bag two MI6 personnel files, one held the name Neil Lamb and the other Nicola Cartwright.

Pimm lifted his eyes, from the photograph, knowing Bull's people were, for the most part, not tactical field agents like himself.

"Where exactly was this?" he said, handing them back and taking a drink.

"That's the thing, bold as brass in the daylight can you believe, in the bar from that song Ipanema the girl from." and Bull hummed a couple of bars of the chorus from the song, "The Girl from Ipanema" by Antônio Carlos Jobim and Vinicius de Moraes.

"I know it, I took June there, as you know, Montenegro Street, Veloso bar-café, she liked the steak dish, we went twice," Pimm's eyes glazed over as he remembered a steal band arriving outside their window as they ate their meal and June making him hand over a tip, "I can't believe you thought I'd want to go back without her. Send someone else Bull, I'm a fucking Sandman last time I looked unless they've dropped my service level?" Pimm stared ahead at the willow remembering times when he and June sheltered from light rain in its shroud on the old wooden bench at its trunk, holding out to the last moment before the heavens opened to dash inside.

"Yes BP you are, look I knew you'd be like this and I'm sorry old fruit. You know how desperately sad I was about June. But here's the thing, I did send someone else, on the QT, someone from Scott department, he was in the area tying up a loose end with some Cubans and the Argentinean arms dealer Lucas Santiago again some shit the French have been stirring up about the Falklands, starting their own private arms race down there. I seem to remember you caught a whiff of him in Portugal in 1970, 71." Bull watched Pimm's eye's and saw for the first time since arriving, a spark of interest.

"I know Santiago, low-level was trying to make a buck with the MFA *(Portuguese military)* tried to throw out the replacement to President Salazar after his death, I remember then he had backers, friends in DGSE." *(French secret service)*

Pimm turned back, looking at the house, it seemed to Bull that his old friend was waking from a dream as he studied the home that had once so pristinely been kept by his wife and since her death had been allowed by him in a short time to become untidy in appearance. Pimm began to pull bindweed vines down from the backroom porch that entwined the wrought iron detail to the post. Bull took off his jacket, and his shoulder holster sidearm, wrapped it in its leather sling and lay it on the table and then loosening the buttons on his tartan waistcoat, he joined in the gardening, as Pimm detailed an operation just over two years earlier, where he had helped thwart a military coup, by assassinating two of the principal instigators involved with the arms deal.

"He may have run with big boys once, but I clipped his wings," Pimm had intercepted the delivery of Russian weapons Santiago had arranged, and an arms dealer who fails to deliver soon loses his reputation. He was now considered a low category subject and both Pimm and Bull had heard behind closed doors whispers that the CIA had him in their pockets as an informant. It was the last major field assignment Pimm took before taking time to remain in service in the UK while he helped nurse June through her short chemotherapy period.

"I miss this, gardening, having the flat." Bull said as he wiped the sweat from his forehead on a tea towel, Pimm offered him.

Bull lived alone apart from his cat Dave, that was in fact female, in a gated two-bedroom apartment formed from a converted Georgian four-storey detached building called Mansion House on Abercorn Place, just off Abbey Road, St. Johns Wood. Unbeknownst to the other tenants who jointly shared the responsibility of maintaining the walled communal garden according to their lease, Bull owned the freehold of the building. He was happy with the penthouse, which amongst other things, could if need be accommodate the landing of a helicopter on its reinforced flat roof. He had not ventured into the gardens for many years as he considered them no longer private, with any plans for design or care being overturned by another tenant, irrespective of their good intent. The only gardening he ever did now was watering his precious cacti collection in his office.

But both with sleeves rolled up and joining each other occasionally whistling the same tune, the two friends soon made short work of the overgrowth and bundled it at the end of the garden. Whilst all the time Bull kept one eye on Pimm, seeing he was thinking over the conversation earlier.

"So who did you send, who was on Santiago?" Pimm knew Bull had let him take stock, as his mind began to reboot during the physical exercise, lighting a cigarette he tossed a match into the bracken that immediately began to flare and crackle.

"Well again, that's the thing, it was your boy." Bull took a step back as the flames briefly raised high sending flakes of ash twirling to the sky, Pimm tilted his head back and took a deep breath, realising the reason behind Bull's visit.

"Of course it would be." he shook his head, and once the fire died down, he headed back to the deck chairs.

Although their paths had crossed at Century House, he had not seen Bob Gregory for two years. After Cyprus Bob had breezed through SAS training at Hereford and then went on to the Mi6 tradecraft base on Guernsey and joined the ranks of the "No noise" brigade, becoming an assassin, Sandman just like his recruitment officer Oliver Pimm.

Because Pimm had been responsible for his Mi6 enlistment, irrespective he and June never had children of their own, Bob Gregory would always be referred to within their company as his boy, his own *"Lost boy"* There was for some in the service no higher professional respect than that held between members that shared this relationship. But for Pimm, as with Bull possibly because both having never had children, there was a closer bond, hardly ever touched on by another or called into question except at times such as this.

"Your people, how long have they been AWOL?" Pimm asked spooning out the last small pebbles of ice from the bowl he had used then refilled his glasses with fresh lemon.

"About a week, understand I'm not running with boys like you these days, this was a courtesy, I called Bob answered, London had little to say in it, kept his handler informed of course Pete Wakefield is Shackleton Department now, it could have been yours if you wanted it, anyway, you've worked with him before in Paris, top man."

"Yes, he's a tidy sort, not one to let the baton slip. So he was running this thing, the Santiago Op. in Chile and where was Bob when you called on the favour?" Pimm scratched at his chin and tried to check his reflection in his glass realising how he must look, unshaven in an all blacks rugby shirt he had not changed for over a week, he wiped the sweat from his brow catching a whiff of his armpit body odour, Bull caught his reaction, but his frown held back his own embarrassment.

"He was waiting with a snatch team at the warehouse in San Bernado. Santiago never showed to take the arms on the exchange, last I heard the Cubans are still sitting on the guns at the docks in Valparaíso. Apparently touting word to an interested South American drug cartel as we speak, the Yanks have pulled rank, so Bob's absence to do a bit of moonlighting for me was no biggie." he said expecting a reprisal of some sort, which he received.

"Well, it's hardly round the corner Bull." Pimm tried not to sneer, but it still came out sarcastic, and he knew it. "Sorry, you're the first I've spoken to, apart from the Turk that runs the Café. Come on old man, you can buy the fry up and tell me which ways up on this thing and when I'm leaving. Then I'll tell you how I want this place tidied up while I'm away. Control's been on at me to upgrade with some cameras for years. I didn't want them here working while June was ill, while they're here they can give the frames and sills a coat."

Bull pulled into the small lay by of shops and parked directly outside the A1 café on Muswell Hill, before the entrance bell had stopped chiming the owner Boris had poured Pimm his black tea, giving the bag just four dunks and thrown three fresh rashers of bacon on the flat grill for Pimm's usual all-day breakfast configuration.
"Mr Pimm," he gestured welcoming with a nod "And you?" he said, looking to Bull, who studied the menu board briefly then, smelt the bacon already crisping,
"The same with a black coffee, no sugar."
"Please, take a seat gentleman, sugars on the table." he then reached below his counter and handed Pimm a bottle of Grouse whisky.
"The usual?" Bull raised an eye to Pimm.
"I'm off sugar, and I hate sweeteners." Pimm acknowledged Boris, who then shouted passed them in Turkish to an old man smoking at a window table to give up his seat for them. Which his father did muttering a welcome to them, "Please Sir, sit, sit" he said picking up his ashtray and Boris's oldest daughter arrived and having wiped the table down first replaced it with a clean one before they had settled in their chairs.
"Morning Mr Pimm." she smiled as she laid the cutlery and a copy of the Sun newspaper.
"Morning Alim" Pimm thanked her in Turkish as she placed their drinks down.
"Family business, ex-army they came over from Antalya before Cyprus he married a Brit holidaymaker in his teens." Pimm said as he poured a splash of the grouse into his cup ad then offered it to Bull, "still got a brick through the window, the foods fresh and we can talk of sorts, just make sure you leave a little on your plate, or he'll force you to have more, that's unless you want more, but you won't." Pimm was clearly was a respected regular customer and looked out of the window watching the people drift by. He felt uncommonly out of sorts like a fish in a glass bowl but realised by the way Bull sat comfortably with his rear to the glass he still trusted him to cover his back, then he remembered the large mirror behind Boris.
"First, I need to know something." Bull raised his eyes briefly scanning the room behind Pimm and Pimm immediately knew what was coming as he lifted the edge of the paper pretending to read.
"The old man that got up what brand?" Bull quizzed.
"Number 6, two left in the packet" Pimm answered in a snap and carried on looking ahead but gave a slight shake of his head.
"Just the people?" Bull checked the second hand of his watch as he took a sip of coffee.

"Three women 2 blonde's, 1 brunette, five men 3 dark hair, 1 grey, 1 bald including the old man, all sitting, 3 women all brunettes, 2 men both dark hair, standing," Pimm recalled who was behind him without turning around

"Two tables over your right shoulder the woman?" Bull tilted his head, showing he was taking a better look over Pimm's right shoulder.

"Early thirties, white, grey sweater, pink t-shirt blue jeans, black trainers, blue nail varnish reading her star signs in the Express, she's a Gemini, and she's over my left shoulder in the aisle seat on the third row back her order number is twenty-three." There was a ping of a bell

"Twenty three," Alim called, and Pimm could not resist a smile as the women raised her hand to receive her lunch.

"What did she order?" Bull asked, looking at the plate being served.

"Beans on toast, it was the only thing Boris was cooking when we came in, we were number twenty-four," Pimm said, holding up his ticket.

"Last thing, your friend the chef what's strange about the third knife on the rack beside his work station." Bull watched Pimm's eyes had no tells as Pimm gestured he already knew it was a Kukri fruit knife from a Ghurkhas knife set.

"He uses it to sharpen the yellow pencil behind his right ear." With that as if on cue, Boris performed the action.

"So you haven't totally fallen asleep in civvy land," Bull said and without being announced their order was served to the table.

"Teşekkür ederim," Bull said to Alim, she already knew Pimm spoke Turkish but was surprised to hear another westerner use her language and curtseyed.

"This is an old friend, Bull, this is Boris's oldest daughter." Pimm introduced her in Turkish.

"He keeps the main blade of that Ghurkha set resting on two screws to the right beneath the till counter, to deter unwelcome suitors for his daughter and in case those that broke his window are stupid enough to decide to return when he is in." Pimm watched as Bull began to tuck into his meal as the girl deposited two plates each with two slices, half with toast and half with bread and butter.

"Tell me about Bob," Pimm asked.

"Gregory not much to say, he's" Bull rechecked his watch, "Three days, eight hours of reservation and the embassy have not seen hide nor hair of him. His agreed contact window to report on the operation in Cuba is closing. Could be he's still in the field, but then I have my youngsters that are missing, they were just to get eyes, no contact, on our German friends, it's ten days since their line dropped. Brazil's a funny old place to get lost as you know an hour bus ride from Rio and you could be on the moon, I'd like to hope they are all tip-top, it is their rainy season." Bull

restrained showing his concern, but Pimm knew two streets back from the beach in Rio, a westerner could disappear up the stairs to the Favela never to be seen or heard of again. Each had their own street gangs warring with each other over territory control, as much as they did with the authorities while also vying to act as a protection support service for criminal groups visiting the country such as members of the Nazi Spider organization. Pimm considered it could be that one of the gangs was responsible for the disappearance of the Mi6 operatives. But Bob Gregory was a Sandman, a one-man army that would have caused hell before being taken down. The local authorities would have been counting bodies. Something would have been reported if he had been caught in an exchange. It didn't make sense to Pimm.
"I take it from that little teaser you think six will want me to go prove I can still shoot straight up on the hill if I agree to go for you," Pimm asked between mouthfuls.
"No, that won't be necessary, I had you signed over to my section the first day your convalescence ended." Pimm stopped making a sandwich with his bacon and a half slice of bread, clearly surprised at Bull's statement of covering for his unauthorised extended absence and raised two fingers and pointed to their cups gesturing refills to their cups to Boris.
"Monty has been filling in your weekly's, at the moment you are up in Edinburgh castle checking out a new safe site, something Control stuck on my desk, the old prisons has been earmarked as a retreat just in case someone decides to press the button. The jobs on the books, but she really has a flair for the imaginative anyway your pensions covered." Bull smiled.
"So why now, Bull? Why have you left it three days, you could have picked up the phone, called me to take a look-see, left Bob out of this, especially as I have experience with Spider." Pimm studied Bull's face.
"You know why, June, standard bereavement period of four weeks to get over the love of your life seems hardly cricket in my book. As to why now, well, that BP is a little simpler. It's because our Israeli friends have sent another team down as of yesterday, they are planning another snatch and grab like Eichmann, I got a heads up from an old sort on their board, General Zavineski, who got wind I already had a hunting party in the area, he was just letting me know, avoid any blue on blue." Bull held up his cup towards Alim requesting another coffee, but she missed the eye contact.
"Me too please." Pimm held his like he was ringing a bell and Boris gestured his daughter to replenish their drinks.
Once she had stepped away taking the empty toast plates Bull explained his contact Zavineski as a member of the Mossad Israeli intelligence executive and had reached out as a professional courtesy to inform him that a team of four agents

were in play to capture the Germans, but if it turned out to be Josef Mengele an assassination was authorized, Tel Aviv, his call to Bull was to avoid any conflict with the three Mi6 agents they had discovered were already in Rio.

"So what did my sector chief say when you seconded me four weeks ago?" Pimm asked, but he already knew there were few in the service that would refuse a request from Bull.

"What Berni Martin, we had a chat as you do outside the Spaniard's pub, he's made the move north of the river, Hampstead now did you know, not a million miles away from the Yanks safe house which is handy."

He caught a look of recognition from Pimm, "Of course you do, anyway I told him as you said, given your past history, I had these two Nazi's that would probably cause a stink rather than come over to clean up and settle in Blighty, the type that doesn't care about protocol. Too old, nothing to lose, the type that makes us all look bad in the papers, he understood I needed someone I could trust to handle it, with Sandman skills." Bull raised his eyes as he mopped his plate with the last piece of bread and then remembered Pimm's comment about the café owner Boris and left it, folding his knife across and pushing his plate to the side.

"The bloody thing should have been just a sightseeing jaunt for these two, check out the heads in the picture and then we'd have pulled in the locals along with our own heavies on the ground to pick them up, Mossad would have been none the wiser before they were back home to Blighty, Christ BP between you and me I'd have let Mossad or the Yanks have them if I had thought these two cherries were at risk." Bull appeared to show real regret at choosing two lower-ranking analysts in his team to send out to Rio and Pimm was surprised it was not like him to underestimate the opposition.

"And what of your people if they are six they must-have skills, surely they can think on their feet, they wouldn't have steamed in without clearance." Pimm was trying to picture how this had escalated from a simple stakeout to possibly three missing presumed dead Mi6 operatives.

"They've been in my team two years, bright enough, know the score, sit and wait, plenty of patience. Both have thrown a few punches, can hit a target on the run and stood their ground on past acquisitions. but neither has done any wet work, we are still mainly trying to trace the treasure unless it's a big hitter, of course, The angel of death Mengele would be, but they know better than to tangle with a fish like that, the girls the lead and she's not the excitable type." In Pimm's eyes, Bull appeared to be justifying his assessment that his team had been up to the task he had set them.

"You talked of letting the German's go have you reached out to anyone down there apart from Zavi's people, the yanks, you must know people." Pimm started to run through his own list of contacts in his head that operated in South America and got a look from Bull that told him if anyone had come back, he would not be sitting there with him.

"Ok, so you have squared this with Martin, when we're done here you can wait as I pack then you can drop me at Heathrow. I'll catch a red-eye." Pimm sat back considering what he would need, "have the embassy get a pack up ready for me to pick up, I'll call the Othon if it's the same concierge, he's a useful chap, I take it Mrs T already has a seat for me."

Pimm began to remove his spare house key off his key ring and seeing it held a dab of red nail varnished placed there by his wife so that she could recognise it instantly from the other keys, Pimm pushed it around and unlinked his own key and slid it across to Bull.

"Everything you needs in my bag, including the contact safe words for my people, their bio, get them to the embassy. I'll get them home, as for Bob if he surfaces tell him to call Wakefield, remind him of his prior engagement and thank him for me. FYI so you know, your people at Drake have sent two along with a Scalphunter from Raleigh to assist Department Speke in Cape Town, turns out there is a group of mercenaries, seven are Yanks, running around selling their skills in Rhodesia lead by an ex-pat Marine Colonel, the American's want to try to get Jem Stapleton to pull rank, remind him of his past loyalties before it hits the Sunday papers and we all get accused of destabilizing another communist African state, that's part of the reason he let me borrow you and as your jab dates have expired." Bull smiled as he watched Pimm scanning his medical record in his mind.

"No, they're not?" Pimm said quizzically.

"That's what I told him, I get the impression Martin has a soft spot for old boys like us. He's sharp, but he does love his technology, computers, personally I hate them he's one of the new breeds of analysts a flick of a button and a date can be changed in a microsecond allegedly, perhaps they do have their uses" Bull gestured feigning his disapproval having had one of his team adjust Pimm's medical file by accessing the new Mi6 computer mainframe.

Good to his word Bull Gordon settled the £3.50 breakfast bill with a tip in the café then waited as Pimm packed light and grabbed one of his cover passports and a dozen business cards as this was off the record, he would use personal legend rather than travel as a member of the Foreign & Commonwealth Office.

"I'll shave on the plane, you lock up." Pimm walked to the car then sat watching Bull close the door to his house as he pushed a couple of business cards into his wallet.

OLIVER MARTIN PIMM

Executive Insurance Loss Assessor

NEWMARKET INSURANCE COMPANY LTD
International Insurance Solutions

At Heathrow, Pimm slipped into the frenetic world of airport terminal two, amongst the fellow travellers, some stood around almost mesmerized watching the flight information boards update while others searched the myriad of signs for the right booking-in desk, rushing back and forth with younger family members being dragged across the slippery tiles. As the tannoy ping pong tone announcement heralded another inaudible nasal accented attention notice that clearly was in English but so wasn't.

Pimm moved through the bewildered civilians, tradecraft instincts already firing like the beat of a Ferrari engine. They had been asleep in Muswell Avenue for the most part, all but the instinctive, with no element of risk. Now amongst the world again, his eyes scanned reflections for possible tales and gauged any person, male or female, with a jaundiced eye, to see if they appeared remotely interested in his presence as he strolled casually up to the British Airways desk.

"Gate 8, boarding will begin thirty minutes before the flight sir, there are no delays you may proceed straight from club lounge." The two young ladies at the desk handle his passport and flight documents with meticulously manicured talons, both presented in full makeup as if they were going on a date with Robert Redford. The one that handed him his stamped first-class ticket, gesturing him towards the VIP lounge, sounded like she had just stepped off a polo field as she gushed a smile. Going first class was somewhat high profile, but it was the one luxury he would allow himself. He had promised to return to Rio with June one day, she may not be there at his side during the flight, but he would be riding high in first class and she'd be there in spirit, at one point he even bought her favourite tipple, a gin and orange and had left it untouched so far throughout the flight, it is how he wanted them to return, it was all he could do to fulfil that dream. Up there alone in the seat as he watched other affluent couples enjoy the opulent setting of first-class, he felt truly a lost soul, then gritted his teeth downing her drink in one and banished his thoughts of self-pity forever.

Chapter 13: The Little Disgorger

Serra Negra, Brazil
May 1974

Two months prior to Pimm being dispatched by Bull Gordon to Rio, deep within a cleared area of the forest in the remote hills near Serra Negra. Doctor Merill Nestlar pointed to the marker flags on the brow of the hill in the east, that tracked at given points, along the edge of the dense jungle and across the length of cleared farmland of the valley to the far side, just under 3 kilometres wide to the west, then pointed to a similar flag above their heads.
"We will be quite safe here, but in case the wind changes direction, we will arrange suitable safety equipment for the demonstration tomorrow," he said, accepting a bottle of water from one of his support armed guards that swarmed in defensive positions around their principles.
"The General was expecting Dr Mengele to be available for consultation, regarding deployment of the weapon for demonstration." With finger length, parallel warrior brand scars tracked across both cheeks General Musse, *"Moses"* Bin Abokkor, second in command to the Somalian warlord Mubarak Ali Hassan, was a fearsome individual, towering a foot taller than the 54-year-old ex-Nazi scientist.

Moses was the only surviving son of a chieftain, who was once the leader of a 13th-century Somalian Isaaq clan, natives of an area bordering the Ogaden region within Somalia in East Africa. After his village was wiped out by an opposing warlord who held allegiance to President Major General Siad Barre, the dictator of Somalia, Moses swore a blood allegiance for himself and on behalf of the handful of Isaaq clansmen survivors, to support Mubarak Ali Hassan, whose family also hailed from the Ogaden region and was intent on overthrowing the dictator and killing those responsible for the massacre of his people.
The nerve agent chemical weapons they were inspecting that would aid their goal, were produced at a chemical factory located on an abandoned coffee plantation purchased by the Nazi Spider network, adjoining Mengele's own farm near Sierra Negra 150 kilometres north of São Paulo.
"Our people will arrange transportation from São Paulo. Unfortunately, Josef will not be attending the demonstration, but I can assure you my colleagues, and I will be able to answer all General Ali Hassan's questions and have the full authority of the

senior executive to oversee the specifications for delivery." Nestlar removed his Panama hat and patted his forehead with a folded cotton handkerchief.

"Thank you," he said as he was handed an iced lime cordial from a tray by one of his men as he stood in the shade trying to get relief from the harshness of the sun under a refreshment marquee. The armed waiter offered the tray of drinks to the Somalian's as they stepped back from the edge of an observation plateau of the lower fields and valley.

Nestlar turned back to the field and smiled as four heavy cattle trucks tore down the track alongside the small private grass runway where a sleek Piper Navajo executive turboprop plane sat alongside a Grummer bi-plane crop sprayer.

"Here come the rest of the test subjects now." Nestlar gestured to the trucks entering towards the open fields that had been set in corrals, once parked up they began to unload their livestock, cattle, pigs and box crated hens each into their own segregated areas,

"You are welcome to inspect, they are all in good health." He held his empty glass out, and it was removed from his hand as he wiped his lips again, studying their clients.

"No, that will not be necessary. I know nothing of animals, other than how to track kill and butcher them." Moses stirred the remains of the ice in his glass, then threw to the dirt, "you appear to have a small army of your countrymen here, how do they like the heat." he said noticing, like the waiter and armed guards stationed in strategic vantage points around them, most of the men driving the trucks were of European descent, and he presumed, predominantly German.

"If they complain I have never heard it, but myself I appreciate the air conditioning of the plane. So if you are satisfied with the security arrangements for the test tomorrow. Please this way, I have prepared some further refreshments at the factory, where you may inspect the inventory of your shipment and our production laboratory." Nestlar watched Moses look to his equally aggressive looking countrymen bodyguards, as he grunted a command in Somalian, to which they fell in line at his side, immediately.

"Good, please this way." Nestlar turned back towards two Mercedes saloon waiting to drive them down to the small grass runway.

With Moses and his bodyguards aboard the aircraft, Merill Nestlar noticed something about the selection of animals.

"One moment, gentlemen please," he said and approached one of the Lorries as it was about to leave the site. "Where are the donkeys and horses we were promised?" he called to his personal bodyguard Klaus Ritter who was checking the arriving inventory. Klaus shook his head looking towards a lorry being driven by one of the few local farmers, who having parked up stepped down from his cab and appeared to be having a dispute with one of Klaus's subordinates.

"I am sorry, Herr Doctor, our man over there tells me the farm manager says he will not release the animals he has brought or bring the rest as agreed, without additional funds. I was going to speak with Herr Bouhler when I get back to the facility." Klaus spoke in German.

"No, no, in English or Portuguese, please Klaus, you know the orders." Nestlar looked over at the Brazilian farmer, gesticulating and red-faced, arguing with now two members of the German team.

"Not to worry Klaus, for now, agree to his demands. Tell the greedy scoundrel we will buy whatever he has, agree his terms, and tell him I go now to get more money, he will be fully compensated. Tomorrow, first light go back, collect the man and his family and any other animals you think may aid our demonstration. I think the presence of him and his family may impress the client, an extra bonus, yes. I never renegotiated a deal, you should know this, I am not about to start now, you understand Klaus, his family, bring them all out here." Nestlar squinted at the man then waved a hand to him as if in friendship and agreement.

Without giving him details, Klaus knew what was to be done as he watched his master drive back towards the Piper aeroplane.

"Doctor, can you come forward please." hearing the pilot call to him in German over the intercom, less than a minute into their journey, Nestlar raised his eyes in frustration, but smiled apologetically to Musse and his colleagues.

"What is it, Captain, why are you circling back?" Nestlar asked, looking forward of the cockpit, through the screen.

"Sorry doctor for speaking German, I understand your guest's do not." The pilot's eyes gestured back to the Somalian's enjoying their drinks.

"On take-off, Herr Doctor I spotted intruders, behind some of the old buildings in the southwest corner, over there!" The co-pilot pointed as they swept low over the site again, Nestlar leaned over his seat to get a view.

"Radio our people on the ground, have them picked up, immediately!"

He said and swore in German under his breath, then returned to the cabin and his guests as if nothing was wrong.

"My pilot thought you may appreciate another aerial view, so circled back, we shall continue now," he said, as he took his seat.

Bull Gordon's two young Mi6 observers, Cartwright and Lamb, had followed leads from the Ipanema restaurant, where the ex-RAF Captain had first spotted the Nazi doctor's, down to the southern Brazilian city of São Paulo. Where posing as coffee pickers and speaking to lorry drivers, they learnt of a construction project at an abandoned coffee farm and mill in the north, where no coffee grew since the river had been diverted towards a hydro dam.

The pair then drove 130 kilometres north, and outside the village of Monte Alegre du Sul, they stumbled on a pharmaceutical factory. It was originally set up by Dr Mengele's Fadro Forte chemical company, which was, amongst other legitimate more process's, secretly conducting experiments with the refined nerve agent that remained non-toxic until added to its catalyst. Having succeeded, they were now offering it for sale worldwide through the Spider network to the highest international bidder. This was in total contravention to the exclusivity agreement they had in place with members of the CIA. Who had been sponsoring Fadro Forte and turning a blind eye to their founder's notoriety and history.

All financial transactions had been negotiated in Geneva and payments were being diverted and cleared through First National Geneva Bank and Peter Salter-Kingsley.

"Shit they're on to us!" Nick Cartwright watched as Klaus pointed in their direction, and watched him climb aboard a Land Rover with other security personnel, while other members of his team opened fire. The leaves and branches that had camouflaged the position above the Mi6 agents cover were stripped from the trees and bushes, as tracers strafed across the field. Turning tail, the two Lamb and Cartwright grappled over ancient vines and through the dense vegetation struggling to find the path they had used.

"I see it, this way" Fortunately Nick Cartwright caught a slither of the distinctive red of their E3 BMW amongst the broadleaf green foliage, and they found their car parked up on a dead-end path ten meters in from the main dirt road.

"Drive! Don't stop till you get back to the city. We'll call London, speak to Bull get some heavy guns out here, this is above our pay grade." Lamb screamed as the cars air vents filed with the smell of burning clutch, and their tyres slipped on the soft soil while the engine revved and they remained stationary for what seemed like an age waiting for the tread to grip the earth, Nick threw the car into reverse briefly rocking it back and the immediately into first and thankfully they bucked forward skidding onto the main track.

"Nick!" Lamb shouted again, as around a distant corner from behind them a vehicle appeared, flashes of gunfire peppered the road spiting earth over the back of their cars boot and an indicator shattered. Then as the Land Rover chasing them

received a clear line of sight the back screen of their BMW was hit by bullets and imploded showering both agents with glass fragments.
Neil Lamb turned to face their pursuers and pitched himself low, firing between the headrests through the back of the car, but the heavy Land Rover did not falter from its advance, barging its way through the undergrowth and able with its four-wheel drive to hop in and out of the dirt road ruts, to avoid Lamb's shots.

For three kilometres the Mi6 agents were hounded by the Land Rover and another vehicle that Lamb occasionally caught sight of bringing up the rear until they hit the tarmac of the highway. Then they were able to outpace the four by four, in their BMW as they zipped in and out of the traffic heading back towards São Paulo.

"Scheisse!" Klaus Ritter swore as he watched the red BMW disappear amongst the other traffic heading towards the coastal cities.
"Turn around, take me back, I must report this to the doctor, we can arrange our people to be on the overpass, they'll pick them up."
The SP 381 was the only main road into the city from the northeast at this time, and so the red BMW was easily picked up from some distance away in the binoculars of Klaus's colleagues, waiting on the main overpass before São Paulo. The Spider operative's instructions were clear, prevent them from getting to a telephone at all costs, and if possible, kidnap them alive for interrogation.

With one call from Klaus, the Spider network had gone into overdrive, and with its sources of informants amongst the Federales, they had already located where Cartwright and Lamb had discovered the leads to the Serra Negra farm. The Pousadas Cantinho Ocian, a beach motel situated on the outskirts of São Paulo just over 50 kilometres south from Ipanema. The area was in lockdown, and they had cut the phone lines with a team already waiting in the agents motel room, while those that followed them across the city hung back and seeing the red BMW park up in the main street, instead of the hotel car park they followed suit a few cars behind o the opposite side
It was Nick Cartwright idea not to use the motel car park, on edge from being chased from the jungle, true to her tradecraft she assumed all exist were compromised, staying in the open was as good a place to hide and having parked up, the pair went into the busy Cantina across from the motel, before checking to see if their room had been discovered.
They had been driving for just over three hours, the sun was already down, Samba music filled the air, as ice-cold Caipirinha cocktails were being drunk faster than the

barman could make them. With no air-conditioning, most of the customers sat outside on the shady rear porch, two large propeller sized ceiling fans swept through the air slowly their dry bearings humming like the soft brush on a snare drum, Cartwright opened the top button on her shirt and blew air down her front and smiled nervously at Lamb as they approached the bar.

"Two beers" Lamb ordered as they sat at the barstool, both were drenched in perspiration.

"I'll get those, nice to hear another Brit!" from behind them, Bob Gregory slurred pretending to be drunk and threw a note to the barman, as out of sight Cartwright's hand went instinctively to the hilt of the revolver she had hidden in her hessian bag. Bob's hand caught hers holding it firmly in place, as Lamb stepped in to defend her. "Don't, I'm a friend, Bull sent me," he whispered, releasing his grip and then spoke the safe phrase, both agents would know that marked him as Mi6 as he lit the thin reefer behind his ear.

"Glad you're here can't get the cricket results, nothing but the world cup, I heard we lost two six's in the slips at Wembley." he looked for their acknowledgement at the code.

"You mean Lords" Lamb looked at Cartwright who kept her hand on the gun waiting for the correct words

"No, I don't" hearing Bob confirm the wrong venue for a cricket match, she released her hand.

"Come on, tell us what's been going on back in Blighty apart from the rain?" Bob said loud enough for all to hear, dressed like a beach bum that had just slipped from a hammock he led the way back to a corner table that held a collection of his empty bottles aiding, his image of a lonely British drunk backpacker.

"You two look like you've had sand kicked in your face, I take it the locals have been playing rough." Gregory kept his eyes low, "I've been coming here for two nights, trying to get a whiff of you buggers, old father Bulls not happy you've been off-reservation without keeping in touch, and you left nothing at the Rio safe house." "She wanted to get closer to the restaurant in the photo, we found an apartment a few streets away, she kept feeling watched at the regular hotel, there are yanks in the city." Lamb looked to Cartwright as she took one of Gregory's Marlboro cigarettes.

"I know someone was watching us, not the German's maybe the Yanks but someone, as soon as we got off the plane, every time we stepped on to the beach, I sent a message to Bull we were going to relocate. That's was before we found this place and the hotel over the road, things moved on quickly after that, that what happens when you go fishing, the line runs." Cartwright kept an eye on the front door as a group of six-holiday makers entered, they sounded Italian, and the girls began to line up Latino songs on the Wurlitzer bubble tube jukebox, then began to shuffle to the music, oblivious to the tension in the air.

"A pretty girl gets attention stepping onto the beach in Rio, you were not hard to track." he smiled at one of the Italian girls but looking to his new companions Gregory saw neither of them was up for making light of their situation.

"Ok, a bit harsh, but you two have made me come down here from an OP. I've been working on with Drake for three months if it was not Bull that put in the call you'd be facing the twats that pulled up outside behind you on your own." Bob eyes switched back and forth between the barman and the door, not absolutely sure or not if he was in the payroll of the Spider team.

"Look, we know we are out on a limb, the Germans, Mengele and others, they are dealing with African's we don't know who but they are serious people, and I am telling you someone was watching us in Rio, someone knew we were there." Cartwright stared at Bob Gregory defiantly, her tone was agitated

"Ok sorry, like I said I've been sleeping on the rock and roll bed in my camper for the last seven nights, terrific if you are only five foot tall. But for the record, your eyes are good, I caught three Mossad outside in the park where you set your new pitch." Bob said referring to an unregistered safe house Cartwright and Lamb had taken it upon themselves to find, without first informing London, "off the range, with no heads up to London, that was naughty, Bull was not impressed you'll have Monty after you."

Nick Cartwright smiled at the thought of Mrs Thompkin, who she could just imagine was wearing holes in the carpet tiles in their office at Century house, pacing, vexing at the fact they had gone dark.

"Trust me that old bat will bend your ears for a month of Sundays when you get back speaking of which, by the way I found your safety stash under the cat litter, I don't expect you to nick a stray off the streets, although the shit in the kitty litter was a nice touch, but you might think about buying some whisker's and putting some empty cans in the bin. I lifted your passports and the photographs you have taken relocated them off-site."

"We sent a non-priority postcard through the embassy drop before we got down here, it gave the details of our nest, you must have missed the update on the cross over, but you're here now that's all that matters, I take it you're a sandman and can came prepared to dig us out of this shit." Lamb's tone held a wish from reassurance from Gregory that all was going to be well now the cavalry had arrived.

"I came to party hard, but you two have drawn them out like mackerel to baking foil in a Scottish Loch and speaking of uninvited guests, two of the Germans are over there as we speak, your room, looking through your draws and they have people in the local Federales on their payroll, there was a Captain asking questions about a red BMW in here two hours ago, I take it that's yours. Shortly after he left, the phones went down in here and over at the hotel. They must have hit the exchange in this area, I already tried elsewhere one-click outside the town to the south, no joy. So what's up, what don't they want you telling London about, what have you two stepped into apart from a few old Nazi's?" Gregory sat silently as Cartwright explained all that they had seen and how they had only just managed to escape from the fields of the planned nerve gas demonstration.

"So, the photographs from your apartment is that all the Intel you have? It's a big thing for six to get involved down here. We have to be careful there are many feet you can step on if you want to samba. More spooks down here these days than Berlin." he said eyeing the Italian girls dancing to which one of their muscular companions noticed him looking. Bob Gregory raised a glass and smiled, but the girl's boyfriend seemed unimpressed, not that it bothered bob with his skills.

"Like I said Mossad had you in their sight, to be honest, that's not of any real concern on its own, but with the CIA, Russians, and Brazilian Federales, not to mention the drug cartels, no wonder you felt nervy, that's Rio for you everyone loves to party. To be honest, I would have bet a month's pay, you two were already shark bait, but you're not so good for you, so you think, they are making some kind of poison gas, now we get you back to your nest and I'll get on to London get some of our blokes from Porton Down over, good work you two, I'll smooth things with Bull, you'll find your passports and the stuff from the cat tray along with some snaps I've added off-site, look to the fridge…" Bob stopped mid-sentence as Nick placed a hand on his, as two blonde-haired men in their early thirties entered, they were part of the team that had followed them from Sierra Negra. Both wore an open short sleeve shirt that covered their waistbands and each, to the trained eye, had a sweat crease across their shoulder from where they had removed their shoulder holsters.

"I see them, give me the keys to your BM. mines the blue camper van outback. like I said I've been dossing in it a while waiting for you two to show up, so it's a bit funky, what can I tell you gives cred to my ledge."

Gregory tapped Cartwright's knee under the table, and they exchanged keys.

"Help yourself to what you like just don't touch the milk, you'll find some handy tools under the bed, I take it there's nothing in the hotel you can't walk away from." Bob looked again at the scantily clad Italian girls, dancing suggestively and an idea began to percolate in his mind.

"Clean as a whistle, what about these jokers?" Lamb went to finish his drink as Cartwright, now calm, watched the seasoned field officers eyes. He was everything she aspired to be, confident and deadly, she had no doubt if he wanted he could kill everyone in the room before the next song cued on the jukebox.

"Leave them to me, when it kicks off-take to the back door and don't look back, get to Rio. Send Bull your report and my love. I'll deal with your pals and take a look at that field up north, see if I can find out for sure what African's are in play and what they are buying. You're probably right it can only be drugs or guns, especially if Uncle Sam's involved, but it's a long way to come for guns."

"I know what I saw." Cartwright insisted, "Good luck."

Gregory watched the body language exchange between the Germans and the Italian group, as the girls continued to dance and flirt around the room and the two German's received some glances from the Italian men. Neither was impressed by their sniggers when one of the Italians referred to them as possibly being gay, and they continued to focus their attention on Cartwright, Lamb and Gregory with the occasional furtive glance through the reflection of the back bar mirror.

"Fuck it, let's have another, my shout!! Gregory shouted as he launched himself suddenly from their sides, sending the empty beer bottles from their table like skittles across the floor as he staggered towards the bar. Both German's looked up and appeared to Cartwright to brace themselves for an attack, then within three steps Gregory turned towards the Italian group and the Jukebox

"First I'm going to put on something proper, better than this shit, haven't you got any Elvis, I love Elvis, play the king." Gregory headed towards the jukebox scattering coins across the floor, one of the Italian girls bent down to pick up the money as it rolled across towards her, by now most eyes were on Gregory accept the German's still concentrating on Cartwright and Lamb.

"Do you know this fool?" one of the Germans asked the barman.

"He's ok, harmless, gets drunk sleeps out the back, on his way to Iguazu Falls looking for someone to share the ride when he has money, they won't get there the amount he drinks unless they have plenty." The barman nodded towards Cartwright, then with the sound of the record being scratched as Gregory barged into the jukebox the barman changed his tone, "Hey you Mr mad, take it easy."

The German's dismissed Gregory as a drunk, one made a loud joke, and they began to laugh.

"Fuck me mate, are you going to stand for that," Gregory turned on the largest Italian boyfriend gesturing towards the German's "That fucking Kraut called your Mrs a tart, wait no no.....let me get the translation right a prozzie!"

At first, the Italian was unsure what was going on, and then one of the girls who could obviously speak English but not German began to gesticulate aggressively pointing towards the bar, translating what Gregory had said.

"Prozzi?" the Italian asked smiling, still was trying to make sense of the situation "Prostitute you thick Wop!" Gregory goaded, as the girl continued to act offended. With that, the Italian swung wild as his friends joined his side.
"Not me! You idiot, them over there Blondi" Gregory ducked and then stepped back with his hands held up in peace, and the girl stepped in and backed up his words with an accusing finger, encouraging her girlfriend to join in the attack on the German men, all three Italian men turned away from Gregory towards the Germans.
"Go to toilets open the back door and get ready, I'll be with you soon." Lamb could see what was about to evolve and casually pushed his chair out, allowing Cartwright past gesturing her free path towards the back door that Gregory had now created for them, by surreptitiously moving chairs and tables with his swaggering antics.
Cartwright was sure she saw Bob Gregory give her a sly wink as he finished his bottle, and she passed by, while the German heavies exchanged a glance and looked to Lamb, one shook his head looking to the toilet sign as the three Italian boys drew up confronting them, with their girlfriends barking at their heels goading from behind, like a pair of Chihuahua. It took another simple stagger forward and deep push forward from the back by Gregory, and one of the Italians barged ahead into the nearest German. Perplexed he instinctively raised his fist, within seconds a brawl ensued, with Gregory bringing up the rear between the girls adding fire to the situation and aiding the Italians while preventing the German's breaking free as Lamb made a dash to the back in Cartwright's footsteps.
The Camper van was as expected, looking like it belonged to a surfing bum with a large yellow smiley face and an original Al Merrick lightning board strapped to the roof with bungee cords. But it started like a Porsche 911 and by the time they were on the coast road back to Rio Cartwright had found two hand grenades and Gregory's compact 45ACP Mac-10 machine gun in the fold-out bed void.
She settled back, grabbing a cold beer from the gas fridge and pulled the concertina windows open allowing the breeze to wash over her, face pushing her hair back from her face she felt a fine cut and welt on her face she had noticed before from when they had run through the forest to escape the Germans. She noticed Bob's leather travel shaving bag and checking her face and neck in its small lid vanity mirror she examined his shaving brush, it smelt of soap, musk and him. As her thoughts turned back to their encounter with the sandman in the canteener, she realised her nipples were erect, was it the danger of their confrontation with the Germans that exited her or him, she thought as she took another sip. She rarely drank beer, but it was the most refreshing drink she had ever tasted.

"He was something else back there, have you seen him about before Dave? I hope he makes it." She asked, handing him the bottle.

"No, but I wouldn't worry about that guy, the way he set that up was better than Shakespeare, get some sleep, I'll give you a shout when we're close to Rio, I won't be happy until I'm back at my desk, being caught by Mrs Thompkin for pinching too many Jaffa cake's from her tin is enough excitement for me.

It was a seven-hour journey back, and unfortunately, tiredness had dulled Lamb's senses, he missed the car that had trailed them from the moment they left the cantina after hearing the shots from within. The Germans, inside the bar having been jostled and punched, had finally resorted to their weapons to break free from the disturbance, firing into the air to disperse their attackers.

Gregory allowed himself to be floored in defence of one of the Italian girls as they vented their anger at losing Cartwright and Lamb and for a moment as one of the German's thrust his gun forward there was a second Gregory thought his time might be up, and then there was a distinctive double click from behind the bar.

"Leave the drunk and go!" The cantina barman grunted, pressing the barrel of his side by side AYA shotgun against the cheek of the other German.

Outside the other member of their team had seen Lamb pull out from the car park moments earlier and followed.

"Now you English, you fuck off, don't come back!" the barman turned his gun towards Gregory once the German's had left as the Italian men were praised and preened by the girls for their bravery in defence of their honour.

Bob hovered around the streets and wandered up to the next bar from where he could watch Lamb and Cartwright's hotel but once the two German's from the Cantina took off towards the city, having found the telephones in the area still down, he used the red BMW to get back into the town and then parking up in a square, located a little rusty blue Fiat 127 he had previously hired and left safely parked up. Inside, under the passenger seat, a Smith & Wesson Special and five spare rounds in the ashtray and a small backpack stowed under the seat.

Gregory gave a quick glance at the map from the glove compartment provided by the hire company and headed directly north towards Campinas, it would add another hour to the journey to Serra Negra, but he figured it would save him worrying about the German's who would be watching the main highways from São Paulo.

Gregory pulled over at a narrow vehicle passing point, perilously close to the ravine edge of the dirt highway less than a kilometre across the valley. Below him, the strung street lamps of the small jungle town of Monte Alegre du Sul and the few buildings with electricity pin-pricked the darkness. Ahead of him, he noticed a narrow path set into the trees, just wide enough for a cart, as he felt the earth ground the underside of his vehicle, one of the wing mirrors caught a branch and smashed as he pulled off the road to hide the car amongst the thick undergrowth. He checked his map, Sierra Negra was an eight-kilometre hike the other side of the town, where he expected the German's would have men waiting.

Grabbing a small rucksack he used whenever on foot filled with items that made him appear like any other backpacker, he began to trek along the road, the air was steamy and the night full of the animals of the night, occasionally a bat would catch his eye in his peripheral vision, looking up the jungle canopy silhouetted against the bejewelled sky, like the sunlight hitting quartz sand grains in the surf.

The road gave him ample warning of any approaching vehicle, and he entered the town and skirted along the first derelict buildings towards the small centre square, where Bar de Fonte *(Fountain)* was the only watering hole for the truckers that dare risk the roads.

Gregory immediately noticed three large trucks parked up and their owners sitting separate to a group of Europeans in the open-fronted seating area of the bar, watching football on an old television hung from a shelf. As he approached, he could see the Europeans were all armed, but they appeared relaxed with a collection of bottles on their table.

Gregory checked the buildings as he watched a women in an upstairs room across from his position close the curtains of her room, he could see looking up the road many of the other houses in the street had no lighting and those that did had their shutters closed, to prevent the night bugs entering. Gregory slipped through their gardens and down the gaps between them, then ducked through the gates into the yard of a wheelwright and climbed up over a horse cart under repair and on to the flat roof, to get a better vantage point and was now close enough to catch the odd word of the Spanish football commentator when the wind blew gently his way. Bob used his miniature standard Mi6 issue telescope and scanned the seating area of the bar as the waiter came out again and he watched as he served a suited man sitting alone in the corner away from the Germans, smoking. As the waiter lit a table lantern, Bob was able to see the man's face, he was a white chisel jawed westerner and something about his manner, more than the way he appeared disinterested in the game of football, when occasionally one of the other men nearest him would comment on the action on the television, screamed CIA to Bob. Squinting Gregory zoomed his lens into the dimly lit area and fixed the image of the man's red and white cigarette packet, next to the edge of the lantern, he recognized as the brand

as Marlboro, to bob, that was as good as a smoking gun. *"But what was a Langley farm boy doing out in these woods"* he thought.
As he strained to listen for the accent of the man, his eye caught from behind, the beams high in the air of an approaching vehicle along the road down which he had just come. Bob turned back, watching as it approached the town, Gregory held his breath as he judged that where he had parked up, they appeared to slow. He had thought his Fiat was far enough off the road to be seen, but in the pitch dark of the jungle, anything reflective hit by a headlamp shows up like a lighthouse beam, normally it is the eyes of the creatures of the night, this time It was the wing mirror glass that Klaus saw on the road, he slowed and wound down his window.
"What is it?" his driver asked, as he wound down his window and looked at the shards of broken mirror, then lifted himself in his seat stretching his neck, looking into the darkness of the jungle either side of the track, then noticing the mirror of their own vehicle had at some time been smashed under similar circumstances, he sat back down and ordered the driver to carry on.

Gregory ducked low as the jeep entered the town and he watched them pull up alongside the bar and beside a Volkswagen Fusca estate car, Klaus appeared to hover at the car, he was checking to see if it was the one that had left the mirror glass on the trail, when one of his colleagues called to him from the bar and he was immediately handed a bottle of beer, and he spoke briefly in German with the other Europeans, almost ignoring the Brazilian drivers and then turned to the back of the room and sat for a while smoking talking with the man that sat alone at the back, after a few minutes the man got up and left. Bob Gregory ducked low as he drove the Volkswagen passed his position heading out of the town, he watched for a moment as the brake lights disappeared into the jungle then turned back to the Cantina and could see Klaus had now standing having joined his colleagues.

"Take it easy tonight, tomorrow first thing you two, with me we see the farmer before the blacks arrive." he gestured to the men across the table from him, but as he watched the game on the screen, he looked over at the trucks, the broken mirror glass he had seen on the road bothered him. Gregory watched Klaus get up and look around their trucks and vehicles, checking the wing mirrors of each and tying up the cord binding that held the canvas truck canopies in place.
A dog in an adjoining yard to the wheelwrights must have sensed Bob's presence and began to bark. Hearing the disturbance Klaus wandered to the back of one of the trucks and looked back down the street, a light came on in the dog's yard, and the owner began to scold the animal while Klaus continued to watch while lighting a

cigarette, and saw the light turn off. Satisfied it was nothing he then turned back to his colleagues hearing their cheers as a goal had been scored.

In 1974 the 10th FIFA World Cup was hosted by West Germany who along with East Germany were in group 1, the tournament would come to be dominated by the Germans. Some believe this was the catalyst of the reunification of Germany and the end of the Berlin wall, a divided nation united by football, the beautiful game, even though they were on opposite sides.

In spite of Klaus's instructions, with both the East and West German teams winning their first game on the 14th June, the Germans celebrated hard but were still on parade by first light.

However, sitting in his jeep watching his men climb aboard the trucks, Klaus's own hangover was heightened by the oppressive humidity of the jungle, alcohol sweat pooled stinging his eyes and he doused his head with water from his canteen as the beads of water cleared his vision, he noticed the back of one of the trucks as it pulled away and frowned, replaying his examination of the vehicles the night before and remembered specifically he had tied that particular rope fastening with a stronger loop.

He made sure his driver remained in the jeep with a gun covering the back of the truck as they rounded up all of the farms' livestock including his own horses. As soon as the farmers own grey mare was loaded into his horsebox, the farmers began a vehement protest, that it was not included in the deal, his expression soon turned to curiosity at seeing two of Klaus's men escorting his wife and children from his villa. He stormed up to the German, demanding an answer and raised a hand, swearing in Portuguese, this was met with a brutal battering from the butt of Klaus's Colt revolver. The farmer was then dragged along the floor and thrown in the back of the horsebox along with his family, but before his nine-year-old daughter was placed inside Klaus pulled her to one side and stood in front of the truck that he believed held a stowaway, as her mother began to scream and plead for mercy.

"In the truck! Whoever you are, come out now!" Klaus shouted in English, his men braced themselves, each aiming their weapons at the vehicles canvasback. Inside Bob, Gregory looked around the supplies for additional weapons, but the truck contained only empty sacks and some full of coffee beans, nothing that would help. Klaus repeated his order "In the truck! Out or girl dies."

Bob froze peering out from the rope canvas eyelet holes to gain a vision of the number of men he was about to battle as he heard the clicking of gun safety catches and the Germans surround his vehicle. Then above the snivelling and cries of what he took to be a little girl and her mother's calls to her defence, there was a gunshot, and the girl screamed.

"That was her dog, the next is for the child unless you come out, in this heat, I'm not even going to count, come out now, or I will shoot." Klaus chambered another round in his revolver with a sharp click.

"Ok. Ok! I'm just looking for a ride, please don't shoot, I'm just looking for a ride, I'm English." Bob called out surrendering as he hid his gun and ammunition deep within in a sack amongst the coffee beans.

"English, any shit, I'll shoot both children first, before you" Klaus barked and gestured to one of his men to untie the back allowing Gregory to come out. Bob threw out his backpack first, then shielding his eyes from the morning sun dropped to the dirt and was pushed forward before Klaus.

"Who are you?" Klaus discarded the child shoving her into the arms of one of his men, and she was placed into the horsebox with the rest of her family.

Bob continued to hold his hands up and tried to look shocked at the sight of the farmers Alsatian laying in the dirt minus the back of its skull.

"Oh! My God, I'm just a backpacker, I saw the lorry, I just needed a ride." Bob was shunted forward and relieved of his bag, Klaus's man began to throw the items out on to the floor and coming to Bob's passport, along with his wallet threw them to Klaus gesturing there was nothing of interest,

"William Grey! This is you?" Klaus looked at the photograph of Bob Gregory's Mi6 pseudonym legend and then at Bob.

"He was the fool in the Cantina, the drunk who started the fight." Bob recognized the blonde German sporting a split lip and bruised cheek as he stepped forward gesturing to him, but pretended not to understand as the man spoke with Klaus

"Was he?" Klaus said, "Did he do that?" Klaus pointed to the man's face

"No Italian's, as I said he's a drunk." The man was waved back, by Klaus.

"Is he, perhaps, perhaps not?" Klaus looked again at the passport.

"Hi, I remember you, I was drinking somewhere," Bob took a step forward as the man took up his position again, then halted as the other guard's guns bristled in his direction while the man with the cuts to his face offered no sign of recognition. Bob continued to claim his innocence, "I can't remember when, but I remember you, some problem at a bar with Italians, was it over football, hotheads, eh." Bob played on what the man had told Klaus, "I'm Billy, my friends call me Billy" he gave a nervous smile ad held out his hand in friendship.

"We are not your friends William" Klaus said and Bob, caught the flick of his eye gesturing to the man at his back, knowing what was coming he braced himself.

It was the last thought he had before the darkness fell across him with a numbing pain as the guard behind that had searched his bag slammed the butt of his

Kalashnikov into the base of his skull and Bob buckled forward, falling inches from the dead dog.

"Put him in with the others, when we get to the fields search the truck, burn his shit," Klaus ordered then climbed aboard his jeep.

Before he felt another kick from the grey mare on the other side of the timber guard rail he had been tied to, Bob heard the sobbing of the children as he regained consciousness. Immediately his arms, pulled high above his head began to ache as the muscles under his armpits had been torn by his captives binding. His legs spasmed kicking across the floor and as he jerked the farmers grey mare behind him bucked again. This time he felt the full force through the timber on his back, winding him.

His neck felt greasy from his own blood, and the wound to his head throbbed, but it was his arms that concerned him most and considered his right may be broken. He tried to raise his backside from the floor, taking the pressure off his arms to relax his shoulder muscles, enough to rotate them and check to see if they were dislocated. Fortunately they weren't and fortunately for Bob when they arrived at the field with the farmer's animals, events had overtaken the full search of the truck he had been hiding in, Klaus's men did not carry out a thorough search of the bags of coffee and find his revolver.

Bob looked across at the farmer's family, they were all bound similarly to him, but the children had slightly more play on their tethers so that they kneeled against their mother as she tried to comfort them. It appeared that the father was still unconscious. The wounds to his face and blood on his clothes were from the additional beating he had sustained for his expression of greed to Doctor Nestlar. Bob considered it was unlikely he was going to be of any assistance in any escape.

"Mother, we need to get out of here," he whispered softly in Portuguese, "I cannot move my hands, can you?"

Her eye rose from her children, then she held her palms out, her wrists were swollen and ripped by the coarse rope, where she had apparently tried to loosen them, and her children clutched her close wary of him.

As Bob received another smash to his back from the farmer's grey, he cringed with pain and the little girl joined her mother in calls to the mare to calm. Bob looked again at the farmer, but he had not stirred, then outside somewhere in the distance he heard the sound of a plane engine, coming into land.

It was the Warlord Mubarak Ali Hassam arriving to witness a live demonstration of how the deadly nerve agent Mengele and Nestlar's team of scientists had produced would affect the victims that he intended to kill in his own country.

Like the animals corralled in the field, Nestlar had decided Bob and the farmer's family would allow their client to experience firsthand the effects of the poison gas on human subjects.

Bob looked at the children's bindings, the rope was coarse and thick, and against their tiny hands, it was like trying to tie a noose around a strand of hair. "Mother, can you ask them, your children, can they free their hands?"

"Mamma?" The little girl cuddled close to her mother lifting her top and Bob saw that already the little boy had one hand loose.

"Mother, we must leave this place, they must help us, they must help me," he said gesturing to her son.

The woman looked first to her husband and then calmed her children, speaking softly at his protest she explained to her son to try and untie the ropes above her head, but as he stood, it became apparent the knots were too high for him to reach. Bob gestured to his sister, hers were bound lower.

In preparing the scene of his captives within the horse truck, Merill Nestlar had even considered given the freedom of their movement how the children would appear in death to his client. Thereby replicating the scenario he imagined would occur when Ali Hassan released the nerve agents on the villages in Somalia that supported his enemy.

As the horse shuffled behind him, Bob sensed the prelude of another kick and arched his back away from the timber boards before it arrived. He was right, but it gave little relief, but as the steel hooves slammed into the timber Bob stopped struggling hearing something in the wood, a splintering crack, he turned his head seeing the timbers he was attached to were weathered and in places well worn.

"Shush Glaucio" the girl called to the horse, and Bob smiled, seeing she was trying to help him.

"What is your name?" he asked, and the girl received a gesture from her mother that it was alright to answer.

"Ofelia," she said and bit her lip holding back her fear, her cheeks held the tracks of her tears.

"That's a pretty name Ofelia, We need to leave this place away from the bad men that put us here, I can help, if you can free me, Ofelia help your brother." Bob nodded his head reassuringly as the child's mother coaxed her to do as he said. Bob watched with hope as Ofelia held her hands forward while her brother began to pinch at the rope, and she grimaced as he fumbled while twisting her wrist. Finally, she pulled one hand, and it slipped free, but the other knot was even too tight for her to loosen.

As she got to her feet, the horse bucked again, and again Bob felt the sound of timber snapping inside.

"Ofelia listen carefully. I need you to be brave, I need you to do something, pick up that end of the rope," he said gesturing to the extended length that now hung free, which still held a large knot where her hand been tied.

Her mother nodded as Bob turned his head looking upwards to the rear of the horses grey haunches, visible above the timber stall guard.

"Do as he asks" her mother said as her son held her tight, she appeared to understand his plan.

"It is an impressive selection of test subjects you have organised for me, and once the demonstration is over, we may examine them, when?" Ali Hassan looked out across the fields dotted with corrals, through his binoculars and noticed the horsebox in the centre, that occasionally shuddered.

"Following the deployment exercise we will arrange a flyover today, and then within twelve hours the nerve agent should have dissipated enough for a ground-level examination, however, we recommend twenty-fours to be sure unless you wish to wear the suits we have provided. I must tell you in this heat they are extremely uncomfortable, but then without them, exposure to the nerve agent, is I assure you far less palatable."

Nestlar watched the warlord walk over to the bag marked up like coffee. On close inspection, the brownish pellets of a similar size were not coffee beans.

"And it is safe to handle in this form?" Ali Hassan looked to Nestlar who gestured yes.

"Show the General," Nestlar ordered.

With that Klaus rolled his sleeves up and drove both his arms into the Henna coffee bean bag halfway to his elbows, removed them holding two handfuls of the pellets and then let them fall back and smiled reassuringly. Ali Hassan received a gesture that his man Musse Bin Abokkor was suitably impressed.

"In its dehydrated form it is perfectly safe to touch, however, I would not recommend eating it." Nestlar watched as Ali Hassan cautiously took out one pellet and held it up to his eye.

"Good work, Moses," he said, throwing it across to Bin Abokkor.

"So they will be hidden amongst a shipment of coffee, excellent, and that is the catalyst, to makes it active as an aerosol?" The Somalian gestured to a large gas container, similar to those slung under the wings of the crop duster that began to taxi ready for the signal to start the demonstration below in the valley.

"Yes, highly combustible but on its own, it would give you a migraine for sure, they will be marked as a shipment of acetylene."

Nestlar then turned from the group and cast an eye over the wind flumes blowing lightly in the opposite direction as he heard the pilot of the crop duster announce on his radio he was ready to begin the display.

"So we begin, and with some refreshment, I think, please Klaus some water for the General to wash your hands first, purely precautionary, you understand." Nestlar smiled and gave the order for the plane to take off.

Inside the horsebox, the little Portuguese girl stood, her eye streaming tears as she pleaded with her mother, refusing to carry out Bob's wishes. Bob sensed timing was not on their side and now changed his tone speaking directly to the woman, in sharp, single instructions.

"Those men outside will kill your children, she must do this, I must get free to save you." Bob tried to stem his tone, speaking clearly.

The mother scolded the girl "Look at me Ofelia Look at me, your father, you brother Paulo will die here, I will die, unless you do as this man says, now Ofelia! Now!"

With that Ofelia began to lash the rump of the horse, causing the horse to buck more violently than before, while Bob tried to push his body off from the timber boards. By the third kick, Bob's back was racked with pain, and he growled cursing. This intensified the tension in the horsebox which the animal sensed as Ofelia continued to cry out with each lash, she delivered.

On the sixth occasion, Bob fell forward and hung off a broken slat, as exhausted the little Brazilian girl stepped back. Bob was now able to turn to face the slats and his bindings, he braced his feet against the wood and broke the timber further releasing his ropes, and he Immediately loosened Ofelia's remaining bound hand and cupped them together praising her efforts, she went to the horse and began to calm it and then joined her mother's side as Bob freed himself.

Looking to the farmer, Bob felt a very light pulse in his neck he realised his condition was grave and he could do nothing for him, at that moment his priority was the women and the children. Suddenly he heard the roar of the crop spraying plane as it took to the sky and buzzed low overhead. He scuttled over to the rear doors which had been left partially open to allow the poison gas full access.

Keeping low Bob looked across the field at the corrals full of various penned livestock and realised he was in the field Cartwright and Lamb had spoken of. High on the hillside, the German scientist's had created a small plateau that had been cleared as an observation platform, where a number of the trucks he had seen were parked along with other vehicles. Too far away to identify their faces he could see the Somalian's and a group of suited men, surrounded by at least ten heavily armed guards, but at the centre, he saw two blonde-headed men the taller of the two he knew to be Klaus.

Bob ducked back into the shadows, hearing the plane circling around and looking up he recognised it as a crop duster, his heart began to race. Watching it for a moment, he then noticed the orange wind flumes stationed along the headlands of the field and his eyes drifted back to the animals, and he knew precisely what danger they were in, he judged the forest to be 100 metres from the horsebox, that was the only route to safety.

He spun back to the Brazilian family, "We must go now, get up all of you! You must leave him." Bob tried to hide his fear for the family as he spoke fiercely gesturing to the farmer, but the mother and small child were huddled around her husband as she began to tend his facial wounds. Bob shook his head in frustration, then seeing the horse was tethered by it bridle loosened it,

"Glaucio, yes?" he gestured to Ofelia, "We go now on Glaucio, quickly you must jump on."

Then Bob heard then heard the high pitched whine of the crop dusters engines as it swooped in low on an approach run he took one glance out of a gap in the horsebox side's slats and saw the first barrelling plumes of white smoke jettisoning from under the fuselage as the aircraft began to release its evil toxin. Grabbing the girl he threw her to the horse's mane and then pulled at the little boy, but the child kicked out and clung to his mother, who now saw Bob's eyes held pure fear as he shook his head in frustration.

"Go! Save her" the woman cried, pulling her son into her breast and seeing the girl was about to dismount, Bob leapt onto the horse bareback throwing himself across Ofelia barring her escape and released, the grey mare bolted down the trucks loading planks onto the field.

"Doctor?" Klaus pointed seeing the horse and riders appear, all other members of the party until then had been focused upon the plane. Nestlar trained his binoculars in the direction Klaus was pointing and saw Bob struggling to pin the girl down around the horse's mane, he gestured to Klaus.

"Well, what are you waiting for kill them, you idiots!" Klaus snarled.

"I am sorry General, it was to be a surprise, I had arranged additional specimens for you to examine, there are more in the box, I assure you, you will not be disappointed, and my men will get those two for sure." Nestlar looked to Klaus, who stepped away from their group and snatched at one of his colleague's rifles. As bullets cut across the field spitting earth and grass just shy of the horse's hooves as it thundered towards the forest, Klaus settled himself and pinched the meagre image of Bob Gregory and the girl in his sight judging they were almost out of range he held his breath and let off a single round.

"If your gas is as good as you say, there should be no problem." Ali Hassan shrugged and then they saw it appeared Bob slumped forward, just as the horse disappeared into the tree line.

"Tell the pilot to take in that forest on his next pass," Nestlar ordered.

Inside the forest, the grey mare continued at pace having found an open animal track, both Bob and the girl were slashed by branches as they cut through the overhanging undergrowth. Bob's side was burning, he had been shot before and knew he had been hit, but as the horse slowed in an open area, he looked up and heard the crop duster again, immediately he dug his heels into the horse's flanks as Ofelia fought with his arms scratching at Bob's wrist.

"Cover your mouth!" Bob ordered her as the mare began to barge ahead, while behind them the white dust began to settle drifting down through the trees and a sound like the start of a heavy deluge filed the forest, growing in intensity as if chasing them, as birds began to drop from the trees to the floor, along with any other creatures caught beneath the canopy.

Bob heard the rushing water before he saw it and both he and the girl were thrown around the grey's neck, almost catapulting down into the ravine below and the rapids of the river as the grey mare pulled up sharply bucking back. With no concern of the force required and it hurting her he grabbed onto the girls arm fiercely as they heard the plane coming their way and the sound of dead birds pelting the broad leaves of the jungle became like a crescendo of a hale stone. Bob took one glance below and pulling the child into his body, "God save the girl." he whispered and flung himself out into the air spinning so that she was held above him and his back would brace any impact from below.

With the first exhausted breath of the white cloud touching his lungs, the mare Glaucio's front legs buckled to its knees, white froth spewed from the animals mouth and nostrils, it gave a hoarse groan and collapsed, writhing as if its body had received a massive electric shock for just over twenty seconds and then the horse was dead. The gas was indeed as deadly as Doctor Nestlar had informed the Somalian's and Mubarak was satisfied with the demonstration and that evening ordered the release of the deposit funds from Geneva for the transaction to proceed.

Chapter 14: The Calm Tangler

Rio De Janeiro, Brazil
1974

The day after Pimm had his breakfast at the Muswell Hill cafe with Bull he arrived at Galeão airport 13.43 local. The afternoon sun baked all standing in line for passport control, under the thick modern glass plate windows of the arrival lounge. A small ineffectual desk fan span as if every rotation would be its last, wafting humid air into the face of the Brazilian uniformed officer stamping the passports, he raised one eye and gave a cursory glance at Pimm when he announced he was on business to verify the demise of a racing yacht, only just catching the edge of his passport with the stamp he waved Pimm through. "Obrigado." *(thank you)* Pimm said and got less than a grunt of acknowledgement to his Portuguese. "No wonder the Nazi chose Rio as one of the first ports of call after the demise of the Reich." Pimm thought and remembered that what he had thought the last time he arrived at Galeão with June at his side.
Letting the breeze from the open window taxi take his breath he checked the driver's face against his registration card stapled to the back of his seat, in no mood to talk he lapped up the sublime landscape occasionally catching the sound of a Bossa Nova track from a radio each time they paused for traffic and at lights. The air was filled with the sweet aromas of street food vendors cooking and exhaust fumes from the wining motor scooters that zipped in and out of the traffic while a ferry horn called to the Corcovado as they dropped down into Copacabana beach.

An hour later, with his case open on his bed, outside on his balcony, he turned to the sun, watching the beach hustlers. Each master of their own dominion of beach turf had assembled their chairs at sunrise that morning, like spiders setting webs, waiting to capture passing tourist trade, with promises to service your every whim. They could get you anything your heart desired and with hawkish eyes watched for the slightest rise of a client's finger or an empty glass to refill.
Pimm located a tall, bulky black Brazilian in black Speedo's, "budgie smugglers" as Bob Gregory had once referred to them to Pimm, they left nothing to imagination to why the man held one of the prime sites on Copacabana beach and although he wore a stretched M&S string vest and West Ham cap, with Havana flip flops on his size thirteen feet, he was probably pulling in more money a day then most of the local city officials were being paid weekly. Pimm knew him as a friendly informant,

and even from the seventh-floor balcony of room 61 of the Othon Palace hotel, Patrick's wide white-toothed smile set a reflective glare in Pimm's camera lens, he heard his booming laugh in his head as he remembered the last time he was in Rio. Less than a snatch away he sat the camera next to the 9mm hi-power Browning revolver that had been waiting at locker 88 of the airport along with a silencer two full clips and assignment documents.

Studying the headshots of Cartwright and Lamb he sat for a moment planning his search, the beach hustler Patrick, may know something and if Bob Gregory had made it to Rio, he would almost certainly have contacted him.
"Where the fuck are you, Bob?" he whispered, looking down Copacabana beach towards the old fort and beyond to Ipanema, looking out and seeing the sun drifting down towards the sea, his eyes search below his window down towards Patrick and he saw like Fagin the beach master had already set a team of his urchins to task restacking for the night any of the sun loungers no longer in use and
Patrick was in full swing for his second mode of employment, ingratiating, flirting and chatting up two middle-aged western women that sat at his private bar, no doubt drinking spiked drinks and who no doubt had caught sight of Patrick's package and wondered.
Pimm knew he would most likely pick them up later that evening and take them to the Samba bar, Carioca da Gema, Lapa and wine and dine them all night.
In the morning, both women would be considering dumping their husbands and selling up their suburban semis in Richmond or were ever they had come from to live in Rio. Patrick, Pimm knew he would be counting the money he had managed to fleece from them with whatever hard-luck story he had decided to peddle that night, most women knew he was just a gigolo, but they didn't care, the man had charm an easy smile, and his cock was in double figures.
Pimm decided not to disturb Patrick's play, he would start in earnest tomorrow looking for the missing Mi6 agents, considering once this thing started who knows when he would get a chance to rest so after priming the room per his tradecraft for no rude awakening he turned in for the night.

The next morning at the front desk, Carlo the Othon Palace concierge handed Pimm a telex from London.

BP,
Your boy found a new roost for my chicks, before going to ground
Bull

Carlo told Pimm he had not seen Mr Grey/Bob Gregory but promised to make inquiries when Pimm handed over his room key and then arranged for his cousin to drive around to the front of the hotel and act as a daily taxi service during Pimm's stay.

"He has only been in Rio a month, but he knows the street like the back of his hand, he won't mess you about taking the long route, like some cheeky buggers, he's a good man Allan, reliable unless you're his wife and quiet like, just you like Mr Pimm, he'll be outside every morning, and I will organise a bed here, so he is on call in the night." Carlo raised a hand of no, as Pimm drew some money from his wallet, "Not necessary Mr Pimm always a pleasure."

Pimm had stayed with June in the Othon once and noticed Carlo not once asked after her, someone had told him of her death, and the concierge had remembered. Alan hardly raised his eyes from his newspaper as Pimm stepped down from the hotel lifting a finger gesturing a moment then crossed the street and walked down the beach promenade road.

Each day the dual highway nearest the beach in Copacabana is closed to traffic and becomes a wide pedestrian walkway, for joggers, roller skaters cyclist and couples who amble slowly up and down enjoying the fragrance of the many food stalls the beach master operate. Set along the four-kilometre stretch of white sand, occasionally there are toilets and free showers, some local families bring their children and washing down to the beach to use the facilities. The beach community of Rio has a vibe and atmosphere that has marked it, along with the remarkable sights that surround the city into the bucket list of many across the world. Most that make it there go back, at least once, however, many who live there would do anything to escape.

Even before Pimm had stepped onto the pavement Patrick's wide-open gape signalled he had caught Pimm's image,

"Mr Pimm, Mr Pimm how the devil are you, Sir? May I get you a beach chair? Get Mr Pimm a chair Junior." before Pimm had answered a young street urchin was already at Patrick's side with a clean folded sun lounger and fresh towel.

"Not today Patrick, thank you, it is good to see you are well, you have moved up to a new spot I see, very nice and I like the hut and bar, maybe later. I have business first." Pimm acknowledged with a wave an elderly lady with a colourful hair scarf and matching sarong, whose head only just peeked over the counter, preparing food on a single gas ring that infused the air with an exotic aroma.

"How about nice bacon butty, mama, make some bacon, for Mr Pimm."

Copacabana beach is set as a cusp arch the closer a beach hustler is to the centre the higher the ranking of that beach master and to get to the centre, demands respect earned with muscle, Patrick had all this and more, that belied his true nature. He snapped his fingers again, and the skinny boy with the chair was gone attending Patrick's mother, but not before thrust out two bacon rolls, Patrick handed one to Pimm "Please." And Pimm thanked him, "You see, mama remembered you, even put the sauce you like."

Pimm raised a hand to the lady, and she gave him a gap toothy smile.

"How may I be of assistance for you today, Sir?" Patrick realised Pimm required his more nefarious talents. While Pimm, having made no attempt to conceal his nationality wearing a straw trilby, Burton's striped shirt, Khaki long shorts and white socks with open toe sandals appeared to all passing by as just another English tourist haggling the rate of a seat.

"You know my colleague, I introduced last summer, Mr Grey."

"Yes, I remember a nice man Mr Billy." Patrick's keen memory was his stock and trade, and if asked, he would probably even remember Bob's favourite tipple as Bacardi and Coke. However, he informed Pimm he had not seen him that season or Cartwright and Lamb when shown their pictures. Pimm looked back towards the taxi then considered the image of what was believed to be Josef Mengele.

"Patrick, I know they are always in town but are there any new Israeli's stirring the water for old friends of Adolf." Pimm saw Patrick's eye snatch an image of a couple of young bikini-clad western girls in his peripheral vision, turning away he snapped a bark at his young worker to attend to their needs.

"The German's pay well, they have many, many friends especially with the Federales, it's not wise to get involved in their business as you know, they are not like your bobbies on the beat in London and the Jews don't pay well enough for my people to help them with that sort of information."

Just talking openly in a bar about the Brazilian police could lead to a closer introduction conducted in a back street alley.

Patrick in his time had received his share of beatings from the end of the long batons, the beach patrols used to enforce discipline amongst the young men that came down from the Favela's to earn from the tourists, irrespective if it was an honest or dishonest crust.

Patrick lowered his tone, showing no teeth as he spoke now to Pimm, "That said only for you, Mr Pimm, try the JB building you know it?....Jornal do Brasil opposite the church Nossa Senhora da Candelária, a new girl arrived this season, Greek papers, she's not Greek." Patrick was referring to the newspaper building opposite the Catholic church to the east of the city, he could not resist a wide smile remembering the girl, "she's a looker, has been down to the beach a few time with a young man, vermelho, *(red)*." he touched his head, "like the sun when it sets you can't miss her, drives a motorbike with a white helmet."

Rio has a sprawling population in the millions, but those out of place stick out like a floater in a swimming pool to those that were born there. However, such excrement would attract fewer flies than the beach hustlers of Copacabana, when a pretty young western girls feet touch the golden sand.

"For you're the bacon" Pimm thrust a couple of notes into Patrick's shovel sized hands and thanked Patrick, allowing the big man to do what he did best and entertain and service his latest scantily-clad clients.

"Come soon and rest in a chair, Mr Pimm have some of Ma Ma's Shrimp before you return home." he crowed, skipping backwards across the sand, like a premier footballer.

Pimm smiled as he crossed back to Allan's waiting taxi, recalling that as big as Patrick was, his mother, a tiny lady, who spoke perfect English, used her ivory fan to rap across her son's knuckles on each occasion she felt his language was inappropriate.

The mention of the Catholic church was something Pimm had already known for years Mossad, had been using Catholic churches as drop boxes, where better to pass secrets than in a confessional and where better for a Jew to hide than amongst Christians at prayer. But first he would check out the safe house address Bull Gordon had given him for his two young observers, it was where Bob Gregory would have started.

"Mr Pimm I am Allan, Carlo is my family I am with you today all day no problem," Alan said, as Pimm stepped into the back of his taxi, then his eyes raised from his paper in surprise as Pimm answered in Portuguese with hardly any accent.

"Morning Allan, hopefully not all day, please take me to the gardens at Praça General Osór

Allan immediately slapped his paper down to the passenger seat, now considering Pimm was not like the regular executive guests his cousin Carlo recommended.

"You know Rio well then, the craft fair it is," he said, starting the car he glanced back across at Patrick who he knew as a beach player and by now was delivering two cocktails in coconut cups to the girls, then Allan turned down the side street heading towards Ipanema.

Pimm left Allan in the shade parked on Rua Jangadeiros, facing the hippie craft fair in the garden square and mingled with the other tourist's snapping with a "Wow!" at any vague interest with his oversized Olympus camera strapped to his neck. All within earshot knew he was English, none knew concealed in his lens case was a Browning revolver and silencer.

Allan watched as he ordered a coffee from one of the street vendors, Pimm sat and let his camera lens drift along the skyline apartments to the far side of the square and to the apartment windows off Rua Teixeira de Melo finding the third floor windows of the Mi6 safe house, he saw the two empty milk bottles in the window, a visual Mi6 code, sometimes used by field agents to alert colleagues that the safe house is vacant. Pimm considered for a moment regardless of the significance of the milk bottles the apartment, Bob Gregory had left word about at the British Embassy, may contain the bodies of the missing agents and Gregory himself.

He watched as the window was open, and the cotton curtain drifted in and out with wind-blown by the passing buses, and he noticed as he scanned the street-level shops and café barsas, that as a bus passed by it shielded the apartment's street entrance below from onlookers.

Finishing his coffee, he joined those examining the handmade craftwork of trinkets and souvenirs. As he slowly made his way across the square, he focused his attention on other apartments in the square overlooking the Mi6 safe house apartment, to see if anyone else was interested in the apartment.

Judging his pace on the street as he watched the approaching busses as he passed those hovering in cues by the bus stops in front of the entrance, in a straightforward movement as passengers pressed forward to board the next bus he darted off the pavement and back behind the steel gates and towards the main apartment lobby doors, with a flick of a lock pick he was inside the main lobby, before the bus outside had pulled away.

With the tall oak panel door closed the noise of the street seemed calm and the coolness of the stairwell was a relief as he pitched his head upward towards the glass roof, refraining from holding the stair rail and listened, with nothing but the call of the street he took swiftly to the stairs his Browning was now in his right hand with silencer attached.

Finding the third-floor apartment he listened through the door, a radio was playing somewhere in the rooms beyond, there was no damage to the door or the frame. Again with a flick of his wrist, he picked the lock, as easy as if he was pulling the ring pull of a can of Coke, he checked for any improvised explosive trigger wire before slowly entering.

Although on entering he could hear the radio on somewhere in a backroom, he sensed the apartment was empty.

Entering the main lounge there were signs of a struggle of some sort altercation and possible abduction, furniture was pushed against the walls a lamp having been used as a weapon, smashed. Picking up pieces of furniture, he noticed scuff marks and what appeared to be lines on the linoleum floor, from where shoe heels had been dragged backwards.

As the wind caught papers on the table in the kitchen, he span low with his Browning in his hand, "Easy Pimm." he whispered and turned the radio down to a murmur as he studied the cat litter tray, most of its contents were spread across the melonium floor.

Having established the flat was empty, his attention turned to the main bedroom which it appeared the two Mi6 agents had been using as an HQ, gathering Intel on their German targets. The walls held pieces of tape and fragments of photograph paper, from those that had been stripped away, a map of Brazil had been torn down from the wall, only its corners remained. With nothing of value in the room on the first inspection, he turned his attention to the few personal items left by their abductors looking for signs of tradecraft.

They may have been young but they had been trained by the best and he viewed each room as if he had been there and needed to leave a hidden gift for any following Mi6 officer that followed in behind, at the same time he looked for signs Bob Gregory had also been there, in secret coded hints they left for each other on such occasions, a painting turned to face the wall, any book left upside down amongst others on a shelf, just two of five innocent things that any household might hold that would reveal to him, Gregory's presence. But there was nothing and nothing to show from Bull's team members, even after checking air vent covers and pulling all the kitchen appliances out, but interestingly there was no sign of a cat. He looked at the kitty litre on the kitchen floor and then checked the cupboards and then rubbish bin for empty cat food tins and summarized that under the paper of the cat tray was where the agents had hidden anything of value, and it had been found, but by who?

He sighed and grabbed a bottle of gin from the lounge and an aluminium ice tray from the small freezer and sat at the bedroom desk looking around the wall speculating what had been held there, and taken by whoever had abducted the two agents. So far the only good news was there was no blood on the scene. Whoever it was they had attacked with overwhelming brute force, there was no exchange of gunfire.

As his eyes looked at the residual cotton still tied to pins that had once connected the information map together that had been displayed on the wall Pimm's eyes noticed the pinholes in the wall where the map had been hung, as well as those that had once been set in its corners that kept it up in place, they would have signified points of interest to the Mi6 team. He rubbed his finger over the tiny indentations and then looked at a torn piece of the map corner still pinned to the wall it held a part of the map company's logo. Pimm had seen this style of map many times in the airport, in tourist shops and on sale in the fair in the streets below. He gauged the size of the map and taking the corner piece headed back down to the street and purchased a copy of the same map.

Unfortunately, Pimm's exit and entrance this time were observed by the red-headed Mossad agent who had been staking out the Mi6 safe house from an adjoining building.

Having taped the map on the wall exactly in the same position as the original Pimm felt along with his finger gently until he could feel the indentations and then pushed four pins into the map then stood back, they marked Sao Paulo, Caieiras, the town of Serra Negra and an area north approximately 13 kilometre off the SP 352. Pimm sipped the remains of his glass of gin, it was warm, so he went to grab ice from the aluminium ice cube tray, it was then he hit pay dirt, amongst the melt water a small locker key with the number 404 that Cartwright had concealed within an ice cube. Pimm glanced out of the window it would be somewhere close, Bull had taught them well from the window he could see across the street beside a tattoo parlour a public notary office, they would have secure lockers within the building.

Pimm double-checked the map and folding it up, went back to the square. As his sandals touched the clay path into the gardens, this time Pimm sensed he had a tail. Even without the heads up from Patrick, the beach hustler, that Mossad had a red-headed agent stationed in Rio, Pimm had spotted the girl, catching her tied up ponytail as it swished from side to side in the refection of an ice cream vendor's tall steel fridge unit. Pimm pulled up abruptly and ordered a raspberry ripple ice cream as he watched her make a play of checking out a bookstall on the market.

Questions now rose in his head as he led a dance through the hippy market, buying two postcards, why was Mossad staking out their safe house, did this agent know anything about their missing agents?

He gave a slight gesture of No! to Allan, as he looked up from his paper still sat behind the wheel of his taxi and Pimm passed him by and carried then entered the public notary offices. Inside he showed the guard the locker keys and was directed to an open area at the rear of the building where the general public could rent a small luggage locker.

Opening 404 he found an A4 sized envelope inside, it held two spare passports for the agents, a small bundle of Real notes and a collection of colour photographs. Pimm used the locker door to shield his examination as he quickly flicked through them, immediately he recognised the image of the girl that had just tailed him, from two of the photographs, alongside a man Pimm judged to be in his late twenties

early thirties with dark curly hair, who he presumed was also Mossad. Both were in the company of General Daniel Mier Zavineski, "Zavi" a senior Mossad commander, in one photo and in another with a light blue-suited tall westerner, Pimm took to be a company man, CIA.
Pimm was not to know it at the time, but the man in the suit was the same individual Bob Gregory had witnessed meeting with Klaus in the canteen Bar de Fonte *(Fountain)* in Monte Alegre du Sul, a member of Carter-Wallis's rogue CIA operation, playing a fine dance between The Spider Organization and Mossad.

Pimm had first heard of Zavi through Bull who had met him in Berlin. He had worked with British intelligence after the war. Like Bull Gordon and Tom Quinn, Mier Zavineski had been on Omaha Beach with the Americans on D day.
At the end of the war he had worked for a time with Berlin SIS, Zavi had used his last days in Berlin trawling as much information as possible from both sides of the iron curtain, so that when he left to join Mossad, he caused security mayhem for not just the American's but also the British team that was stationed at Neukölln where the 450 metres surveillance tunnel to the east to spy on the Russians was well into construction, for a time there were calls by some that it had been compromised by Zavi's departure. At that time the Section Chief was Simon Lunn, and Bull Gordon was his second in command, Pimm was working in the field, where for many it was tense days as a witch hunt ensued believing the Russians had captured Zavi, until he turned up in Tel Aviv wearing his new Aluf, *(General)* insignia.

If Zavi had been caught in Europe by either the American's or British, the fact he had been at Omaha on D day would not have helped.
As Pimm studied the image of General Zavineski, he considered how deep the American's may be involved in whatever operation, Bull's people had stumbled on in Brazil looking through the other photographs taken by Lamb and Cartwright he searched for images of CIA presence, saw none and although there were no images of Dr Mengele he also recognised the image of an unidentified male in his fifties that had been originally captured RAF Captain's family snap at the Ipanema café restaurant, Pimm had no name but it was Merill Nestlar.
As Pimm flicked through the other images two photographs set him on edge, both holding images of a black man, who Pimm recognized as Musse Bin Abokkor, Ali Hassan's, chief enforcer.

Pimm considered his options with the redhead outside, it was too hot to run around, so he decided to play a hunch and walking back outside, noticed the girl had withdrawn to the other side of the street as he climbed back into Alan's taxi.
"Hold for a while let the girl get her ride, then back to the hotel, take it easy," Pimm told Alan, as they pulled away from the square, Alan spotted the girl following them. "She's got a scooter, two cars back," he said and now knew exactly what sort of client Pimm was.
"Drop me at the hotel, and then wait for me by the side entrance," Pimm said as they arrived outside the Othon Hotel. He then dallied in the entrance lobby looking at the papers, allowing the girl to follow him in and witness him retrieving his room key.
"The redhead behind, let the girl hear my name," he whispered to Carlo.
"That was quick work I wish I managed that when I go fishing," he muttered under his breath
"No messages today, Mr Pimm!" The concierge announced turning away from the key box, and the girl caught the room number and name then watched Pimm step into the lift with other guests, he got out at the first level and darted to the stairwell. Allan watched the girl pass by him on her scooter in his rear-view mirror, then started the engine as he saw Pimm bound down the steps from the side entrance.
"I take it we follow," Allan said and span the car in a wide U-turn then joined the other taxi's headed towards the city centre, travelling north along Copacabana, occasionally receiving hand gestures and swearing from other drivers, as they kept up with the girl as she weaved in and out of the traffic. The beach vendor Patrick had been right, the girl pulled into the bike park below the Jornal do Brasil, parking up they watched her go inside holding a camera, Pimm sat in the open window of the café opposite obscured by a large yucca plant.
"Bless you your heart," he told the waiter who brought him a cup of tea and single J & B Scotch. Dabbing his forehead with his handkerchief, he scanned the windows of the newspaper building through his camera lens.
By now, it was midday, and some of the workers were heading from the buildings for lunch break. He watched most wind their way towards the beach to steal relief. The young redheaded women emerged and with others drifted alone amongst the main group of pedestrians that were called by the bells of the midday Catholic mass to cross the road over towards the church. As the first chime of twelve rang down the bustling streets, she stubbed her cigarette out on the steps and filed behind the bent heads of other parishioners that disappeared behind the Norman styled doors. Pimm checked the street both ways downed his scotch then gestured to the waiter as he left a note under his mug that held a peace logo.

Instantly on entering the sanctum, the oppressive of heat slipped away, as if taking off a heavy coat and the still, cool scented air held familiar dampness. It could be any Catholic church in any city, he touched the font's holy water making the sign of the cross. Taking a pew three rows from the back, beside a column he watched the girl on the opposite side, eight rows down listening to the Padre as he began the service in Latin.

The congregation of forty or more sat, occasionally muttering the response's to the service, overseen by the mesmerising stare of a life-sized authentically gruesome crucifix that hung from ancient chains from the vaulted ceiling. As the pale suited man Lamb and Cartwright had photographed with General Zavineski drifted casually down to the pew in front of the redhead and placed himself in front, it wasn't just the fact that he failed to remove his standard-issue Ray-Ban sunglasses that screamed CIA in Pimm's ears. When next the mass prayer service called for the kneeling for prayers, with all heads bowed except Pimm's the girl shuffled very slightly forward, and when she raised to her feet she no longer held her Bible. As some of the faithful took their place in the line for communion, she turned back towards the door and slipped to the street. The drop was that quick that simple, Pimm considered staying with the American in the pale suit, but seeing the man's vision to the rear obscured, decided to follow the girl.

On the steps with his camera raised to his eye, he caught sight of her hair a street away, Pimm passed by Allen's taxi he dropped the camera to his lap, through the car window

"Wait here" he ordered, and Allan and the taxi driver got the briefest glint of the silencer on Pimm's revolver as he folded his gun within the pages of his newspaper as Pimm began to follow the girl on foot.

Trailing back he occasionally stopped to watch her reflection in shop windows, and while pretending to be choosing postcards from a vendor's carousel, at one point he removed his shirt and hat, laying them at the feet of a beggar, this effectively lowered and altered his profile amongst the camouflage of other pedestrians. Unlike so many that get caught up in a mouse chase, Pimm checked behind and to the opposite street, to make sure he himself was not being tailed and as her sandals clipped inward to the city, along taller darker streets, he began to feel more conspicuous receiving the occasional glance from young men who obviously were sizing him up as a mark.

Turning down a residential street, he held back, watching her in the reflection of a parked van door mirror and saw her scan briefly back and forth, then crossed the street and pressed one of the many buttons on an apartment block.

Pimm could not see the number but saw it was one of the highest buttons on the bell board.

Looking up to the top floor balcony, a mop of brown curly hair appeared belonging to the man that had been captured in the photograph by Cartwright and Lamb. He whistled down to the girl and threw her a set of keys, looking along the street the man appeared drawn to the noise coming from a group of street urchins who were playing as they kicked a battered tin cooking oil drum, back and forth across the street.

Pimm ducked into a doorway and waited until the man at the balcony disappeared, and the girl entered the apartment block, crossing the street he hugged along the doorways of the buildings on the same side as the building. His gun was now held ready within the folds of his paper as he slipped down a tight municipal service street until he came out into two diverging alleys one backed along the rear of the apartment block the girl had gone inside. Cautiously pushing forward, he heard three of the teenage gang members, were now stalking him from behind four meters back. He gave them a sideways glance, then briefly let his revolver slip down from the newspaper into the grip of his hand, with the faintest glint of the barrel in the light the boys disappeared into the nearest rear garden doorway, cursing at each other.

In an adjacent apartment block back yard, skulking behind the rusted wreck of a truck, Pimm sensed someone was using as a home, he scanned for the corresponding rear balcony area to the girls flat, counting along, he noticed theirs like so many others, was cluttered with timber crates and general household rubbish. The probability was high; it was either a Mossad safe house or a stakeout for another building opposite.

Pimm span back on himself, ducking low, checking behind and up to see which building they would have a good line of sight of from their balcony. He immediately realised it was the larger six-storey apartment building, behind and to his right, but there were too many windows for him to work out which they were watching. There was only one way of finding out, and that meant getting inside the Mossad apartment.

Mossad and Mi6 were not adversaries at this time, but sharing of information and assets was frowned upon and only occurred amongst the highest levels between individuals that had history, often from service in the field together. Although each operated their own clandestine foreign assignments, both security agencies took their lead from the Americans, who often acted as an intermediary.

Pimm could not be sure what sort of welcome he would receive.

Standing on the external iron staircase he realised the teenagers were still watching him, he whistled calling them over and holding up four twenty Reais notes, slowly they approached.

"I need to play a trick on an old friend, in the flat up there." his fluent Portuguese took the boys off guard, as he gestured to the building and they listened to his orders like the street commandoes they were.

Once he had instructed the group what they were to do, he handed them some of the money, and with the rest, he tore the notes in half, giving them one part. "You get this when I come out, go!" again he flashed his gun, to dissuade any surreptitious plans they may have for him, with their friends, who he had no doubt were waiting close by. Watching them turn tail, Pimm then climbed up an external fire stairwell that in places had missing ladder rungs. It would have been a death trap to anyone seeking to exit the building in an emergency.

On the roof of the apartment, he found more signs of the street urchins, a mosaic of graffiti gang tags and timber boards that allowed them to cross back and forth between the flat-roofed buildings.

Having picked the door lock, Pimm crept inside the access stairwell, immediately sounds from the flats echoed up and the smell of cooking was overpowering, bags of garbage sat in some of the halls, and he watched a rat having been disturbed following his run disappear into a crack in the skirting.

From the landing window, he looked down to the main street and saw the children begin to run between the buildings, making a nuisance by repeatedly pressing the apartment doorbells. It was followed soon by the irate curses of the tenants, and he began to hear the sound of door buzzers in his building, within minutes there was an eruption of foul language and threats from the front balconies to the street urchins below, the occasional bottle was heard smashing in the street. He then heard from the Mossad apartment front balcony the man's voice swearing in Hebrew and English,

"Fucking rats....fuck off now, I'll call the police, fucking vermin!" he shouted and tossed down an empty can of Pepsi.

On hearing the man speaking English and as instructed by Pimm, the boys he enlisted began to challenge the Israeli goading him further, focusing their attention on that building.

Inside the stairwell landing, Pimm dropped to the other side of the apartment door with his ear pushed against the side, listening it appeared the girl was arguing with the man, who was getting increasingly worked up as their door buzzer was by now almost constant, There was a brief pause and Pimm braced himself ready as the buzzer sounded and the shouting continued outside. Hearing footsteps approaching the door from inside, he drew his hand back with his revolver clasped across the handle.

Full of furry, totally distracted, the cursing Mossad agent removed all the door latches. The jangle of the latch chain signalled Pimm like a starting pistol, and with the faintest opening, he barged forward. Immediately following through with an upward punch ramming his gun into the face of the Mossad agents nose knocking him backwards with such ferocity that he doubled back smashing his head on the door frame and wall behind and collapsed in a heap, blood gushing from his wound.

"Don't!" Pimm warned the girl standing in the far doorway and raised his gun, "I'm Pimm, Mi6 London." he showed her the side of his gun and sliced back the safety.

The girl stepped back as Pimm checked the man's pulse, placing a hand on his throat.

"Is Mel dead?" she was frozen with her hands stretched out, aware Pimm could cut her down before she reached her Glock revolver sat next to a bottle of Pepsi on the coffee table.

"He's alive, stay where I can see you." then he gestured for her to back up, "sit in the chair now….on your hands."

The girl did as he ordered, "If you are Mi6, why this?" she looked at his gun.

"Your people have a habit of shooting first, I know from experience, I am sorry about your friend." Pimm removed Mel's gun from its holster and felt his neck for a pulse, catching some of the blood coming from his nose on his fingers he wiped it off on Mel's shirt and stepped forward into the lounge. His gaze went straight to the far wall examining their own operation plans with maps of Brazil, Rio and photographs that included images of the two Mi6 agents Nick Cartwright and Neil Lamb.

"These are why I'm here Lamb and Cartwright, my people." Pimm looked to the girl and retaining one of the Glock revolvers removed the magazine from the other and placed the gun on the table as he heard shouting outside from the street urchins calling up and the door buzzer sounded again.

"Hey, mister, mister! English where's our money English!" One of the boys called up.

Pimm went over to the window but looked first to her, "You calm now Red, what is your name?"

The girl gestured with a nod "Yes, Ruby." She studied his clothes, the ridiculous unfashionable socked sandals, how the hell did she not catch him trailing her, she cursed herself.

"Believe it or not, I'm a friend Ruby, go, see to your colleague and please no problems, I am who I say I am. I know you work with General Zavineski, I worked in Berlin in 68. I have no idea how ling a leash your people have you one but the company man you met in the church will confirm my identity, I followed you from the church. If I wanted to harm you, I would have when I entered." Pimm picked up a cushion from the sofa and turning back to the window took the torn banknotes from his pocket poked them inside the cushion and threw it down to the street, it was greeted by whistles from the boys, he saw the girl hesitate, "and if I was not a friend would I do this." he threw the gun magazines to the empty seat, "Listen Red, I'm just here to take a look-see, find out if you can help me with my people, that's it, whatever you have here, is not my concern today, unless you know different and something has happened to them?"

There was a look of guilt in Ruby's eyes as she looked to the kitchen and he turned his attention back to the wall of information, studying the images he looked through the kitchen and to the open rear balcony door where a high powered sound recording antenna was set alongside a tripod holding a telephoto lens camera. Pimm pulled one of the photographs from its wall pins, it held the image of Bull's missing officers, they appeared to be being escorted from a white van into a building, the body language was wrong, and the expression's on the Mi6 operator's faces especially the girl Cartwright indicated to Pimm they were being forced. Pimm walked through to the camera and looked through the lens,

"He's out cold, you really did a number on him, his nose is broken, I need a hand," she called as Pimm squinted through the viewfinder of the camera and saw the Mossad agents had been watching a top floor apartment with curtains drawn in the building backing on to the rear alley and backyards.

With apartments having ineffectual air-con closed curtains during the day raised little suspicion amongst other tenants. With a metallic click Pimm raised his head from behind the lens, Ruby had returned to the lounge and had already loaded her magazine into her Glock, which she now held at her side cocked, for a moment there was a tense silence then she slipped the safety back on and tucked it into the back of her jeans' waistband.

"It would have been a problem if you had killed him, you say you know Zavi, he's very protective," she said and as Pimm helped her carry Mel through to the lounge placing him on the sofa with his legs raised.

Pimm's eyes could not help drifting to the girl's chest, she wore no bra her olive tone blended with the sweat of her body and her small breasts clung to the fine orange cotton of her short sleeve shirt. As she brushed her auburn hair back over her ear lobe, something stirred inside Pimm, he put it down to the rush of the action and stepped over to check the damage he had inflicted on her colleague, weary that he might wake at any moment and continue to fight him.

Pimm knew it was a stretch to say he knew Zavineski, but he had no time for explanations, to establish trust but knew the Mossad chief would have taken it personally if he had killed one of his agents and listened to Mel's breathing, while feeling for a pulse, then checked his pupils.

"He'll be ok, get some ice for his head and some water for when he comes round, where are my people?" Pimm pulled another photo off the wall, Ruby looked back towards the surveillance equipment.

"As of forty-eight hours ago they were in the room with the yellow curtains, we have seen no movement since, they are being held by three maybe four, Germans, our brief originally concerned an arms sale. That was until we had confirmation of Mengele, from a picture taken by one of your people in Ipanema." she gestured to a copy of the Mi6 photograph Bull had originally showed Pimm at his home in Muswell London, the holiday picture that was taken by the ex-RAF Captain showing Josef Mengele, Merill Nestlar and another elderly looking European sometimes pictured with the younger man tall blonde man, Klaus Ritter.

Bull gave noting away as he examined the print as he considered either Bull had passed the photograph to General Zavineski, without informing Pimm, possibly reaching for assistance regarding the missing agents, or there was a Mossad mole inside Mi6. Pimm chose to ignore the burning questions in his head, where and when did they get the photograph, focusing on the lost agents and part of him considered he may already be too late.

"You mean to tell me you have been sitting on this? How long have our people been over there?" Pimm shook his head in disbelief as the other Mossad agent Mel began to moan, regaining consciousness as Ruby comforted her colleague.

"Fuck, my head! " Pimm heard the man say as he returned to the camera and scanned along the building. One of the Germans wearing a shoulder holster came out onto a balcony and was smoking with a bottle of beer in his hand. It was Nestlar's bodyguard Klaus, at times to Pimm he appeared to be looking directly across towards the lens, another man appeared on the balcony and directed Klaus back inside, Pimm tried to read his lips, he appeared to say the word "Doctor." Inside the Spider apartment Klaus took a phone call.

"Yes Herr Doctor, I can confirm the shipment is on board the vessel, the Somalian Abokkor witnessed the loading and he and his men will accompany it. Departure is 06.30 tomorrow morning, they remain in place guarding the dock, our end of the agreement has been fulfilled." Klaus, looked at his men watching the opening

ceremony of a football match on the television and held his hand over the mouth piece as cheers went up on the screen with the arrival of the players on the pitch, "Turn that down!" he growled.
"And what about your guest, did they report home?" Merill Nestlar asked
"I do not believe so Sir, they are from a British newspaper apparently they were investigating information regarding a photograph taken in Rio" Klaus looked towards the kitchen.
"And the one that got away, was he with them?" Nestlar asked concerned about Bob Gregory's escape from the gas killing field.
"No, I was thorough, if they had I would know I believe, he was some bum."
"You believe or you are sure?" Nestlar sounded unsatisfied with Klaus's report.
"I am sure, Sir," Klaus raised his eyes to his colleagues in the room, seeing the football game was about to start.
"Well let's hope so, it is a shame we could not find the body. Perhaps it is as well we are leaving for a while, be sure and pick me up from the hotel tomorrow early. I would be happier if we were flying direct, it's a long way round to return home, but I think necessary under the circumstances." Klaus could hear Nestlar was unhappy in the manner in which he was being forced to travel back to Europe.
"Yes for sure, I have informed, the Executive Committee of our travel arrangements and they have the bank in Geneva standing by for our arrival." Klaus made a gesture indicating to one of his men to fetch him a beer.
"Good, deal with your guest, understand." Nestlar's tone was callous and unemotional in ordering the disposal of the Mi6 agents.
"I will do it myself." Klaus answered and hung up.
"So, they are for the bin," One of Klaus's men went to stand reluctantly.
"Yar, yar, but it can wait, they're going nowhere, turn it up." Klaus raised his bottle and slouched down on the sofa, as supporters waving German flags in the stadium pictured on the television erupted in cheers at the action on the pitch.

Behind him, Pimm could hear Ruby Struggling with her colleague, as he began to swear at him. "You fuck, you broke my nose, what are you doing here you're screwing up months of work." he shook his head, and now upright more blood began to drip from his nose, he held his head back.
"My fucking head I should kill you, why the fuck did you let him in, how the hell do we know he's from London?" Mel glared up at him, and Pimm took out the two Mi6 agents passports from his leg pocket.
"You would be dead, and I would not have these, now answer the question, how long have they been over there and why have you not reported this to your people

and mine?" Pimm glared at the man with little sympathy for the injury he had caused.

As they spoke, Pimm saw in both their eyes the truth, Tel Aviv already knew about the British agents, "What about Langley, I know you're getting help on this party from the farm boys." Pimm considered the company man at the Catholic Church.

Mel shook his head, "This is too much you need to leave, I need to contact the boss, you have no business here Mi6 has no jurisdiction, something is happening you know nothing about."

The girl could see Pimm's eyes recording every detail of the information on the walls, he recognised their map held the same pin locations like the one he had made from the holes in the wall of the Mi6 safe house.

"Who are the old men with Mengele, and other Nazi's?" he asked pointing to photographs that included shots of the men first recorded by the RAF pilot in the Ipanema bar Bull had given him in England.

"We believe Mengele has been recruited working with those he knew in the war, from the Kaiser Wilhelm in Berlin, now they work on this, we want Mengele, but there is so much more going on" Ruby tapped a photograph that showed cattle lying dead in a field, blood appeared to be emanating from their eyes and mouths

"Gas?" Pimm whispered

"Ruby shut the fuck up! This has nothing to do with him" Mel whined.

"One we think has already flown the nest headed back to Europe, Merrill Nestlar a scientist like Mengele in the war, ex-RPA, Aktion T4." she ignored Mel and continued, "this is his bodyguard, Klaus Ritter, the doctor goes nowhere without him, until now, he is over there, East German military we think." Ruby tapped his image in the Ipanema photograph.

"Spetsnaz?" Pimm asked recognising Klaus Ritter from the original photograph from Ipanema

"Possibly or Stasi, Tel Aviv is checking on him, this Philipp Bouhler, if you are who you say Pimm you know he is a senior Spider Executive Director and was head of Aktion T4, we think he is the one recruiting for Spider over here, you know this ?" Ruby's answer was reprimanded again.

"Yes, I know of Philippe Bouhler." Pimm nodded.

"Will you please just shut the fuck up Ruby, it's bad enough we deal with the Yanks the Brits will screw us!" Mel snorted as if he had swallowed dirty water.

Pimm probably as much as they knew about Aktion T4 and Spider network and remained calm, that was not his mission, and he had already decided his next move.

"One last thing, we had another man from six come over, six, four, younger, dark hair, if you saw him you would remember." Pimm looked to Ruby, she shook her head.

"No, we caught your people on camera entering three nights ago, no one else, the men holding like them take their orders from Ritter all are members of Spider. Most are too young to have served the Reich except him maybe?" she pointed again to the image of the man Pimm had just seen smoking on the balcony.

"He's defiantly in charge of the muscle," she added.

With that, Pimm gestured to Ruby's Glock revolver and magazine he still held in his hand.

"Bill London for this, I 'm sorry about." Pimm tapped his head looking to Mel who clearly did not accept his apology. "If you want any chance to come out of this without shit on your face, use your emergency Evac. Get your people down here now! If they ask about me, tell them to speak with Bull Gordon he and General Zavineski go way back. Whoever is over there that lives, you can have, I just want my people back." Pimm left to the sound of the Mel cursing at Ruby.

In the street, he got a thank you wave from one of the street kids he had employed for his distraction, Pimm flashed his gun, and the urchin acknowledged and backed away. Pimm followed the back yard walls towards the parallel street that held the Spider apartment block. He noticed a woman pushing an old supermarket trolley full of bags of clothes and then others, similarly laden with laundry, some with children that entered the public laundrette a few doors down. Grabbing a small sack from the side of overflowing garbage bin, he wandered down the street with the bag held up it stunk of rotting fish and maggots dropped to his shoulder, but he kept it covering his face as he passed the main ground floor entrance the Spider apartment building. Inside the lobby, he glimpsed briefly a middle-aged European reading the newspaper Die Welt, sat at a desk while listening to what sounded like a football match on a portable radio.

Pimm continued on and entered the laundrette, receiving the odd look from the women, especially one who sat nearest to the door where he dropped the bag of rubbish, she noticed the maggots he brushed from his shoulder and let out a scream, as he headed through to the back room and toilet.

"Ignoring the commotion ensuing inside, Pimm studied the rear elevation of the building. As with the Mossad apartment block, there was a fire escape servicing the two adjoining buildings, this one was in better order, and although the bottom had a chained padlocked gate, he climbed over and took to the steel stairs. On the roof Pimm found some of the people of this block had made the area a communal cantina area with a barbecue, homemade Jacuzzi with seating and as with many of the flat roofs there were signs of children with graffiti to the walls and scaffold boards used to access across from one building to the next.

Mel nudged Ruby from the eyepiece of the camera in the Mossad apartment kitchen.

"What the fuck's he up to? He's going to blow this deal." He said, watching Pimm peering over the edge of the rooftop down to the two balconies of the German apartment three metres below. While Ruby turned back to the lounge and looked at a photograph that contained the image of Nick Cartwright. Ruby had questioned why they were not helping the Mi6 agents to Zavi, but Mel was lead on their assignment and had convinced Tel Aviv, with Mengele, and Bouhler circling the area there was the possibility to bring the whole Spider network down, not just in South America but also in Europe if they could trace the source of the money. Sacrificing two British agents was a small price for justice for the millions lost in the holocaust.

Mel was born in Kamianets-Podilskyi in May 1941, his mother worked in a poultry factory, with a neighbour who was still breastfeeding, they took turns watching over each other's child during their alternate work shifts, the neighbour was Christian. On the 27th August when Einsatzgruppen C rounded up over 23,000 Jews in the area and began a three-day massacre, it had been the neighbours turn to look after the infants, and she claimed to the soldiers Mel was her child.

All of Mel's family were killed in the massacre at Kamianets-Podilskyi, and he had no recollection of their existence, his surrogate mother brought him up as her own, in the Christian faith along with her own child, who he still called sister. But on the day of his sixteenth birthday the women he had always known as his mother told him the truth as she wept, two years later he changed his name from Michel Gyuri to the name he was told he was born with Melvyn Aronov and joined the IDF *(Israel Defence Forces)* from where he was recruited to Mossad, now ranking as a senior field agent.

From the roof edge, below him, Pimm could hear the television turned up loud and the sound of men cheering coming from the main rooms separate balcony. One of the French doors had been left open, and a long nylon net curtain drifted in and out caught occasionally by a soft gust.

Pimm stole a breath and looked down at the smaller kitchen balcony with its doors closed and then looked back across the rear yards towards the Mossad apartment and shook his head. He was still vexed that they had done nothing to inform Mi6, but he cast thoughts aside and focused his intent as he gently shuttered the slide on his revolver, pulling it into his body to muffle the sound and then turned back to the contents of the roof, taking every detail in of his environment as he walked back over to the internal stair access and gently tried the metal door. The handle was rusty, the sound it made as he gently turned it was no louder than the squeak from a bicycle's brakes, to Pimm it sounded like a steam engine's whistle and he bit his lip finding the door held a heavy internal chain and padlocked, that was too far from reach to be picked. Perspiration rained from his forehead as he closed it softly and went back to the roof edge to check his access to the separate kitchen balcony bellow, looking to the large gutter and drain pipe that serviced that side of the building he judged it would take his full stretch with both arms out to reach across the balcony, if he climbed down. Recognizing it was the only assault option available he began removing his sandals and socks.

"Can you believe this clown" Mel cursed as he watched Pimm gingerly scaling down the outside of the building. At the same level as the balcony with one hand wrapped around the pipe and his toes clawing to the fixing bracket Pimm stretched out, reaching over the clear drop to the back yard below. Pimm's fingers were only just able to grip the edge of the concrete balcony, and he had to spring away from the pipe to take a firm hold, before hurdling over the edge and landing gently on the other side.

He stayed his approach and took a breath listening, there was no sign he had disturbed the occupants as he heard, what sounded like a dispute between the men over a referee decision regarding a foul, in the football game they were watching. The smaller separate kitchen balcony held a simple twin chair set and table. Crouching below the handrail Pimm looked through the open metal guard bars that faced out, knowing Ruby and Mel if they were watching would be able to see him, he hugged the wall listening to the sounds of the German's football banter coming from within the apartment, the kitchen was quiet.

Across from the backyards In the Mossad apartment Mel had seen enough and held out his hand expectantly to Ruby,

"That was your gun he took." He snapped his fingers and Ruby shrugged bowing to his seniority removed his revolver from her waistband which he snatched from her hands.

"This operation is blown we need to contact Zavi, get your shit together and get back to the newspaper, until I get new orders" he barked as he began to strip their rooms of any papers.

"And what about him and them, we still have no idea what the Africans are buying and I don't trust the Americans treating us like a yoyo, something is not right there, I don't know where Zavi's getting his Intel, but I just don't see how this works with the Yanks knowing about the Brits over there, it makes no sense they didn't tell London.

Our people Zavi, I can understand, but the Yanks, it makes no sense, Washington and London are joined at the hip."

Ruby returned to watching Pimm's progress and could see he was still on the kitchen balcony, through the metal guard.

With his face against the glass, Pimm looked through a slit in the curtain of the patio door, it was worse than he had expected, he ignored the sight of the agents, and as he pushed his face to the side, he saw the kitchen door to his right was closed. He moved further forward, and Nick Cartwright looked up, seeing his shadow at the window. Her face was badly bruised, her right eye bloodshot and as puffy as a Sunday roast Yorkshire pudding, her cheeks were badly scratched and cut from the gold signet ring on the fist of one of her assailants. Having removed her bra, they had stripped her down to a vest shirt vest torn to one side it barely covered her breasts. Pimm could see blood to her spit lips had soaked into the fine white cotton of the gag across her mouth which had been made with the use of her own bra and pulled so tight it was cutting the blood to her cheeks.

Her eyes showed pure fear as she looked at him, closing them in pain, she winced as he watched her raise a single finger from her bound hands and arms tied behind her back and pointed in the direction of the main room. Pimm recognized how some of her fingers were twisted back and obviously had been deliberately broken, during her torture, but the one Cartwright raised flicked four times signalling to Pimm there were four combatants to deal with, lifting her head she looked across the table to her partner and tears streamed burning into the wounds on her cheeks.

Neil Lamb did not move, his battered head remained down, hair thickly matted with blood. One of his hands was untied and pinned to the table with a barbecue meat skewer, at its side three of his fingers lay in a pool of blood having been cleaved off, the wide butcher's knife rested upright with its blade embedded in the tabletop, next to what appeared to be photographs. Pimm could see both agents had their ankles tied to their chairs as he looked at the blood pool on the floor below Lamb and knew there was too much, it was likely he was already dead, if not, then close to it.

As per his training, Pimm's eyes began to scan the room, before entry, looking amongst other things for obstacles that might impede his progress or be used to assist in defence of the environment and for any weapons that might aid his assault. His eyes were immediately drawn to the back of the room and a stack of black plastic bags, wood saws and other butchering equipment, clearly, at the ready for the dismemberment of his colleagues, they were going nowhere except out of the door in pieces, without his help.

This was going to be a hard exit to accomplish, but he gave no inclination in his expression to Cartwright of his misgiving of the likelihood of success as he raised his hand and made the sign OK.

He rested for a moment with his back against the window, his mind began picking up on every detail of his surroundings since arriving on the rooftop. Irrespective of Cartwright's gesture he knew there were at least three or four heavily armed men from the photographs he had seen in the Mossad apartment, he could expect no assistance from Lamb or Cartwright in their escape, and at first glance it appeared neither could make it back the way he had just come, the only way out was through, them, his only advantage to date, their distraction by the football game, but if he was going to get his people out, he would need to kill all the Germans and to do this he would need a monumental distraction to maximise his element of surprise.

Pimm turned back briefly and felt the door handle it opened, then on hearing movement in the main room, he ducked back, dropping over the metal guard and hanging off the lower rail in mid-air below the balcony floor.

Watching from the Mossad apartment Ruby was amazed, she had miss-judged Pimm's agility totally, and his athletic strength, his strange quirky almost comical caricature of middle-aged Englishman had thrown her completely.

"Only ten minutes to half time, maybe we have a quick fuck you and me Brit bitch before I chop you up!" Pimm heard one of the German's blood-curdling threat to Cartwright, as he came through from the lounge and passing her by having retrieved four bottles of beer from the fridge for his colleagues, he paused and pulled her hair back, for a moment Cartwright thought this was her last breath as he pulled the meat cleaver free from the table, dripping with Lamb's blood he brandished it at her neck and she felt the fine steel blade's cool touch on her throat, then hearing a cheer from his cohorts he slapped her lightly on the cheek and dropped the knife on the table, then rushed back into the room with the television, leaving the door open. Realizing this would hamper Pimm's entrance into the kitchen Cartwright began to deliberately moan, and one of her other captives scolded the man who had fetched the beers. "Shut up, bitch!" he swore before pulling the door shut.

Pimm pulled himself up onto the balcony, moving quickly inside he grabbed the bloody cleaver from the table first cutting Cartwright's restraints, then getting no pulse from Lamb, he left him tied and gently wedged the thick meat cleaver blade into the door jam, with the expectation of it hindering the opening of the door from the other side.

"Bull sent me, I'm Pimm, I know you're in pain, be strong, Lamb is dead, but he can still help you." Pimm took her weight and helped lay her to the back of the kitchen, propping up with her back against the far wall on the other side of the fridge, then opening its door he removed a bottle of water and held it to her lips, having to cover her mouth as she went to splutter and cough.

"I'm ok" she breathed as the blooded water trickled down to the bra gag still hanging off her neck, Pimm nodded and then carefully balancing the weight of Lamb's body on the legs of the chair, lay the agent down so that his body wedged the fridge door open and partially shielded Cartwright on the floor.

Pimm looked at her hands, there was little to distinguish between them in damage as he took the safety off the Glock he had taken from the Mossad agent, he cocked it, she knew what he was going to try and do and signalled she was ready. Pimm allowed her to muffle her cries into his shoulder and as she bit into his flesh, he had to grit his own teeth with the pain, while gently he opened her hand and placed the gun in her mangled grip, with the one unbroken finger resting on the trigger ready to fire.

"I need to go to work in there and have to leave you, he pointed up to the roof, keep down, shoot anything that comes through that door, even if I am not ready." As he spoke, her eyes appeared to register her understanding he was her only hope. Working purely on his tradecraft training, with instinctive precise moves with each breath as he passed by the table again his hand snatched up the photographs from the table, and gave them the briefest glance, two showed clear headshots of the Mossad agents Ruby and Mel and also alarmingly one showed Bob Gregory who appeared bound and unconscious. Pimm stuffed them in his pocket then froze hearing the men in the lounge thunder a tremendous cheer as a goal was scored. Fortunately for Pimm and Cartwright, the men in the other room were not just watching any football match, it was Bayern Munich v Atlético Madrid, the European cup final and it had completely distracted them from completing their instructions. Having been given the green light by Merill Nestlar to dispose of the Mi6 agents following Lamb and Cartwright's torture.

It had been an effective sequence of inhuman acts of barbarity by Klaus Ritter that had precipitated Lamb informing them that no report concerning the nerve gas experiments had been sent back to London. Having had his third and fourth finger from one hand removed and watched while each of Cartwright's fingers had been broken in turn, bar one. It was only when the cleaver rested on her knuckle that Lamb looked up into the bloodshot eyes of his female colleague and friend that he broke.

Nick Cartwright lay hunched back in the corner behind the fridge, she tried to avoid looking at the plastic bags and paraphernalia that had been assembled for the disposal of her body and watched through tears as the last part of Pimm's shadow disappeared from the balcony as he leapt across to the soil pipe and began climbed back to the rooftop.

The first thing Pimm did when he reached the roof and prayed to God the Mossad girl was still watching him and then pulling from his pocket one of the photographs that held her image and her partner, Mel and Pimm clipped it to the gutter fitting, facing it towards the Mossad apartment and then pointed to his own eyes and then down to the photograph.

Ruby was watching, curious, she zoomed in on the photograph and could see it held her own image and while Pimm went over to the barbecue area and began examining one of the larger gas propane cylinders, in her ear Ruby heard Mel say he was leaving,

"I'm going to do as he said, send an evacuation call. General Zavineski may order we round them all up now, without talking with the Yanks, we could lose Mengele, and God knows what else with this shits interference... are you coming." Mel struck a match and set fire to their paperwork in the small apartment fireplace.

Ruby shook her head and gestured with her hand, "First come here, look at this, what you make of it?" Ruby called him over to the camera and squinting he recognised himself and Ruby in the photograph set on the gutter by Pimm.

"They knew we were watching them?" Mel whispered as he stepped back confused by the image.

Ruby pressed her eye against the eyepiece, scanning back to Pimm and watched him disconnecting the gas cylinder and begin rolling to the flat roof edge. She could see his shirt now had fresh blood on the shoulder from Cartwright. Ruby's eyes cut down to the kitchen window, and she shook her head, someone was still alive inside she thought and watched Pimm slip just his sandals back on.

"You know, if that was me over there, I would want someone to come for me orders or not, warn Zavi if you want to and the Yanks will need to know about this, leave the case, I'm going to help him if I can." she gestured to Mel to leave the long gun case containing a sniper rifle.

"Fuck! Out the way." Mel barged her from the eyepiece again and confirmed in his own mind, it was definitely them caught in the photograph. "Fuck!"

He threw his bag to the couch and began to assemble the sniper rifle.

"Give me your extra magazine, I'll go see if I can salvage something of this if it goes to shit tell General Zavineski it was my idea, fucking Brits. You know I've seen your record Ruby, I know they killed your father in 59....Shalom" he said and grabbing her extra gun magazine darted out the door.

Now with the sniper scope, Ruby began to shadow Pimm's movements even closer, she shuttered a bullet into the breach of the rifle as she watched him ease the gas cylinder over the low roof parapet above the German's main balcony. Briefly, she flicked down to the main balcony.

"Fuck you know how to party English," she said as she focused back on the open French door where every so often when the wind caught the curtain she had a full view inside of the four German's all seated, with one at a table with his back to her, she focused the crosshairs on the centre of his back, knowing that was not her first target, Pimm had something else for her and she readied herself to fire.

On the roof, Pimm went back to the television aerial and taking out his knife cut through the television cable. Immediately below Ruby saw the German's reaction, as at the same time within the other apartments sharing the signal from the aerial, the TV screens switched to grey static. All four Germans let out an angry cry, and the man nearest the door stood up and appeared to move forward towards the television, the curtain fell back in place as he began tapping the side of the television.

On the roof Pimm dropped the gas bottle down onto the lounge balcony, it made an almighty sound as it shattered the glass from the open French door and pulled the curtain from inside down crashing into a pair of small deck chairs it came to rest partially on and off the balcony rail.

"What the fuck!" One of the German's screamed as Ruby through her telescopic sight saw the Germans inside scramble for cover as they grabbed their sidearm's. Pimm looked briefly to the Mossad apartment and with no reaction, leaned out from the edge of the roof and began unloading shells, the first two clipped the side of the bottle giving Klaus enough time to instruct one of his colleagues to check the kitchen. As he pushed against the jammed door swearing Pimm went to fire but was beaten to the shot, with the cylinder fixed in her crosshairs Ruby fired, the punctured gas bottle erupted like a bomb, the blast wave blew Pimm back across the roof and sent a ball of flame and metal fragments from the cylinder slicing through the air, directly into the lounge forcing all the occupants to dive for cover as lounge furniture and material was engulfed in flame and began burning. The man who had previously threatened Nick Cartwright and was trying to enter the kitchen had been blocked by Pimm's use of the cleaver as a door jam and with the full force of the explosion was propelled through the door landing face down with gun still in his hand and his back smoking cut to ribbons, while Lamb's body was blown still attached to the seat further towards Cartwright almost wedging her behind the fridge door. Inside the lounge, the German's began to fire indiscriminately out towards the balcony and towards the kitchen.

On the Mossad apartment kitchen balcony, Ruby now pushed the camouflage rubbish off the edge, and it tumbled to the yard below as she fixed her rifle rest firmly in place while watching Pimm through the scope. Getting to his knees he found his revolver and immediately began climbing back down to what was left of the balcony's as his foot reached almost level with the top f the balcony parapet and was about to leap across when the first of the remaining Germans emerged outside through the remains of the French door, seeing Pimm and ducking low he went to shoot. Ruby stole a breath and fired catching the man in the shoulder sending him back into the lounge, she loaded another shell and fired without a clear target into the centre of the room, pinning those inside down.

Pimm snatched a look back over towards the Mossad apartment before diving inside the kitchen, and immediately heard the German's calling to each other and sent a couple of rounds into the lounge through the open kitchen door.

"Ok?" he whispered to Cartwright, and she managed a half-smile.

"Scheisse Scheisse… Raimund, Raimund!" there was a call from the lounge towards the kitchen and the man face down, in the doorway.

"Raimund is toast. Time you say Auf Wiedersehen and fuck off! " "Pimm shouted back in a confident manner as he checked on Cartwright, pulling her back up and pushing Lamb's body off her feet, just as a hail of bullets cut through the thin walls. "Stay down, we have help outside, you are getting out," he said realising the Mossad agent was still be covering the action, as Ruby set another two rounds from her sniper rifle into the lounge. Pimm considered they stood a chance if between them they could make the German's flee and considering by now Brazilian law enforcement would have been contacted about the explosion and gunfire.

Cartwright watched as Pimm prepared to make an assault from the lounge balcony and he had his back to the kitchen, suddenly seeing the injured Raimund begin to raise himself from the kitchen floor, "Pimm!" Cartwright screamed in pain and fired three shots into Raimund's head, it disintegrated, showing Pimm with brain matter and blood. Hearing this the Germans opened fire again turning their attention back to the open kitchen door where the timber door lining splintered off in needle-sharp shards, while Pimm jumped across from the kitchen balcony to the bomb-damaged lounge balcony, again Nick Cartwright fired, diverting their attention and it gave Pimm time to dive to the side of the remains of the open French door and set a shell in the exposed leg of one of the men hiding behind the lounge furniture, the man he hit spasmed in pain, as he pulled back, breaking cover Pimm caught him immediately with a round that entered his cheek and he dropped back behind the upturned sofa, they, were now three against two, but for all the German's knew there could be more.

"Shit! Come leave them, fuck it, the Police are coming, we go now!" Pimm heard one call to his last colleague and hearing movement Pimm pressed forwards and

caught one man square in the back as he was about to disappear down the hallway to the main door, his body flung forwards landing at the bottom of the door, preventing it from opening, Pimm fired another shot into the back of his neck as he stepped over the body and then turfed him over away from the door with his sandaled foot, as the door sprung back now released Pimm dived for cover as two shots echoed in the hallway and bullets ricocheted, at knee height off the concrete wall of the apartment entrance, fired by a shooter located on the lower stairs.
Pimm caught his breath and then heard the distinctive sound of the building's main door to the street clatter open and then shut in the lower lobby, somewhere in the distance on the street outside he heard three shots.
Pimm looked down the stairwell and then back down the apartment hall towards the lounge that was becoming enveloped in flames. Quickly he went back inside, and as he went to enter the kitchen from the lounge, Cartwright fired, the bullet only just missed Pimm, if it had not been for her hand injury he would have been dead.
"Hold, It's me Pimm, their dead, we have to go." slowly he showed his hand and gun, then his face, her eyes were streaming tears, and the relief in her face was still marred by the pure anguish of her ordeal.
"Come on, girl, we need to get you out of here, there's nothing we can do for him." Pimm caught her look at Lamb's body as he calmly pulled her up and led her out through the lounge, grabbing a jacket from the hall pegs he threw it over her shoulders and clutched her close as if they were a couple as they hobbled down the stairs to the street, while other residents of the apartment block had begun to appear on the landing and stairs making their escape from the building and threat of fire.
Already they could hear emergency alarms heading their way, but both of them looked to an open group of people circled around a body that lay face down arms splayed, his blood flowing into the gutter, where a sparrow sat dipping its beak.
It was Mel the young Mossad agent, he had run straight into Klaus Ritter and was cut down before he had pulled his revolver.
"Keep your head down," Pimm said, pulling Cartwright in close as she hobbled forward.
"I heard the bomb, come!" Allan called and for a moment seeing his taxi pull up in the side street Pimm relaxed, then with a screech of tyres from the far end of street two white panel vans appeared and raced past him towards them.
Pimm looked at Cartwright he saw the life drain from her eyes, he could not leave her, as five heavily armed men each in black camouflage scattered the crowds with gunfire into the air. Allan gave Pimm an apologetic look and Pimm gestured with a

flick of his head for him to go and the taxi driver hit the gas with the car in reverse and disappeared from sight as another hail of bullets scattered all from the streets
"On your knees, show me your hands!"
"Your knees now!" They were screamed at by two of the camouflaged team, and Pimm gestured to Cartwright to comply, and as she slumped down, her jacket fell from her shoulders.
"Drop the weapon." As Pimm did as he was told, his hands were pulled behind his back and cuffed, loose with cable ties, hoods were thrust over their heads, but not before Pimm caught their attackers pick up the jacket Cartwright had been wearing and his gun. He then heard her cries as they were bundled into separate vans, then driven off at high speed away from the scene, passing many approaching police and emergency vehicles.
As they travelled across the city and he was bounced back and forth on the bench Pimm tried to recall the details and voices of those that had captured them, the fact they had picked up Cartwright jacket signified an interest in their well being, but none spoke once they were in the van, however by the time they came to rest Pimm had decided they were American's and not Mossad.
Pimm heard the engines of an executive jet humming as the van swung past into an aircraft hangar and the doors closed behind. He was helped, still hooded from the van and sensed Cartwright was no longer with him and also that there were was a security detail watching him as he was led through to an office and sat in a chair, the hood was pulled from his head, and the hand ties were cut.
"Mossad," he thought as his eyes adjusted to the glaring overhead strip light and he was greeted by the image of General Zavineski's unblinking stare, as the soldier that had escorted him left the room.
"Believe me, Mr Pimm, if I was in charge you would be on your way back to Tel Aviv by now," Zavineski looked at the conference call telephone speaker.
"You gate-crashed a party, one of my people is dead, I don't know yet if it was you who got him killed, but I think probably he would still be alive if you had not come calling." Zavineski's tone was fiercely abrupt.
"Ask your girl, the Germans were already packed, they had enough body bags for your people, once they were done torturing ours. You ordered them to sit and watch. But they were already on to you they would have taken out your nest, you are lucky I came along when I did" Pimm's adrenaline from the fight had sapped his patience, he blamed the man in front of him for the death of Neil Lamb and held back, for now, the question if he knew the whereabouts of Bob Gregory.

"So you say, I am a shepherd of one flock when the wolves come. Now the flat was destroyed, we will never know, there is no evidence to substantiate your claim." Zavineski brushed his hands as if washing them.
"I said, ask the redhead, Ruby, I showed her the image and while we're at it where's our agent, the girl I rescued?" Pimm was in no mood for a challenge, from someone he considered had once, nearly had him and a host of other agents killed in the field, when he left for Israel.
"And as I already told you Pimm, lucky for you this is not Tel Aviv's show." As he spoke the door opened, and an American black-ops seal officer walked in and pressed the zero button on the conference phone,
"Line secure, you are on speaker, sir!" he said then stood back against the wall at ease.
"Mr Pimm, Carter-Wallis, we have a mutual acquaintance Bull Gordon, time is pressing so I will be brief. First, your girl Cartwright is on a C130 back to Heathrow, I am told she will be fine, second, this party is over the guest will be leaving, the gentleman with you is Colonel Blake. He is leading special ops. Seal team about to depart to San Paolo on the jet outside, where we have three Black Hawks and two AH-1 Cobras on loan to the Brazilian government. They are taking part in a joint operation our government are undertaking with the Israelis to terminate a major drug cartel operation we believe the Germans you encountered were associated with. General Zavineski, you know, of course. He and his agents were assisting in our surveillance in Rio, I am sorry to hear of the loss of your man General and the British operative Mr Pimm, I have notified London. In the spirit of international unity between our nations and agencies I am authorized by the President to invite you to join the Colonel as guest observers, you leave immediately, but I repeat you are guests with no authorization to engage combatants do you understand Mr Pimm?"
"I understand Sir." Pimm looked to Zavineski as he got to his feet realising the General was not going with them.
"Also understand this Mr Pimm, my agent informed me she had the opportunity to terminate your intrusion, she has been reprimanded, I assure you if that situation should arise again I will personally correct the outcome." Zavineski's threat was emotionless.
Pimm, felt inside his back pocket and pulled out a single photograph with the image of Ruby taken by the German's and placed it on the table, said nothing then followed Colonel Blake with one foot on the ladder the jets engines began to race, and it started moving before the door was locked preparing for take-off. "Here, we're a bit tight for space but change onboard sorry no time to get boots." The Colonel looked at Pimm's sandals as he handed Pimm a black boiler suit.

"Are those British issues?" he smiled and handed him back the Glock revolver Pimm had taken from Ruby earlier.

"Keep that in your pants let my boys do their thing, the boss knows your record, so do I, he's hardly going to let you play with the big boys with just." he made a finger of a gun with his hand.

"Gentlemen this is Mr Pimm, he is here along with our Mossad guest just to watch." The eight-man team bulged from their seats, already armed to the teeth, wearing black rub on their faces there was little distinction between each man in contrast to the bright auburn hair of Ruby, who sat up front wearing a similar outfit as he had been handed and although it appeared to be of the same size and too large for her, she made it work.

"You can change in there." Colonel Blake pointed to the toilet.

"Let's do this, Captain when you're ready." He ordered the pilot, and Pimm noticed although it was a civilian chartered jet the pilots wore U.S. Air Force uniforms and insignia.

"I am sorry about your colleague," Pimm said as he sat beside Ruby, after changing and then thanked her for covering his back in the apartment.

"I see you still have my gun." she gestured to his wrist, "Keep it, I have another, courtesy of American friends."

"I understand Zavineski gave you shit for not taking the opportunity to try and stop me." Pimm gave a nod of appreciation.

"And me the loss your man, I am sorry, but if I wanted to stop you I would have. Now we put that aside, I understand why you did it, but I will be surprised if we bag any of the prize players, the yanks promised us, this is a showboat, why I have no idea?" she handed him a bottle of Perrier. "Did you find anything about your other man, Mr hansom?"

Pimm shook his head, "There were photo's, our German friends had run into him, he is in this somewhere, I had no time to check with Cartwright, but I believe he's compromised, his identity was something they were trying to verify, Lamb, our man, he was a bloody mess, I have no idea what he told them, but our girl was alive so no doubt he told them everything, I think her tits bought her time, but she was destined for the bins, as I think so were you." Pimm watched Ruby's head drop, and she stared out of the window and sensed her regret as they listened to the banter of the Seal team preparing themselves, checking and rechecking their weapons.

"But, as you said that's behind us, I take it from that you are just a tourist too," Pimm said, gesturing to her compact Kodak camera.

"Yep, we're in the same boat, but I still have orders to capture heads, but only with this." she raised the camera.

They arrived in Sao Paolo just after five; it was a seamless transition for the Seal team to move to their own Black Hawk helicopter while Pimm and Ruby along with two medical staff and the main gun crews boarded a separate Black Hawk helicopter. Pimm gestured to the occupants the third Black hawk, three individuals sat in biological protective suits with their hoods down, the one closest looked directly at Pimm, and he could see it was a woman, Ruby managed to take a photo without being seen just as their doors slid shut.

The journey to Serra Negra took a little over an hour, and they passed over a convoy of Brazilian security forces and army personnel parked up, blocking the main road south waiting for instructions to move in, once the American's had completed their mission. At the given signal the two Bell Cobra attack helicopters split from the formation and raced ahead, in Pimm's headset he heard them count down their approach as they ducked below the densely forested hills into a deep gorge travelling below the tree line of the hills until they pulled up sharply over the ridge and dropped down into a cleared area of fields of coffee. Pimm heard first the explosions as the Cobras took up their attack stations and engaged taking out two guard towers at either end of the vast complex of industrial buildings with tanks and cooling towers of what appeared to be a chemical facility,

Almost immediately their pilot set their chopper down furthest from the action, and as the nearest gunner began to strafe the roofline, Pimm and Ruby watched as the Seal team deployed and launched their assault, as the facilities security forces started to repel their advance.

Instantly it was apparent those defending the facility, although heavily armed, were outmatched by the Seal team, within minutes of the first shots being fired the externally the guard combatants were neutralized, and the American team moved forward into the internal structure, where the sound of gunfire recommenced along with the sound of small grenade explosions.

From landing to the last shot fired, it took twelve minutes, but with the sound of silence, the side gunner of Pimm's Black Hawk held his hand across the door.

"I have orders for you to hold Sir until Colonel Blake gives the clear signal," he said. Pimm and Ruby watched as the three scientists' wearing biohazard suits headed into the facility building, and the Seal team began to regroup taking up stations as a group of civilian workers began to emerge from inside.

Colonel Blake approached signalling the gunner to allow Pimm and Ruby to join them as the civilians were lined up.

"Ok, guys, Mr Pimm, Miss? give the boffin's a few minutes then you can take a look, not a bad away game fifteen nil, no own goals" Blake smiled at the body count then looked at Ruby's Kodak, "some are none too pretty, we'll get them out for you, my orders are to dust off in five, so make it snappy and only the dead." he tapped her camera with his finger.

"So what about the ones you captured, will you release them?" Ruby looked at Pimm as she went up to the line of farm workers and began quizzing them in Portuguese.

Blake's blank stare told their fate, "Those are not my orders, Miss. You have four minutes now." Pimm and Ruby knew no one that worked within the compound was leaving, even the forced workers.

Pimm watched as the scientist emerged, two were carrying what looked like a long acetylene torch gas cylinders, similar to the butane cylinder Pimm had used in attacking the German's apartment, except it was black and not orange and had a double sealed protective bell housing to the valve.

"Colonel Blake, can I ask them if they have seen my man?" Pimm took out the photograph of Gregory. Blake bit his lip clearly wrestling with his authority.

"Three minutes! Go ahead, the Federales are inbound, they'll want to take this lot in, and that's not happening, some have been involved in the drug production, seen too much I guess."

Pimm went quickly through the line of peasants, talking to them in Portuguese, most explained they were seasonal pickers that had been lured away from local farms, initially by promises of higher earnings, but once they had arrived things had changed dramatically, and they had been forced to work at the facility under guard and kept in a detention block, some soon spoke of other sites that they had been forced to work on, in particular, they mentioned over the past few weeks being involved in a field station, where Nestlar had carried out the weapons demonstration, and one man told Pimm that he had heard talk of an intruder their captors had discussed and believed he had been killed at the test site, where he had helped deliver tanks like the one the scientist were loading,

"Death gas" he called it

Pimm watched as Ruby went along the line of bodies taking photographs of those killed by the Seal team, most were security personnel, there were half a dozen that wore laboratory coats, Pimm followed Ruby into the main courtyard where the remainder of the Spider team had been dragged out as the Seal team began to withdraw.

"What is it?" Pimm asked Ruby as she stepped in close taking a number of headshots from various angles of one of the oldest men in grey flannel trousers and a short-sleeve shirt who had been hit twice in the chest,

"I'm not sure, but this could be Philipp Bouhler, dentals would confirm it, look SS." She pulled his arm up, revealing the blood tattoo on his underarm.

"Colonel I need this one, for my boss." she called to Blake, to which the Colonel whistled, and two of his men brought over a body bag and rolled the dead man to its side, Pimm knew what was coming next "Ruby you might want to look away." "Heads and hands only, we have a weight limit, sorry Miss." Blake said and with that one of his men pulled a machete decapitated the corpse with a single stroke and then with two more took off the hands and threw them into the bag with the head.

"Ok time we go! Signal the local Federales." Blake made a circling motion with his hand for all to see and began to walk back to his helicopter as his men followed suit.

"Colonel, I have no idea what your people are looking for, but they say there is another site 10 kilometres to the west, Itapera, this man here has seen it," he pointed to the worker, "he says the doctor's here were conducting some sort of test, they loaded an aeroplane, I think he's talking about a crop duster with whatever they just loaded." Pimm gestured to the scientists.

"I have my orders we have to terminate this site now, get aboard this place will be toast along with anyone on the ground." Blake stood firm ready to close the chopper door.

"I understand your orders, Colonel. However, Intel updates change operational procedure in the field and can override original objectives, as we all know. I'm just thinking if you have come all this way, someone's pulled some long strings, I recognise a clean-up when I see one, I don't know this Carter Wallis that has organized this shin dig but I would bet you a month of Sunday's he won't be pleased if the Brazilians discover something you left behind." Pimm looked to Ruby and then at the workers.

"Get aboard please, Mr Pimm!" Colonel Bake spoke firmly as he climbed in, and Pimm heard static clicks on his headset and assumed the Colonel was relaying the information to the American scientists. A split second from taking to the air the Cobra's unleashed all their weapons, while within the facility strategically placed radio-controlled explosives detonated obliterating the site, then as they turned to go there was a buzz on their headsets.

"You say Itapera Mr Pimm that's 20 kilometres, can you do that Captain?" Blake got a thumbs-up gesture from his pilot.

"We don't have fuel to cover you for that Colonel." the lead Cobra pilot interjected, and there was a pause.

"Thank you for your support, get back to the city, we can take it from here," Blake ordered.

Pimm looked down at the peasant workers bodies, none had tried to run, and all were now dead. Then as the Cobra helicopters streamed over the heads of the approaching Brazilian enforcement team, the three Black Hawks headed north.
"What do you make of that?" Pimm pointed through the window at a large smouldering blackened area that appeared to be moving in the centre of the fields that Nestlar had corralled the test animal subjects in, but now there were no animals, only what looked like the scorched area with the remains of a large bonfire and the Brazilian farmers old animal box wagon, that had held his family and from which his daughter and Bob Gregory had escaped.
Only as the three Black Hawks dusted down on the cleared area of the observation plateau, that had held the refreshments tents and been used by Nestlar for the demonstration, did the black movement become clear as hundreds of blackbirds took flight from the burnt area.
"Please remain inside until our people give it the all-clear." Blake hailed them as his men deployed a security perimeter outside the helicopters with their blades still turning and the scientists holding a number of instruments began to make their way down the to the site.
As Pimm and Ruby watched them approach the dark region that appeared like the remains of a large bonfire. Pimm's eyes caught sight at the eastern edge the field before the landscape became thick with the green of the lush forest, a man wearing a straw hat sitting watching them from the back of a mule.
"Colonel, nine o'clock." one of the Seal team had also seen the local farmer.
Then as two of the scientist began to take samples from the burned area, one of them gave the signal they could approach, "Colonel we need some bags down here." He called on his internal suit speaker.
Pimm and Ruby began to walk down the track, shadowed by Blake and two of his team members, Pimm noticed the deep wheel ruts from the many lorries.
"Go see what he knows" Blake ordered one of his men, pointing to the man on the mule.
"Those are for planes?" Ruby gestured to the numerous windsocks
"Maybe?" Then Pimm stopped short as both he and Ruby realised at the same time what the scientists were pulling from the bonfire, It was the charred remains of the Brazilian farmer, his wife and their young son, amongst the bones of the test animals that had been tied up and all, killed when the crop duster had unleashed its deadly cargo on the fields.
Pimm turned his attention to the cattle wagon and examined the ropes that had held the prisoners as Colonel Blake went over to discuss what the local on the mule had to say.

"Three bodies in the fire, but there were five in here, look at the ropes." Pimm said to Ruby as she came up behind him and kneeled at his side, studying the broken slats of the horsebox and reached in and felt the horse dung, breaking it art in her hands, it was still moist "And a horse."

"Mr Pimm," Blake called him outside, "there is a river in that forest somewhere, that local man says his village is located downstream, two days ago they pulled a young girl and white man out of the water." Blake read Pimm's disappointment and concern. "Badly injured half-drowned but alive, you got that picture of your man?" Pimm followed him over, and the man confirmed it was Bob Gregory that they had saved, but the girl that they had found with him he informed he recognised as belonging to the family of a neighbouring farm which he had already visited and found abandoned.

Blake got the word from the team of scientist that they were ready to leave.

"Escort the scientist back; I'm going to take Mr Pimm to see if this man is his, in for a penny in for a pound, isn't that what you Brits say" Blake smiled at Pimm.

"Miss Ruby, you coming with us?" Pimm asked

Ruby looked at Pimm and the body bags being loaded, Pimm sensed she was torn between joining him and her duty to file her report and get the pictures in her camera back to General Zavineski so Mossad could get to the bottom of what the Germans were doing out there, which she and Pimm both knew had nothing to do with a South American drugs cartel.

"Good luck Pimm, I hope it's him," she said and climbed in the helicopter with the rest of the Seal team. As the door slid closed somehow, Pimm knew their paths would cross again.

Chapter 15: The Loosefeed

East Finchley, London
1975

Pimm stood discreetly back from the side of the grave as the mourners paid their last respects to Neil Simon Lamb, "Lambo" as his university pals called him and had written on his wreath.

There was a good turnout; he was well-liked and had many friends who helped console his mother and father, who now stood at his graveside of their son, quietly sobbing.

He was not an orphan, a *"Lost Boy"* and not destined to be a Mi6 field operative with Sandman status, he was among a new breed of Mi6 analysts recruited while at University, because of his academic qualification including language skills and the increasing demand within the service for computer programmers and IT consultants, and had previously been mainly an office-bound agent working with Nick Cartwright on the computer mainframe, building up a data bank for Mi6 while working within Bulls department.

Someone on the top floor of Century house had thought it would be wheeze handing the job of overseeing the creation of the first Mi6 supercomputer intelligence bulk data gathering system to Bull and although it made Maurice Oldfield who was now running things as Control, chuckle knowing what a technophobe Bull was, Oldfield, considered some of what Bull had learned during his thirty years in the service would be imparted into the foundations of the system they were now calling "Ebla" The name derived from the Sumerian library discovered in 1964, dating back 4,500 years it's considered to be one of the oldest, again Control chuckled at the idea that their oldest serving agent being put in charge of its installation. Bull, on the other hand, saw no humour in this assignment and once commented to Oldfield he was only three years his senior, both having come up through the ranks, so to speak, to which Oldfield remarked, "You do, so I don't have to."

Although at one point Bull Gordon seriously considered retirement, having reluctantly accepted the additional workload, Bull relied heavily on Mrs. Thompkin to delegate the workload of the tedious programming, to a team that included Neil Lamb and Nick Cartwright.

It had been Nick Cartwright that had pushed hardest amongst the two, for them to be assigned to take on the reconnaissance mission and confirm the identity of the individuals captured in the photograph taken in Ipanema, "it was only meant to be a look-see" as Bull had put it, failing to take into account his young agents spirit and tenacity. Like all Mi6 operatives Lamb completed his advance training studied the technical side of tradecraft, he knew how to fire a gun, but he had none of the instinct and focused discipline required to be a field operator, a Sandman predator like Pimm.

"Good of you to come, Pimm." Bull pulled Pimm to one side as they stepped away from the group and began to shuffle away from the graveside, leaving Lamb's closest family alone and perplexed as to how their son a Foreign office assistant statistician had been killed in a freak climbing accident while attending a four-day assertive team leadership course in the Brecon Beacons. They would never know he suffered at the hands of Klaus Ritter and the other Spider operatives Pimm had killed in Rio.

Pimm lit a cigarette and caught a look in his direction from Cartwright. As she lifted her hand to acknowledge his smile, he noticed the finger splints.

"Just a shame I was a day out, I read your girls brief, the bastards put the poor lad through the mill," Pimm said, remembering vividly the sight that greeted him of the kitchen torture chamber.

Bull matched his whispers occasionally acknowledging the other passing mourners heading back to their cars.

"Yes she blames herself, he held out till they turned on her, makes you wonder faced with watching someone else suffering how many of us would crack." Pimm followed Bull back to his Austin Wolseley

"Well, I guess that's why us no noise boy's are all orphans." Pimm shrugged his shoulders.

"Speaking of which I hear Gregory's on the mend, he'll be missed back out in the field even though Scott has filled his spot, to finish off the assignment in Cuba. You should know I have already set the seeds in place upstairs and thought when you feel the time is right, you might have a word, see if he's up to a spot at Hereford or Guernsey. You're far more tactful at that sort of thing than me, and he is your boy after all. Yes, Siree! Your eye was sharp with that orphan BP, he had some of the highest stats, would make an excellent training officer. Explain we use our best and like to keep it in-house, none better that one sponsored by the bad penny....think it over?" Bull then turned to Cartwright as she came down the path "You two coming back to the house, need a lift?"

"No, you're alright Bull, parked outside, as Bob's awake thought I'd take him some papers and grapes have an informal chat. If you know about Scott you know I've requested reassignment from Drake, I had a word with Jem Stapleton. Can you believe it, he had the cheek to ask me if it was personal. I told him I needed to tidy a few loose ends on this gig of yours. So you are stuck with me for a bit, It would seem I'm not so indispensable, his new crew is gelling well, they have an operation cake all divided up, working with the Yanks in Iraq, they were all decent when I checked back in, but no one wants to give a slice up for an old man like me. To be honest, I'm glad, the sand over there, all that weapons cleaning, I told Jem it was up to you." Pimm looked at Cartwright hovering to the side and was glad to see the swelling to her eye was going down.

"I know the feeling well, but for the record, there's always a chair at my table, old fruit, I'll get Monty to do the necessary," Bull said, opening the door expectantly for Cartwright to step into his car.

"I think I'll tag along with Mr. Pimm if that's alright with you sir?" Cartwright looked first to Pimm, who gestured with a nod, it was.

"Well, pick up some grapes from me, ask him to think about the offer, regarding the other thing, I already told Stapleton you were welcome to stay as long as you like, mi casa su case, as always BP and with their concerns regarding Gregory being your boy, they asked me the same each time one of mine was lost, it's just what they do." Bull smiled and watched as Cartwright followed behind Pimm back to his Ford Granada, then noticed how they walked along the graveyard avenue the young agent stuck her arm in his, in the way a daughter might rest on the shoulder of her father.

At the Royal Free hospital in Hampstead, Cartwright felt him come up beside the ward observation window, which held a line of tinsel.

"What's this about an offer for Bobby?" As Cartwright spoke, Pimm smiled inside he had heard from the ward nurses Gregory had been visited regularly by an attractive blonde, it would seem they had become cozy.

"Maybe it's something you can help me with? Tact was never a strength I would rely on, regardless of what Bull may say. You girls, no disrespect intended, can make the most unpalatable situation seem reasonable." Pimm understood Cartwright was not offended and could see she was genuinely concerned about Bob's future. At first, Pimm considered, having read the briefing on the incident in the bar in Brazil, it was from a sense that she believed she owed Bob something, but as she spoke, he realised something else was behind it.

"You always were a charmer Bob." he thought to himself, having never heard anyone call him Bobby before, accept June, he was after all like him, a no noise, sandman, killer.

She appeared to sense Pimm's interest in her attention for the patient and made a tactical excuse. "When I heard you brought him back and about his condition, I thought I'd check-in. I know how you lot are, family, friends, zero. I thought he could use a friendly face, I owe him that much, for what he did in the bar over there. Besides its Christmas, I'd rather be in here than on the streets with the rest of the sheep and if I go back to my Mum's I'll have to make up some shit about this." Cartwright raised one of her broken hands.

"She's the only one I hate to lie to about what we do, Lambo was the same about his parents, they thought he and I were a thing. There was nothing to it except, it helped both of us with our folks, know what I mean?" From Pimm's blank expression, she realised he didn't. However, she need not explain her presence at Gregory's bedside to Pimm, he had spent enough time laying in ward beds over the years recovering from one work-related injury or another. If it was him lying there, he would appreciate the attention and the distraction from the boredom. Especially taking into account the damage Gregory's body had sustained, as it was pulverised by the numerous rock hits, as he was dragged downstream for nearly half a mile before washing up on a riverbank, where he and the girl had been found by local villagers.

"I am sure he appreciates it. And you, how have you been, your hands are healing? Your eye looks a lot better." Pimm asked without turning as they watched a nurse pull a curtain around Gregory's bed, to change his catheter.

"Max Factor." She smiled, and Pimm saw the split to her lip still pained her, "I was never that quick at the typing, and I'm tone-deaf, so there's no loss to the music business." Cartwright gestured her fingers as if she was playing the piano, but as she wiggled them, he could see it still hurt her joints, but she smiled again, and blood now oozed gently from her lip. Pimm reached in his pocket and handed her a clean folded handkerchief, he always came prepared, at a funeral.

"Thank you, I'll be alright, I'm back at the factory, light work, helping on the team's follow-ups, it's an eye-opener one hand filing, how many you can balance between your teeth, but I'm also working with the technical team on the data processing, trying to take up some of the slack since Lamb..." She looked away for a moment and then regained her composure "Well he was just better at that sort thing, I never saw the point of playing computer games, but I've started a course in programming, it's quite addictive when you get into it, a little slow like this, no file juggling though I think paper will be a thing of the past one day, Mr. Gordon's suggested it, he's good like that."

"Yes he is, that's good to hear. I'm not a technophobe like Bull, but space invaders in the local pub is about as good as it gets for me with those things. Good for you though, I think they are the future and anything to save the rainforest. Perhaps we will run into each other." Pimm considered it was unlikely following her ordeal Cartwright would ever make it into the field again, well at least for some time, and honestly he thought that was probably for the best.

"Look, would you mind giving me a few minutes with him." Pimm acknowledged the nod from the nurse that she was finished and that they could enter Gregory's room.

"Does he know about the girl?" Cartwright asked, aware that Ofelia, the peasant workers daughter, Bob Gregory had pulled from the truck and saved from the poison gas, had drowned in the river during their escape.

"No, that was one thing I was going to speak of, but perhaps not today, we'll see." For a moment Pimm considered delegating Cartwright with that duty. But he knew Gregory would feel guilty when he heard the news. He took two fifty pence pieces from his pocket and handed it to her "Look, I saw a coffee machine on the way in, black and no sugar, coffee or tea either is ok, thanks Nick, see I took time to read the personals in your file, you wrote you like to be called Nick by your friends and family, you should know, you're part of his family now, and Mr Gordon won't mind you calling him Bull."

"I know BP, it just seems... more respectful," she said, and he caught a light skip in her step across the linoleum flooring.

"I'm a sucker for shortbread if they have any," he called after her and knew she was going to be alright.

As Pimm placed his hand on the door handle, Gregory turned gently, his instinctive reflexes impaired with his skull skewered with the rods of a cranium brace and plates. Having severely fractured his skull from the many encounters with the rocks and boulders of the river. The impact from one that nearly claimed his life gouged his right eye from its socket. His career as a Mi6 field officer was a thing of the past like his handsome features.

Scheduled to have additional reconstructive surgery to his nasal cavity, for now, Gregory's breathing was being supplemented with oxygen tubes. It appeared to Pimm each breath caused discomfort, and he held his facial expression in check as he greeted one of the few true friends he had. Feeling his body wince inside he tried not to focus on the swelling and bruising to Bob's face, which made him look ridiculously like a cartoon character that had been hit with a steam iron, the bruise colours on his face as vivid as an artist's paint palette.

With his left arm in plaster hung from an overhead support cable Gregory wagged the only two fingers on his hand not broken as Pimm approached his bed, shuffling up slightly in the brace that was fixed along his chest protecting the ribs he had broken.
The fine cotton sheet raised and Pimm could see the fractures continued to his lower abdomen, but miraculously Bob Gregory had received no damage to his spine considering his back had taken the full impact when he leapt from the cliff into the Amazonian river clutching Ofelia to his chest for her protection. Fortunately for the agent who previously could match the Olympic qualifying time for the 100 metres sprint of 10.18 seconds, apart from a fracture to his pelvis, below waist height, only his ankles were broken.
Irrespective of his condition and lying with various tubes feeding and removing fluids from his body and offering pain-relieving drugs, his eyes still carried a familiar sharpness, and he managed a faint smile then took a sip from a straw of clear liquid to loosen his dry throat.
"BP Old man, come to see how the NHS spends your money?" His voice was hoarse before the end of the sentence, and he took another sip.
"Stop fucking about Bob, there are real people that need that bed." Pimm put down the bag of grapes and seeing Gregory struggling to keep his eyes open with the light pulled across the curtain slightly.
"Well at least you have a view, I sometimes think about getting a flat, like Bull, but there is something about going up to bed, I know June hated having to sleep on the ground floor, but then she never made a fuss." Pimm's eyes drifted along the windows of the nearest houses below Gregory's ward, some of which had uninterrupted views straight into their rooms. Realising the occupants had little privacy what with the overlooking hospital and the buses in the street that now navigated passed during the afternoon rush hour, he remembered his times from queuing in the same traffic while bringing June for her chemotherapy. It seemed like a lifetime ago. Ignoring the comment about June, Bob chirped up, before Pimm had time to turn maudlin in his thoughts.
"I think I'll know the number of leaves on the trees by the time they have me up and about. At least I'll have a front-row from up here when Santa does his stuff, next time, bring some binoculars, it's all happening out there, especially at number twenty-two."
Pimm turned back with a smile of understanding refraining from checking which house he was talking about, "Sure thing." Admiring the fact Gregory's tone held no self-pity, but he noticed Bob's eyes flickered as if he was struggling to focus as he watched Pimm place a selection of daily papers on his bedside table.

"Have you been here before, while I was out? I know I lost time, my head feels like it's been stuck in a vice for a week, Doc gave me the heads up on my noggin, I was lucky I guess, especially with the back, wiggling my toes is worse than pins under the nails, but honestly BP I nearly cried" he watched Pimm carefully as if trying to remember and Pimm knew he meant cried with joy, in finding out he had not broken his spine.

"Very funny glad to see you kept your sense of humour, I did come by a couple of times when I got back from Rio, but I didn't want to disturb your fan club." Pimm reached into the bag and broke off a stalk of grapes and began to eat and then gestured to the window, Gregory smiled, seeing Cartwright behind the glass.

"The girl Cartwright, Nicola yes I remember her in flashes from the day I cut her out of the bar with her partner, Bob Marley was playing, I Shot the sheriff, I think I put on some Elvis, you just can't start a fight with reggae in the air, anyway I started a ruckus with some Italians, I think probably the last punch I'll be throwing for a while." He then stopped and looked at Pimm, realising his last comment was unrelated and that he was already beginning to feel tired, "off the record, not for file, I don't want them trying to saddle me as a desk jockey because of this." He tried to gesture to the damage to his eye with his free hand, but it was tied by tubes.

"So that's good you remember being over there, it will come back, as you say give it time." Pimm realised Bob was unaware Lamb had been killed in Rio.

"Brazil is all flashes, maybe the gas they were using, I remember that along with a grey horse kicking me in the back and the farmer's girl." Bob immediately read Pimm's micro expression and downturned eyes.

"She didn't make it did she, shit?" Gregory looked to the window.

"No old chum, to be honest, it was touch and go with you, as you said you were lucky, one more day in the woods the Doc's in Brazil were talking cerebral oedema, brain damage, I told them they were looking in the wrong place." Pimm tapped his head and was pleased to see Gregory recognised his humour, but could see he was struggling with his attention and decided now was not the time for questions of what happened at the Spider nerve agent testing fields at Sierra Rossa.

"Makes up for all the times I've saved your sorry arse." Bob looked on enviously as Pimm continued to eat his grapes and took another sip of water.

"Not me, you can thank a Yank Seal for that and the villagers who dragged your soggy arse from the river. As for the other thing let it ride, I hear these whizz kids talk about computers crashing, rebooting, it's all pish-posh to me, but maybe your brain needs to reboot." Pimm realised he had real emotions for Gregory, next to Bowman's boy he was the closest thing to a son, and Jake Bowman had gone walkabout soon after his wife died.

"If I were not strapped to this bloody machine I'd be breaking a few Krauts' heads, that said BP, one thing I do remember, I don't know about Seals, but the Yanks were there in the field with the Germans before the test, and the Somalian's arrived, I heard one before things went black, I never saw a face, I think that was before they got me, but I can't remember, no that's right, it's fuzzy, but I remember scoping out a factory in the jungle."

Gregory's heart monitor began to pick up the pace, and his face became flushed as he tried to piece together the events that had led him to be captured, realising he had forgotten hiding in the coffee truck when he was first captured by Klaus, a look of panic hit his eyes.

"Forget it, it will come, Bob, take a sip, we'll chat another day." Pimm's concerns grew, questioning himself, had he unintentionally pushed Gregory too far. Although with what he had already witnessed himself and the mention of the American's being on-site prior to the cleanup operation by the Seals, the idea that Lamb, Cartwright and Bob had stumbled on a rogue CIA operation gone wrong orchestrated by Carter-Wallis, began to rise again in his thoughts again. The American secret service was becoming like the Hindu goddess Kali with a number of hands each not knowing what the other was involved with.

Seeing Cartwright at the window, Pimm waved her in.

"Focus on getting strong and enjoy the company, don't worry about Six, Brazil or the bloody German's, but if it helps, I can tell you, I clipped the wings of a few of those you ran in to." Pimm got a raised thumb from Bob, "and Cartwright here unwittingly managed to score a winning goal, which has given us something to play with, I'll make sure she keeps you up to speed, but take my advice enjoy the rest, I know from experience, once Six has its claws in you, it never let's go. Meanwhile, I'll get you some bins." *(Binoculars)* Pimm turned to go, "you ok, for a lift?" Cartwright nodded, yes.

"Take it, easy son, just get some rest, but one last bit of classified, she likes to be called Nick, don't want you starting on the wrong foot." he looked at Bob and winked at her."

Pimm felt an edgy embarrassment to his words but hovered outside the window for a moment and watched how the couple interacted, Cartwright's eyes held a sparkle he recognised and remembered from the way June used to look at him.

"You're going to be ok son," he said and dropped the coffee into a bin as he walked down the corridor.

"What did he mean about the goal?" Gregory asked, even through a blinding headache, he wondered why such an attractive girl should appear to be interested in him. He knew he had suffered facial damage even though he had not seen his reflection as yet.

"When the Yanks airlifted me back with Lamb, you remember Neil?" As she said it she realised Bob probably was unaware Lamb was dead and seeing he was having problems recalling events from Brazil she brushed past it.

"Look it doesn't matter rest as BP says, I can read you the headlines from the paper if you like?" she snatched a grape but let it roll in her mouth, instead of biting it, while Gregory smiled at hearing her call Pimm BP.

"Seriously first tell me, what BP meant please, I need to join the dots when you leave I'll rest," He said and let her hand take his hand which was a clumsy affair at first both wearing splints to their fingers.

"Ok but just this and only this, you look tired. When Pimm rescued me, he placed one of the German's coats on my back. In the inside pocket was a passport for one of them, flight tickets and papers, the American's slipped up, never searched it. As for the other stuff, the Somalian's and the ship that went down, I know nothing only that the German's chartered it and the Brazilians are kicking up a stink."

"What ship?" Gregory asked then groaned as the pain in his head forced him to rest back. "Maybe you're right, tell me later, stick to the footy for now, how are the Gunners doing?.... Nick" He smiled.

Cartwright picked up the paper and began looking through the football details. Even in his battered state she remembered him as the strong uncompromising confident and deadly agent she had met in the bar in São Paulo and as dull as dishwater she thought football was, she would read every result to stay by his side. And even though his head burned, Bob wanted her to stay so he could hear her voice. Later she sat for a time watching him, even after he had fallen asleep and pulled the curtains fully as those in the street fronted houses below did the same before she left to catch a bus home.

The ship Cartwright mentioned to Bob was the Cardigan Bay, a freighter chartered by associates of the Spider network to transport the chemical weapons from Santos in Brazil to the port of Soyo on the mouth of the estuary to the Congo. Muuse Bin Abokkor had secured a place on board and planned to chaperone the deadly cargo along with five of Mubarak Ali Hassan's elite guard.

However, once Carter-Wallis had received word that the shipment was in transit, he had no choice but to arrange its interception. Fortunately for the CIA Section Chief, the American Sixth fleet was 600 kilometres from St Lucia on exercise. It took less than a twenty-minute conversation with a high-level aid to the "Gatekeeper" to

arrange the diversion of the SS Achilles, a Los Angeles class, nuclear-powered fast attack submarine.
The Whitehouse aid, who had studied Historical Criminology and Security Studies with his master's in Business, Law and Social Sciences at St. Johns College Cambridge, England had a fascination for the Jacobean era and smuggled the attack orders on the Cardigan Bay, amongst other documents that were whisked across the oval office desk for Presidential approval signing, listed as,
The termination of target Fawkes 13041950
The reference to Guido Fawkes birthday was lost at the time on President Gerald Ford, who believed he was signing yet another operation sanctioning the destruction of pesticides identified by the reregistration of pesticides that it had been concluded as having risks for humans, wildlife, and/or the environment. The orders were an attachment brief held within a plethora of documents regarding the FIFRA, *(Federal Insecticide, Fungicide, and Rodenticide Act)*, FEPCA *(Federal Environmental Pesticides Control Act)* and FIFRA *(Federal Insecticide, Fungicide, and Rodenticide Act)*, that had been pinging back and forth between the FDA *(Food and Drug Administration)* and the EPA, *(Environmental Protection Agency)*, formed by his predecessor President Nixon a can of worms dropped in his lap.
To the Captain of the SS Achilles, the attack was a CIA presidentially approved operation, and although he got the reference to Guido Fawkes in the target name, he held no hesitation in announcing,
"Launch one!" to his weapons, Chief.

"Look General more dolphins, I hear they eat the shit from the ships." one of the Somalian's guards pointed out to sea noticing a spray of surf wake headed in their direction.
"That's no dolphin!" Musse said, turning his binoculars to see the incoming torpedo that had been launched from the Submarine.
The Cardigan Bay went down in under fifteen minutes; Muuse was one of only three men that made it to an inflated safety raft. It would be two days before they would stray into the main shipping line and be picked up by a tanker travelling back to Porto Alegre in Brazil, by then the Achilles was back, shadowing the sixth fleet as if nothing had happened and because of what was on board Muuse and the other survivors were ordered by Ali Hassan not to report how the ship had met its fate.
"What will you do General?" Musse asked, preparing to leave Brazil.
"This is the second time my plans with this insect at the bank in Geneva have come to nothing and cost me, return home, I will send Cawil he will speak for me over there, he has the reigns, you understand?"

"Yes General, and our men, the two that survived?" Muuse asked.
"I should not have to say, old friend." The Warlord's tone was abrupt.
The following day on the way to Galeão international airport, Muuse picked up the two men he had shared the life raft with at sea. On arriving at the airport he parked in one of the furthest spaces from the entrance to the long stay car park, only Muuse stepped from the car. With the humid heat in Rio, it would be only a matter of days before the smell coming from the boot of the car alerted the airport police to what had happened to the unfortunate men.
On the flight home, Muuse had one thought on his mind, that Ali Hassan would seek retribution for the loss of his cargo on all that were involved and he considered those that would collect him from the airport in Mogadishu would take him somewhere other than home.
In Geneva as sleet melted and slid down the outside of the window of his private office in the FNIG bank, Salter-Kingsley hung up the telephone receiver and swivelled his chair around pitching it so he rocked back and forth in a trance of confusion, while facing the timber panel wall staring up at the Nazi membership registration certificate of his grandfather and contemplated his next move.
He had just received disturbing news from the Warlord, Mubarak Ali Hassan, informing him, with at times an aggressive tone that he would be sending over representatives in eight days, to address the issue of the delivery failure of the materials he had agreed to purchase through the Spider network.
Mubarak's orders were specific, the banker was to halt all transactions on his account, including termination of the remainder of the agreed transference of gold deposits into the new Brazilian account associated with the German Senior Statesman account, because the trade agreement brokered within the conference rooms of the FNIG bank earlier that year had not been completed, satisfactorily.
On the day he surrendered his boardroom to the representatives of Spider that included Doctor Nestlar to carry out the negotiations with Mubarak, Peter Salter-Kingsley had no knowledge of the inventory or materials the Somalian's had agreed to purchase. Dutifully he had, at the CED's request, agreed for the banks premises to be used as a neutral and secure venue for the meeting, even allowing the use of his own private office, in which he remained throughout the meeting, only called back into his boardroom at a specific point towards the end of the negotiations, when he was requested to confirm the sequence of actual financial instructions and arrange the up-front deposit transfer. Knowing enough, that the trade consignment from Brazil to Somalia was illegal, he considered it was most likely to be a traditional arms purchase of some kind and bearing in mind it was occurring five

and a half thousand miles away from his office, was quite happy to accept the six figure retainer and commission the bank was being paid for their service.
However, now it would appear once again his bank was involved in a transaction with the African's that had been affected by outside forces, which ultimately did not look good on the bank or him personally.
Within the halls and the air-conditioned conference rooms of his bank, all that entered acted in a reasonable manner, but he was fully aware this was a thin veneer of persona they adopted, to use the facilities the FNIG bank provided. He had no doubt the true nature of some of his clients verged on the medieval barbaric, Ali Hassan's tone during their conversation reinforced his concerns.
However because the bank had been predominately founded through the exploits of the Nazi's and the Spider network organisation, his allegiance was very much set, like the foundations of the building they occupied as within their underground vault, the vast proportion of gold the bank held was as security on the main SSG account that levied the associated accounts.
Before the call from Mubarak, Salter-Kingsley had been about to act on the contents of a sealed envelope he had picked up that morning from his own drop box at the Metropolitan hotel, having received an anonymous call during the night before, informing him, "You have post."
As before the letter had contained brief non-incriminating instructions and It ordered him to be available on the following Friday, at eight o'clock.
An associate of Herr Wolff, a doctor you are acquainted with will be visiting the bank and require your personal attention.
This was the CED informing him Merill Nestlar was on his way from Brazil, to confirm the completion of the financial transaction with the Somalian's and arranging a distribution of assets across from the SSG account to the associated Brazilian account, that without Salter-Kingsley's knowledge, was destined to be controlled by Doctors Mengele and Nestlar and assist continuation of their work in Brazil and Uruguay.
As far as the CED and Senior Executive Committee of Spider were concerned, in accordance with the original agreement, Mengele's and Nestlar's team in Brazil had signed off and completed their part of the deal with Mubarak, when the container marked as containing coffee beans, that was holding the dehydrated poison pellets and gas catalyst canisters was loaded aboard the SS Cardigan Bay at Santos docks and at that point the deadly cargo became the Somalian's responsibility.
However, to the Warlord taking into account the failed heist of his gold that was brought by Sean McLoughlin/Byrne from Libya, the attack on the freighter and loss of the chemical weapons was one leak too many. If it had been orchestrated by just

his men, Mubarak would have had every one of them shot, to be sure none were responsible, bar possibly one, General Musse Bin Abokkor. On this occasion, he was only spared from his judgement, after a long consideration that included, the Mubarak taking counsel from his only living male relative, Cawil.

It is possible in speaking with the young man on such a sensitive subject, the Warlord was in his own way acting as a mentor, continuing the process of grooming he had already started with his nephew, with the expectation his own flesh and blood would accept more responsibility within his organisation.

So he recalled Musse, Uncle Moses' as Cawil called him, back to Mogadishu, where he would join Cawil and assemble an enforcement team to be dispatched to Geneva with instruction to salvage something from the deal with the Germans or with extreme prejudice withhold the final gold payment to Spider by the FNIG bank.

Salter-Kingsley looked at the inside page of his Swiss newspaper, International news section, the two column story detailed the mysterious washing up on the beach of Copacabana of rotting fish. Locals were blaming the inadequacies on an ageing sewage treatment plant that spewed the cities untreated raw effluent just over 4000 metres out to see off Ipanema.

Now having been informed to make arrangements for both parties to visit the bank that coincidently was to occur on the same day as the event in Brazil, you did not have to be good at numbers to know the two events were connected.

"A dilemma, so the German's believe the conditions of the transaction were completed to the letter of their agreement, and the Somalian's don't. But the bank, you did not broker the agreement, so I take it this is something other than business." Merryman said, having been called into Salter-Kingsley's office and informed of the phone call his boss had received from the Mubarak Ali Hassan. Merryman felt honoured that his boss had chosen him to confide the details of the call. However, strictly speaking, there were few people inside his bank Salter-Kingsley believed he could discuss such sensitive issues with frankly. Plus by association with Byrne brothers, Merryman was already aware of the transaction.

"I take it this means we are not going to Verbier, Skiing?" Merryman said, somewhat disappointed. But he understood the potential seriousness of the issue, that had developed between two extremely dangerous parties, that were likely to be entering into hostile negotiations, regarding the dispute of the terms of the illegal trade, the banks acting as it had for both was fixed firmly in the middle. "A rock and a hard place?" Merryman whispered.

Salter-Kingsley's next statement came as quite a surprise to Merryman.

"No, I will sort this tonight," he said, shaking his head, "I'll swing by in the taxi pick you up at your apartment in the morning around ten. The Africans are not due over until Tuesday next week, and I will have a response from the representatives of the SSG by the time we come back, most likely they will halt their representative, the Doctor from coming and send another in his place with authority to sort it out. There is nothing I or we can do between now and then," he made a gesture of washing his hands in the air.

"If anything the break could not come at a better time for me, the Spaniard can hold the fort for five days."

As Merryman watched him fold the envelope and place it in his desk, he felt he was edging a little closer to the seat of his rival hearing Salter-Kingsley refer almost disrespectfully to Zabala as the Spaniard in his company. He would make sure this skiing break would aid his promotion even if he had to break a leg, knowing Salter-Kingsley was, unlike him, a regular on the black runs as a very accomplished skier. As for his boss, there was only one place Salter-Kingsley could turn, Mengele and his Brazilian cohorts were only a fraction of the Spider network. The initial negotiation with the Somalian's had been orchestrated by the Chief Executive Director and members of the Executive committee of Spider. Salter-Kingsley remembered Doctor Nestlar on the day of the negotiation, he had said little at the time of the meetings within the boardroom and appeared more of a subservient advisor, possibly a technical advisor, but no one of power at least that was the impression the banker got.

Salter-Kingsley decided to make contact using the SSG specific drop box in the Metropolitan hotel, informing him of where he could be contacted and requesting direction, something he had rarely done in all the years he had been acting on their behalf and which he believed the CED would take into account.

He spent most of that afternoon and evening constructing as brief as possible a non-incriminating report of the events and some of the participants involved, including details of the failed attack on the original shipment of gold from Africa and the Byrne brothers part in its delivery. He also confirmed that the date the Somalian's would be returning to the bank was the same date he had already been informed would coincide with the attendance at the bank of an associate of Mr Wolff and requested that, in his respectful opinion given the sensitivity of the situation the presence of a Senior Executive Director would be preferential to represent the organisation with authority as a plenipotentiary to negotiate any final settlement with the Somalian's.

Having completed his report, he delivered it by hand to the drop box, then sat at the hotel bar and ordered a Bombay Sapphire gin and tonic and a packet of Benson and Hedges, breaking his three-year non-smoking vow and prayed that he would get an answer from Spider before the Somalian's arrived. He resisted the urge for a third drink, whilst grabbing some mints from the bar on his way out to hide the smell of cigarettes on his breath from his wife Martha, unaware he was being observed by the Spider operative, Noah Benneck watching from behind the reception and that outside the hotel there was a Mossad agent waiting in the park opposite that had tailed him from the bank.

Chapter 16: The Brackish

Verbier, Switzerland
November 1975

Salter-Kingsley's letter was on the desk of the Chief Executive Director of Spider before the sun hit the dome of the Sistine Chapel in Rome and Walter Thomas had received his instructions from the CED to visit the FNIG bank and negotiate a settlement with the Somalian's, by the time the banker traversed parallel up beside Merryman on a blue run slope in Verbier the next morning.
"Something else up here, isn't it, makes our world feel so small," Salter-Kingsley said, lifting his goggles as they stared out over the vast expanse of panoramic views of the Swiss Alps.
"Reminds me why we do what we do down there." His expression was totally at odds to the man Merryman had got used to serving in the bank and for the first time, he considered his boss as someone that had aspirations and interests outside the bank.
Then as a yodeling group of six skiers slalomed by, Salter-Kingsley nudged him, "C'mon, last down buy's the hot dogs," he said and sped off, slicing through the fresh powder snow.
"They're on their way daddy." Suzy lay back in a bikini top wearing jeans instead of ski salopettes with her feet pinned up-right in the snow, still in her ski's as she sat in a deck chair, at the edge of the restaurant deck watching the approaching skiers through binoculars with a sun catcher resting under her chin. Copeland approached and leaned over the timber decking as if waiting to land a large fish.
"My god I thought that was you, Charlie Merryman!" He called down as Salter-Kingsley clipped off his ski's and stuck them upright into the snow, then hook his poles and loosened the top clip of his Nordica ski boots. He looked up confused and gestured at Merryman to the man addressing them in the bright woolen sweater that displayed the Jamaican flag colours and smiled even though he did not recognise him.
"Do you know this guy?" He asked as Merryman drew up beside him and tried hard to hold back his own surprise as he received a wave from Suzy.
"You're on," Copeland said under his breath as his smile widened at Suzy and the girl she had brought from the club, to entice Merryman's boss.
Copeland thrust his hand forward to a bemused Merryman as the bankers kicked the snow from their boots stepping up the outer timber steps to the decking,

Merryman felt his face flush as he tore his glove from his hand and accepted Copeland's firm grip.

"My God, what a welcome surprise, Hong get these guys a beer." Copeland gestured and moved back to a reserved seating area he had arranged, that was guarded by two of his men, Salter-Kingsley looked to Merryman for an introduction.

"Mr Salter-Kingsley may I introduce Mr..." Merryman was unsure if he should use Copeland's real name.

"Frank ...Frank Copeland, pleased to meet you, come join us, Peter is it, I am up here with my daughter Suzy and a couple of her friends. JoJo and Lilly, girls move along, let these guys in." as he spoke he noticed a softening to Salter-Kingsley's approach, his smile widened and even shielded behind his mirror sunglasses Copeland knew the banker's eyes were wandering across the girl's flesh as he introduced himself.

It's not unusual to see young women basking at the high altitude for a tan, wearing little under their snowsuits, with the additional glare reflected by the snow, it's possible to get a tan faster than if you are on a beach in the Caribbean, and there is often plenty of flesh on offer for those that wish to ogle.

Copeland leaned into Merryman, "Play nice and I'll keep things social, I also brought my own snow, here's a taste and JoJo will keep you company." he winked, slipping a tiny postage stamp-sized polythene pouch into Merryman's hand, his under breath sneer may have sounded light, but it was still serrated with a threat, as Hong arrived with a tray of stein beers, followed behind by a waitress, who deposited a basket full of long frankfurter hot dogs and French fries, with a selection of bottled sauces.

"Dig in I always order too much, what can I say, I'm a feeder" Copeland held the banker's shoulder as he moved around their bench table in a friendly almost fatherly manner. The American's relaxed manner was all beguiling, as he grabbed a hotdog for himself and offered the basket forward

"Thank God for some male company, this lot twitter like birds," he said, licking the sauce from his fingers.

"Thank you." Salter-Kingsley accepted his offer, as the girls appeared to railroad him on either side. Soon he was settled back within the group of strangers and onlookers would think they had known each other for years, that was Suzy's skill and as they sat laughing and socialising about the snow and the runs each of them had skied that morning, while enjoying the spectacular landscape and weather, Hong kept the drinks flowing at each snap of Copeland's fingers, that soon included warm plum schnapps all courtesy of the bankers new, worldly-wise and generous American friend.

Earlier that same day as Salter-Kingsley and Merryman had been queuing for their lift passes, on the third floor of the FNIG building in Geneva, behind the smoked glass door etched with the name, Managing Director Plácido Zabala his intercom buzzed once on his desk.
"Mr Zabala, I have Mr Lansford in reception, he has one of Mr Merryman's cards and wishes to discuss some arrangements for an account." Was how Miss Bishop announced Günther Brahn's arrival, as the old German sat almost relaxed in the leather seats and waited expectantly for his water with a lemon slice, from Francesca.
Having pressed reboot on his computer for the third time that morning, Zabala threw the paper manual to one side and looked through the glass partition office towards Merryman's empty office, across the heads of other staff members, sat in computer pods watching numbers flicker on green screens in the open-plan office area.
"Send him up room one please," he said switched the computer off, then adjusted his desk straightening a recent addition of a simple photo frame that showed an elderly couple, huddled together, both wearing matching jumpsuit tops Their expressions showed his parents happiness in each other's arms, but there was something awkward in their posture as if not posing for the cameraman, or as if they had done it out of duress, something more than if they were just camera shy.
"Mr Zabala is handling Mr Merryman's clients today. Please come this way, Sir." Miss Bishop recognised Günther although it had been many years since he had first visited the bank.
Having deposited Günther in room one, Miss Bishop then entered her boss's private office and started the videotape machine to record the meeting, which she had been instructed to do if any of Mr Merryman's or his own clients visited the bank in his absence, by Salter-Kingsley before he left for Verbier.
Günther's unscheduled visit to the bank that morning marked Sebastian's next stage in the evolution of the Westerberg Pharmaceutical Company. With a product that provided such outstanding results, word had soon spread, and order books were filled, by an expanding international beauty and cosmetic surgery industry, in particular through the United States.
Initially selling through a mail ordering system to specific high-end trade outlets supplying cosmetic surgery clinics and therapeutic retreats and Spa's, when the word Spa meant you would be likely to be rubbing shoulders with a film star.
Having withheld some of the more aggressive variants of the skin rejuvenation products Sebastian had developed, they moved into the creation of the Westerberg Retreat, an exclusive life spa's of their own where the more restrictive products

based on Sebastian's and Lenora blood were administered to highly selective clientele. Some of whom would fly in, via their grass runway for their yearly infusion of the secret life-giving properties that assisted their youthful appearance. The treatment for some included direct plasma transfusions, and they paid vast sums for the therapy through offshore banks into the Westerberg account at the FNIG bank in Geneva, thus allowing the Westerberg's to avoid the heavy Swedish corporation tax levies.

Merryman had kept a personal eye on the account and was impressed to see how quickly it grew in funds, still unaware of exactly how the Westerberg's made their money and as yet had not met Sebastian Westerberg, or seen Mr Lansford, Günther, since his original meeting, all contact had been a third party offshore Cayman Island bank account and confirmation of instruction through coded transmissions carrying the verification of the account details held at the FNIG.

As The Westerberg Pharmaceutical Company had not moved into the retail sector, for the time being, the products sold were not for the general public, so unless you were involved in that business, it would be unlikely the name would be familiar. Even after a particular Hollywood star and member of the rat pack, although he had been warned treatment would be withheld if he revealed the nature of his youthful appearance, had started to drop hints during a talk show interview that he received treatment in Finland. Fortunately, like many American's even though he had flown to the Westerberg retreat in his private jet, he did not know where Sweden was.

Set over a 500-acre site along with their own runway and helicopter pad, a cluster of self-contained hi-tech complexes expanded to facilitate the spa and commercial production factory, that included the "Strictly off Limits" underground laboratories. Aunt Krysia's original house and barns were totally refurbished, and she remained there while Sebastian and Katrina had a six-bedroom house and two separate annexes built on the site overlooking the lakes. Although Vincent remained in the main house, Günther lived in one of the annexes when he was not at the hunting lodge or staying with Aunt Krysia.

Soon within their exclusive clientele of internationally famous and mega-rich, royalty began to court their door and with their unique social acceptance, came power and the need for anonymity. However, the remoteness of the location was soon not enough to guarantee the privacy of their clients or their family even though Sebastian purchased additional land which allowed them to create a modest hydro-electric plant, making the site totally self-sufficient.

It became necessary for Vincent aided by Günther to take charge of a small security team that ensured their safety and that the location was off-limits to the prying eyes of the new scourge of the media they were now calling the "Paparazzi" the increasing risks of industrial espionage.

The concern, in particular, was for the discovery of Sebastian's highly secretive work with a select group of scientists that worked on the separate off the books operation, devoted to deciphering the Vor Elle journal and reproducing the serum, this included the analysis of his and Lenora's blood.

But with all their success, he had to admit that without the same recourses utilised in the original experiments that took place in the secret Aktion T4 underground laboratories in Sardinia that included above all an inexhaustible supply of human guinea pigs, their search would take many years and meanwhile, the gulf between his and Katrina's physical age continued to widen.

There was only one option, he had to retrieve a copy of the Nazi codebook used to access the information contained in Professor Heikkinen's private journal, that held the encrypted equations and notation of the final successful Vor Elle experiment that he was subjected to.

As always Sebastian's programmatic brain went into overdrive analysing every scenario and plan to achieve his goal and the possible repercussions of coming forward into the light from individuals from his past.

"So when were you going to tell me you sent Günther over to the bank in Geneva, I thought we agreed we run everything through the Cayman island accounts, it has been working well why try and fix it?" Katrina raised an eye over her glasses from the page of company trading figures she was reading in bed, watching him in their en' suite bathroom at the basin. She still marveled at his lean physical torso, his back strong and broad, skin-tight overstretched muscle that showed no sign of his true age, her eyes drifted down to his firm rump and she licked her lips, then felt a pang of pain to her wrist as she placed the document she was holding, down on her nightstand.

"I thought the old man had gone back to the wilderness again, I had to learn from Vincent." she sounded a little miffed that she had been kept out of the loop.

Sebastian looked up at her reflection in the mirror, "I know how busy are, I didn't want you to worry, but, I must contact our people, I mean from our days in Berlin, It is the only way, my love, I hate to tell you, but I'm not as smart as you thought," he said seeing her rubbing her wrist.

"I need the secrets of that devil's book." He cursed lightly under his breath as he washed a cut to his hand, caused by smashing a laboratory glass flask in frustration earlier that evening.

He lay beside her and looked casually across the paper she had been studying, she was in charge of all financial aspects of the running of the company, day to day he focused on the production and his special project.

"All ok?" he asked.

"Yes, at the rate the American distributor is buying, I think we will need to set up a production facility over there, maybe Canada, it will cut down the shipping cost, of course the "baking powder" will still need to be sent over." she winced again, feeling the arthritic pain to her hand and seeing his wound was still weeping he placed it over her hand and rubbed some of his blood into her skin.

She had no idea how it worked, but as it was absorbed into her skin while he massaged her hands, she felt the suppleness return and the pain ease.

"Do you have enough, can you do my feet," she smirked.

Sebastian tutted with a mischievous smile and did as commanded.

After they had made love, they sat holding each other as she spooned behind him, discussing his plans into the early hours and Katrina recognised the dangers in what he was proposing.

Even though the war had been over for thirty years and they were no longer the individuals the Nazi made them, he was once an SS Colonel and had shaken the hand of the Führer, many out there, beyond the safety of their home, would wish to use his past for their own aims, while others would seek retribution for his sins.

But Katrina knew all Sebastian was doing, ultimately was because of his love for her. As she felt his slow heartbeat on her palm, she wondered how Günther was, such an unlikely individual to be walking the halls of the corporate international banking world, but perhaps that was just as well.

The first blindside to hit Sebastian's plans came in the form of the coincidental recognition by Plácido Zabala of the name Westerberg, when agreeing to handle Merryman's client list in his absence during his Skiing trip with Salter-Kingsley in Verbier. In taking the meeting with Mr Lansford/Günther and scanning the accounts, he recognised a transaction on one of the statements of twenty thousand dollars from one of his own clients into the Westerberg account.

Zabala recalled how the long-haired front man of a heavy metal group, that shall remain nameless, who was also the same individual who had confused Finland with Sweden during a television interview, informed Zabala the money at the time he was transferring was part of a rehab process he had agreed to undertake at a Scandinavian clinic in accordance with the demands by his record label and by his wife who had been visiting the clinic for some time. During their meeting Zabala had paid little attention to the aging rockers mumblings, who had a reputation for biting the heads off mammals of the chiropteran order *(bats)*, and handled the request for the transfer, even though at the time Zabala remembered considering the gentleman looked good for his age, bizarre, but good.

However after Günther left the building on the morning of his meeting with the Spanish banker, Zabala started to look into the Westerberg's and having made the connection with the Swedish clinic, he made some enquires, possibly with the view of stealing the account from his junior. If he could make a case to Salter-Kingsley that the value of the account holdings appeared to be heading above Merryman's account threshold, there was a good chance it would be handed to him, which had happened in the past. That said, as he looked at the image of his parents in the small photograph frame on his desk, there were other issues regarding some of the bank's main accounts that played on his mind.

For the time being, reluctantly, as it had been less than a day since his boss had departed, he decided to contact Charles Merryman and inform him of the meeting with Mr Lansford and the clients demands, not because of Günther's transactions, which were not of an excessive amount for Plácido to handle on the existing account. But because the German had requested an introduction to the in-house security team, detailed in a letter, Merryman had deposited many years earlier in the drop-box numbered 555 located at the Metropolitan hotel and in addition Mr Lansford had informed Zabala, that Mr Sebastian Westerberg would be visiting the bank himself to access an associated account. Reading the account code number, Zabala considered this could only be a SSG account that held funds above his own threshold and were associate with clients handled by their boss Peter Salter-Kingsley personally.

Zabala's call to Merryman went straight to the voice mail tape cassette of a newly installed Sony telephone answer phone in Salter-Kingsley's 3000 square feet luxury apartment in Verbier, which the Spanish banker half expected, as he held his breath waiting for the tone.

"Message for Charles, hope you guys are settling in, nothing urgent, an older gentleman from Germany has paid us an unexpected visit an acquaintance of Mr Wolff. I have assisted with his request that included security facilitation and have organised per your previous recommendation an introduction to the two gentlemen from Ireland you are acquainted with. On a separate note, t would appear there is a connection with one of my own accounts, which we can discuss on your return. Additionally, the client has booked another appointment for his employer that may concern SK. Please, can you inform him and give me a bell when you get a moment, I am presuming you are on the slopes hope the snow is good.......god, I hate these machines." He could be heard saying just before the tone cut in again and the line went dead.

In Verbier, Charles Merryman and Salter-Kingsley had eventually left Copeland on the sun deck of the Le Rouge Restaurant & Après-Ski and continued skiing in the company of Suzy, Hong and the girls from the club. JoJo, Merryman paired up with quite happily, he had already met at the club and although he had never had sex with her, had already seen most of her talents when performing her exotic dance routine. The same was true for Lilly who Copeland had deliberately chosen to enchant Salter-Kingsley, having found out what his wife had looked like when she was very much younger, before their children. As for Suzy and Hong, they acted for the most part as chaperone's but were Copeland eyes and ears, there to document everything for her father.

It would not be until later that afternoon when the bankers returned to Salter-Kingsley's chalet, that Zabala's message to Merryman would be played and after having enjoyed the spa and sauna facilities of the world-famous five-star, Hotel W Verbier, where Copeland was staying, followed by another few rounds of après-ski drinks by the lounge log fire, where Salter-Kingsley took little persuading and accepted the Americans invitation to join his group for a meal at the hotel.

As his boss waxed his ski's ready for the next day outside and having entered the chalet first, Merryman was Intrigued by the telephone answering machines red flashing light and pressed the play button, hearing Plácido Zabala's voice he turned the volume down and continued to listen and when it had finished the message he pressed erase, just as Salter-Kingsley entered.

"Come on, Charles, never keep a lady waiting, that Yanks something else, now I see why your expense bills are so big, joking, forget work, we're here once right!... know what I mean?" Salter-Kingsley gave Merryman a knowing wink, which he took to be a reference to the girls.

"Yes, of course, Sir." Merryman checked the machines light had gone green.

"Peter up here, come on, tick-tock." Salter-Kingsley dashed up the open tread stairs to his bedroom to get changed.

"Yes, Peter, right away." Merryman smiled, nothing was going to interfere with his private bonding time with his boss, especially the man whose job he had his eyes on. The only concern he considered as he wiped the cocaine from his nose and checked himself in his bathroom mirror, was what Frank Copeland ultimately had in mind in turning up unannounced In Verbier.

"Coming Peter!" he responded to hearing the taxi had arrived and as they drove the short distance back to Copeland's hotel he stared into the winter wonderland Verbier becomes at night, but his mind he kept revisiting his recent conversation in the study of the American's chateau, following the failed container heist and he presumed whatever he had planned it was nothing good, but he had no choice but to go along with it, and as the drugs kicked in he smiled at something Salter-Kingsley said without catching his words about the revellers spilling out of the small bars, still in their ski wear partying in the snow.

During the meal, Merryman slipped from the table after JoJo and having shared another line of cocaine in the gent's toilets with her she, pushed him into a cubicle and gave him a blow job. Only Copeland noticed their dual absence and return, Salter-Kingsley was by now firmly besotted with Lilly like some gooey eyed teenager, having just had his first French kiss behind a school bike shed. All was going according to Copeland's plan and after the meal, the American announced he had a surprise for the bankers and handed each of his guests a small torch as a minibus arrived to take the group up to a toboggan run, where hey divided into pairs per wooden sledge for a spot of night sledging.

Night sledging is a chance for any adult to revisit childhood memories and emotions, in much the same way as the rides of a funfair do, playing on our expectations and fears, but unlike the fairground ride there is no strapping-in no safety net, just snow rushing past under the rails of the sledge in the night and although at times you appear to be travelling in almost pitch dark, the course is lit along the run at various intervals and with the high banks and snow walls there is little chance of doing any real damage, to your selves. That said in the dark, the half kilometre run feels like five and is exhilarating as you chase the yodeling next sledge in front of you, while aware of the presence behind of another bearing down. Salter-Kingsley laughed like a teenager using his heels to break from the back as he held Lilly tightly while she steered, pulling the rope at the front of their wooden toboggan.

"You should know better than to let the woman drive Peter!" Copeland said, as Salter-Kingsley finally arrived at the bottom of the run, covered in snow, smiling like a hyena and although they crashed off the course a number of times, nothing was going to stop him attaching his sledge to the next in front, as they were dragged back up to the top of the run in convoy by the organisers snowmobile while he and Lilly began to get intimate, just as Copeland had ordered.

"Relax Charlie! You're having fun with JoJo aren't you, I just wanted to meet the man you work for." Copeland pulled Merryman back before they set off again from the top as Salter-Kingsley's torchlight disappeared into the dark. "But one thing, don't forget what I said, any news I want to know," Copeland said, handing Merryman his hip flask, topped with Talisker whiskey from the Isle of Skye.

"You should know the bank has made contact, I should tell him, it's nothing important, but I believe it may involve a cash withdrawal, a client of mine, nothing I think you would be interested in." Merryman took a gulp and felt the warmth of the alcohol steel his breath, the handed the flask back.

"Let me be the judge of that," Copeland said and laid his sledge ready to shove off. "No problem, I'll know more when I get back unless you think I should call." Merryman drew up reservedly alongside him to race.

"No he seems to like the girl, let him have a good time, I want no distractions; what did you tell him about me?" Copeland said as he removed one of his gloves.

"Just that you were in the hospitality business and that Suzy owns the club, he knows it but has never been, you know he's married, Martha his wife, two children, boys."

"Yes, of course, I also understand his in-laws, the Salter's are quite religious, I should imagine he doesn't get much time off the leash, let's see how far this puppy will run." As Copeland and he watched the girls climb on behind them, Merryman now realised precisely what Copeland was up to, having the girl Lilly in play. But with a wide grin like the Pied Piper of Hamelin, Copeland offered him the remains of the white powder inside a glass vial Suzy had been wearing around her neck Merryman ignored the alarm bells ringing in his head at this forced introduction by the American and smiled as he sniffed the cocaine from his clenched fist, like Copeland was handing a treat to a dog.

"Good! Just remember Mr Merry-Merry this place may be a playground, but people go missing every season, some never get found." Copeland growled like a ghoul playfully, holding his torch so that it pointed up at his face making him look ghostly and then got a slap on his back from the giggling Suzy as he kicked off to begin his sledge run. Merryman gave a nervous laugh as he felt JoJo squeezed him from behind egging him on, then looked to Hong who sat alone on his own sledge, he gestured with his hand, as if to say "After you."

The following evening, Sebastian Westerberg, having driven down during the day stood looking out on the double-length balcony in the Pregny-Chambesy district overlooking Lake Geneva, with a bottle of coke in one hand and a Gauloises, Disque Bleu cigarette in the other.

"I like it, being on end here, there is potential to exit to the adjoining roof if we install a rope of some kind, the secure underground parking is good, and the view of the lake is excellent. I'm not sure how often she will come, but I am sure Katrina will appreciate it. Well done Gunt at such short notice, Vincent can I leave you to organise the rope and examine all emergency exit strategies."

Vincent looked up from his card game as Sebastian leaned over and placed another two of hearts on the ace. Vincent had become quite skilled as a magician of street magic, he never went anywhere without at least two packs of cards and constantly practiced elaborate shuffles that defied the laws of gravity and physics while entertaining the girls.

"Maybe look at a cheap car, nothing flash just park it in the basement, just in case and at some time organise some linen and household stuff, staying at the hotel is too high profile for me, make tonight your last, but don't go mad your Aunt will want to get new, when and if she comes to visit. No, this is good well done both of you."

Sebastian went to move another card the seven of diamonds, and before his hand had touched it with sleight of hand just by passing his own hand over it, Vincent changed it the joker and Sebastian backed away with acknowledgement of his skill and apologised for interfering.

During the meeting with Plácido Zabala, Günther had cashed in two bars of gold they had deposited initially to raise funds and had already withdrawn ten thousand Swiss Francs, put down a deposit on the apartment and paid a year in advance on the lease. To Sebastian, the apartment was a necessity for the second phase of their banking facility arrangements in Geneva and to be used to conduct interviews of any individual from the scientific community the Spider organisation were willing to introduce, effectively it was their own safe house.

First, he intended to access the personal account Count Erichh had set up during the war, which he believed would confirm his status and lead to his acceptance by whoever was running the Spider organisation. At this point, he had no knowledge of the value of the account. Whatever was there as his successor, and with the correct access information, he was well in his rights to withdraw the entire contents.

However he assumed this may bring him into contention with any individuals, ex-Nazi's that had associated accounts, irrespective of Salter-Kingsley's assurance all clients account remained strictly private and all he knew was that he would need to deal with these people, even though there was no guarantee they would have the answers for him to fulfil his goal.

For now, he wished to keep them separate from their home in Sweden and his family, the apartment would work well for his plan.

"So you have never met this new fellow Zabala?" Sebastian asked as he looked at the image from Time magazine clipped to the research he had managed to uncover about the chairman of the First National and International Geneva Bank, Peter Salter-Kingsley.

"No, never met, Mr Merryman is away, he let me know, informed me" Günther held his spoon up and then began to recite Zabala's words verbatim,

"For accounts of this distinction the Chairman normally overseas new access arrangements and future transactions, including withdrawals but he will be able as long as you provide the correct information as we are an existing account with the bank he will able to verify any access arrangements with you personally and have any transactions them authorised before completion, I think that was it?" Günther smiled to himself, pleased that he had remembered what he had been told and poured himself another bowl of Kellogg's cornflakes,

"The Chairman, so I think we are talking a great deal more than a few gold bars, and you have never met this Peter Salter-Kingsley, the Chairman either?" Sebastian asked as he picked up a backdated financial magazine, that carried a biography of the FNIG Bank and its Chairman, then tutted as Günther moved to the balcony table and plunging the spoon to his bowl with one hand while stuffing a blackened piece of burnt toast into his mouth, allowing some of the crumbs to mix in the cereal bowl.

"Him I could understand," Sebastian gestured back into the room towards Vincent "Lenora she's the same, eating cereal in the middle of the night, but you, why don't you make a sandwich or something. It's like having another child, and while we're on the subject, you know, honestly Gunt you are spending too much time on your own in the woods, my girls have better table manners. You should really start to look after yourself."

"If you say act your age, I'll split my sides, with that shit running through your blood, the people back home will be calling us vampires soon, that's half the reason I stay away from the town, the bloody widows are queuing up, and they look at me, like I'm a fresh pound of veal." Günther shook his head, considering the advances from some of the older women whose husbands had passed away, while Günther with the aid of Aunt Krysia's products and Sebastian's serum remained spritely for his age.

"Well that's as maybe, but Katrina said she will give you a list of things you should begin to avoid…… at your age," Sebastian said, ignoring the raised bushy eyebrows Gunt gave him before shoveling another heap, of sugar covered flakes into his mouth,

"I read somewhere they fed rats cocaine and sugar, they could wean the rats off the cocaine, but not the sugar," Sebastian said remembering a column in the Lancet, medical journal he had subscribed to for some time now.

"Really! I'm eating here! Next, you'll be drawing me diagrams!" Günther sploshed his spoon in the milk, then placing it to one side lifted the bowl in both hands and drank from it.

"I never had a sweet tooth apart from Ma Lansford's strudel, now since we have been here, I can't get enough, chocolate, that choux pastry cream cake thing, they do here, I think it's something to do with your blood, what do you call it..a reaction?"

Günther stopped, "anyway there it is, I have a sweet tooth, and I don't want to wake up with a stake in my heart because some batty Swede window thinks I'm a vampire, just because I can still" Günther raised his forearm with his fist. "Like rod of steel."

"Fuck me, old man, I have to eat sometime this week, you're lucky it hasn't fallen off, why don't you settle down with Krysia, I thought you two were getting on." Sebastian flicked his cigarette off the balcony.

"Yes, yes, but what would that make Eliza...I mean Katrina, I'm your father so she would be what, your father's niece? It's too confusing, beside's Krysia and I are fine, no point rocking the boat, you stick to your plan, I'll stick with mine." Günther could see somewhere during their conversation Sebastian had drifted off with his own thoughts. He was now concentrating on the details of Peter Salter-Kingsley again, he watched him light a cigarette and brush his hair back, Günther could still not get used to how young he looked, he tapped the image of the banker on the magazine, "Like I say I never met the man, if that is him, Merryman said when we talked of looking into recruiting a permanent security detail they would be in touch to finalize any details, that letter I picked up from the drop box has been sitting there for years, perhaps they want to just check these are the right type of people, maybe this is to do with that" Günther rubbed his thumb against his index and forefinger gesturing money, "it's not like the army, this is all people respect now, ..and this" he said taking a Glock 9mm from under the rear of his waistcoat and placing it beside his plate

Sebastian put down the magazine, "For Christ sake put it away and mind you don't shoot your balls off, or no Swedish widow will want you." Sebastian shook his head looking at Vincent, who then showed he had the same style gun,

"I have hidden two more, behind the toilet cistern and behind the pipe under the sink." Vincent signed gesturing toward the kitchen unit.

"You two are like Bonny and Clyde, I haven't decided which of you is the girl." Sebastian opened the sink and found the spare Glock wrapped in a duster.

"I love that film the actress she reminds me of Aunt Katrina." Vincent made an action with his gun as if shooting and then twirled it.

"Really?" Sebastian gave Vincent a stern look.

"Well he's right; she is a bit like Kat and not just in the looks." Günther defended his nephew.

"You know I had hoped we left all this shit behind us in the old days Gunt, I guess we will know more tomorrow." He picked up to the Metropolitan box key sitting on the envelope Günther had retrieved with the details of Sean and Connor Byrne "this was the only thing they left in the hotel drop box?" he tapped the envelope, and Günther r nodded yes.

"Why do we need more muscle? We have our people." Vincent signed.

"I want to keep the two things separate, we are heading into an unchartered area revisiting the type of people your uncle, and I knew from back then. There is no guarantee they will wish to see us let alone help us. But if they have what we need, then we must persuade them, hopefully, the money in the bank may help, but if not we must still persuade them and using our people at the spa in Sweden could complicate matters, in the long run, it's too close to home."

Günther then spoke out, he tried to sign but gave up,

"What Stef...Sebastian means is, the men in Sweden we use are fine, for what they do, guarding, this may require something else." Günther put his gun away,

"You mean, like the two from the shop in Stockholm I put in the lake?" Vincent signed back

"Yes, exactly." Günther nodded.

"Ok so Gunt, you go back to your comfy hotel room tonight and go to the meet their security people in the morning, for now, I don't want them to know of this place exist or that he and I are in town. I suggest you take these Byrne... brothers out for dinner or something later on in the week give us time to learn something about them. I will have had a word with our friend the police chief Nilsson, he is already going to speak with someone in the Swiss guard, find out if there have been any problems, moving money from this bank in the past. I will stay here with Vincent. Vincent grab us something hot to eat once you have dropped your uncle off, anything but Chinese, without her it makes me sad, I have no idea why, it's just food, anyway, your choice."

Sebastian watched the old soldier move back indoors to the sparse kitchenette and wash his bowl and cutlery, then dried them placing each item in a cupboard that could easily be mistaken for someone with O.C.D.

"You know I will solve this thing just as they did, especially now we have Dieter Myher's original diagrams for his expansion vessels. It is my fault we are going through all this shit now, I know that. I should have known they would use a codebook for encrypting some of the main equations. That fucking boy buggerer Heikkinen, it was probably in his safe all along, but we can't go back. Let us hope the Jews didn't get all the scientists that worked at the Kaiser Wilhelm at that time, one of them will know what book they used. That's the only reason I want to contact some of the old guard from Berlin, and this banker knows where they are." he tapped the image of Salter-Kingsley, standing alongside his family in the article.

As Günther and Vincent drove out from the apartment underground car park, the Bennick, the Spider operative that had also witnessed Salter-Kingsley at the hotel had and begun tailing Günther since first arriving in Geneva and picking up the envelope from his Metropolitan drop-box before going to the bank, for his meeting with Zabala. Bennick waited before pulling out in his car and followed them back towards the Hotel, Le Richemond. He had already made a report that was on its way to Rome and the CED of Spider, informing the Executive committee of Günther's visit to the bank and then to a local Immobilier agent, where under pressure from Bennick the estate agent had released a copy of the lease agreement on the apartment Mr Lansford had signed. Although Bennick had not seen Sebastian he included details of Vincent and the vehicle they were driving, this was the second blindsiding to Sebastian's plans.

"They're here, Sir." Francesca's voice came over the desk intercom of room one in the FNIG bank in Geneva, where Plácido Zabala sat opposite Günther.

"Good! Send them up would you please Francesca." Plácido looked at Günther's empty cup. "Can I get you another coffee, Mr Lansford?"

Günther gestured no, and stood up stretching his legs, walking past the bankers chair over to the window and looked across the road at the gardens, where Vincent sat in the distance, seated by the café near the central park Anglais fountain and appeared to be feeding the pigeons from the remains on his plate as he played cards by himself.

"Mr Lansford, these are the gentlemen who will accompany you back to Stockholm, Sean and Connor Byrne." Zabala gestured to the brothers, reverting to speaking English, as they entered the conference room, where, all but Günther knew their proceeding was being recorded by the hidden surveillance camera, installed in the air-conditioning vent, Mrs Bishop had as always, "Done the necessary" on behalf of Salter-Kingsley in his absence.

"Gentlemen Mr Lansford, he acts for the principal client," he said, as Günther turned back from the window to greet them, and then sat down, and after introductions he began to outline the procedure for the withdrawal Günther had informed Zabala, Sebastian was going to arrange, however the exact value and currency of the withdrawal would be confirmed by Sebastian.

"So once the arrangements are in place, any shipment will be ready as per Mr Westerberg's instructions, you indicated this coming Friday is likely to be the day of the transaction, and so these gentlemen have agreed to remain on standby for seven days, anything beyond that we will require additional notice," Zabala confirmed in front of Sean and Connor, who both agreed with a nod of their heads as they sat looking at Günther.

"Yes that is correct, Mr Westerberg will confirm the details of the exact transaction and the day, but I believe Friday is what he has in mind, he is due to arrive in Geneva tomorrow afternoon, I inform him you have booked his appointment for ten o'clock." Günther smiled and turned back to the boys.

"Can I ask, you will be armed, yes?" he looked at Sean for the answer.

"Yes Sir, but hopefully it is just a precaution, we are not expecting any outside influence to affect your consignment arrangements. It has been some time since Mr Merryman first discussed that you may require are services, but he indicated you wished to adopt a low key approach for any transportation." Sean studied the old woodsman, noticing although he appeared somewhat out of context in the banks surroundings, he was calm, and Sean sensed Günther was someone familiar with situations that required extreme focus and determination, but his English had the unmistakable guttural fleck of a German accent that made him sound as if each phrase had been plucked from a Hans Christian Anderson fable.

"Good, it is two days until then, I appreciate your recommendation of these gentlemen, but we are talking about transporting a considerable asset some distance. we will be required to spend a great deal of time in each other's company, can I ask that we at least spend some time becoming acquainted, before our journey, perhaps a meal, nothing formal, a place of your choosing gentlemen, my only request they serve good beer." Günther saw a sparkle in Connor's eyes.

"That is unusual," Plácido said, but Sean held his hand up signaling it was alright

"No, that is an excellent idea, quite understandable, I know just the place." Sean said, looking to Connor "My brother will pick you up from your hotel, Le Richemond correct? Is eight o'clock this evening good for you, Sir?"

Günther turned back to Plácido "Günther, please, yes, that is good."

"Unfortunately I have a previous engagement, with Mr Salter-Kingsley away I must run a few additional errands." Plácido shook his head.

"That is not a problem; after all, you will not be joining us on the journey." Günther had not considered inviting the banker to join them anyway.

"One thing can I ask, Mr Lansford, will your employer Mr Westerberg be present during the withdrawal and the migration to Sweden?" Zabala asked.

"Migration? You mean the car journey. No Mr Westerberg will not be with us. My ...boss has what you might call a hectic schedule and time as you know, gentleman waits for no one." Günther smiled and shuffled forward in his seat, getting ready to leave as Sean gave a look to Plácido that indicated their business was done and held out his hand to Günther.

"So, I will see you tonight, I am staying in room 44, will be fine. I will wait in the reception gentleman." Günther then stopped and looked to Connor in his new three-

piece suit, "perhaps, maybe later you can tell me where I can get such a fine suit young man, my son is always telling me I must move with the times." Günther said and then shook Zabala's hand, while Connor found it hard to hold back a grin.
As they walked back to their silver series 3, BMW Sean threw Connor the keys.
"You drive, let's hope this thing runs as smoothly as this Spaniard, believes, I would feel easier if we had dealt with Salter-Kingsley even Merryman."
Connor sat for a while looking at the street and watched the municipal trucks criss-cross the main road as the city workers installed the Christmas lighting to the street lanterns.
"Yer I know what you mean Seany it all seems up in the air not nailed down as usual. We don't even know what we are transporting, how much, looking at that old man, Günther, you wouldn't think he hadn't two pennies to rub together, how old do you think he is?" Connor said as he started the car up
"No idea, bugs me that we're not dealing with his boss, whoever they are, they must trust him, that or we should keep an eye out for a second home team like the Africans. These bankers live in a paper world, they make a mistake rub it out add a number here or there, it's too ficking iffy, and I don't trust Merryman. I'm thinking maybe it's time we up anchor found another gig. We have plenty of tucked away, for now, kid, head somewhere south, see the winter out on a beach." Sean looked over to the gardens across the street, he sensed something out of sight as he watched the beads of fountain water sparkle in the morning sun and also noticed the increase in the number of vans and workers preparing for the festive season. "I hate Christmas, people turn into lemmings." Sean snarled as they pulled away.
"I like this old boy, perhaps this trip will be better than I thought, I heard its fucking cold in Sweden if that's what you're thinking." But Connor was still feeling upbeat, pleased someone had finally remarked positively about his James Bond-style suit, which his brother had deliberately avoided the subjected of, having seen the invoice and the fact he had bought the heat *(gun)*, from two old Jewish tailors they knew nothing about.
"You know Abba is Swedish and all the best porn is Swedish." Sean knew his brother had a thing for Agnetha.
"I heard that maybe that's why they spend so much time in bed, any way you have your china girl, looky-looky, no touch-touchy, for you from now on," Connor smirked. Sean shook his head, he liked Suzy, but the more he considered Copeland's past and present connections, he began to speculate Suzy knew more about her adopted fathers business than she let on and part of him realized his sense that their time in Geneva was coming to an end was probably based on his own feeling about becoming attached to the girl. Although he was both curious and concerned

where her loyalties would lie if he and Copeland's paths should cross again during the performance of his duties with the bank, the man reminded him too much of Uncle, and he remembered how that had turned out and how long he had been fooled.

Less than a two-hour drive away, on the slopes of Verbier, Copeland's matchmaking plans were developing well, as the last couple of days had fallen into a routine. Salter-Kingsley was enjoying the time talking with new friends about anything other than banking, and Merryman had turned out to be an ideal skiing companion, even if he did have to stop and wait for him occasionally on the slope to catch up, but then the girl Lilly, was an enchanting partner and on occasion, as requested by Copeland, Merryman and the other girl JoJo, with Hong and Suzy would hang back or take an alternative run down to the chair lift so that Lily could work her charms on Salter-Kingsley while they shared the chair ride back up to the top again. Although he had not made any advances on her, the banker was clearly attracted, and even the occasional cuddle he received, from Lilly, would have been frowned upon by his wife Martha and her parents, but they were out of sight and mind, and for once Salter-Kingsley allowed his life to be organized by others as they drifted into a casual routine.

They would all meet up and ski first thing as soon as the lifts opened, then break for mid-morning coffee or chocolate at a mountain Ski rest stop where Copeland, feigning age and past injuries would hole up and relax waiting for the rest to turn up at midday for a pre-arranged lunch he had already organized and then again later for après ski, he was true to his statements, "a feeder."

"I hope you guys like fondue I have fixed us a gondola for this evening an early Fondue in the Sky, you get to see the sunset, have you ever done it?" he asked having organized one of the most exclusive and sought after set meals onboard an individual Roc d'Orsay-Villars gondola, rising 2000 feet it offers the diners of forty individual tabled cable cars just under two hours of spectacular views of Mont Blanc, the Muverans mountain range, Villars and the Vallée du Rhône, while they enjoy their meals, six people to each car.

"I have heard about it but not done, you have to book well in advance. I never have time, you must know people." Salter-Kingsley looked impressed as his escort as she squeezed his leg with excitement.

"Daddy knows everyone." Suzy butted in jokingly.

"Sound's fantastic; what time?" Merryman asked, catching a look of discontent at Suzy's remark from Copeland.

"Well, we have to meet up at six at the cable car station, just us six my boys will wait." He said gesturing to Hong, and not for the first time Salter-Kingsley looked intrigued at the two companions Copeland appeared to go everywhere with who jumped at his every command.

"I understand you bring your own wine, they supply only the food, three courses, I am famished, from this skiing, sounds a great idea, well done Frank for organising it," Salter-Kingsley said.

"Yes, they sell some stuff at the cable car, it's not the best, I generally take my own. I will get Hong to get something for the meal from the hotel." Copeland said, and Hong nodded he understood, then Copeland received his first real bite that the banker was on his hook.

"Nonsense, we will do that won't we Charlie, maybe if the girls know what you like they can join us choosing the drinks, there is a very good off-license near my apartment, please whatever you want it's on me." Salter-Kingsley raised his bottle, "That's dammed decent of you, Pete!" Copeland chuckled, and they clinked bottles with the others joining in with a collection of different toasts, "Cheers! Prost! Gun bae! Chin Chin! Skål!" with Merryman bringing up the rear, remembering Connor Byrne's Gaelic toast "Sláinte!

Parked in the side street opposite the FNIG bank in Geneva, the shutter clicked on the Praktica camera as the lens zoomed in on the image of a man dressed in a dark blue Crombie coat.

"New face," David announced in the back of the Mossad surveillance van, as he watched Sebastian approach and stand for a moment staring up at the outside of the bank as the security guard on the other side of the door stepped forward and released the revolving door, allowing him to enter.

"Did you get anything on the guy that entered?" Ruby asked, as they let her in, having heard the correct sequence of coded taps on the sliding side door and she began divvying up the fresh coffee and croissants.

"No, his face the scarf the hat, nothing, maybe when he comes out," David answered.

"Could be whoever it is they are just cold, it's freezing in here, run the engine Leon, get the heater on for a bit," Ruby said diving under an open sleeping bag on an upturned empty plastic milk crate.

"Does Zavi know who the American's have inside the bank yet Rubster?" Leon turned around from the driver's seat as she passed him his coffee and pastry.

"No, they won't share, only that he is someone they have a stronghold on, maybe a secretary for all we know, the word is they dropped a connection to Brazil with the owner of the bank Salter-Kingsley, the details are sketchy but the banks up to its neck in the middle of the exchange, with the boys from Brazil and the African's the Brits are hunting. Zavineski informed me whoever it is they are trying to buy family out of some Yank holding pit." Ruby began to look through the dates of the undeveloped films, "I'll take this lot back to the flat, get it developed and check it against the headshots on file." she said scooping them up and placing them in a small leather bag that held her revolver.

"Zavi also got word from our people in Mogadishu, chasing down the identity of the two Somalian's that turned up near the airport in Rio, the word is Mubarak Ali Hassan has people headed this way, so keep those greased," she said gesturing to a cloth bundle in the corner of the van where three Uzi machine guns lay hidden, then sat back cupping her warm hands around her coffee cup.

"You know the kicker; I staked this place out with Mel in this bloody van before, we got pulled to Rio just after Wiesenthal confirmed Eichmann was in Buenos Aires. It would be fucking great if the one that shot Mel and got away in Rio turned up here amongst the head shops, on file. I'll be back to cover one of you later, draw straws. I don't care if we sit here to doomsday, something's not right with this place. The banker's grandfather was a Nazi, and I bet the three of you a dance in your sandals, there's a ton of gold sitting in their vault made from gold teeth, carrying the eagle. So you schleps sit tight freezing your tuches's until we get something, we owe Mel that much."

The presence of the Mossad agents was the third blindside for Sebastian's plans, and although when he emerged from the bank an hour and a half later having completed his business with Plácido Zabala. As he stood on the steps, he felt that their future had taken a sizable step forward with the information he had been given. His image was once again caught in the camera lens of the Mossad van; albeit, he had deliberately as a matter of course, pulled his scarf high up over the bottom of his face and turned his collar up.

Unfortunately, this was not the last variable that was going to affect the plan's Sebastian eventually put into place, as a number of opposing forces and wills began to converge on the city of Geneva.

Inside the FNIG bank, Plácido Zabala checked with Miss Bishop again that there had been no word from Merryman or Salter-Kingsley. Sitting at his desk, again he looked towards Merryman's empty office and wondered if he had known in advance that Lansford and Westerberg were planning such an important visit and if he had intended it to make it appear to their boss that he was unable to handle things in his absence. He looked at the statement balance of the SSG account Sebastian had just accessed for the first time, it showed him details of the account General Count Erichh Von Stieglitz, his guardian had set up during the war, including side notes that the account was attached indirectly to other SSG accounts that Salter-Kingsley dealt with personally.

Having already established that Sebastian was the same Westerberg from the Swedish Westerberg Pharmaceutical Company, he found it hard not to comment when he divulged the value of the portfolio of assets that belonged to the account. Although Sebastian gave a meagre reaction, he took his expression as a surprise and realised he had no idea about the considerable funds now available to him. Although the SSG accounts were the sole domain of the Chairman of the bank and explicitly assigned as clients of Salter-Kingsley, strictly speaking, and acting on behalf of the FNIG bank for Plácido as managing director of the bank, because Sebastian had given the correct access code name and code word, he now had the legitimate right to walk out with the total amount, and the total assets of Count Erichh's account not totaled just under forty million U.S. dollars.

After Sebastian had left the building, Plácido called Miss Bishop into his office to confirm the details he had been given and to begin orchestrating the dual asset withdrawal Sebastian had requested, which was just a small proportion of the funds in gold and US currency, but still a considerable sum on its own. Westerberg had confirmed it should be ready and available for withdrawal by Günther and the Byrne brothers for transportation and that it would be collected on Monday. This was the day before Salter-Kingsley was due back in the office.

"Yes Sir it is correct, shall I prepare the paperwork and make the arrangements Mr Westerberg had requested with the teller in the vault" Miss Bishop, asked

"Yes, if you will, I shall sign the internal withdrawal papers," he said, then immediately placed a call to the number for the Chalet in Verbier but found the line engaged. With that, he routed through his Filofax and decided to contact the concierge at a nearby hotel to the Verbier apartment, who he had met when he had been honoured by Salter-Kingsley to join him in a skiing party with clients of the bank one year.

"You understand, I need you to contact Mr Salter-Kingsley himself, ask him to call, please take this down, it concerns SSG, you understand SSG."

"Yes Mr Zabala, I will go myself straight away, if there is no response I will leave my card and call you back." Bernard, the concierge at the exclusive W hotel, remembered the banker and his boss.

"Good thank you. I appreciate this, Bernard." Plácido then told his secretary to hold all his call and pouring himself another coffee he lit a cigarette, staring for some time at the requisition forms before filling them in to arrange the withdrawal from the account named Arno a combination of his brother and his sister-in-law's name and the date that Leopold was born.

In the main lobby of Salter-Kingsley's apartment block the desk receptionist gestured Bernard towards the taxi outside in the car park as it was leaving, saying "You have just missed them," but he had no idea where they were off to.

The girls had just arrived taking Salter-Kingsley to the off-license and then on to the cable car and Fondue in the Sky, to meet up with Copeland, Suzy and Hong.

"No matter, please give him my card when he returns, I will be on duty this evening," Bernard said and reported back to Plácido in Geneva when he returned to his desk and informed him that having recognized the taxi firm they had used he had placed a call to ascertain where they had gone.

"Good thank you; this is most urgent if you will keep me informed I will be very grateful Bernard," Plácido said then gave the receptionist his home number and asked him to pass it on to Salter-Kingsley. Twenty minutes later at 18.20, Bernard received word that the taxi had dropped the group at the Cable car, the group were already popping corks of champagne onboard one the Fondue in the Sky cable cars as the sun began to fall from sight.

Bernard meanwhile placed a call with the restaurant and was informed that although the cable car usually took ten minutes or so, for the meal they slowed it down for the diners, they would not be returning to Verbier for another hour and a half that was if they did not decide to stop in Le Châble.

Around the same time In their apartment in Geneva Sebastian considered calling Günther to discuss his meeting at the bank but believed it would distract him from their schedule, he loved the old man dearly but the idea he might blurt something out having learnt they had just come into a fortune that rivalled the gross national product of Sweden's nearest neighbour Norway, was too much of a strain He held back a chuckle as he wrote the sum of the account holdings down, mesmerised by the line of zero's, knowing Günther when he found out what the Count had done would chuckle for a month.

In the lounge Vincent practised card tricks while watching the portable television Sebastian had sent him out to buy, while Sebastian began to plan how Günther would take the Byrne brothers to Sweden, he replayed the route in his mind, looking for the most likely locations for any raid to take place. At this point, they had already agreed without notifying the Byrne's brothers he and Vincent would act as out of sight armed chaperones.

It was not until Vincent came through and tapped the table gesturing to his collar, having donned a black suit and he stood in front of him that Sebastian recognized it was almost like staring into a mirror of his younger self, accept Vincent had no scar to his chin and dark hair.

"So you know what to do, stay out of the way, these guys are smart, just watch and read." Sebastian pointed to his lips as he stood behind him in front of the hall mirror showing his young cousin once again how to tie a Windsor knot.
As the Roc d'Orsay-Villars gondola carrying Copeland's inebriated guest began its descent to Verbier, Sean and Connor picked Günther up from the Le Rosselle hotel in Geneva it was just before eight and they drove to an Indian restaurant where they were regular customers.
"I have never had, so you must order, we have few in Stockholm." Günther answered to the question from Sean, "Curry, alright with you tonight?"
At the Red Fort curry house, having ordered a range of dishes varying from mild to very hot. The Irish brothers spent some time preoccupied with working out the age of their guest and understanding, since he was not used to eating Indian cuisine how he was able to demolish most of a chicken tikka phaal without breaking into a sweat and having few breaks from eating apart from ordering another IPA, *(Indian Pale Ale)*.
"I thought you Irish drink a stronger beer ... stout yes?" Günther looked at the beer in his glass.
"There be plenty of time for the black stuff if you like, after this, have you tried it Mr Lansford, Guinness?" Sean kept getting the sense that he had met Günther previously becoming interested in the old German who spoke with non-condescending wisdom on most subjects.
"Günther please it's a long journey we will be making together, as for the black stuff, no again I have never had, but we have dark beer similar, I think, I have heard your people drink nothing else. Do you ever return to your homeland, Ireland to family?" Günther watched Sean's eyes and noticed Connor shuffle back, and he sensed immediately the boys were uneasy talking about their past.
Connor was surprised how candid his older brother was with someone they knew little about. That said he too felt Günther had a calm, relaxed presence, like so many he came into contact with appeared to appreciate. He was a big man still, but Connor gauged from the size of his weathered hands and titan wrists he must have been of formidable strength in his youth.
"No we never go back, that is something many of our race believe is a law of life." Sean eyes glazed for a moment as vivid images of Cork swept briefly into his mind, and Günther noticed a sign of what he took to be regret.
"You don't miss it then." he pressed to see if he could catch a glimpse beyond the facade of strength Sean wished to display. For the first time that evening, Sean was reminded this was work, and the old man who sat before him was part of something that could prove dangerous for them, as Connor ordered another round of drinks.

"I don't know if you would say I miss it, but like most things when the choice is not yours, it can make the wish to obtain it stronger." Sean found himself offering up a piece of his true nature, hoping it would satisfy his inquisitor, and he watched Günther stop chewing and stared into his eyes with a glint of recognition.
"Huh, I know how that is, my friends." he said softly, "so what have you planned for me, it is still early, I have a day to recover before our business," Günther said, polishing his dish with the last piece of naan bread.
Connor pulled his zip up and washing his hands checked his hair in the toilet mirror, "I know what you're thinking, you want to take him to the club, if you fuck off with your chinky bird and leave him on my lap I won't be happy, he's a good old boy I think, but he will cramp my style, I fancy a shag myself tonight, I didn't buy this suit for nothing." Connor checked the condom machine and then bought two packs of ribbed.
"She's Taiwanese, but whatever, I figure the old man will be happy with a nightcap, if he wants any more, sure we'll treat him to a flash of a few tities. He must be 102; he'll be off in a taxi before midnight, either way, then Mr dandy pants you can impress the girls with your threads. I'd just like a little more time with the old boy, find out about his people. He gave me the route, if he's not ex-military I'm a Dutchman, but there's something else going on, I'm just not sure what, just keep an eye out Kid, did you take a look at his mits, I recon they snapped more than a few breadsticks."
In Verbier, at the cable car station, the concierge Bernard had arrived looking for signs of Salter-Kingsley. He paid little attention to Hong and Tang, who were also waiting in the main reception as the sound of the arriving gondolas clanked somewhere above in the machinery of the building and groups of disembarking satisfied dinners came down the steps.
Seeing Salter-Kingsley, unannounced he moved forward, approaching the group and immediately, unaware who he was, Hong sprang defensively and was about to floor the concierge when he received a gesture to withdraw from Copeland standing behind Salter-Kingsley.
"So when did he call?" The banker asked Bernard taking him to one side as the concierge explained the circumstances of his presence. "And you are sure he said SSG?"
Bernard showed him where he had written it on a hotel business card, as he called Merryman over "Problem Sir?" Merryman tried desperately not to slur his words.
"Possibly, I am not sure, Plácido Zabala has been trying to contact us, something with one of my clients, for this guy to come out here must be something. I must attend to this right away." He turned back to Copeland who stood waiting with the

girls, trying to gauge what was happening and disliking the interruption to his evening he glared at Bernard who was still hovering in the background.

"I am sorry I must check in with the office now, unfortunately, if I can get to a private phone, it may be nothing." Salter-Kingsley apologised to Copeland.

"Peter don't worry, look we can go back to my hotel, organise some drinks and you phone your people there if there is a problem, my boys can sort out, we are less than two hours from Geneva after all."

Twenty minutes later, having spoken with Plácido, he called Merryman from the group that once again occupied a prime window location of low slung seating area in the sky lounge of the hotel.

"I have to get back to the bank, it would appear your man Lansford, you remember the old German, his boss arrived he is here in Geneva, he has accessed a very important account, very important and arranged a withdrawal for Monday.
I must deal with it personally, now, tonight. Can you organise a taxi and have my things from the hotel brought back, first I must thank Mr Copeland here, you have interesting friends, Charles, I am impressed, you stay, keep them entertained pick up the bill here, we will speak when you get back, one thing Zabala said he left a message on the machine in the apartment, you didn't it pick up, did you?" Salter-Kingsley asked, while looking over Merryman's shoulder and regretting his departure, he had planned to make his move on Lilly later that night and was even going to suggest Merryman get a room in the W hotel for the night so he could be alone with the girl in his chalet.

"No, I hate those things." Merryman felt his face flush.

"No matter, look you just, do your thing, buy them a nightcap, I'll take care of it, perhaps when this is all done you can arrange a revisit, with the girls, understand, we'll talk when you get back," Salter-Kingsley said and then informed Copeland that he had to leave.

"Yes Sir, of course, I'll take care of it, if you are sure you don't want me to accompany you?" Merryman caught the look of disquiet in Copeland's eyes and then with a blink of an eye, the American's expression changed as Salter-Kingsley approached the group to make his excuses, for breaking up the party.

"Nonsense, my man Tang will drive you back in my Porsche to your apartment and then back to Geneva, it saves waiting for a Taxi." Copeland was all smiles and magnanimous in their parting. However, as he watched from the glass windows of the hotel doors as they drove off and having told Tang to stay with him, Copeland pushed the girls from his arms.

"Merryman! Explain what has happened?" He said sharply drawing the banker to a side table in the hotel reception by tugging at his elbow, as Hong sensed it was now business as usual and stood to one side awaiting a command.

"I am not sure, but it may be something that will be important, I think a large transaction is being organised soon, Monday or Tuesday, this must have something to do with the meeting with the Irishmen, Sean...the Byrne brothers."

"Shhh..." Copeland gestured he lowered his voice, seeing Suzy looking at them, then his eyes glazed over as he watched the girls begin to walk back towards where they had left their drinks.

With a loud clap of his hands, all eyes turned to him. "Ok people parties over, we go back to Geneva tonight, I want you in the minibus within twenty minutes!" There were groans from the girls, but obediently without asking for an explanation, they grabbed their room keys and headed to the hotel lift as Copeland turned back to Merryman.

"We will drop you at your office, you make out you are a conscientious employee and didn't think it was right to stay, buy yourself some brownie points, and you find out everything, you understand, everything! Then come on to the club, Tang will be outside the bank waiting for you and don't worry old chap, I will make it up to you when you get back if you do as I ask. I saw how you looked at our Lilly" he gestured to the girls as the elevator door closed, "fancy fucking something your boss wanted first, why not, you can have both of them if you bring me the goods tonight" he snarled, almost relaxed now he no longer had to continue with the pretence he had played for Salter-Kingsley.

"Hong take Mr Merryman back and help him get his things in our mini-bus then come back," he ordered then settled their bill at the reception.

About the same time that evening in Geneva, as they left the Red Fort curry house, once again, Sean felt uneasy. As he pulled the driver's seat forward to let Connor climb into the back seat of his BMW, he caught Günther's questioning eye over the roof of the car. Günther realised Sean was scoping the area and looked over his shoulder then up and down the street, he gave an understanding shrug,

"Something?" Günther said, even though he knew there was a legitimate reason for the Irishman's sixth sense.

"Just doing my job, Mr Lansford." Sean strummed the roof and seeing no one out of place in the street, shook his head. "habit." he said and got a nod from Günther

"I know that feeling." Günther gave a disarming smile and then clambered his large frame into the front seat.

Wilderness or city, the old woodsman had taught his nephew well, as a child he had tracked 200 Kg adult bull Reindeer to the edge of the Swedish tundra, before taking the kill shot, without them getting his scent, neither Sean or Connor noticed Vincent skillfully trailing five vehicles behind obscured by a van while riding a Suzuki trial motorbike as they drove to the first watering hole, the Irish bar and introduced Günther to a little bit of plastic paddy magic and his first pint of Guinness, while Vincent waited outside.

"So Günther what do you think of the black stuff?" Connor asked as he made a show of downing his pint in one, Günther raised his eyes then Sean followed his brother's lead and also cleansed his glass before Günther had taken a sip. Günther smiled widely and raised his glass then opened his mouth, and as the last few drops slipped down his throat, Sean and Connor slapped the table in applause.

"No, but I fancy I can get used to it," he said, wiping his whiskers, "and I like the music, reminds me of home, the violin." He said, looking at the little four-piece band that would occasionally startup, as they sat drinking amongst friends, two of the girls began to dance a jig, with no rehearsal or conformity to their routine, just as they do in Temple Bar in Dublin.

On the other side of Geneva, the Mossad surveillance van had already departed for the night, not long after the bank had closed its doors with Claude Dieppe waiting for the last employee to leave before locking the main entrance with the night guards stationed inside at the reception.

Copeland's man Tang now sat in the same side street as the Israeli team had been parked. He watched Salter-Kingsley punch in the security code for the electric gate and enter the bank via the underground car park, where he used his private key to access the main lift. A few minutes later Tang saw the security guards standing to attention as the banker signed in at the reception and then watched as the strip lights on the third-floor flicker on and the shadow of the banker moving back and forth between the rooms.

Salter-Kingsley called Plácido Zabala from the Spaniard's office as he gathered all the paperwork and the account books together for both the Westerberg's and the SSG account Sebastian had accessed.

He stared for some time almost in a trance at the small photograph of the elderly couple in the frame on Zabala's desk and questioned in his mind who they were, having previously confirmed with Miss Bishop Zabala's parents were listed on his file as deceased, finding it a distraction he laid the frame flat.

Having confirmed for himself that Westerberg had used the correct codes, he contemplated the enormity of the legacy Sebastian had now inherited and the power it represented, not just against the other associated GSS accounts but with the bank itself, effectively he had become one of the banks most affluent individual account holders.

Reading up on the particulars Zabala had researched concerning the Westerberg pharmaceutical company, he discovered there was little about Sebastian himself, Katrina and the girls received a single mention, and the article spoke of a cottage industry that had grown from herbal health products and carried an image of Aunt Krysia's small timber house as the place where it had all begun.

It was the granting of the joint royal warrants by the King of Sweden and Norway that generated the attention of the financial journalist's article, and although there was an image of Katrina cutting the ribbon of a new kelp processing plant in Stavanger, with Sebastian at her side, both were turned in such a way from the camera lens that their facial image was not clear, the photographer choosing to focus on the royal dignitaries inaugurating the opening of the building.

As he read the article, Salter-Kingsley found there was something intriguing about the couple in their lack of self-promotion.

He returned to his own desk and opening his draw, turned his attention to the videotape recordings that Miss Bishop had made of Günther's visits including the one with the Byrne brothers. He was replaying the one with Sebastian when he heard Merryman in the back office, at first he thought it was one of the guards doing his rounds, then there was a knock at his door, and Merryman poked his head round. "It didn't feel right staying up there, I made my apologies to Frank Copeland and the girls, I put a bottle of bubbly on ice at the bar before I left, the good stuff, they understood. I have dropped your skis and bags off at my place. I was not sure if you needed a hand, with organizing the Byrne's brothers, but here I am, what was the panic with Plácido."

Salter-Kingsley was surprised to see him, but also suitably impressed, and gestured to the chair in front of his desk and pushed over the documents Zabala had gathered on the Westerberg's, as he explained about Günther and Sebastian's visit. "So that's Westerberg, and he owns this health product company in Sweden, figures they have some crippling taxes. I am surprised we did not make the connection between us." Merryman said, looking for confirmation his boss was not looking to him for miss-judging the client's status.

"Well now he need never work again, although from the look of the transfers they have been making from their Cayman Island account they appear to be quite fluid, I can see how this would fall under the radar, it's just been ticking over nicely, with regular payments, apart from the initial guarantee of funds we hold you issued through the telex to the Cayman's you have had no contact, personally, all the paperwork is good, I quite understand Charles, but still now we may have a problem," Salter-Kingsley said and handed Merryman the SSG statement.

"I see, so he is German you think, not Swedish? But either way presumably he will keep this here, there is no reason for him to move the money from Geneva, from as you say from the looks of this his business is sound." Merryman's eyes then drifted down to the withdrawal Sebastian had arranged to be ready in two days.

"Yes, perhaps, but it's a little more complicated than that, I wish I had been here. Look Merryman it's very good of you to come back, I am sorry we had to cut the trip short, but I really need time to sort this out myself. You get off now home, I'll see you tomorrow, we will talk then?" Salter-Kingsley said, without looking up from the papers and although something Merryman had said was troubling him regarding the Byrnes brothers, he was so deep in thought he did not notice Merryman slip back into Zabala's room and check the paperwork regarding the withdrawal arrangements before he left the building.

Salter-Kingsley thoughts were preoccupied with how the CED and Spider executive committee would react to the news and realised regardless of the authenticity of the account accessed by Sebastian Westerberg he needed to inform the CED immediately and began preparing a letter for the drop-box, this time he included the details from the article identifying Sebastian as the owner of Westerberg pharmaceuticals and gave details of the withdrawal, he had arranged, including the route.

Salter-Kingsley requested an immediate attendance by a senior member of the executive committee and confirmed that unless he was informed otherwise, he would be forced to comply with Mr Westerberg's request and signed off by stating; I can confirm this individual used the correct access requirements for the account in question and is the legitimate account holder.

He made six drafts of the letter and shredded the ones he did not use.

Across from the bank Tang flashed his headlights to Merryman as he emerged and drove him to the Senkin club, where before he was allowed a drink, he was taken up to the private office and made to call Copeland who had been sat waiting in his study at his chateau. Suzy sat smoking in the corner swinging her leg, watching her father taking the telephone call as he pointed to his drinks cabinet and Hong did the honours looking at Suzy, he raised the bottle of Chivas to an empty glass, and she gestured yes.

"Well it looks like the banker was right, he has another apple for you to bob for Hong, I've told him to wait at the club, I'm going to meet him tonight, discuss the arrangements in detail, apparently it's another businessman smuggling their ill-gotten gains out of the city, a German, I want no fuck-ups this time, put him in the back suite of the club", he looked at the time on his wristwatch, "I'll be there by

twelve-thirty, keep him off the coke before I get there, go now before he gets loaded." he gestured to Suzy and she stubbed out her cigarette.
"I told you that the skiing thing was a good idea." She smiled.
"Tell that to my calves," He said, placing one leg across his desk and began to rub the muscle. "Listen, Suzy, tonight, I want it all on tape, if it works out we have him for life, if not one less bean counter on this rock won't be missed, either way, the tape will keep him on a leash."
"You want I should make it a private party for you and him, with the girls, Daddy?" She understood exactly what her father intended to do in having a blackmail tape made.
"Once we have finished our business fair enough, I promised him, JoJo and Lilly earlier if he comes thru, I'll leave that with you, two minutes with the man makes me want to reach for a gun. But perhaps hold back Lilly for now, use Katie after I am done with him. The coke loosens his tongue, and she knows how to tame him and will be more attentive this time. But Suzy, you! make sure he's straight before he turns up for work, he's just the sort of fuck up to screw up a plan at the last moment, I don't want him anywhere near that bank if he's toast in the morning."
She downed her drink and called to the dog Binki, getting ready to leave, as she went through to the hall and once out of earshot, Copeland looked at Hong.
"Drop her at the club, then sort out who you want for this thing and make the arrangements then come back to pick me up. Close the door on your way out,
"Hong tonight bring some chain, in case I have a change of heart, that sack of shit Merryman can do his bit for the environment, feed the lake fish."
Having showered and changed into one of his trademark Hawaiian shirts Copeland looked up at one of the four world clocks on his study wall and saw it was 18.23 in Washington D.C.
Then he opened his top drawer and placed the receiver into the phone scrambler placing a call with Langley and operator 4452790 who patched her through to Craftwork, he heard the voice on the other end of the line struggling, out of breath.
"Got you at a bad time?" Copeland asked.
"I'm on the tenth finishing up a late-game at Lowes Island with some of the chiefs. I just had one of those new mobile phones fitted to the buggy, so if I lose you don't sweat, what's up Frank?" Carter-Wallis waved his caddy away as he rifled through the back of the golf buggy and having chosen a three-iron, held it up and received a nod from the caddy signaling he had chosen correctly.
"Nice, just watch that dogleg on the twelfth that water comes up fast just like the falls, must have lost a bucket of balls down there next time I'm stateside I'm going to bring some scuba gear or stick to rafting the rapids, that was a hell of a trip in

68." Copeland pictured the golf course in his mind and how the weather would be hot and looked out through his study window at the snow-covered mountains in the distance.

"Well, that was when you still had a visa. but I told you if you drop your oriental friends, I'll have another go with the farm, see if they will allow a prodigal son back home, we could do this every week, but the rafting is out for me, old friend, my piles would swell up like a May West." Wallis looked across at the three players that made up his four-ball and received a glance of irritation from the Secretary-General. "But I guess we both know that's never going to happen, look I'd like to stay and shoot the breeze. Unfortunately, the Gatekeeper's got a corn cob up his arse. The Brazilians are curious why ten tons of fish are stinking up the beach at Copacabana, the fuck up with the Somalian's and Mossad are going to cost me, I'm going to have to let him win, and you know how I hate to lose to the top brass." The Gatekeeper is the nickname of the White House Chief of Staff. Some judge that he is in a unique privileged position, as the highest non-elected official of the Whitehouse to discuss with the President topics that may be brought to his attention by black operations. Orchestrated by divisions of the U.S. security services including the C.I.A. and although Wallis had sunk the freighter Cardigan Bay out at sea at one of the deepest points, the neurotoxin loaded by the German Spider team and Somalian's had interacted with the seawater and had killed all the marine life in the area. The smell of the decaying fish was still affecting the tourist trade in Rio. "Again sorry on the FUBAR *(Fuck up beyond all recognition)*, did you get the Concorde tickets and reservation details for London?" Copeland swallowed hard, for him to apologise was as rare as hen's teeth, but Wallis was the only bridge he hadn't burnt when he was disavowed by the agency.

"Yes and the Swiss chocolate you sent Meg, her hips say thanks." Wallis looked down the field and saw their strategically placed security detail was getting pushed up by the next group of gophers

"Greens are kind of getting backed up here Cola, cut to the chase." Wallis caught another look from his group of players.

"Yes, Sir General! But perhaps this may improve your swing. I'll be able to make up that shortfall we spoke of, it will be waiting in London by the time you get there with Meg and no promises but also a bonus. Two Irish poachers have strayed onto my patch, with all that shit they are giving the Brits these days, may buy you some love over there. Who knows a knighthood, I heard they gave one to Charlie Chaplin, you watch they'll be giving one next to Steven Spielberg for Jaws, bloody film, put me right off my morning dip in the lake over here, anyway I'll keep you in the loop and see you and Meg at the Grosvenor House hotel."

"That sounds swell Frank, but you'll have to excuse me, if I don't give it a yippee ki-yay brother, I'll still take a dive on the twelfth to the chief, hedge my bets, until you tell me you have reigns around that colts neck."
"Well General, as sure as shit, if this one goes to the wall, I'll seriously consider hanging up my guns, Cola out."
Copeland believed it was unlikely he would ever return to the States without the risk of detention. If it were anyone other than Carter Wallis, he would not make an effort to get on a plane and would make them come to him, but London was considered neutral ground. Some in the CIA may wish to use the opportunity for a full debrief and call him to account for past sins, but they knew of his status in the Japanese crime syndicate, and he felt relatively safe with a strong protective Yakuza presence in the city. It was worth the risk to keep at least one finger in the pie of the C.I.A. and besides he was a sucker for a good stage show.
"Sorry about that Gentleman, the Kremlin never sleeps." Wallis made the call interruption appear more critical than it was, before swinging a Mulligan, sending his ball deep into the rough, which as he predicted brought a smile to the lips of the Gatekeeper.
Having taken to a bar
Meanwhile, with Copeland and his group already returned to the Senkin club, having realised that the old German still had some spirit in him and because Sean had begun to feel somewhat frisky himself, they drove across town to the club.
It was just after twelve and the bouncers on the door had already turned away a number of over inebriated unwanted visitors, they gave Günther a second look then one of the Japanese bouncers recognized Sean and with a flash of their Platinum membership cards irrespective all three smelt like a Liffey distillery they were ushered inside
"It is good to see you again Mr Byrne" Don the Maître D welcomed them and escorted them to a private wall booth and returning to his station used his house phone to inform Suzy who was upstairs in the private office suite listening in on a headphone as a tape recorder turned slowly, and the voice level needles pinged back and forth, recording the conversations Copeland was having with Merryman.
It was still early for the Senkin club, the action did not get going until after one and a queue had yet to form for the exclusive basement disco.
This is possibly why a smartly dressed young newcomer was allowed into the club a few minutes later with only a brief demonstration of his card street magic. Vincent first bemused the bouncers with some elaborate gravity-defying shuffles and then when one picked a card, the four of hearts from those Vincent fanned in his hand, having placed it back and watching it disappear with a shuffle back into the pack,

both men were left disarmed in laughter to find that with a gesture from Vincent it reappeared in the top pocket of the bouncer and had changed to a card that read three simple lines,

Hi! I am Vincent
I am mute
Do you like magic?

Who doesn't? Vincent then offered them to choose again, when one turned over his card, it revealed a single ten Franc note, which they assumed was a bribe and gauging his attire to be within the accepted parameters of the club gestured him forward. "Go on in boy, if I find your quick hands have been in our clients pocket, I'll show you a fucking trick, cut your fingers off." the bouncer whispered with a cheery grin, shrugging dropped the rope allowing him to pass inside, having welcomed the few moments of light relief to the boredom of his job entirely misjudging the light-framed individual that stood before them.
Inside Günther gave nothing away as he watched Vincent carry out the same routine on Suzy at the bar, she gestured to Don that she had said "yes" allowing Vincent to move amongst customers showing them some street magic.
"Just don't make a nuisance of yourself," she said and gestured to the barman to give Vincent a drink on the house, to which he pulled a yellow rosebud from the air and handed it to her.
"You're good kid, but remember most are here for the tits." she smiled and toyed with the stem as Vincent turned to a couple sitting at the bar and began to astound them with his skill, whilst all the time using the reflections cast from the rooms many mirrors to watch his Uncle and the Byrne's brothers in the wall booth, as three pints of Guinness arrived at their table.
"You sure you haven't any Irish in you Günther," Connor said as he watched Günther take a large gulp that left his glass half empty.
"Maybe, I think we all have when it comes to having a good time, this is some place you found here, I take it from the gorilla's you are not allowed to touch, yes?" Günther gestured to the black-suited bouncer's strategically placed around the club.
"These places are ok, but it's a bit like paying to go watch a man eat, you get hungry, but your belly is still unsatisfied unless you know one of the girls privately," Connor said.
"And you know one of these girls, lucky dog, which one," Günther smirked giggled.
"Not me this fellow here." Connor gestured to Sean with a nod.

"Some of the girls are allowed off their collar, upstairs, but nothing is free, I can probably arrange it." Sean gestured up to Hong on the top deck of the VIP area.
"He decides?" Günther asked, weighing up the tall Vietnamese.
"No her," Sean said, spying Suzy.
She was about to go over and replenish their glasses when she caught a signal from Hong on the upper VIP level balcony, who had noticed Günther looking at him.
"Who's that?" Hong asked, watching Vincent entertaining another group of people at a table.
"Some guy off the street, he's classy don't you think a magician, I like it, pretty good and free. If it works, I might offer him a regular spot as long as he doesn't fleece our customers. Someone with his skill could pick up some fat wallets in a place like this. I'll keep a check on him, just look after the banker." She noticed a group of her customers appeared completely enthralled by Vincent.
"I'm doing my job." Hong nodded and then gestured down towards Sean's table "and the old man with your boyfriend, did you know he was coming in tonight?" Hong then looked back at the closed door of the executive suite where Merryman and Copeland were finishing off their discussions regarding the Westerberg's withdrawal from the bank.
"He will not be happy if these clowns interfere with his plans, keep them out of Franks way." Hong always referred to Copeland by his first name.
Suzy looked at the other patron's in the select lounge areas on the balcony, checking all were being serviced well by her staff.
"No I didn't no Sean would be here, no idea who the old boy is could be his dad for all I know, I'll find out and handle them. But let Daddy know they are here, try and keep the banker up top until I have spoken with them." Suzy said and began to descend the stairs as the music started, and a new group of exotic dancers began to strut across the main, narrow catwalk stage.
Günther could not see Hong and Suzy's exchange from his vantage point in the booth, but Vincent noticed and read their lips even in the rouge filtered half-light of the club and while still using muscle memory to carry out his act.
Suzy slipped unnoticed by Sean, back to the bar as the first confident party-goers stepped down to the small disco area and began to gyrate to "blockbuster" by the pop group Sweet.

She gestured to the bartender that she would carry the boys' next round of drinks over and added a bowl of pretzels and olives.
"So looks like you boys are on the tear-up tonight, nice suit Connor, it is Connor your brother has yet to introduce us and your guest Mr.?"

"Günther, Günther Br...Lansford, what is tear-up?" Günther asked as Connor gave Sean a look hearing Günther was about to say his real name, but he glossed over it, after all, they were not the Byrne brothers, and he doubted Suzy's real name was Suzy Bell.

"It means on the razzle, on the Craic, on the beer...Seany's been teaching sexy Suzy here, some of our native tongue isn't that right Seany." Connor gave a friendly grab to his brother's shoulder, but Sean flinched back and gave him a stern look.

"I can see why it's a pleasure, Miss Suzy." Günther stood, ignoring Connor's double entendre and kissed Suzy's hand.

"A gentleman, a refreshing change, nice to meet you Günther, don't let these two eejits! Lead you astray." Suzy winked with a tease at Sean, remembering the Irish word correctly.

"Watch it boyo, this old fella will shanghai your Suzy here, if you give him half a chance." Connor settled back in his chair and dived into the bowls of table snacks, demolishing the pretzels before anyone else got a look in.

"Jeese! Brother, you can't still be hungry, I swear you have hollow legs?" Sean raised his hands, gesturing an apology for his brother as Suzy leaned over and kissed Sean.

"Well, welcome Günther, I hope you enjoy your visit to the Senkin, and if not you let me know, I will sack someone." she cleared their empty glasses from the table and turned back to Sean, "maybe if you are still about when I finish we can have a drink."

Sean played cool and gestured with a slight nod, "In the meantime, I will send some company for you, look no-touch, she tapped Sean on the nose playfully and I'll send over some more snacks Connor."

"Your lady?" Günther asked as he watched Suzy glide back to the bar, stopping to welcome the odd patron she recognized as regulars.

Sean felt a pang of commitment at the term, it was a little strong for how he considered his relationship with Suzy was developing, "An acquaintance." he said.

"A very friendly acquaintance, eh! Seany." Connor butted in.

"Well, she runs a very interesting club," Günther said, and they raised their glasses in a toast, as two of the clubs escort girls came over to their table.

"Is this ok for you, Günther, I don't want to get you in trouble with Mrs Lansford." Sean joked.

"No, Mrs Lansford, never had, and now I think I am a little set in my ways, that said, I can enjoy the view." he smiled and moved up allowing one of the girls to sit beside him, while Suzy went back up to Hong and informed him that the man sitting with Sean and Connor was Mr Lansford.

Across the room, Vincent had to sip his drink to cover the smile forming on his lips from watching his Uncle with the half-naked girls, and for a moment he was concerned Suzy had caught him watching Sean's table, then noticed as she looked up to the VIP balcony where Copeland had appeared.

"So, he is the Swede, German, Merryman talks about, is his boss here?" Copeland asked Hong while watching Connor revelling in the girl's attention at their table.
"No, just the three of them," Hong answered.
"Ok, check with the girls after they leave, find out if they heard anything, keep it friendly, you have to learn in this game, no one picks a bruised peach," he told Hong.
"Does she know about the plans for the Irishmen?" Hong asked with a sneer.
"No, and I want to keep it that way, you know how she is. She will get distracted soon enough when he is no longer around. Just make sure there are no comebacks, I want no fuck-ups on this one Hong, do you think you can handle that for daddy?" Copeland said as he stood surveying the club below like a ship's Captain, standing proud as Sean walked through to the toilet's and acknowledged him, gesturing with a tap to his head.
"Yes, I can do that, Frank." Hong glared down with disdain as Sean passed by below.
"What about your guest?" Hong gestured back to the VIP lounge where Merryman was already enjoying his second line of cocaine.
"Stay with him, keep them apart, I'll speak with Suzy on the way out. Use your judgment, if he looks like he might shoot his mouth off gets one of the girls to sit on his face, that will shut him up and remember if he is fucked up tomorrow morning I want Tang to sit with him, until he's sober, he's not important on this thing now, but who knows if this works out, maybe we get another bite before we throw the bad apple away." Copeland then gave Vincent a quizzical look as their eyes locked, Hong caught his expression.
"Don't ask Suzy's idea, she thought it might take the pressure off the girls, he's behaving himself, so far." Hong secretly wanted to leave his station and see what all the fuss was about with Vincent, in spite f his misgivings of his men allowing him in Hong was secretly fascinated by magic and was hoping later to learn a few tricks.
"Well keep it like that, as long as the punters are happy, but I think your sister forgets who owns the building, sometimes." Copeland lit one of his cigars and began to step down from the balcony.

Having caught most of what they had said from their lips, Vincent watched the club owner, chaperoned by two of his bodyguards come down the stairs and walk over to Suzy at the till.

"Keep the Irish away from the banker, I mean it Suzy, no screw-ups, if you decide to shag, find somewhere else, not the club tonight and not home." He whispered as he left.

Unfortunately, Vincent could not see their faces clearly enough to read their lips as one of the erotic dancers on the stage came in close to his seat and began to perform her routine for him blocking his line of sight. Distracted by his wish to see what Copeland was talking about he failed to hear the dancer addressing him directly and one of the members of a group of American executives beside him that had been ignored by the girl appeared to take offence at his lack of response.

"Hey buddy, give up the seat if you're not interested in the girls." he slurred, "Hey Buddy, you deaf!" he repeated, and when Vincent did not turn, he placed a hand on Vincent's shoulder roughly. With a snap of his hand, Vincent placed the man's wrist over in a judo pressure hold pinning him to the tabletop.

The pain of the hold was excruciating, and the man growled, then gasped as Vincent released his grip and as the man raised his sore hand he revealed beneath it a playing card had been placed without his knowledge into his palm, amazed by the sleight of hand skill, his anger was culled as Vincent took a sip from his drink and got up from his chair, while the American revealed the card to his companions as the Joker of the pack, which they roasted him about.

"Hey buddy, how did you?" he said, passing it to them. but Vincent was already on his way across the floor towards the restrooms.

"Must be part of the club entertainment." he said confused and totally disarmed feeling somewhat foolish as he rubbed his sore wrist, as one of his friends taunted "Got your number, Bob".

The exchange was over in a moment and lost to most including those on Sean's table and seeing the card in the American's hand Suzy assumed it was part of Vincent's act, but had already noticed the American's vocal comments were becoming more offensive, towards the girls. As Vincent walked through to the rear toilets, Suzy raised an eye and gestured to one of the girls to go over to the group of American's and offer them a private side booth.

In other clubs of a similar nature, even though the American's were spending well, they would have been reproached. Suzy had learnt from the master of control, Copeland and would entertain them with private dancers where their behaviour would not upset other patrons and where she would ensure by the end of the night they would leave with empty wallets.

"Give them enough rope to hang themselves." Copeland had repeatedly told her in the past.

A few minutes after Vincent returned to a seat by the bar, he read the lips of one of the waitresses who went up to Suzy,

"The Gents toilets something is wrong, they are flooded again!" she whispered.

"Fuck! Go tell Hong to get one of his boys to sort it, this is the last thing I need tonight, talk about back to work with a bang, I'm still in vacation mode." Suzy scowled and accepted a glass of Martini Asti spumante poured by the attentive Don who noticed her frown, "This will help some," he said then returned o his station at the check-in.

Günther watched as Hong disappeared down the rear hallway towards the toilets just as a group stepping down to the lower dance floor masked Vincent's movements as he slipped around the VIP guard rope to the stairs and at a two-step, stride climbed up to the balcony within seconds.

At first, he began to entertain a few of the guests partying in the outer lounge seats, while keeping an eye on the rear corridor that led to the two main private entertainment suites. In front of one of the doors stood another of Copeland's bouncers, who assumed as he watched the magician working that Hong must have allowed Vincent up to that floor.

With the arrival of a waitress on the landing, with a tray containing a bottle of Crystal in an ice bucket, the bodyguard opened the suite door and followed her inside. Vincent moved further down the corridor and through the open door caught a glimpse of Merryman sat lying back laughing, fielded on either side by JoJo and Katie, gyrating over his lap topless, wearing only knickers and suspenders.

"Can I help you?" Suzy asked, and Vincent twisted back feeling in the wrist of his jacket for his safety net card pack and fanned them out for her to take a card, gesturing to the room, but she did not smile.

"No! Not up here, this area is reserved," she said, handing back the playing card without turning it over. Vincent nodded his understanding signing he was sorry and made the pack disappear from his hands as he caught a questioning glance from Hong who drew up behind her.

"Problem?" Hong asked gruffly.

"No problem, have the guys fixed that mess downstairs?" Suzy asked, taking a quick peek inside the VIP room.

"One of these white boys thinks it's funny, someone blocked the sink and left the taps running, it's done, my bet it's the trappy Yanks." he said, allowing Vincent to pass by, but he watched him until his descended down the stairs as did Günther who breathed a sigh of relief, and caught the hand sign gesture across the room from his nephew which meant, "I'm off, we need to talk." as he headed for the exit.

"So boys, I am sorry, but I must leave you now, as much as I would like to stay and enjoy the company of these young ladies, I think an old dog like me is cramping Connor's style and honestly, I know I will suffer in the morning, for this tear-up." Günther smiled in using their words, "it's something you will learn when you get to my age, the spirit is still strong, but unfortunately, the body is weak. Besides as much as I know you enjoy my company, Sean, others may hope I do not monopolise your evening." He looked towards Suzy and went to stand.

"So thank you for the ...Black stuff and company, I believe we shall have an interesting journey back to Sweden and when we get to Stockholm, and our work is done, I will show you how the Swedes provide hospitality." Günther noticed Suzy looking down at them and finished his drink.

"I look forward to that," Connor said with a genuine tone.

"Me too, let's hope for that." Sean agreed, but in the back of his mind, something was still niggling his ability to completely relax in Günther's company, even though he also liked the old woodsman manner.

Chapter 17: The Trolling

Geneva, Switzerland
1975

Thursday morning the Mossad surveillance van was once again parked in the side street opposite the FNIG bank, the team had already captured a couple of headshots before Ruby had arrived on her motorbike with no news from Mossad headquarters on the identities of Günther and Sebastian or Sean and Connor Byrne.
"Shit weather, what's new," Ruby asked as she removed her motorbike gloves and slipped her revolver from the rear of her waistband as she sat down, placing it inside her helmet.
"Four new faces inside, early, the weather's not helping with the camera, it will be better when we get the upgrade surveillance van with the roof telescope if we get it?" David said looking through the bank one way glass of the van as an April shower drenched pedestrians running to the nearest shop doorways.
"You and your gadgets, but your right the video system will help….when we get it, Zavi told me it's on the next transporter from Jerusalem."
"Well I believe it when I see it the heaters packed up in this heap of shit, I had to go buy a couple of tourist stickers to cover up where the one-way mirror is peeling away." David gestured to four plastic Geneva tourist stickers, he had stuck inside at the corners of one of the doors windows.
Inside the bank's main lobby, Klaus Ritter looked up from the seats opposite the reception desk, over Merill Nestlar's shoulder towards the entrance, as Claude Dennee pressed the security door release.
"What's he doing here?" he asked, recognising Max Binder as he entered through the banks revolving doors first, followed by Walter Thomas.
Merill Nestlar had been waiting outside the bank, shielded from the rain by an umbrella held by Klaus, as the security guard had pulled up the guard rails and unlocked the doors dead on eight, even though Claude had noticed the doctor waiting on the other side of the glass, while the girls at the reception prepared for the day. Nestlar's expression of irritation was unmistakable as he checked his watch again, having arrived twelve minutes early, before the banks official opening time.

The doctor's meeting was scheduled with Salter-Kingsley for eight-thirty, and at this point, he knew nothing of the Spider organisations executive committee's revised plans for him.
As far as he was concerned he had followed the protocol instructions since leaving Brazil as relayed to him via Ritter, following the bodyguard's altercation with Pimm in the apartment in Rio.

Having learnt that the weapons laboratory at Serra Negra had been destroyed by the CIA, the CED and Spider Executive Committee in Rome considered the attack by Oliver Pimm on the apartment, used torture the two Mi6 agents Lamb and Cartwright, was likely to have been part of the same operation, as yet they had not received the full details from their operative within the CIA.

However as Josef Mengele had already earmarked a site in Uruguay for a similar weapons factory, the Executive Committee's original plan was to have Merill Nestlar travel to Geneva, to confirm the final tractions regarding the Somalian's trade agreement at the Bank and arrange funds to be dispersed to the new Brazilian accounts, that would be used to create a new laboratory in Uruguay, Nestlar was also in Geneva to meet with representative that had been supplying some of the raw material they had been shipping to Brazil, required for their work.

Ritter was to act as his chaperone and escort him back to Uruguay when their business was done.

That was until they had received Salter-Kingsley's letter and the information that the ship transporting the neurotoxin had been sunk and learned from one f their operatives that it had been under the orders of CIA Chief Cater-Wallis.

As Max Binder and Walter Thomas approached the reception, Nestlar looked up through tired eyes, already in a disgruntled mood from having to wait in the rain outside the bank, he began to tap the armrest of his chair, watching to see if these people that had arrived after him were about to be seen first. His patience when dealing with other individuals outside his work was limited at the best of times, having just completed an exhausting and arduous, 1500 kilometre drive from Madrid to Geneva, travelling incognito, at times using alternative routes, rather than those that would be more direct, while staying in low-key hotels with poor facilities, he felt his pulse race and a burn to his neck, but he held his tongue and remained seated as Walter walked up to the reception desk and looked on with some suspicion, the man had a manner he recognised, and he caught the German guttural tone of Walter's voice as he spoke.

"Francesca isn't it, good morning. I have no scheduled appointment, but please inform Mr Salter-Kingsley, a Senior Director of the SSG is in your building." As Walter introduced himself, Francesca, had a vague recollection of the distinguished-looking immaculately dressed elder businessman in front of her, knowing he had been to the bank before. But it was many years ago, not long after she had started working there and since she was not wearing a name tag, she was pleasantly surprised that he remembered her name, although she could not recall his.

"Yes Sir, he has a prior appointment with these gentlemen," She gestured to Nestlar and Ritter and Merill Nestlar caught the action and strained to hear what was being said as Francesca spoke, "but I will contact his assistant, Miss Bishop and have her inform him you are here." she gestured to the leather seating area, and Walter looked briefly back over his shoulder towards Nestlar, knowing exactly who the doctor was and why he thought he was there, but gave nothing away.

"They will wait," Walter spoke with an uncompromising authority and certainty, without acknowledging Nestlar or Klaus.

His statement surprised Francesca; however, her elder colleague at the desk in hearing the words Senior Director and SSG immediately picked up the phone and called Miss Bishop.

"I'm on it, Francesca." she snapped in a whisper and caught a brief smile from Walter's lips at her acknowledgement of his importance.

"Oh! Certainly Sir, please take a seat, may I get you some refreshment while you wait?" Francesca now felt a little flustered.

"That is kind, but will not be necessary young lady, thank you all the same." he smiled and remained in front of the reception desk as Francesca now realised she was in the presence of one of their most important clients the bank had. While Max turned back to the seating and stared down Klaus.

"Who is he?" Nestlar asked his bodyguard, turning his face away.

"The suit, I don't know, but he must be important with the organisation, his man, I remember him from the training camp in Cape Town, he was a senior instructor, I believe he was once Stasi, I never met him, but I know of his reputation, he is old guard, I was not told they would be present, perhaps there has been a development, since Rio." Ritter shook his head and glanced to the entrance to see if there was an additional protection team for Walter stationed outside the building, but could see only the Volvo car they had arrived in.

"Where? Here! Christ that was quick! Fetch him up Miss Bishop, immediately in here, please. Show the other gentlemen and his colleague to room two, for now, explain I am delayed on an issue, that has relevance to their meeting this morning, say exactly that and when the Somalian's arrive, please inform me at once." Salter-Kingsley ordered, presuming the visit from Walter could only be because of the letter he had dispatched in the early hours of that morning regarding the Westerberg's accessing the SSG account.

Walter walked around Salter-Kingsley's office and opened the adjoining door through to the main boardroom, knowing it had been the venue for the negotiations with Mubarak Ali Hassan, seeing it empty he left the door open.

"No, as you may be aware I was not involved in the particular arrangement, with the Somalian's and our people in Brazil. This was negotiated by the representative of the Chief Executive Director, I believe here in your building, again I would like to thank you on behalf of the organization for assisting in these proceedings and such like." Walter watched as Miss Bishop closed the door as she left the room.

"Not at all, please come sit, coffee, tea?" Salter-Kingsley gestured to the seats before his desk, but Walter remained standing as he took off his coat, hat and gloves and handed them to Max, who took them through to the adjoining boardroom and placed the coat over the back of a chair and glove and hat on the table then returned and hovered in the doorway.

"So, good I believe this will do fine if you would please Peter." Walter gestured to Salter-Kingsley's desk, and the banker realised Walter wished to use it and relinquished his leather executive chair,
"But of course." he said and watched Walters' eyes drift briefly over the Nazi membership certificate, "I remember your grandfather, I was sorry to hear of his wife's passing, my condolence's."

As Walter tapped the picture frame glass, Salter-Kingsley got the impression Walter had always been there in the background of his life and somewhere deep in his memories he remembered a visit to the bank at the weekend, as he often did a child with his grandfather and being introduced to a distinguished German, who he now considered was Walter.
"Yes, she was eight-six, very active, she was at the old chalet we have in Verbier when it happened, had been skiing that morning." Salter-Kingsley gave a reverent smile.
"So, she was doing what she loved and where she wanted to be." Walter studied the banker as he sat before him and remembered his the death of his wife Greta under similar circumstances at their home, but decided not to share and patted the leather top of the large antique partner desk as he sat, realising that it was the same desk that he had sat before when first arriving at the bank in 1943, when he escaped Germany, and he looked at the neatly arranged documents.
"So to business, you understand I am here at the request of the Chief Executive Director for a specific task. As yet I have not received any additional notification from Rome; perhaps they will make contact today, in which case we will resolve at that time any alteration that may have been decided by the Executive Committee. In other words, we deal with what we know and such like, you understand."
Walter looked to Salter-Kingsley and smiled widely at his affirmation "yes."
"Good and so first, you will excuse me, Peter, possibly my age, but I find it easier if I focus on one topic at a time, it is less likely to lead to mistakes. First, I will address the situation that has developed between our African clients and our colleagues in Brazil, I believe they are the gentlemen I passed in your reception, correct?" Walter had never met Klaus Ritter or Merill Nestlar, even when he had chauffeured Stefan Keplar/ Sebastian Westerberg to meetings with the doctor at the Kaiser Wilhelm University in 1943.
"Yes Sir, I have had them placed in another conference room, Miss Bishop will notify us as soon as the Somalian representatives arrive." Salter-Kingsley check over his shoulder as he sat down, looking somewhat nervously to Max as Walter studied the pile of account books and documents regarding Sebastian's transactions but did not touch them.
"In light of the fact you have not acted on Mr Westerberg's instructions, this can wait, and like you say, you have already passed on these details, so as I have explained it is possible my colleagues in Rome may already be dealing with this issue and update us in due course," he said, tapping the top red account book and

about to hand him the separate envelope Sebastian had written, Salter-Kingsley placed it on the top of the documents and sat back.
Walter looked at it but allowed his methodology of work to override his curiosity. "So, you mentioned tea, a cup of Earl Grey tea would be appreciated, black no sugar, Max I am sure will appreciate coffee, please Max open the blinds and sit, I want these people to see my eyes, even though they are tired." Walter smiled at his man.

"So we agree we deal with this first then I will look at the information and such like, you have on this Westerberg chap and this fellow Lansford, I know not why but the name is familiar, somehow.." Walter appeared to confirm to himself then gestured to Max, who opened his briefcase and passed him the documents he believed would assist him in his negotiations.
"Can I confirm please Peter; the details of Ali Hassan's account status, the balance of the funds owed to our organisation as we speak is still held within the bank, yes?" Walter looked over the rims of his glasses at Salter-Kingsley who now sat on the other side of his own desk, while Max sat through in the open boardroom watching from the nearest seat.
"Yes that is correct," Salter-Kingsley answered then confirmed the details of the conversation he had with Ali Hassan, and as he finished, Miss Bishop announced Cawil and Musse Bin Abokkor had arrived in the reception on his internal phone. "Do you wish to speak with Doctor Nestlar first?"
"No that is not necessary, he will do as requested." Walter paused as a memory was triggered "Doctor Nestlar?" he repeated, and the banker noticed as Walter's eyes glazed as the name began to filter through the years of his memory back to Berlin in the 1940s.

With the emphasis on his own anonymity and not being involved in the original transactions with the scientist's, Walter had been unaware it was Nestlar that had come over from Brazil. He had been informed by Friedrich Fischer, only that it would be an associate of Doctor Mengele who he knew was involved in the development of the facility in Sierra Negra because he had in the past arranged for funds to be transferred from the main SSG accounts to Brazil via an account Count Erichh had set up for Herman Goring, four years earlier that because of his demise at the end of the war and with no airs had been scooped into the collective pool of the SGG accounts, much in the same way Count Erichh's account had been used as a guarantee of funds, held by the organization.
"So, that's Merill Nestlar, how things circle back." Walter gave a churlish grin, remembering the times he had waited outside the Kaiser Wilhelm University in Berlin, while Stefan Keplar while he met with Nestlar, who at that time was a Senior Director of a Third Reich special project division, that included the Vor Elle facility in Sardinia. In all that time, Walter had never met him in person, and back then he would have been Walter's superior, now with the tables turned Walter controlled the doctor's life.

"Sorry Herr Director, do you know the doctor?" Salter-Kingsley looked back to Max, then again to Walter.
"No, but I know his work." Walter looked up at the banker and considered how impossible it would be to explain the past and how he and Nestlar were linked by just the handshake of an old friend.
"I can have him brought here if you wish to speak with him first?" Salter-Kingsley asked and looked through to Max Binder.
"No that is not necessary; Doctor Nestlar will do as he is requested, by the organisation, by me, but." Walter looked through the open door leading to the main boardroom, "That room has separate access and is free this morning, yes?" Salter-Kingsley nodded his agreement.
"Good have the doctor placed in there for the time being, please, and close this door, until I am ready for him. Once you have done this, then please ask the Somalian gentlemen to come up, I will speak with them first, when he arrives I would appreciate it if you can give me the room for a short while and wait in there with the doctor and Max."

Leaving two of his bodyguards in the main bank reception, Cawil entered Salter-Kingsley's office along with Musse Bin Abokkor. Immediately Walter made a point of moving back from around the main desk, gesturing to the two seats in front, Cawil then took his lead from Walter when he asked Max Binder to wait in the boardroom and motioned for Musse to follow suit, and they joined Salter-Kingsley, alongside Merill Nestlar and Klaus. Walter found it hard not cast an eye in the direction of the boardroom as the interconnecting door opened, he considered the fleeting image he received of the doctor was a distraction from his task and looked away.
What then followed between those exiled from the room was an uncomfortable silence that appeared at times inordinately long as they occasionally caught the muffled voices coming from the main office. As Walter explained to the young Somalian the arrangements that the Chief Executive Director and Spider executive committee were willing to put in place for Cawil's uncle, to make up for the loss of the chemical weapons at sea.
"But before we talk on that you must be made aware of certain external forces that have brought us to this point that were not initiated by my organization, your Uncle was betrayed by another, suitor, someone your Uncle I believe has previously been discussing alternative arrangements, regarding equipment he requires to carry out his endeavours in your home country." Walter handed Cawil a folder containing evidence obtained through an undercover Spider's agent within the CIA proving it was Carter-Wallis that had organised the USS Achilles to torpedo the freighter Cardigan Bay.
"That is the manifest from the Achilles, as you see, the inventory shows a discrepancy in their arms manifest. Also unlike the tampering of an automobile mileage clock by some unscrupulous car dealer, the Achilles is a nuclear hunter-killer submarine. You have the records before you, showing the distances it covered during a local exercise in the Caribbean with the sixth fleet and the distance

covered corresponding to other vessels of the same class operating during the same exercise, the discrepancy is an increase in nautical miles that matches the point at which the Cardigan Bay was reported sunk by your people, I believe." Walter paused, allowing Cawil to process the information on the pages, as he stirred his cool earl grey tea.
"That does not explain who leaked the details of the shipment, when all is said and done we are still without our weapons, for our plans to succeed and if our plans do not succeed, then the additional requirements your organization has requested that General Mubarak make available in our country will not be forthcoming." Cawil had strict instructions not to return empty-handed, but for him, it was a matter of honour that he made a good trade with the German, to show his Uncle he able to handle such responsibilities.
"Yes, yes I understand, but please so we are clear, and there is an agreement between us to who is responsible for the loss of the shipment. The pink pages, they are confirming radio transmissions that were redirected through the U.S. Naval base at Guantanamo Bay, they originated in Langley, to be precise, from the secure line of a CIA chief known as Craftwork, General Benjamin Carter-Wallis," Walter saw a look of recognition of the fact in Cawil's eyes.
"Who, we are reliably informed your Uncle had been negotiating additional arms through one of his own shadow operations. My organisation the one I represent, Spider, consider this....action was his sole initiative. That said we have experience with the Americans as do the Russian that they are less predisposed to a free market economy, when it comes to such weapons and wish to have the monopoly or at least have a finger in the pie, so to speak. Your Uncle may wish to resolve the matter with Carter-Wallis personally. However, you may inform him of the option that we can obtain suitable replacements for any arms he requires, if he wishes to end his association with the Americans, having received this information." Walter then handed Cawil the details of other relevant Spider recourses and contacts on the African continent, in particular within South Africa, where many of his own countrymen had found a place to reside since the end of the war and with some of whom he had already agreed with Josef Mengele, who had already relocated to Uruguay a plan of a settlement with the Somalian's, involving without his knowledge Merill Nestlar, that Walter considered would appease the Warlord's loss of chemical weapons.

Walter watched Cawil rise to his feet and walk over to the window, the young man had a lean, hungry look about him, but Walter sensed he had been educated in Europe, his English had perfect diction, and as he watched him perusing the documents Walter could not help notice that his nails were manicured except for a long thumbnail, like the type a guitarist might have.
"With respect, can I ask do you need to contact your Uncle to make this agreement?" Walter's tone was sincere.
"No, if I say no to your proposal, will you need to go back and talk with your people?" Cawil smiled.

"No." Walter shook his head.
"So it would seem we are the ones to do this, you are offering one of the scientists my Uncle has already met in Brazil as a sign of good faith, yes," Cawil considered how angry his Uncle would be once he received the information regarding the CIA and Carter-Wallis and what he was likely to do, in one respect it added to the importance of securing a positive outcome with Walter.
"Yes, we will make all the arrangements for the raw materials and machinery to be in place and supply the technical personnel to satisfy his needs. He has only to supply a suitable secure facility and the necessary security elements for its protection. These are schematic's for the design of the primary buildings that will need to be constructed, however Doctor Nestlar, I believe, would be in a position to approve any existing structures and such like." Walter pushed forward a set of architectural blueprints.
Cawil looked down at the papers and without examining them held out his hand, and Walter stood and shook it.

"So now you meet one of the men that will return with you." Walter opened the door through to the boardroom, his aid Max immediately raised himself from the board room table in respect at Walter's presence and Walter stood for a moment looking at Nestlar knowing the doctor knew nothing about their history, and watched how he and Klaus Ritter appeared to squirm in their seats, before they too began to stand.
"Please come through Doctor Nestlar." Walter gestured, and as he saw Klaus make a move, he raised a hand. "You stay, just the doctor please."
Klaus received a glare from Max and settled back in his chair, as Nestlar left the room.
"And you Peter if you would," Walter placed a hand on the banker's shoulder.
Salter-Kingsley felt an unusual sense of privilege to be called back into his own office.
"Will two day's suffice for your preparation for our return to Mogadishu?" Cawil looked at Nestlar who sat in partial disbelief, but obediently quiet, having just discovered he was being offered up by his lifelong friend and colleague Mengele and the Spider organization as a sacrifice for the loss of the chemical weapons, in a forced relocation to Somalia to oversee the creation of their own chemical weapons factory. Seeing Walter sitting behind the banker's own desk had reaffirmed his belief Walter was a Senior Executive of Spider and he had said very little as he was informed of his new assignment.
"Two days is fine, the doctor will be ready, you will collect him from here, he has his own security guard who will accompany him, I trust you can arrange suitable security, for his transportation."
Walter used the word transportation, rather than journey, as if Nestlar was a commodity that he had sold and in actual fact as he sat and witnessed Cawil authorise the transfer of the remainder of the gold funds to the SSG account, he realized the man meant nothing to him, his association with Stefan Keplar during the war had no impact on Walter.

As Salter-Kingsley organized the transfer within the bank's system and co-signed the documents he suddenly looked up towards Walter, "Sorry, two days that would make it Sunday, the bank is closed on Sunday, and also the street outside this building becomes pedestrianized for the street market."
Cawil was at the window and turned back, "The Park over there, we will pick him up from there." Cawil gestured down, "ten o'clock, Sunday morning."
Walter looked to the window and saw a questioning look from Nestlar as if waiting for Walter to answer on his behalf.
"Ten o'clock on Sunday. Good, I will have the arrangements in place, for the doctor and his man to be there." Walter gestured back towards the boardroom.
"Thank you, I believe this will satisfy our needs, I will inform my Uncle of your assistance I this matter, thank you, Sir, it has been a pleasure." Cawil shook Walter's hand again and then looked at Merill Nestlar as if he had just bought a cow and refrained from shaking his hand, sensing the doctor was not impressed with his part in the negotiations.
"Impress upon your Uncle the benefits, once Dr Nestlar here has produced the first successful results and trained your people, you can make as much as you require, even sell to your allies and this way he will be in charge of his own destiny, and that of your people. This is I believe what he would wish, not to have to go cap in hand to the CIA. Please also respectfully remind him, my organisation will require the land he has agreed to be released for our purposes as soon as the land is available, it will if anything strengthens his bond with Spider, which I am sure will be of benefit, to both parties."
Cawil nodded his understanding, looking to Musse who also showed he agreed and the pair left the office, escorted to the lift by Miss Bishop.
As he did, he was observed by Plácido Zabala who stopped talking with one of his juniors as he examined the market trading data on their green computer screens and began to make his way across the open trading floor of the bank towards the corridor and side door access to the main boardroom. Seeing it empty, he slipped in unnoticed and stood behind the adjoining door to Salter-Kingsley's office that was slightly ajar, listening.

"So now doctor you will wait within the hotel suite we have provided until the day of departure, for your own protection, as you are aware the recent events in South America call for us all to be vigilant. Your man will see to your needs, and I understand it is very comfortable. I will have all your documentation made available before your departure, and Mr Salter-Kingsley here will arrange a new Somalian account which you will oversee personally, the initial funds will allow you to purchase any personal provisions, clothes and such like, which Klaus can organise." Walter held back the smile he felt forming on his lips, like Cawil he had noticed how quiet Nestlar had been. He tried to remember some of the things Stefan had once told him about the old German that now sat in front of him, but found it hard to make the connection. Then his eyes settled on the unaddressed

envelope Salter-Kingsley had placed on the documents on the desk he knew he still had to look through concerning the Westerberg's.
In closing, he chose for the sake of his position to make a minimal effort of consolation towards Nestlar for his actions.
"Think of it this way doctor, you are doing great service for our organisation, six months maybe a year at most. I do not know the details of the product, but I understand from talking with the Chief Executive Director you have already the formulas in place. Surely it is not like starting from scratch, and such like. We will ensure Ali Hassan honours the agreement, you and your people will live like kings over there, and you will have your man here to keep you company." Klaus had been invited back into the room to hear the part he was being ordered to play, and like Nestlar knew he had no choice, Max's Binder's stern expression amplified the power of Walter's authority.
"I am aware of a number of our comrades who resettled through choice in this region, who knows you may find some of the people who join you from Cape Town are individuals you have worked with in the past?"
"So, Klaus just make sure you have him in the Park before ten on Sunday." Walter looked to Klaus and waited for his acknowledgement.
"Good now that is settled, I still have work to do with Mr Salter-Kingsley on another matter. It is unlikely we will meet again before your departure, I wish you every success in your endeavours, May our path be as our hearts, strong and true" Walter, raised a hand and gave the Spider oath.
"May our paths be as our hearts, strong and true!" Both Nestlar and Klaus responded placing their right hand over their hearts, then with a dismissive wave of his hand Walter watched as Nestlar left the room and found it strange how he could still not get a sense of the man or raise a negative emotional response, towards an individual his friend Stefan Keplar during the war had spoken often about in disparaging terms, a man who had ordered Grethe and him to be killed, and caused the death of his master, Count Erichh, back in 1943, had he changed so much himself, he thought as he took a moment before attending to the Westerberg documents.

Having requested a fresh cup of tea, Walter began to read the sealed letter from Sebastian Westerberg, while out of sight in the boardroom Plácido Zabala made his way back to his desk and sat behind his own desk looking at the image of the older couple in the photo frame and contemplated his future and theirs.
In the street outside the entrance of the bank, Nestlar waited for Klaus to open the umbrella shielding him from the rain, as he transferred across the pavement to his car, he paused briefly, watching the group of Somalian's drive past in two black Mercedes.
"Fuck! Untermenschen!"
Nestlar snarled as he got into the back seat.

"Well, at least I doubt we will see much of this weather where we are going," Klaus replied with a tut as he shook the water from the brolly and closing it, the back of his car seat received a fist battering from Nestlar in his frustration.
Across the street, the team in the blue Mossad surveillance van were running out of camera film, having snapped numerous pictures of all the individuals that had entered, two of which Ruby recognised immediately.
"I'm going to follow them you stay here, no break from now on we sit outside this bank, twenty-four-seven! And when the old man comes out one of you follow him, I'm not going to let that shit over there get away."
Ruby stared out of the one-way screens of the rear doors at Klaus, as he got behind the wheel of Nestlar's car. Then she darted out of the back of the van, kick-starting her Suzuki motorcycle she began to follow them.
Later that evening she would make a full report to General Zavineski in Tel Aviv sending him the most recent photograph images from outside the bank entrance and requesting a snatch team to be in place, with logistics to smuggle two individuals from Geneva to Tel Aviv.
However, Zavineski would prove to have by then his own Intel on the activities of the FNIG bank, having spoken with Tom Quinn of the CIA, who in an exchange of intelligence information had informed the Israeli Mossad chief without giving up the name of his source, what Plácido Zabala had informed his CIA handler in Geneva regarding the Somalian exchange taking place in the Park on Sunday. Zavineski immediately set his team the task of capturing the Nazi scientist Merill Nestlar and his guard Klaus Ritter.

On the third floor of the bank, satisfied with the business completed with the Somalian's, having turned his attention to the Westerberg issue and re-read the letter Sebastian had given Salter-Kingsley, he took the banker by surprise as he suddenly laughed out loud, "Priceless?" Walter said, in realizing the fact the very type of person Mr Westerberg appeared to be seeking to be introduced to by the Spider organisation was like the individual he had just ordered to go to Somalia, Doctor Nestlar. Walter held the letter in his hand and teased the end of the glasses in is teeth, and then placed it down.
"Friedrich Fischer tells me you have a recording machine of some such like, show me." Walter was beginning to feel tired and received a look of concern from Max as Salter-Kingsley moved round to his side of the desk and opened the built-in surveillance control drawer. As he opened it, Walter smiled to himself thinking, That wasn't there the last time I came here and seeing the banker struggling at the angle he now stood fiddling with the buttons and switches as the false wall behind slid to one side revealing the security monitors, Walter got up from the seat, "Please." he gestured and then went and sat around in front of the desk and watched with some interest at the marvellous technology, his eyes again focusing while he waited on the Nazi membership as he held his chin as if deep in thought.
"You are very proud of your heritage Peter, that is good, not everything they write about, regarding those days was bent on destruction. Some of us rightly or wrongly,

maybe even foolishly believed we were building a better world. That said, many that were once proud, hide such a thing in an attic, I myself.... burnt mine." his smile appeared to hold regret to the banker, but Walter knew Salter-Kingsley did not really understand and moved the subject on before he could offer an opinion, enquiring about the type of videotape player, and where one might purchase one, confused like many at the time by the difference between VHS, Betamax and Philip's.

"Show me first this man, who has asked for this list of scientists, we have in our membership, this Westerberg fellow." Walter manoeuvred the cork coaster on the desk as he placed down his china teacup, as Salter-Kingsley loaded a paperback book-sized tape into the enormous tape machine and zipped back and forth with the images, by pressing the buttons repeatedly.

"As I explained in my report, unfortunately, we had no prior knowledge that Mr Westerberg or Mr Lansford were to visit the bank, I was absent from the bank, it is my managing director Mr Zabala, that dealt with their enquires. I should mention, he has no access to additional accounts of the SSG, and if I had been here, I would have dealt with it personally."

As Salter-Kingsley spoke, he watched Walter begin to lean forward slowly and a curious expression cross over his face as if he had just drunk sour milk and he pushed his glasses back firmly on his nose as he studied the image flickering in the centre of the screen. He raised his hand in a halting gesture, as Salter-Kingsley recognized the image on the screen as that of Sebastian Westerberg and then offered forward the biographic article Zabala had unearthed regarding the Westerberg Company.

Walter felt like he someone had thrown a pale of ice cold water over his face and he looked to Max and then through to the open boardroom, his mouth dropped, and he shook his head as if looking for an explanation and felt as if he had been set up in some way. Then he stood and placed his hand over his mouth, as he coughed choking on his tea.

"This is a joke, a trick yes, with the doctor or such like, I have no time for this?" His tone was harsh as he gasped looking again at Max and then pushed behind the seated banker with his nose up against the screen and removed his glasses and wiped the lens then peered closer again.

"Are you alright Director, may I get you something, this is the man Westerberg, and this is Lansford." Max stood, seeing the colour from Walters face drain away as on another screen, the image showed Günther Brahn entering the room on a separate day.

"It can't be? He died, they both died in the war, it can't possibly be them." Walter looked at the Sony Betamax machine as if it was made using some sort witchcraft. "Play it from when the first man comes in the older one... Lansford, his very first visit, now if you would please. This is not Lansford this Brahn, Günther Brahn? Do you have sound, I want to hear his voice, this is Günther, my god, my god this Günther!" He turned to the banker with a look of pure disbelief then cleaned his glasses again as he studied every gesture Sebastian Westerberg made, then became irritated as with a switch of the button by Salter-Kingsley the screens went blank for a moment.

"Yes please Max water, it can't be him, Max, he has not changed he has not changed a day, bring it back show me again, now!" Walter sat back and began to flick furiously through the files, looking for anything that might explain what he was watching.

"Is there a problem, Sir, he confirmed the correct code word and account details, has that been compromised." Salter-Kingsley looked at the black and white image as it reappeared in the screen

Then Walter smiled "It must be Elizabet, she was pregnant, she must have survived, this must be her son... of course, but?" Walter's mind began to overheat as it tried to make sense of the images.

"I must see everything you have, including paperwork signature and such like, you have a permanent address record now, show me now, I must understand for sure yes, how this is possible?" Walter felt his heart race with expectation and Salter-Kingsley was further surprised as his smile widened, as the name Lansford suddenly stuck its chord in his memory and he the housekeeper at Schloss Klink the Bavarian castle of his master Count Erichh Von Stieglitz,

"My god, fool Walter." he cursed himself, how had he not remember it the first time. "My tablets." he looked to Max as he felt his heart palpitation begin to cause pain to his chest.

"The Director suffers from low blood sugar, perhaps your women can organise something to eat, a sandwich?" Max looked to Salter-Kingsley, who noticed there was something more to the way Max attended his master other than that of a servant, there appeared to be a real concern for his health.

"But of course, immediately, I will arrange it." And remembering a Mars bar he had his drawer, Salter-Kingsley offered it across to Walter "I this while you wait." Walter almost snatched it from his hand and began eating it,

"Thank you, Peter, continue please," he said with a mouthful of chocolate.

A few minutes later they sat eating, in silence as having now been shown how the machines worked Walter replayed the tapes over again, pausing the images at certain intervals.

"My God in heaven Günther you old rascal, I thought you'd be dining with the devil by now." he began to chuckle to himself at times forgetting there were others present in the office, now feeling somewhat calmer having now reasoned the events that must have taken place after the war and now believing that Westerberg was probably Stefan Keplar's and Elizabet Kempe's son. However, there was no mistaking Günther, as Salter Kingsley fixed the image of the old woodsman shaking the hand of Plácido Zabala.

"Your man, may I speak with him before I leave, he need not know why, or our other business." Walter looked at Salter-Kingsley.

"Yes, of course, I will arrange it, but it is Mr Merryman that really knows more he is the executive that has been dealing with the Westerberg accounts, again I can arrange it if you wish to speak with him." Salter-Kingsley volunteered as he watched Walter begin to doodle, jotting down figures that represented the ages of Stefan and Elizabet and how old their son might be if it was him that was calling himself Sebastian Westerberg.
"It's perfectly possible and strictly speaking he would be the heir to this account?" Walter said aloud.
"Herr Director regarding the account the withdrawal scheduled for tomorrow, do you wish me to halt this transaction?" Salter-Kingsley held forward the paperwork.
"Tomorrow," Walter echoed, looking at the details of the withdrawal documents; it amounted to 1.2 million in gold and American dollars.
"No, let this proceed, but I must speak with the Chief Executive and other committee members. Remind me please, when did you send these details to your drop-box in the Metropolitan Peter?" Walter began to see a potential problem with the Spider Executive Committee now knowing the identity of the Westerberg's and threatened by the loss of assets, may have already assigned operatives, whose actions would safeguard their position, using extreme measures.

Walter was well aware of other members, including the Chief Executive Director himself who favoured more decisive action, often before they had all the facts.
"Walter felt his concerns begin to cause him indigestion as fear began to grip him, in standing his plate was nudged to the floor, ignoring it he snapped his fingers and tapping his head gestured for Max to get his coat, they were leaving.
"Ok, we must get back now, at once."
"So do you want to speak with Zabala and Merryman?" Salter-Kingsley began to tidy the documents together.
"Yes I will, but another time for sure, but now I have many calls to make. For now, you organise the withdrawal for Günther Brahn....Mr Lansford, he has my total support with this and in the meantime give Max everything you have, the tapes all of it. I hope to be available to come back before they depart in the morning. But Peter, please understand, do not mention my visit to Mr Brahn... Lansford or the Westerberg's, I don't want the old boy having a heart attack, or doing something rash." he watched Salter-Kingsley take another sandwich as he spoke.
"Now Peter, please if you will the tapes and if you may, also inform Max where we might purchase one of these machines, today." The feeling that time might be of the essence began to peak in Walter's mind as he closed the accounts page that held the figures of the SSG account Sebastian had accessed, knowing the CED would react in a preventative measure to stop that account being plundered. Walter would have to gather support amongst other members of the committee before he offered his own evidence that Mr Westerberg had a legitimate right to access the account set up by Count Erichh, even though he had many questions himself.
As he sat in the back of his car waiting for Max outside the Laskys home audio shop on Rue Du Rhone, one item in particular played on his mind, why Günther and

the son of Stefan Keplar would want access to scientist of the Reich and the possibility that the man he had just ordered to go to Somalia may be the only person that could fully answer that question.

He watched the pedestrians pass by outside and checked his watch, becoming impatient then saw the store salesman aid Max in opening the shop door as he struggled with the large video machine box. As he crossed the wide pavement, a tram went past, and as Max stood for a moment in the street waiting, Walter noticed his expression changed. Walter turned in the rear seat of the car, looking behind through the back screen and saw on the opposite side a figure on a motorcycle. Having followed Nestlar the short distance back to his hotel, Ruby had arranged for one of her team to take her place across from the entrance and then returned to the bank in time to see Walter and Max leave and then follow them.
"Across the road, I am sorry, Herr Director, I think they followed us from the bank, I will need to lose them before we leave the city," Max said as he got back into the car adjusting his wing mirror to take in Ruby's image, he then started up and moved off as if about to drive away and watched her begin to follow suit, then stopped and indicated as if about to turn back against the traffic and saw she did the same. Seeing another five carriage tram headed along the road towards them he sat stationary, then as it pulled past blocking her view he turned back immediately and skidded ahead darting up the first side street, it bought them enough time as Ruby had to wait for the tram to pass and then cross the road.
Walter held onto the side of the door as his papers fell from the rear seat into the foot while Max thrashed their car around Geneva's tight, narrow medieval streets heading first uphill towards the Bastion fort, then pulling back down before taking the north road tunnel towards the airport to lose their tail.

"What do you think?" Walter asked when finally Max began the ascent up the mountain back towards his home.
"I think I will change the car, perhaps we stay away from the city until I find out from our people who it is that is snooping about, possibly it is the Israelis, this is no coincidence coming so soon after Rio and with respect to the young gentlemen you met today, the Somalian's have a habit for drawing attention. It may be wise to alert the banker, I can do this if you wish Herr Director, and I can slip back on my own and leave a message in his drop-box in the hotel, later tonight." Max looked at Walter through his rear-view mirror for confirmation.
"Possibly yes I need to contact the Executive committee first, have some of our people come up and watch the house, only those you know, Max. I need time to sort this thing out with the Westerberg's. Without worrying about who may come knocking at my door. But first Please set the machine up in my study and explain how it works." Walter allowed himself a smile, "You know what I am like with machines and such like."

On entering his house, Walter immediately placed a call via the senior executive offices to the CED, by now it was a little after eight o'clock in Rome, and he was informed that the Chief Executive Director was attending a function. La Traviata at the Teatro dell 'Opera, as a guest of a senior Italian media mogul and the existing leader of the Italian national socialist party, he was also in the company of two other members of the senior executives of the Spider Organization, and although they were not to be disturbed, Walter requested the CED personal financial assistant Friedrich Fischer contacted him as a matter of urgency.
While he waited, Walter unearthed a well-hidden battered shoebox from the attic which contained the last remnants of Grethe and his previous life in Germany. He began to hunt through some of the photographs they very rarely dared look at when she was alive. Amongst the images of young men in black uniforms, wearing the Swastika armband, arm in arm with two young women, he found it hardest to recognize himself as being one of them. He placed the small collection of cine film Grethe and Elizabet had taken many years earlier while staying at Count Erichh's, Berlin Villa, to one side and collected a few photographs that held the image of Stefan Keplar, "There you are my friend, your boy is the spitting image of you." He smiled at the picture and set it propped up against his brass desk light as he began to operate the videotape machine as Max had shown him. At certain intervals, he compared the image of Sebastian Westerberg with that of photographs of Stefan Keplar which he held alongside the television screen and while again reacting with astonishment of how remarkable their shared likeness was, the telephone rang, it was Fleischer returning his call.

"So what you are telling me is the Chief Executive Director has sanctioned an operation to go to Sweden," Walter spoke openly and plainly over the telephone, breaking every rule of their organizations code, in frustration, by talking directly over the telephone about the arrangements of a specific operation, even though he was allegedly speaking on a secure phone line set up by one of their contacts at Interpol. He felt a cold sweat bare down on his body and loosening his tie he removed it and unbuttoned the front of his shirt as he listened to Fleischer.
"I cannot confirm this Herr Director at this time, only that we received news from Geneva and that following discussion with other on-site senior directors, the CED authorised a serious assessment of the intent of those responsible, this has been actioned and is operatives are now in play, only the CED can cancel the orders."
It was only that Friedrich was well known to Walter having taken up many of his duties, working within the organisation since Walter's semi-retirement that Walter was able to get even a vague understanding of what the CED had done since receiving the report from Salter-Kingsley, that a main SSG account had been accessed.
"Friedrich this is important can you at least tell me the schedule of our people and how many." Again Walter was breaking all protocol using Friedrich's first name. There was a long pause on the line "The rally point is Munich, tomorrow first light, I have no specifics of the team's schedule, thereafter."

Walter thanked Friedrich and hung up and began to consider his options and looked again at his television screen, as a wave of conflicting duties to his present status began to flood back.

With his mountain retreat now surrounded for the first time with armed guards, individuals who were totally loyal to Max Binder, from his study window Walter watched two exchange a cigarette, as Max entered with a cup of hot chocolate.

"Herr Director, I have placed a man at the main road up towards the house, they all report directly to me, as yet there is no news from Geneva, this is radio fixed to their frequency, if you hear the words lockdown, please make your way immediately to the safe room in the basement." Max placed a Sony walkie talkie on Walter's desk, "It is just a precaution, sir."

"I understand, good work, I will need you to take a letter for the banker Salter-Kingsley, then I think without wishing to panic you, Max, we make plans just in case, things escalate, the children are safe enough, but I want nothing that could act as a compass."

"Can I ask Herr Director, these people, this person Westerberg, he is important enough to risk everything?" Max studied Walter's face as he looked at a single photograph of himself with Stefan Keplar and Elizabet between them holding up her ice-skating boots in the park in The Berlin Zoological gardens, taken by Grethe in 1943, only months before they made their escape.

"This man, his family, yes." Walter smiled.

"I hope I have the honour to meet with them, Sir." Max nodded his head, understanding, the nature of the loyalty his master was displaying.

"Yes, if possible we must make that so Max," Walter said, then began placing calls with individuals within his organisation he knew he could count on for support to levy the Chief Executive Director to cancel his instructions to the Spider field operatives he had dispatched.

During the same evening, 250 kilometres away in a disused factory outside the border town of Basel, Sebastian Westerberg and Günther waited as the back of a box lorry was opened and a police car was reversed down the ramps, followed by Vincent riding a police motorcycle.

"Captain Nilsson said everything you requested is in the boot of the car Sir, are you sure you don't need me here, Mr Westerberg." Luke Sandberg, one of the trusted guards from the Westerberg facility in Uppsala, had brought the lorry across on the ferry.

"No, Luke, get home to your family, we can take it from here." Sebastian handed him the keys to his red VW Beetle.

"Second is a little temperamental, look after her, I think Lenora has her eye on it for her first car." he said then watched as Luke acknowledged Vincent with the sign language, "Happy hunting."

"I hate using our people, for this kind of shit." Sebastian opened the boot and examined the uniforms as Luke drove off.

"He won't say a word, with what you have done for his mother, that's why I chose him," Günther said as he closed the back of the lorry up, reminding Sebastian that as in the days when he commanded a troop of men in the Waffen SS and had always been attentive to their needs, sometimes above his own, like then, today his actions had born the fruit of unquestioning loyalty by many of those that now worked within the Westerberg Company.
"Come on old man, you can sleep on the way back to Geneva." Sebastian whistled to Vincent to lock up and then follow them on the motorbike.
"I know what you're thinking, this is over the top, and personally I hope you are right Gunt, but you know me, *Just in case*." Sebastian looked at the fake police identity card that held his picture that lay on the dash, and as the lights in Geneva came into view he wondered about the following day, and if he was expecting too much from his young nephew and father, but Günther had always been there, always.

Bull's battered Wolseley looked out of place sat next to the three new black Grand Cherokee four by fours, parked in the drive of "Collingwood" the American Safehouse on Highgate Hill as a security guard used a mirror on a rod to check underneath for explosives, it was the era of car bombs, soon the people of London would become used to the "Suspect Package" warning posters and tannoy messages on the underground as the conflict with IRA escalated on the mainland.
"Way of life," Tom Quinn said as he met Bull on the steps as three bodyguards carefully watched each car that passed by the closed metal gates until both men were inside.
"Perhaps, but I didn't expect it to come in my lifetime." Bull handed Quinn a paper bag with the name "Fitzbillies Bakery" containing four Chelsea buns he had couriered down that morning from Trumpington Street, Cambridge, Quinn had got a taste for them when stationed in England prior to "D" day.
"Remind me again why you won't come and work for us, I'm joking Bull, I'm just glad you're not with Moscow, come on I think I heard the kettle whistle." Quinn smile was already wide in seeing his old friend, but he positively beamed with a look in the bag.
Not having spoken to each other about the fiasco in Brazil, Bull had called the meeting in the first place to hand over the information Nick Cartwright had unexpectedly recovered in Klaus Ritter Jacket, a wallet that contained a selection of currency including two hundred Swiss Francs, Klaus Ritter's passport, who they had now identified as Henri Krause, an East German who had been a Stabsfähnrich, *(Staff-Warrant Officer)* of the Fähnrichkorps, Berlin border control assigned within a specialize attachment of the Stasi East German intelligence security service. Also in the coat were two flight tickets to Madrid, one of which was for Doctor Merill Nestlar, who although he was on the list Orran Danis had given Pimm in Cyprus in 1943, was not on any war crimes warrant, in spite of the fact from the few records recovered from the RPA after the war there was clear evidence that he had an association with other high-ranking Nazi's such as Josef Mengele and Philipp

Bouhler, who along with most that had worked within the Reich RPA and Aktion T4 had been designated as war criminals in their absence.

Regardless of the bounty that had fallen into the lap of Mi6, the top floor were treating Bull's team stumbling on to a Mossad/CIA operation in Brazil like a can of worms they wanted to bury in a place the sun never shines, especially by those that knew more and said nothing about the fish washing up on the beaches of Rio.
The fact it involved a group of ex-Nazi scientist did nothing to the appeal for further investigation, Bull's Operation Turkish Delight, was seen by many that sat alongside Control on the top floor of Century House as overindulgence of a man that they would rather have no longer in the building.
The fact he had Pimm carryout some moonlighting in Rio, having already unofficially involved another *Sandman*, Bob Gregory, who was now decommissioned, helped those that were whispering in Controls ear it was time to let him go and he did receive a rap on the knuckles by way of a private talk between himself and Maurice Oldfield at the SFC *(Special Forces Club)* in Herbert Crescent, behind Harrods in Knightsbridge, where he picked up the drinks tab.

Fortunately for Bull over the years, he had always stayed at arm's length distance from the politics of the top floor for many years and watched as other long-serving agents had burnt their bridges, either making a play for the top slot themselves or by supporting the wrong candidates. Since Dickie White, there had been two new Mi6 heads, and already there were clouds circling above the head of Maurice Oldfield. Waiting in the wings was his successor, another ex-member of the signal corp. in 1940, Arthur Temple "Dick" Franks, someone that had worked in the field alongside Oliver Pimm in one of Pimm's first assignments as a Sandman during the joint Anglo-U.S. coup d'état to overthrow Mohammad Mosaddegh, the nationalistic Iranian Prime Minister in 1953 Mi6 codenamed as "Operation boot."
Like all the previous Mi6 heads when Franks became Control in 1979, he would retain Bull's services. Like those before him seeing Gordon as a foundation stone of the service that it would be better left in place, like that at the bottom of a water dam.

For now in 1975 with Maurice Oldfield still at the helm of Mi6, those that considered Bull, a fossils from the second world war, could not disagree with his decision to keep Gordon on for the sake of having additional ballast to hold their ship in check, this was especially true with the teething problems of the new computer mainframe and networking system Ebla having Bull around often brought about a sense of relief, the kind you get when eventually you find a plug fuse that works in the back of a draw, when you desperately need one. Bull Gordon's history with the service and long-established global networking ensured him the reputation, if the lights ever went out in Mi6, he would know what draw to look in first.

However Bull was Bull, old guard he may never overestimate his importance or the fact that he was not indispensable, but a rap on the knuckles and the paying of a forty-pound drinks bill at the SFC was not going to stop him doing things his way. Circumvent the old boy network of Mi6 rather than creating waves to get to the nub, was something every Mi6 head since Dickie White had understood was part and parcel of having Bull on the payroll and Maurice Oldfield had no doubt with an operation, such as the follow up to the Rio incident and death of Neil Lamb, which appeared to have been prematurely dropped, probably by someone pressuring Whitehall from the American's side, Bull would charge ahead and discover the truth, but with the delicacy and precision of the men that served within Explosive Ordnance Disposal and Search Regiment, that were called to investigate every "*Suspect package*" reported during the 1970's.

When Bull arrived in Highgate to meet with Tom Quinn that morning, he knew only what they had retrieved from the coat Cartwright had worn and from Pimm informing him, that he had spoken directly with Carter-Wallis on speaker phone while sitting opposite Zavineski, Bull had no idea who had been the instigator of the operation in Brazil, from Langley.
Seeing no mileage in escalating his own meagre section resources and knowing his superiors above him would do nothing accept bury the information, Bull chose to share his Intel with Quinn and possibly learn something about what exactly had been going on in Brazil and how involved the CIA was, with Spider, the Somalian's and Mossad.
"Pass on my regards for looking after our man Gregory, sending over a team of brain surgeons was a good call, he'd have been as useful as a Halloween pumpkin if the Brazilian doctor's had got their hands on him, same for our girl she was lucky Pimm came along, even if he had to butt heads with the Israelis." Bull then handed over the file containing Klaus Ritter's wallet and everything he had learnt from its contents and watched Quinn's face as he opened it while tucking into his first Chelsea bun.
 "Mmmmm, I can almost smell the grease I use to wear in my hair to make it straight back then when there was a little more of it." Quinn patted his flat top hairline.
"Not wanting to put a damper on your generosity and those kids of yours involved, but you might want to have a word, our girl had this on her without knowing, some souvenirs pulled from the fire so to speak," Bull added hoping Quinn would feel open enough to blame the team leader by name, but he said nothing as he examined the wallet.
"Yep, shame about your man, at least you know Zavi's people are on the case, I'll pass this down the line if that's ok with you, tell him you are thinking of him." Quinn's tone was lightly touched with sarcasm, as he knew both men respected each other, even if their governments didn't.
"No problem I hear Zavi has a team as we speak in Geneva, watching every watchmaker over sixty. Feel free with my compliment, I know how it is, one hand

washing the other and all that, one day you can tell me what you get back." Bull sensed Quinn was building up to something but was not expecting him to immediately turn the tables so sharply and he listened while chewing on his pipe, coming up to eight weeks without having lit it, soon he would need a to replace the mouthpiece, having a habit of brushing it back and forth gently across his teeth when in deep thought, which made the sound as if he was eating a Murray mint. Not that non-smoker Quinn minded, having referred to it on a previous occasion as a portable incinerator, "What the hell is in that thing cactus compost" he had once exclaimed, then proceeded to open the bulletproof French doors at Collingwood which at the time made his security team nervous.

"So cards on deck time, there a shit storm brewing back home over this, your man Pimm spoke with the prime suspect Deputy Director General Benjamin Carter-Wallis, It was his show your people stumbled into, he's been playing fast and loose with Zavi's people, keeping them at arm's length from members of our German friends in Spider, scientist left over from the war, he had brewing up some a replacement for agent Orange, When Mubarak Ali Hassan came on the scene, he knew it wouldn't be long before the rains came back home so he decided to shut up shop, unfortunately he left a yellow brick road all the way back to Kansas and now questions are being asked in the big house." Quinn smiled as he watched Bull rub his pipe tip across his teeth.

"I can see how things might be a little difficult with your kin, you have my apologies if my people had aided your stress, it was not my intention."

Quinn shook his head, "I know that, but you see it was in the cards, would have happened sooner or later, you see Carter-Wallis is not the only one that has been running a play, the things is I have a seed that I have been tending for some time, all above boards and it has the possibilities it will bear fruit that will feed many mouths for years to come, and I'll be dammed if I'm going to have it blown out of the water, by a man who thinks using people like Josef Mengele and his cronies is good for business, long story short, he's on the edge, he just needs a push and that's where you come in old pal of mine." Quinn wiped his hands on a clean handkerchief he pulled from his pocket and patted the beads of sweat from his brow, formed by a reaction from the sugar he received from eating the cakes.

"This is quite an ask Tom, it's not the usual way you guys have shuffled your new deck in the past. You must really rate Carter-Wallis as a pain in the arse, is that why you don't want to use our own people, or am I missing something?" Bull said and thanked him as he shoved a gin and tonic in his hand, they had been talking for over an hour and moved on from tea to something more befitting the subject, but Quinn could not resist having his second Chelsea bun.

"American strange taste buds, each to his own" Bull thought.

"I feel there are no safer hands for something so delicate, but you're right as usual, If I go for him direct, use CIA recourses, I will lose support at home, you know how it works, turn on your own, you'll watch your back for the rest of your time." Tom Quinn's flattery was met with a raise eyebrow from Gordon as he watched Tom Quinn remove a blue folder from his aluminium briefcase.

"I thought your boys tied up all the loose ends over in Brazil when Pimm was over there." Bull watched the deep creases on Quinn's forehead ripple deep as he frowned, shaking his head and licked his fingers.

"Yes well, so did we, what can I tell you, today his face doesn't fit, all I know is the orders come down, they would rather he jump from his position as a CIA chief than being pushed, and this buddy of his go way back, he's bad news from Saigon days, someone above my pay grade believes if Copeland is sat down with a polygraph then Carter-Wallis will walk away, without upsetting the apple cart." Quinn handed Bull two files

That's everything we know about Copeland and Four Star Army Marine General Benjamin, *Ulysses* Carter-Wallis." he smiled, with slight embarrassment as Bull held up one of the thin folders.

"Tommy boy you're kidding me, two LRRP U.S. rangers, one of whom is a disallowed Yakuza, Oban, the other one of only two four-star Marine Generals, I've seen more meat on my postman's file. Fortunately, we have our own computer, just don't ask me to switch it on." Bull examined the picture of Frank Copeland as a young Ranger and then a more recent surveillance photo sat as usual in a flamboyant Hawaiian shirt amongst a group of elderly Japanese men opposite a sumo domo in Tokyo.

"What can I say, Bull, it's all I can give." As Tom spoke Bull regretted questioning his word, they each knew that the other would give as much information as they could, it would be rude to question the authenticity or quality of information passed. Bull looked to the separate photo's Quinn had taken out of the same folder of Sean and Connor McLoughlin, taken by the Mossad team outside the FNIG bank in Geneva.

"What do you think on that loose end, you always said all prodigal sons' return home, eventually?" Quinn tapped one of the photos with his finger.

"I know it's not your department and you Brits have a cease-fire with the Irish in play but, with all that's gone down over there and here, our analysts say it won't last and figured this may help you square this away upstairs. I didn't give their names to Zavi, they have the pair down as an Executive security detail for the bank, going by the name Byrne. You can use it as you like, just don't upset things around the bank and FYI the Irish hold accounts but have left them dormant, they seem to prefer the Cayman's if that should change then I will come to you first."

Bull looked at the image of the service record of Copeland again.

"And you say Zavineski has no knowledge of the heritage of these boys?" placed the file to one side and considered what Tom had just asked him to put in place In Geneva, "So as I see it Wallis-Carter is not my concern, as long as I can guarantee my people won't get caught up in some CIA internal squabble over this asset you have in play, if things go south over there, that's what you are saying."

Bull studied the file

"As I said a big ask even bearing in mind, Frank Copeland has been on Six's radar for some time, of course, we knew someone in your lot was playing fairy godmother, there were questions why you would keep such a loose cannon out there, but I dare say he's not the worst you or we have on a very thin lead, last I heard was he'd hung up his guns, local drugs and some bars and keeping his ear down for you guys that's it." Bull closed the folder.

"Yes well, looks like he got a second wind, not sure if Wallis-Carter pulled him back in, to be honest, but he's sniffing around a honey pot, we are hoping will draw in a lot of bees and just maybe a big fucking bear." Quinn smiled widely as he saw Bull looking at the images of the McLoughlin boys and the bank in the background.

"The bank, of course, I should have guessed, that's why you wanted the introduction with Franco Perri at the CNI (*Centro Nacional de Inteligencia*) in Barcelona." Bull nodded, remembering one of their past exchanges.

"I remembered you worked with him in the Sahara," Quinn went to take another Chelsea bun then folded the bag closed. "Look Bull I guess I owe you this much, we got wind your Spanish amigo has been holding the parents of a principal player at the bank without knowing it, they got mixed up with Eta. When he was just a babe, fostered to an uncle who shipped him to the UK for schooling, apparently, he thought they were dead, the Managing Director Plácido Zabala, he's our in." Quinn held his palms up.

Bull allowed the scenario to percolate in his head, "Basque separatists, so you did a deal with Madrid, got them stateside, witness protection to keep your player on the line at the bank, it all seems very cozy." Bull could now see the dots joining in his mind and where he and Pimm fitted in Tom Quinn's plans.

Negotiating a deal with the Spanish Secret service to have Plácido Zabala's elderly parents who had spent over fifteen years in a maximum-security prison, so that he could have an inside man in the FNIG bank, was one of Tom Quinn's personal black projects, and he was not going to have Frank Copeland or the Yakuza poison the well, especially since Carter-Wallis's involvement in setting up a chemical weapons factory and diverting a nuclear submarine in a cover-up mission appeared to have terminated not only his vision of becoming DCIA (*Director of the Central Intelligence Agency*) but also a forced retirement and effectively pushed Tom Quinn further up the ladder, it was unlikely as a black man he would make Director, but assistant Director would be a start.

"Will you inform Zavineski, Six is sending a team to Geneva," Bull asked.

"No, I understand Jeremy Stapleton's team, Drake is handling the Irish situation these days, I'm assuming you'll talk with him regarding the McLoughlin boys. I suspect Mossad will let you do your thing if you let them do theirs, they are only interested in the German's, they have no interest in the IRA or the bank, and we want it to stay that way. That's why I don't want our boys over there, or Zavi will smell a rat and be like a dog with a coacher bone. As far as the farm is concerned they would like Copeland stateside, he has more than rotting fish to bury Carter-Wallis up to his neck with, if they get him to sit still. The Somalian thing is just one nail in the coffin they are getting ready for him." Tom Quinn was well aware Carter-Wallis had friends on the Presidents Chief of Staff, and it was likely had a few safety nets in place, the key was to get him bang to rights so he would be as toxic as Ebola.

"So, you want me to sell a bird watching team to Six in Geneva, with the possibility of capturing and turning the McLoughlin boys, and you really expect they will not make it personal, knowing the Germans you say Mossad has eyes on this guy Klaus Ritter, the one that killed our man Lamb. But what you really want from me is a Sandman, one of my own, to keep an eye out for Copeland and be on hand to deal with him if it appears he's going to rock your boat. To put it, in a nutshell, you want me to land the fish and gut it for your private barbeque, which I won't even get an invite for." Bull chuckled.

"That's about the sum of it." Quinn shrugged. "You can let Six know regarding the German's, Zavi says he will share whoever they pull from their operation with us before they hang them, I can promise you I will pass that down the line to your lap, but I can't promise you won't trip over each other's feet while over there, like in Rio, who will you send."

"Well, you know my office doesn't have the views, but fortunately I have someone in mind, but I guess you already knew that being as we are making this personal, someone that has history with Mossad and they will recognise rather than shoot." Bull realised Quinn had already worked out the finer details and had come to him knowing Pimm was temporarily assigned to his department, making it possible for Quinn to use a Mi6 Sandman to get some CIA house cleaning done.

"What can I say, if the shoe fits?" Quinn smiled.

"Pimm is the best there was, but he won't appreciate being chucked in the deep end again." Bull briefly thought back to June and his time in Muswell Avenue before Rio.

"He was?" Quinn looked for a gesture of confidence that Pimm still had what it takes.

"Is..... he'll get your man back." Bull then caught a look from Quinn

"God, this is why they dropped me four floors, you never said you wanted him back," Bull sighed

"I can leave it with you then, mate," Quinn said with an English accent as he raised his glass.

"Christ this things got more wingmen than the red arrows." Bull raised his eyes, contemplating how much he would tell Pimm.

The next morning Bull called Pimm up to his office from the basement firing range in Century house.

"How's she settling in?" Pimm asked, looking across at Cartwright, showing Mrs Thompkin how the latest computer system worked.

"She's a whiz with that thing even with fingers still in plaster, you wait, we'll be working for her one day, well you will, computers and camera's that's the future, and I'm crap at both." Bull chuckled with a glad eye.

"Good for her, she let me know Bob's accepted a posting in training, Guernsey, she looked a little upset about it, perhaps you can see if Hereford has a spot when he gets the all-clear from the Doc, at least until they get hitched." Pimm went over to the window and examined the line of cacti and noticed one was in the shape of a Star of David.

"I hadn't realised they were getting along so well, I'll have a word." Bull sat back behind his desk, he was still waiting for Pimm to give him a reaction to the folder he had handed him.

Pimm held up the image of Nestlar, "You say this one, Doctor Merill Nestlar is on Orran Danis's original list, that's confirmed, but nothing on Interpol, no surprise there." He then flicked through the other photos,

"This is definitely the guy I winged on the stairs, and killed the Mossad boy outside, but you don't want me to touch them."

"Yep that's it, Drakes surveillance team will watch out for Harry McLoughlin's boys they're sending a team over today, I'm sure they will appreciate your eyes if you drop in on their nest. The rest is between you and me, but really this is wheel within a wheel with Tom Quinn, just for your ears, I can tell you he has a man in the bank, no name. Tom informed me this morning he got word last night, a meeting of some kind involving the German's and the Somalian's is taking place on Sunday morning, in the park opposite the bank. So I think grab your hat and get down to Luton, you have a day or so to settle in, nose about, while I'll square it with Jem Stapleton, make up some BS you're on a fact-finding hunt, Nazi gold lead, they all know it's over there." Both he and Pimm knew that would be looked on with a jaundiced eye.

"There are a lot of players on the court; this could end up a real bun fight, especially with the Somalian's in tow, do we know who?" Pimm shook his head but considered the idea of being involved in squaring things with the one that had killed Lamb and indirectly ended Bob Gregory's career was an opportunity to good to create waves around.

"No, you are going to hit the ground running over there, the only thing I know for sure, is the Farm are giving the city a wide birth, so if they have Yankee accent and pull a gun, don't stop to ask them how Dorothy got back to Kansas, consider them hostile."

"Great, I'll bring you back some cheese," Pimm said, lightly.

"As long as it's the only thing that has holes in it." Bull handed him his flight ticket to Geneva from Luton.

"I'd expect nothing else, I suppose Mrs Thompkin has a travel bag ready?" Pimm asked.

"No I thought you'd appreciate something a little modern, I had Cartwright here run by C&A's, you can blame her if she got your size wrong, pick up what you need over there just keep the chits." With that Bull produced from behind his desk a cabin holdall bag.

"This thing must have really rattled Tom Quinn's cage." Pimm felt the bag weight and looking at Cartwright in her all in one flared jumpsuit wondered what she may have bought for him to wear.

Chapter 18: The Jigging

Geneva, Switzerland
May 1975

Early, Friday morning the day Günther and the Byrne brothers were scheduled to make the withdrawal from the FNIG bank, Hong and a team of five men met in Copeland's study to go through the final details of his plan, to intercept the Westerberg gold shipment, having marked various positioned along the route Merryman had confirmed they would be taking between Geneva and Travemunde ferry dock.
Frank Copeland looked towards the window hearing the skid of Suzy's black, Pickford 1275 GT Mini Clubman on the gravel outside, and gestured to one of the men to close the study door as the dog Binki came yapping into the hallway, closely followed by Suzy. Nursing a hangover from staying out with Sean all night she threw her bags and shoes to the floor, grabbed the dog and without a glance to the study, headed straight to her room, leaving the front entrance door open.
"Alka-Seltzer, ice, champagne someone, now.....now!" She groaned loudly as she disappeared up the stairs.
Copeland raised his eyes from the map, and Hong shrugged and went to her aid. "Keep schtum about this," he tapped the map, "See if you can find out what state her Irishman's in, with a bit of luck he'll be as dozy as my tart of a daughter." He smiled sarcastically and waved him away.
In the FNIG bank basement car park, Sean was present in mind and body, if not in spirit, for the start of their escort duty with Günther. He sat in the front passenger seat of his BMW as he watched Connor kicking the tyres as he looked over Günther's Volkswagen camper van, while at the back of the underground car park two of the banks security guards stood stationed either side of the lift awaiting the arrival of the bank teller with the funds they were about to withdraw.
Head pounding Sean's mouth tasted like an ashtray, as he looked wearily at the wrapped bacon and egg roll on the dashboard Connor had picked up for him when he showed up to drag him from his bed at the Metropolitan at six-thirty, where he had left Suzy sleeping.
"Well Seany me, old son, it's kill or cure?" Sean told himself, and then took the plunge, taking a large bite of the roll, he was surprised and relieved when the grease hit his stomach and stayed there.
"Cure it is" he said, reaching instinctively for the packed of Marlboro cigarettes still on the dash, but at the last moment changed his mind and moved and grabbed the

bottle of water alongside, "Maybe that's pushing it." he thought taking another bite, then grabbing four Anadin tablets from a packet in the glove compartment took a deep swallow and braced himself.

It was not the start he had wanted for the arduous journey over to Sweden, but then he could not resist lying between Suzy's thighs, cocaine sex with her was almost as good as a front-row ticket at Anfield to watch the Reds, almost because he remembered little of the experience of the night before, Suzy had a higher tolerance for the drug than he did and without doubt he knew she was bad news long term, a "tear up" on the black stuff was one thing, this was something else they don't call it "marching dust" for no reason, and he felt edgy, knowing only sleep or another line of Coke was the answer, neither suited the moment. In his mind, he had already decided Suzy was a recreational drug his lifestyle could not afford, and he was still not a hundred per cent sure her father wasn't a silent partner in their relationship.

"Get your shit together for fuck sake!" he growled and using the bottled water placed the opening tight over each eye in turn and bathed his eyes. He sniffed and got a sense of his own sweet aroma, realizing even though he had doused himself in Brut aftershave, he could still smell the alcohol oozing from his pores. Rolling down his window, he placed a hand on the door handle and prepared himself, to join the others.

"Well at least we can make a cuppa on the way, but I don't fancy our chances of making a quick getaway if things get sticky." With the door open, Connor sat up front in the driver's seat playing with the large steering wheel and flicked at the blue and white checked curtains.

Günther smiled as he watched Sean raise himself from the car, then turned back to Connor, "It will help when we cross the border, as for speed." Günther raised a finger gesturing him to the back of the camper, where he lifted the tailgate of the engine bay to reveal a pristine engine that appeared totally out of place.

"An upgraded Porsche," he said, pointing to a 3-litre turbo engine.

Sean got as far as the bonnet of the BMW where he rested back trying to look casual and nodded as if taking in what Günther was saying, suddenly there was a high pitch bell ring, signaling the elevator had arrived on the basement parking floor, the built-in speaker gave a high pitch screech, "All clear?" a guard from within the elevator asked and waited for a response from those outside before opening the doors, the banks security guards gave a look around the basement again, Sean pushed himself off the bonnet and looked towards the closed car park security entrance gate and nodded.

"Clear" one of the guards stationed at the elevator pressed the wall microphone, and the doors to the elevator opened, and a bank clerk emerged with a trolley laden with twenty gold bars flanked by two security guards.

Günther closed the engine bay, "She handles like a boat, but quicker than you would think in a straight line, besides there are other benefits." Günther opened one of the side doors, rolling back the rubber floor mat he pulled on two ring pulls and revealed a hidden sunken hold into which the clerk began to load the gold.

"Even with your upgrades, I would prefer to have a second vehicle for protection, just in case." Sean leaned back and patting the bonnet, then looked passed Günther towards the elevator expecting to see Merryman, who had handled the signing off, paperwork on all previous assignments.

"No, well that's as maybe, but we will go like this, the bench in the back is remarkably comfortable, and there is good visibility. No one raised an eye on my way over, people come and go on the ferry in these all the time, just another fishing group, look." Günther pointed to the fishing rods on display in the back placed in plain view to aid their disguise at border control.

As Connor grabbed a rod a began making out he was fly casting, somewhat disturbed by Merryman's absence Sean began to feel his apprehension rise, Günther's attitude appeared too relaxed and out of sight he shook his head at Connor but secretly considered it was probably just the drugs adding to his nerves, he'd be ok once they were out of the concrete bunker style car park.

"Put it back, kid." He told Connor as they watched Günther eye up Miss Bishop with a smile, as she approached with a clipboard in hand admiring her fine legs in heels. "Now you understand why I asked you to dress down, as much as I like your brother's suit. Stack your bags in the back there is plenty of space, and when you are ready, we go, it's that simple." Günther said, opening up and checking the two cases that the bank clerk then handed him, each held 500,000 American dollars in bound bills. Taking out two hamper sized wicker fishing baskets he removed a top tier shelf that held floats, hooks and baits boxes and began stacking the money inside, the total value of the asset withdrawal Sebastian had arranged with Plácido Zabala was 1.8 million dollars.

"Who knows maybe we'll stop on the way and catch something? It can only help, you told me you boys, live on the water." Günther smiled as Sean began to help him, then they stacked the baskets amongst the other fishing paraphernalia. Günther watched as Connor sat in the back and checked how easy the doors opened from the inside. By now he had become used to wearing the Walther PPK revolver he had purchased from the Jewish tailors, but his heavier Colt had never

let him down and removing it from his bag he found a convenient niche to hide it in, the drop-down flap below the cooker grill and gestured to Sean with a smile,
"This is not so bad, I might get me one of these." he leaned back and found the two large tartan flasks of coffee Günther had prepared for the journey, used to the cabin in the Helena, there was a familiarity to the inside of the VW Camper van, Connor liked.
"There is water, juice in the fridge and some beer." Günther sniffed the air, and as Sean stepped forward, he sensed Günther could smell the alcohol on his body, and he turned briefly back towards the banking team.
"No Merryman today?" Sean asked Miss Bishop as she handed him the consignment acceptance document copy for Günther to sign.
"He has called in, I understand, he is unwell, Mr Salter-Kingsley oversaw the vault withdrawal early this morning, but was called away from his desk, Mr Byrne, is there something else you require or a message you wish me to pass on?" She saw no ulterior motive as to why one of her superiors might not be there for the withdrawal and Günther looked at Sean, who noticed again how the old German appeared unconcerned to the change in the agreed arrangements as he scratched his signature across the paperwork on behalf of the Westerberg's
"Mr Lansford!" He mouthed to himself, remembering not to sign in his real name.
Salter-Kingsley had organized the documentation that morning and had scheduled to be present with Merryman, for the withdrawal, but had received a telephone call in the early hours at his home. As always, the caller remained anonymous, but instead of the briefest of code instructions "You have post."
On this occasion Salter-Kingsley recognized the voice on the other end of the telephone line to be that of Max Binder and he directed him to pick up a letter from the Metropolitan and to ensure Mr Lansford received it before his departure, adding that he should take his time in making his way to the drop box and look for any possible tail.
From the Bank to the Metropolitan was a twelve-minute walk at most, that morning the paranoid banker had doubled back through the main food hall arcade twice and taken a tram ride to the Pont du Mont-Blanc, where he had a double espresso in a café window seat while watching the street, before walking back and entering through the rear of the hotel on Rue du Rhone, it had taken him forty minutes and his shirt was damp from sweat, but he felt satisfied if not a little excited in the role he had just played as he opened the key safe to retrieve the sealed letter, scribbled with the name Lansford.
Max Binder considered the banker would in all probability fail to lose any specialist surveillance team especially if they were Mossad or the CIA, but as long as Salter-

Kingsley was able to make the pickup and deliver the letter, that was all that mattered.

"Pick up before the bank opens, understand, you hand it to the man yourself!" Were his instructions with the strictest secrecy of a protocol that had kept his master, Walter Thomas safe and which he had lived by for over thirty years being bent, in an effort to warn Günther Brahn and Sebastian Westerberg, who he believed to be the son of his old friend Stefan Keplar. That was a much as Walter could do at this point having been forced to remain at his chalet, fielding calls with other members of the Spider network to prevent a calamity befalling the Westerberg family in Sweden.

Confirmation came through in the early hours to Walter, the team of three Spider operatives dispatched by the CED from Munich were already in play, their assignment was to kidnap the Westerberg family using *"extreme prejudice"* and their orders were precise, anyone that stood in the way and anyone that resisted were to be eliminated. Only the Chief Executive Director had the power to recall the group he had sent to Sweden, and following the La Traviata at the Teatro dell 'Opera, he had left on the Italian media mogul's Learjet along with some of the cast for a private audience at his villa on Lake Como. The two other Senior Directors of Spider had not been invited, with limited space on the jet and had returned to Rome, Walter had already spoken with them regarding what he knew about the Westerberg's and while they understood the possible fallout or the precipitous action taken by the CED, neither of them wished to be involved in sanctioning a second team to be dispatched to intercede those that the CED had sent to Sweden, this was an option Walter had been exploring, with the other seven members of the Spider Executive Committee. Walter's only hoped was that the banker would do as ordered and be at the bank before Günther made the withdrawal.

In the basement of the bank, Günther turned and winked back at Connor as he started up the VW camper, and its modified Porsche engine growled like a tiger.
"Good all fit, so we will be off, thank you Florence." Günther smiled churlishly.
"It's Miss Bishop" she corrected him, noticing his eyes wandering to her legs again.
"Sure, sure thank you, Miss, you have a nice day." Günther acknowledged his mistake as he rested his arm on the cab, window sill.
Sean leaned into the passenger side window, "Ok so we do it your way old man, I will park this on the street." he said gesturing to the guard to get the gate.
While he waited in the BMW for the basement security guard grill to rise, across the road, the Mossad surveillance team huddled around the TV monitor. General Zavineski had come through with the goods, and they were now sitting in a

purpose-built surveillance truck camouflaged as a baker's delivery truck, complete with advertising hoarding and containing the latest technology, including a panoramic external telescope camera lens that fed the monitor inside.

Seeing Sean's car in the shadows on his screen, Leon gestured to David sat in front of a tripod zoom camera watching through the one way glass windows of the back door.

"Busy, busy this morning, where the hell is Ruby, she won't want to miss this, do we follow them?" Leon said, checking the tape machine was recording.

"No! You heard what she said, we stay put." David snapped another image.

Ruby had been ordered they were to stay on the bank and only chase down any leads that involved the principle players they had on file and those from Rio. Even though they were probably witnessing events that were involved with the Spider Organization, they simply did not have the resources. In the end, Salter-Kingsley had not been under surveillance when he had made his pick up from the Metropolitan hotel.

"Look here's the boss Salter-Kingsley, Late today?" David said, as suddenly red-faced having run a non-direct route back from the Metropolitan hotel Salter-Kingsley arrived, holding up the letter, he called to Claude Dennee the security guard as he stood to one side allowing Sean to drive passed. With his face a blotchy red complexion and suit somewhat ruffled shirttail hanging over his waist for a moment Sean had to check it was the owner of the FNIG bank and watched him in his rearview mirror as he drove out from the bank to park across the street, where the Mossad team froze in the van "Everyone quiet!" David hushed, then held his breath as Sean locked his car and stood looking directly at their van for a moment, then seeing tradesmen in a boiler suit working in a building further along turned back to go.

"Smile," David whispered and his camera rattled away as he pressed the button on his camera, taking multiple pictures.

Before the end of the day, fresh images of Sean's image alongside Günther and Connor were sent to General Zavineski and the Israel Chief, as per their security detente with the American's, handed them to Tom Quinn of the CIA, who in turn passed them on to Mi6 via Bull Gordon in London.

In the Surveillance van, David caught in his lens as Sean acknowledged Salter-Kingsley before stepping into the passenger side of Günther's VW Camper and the banker holding up the white envelope.

"Mr Lansford, Mr Lansford, I am glad I caught you, a letter for Mr Westerberg, from associates of Herr Wolff."Salter-Kingsley's voice was almost hoarse from running as he handed the letter through the window to Günther he stood a while, expecting Günther might open it there and then.

"I will make sure he gets it." Günther looked at it and then threw it onto the dashboard.

"It is urgent, I believe, I think something to do with your employer's request." Salter-Kingsley had no idea what was inside the envelope, and although he was sure it was Max Binder's voice on the other end of the line that called him to visit the drop box at the Metropolitan, he recognized this was an exceptional event, totally out of character in all the years he had been dealing with the GSS accounts.

As they pulled away from the bank, Ruby arrived on her motorcycle in time to see Claude Dennee standing at the security grille of the basement car park as it closed.

"What did he want?" Sean asked as he watched Ruby drive down the same street he had parked on.

"A message for the boss." Günther shrugged gesturing to the letter on the dash.

Sealed off once more in the basement, Salter-Kingsley tucked his shirt into his trousers and brushing his hair back looked around at his people, then bent over feeling a stitch to his side, "All go ok? Good" he said, as he looked towards the members of his staff getting back into the elevator.

"Miss Bishop! Where the fuck is Merryman?" He said, throwing his hands up in the air.

"He called in sick Sir, he informed me he will be in later today." Miss Bishop had rarely heard her boss swear, but she felt there was nothing unusual in Merryman's absence."

In fact, Merryman had been on a tight leash by Copeland that morning effectively under house arrest with Tang the Japanese guard sat in his kitchen awaiting word that the withdrawal had been made from the bank and Copeland's heist operation was now running. Tang was under instruction only then to drop Merryman at the bank so that he could monitor the situation and alert Copeland of any news, during the day, but only if he was sober.

"You! Go take another shower" Tang ordered Merryman who was already dressed, as he waited for the call from Copeland while watching the small portable in his kitchen.

As

Günther drove over the Pont du Mont-Blanc heading North out of the city, the market stallholders had only just finished setting up their wares and the air had a milky feel that hinted winter was over, spring had arrived.

"So how long have you worked for the Westerberg's?" Sean said, checking his gun and placing it into the open glove compartment hidden by his map as Günther headed along the Lake Geneva shoreline road northeast towards where the Swiss, German and French borders converge.

Günther smiled and winked, "a long time, like family." he said handing him the map from the dashboard detailing the 2000 kilometre journey route,

"I have already," Sean said tapping the glove box lid down and Günther noticed as Sean unfolded his own map he had their route already marked with X's that he considered were likely locations for an ambush.

The route Günther had chosen and agreed with Sean would take them over the border into Germany at the town of Basel, the border control here is less commercial and between the two countries by now had evolved into little more than a drive-through window kiosk, passport check. From there they would travel north along the autobahn to Travemunde again at the car ferry dock, in keeping to their roll on roll of schedules the passport control for general passenger vehicles was verging on a casual affair, mainly looking for those buying cheap wine, spirits and tobacco to avoid the heavy Scandinavian tax.

However it was not the official border control Sean was concerned about as Günther watched with curiosity as the Irishman stuck a suctioned cupped additional rearview mirror on the windscreen so that he could check for cars behind without disturbing the driver, Merryman's absence had set him on edge over and above the caffeine now racing through his body, fighting with the symptoms he was feeling from the withdrawal of the cocaine.

"Keep frosty Con, until we get over to Germany and on the motorway, if that engine as good as you say Günther you can open this baby of your up, one thing you can say about you Krauts you make the best roads," Sean said then tossed their map back to Connor.

"This is true" Günther nodded.

"Call out the spots I picked before we hit them and keep the coffee coming," he said, as he handed him another cup from the flasks.

"Rough night?" Günther smirked remembering Suzy from the club, as he watched Sean take another mouthful.

"We're a long time dead," Sean said, as the sunlight hit his eyes and he fought to keep them open, Christ he picked the wrong night to go on the Craic, he thought as he slipped his Ray-ban wayfarer's on.

Within five kilometres Günther said nothing, as even with the sunglasses in place from his side angle he caught Sean's eye close, but he checked to see Connor was still wide awake as they pulled out of the last the suburbs, heading towards the tunnels through the Alps.

Enjoying the scenery and the radio Günther did not see Sean's reaction in checking himself having realised he had dozed off and surreptitiously check their location but noticed as he checked his own rear mirror when a blue flashing light of a motorbike police officer appeared behind them.

"Kid, I'm getting déjà vue" Sean said to Connor, remembering the attack on the Somalian's and raised a hand slowly and lifted the flap on the glove box, exposing his revolver without saying anything, as Günther watched from the corner of his eye as the Irishman edged forward in anticipation of an attack for a moment. Then appeared to relax back in his seat as they slowed pulling to one side along with other drivers allowing as the motorbike and a single police car passed them on the inside.

"Hope you're not going to be like this all the way." Günther smiled to himself knowing what was to come and gestured no as Sean offered him a cigarette.

They were now heading into the last tunnel that exits Switzerland north, Sean had only taken two puffs when he felt his neck hairs rise catching the first glint of the blue from the reflective flashes pulsing off the tunnel ceiling now ahead and they began to slow to a crawl.

"Fuck, I was joking" he whispered and glanced over his shoulder at Connor. Connor took his lead and slipped his revolver to his side, hidden under a pile of old newspapers.

"Well, at this rate, it will take us two weeks to get to the coast," Günther growled casually and pushed his head out of the window to look down the line of traffic. They were less than twenty Kilometres from the border at Basel about to enter a long remote stretch of road between Eptingen and Tenniken marked by a number of 'X's" by Sean on Connors map.

"Police an accident, I think?" Günther said and then looked at the reflection of his rearview mirror hearing the click of Connors gun.

"Well if I say you boot it, keep your head down and window open. Con cover the back and take the right side." Sean's muscles bristled as he removed his safety belt turning slightly in his seat, making sure all doors were unlocked, in case they need to make a sharp exit, images of how the Somalian's had been slain while still in their car filled his mind.

"Calm young man, no need to get excited five minutes into the journey." Günther got out his license and passport ready, seeing that some cars were being pulled to one side and ahead a policeman appeared to be checking only some of the vehicles having directing them to a side lane.

"Pass me your passports, just in case they ask" Günther asked and held out his hand.

"Why are they checking cars, can you see?" Connor leaned forward, Günther looked in his wing mirror and checked the rearview again,
"Just papers, pass them up, it's nothing I got stopped on the way down," Günther said and collected their documents and placed them on the dash ready.
Four cars behind in a transit van crew-cab, Hong and his team were just as apprehensive as the Byrne brothers and dropped their guns to the floor, then placed them in a duffle bag in the centre aisle.
"Get them out of sight!" he sneered sharply, gesturing to the blue flashing lights then looked to the cars at either side noticing they were becoming hemmed in the slowing moving traffic and soon they were moving forward at a snail's pace. Hong looked across to the opposite lanes of oncoming traffic, flowing freely and could see breaks in the low boundary wall between the two sides with a walkway through to the opposite side of the tunnel.
"Stay here I'm going to take a look," he said and slipped out from his door and crossed over in front of the oncoming traffic. Working his way up slowly while continuously checking the queue, he could see ahead Günther's camper van as it edged forward towards the police that appeared to be stopping the occasional vehicle. Hong got a look from the driver of his car and gestured he was unsure and continued to watch from his vantage point.
"Gentleman, please remain calm, it would appear we have picked up unwanted attention, on the opposite side, it may just be someone taking a look, what is the hold-up," Günther said calmly, as he caught sight of Hong looking back to his car as they inched passed a lorry on their inside through the gap between the drivers cab and the container trailer it was hauling. Tilting his head, he could see the transit van behind and straight away saw the man driving was oriental as one of the police officers signaled for him to pull into the inside lane which was clearly out of the tunnel having been coned off.
Sean's heart raced and his expectations that conflict was about to ensue pushed him to reach into the glove compartment, as he questioned in his mind Günther's next statement.
"Its unrelated for sure, keep cool boys, it's just a vehicle check they have them all the time, tax, I have all the paper here, no problem, stay cool as the hippies say." Günther's over relaxed manner began to have the opposite effect on Sean as he watched one of the officers walk passed their vehicle and begin checking the cars behind further unnerved that both officers faces were almost completely obscured by large mirror sunglasses.
"Con have you eyes on him behind, keep your ficking eyes on him, this is not right, can you see who is on the other side?" he asked continuing to keep his head

forward as the other officer approached their vehicle and then moving some of the road cones signaled Günther to proceed into the free lane that they had blocked off. "You're not going over there, don't go over there, don't go over there... Günther." Sean was now gripping his gun in both hands, held below the dash
"Relax, the lane is clear, over there, we are boxed in here if they were going to start something, look any sign of shit I will boot it like you said, we will be out of here, trust me." Günther gestured with his hand for Sean to keep his gun down.
"What the fucks he up to, you still have eyes on the other one kid?" Sean said but again resisted looking directly back and tilted his own small rearview mirror and saw the officer behind had now moved along the vehicles and was checking the driver's identity in a car just before a blue transit van.
On the tunnels opposite lane walkway, Hong lost sight of his men in the van as the lorry obscured his vision and as he began to gauge the speed of the traffic coming in the opposite direction so that he could cross to middle reservation barrier again he began to walk back, crouching low he received a couple of horn toots from approaching drivers.
Watching the Police officer ahead of him as he handed back to the driver in front of them his license. Hongs driver wound down his window, and while keeping an eye ahead handed out his papers.
"Danke dir, habe einen guten tag." *(Thank you, have a good day)* As the officer spoke he noticed his reflection in the glasses and took back his license then placing it back in his jacket, a playing card fell onto his lap, it was the Jack of spades. He was one of the bouncers that had allowed Vincent into the Senkin night club the first time, he had barely the time to remember the magician from the club as Vincent shot him through the neck then fired over his slumped head into the rear of the crew-cab, taking out the four in the back, when one ducked down he fired three times through the back of the seat in front, none of them had time to pull the guns from the bag in aisle.
Günther had pulled up in the clear filtered lane and was now stationary with one of the Policeman in front as Connor caught a brief powder flash behind them as saw the windscreen of the van splashed with blood,
"Shits going down Sean!" He said briefly turning to his brother and noticed with the sound of the blast of a horn on the opposite carriageway Hong, "One on our right, it's that fucking china man from the club." he said as he saw Hong bobbing up and down on the opposite side of the road, having noticed the car in front of his van had moved forward while his van had remained stationary.

"What the fuck is going on, gun! Floor it old man," Connor said seeing Hong now pull a revolver, but realized he was aiming back towards the police officer behind them near the transit.

Vincent had turned away from his victims dropping his gun to his side and casually walked back over to his towards his motorbike, he was about to lift his leg to climb into the saddle, when the first of Hong shells ricocheted off the side of the tunnel wall behind him, just shy of his helmet.

"Talk Lansford, do you know these people?" Sean glared at Günther as Connor ducked low covering their back, then watched as Vincent, picked up a previously out of sight Uzi machine gun that was hung by its strap over the petrol cap and sprayed a hail of bullets across the line of traffic towards Hong.

"There's some sort of wild west shit going on out there Seany," Connor said and it then he pulled a grenade from his jacket pocket, as the innocent passengers in the other vehicles that were held up in the queue screamed as windscreen shattered and bullets sparked of bonnets.

"Hold tight till I say" Sean ordered with his hand on the door handle, as he watched the officer in front make an exaggerated gesture to come forward past the lead police car to Günther, that showed he should act immediately, then to Sean's amazement he too opened fire on Hong across the traffic, allowing Vincent to climb aboard his motorbike and speed ahead passed them with his lights flashing and siren on allowing them to slip in behind as he cleared their escape, while others car drivers also began to speed away in panic with the less fortunate stuck in the queue blasting their horns and shunted the cars in front and behind them to get away from the incident.

Meanwhile, the lorry driver closest to the lorry laid frozen flat in his cab, causing further chaos blocking the traffic from behind.

Soon tailgating the Police motorbike Günther was in the free lane heading unhindered out of the tunnel, he gestured at Sean to lower his gun.

"You won't need that I hope you didn't drop the pin on that thing," he said, looking over his shoulder feeling the muzzle of Connors revolver at his ear.

"Please relax boys, Mr Westerberg was warned of the problems with a recent transaction you were involved with. He made enquires, it was connected to the people from the club you took me to, the Japanese, not Chinese Connor, although I understand your lady is Vietnamese, to be honest, I am never sure which is which any way Mr Westerberg decided to take additional precaution's, I am sure there will be no problems from now on."

"The paddy wagon is on our case, Seany what do you want me to do," Connor said seeing the police car emerge from the tunnel behind them and speeding to tail them.

"And what about these guys how do you know you can trust them?" Connor hunched down with his gun fixed on the driver of the police car.

"The one behind, he's my son, I would be grateful if you don't shoot him." Günther gestured backwards "and that one there on the bike, showing off, he is my nephew, I will have a word I assure you when we stop." he pointed to Vincent on the motorbike occasionally doing a wheelie as he accelerated away clearing the cars from the motorway road in front of them.

"So now a slight change of plans gentlemen and you get to meet the man you are working for before we continue our journey. Unless you want I should stop and let get out now?" Günther looked to Sean still holding his gun at the ready while Connor held up his hands with a complete look of confusion on his face and showing he had returned the pin back in his grenade,

"Your shout Seany boy, he's right that was the Jap, the big fucker you had a ruck in the alley of the club with, your girl's bodyguard they were shooting at."

"Yer how about it Seany boy? I think I'll have one of those cigarettes now." Günther winked.

"Ok but no more surprises Mr Günther Lansford, or whatever your ficking name is." Sean clicked back the hammer and lowered his gun but placed it in his jean jacket pocket, as his mind began to wonder, had he been mugged off, had Suzy set him up with her father's thugs.

"It's Günther, Günther Brahn, thank you," Günther said as Sean leaned over and lit his cigarette.

Their police escort gave them fast passage along the autobahn until Günther gave them advance warning.

"A mile up we are turning off before Basel centre, nothing to get alarmed about, they will dump the police vehicles and continue on our way." Günther could see Sean was unconvinced.

"And we will meet your boss, man?" Sean confirmed, looking for any sign they were being duped.

"Yes, Mr Byrne, if that is your real name, you will meet Mr Westerberg, my son." Günther saw a look of complete confusion hit Sean's eyes.

"Everything is going to be ok Irish trust me; everything is going to be fine, you'll see."

On the outskirts of Basel, they pulled into a dilapidated industrial zone with the police car racing ahead. In one corner with dual access they arrived at a remote warehouse on the outskirts of Basel, Günther pulled up the hand brake.
"Time to get out gentlemen." By now Sean was living every second as if it was his last and Connor was only a breath behind him, watching for a single hint they were being played.
"If we would want you dead, my nephew would have killed you when the two of you left the club the other night, very, very, very drunk, take out your bags." Günther then stopped and watched as Sean and Connor stepped out of the camper, both stood watching as the older police officer approached Günther and Sean tried to make out what they were saying, still unconvinced they were amongst friends.
"The boss at the bank Salter- Kingl... whatever his name is, anyway he gave me this, said it was important, I must give you, soon as, and you should read it immediately, but ... something else, I think it is not from him. something in his eyes, it was as if he was following orders and wanted to know himself what it contains, I think?" Günther shook his head, and noticed a stray bullet had caught the canopy of the camper vans roof, "Some show you put on back there, I don't know about these boys, but I wasn't totally sure who you boys were aiming at."
He handed Sebastian the envelope from Salter-Kingsley and then drove the camper van up the ramps on to the back of the transporter. Sebastian looked across at the Byrne brothers and removing his helmet opened the envelope and began reading the contents as he walked towards them, Sean was convinced something in the letter made him smile at first, then something turned his expression stern and the colour briefly flushed to his cheeks, as if he held back anger, his eye lifted from the page and fixed on Sean's for a moment as if Sean was not there, then they focused on him.

"I am Sebastian Westerberg, gentlemen, you can relax, you need fear nothing from us. I am sure you have questions, first probably, what that was about in the tunnel and why are you here? So, my cousin Vincent," He gestured with his hand and Vincent waved to them as he began checking the Uzi he had used in the tunnel, "he informed me the owner of the club you took Günther to, planned to have you killed in the raid they staged today, Vincent read their lips." Sebastian said as Vincent handed him a bag with a change of clothes, he had taken from the back of the police car where two petrol can's sat.
"Help Günther secure the Camper before you burn the car and bike," Sebastian said and signed.

"Do we have to burn the bike?" Vincent signed with a frown, and although neither Sean nor Connor read sign language, it was clear from his expression what he was saying as he removed his sunglasses and both boys realized he was the magician from the Senkin night club.
"Help them, kid." Sean gestured to Connor as he watched Günther placing blocks under the wheels of the camper.
"So with respect, Mr Westerberg it would appear, we now owe you and your..... nephew a debt, what now, it would seem you have made another arrangement to return home, I am wondering does a man such as yourself have need of our service?" Sean said gesturing to the lorry and an unmarked Fiat 128, as he watched Sebastian re-read the letter Günther had given him.

"You owe me nothing m Byrne, I had something in mind already, if you wish to continue the journey with us, something a little more permanent than your present employment with the bank, however this letter concerns other business I have with the bank and something else that requires my immediate attention, regarding family. It changes things for me, for us today here." he signaled to Günther he wanted a drink, then turned back to Sean "... and maybe you, Günther may have told you I know about your recent problems with a similar shipment, I know who was responsible."
"Merryman, the banker and the club owner, it would be no surprise," Sean said and thanked Günther as he accepted another cup of coffee from the flask he had taken from the camper van.
"Apologies I forgot the sugar," Günther said, then taking out a small battered tin hip flask, poured some of the contents into a cup which he passed to Sebastian, then he handed the flask to Sean.
This simple act relaxed both Connor and Sean, something he had learnt from his son. So that now both men were totally focused on what Sebastian had to say, instead of watching to see if this was all some elaborate trap.

"Yes the banker, but he is nothing, as is the American club owner, true the men that work for him, men we have killed, belong to the Nakumota Yakuza clan, they will want answers, but that need not concern you. The man Copeland I am reliably informed is ex-CIA if there is such a thing anymore. It was they who did not want the gold you brought from North Africa to reach its destination, they instructed Copeland to make the heist something to do with a transaction with a Somalian you are acquainted with, and an individual that this letter informs me is still in Geneva, someone I must now acquire." Sebastian folded the letter over.

"So Copeland is CIA and his people at the club and at his chateau Yakuza, his daughter, scammed me?" Sean tried to work out what he and his brother had stumbled into.

"Maybe so, maybe she knows nothing of her father's plans, either way if you wish I will ask Günther to settle your fees for the job you were booked for and we part here. You and your brother may leave, and I will inform Mr Salter-Kingsley you assisted in preventing the loss of our money." Sebastian handed the letter to Günther, who began to search for his glasses then realised he had left them inside the camper van.

"Our?

I notice you use that term, so what is this, a family run business, are you the boss or is there someone you answer to?" Sean watched as Vincent began to entertain Connor with card tricks.

"Well Mr Byrne, we all answer to someone, in my case it is my family and those who work for me to some extent. But, yes, I am the boss, when my wife allows me." Sebastian smiled and was pleased to see the brothers appeared to be less on edge.

"As I see it, Mr Westerberg, as I have already said, we owe you and your cousin a debt and besides Günther promised us a meal in Sweden, but first I would wish to settle things with the banker Merryman myself, I am not one for a grudge, but find sleeping in the past has been eased when things that were left undone are settled." Watching as Sebastian removed his police uniform disguise and began to strip changing into fresh clothes in front of them as they continued to talk, immediately Sean realised Sebastian had a strong muscular physique of a disciplined man, he changed as if he was a man used to being in the company of other men, under similar circumstances, army.

"I assure you, Mr Byrne, as much as I can put the skills you and your brother have to work for us, I don't want anybody at my side that wishes to be somewhere else." Sebastian whistled to Vincent, and he came over and took his helmet and the bag, now filled with his uniform, and placed it into the back of the police car

Sean looked at the camper van, "I take it you are still taking that to Sweden?"

Sebastian nodded "Yes but as I say this changes things for me, this is important I need to return to Geneva and locate someone, and if it the person I think, then I will persuade them to return to Sweden with us."

Sebastian noticed the look on Günther's face having heard what he had said as he looked to the letter in his hand and fixed his glasses in place to begin reading.

"So this person, how much persuasion will be required to convince them to join you?" Sean realized his gun was still in his hand and placed it inside his waistband.

"Well it is possible he may require an incentive, but as I said, it is important, maybe more important than that." Sebastian gestured to the camper van.

"That's important, but I take it you don't want to leave that lying around while you go back." Sean watched Günther being helped by Connor to tighten the holding straps and close up the back of the lorry.

"No, that is going back to my family. I have arranged safe passage across on the ferry, we have people in place in Sweden to see it safely home."

"But there is something in that letter, something else?" Sean said, nodding to the paper in Sebastian's hands.

"Quite right, very good, yes, the person who wrote this, I believe, is a friend. The letter also warns me someone else is looking for me and my family, someone who may hurt my family in my absence. I have people, guards at home in Sweden but I would prefer someone a little more capable of handling any situation watching over them, while I organize this and need someone to also explain why my return has been delayed, Günther is...." he saw a look of recognition on Sean's face, "ah, he told you he is my father yes?" Sebastian smiled, "It's true, did he also tell you how old he is, no matter, anyway he will return to Sweden with the gold, but I would feel better if he had company and you would be further compensated." Sebastian raised an eye at Connor.

"And so now you will go to Geneva with Vincent, yes?" Sean received a nod from Sebastian as he went over to the Fiat and opening one of the holdalls he began to remove bound stacked dollar bills as Connor came over catching sight of the money.

Connor brought over Sean's bag "So what's the craic? Is this the divvy up, are we done?" Connor asked as Sean, noticed Vincent was reading their lips.

Sean took his bag and walked past Sebastian and placed it into the boot of the Fiat and saw three oozy machine guns each with a double taped magazine clip of spare ammo, the type you would use if you had no time to change magazines in a fight, Sean knew immediately whoever Sebastian Westerberg was he was without a disciplined soldier and like no other businessman he had ever met.

"No, boyo you go to Sweden," he said without turning back "With the old man, sorry no offence, Günther." Sean apologized as he turned around and saw a look of acknowledgement from Sebastian, who then handed Connor some of the money he had removed.

"What is the problem, we go on now, quickly, yes?" Günther said and looked as perplexed as Connor.

Sean watched as Günther read the letter and noticed his expression became agitated, he looked first at Sebastian, then Vincent and then appeared to reread the words. The woodsman was struggling to understand who could have written such a thing, struck in confusion at the reference, in Walter mentioning that he knew Günther's true identity and spoke of Stefan as if in the past tense, as if dead.

Dear Mr Westerberg,
Please appreciated I write, with a concern that if this letter falls into the wrong hands both your and my position will be compromised, but I sincerely hope you understand the sincerity of my writing and wish to prevent a tragedy occurring.
I had wished to speak in person, but it has become necessary to contact you in this way, so I will be brief, I am an associate of Herr Wolff.
1/ I was a friend of your father and mother in Berlin, many years ago in the army, as proof, I can say that I consider Günther B, the gamekeeper as a friend from those times, who you are acquainted with.
2/. The organization I represent, concerned about your recent activity at a financial institution, have dispatched prior to my knowledge of your heritage, individuals to ascertain the legitimacy of your actions, possibly forcefully!!
3/ I will endeavour to cancel this action, I must stress there is no guarantee I will succeed. You should take immediate steps to address this potential threat yourself.
4/ This is the same organization you demonstrated a wish to make contact with, regarding an audience with members belonging to the 1940 scientific community of Berlin.
5/ A member of this community, who your father Stefan was acquainted with in Berlin is departing Geneva. Sunday 13th April 1975 at 10.00 the Gardens de Anglais.
6/ The individual Dr N will be accompanied by gentlemen from Africa that may resent and wish to prevent a change to his travel arrangements "and such like"
WT

"So, who wrote this, they know me, how?" Günther looked blank at Sebastian and Sean.
"The last sentence Gunt read it again and think of Berlin," Sebastian said giving him a clue, Günther hovered for a moment none the wiser and then read it again.

"And such like, who says that?" Günther asked, scratching his chin
"You know dammed well old man. Walter, he must have realized it was you that activated the account. Walter Thomas, after all these years, the adjutant, he is still involved with all we left behind, like that spaniel at your heels woodsman."
Sebastian's eyes glazed over with a memory of his youth, as he watched Sean go over and explain to Connor why they were to separate.
"I'm going back with them, they have unfinished business and so do we. I wouldn't sleep well knowing the man who had a go at killing me twice was still out there. I'll wipe the slate clean, you know what I mean."
"The boat, shit, I liked the boat, one thing, make sure you bring my suit back." Connor's eye's flashed with concern.
"I won't forget your suit; you follow his lead, he knows the country, but don't let him get you hurt." Sean then turned back to the boot of the Fiat and pointed to a sniper rifle case.
"Will we need that?" he looked at Sebastian, who shook his head, "No."
"I will feel happier if you don't mind." Sean handed it to Connor, who knew exactly what the case contained without opening it.
"I told you it was time we moved on, I'll pull most of our wedge from the bank if I can, when I get to Sweden we can talk about what we do next, for now you do as Günther says and remember what I say, nothing is ever straight forward so when you get over there keep frosty till I join you." Sean patted him on the shoulder.
"So what, you take the Irish, and I should stay, no, if you go back then we send Vincent home, if things don't work out here, he would be more useful over there for your girls, in the long run."
Sebastian looked to Vincent and then at Connor, they were probably only five years apart.
"Ok we do it your way, Vincent put your stuff in the truck you're going home, I have made arrangements with the police Chief Nilsson he has people in place, you will not be stopped on your crossing, with this now I will have him meet you in Malmo when you arrive and I will contact our people on the hill have it locked down."
Sebastian saw a look from Connor at the mention of the police.
"It's ok, the Chief in Sweden is a friend, he will help," Sebastian said, as they watched Vincent push the motorbike outside to be burnt, alongside the police car in the yard.
"No, it's not that, I thought the magic man here was deaf?" Connor said, gesturing to his ears.
"No, no, my friend, Vincent is mute, he can hear as good as you and I, it's just something he's always done, picked up at the special school he went to as a child.

Helped him turn a disadvantage into a skill that has, with respect, on this occasion, saved your lives." Sebastian smiled with a sense of pride, then walked up to Vincent.

"These people whoever they are they are not to make it to our home you understand." He signed but spoke loud enough that Connor could hear.

"I understand." Vincent tapped the watch on his wrist that he had once taken from the Stockholm pawnbroker, the first man he had ever killed.

With Sebastian, Sean and Günther heading back to Geneva passing the scene of carnage they had caused in the tunnel that was still being cleared up by the emergency services, with a tailback stretching out from the Geneva side of the tunnel for several kilometres. Reluctantly Vincent handed one of the petrol cans to Connor and then watched as he poured it over the police motorbike, once alight they began to head north again towards Travemunde.

In the chateau at Saint-Prex on the north shore of Lake Geneva, Copeland had been waiting for news from Hongs team, watching the time and calculating the distance they would have covered on the route map to Travemunde, marking off each location he had marked as being potential sites for the hijack of the shipment to be staged, he looked at one of his wall clocks, it was three-thirty, by now they should be approaching the tunnels of Frankfurt, again a site he had chosen for Hong. Copeland had hoped to have heard something by now and was totally unaware that his team had already failed, yet again, as he heard the familiar steps of his daughter coming down the stairs in the hall.

"So where's Hong, I'm off to the club get it ready for tonight," Suzy asked, as she entered Copeland's study.

"He will be in touch when he's done running errands for me, make sure you take that with you, the bloody thing doesn't stop yapping when you're not here." Copeland looked at the dog in her arms.

"Don't listen to the nasty man Binki," she said, pulling him closer to her chest.

"I was thinking, maybe it's time we get him a friend, maybe a Rottweiler, I hear they get a lot of bad press. Apparently, they are very affectionate." Copeland looked at his phone and let it ring five times before answering, hoping she would leave, but she didn't.

"He's back," Merryman said with a tone of panic as soon as Copeland picked up the receiver.

"Whose back?" Copeland sat forward.

"The Irishman Sean Byrne, I've just seen him outside the bank picking up his BMW across the street." Merryman looked across the trading floor and saw Plácido Zabala looking at him and closed the venetian blinds to his glassed booth office.
"Are the others with him, do they have the gold?" Copeland asked.
"I don't know, I was in the reception talking with our girls, and he just showed up." Merryman held his hand against the receiver speaker as Miss Bishop appeared on the other side of his door holding some paperwork, he gestured her in and directed her to place it on his desk, he could hear an irritated Copeland in his ear calling his name, he waited until she left the room. "Yes I'm here, what do you want me to do?"
"We'll find out you fuck and call me back." Copeland slammed the phone down.
"Fuck, fuck me to Sunday and back those motherfuckers, he looked at his guard. "Your fucking paddy boyfriend has fucked me again, and Christ knows where Hong is." He sat back in his chair, staring at the map marked with red X's, wondering how his plan had gone wrong.
"What you say, Daddy, Sean what's he got to do with this, what have you been doing?" She looked to the guard sitting in the office for an answer, but he lowered his eyes.
"Get her out of here, do I have to do everything my fucking self......shush! shut it "
As he spoke there was a low buzzing coming from his desk, Copeland opened the drawer and saw the red light flashing on his encrypted phone set, picking up the receiver, "Hello" knowing full well who was on the other end of the line.
"General?" he said, gesturing forcefully to his man to take Suzy out of the room.
"Frank, don't speak, just listen, you're name has been tagged onto some shit storm over there, with a bank and those involved with the fuck up with the African's, I have no idea where you intend to lay your head tonight, but my advice and it's the last words you'll hear from me, find a hole and don't ever surface, and if you are thinking of looking to your Yakuza friends don't, you haven't enough fingers to put this one right." With that, the line went dead.
"Benji...General ....fuck!" Copeland looked out of the window as he watched Suzy's mini disappear along the drive,
Having received word Tom Quinn was gunning for him, Carter-Wallis had was busy burning files and cutting all leads to the operation he had initiated with the Spider weapons factory in Brazil, unconnected with Copeland's operation that day it was the last thing he needed to hear. Copeland dialled the number for the Langley operator, but the telephone tone signaled the line had been cut.
"Fuck!" He gathered the map up in his hands and crushed it into a ball and then went to the study window hearing a car arrive outside, it was Hong, who had

managed to evade the rescue services by hiking across the country away from the scene of the attack in the tunnel and eventually flagged down a taxi.
"Those fucking Irish, I think it's time we make a direct withdrawal from the bank ourselves, we'll pick up Merryman as soon as he leaves the bank, tonight, we'll hold him here until Monday morning then pay Mr Salter-Kingsley a visit."

Onboard the ferry at the Port of Travemunde having parked the lorry in the vehicle bay, Connor and Vincent went up to the bar on the second deck and sat playing a game of trumps, settling down for the eight-hour ferry crossing to Malmo, Sweden. With only one company, Finnlines, operating the ferry service, Sebastian believed for those men who Walter had said were headed to their home in Uppsala, because they would be carrying weapons, it was the most likely way they would enter Sweden through this route, rather than by plane.
"Ok?" Connor asked and signed having been taught a few simple sign language gestures by Vincent.
"Not bad, but you can speak, I can hear as good as you." Vincent signed back. Connor had noticed the scars on Vincent's neck but decided not to ask.
"Sorry, you said." Connor apologised, there was something about his travelling companion the Irish boy found a little unnerving, he moved quietly, and it was not just because he did not speak. Twice as they had wandered around the ship's deck searching for signs that the men sent by Spider were on board the ferry, he had turned around to find Vincent standing behind him without realising he had been there.
Connor began to relax as he sipped his pint and he smiled watching how methodically Vincent arranged himself at the table, his lighter stacked just so on top of his cigarettes and then as he produced a pack of cards he placed the empty box carefully to one side. It appeared to Connor that he moved slowly, studying everything around him, except when handling the cards, then his hands and fingers moved at lightning speed, he considered the wisdom in playing cards with him. Vincent noticed Connor's eyes lift from his card hand as he watched, two heavily set men walk in from the side deck and move towards the bar, one was talking in German as they ordered drinks and held a copy of the Münchener Post folded open on a sports page with images of the world cup winning West German team having been honoured in the city.

"Vincent can you understand them" he pointed to his lips and Vincent nodded yes as a slightly older man joined them. Connor downed his beer and got up to the bar and bought two more and some crisps, which allowed Vincent to casually swap places with him so that he now faced the men. As the men turned to step away from the bar and moving to their own table across the room, Sean noticed one had a leather shoulder holstered weapon beneath his bomber jacket.

Connor returned to their table and with his back to the men made a gesture with his hand like a gun "armed" he raise his eyebrows with almost a mischievous smile as he placed the crisp bags down and they began to pretend to play cards as Vincent read from their lips what they were saying.

"So this guy Paul Olsson is local police, he will keep them off our back?" one of the younger men asked.

"Yes, he'll meet us at the dock with a van and the site plan." the older man answered, he wore a shirt and heavy Dockers jacket and appeared clearly in charge.

"And he's sure they have only six guarding the house and factory and nothing heavy?" his younger colleague continued, unaware they were being watched.

"Yes, the principals are the man Westerberg, his wife and two girls, they are our only concern the old man Lansford, the guards, any others we leave, unless they play hardball, if it goes fluid then we torch the site, the factory keeps chemicals, make it look like an accident. It's a fucking long trek eight hours drive from the port, if we arrive in Malmo by eight we should have enough time to do another recon, then hit them tomorrow night, show me the map again," he ordered, then raised his eyes as the man opposite checked his inside pocket finding it empty

"Scheisse, I left it in the car." his companion swore,

"I'll go, order me a burger or something, I'm fucking starving." The older man got to his feet, heading to the door which held above it directions labelled down to the vehicle deck.

Connor waited till one of the other men went to the bar, then followed the older man outside. Hanging back behind their lorry that was parked on the same level but eight cars back, Connor climbed into the driver's cab and sliding across, quietly lowered his window and tilted the side wing mirror so that he could watch the man. When he emerged from the car with the map, Connor ducked down low in the cab as he heard the man pass by, he watched him disappear into the stairwell and then slipped out of the lorry and went back down to look around the car. Pulling off an aerial of an adjoining car he stood on the end flattening it then bent it back to make a catch that he forced down between the rubber of the driver's door, a skill learnt on the streets of Dublin, with a few twist there was a click and the door lock button popped up allowing him to open the door.

He briefly checked the car park then leaned in and searched the car seeing a packet of cigarettes on the dash he took one and then seeing the car had an internal boot release pulled the lever and saw through the back window as the boot popped up. In the boot were three holdalls and then beneath them under the carpet were two gun bags each with a scoped rifle, the men intended to use to take out all the security guards on the Westerberg spa complex.

"Find what you were looking for?" Connor turned to come face to face with the older man wearing the docker jacket having returned to get his cigarettes, who was now holding a flick blade. The German growled and lunged forward, Connor span to his side, trying to deflect the blade with his wrist, but the blade slipped through the opening in his jean jacket and sliced a ribbon of material from his T-shirt that immediately plumed a fine line of red, Connor flinched back as the man slipped on the greasy floor, but regaining his balance smiled and looked at the blood on his blade. Connor felt for his revolver and realised he had removed it when climbing across in the lorry cab earlier. He began to circle round with his hand out as the man swiped the blade through the air towards him, Connor sprang forward and gripped the man's wrist and for a brief moment had control, pushing his arms upward, but the man relaxed briefly, and the pulled the hand with the knife away as his coated wrist slipped through Connor's hand, and once again it cut a fine deep wound into Connor's palm.

"Fuck!" Connor swore and shook his hand, blood droplets were flicked over his attackers face, and he smiled as he wiped his mouth and tasted Connor blood, then stepped forward as they jostled round Connor was once again with his back to the boot of the car glancing to his side he saw the tyre iron and deliberately looked in its direction and the man also saw the wrench, In a fake play Connor dived to reach into the boot, in an effort to block him the man again lunged forcefully forwards as he did Connor reached back with his arm almost falling back with his full body weight on the boot lid trapping the man's hand inside, Connor slammed down hard on his wrist as the yelled in pain, in one movement Connor released the boot lid and then again thrust down while kneeing the man in the side then allowing him to pull his hand free he saw he had released the knife and Connor reached in and grabbing the tyre iron swung it outward catching the man squarely on the side of his head just above the ear, not a deadly blow, the man staggered forward toppling towards the boot bleeding, clutching his head, seeing his blade in the boot he made a grab for it, but now off balance and stunned Connor was able to move to one side then shove him further into the boot with one hand now on his knife and the other on the boot edge supporting himself as he pulled himself upright Connor jerked the boot lid down slicing the man fingers, then immediately swung the iron across the man's temple, he twisted over brought down to one knee and with his head now resting over the boot lip Connor pulled the boot down on his neck repeatedly, until there was an audible crack of bone and as his neck snapped the man slumped like a rag doll to the floor.

Connor dropped the tyre wrench covered in his own blood from the wound to his hand and wiped his palm over the man's back as he pulled a rag from the boot and began to blot the cut to his palm. He closed the boot and stood over the body as he checked the car deck for signs their fight had been witnessed.

In the lounge bar, Vincent got a look from one of the men as he continued to play cards on his own, the man looked to the door and gestured to his colleague concerned their superior had been some time, and Vincent watched them get up and leave their food.

"What are you doing?" one of the men shouted having found Connor inside their car, positioning the man he had killed, so he appeared to be sleeping in the back, and as he emerged, he saw they both had guns in their hands.

"It's not what you think," He said as the saw he was bleeding and tried to look through the rear window at their colleague.

"Ok it is " Connor said seeing that Vincent was approaching silently from behind, then there was the sound of two air bursts like a tyre being pumped up, and both men fell forward, each held the look of surprise and realization this was it as their guns clattered to the floor and they fell forwards onto their hands.

Vincent moved forward and pumped one bullet into the back of each of their heads, and they dropped face down.

Connor staggered back and checked the vehicle hold for other travelers hearing voices in the distance.

"You ok?" Vincent signed

Connor nodded with a wince, "Come on, boyo, let's get these boys inside."

Having made it look as if the men were sleeping in the car they wiped the blood from the floor with clothes from the bags and removed the two gun bags and their passports, then Vincent treated Connor's wounds using a medical kit, which included some of Sebastian's formulated Westerberg Pharmaceuticals antiseptic cream.

"You guys think of everything. Fick" Connor said taking another swig of vodka as Vincent began to stitch his wound.

By the time the captain called the drivers to return to their vehicles the effects of the vodka and pain killers had begun to take effect, and Connor sat slumped in the front of the lorry, as they pulled onto the dock behind they heard the first horns of irritated drivers stuck behind the Germans car.

As organised by Sebastian, Chief Nilsson was at the dock to step in to escort them off, but as it turned out, they sailed through control with no stops.
"Problems?" Nilsson looked to Connor slumped in the front.
"Nothing he couldn't handle" Connor slurred.
Vincent then wrote on a note pad he had on the dash.
"You have a bad officer Paul Olsson? They may send more of them." he then gestured back to the docks
"Leave it with me, you get back to Björklinge and the family, I'll have one of our cars posted on the road up to the facility and get a man up here."
On arriving at their home, Vincent put the site on lockdown, having explained what had occurred on the journey and handed over the letter that Walter Thomas had sent to Sebastian to Katrina, on which he had added the name, Walter Thomas. Connor had his wound treated properly, then joined Vincent on the roof of the main factory building with a sniper rifle, watching the gated entrance, while they waited for news from Sebastian and Günther. Meanwhile, Katrina and the girls, along with Aunt Krysia, stayed within the main house with three armed guards.
As Günther stepped onto the small jetty the lights from Geneva were flickering in a ring from the last ripples of the lakes water spout fountain, that seconds before had been switched off for another day, for a moment as the lake became as still as a millpond, he felt transported back in his mind to the ancient timber pier in Baja Sardinia and the evening when they made their escape from the island in September 1943.
"Stay, behind and wait, till I make it safe," Sean said.
Sebastian looked at Günther as they watched Sean, drop down into the wheelhouse and make his way to the hatch that led to the lower deck berths and living quarters. Less than a minute later he whistled calling them down. Sean had placed the kettle on as they came down the steps, Sebastian pointed to the Guinness can with a guitar string wrapped by its side on the table and then pointed to another similar booby trap set on one of the overhead window hatches, each can was stuffed with explosives and six-inch nails then was ringed with taped nine inch nails.
"Out of tea, coffee only. There are fresh towels on the side if you want a shower." Sean said as he took three mugs from the small locker, having started the boat's diesel generator.
"Coffee is fine, thank you," Sebastian said as Günther picked up a towel.
"I'll go first," Günther said, then paused on the door threshold into the small shower room and watched Sean, as he lifted a cabin box while he waited for the kettle to boil, removing a false bottom he revealed an assortment of weapons including two

Uzi machine guns and additional magazine cartridges, he placed them on the kitchen table, then went back to making the coffee as if he had just laid the table for dinner.

"You appear to have prepared yourself well, expecting company?" Sebastian smiled as he accepted first a cup of black coffee and then the bottle of J&B scotch Sean handed him.

"Well you can never be too prepared, but we are safe for a while I think, if it was the club owner today and I agree it looks that way, I think he will lick his wounds, tonight, he may come but I doubt it, more likely tomorrow and by then we shall be gone, hopefully with this doctor your friend has told you about." Sean raised his glass gesturing cheers.

"You got anything we can eat?" Günther emerged drying his hair, and Sean noticed some of his army tattoos, including the Reich eagle on his arm.

"Some cans, beans, soup help yourself." he gestured to one of the overhead cupboards.

"So you have given up on the idea of getting this man Copeland?" Sebastian asked.

"No, but as I said I owe you, Copeland can wait, if things go smoothly tomorrow for you, then fine I may hang back when you leave and deal with it, we will see, can I read the letter from your friend again," Sean asked.

"I'm sorry I gave it to Vincent, but I have total recall of its contents, I can tell you exactly what it said." As Sebastian then recited the letter word for word as it had been written by Walter, he caught something in Sean's expression when he came to paragraph six. "What is it, Mr Byrne?

"It may be nothing, but these African's, he mentioned, I may know them, we may need those." Sean gestured to the Uzi machine guns.

"Well, as you said, you can never be over-prepared." Günther turned from stirring a pot of beans, "I like your boat." he added as he tasted the sauce.

Chapter 19: The Blade Bait

Geneva, Switzerland
May 1975

As Sean's Silver BMW pulled up parking adjacent to the park, one of the rear markers of Cawil's security team slowed, noticing in stepping out, Sebastian wore a scarf covering his face, and that he had left his door open.
"General!" He called ahead, Musse Bin Abokkor turned, immediately placing his hand on his hip holster seeing Günther, also with his face covered, join the group approaching them on the path from behind.
Then seeing the revolver held low in Sean's hand, Musse pulled his own gun but did not raise it, recognizing the Irishman.
"You are sure of this, Mr Byrne?" Sebastian felt the weight of the machine gun hanging over his back from his shoulder and left it there but placed his hand in his pocket, feeling for the handle of his Glock revolver.
"I'm sure please wait." Sean held a hand out to his side in a calming gesture.

Merill Nestlar and Klaus continued walking with the two lead bodyguards towards the waiting cars, Klaus noticed one of the drivers resting on the roof look past them and stand back to see what the holdup was while the other continued watching the street and pedestrians entering the park.
The two rear members of the Somalian security detail now halted, pulling their weapons free to challenge Sean's advance, as he reached the far side of the gothic bronze Cherubim circular water fountain that is the centrepiece of the park. Hitching the barrel of his gun into his hand, Sean shielded it, as he caught a quizzical smile from a ten-year-old girl sat sharing a sandwich with her mother on one of the nearby iron park benches that ringed the fountain. With hands kept low, he slowed his pace and stood in the open and waited for Cawil to see him.
"Cawil" Musse called and the young Somalian span back, immediately his personal bodyguards, keeping in step at his side, slowed as they were just about to approach the path leading out towards the furthest park exit and the cars. Sensing a problem, Klaus also stopped walking and pulled up behind Merill Nestlar.
"Stay close, something is wrong." He whispered and casually checked his jacket was fully open, allowing quick access to his shoulder holster.
Cawil squinted to see what Musse was referring to and Nestlar noticed the quizzical expression on his face relax and a faint trace of a smile form on his lips.

"Wait with them," Cawil ordered one of his personal guards then slowly strolled back, joining Musse's side and placed his finger on his arm, seeing he had pulled his revolver.

"I know this man wait here, guard the doctor," he said and walked towards Sean, shadowed by one his men as the others began to ring Nestlar, in a heightened state of alert.

"Be quick Cawil we are in the open, the cars are waiting." Musse's tone was edgy as he watched how Günther and Sebastian staged themselves behind, with Sebastian closest to the open BMW rear passenger door. Sean took three steps forward to greet Cawil, and they shook hands. Tilting his head to one side and looking past Cawil and Sean, Musse began to move up, seeing both men behind had what he took to be light machine guns, slung over their back out of sight, apart from the last inch or so of the end of the silencers, visible below their coats.

"Irish you picked the wrong place and time for a reunion, my men are waiting." Cawil smiled gesturing to the lake and then to the streets, as pedestrians filed back and forth laden with goods from Geneva's busy Sunday market.

"Who are your friends they are making my men nervous?" He waved his hand over his face, referring to their face scarf, "why do you not cover your face like them?" Cawil then scanned the park for a sign of Connor hidden out of sight. "Where is your brother?" The young Somalian was as wary as a cat but still smiling widely.

"I wanted you to see it was me and it is just these gentlemen and me, Connor is out of the city. It is good to see Cawil again. I hope your Uncle is well. I think we both smell better than the last time we met." They shook hands as Sean spoke.

He had said less than three words to Cawil at their first and only meeting but chose to use his first name to evoke the memory and establish trust, remind him of whom he was, not that Cawil needed the reminder.

That morning with the side streets leading to the FNIG bank and towards the market closed, the Mossad surveillance van was parked kerb-side at the edge of the park. General Zavi, having received the information from Tom Quinn regarding the exchange in the park, had been authorized by Tel Aviv to carry out an abduction operation and Ruby and her team were on high alert, having received the green light to snatch both Doctor Nestlar and Klaus Ritter. The acquisition of their targets was scheduled to take place at a pre-arranged location where a second team confirmed by radio they were standing by, on the slip road into Geneva airport. Their expectation was with a controlled show of force the Germans would be released to them, and if they decided to resist there was little chance of civilian involvement. The Somalian's had booked six seats on a direct flight back to

Mogadishu, Mossad was going to make sure two of their passengers would not make the journey. With a helicopter waiting at the opposite side of Lake Geneva near Montreaux ready to spirit the ex-Nazi scientist and his guard over the border into Italy where at Turin airport a Mossad Lockheed C5 Galaxy sat waiting on the tarmac to take them back to Israel.

Leon gave the portable TV screen a tap, as the screen grey fuzzed with the occasional passing motorbike and then received a tap himself from David the Mossad surveillance technician.

"What the fucks this?" He said, focusing his camera on the central area of the park display and Sean's image, gesturing to Ruby. She leaned over his shoulder and looked to Leon sat opposite on the milk crate.

"No idea, get in closer, I think that's the guy from the other morning, one of the bank's security team?" She said.

"Quiet there's a lot of chatter and background from the waterfall, they couldn't pick a worse day for this shit." David frowned, pushing his Sony headphones tight to his ear.

Sat up front in the cab pretending to read a newspaper, Marc the driver turned his head back out the window, looking, through the railings as the park foliage was occasionally stirred by a light gust, he could make out Sean approaching the waterfall in the open, looking back from his position he could see Sebastian standing just inside one of the park's side entrances, in front of the BMW parked askew to the pavement, eight cars back from their position. Then as a breeze caught the laurel bushes, he caught sight of Günther for a moment and immediately recognized what was partially hidden hanging off his shoulder.

"It's him from the banks, his car is back there, and he has company, two with Uzi's, these guys mean business," he said and folded his paper up.

Using the manual handle above his head to operate the hidden camera inside the hoarding on the roof, advertising Jacque's Boulangerie et Patisserie, Leon began to pan across the park and zoomed into Günther's covered face then back to Sean, "Any ideas?" He asked Ruby.

She shook her head, "No, Tel Aviv, turned up nothing from the photo's we sent them, this guy is a ghost, and there is nothing on the old man, the other one could be anybody?"

"Yanks, Brits?" Marc asked.

"No, Zavi said the Yanks are on board, the Brits ....no, freelance more like whoever they are if they get in the way of the doctor and the shit that killed Mel, then we drop them, they're not innocents with that much firepower."

Meanwhile, the image of Sean was also caught on the screen in the Mi6 Surveillance van, parked nearest the street that led to the bank and market beyond, on the opposite side of the road from the BMW.

Pimm had arrived in Geneva the night before and stood, hovering over Collins, their own surveillance technician, he glanced down at the headshots Bull had received from the meeting in Highgate with Tom Quinn.

"That muddies the waters somewhat, get a call in with Bull, the Yanks were telling the truth, now all we need to find out is what the hell the IRA is doing with a bunch of ex-Nazis and a Somalian warlord."

"The Israeli's are on the move, Sir?" Collins tapped the video monitor, having picked up the image of Leon stepping from the side door of their van then entering the Park. He took up a position on one of the wrought iron seats set on the main outer path that ringed the central water fountain and watched the meeting whilst pretending to read his newspaper, looking over a flower border full of blooming tulip heads.

"Ok let's keep calm, our Tel Aviv friends can be a little nervy, I have a feeling they are not going to wait for this one to play-out. There are a lot of innocents out there, this could go bad very quickly gentleman, so get ready, if it comes to it, headshots only." Pimm pulled his revolver from his holster and checked the magazine and gestured the other two Mi6 operatives did the same.

In the park nearest the waterfall Cawil rechecked his men behind him and gave them a reassuring gesture to stay put. "Sorry I'm in a hurry Irish, no gold today to move, as you see I have my own people, what do you want my friend?" Cawil's tone was calm even though he also noticed Günther and Sebastian appeared to have guns concealed.

"Your Uncle told me your people are people of honour?" Sean saw Musse appeared to be getting restless.

"So we are, it is more important to our men than anything, money, women even love. What of it?" Cawil looked to the movement of the trees, felt the wind on his face and sniffed, he sensed the tension in the air.

"The man you have, I need to take him," Sean nodded towards Merill Nestlar then gestured back to Günther and Sebastian, "They need to take him."

Cawil looked past Musse who by now was sweating and had begun to crouch low to one side, having thought he saw movement near the Mossad blue van. Leon felt the tall African's eyes on him but kept his cool with his head down and turned the pages of his newspaper, while hidden behind on his lap a Glock rested on his crotch.

In the Mi6 van, Mark Collins handed Pimm a bulky mobile phone,

"The embassy has patched me through to London, Sir, its Mr Gordon."
"Bull, Its BP, Day one, when I get back we need to talk about the deep end, Some sort of exchange is going on down here in the park near the bank, I have eyes on that nasty piece of work Bin Abokkor with a team of six and two of the Germans from Rio. Looks like the Somalian's are going to set up shop back home, with a brain drain. But the Intel from the Yanks was good, about the McLoughlin lambs being in town, Drake will need to be informed." he paused watching the screen seeing Leon sitting alone and looking very obvious.
"Bull the clocks' ticking on this situation, I have eyes on the older boy, Sean, armed to the teeth and in bad company, no idea, maybe an IRA cell over here, no sign of your third man, the American, but it looks like they intend to upset the Somalian's departure arrangements. It's all very, pally-pally at the moment. But Bull, as usual, I'm playing catch-up. Unfortunately, our Israeli friends have an interest in this clan gathering, and one of the German's is the one that killed Lamb and their boy. You know how personal they take that sort of thing. Five will get you twenty this will go south if it doesn't play as they want, we can expect a heavy body count from the locals, I have a trio in play with me, what are your orders, Sir?"
Pimm watched the pedestrian traffic on the monitor, "do a 360 his brother must be out there, somewhere their like Siamese twins." Pimm examined the photograph of Connor as he waited for an answer from Bull.
"Stand down BP." Pimm could hear a reluctance in Bull's tone, then he tapped the TV monitor as it appeared Musse was not convinced Leon was just there to read his newspaper and had begun edging forward past Cawil, off the path looking over the tulip heads, focused in Leon's direction as a couple cycled past oblivious to the threat.
"Let it play, let them have their show, this was a tip from the Yanks, if McLoughlin moves away, stay with him, but don't mix it up with the Israelis, I can't be doing with another trip to Tel Aviv this side of Christmas, my budget doesn't stretch to that, you guys are strictly on a bird watch pass with the Swiss, unless the Yank turns up, Gordon out."
Bull hung up and looked across at the Post office tower still under repair sheeted with scaffolding.

In February 1975 the IRA agreed on a truce until January 1976, but Mi6 were aware they still had ASU (Active Service Units) stationed in England and were continuing to prioritize IRA counter-intelligence. The truce was to be broken with the bombing of the Caterham Arms pub in Surrey on 27 August 1975.

"So it looks like the bank is the key." Miss Thompson said, looking through the glass partition to the operation wall with pictures of Merryman and Salter-Kingsley linked by string guides to other subjects of interest.
"Without a doubt, a ship with many rats. Get me Monsieur Gathon at the Swiss embassy will you duck, I think I should prepare him for some bad news. Then rustle up a complete log covering our time and interest in Geneva. if this goes tits up I want to have our arses covered with Control and last for good measure put in a call with Tel Aviv, General Zavineski, he'll play hard to get they'll tell you he's not there but tell them I need to speak with him even if he's on the moon."

In the park in Geneva, as a sign of good faith to Cawil and the increasingly nervy Musse, Sean placed his gun in his waistband.
"That is what your Uncle told me, so I am here to ask you to let me take this man, just the old man. You can tell him he will be safe." Sean gestured towards Nestlar and caught a stern, threatening glance from Klaus who began to challenge the bodyguards at his side about why they had stopped.
"Cawil! We go now." Musse called, but Cawil raised his hand.
"And these men your people what are they to you, what do they want with the German doctor?" Cawil gestured towards Sebastian and Günther
"I don't know my friend, but I am here asking," Sean said, and he saw a look of recognition in Cawil's eyes.
"I see, so a debt to be paid between you and them, honour tests us all at some times, huh?" Cawil said and glanced briefly back to Nestlar as Musse came up beside him and whispered in his ear, sneering in Sean's direction and watched Günther and Sebastian take a step forward.
"Get the doctor," Cawil stared into Sean's unblinking eyes.
"Cawil! Your Uncle will not be pleased." Musse held his gun to his side, at the ready, flicking his attention back and forth, between Sean and his men behind.
"General Bin Abokkor it was I that convinced my Uncle to spare you when the ship was lost, you will stand by my word now," he continued to look at Sean, "Do it!" he barked.
David in the Mossad van shook his head and looked to Ruby,
"Are you catching this, our orders are to grab the doctor before they get to the airport. If he leaves with these guys, we may lose him. I have no dammed clue who they are, but they appear to be serious." he tapped the screen, pointing at the machine gun barrels, poking out from beneath the coats of Sebastian and Günther.
"Fuck we take them here, I'm not losing this Nazi scum again he killed Mel, I'll get ahead of them take them on the path, wait till I'm in place," Ruby said, uncovering

two similar machine guns hidden under sacking and passed one forward to the driver then checked the magazine in her own.

"What about the people in the park?" the driver said.

"I'll think of something, make it loud, scare the shits away, just be ready, this is on me if it comes to it, the doctor does not leave or that shit from Rio guarding him," Ruby said then ducked low from the back door of their van.

In the park, Musse approached Nestlar and gestured with his gun to follow him.

"Come, change of plans." he nodded towards Sean and the others.

"Nien! We go on we have an agreement, what is the Shit?" Klaus snarled and went to pull his weapon but then felt a gun at his back.

"If he pulls his gun shoot him," Musse ordered his men and Klaus stood back from the group.

"Fuck you!" Klaus cursed defiantly.

"Come, doctor, please." Musse gestured again, Merill Nestlar looked at Klaus then reluctantly stepped away. Moving cautiously forward he cleaned his lens, looking towards the group he did not recognize Sean, but by the time he drew alongside Cawil, he sensed something familiar about the two men behind, in particular, the younger man. Then Sebastian spoke, and the tone of his voice struck a chord in a distant memory of the doctor, he paused and looked to Cawil.

"Into the car Doctor Nestlar, if you will please, you are quite safe, you need not be concerned, you are among acquaintances of Herr Wolff." Sebastian saw Nestlar's eyes flicker recognizing Adolf Hitler's Pseudonym, used within the Spider network, but his expression did not change, and Sean and Cawil witnessed the confusion in Nestlar's as again he cleaned his glasses.

"It can't be," he said, turning first to Sean "Who is that? Behind, it can't be him he's dead?"

"Go doctor now!" Cawil ordered, not understand his reluctance or relationship with the men behind as Sean nudged him forward and then turned back to Cawil,

"What of your Uncle, he'll not be happy?" Sean watched the perplexed Nestlar as Günther stepped forward shepherding him towards the door of their Vehicle "In the back please doctor." Günther said in German.

Nestlar stopped in his tracks at the first sound of his growl, realising the truth, as past memories joined with the present, and he recognised the woodsman was the Adjutant he had first been introduced to in Berlin during the war. He continued moving but seemed to have gone into a trance of disbelief as Günther returned to his station shielding Sean's back.

"My Uncle taught me his code, he will understand, honour is all we really have of our own, everything else we borrow for a time, land, houses, money even friendships sometimes, besides there are others I am sure who can take the German's place." Cawil ignored the look from Musse as he shook his head, almost as confused as the doctor, then focused again on covering the area towards Leon. "He told me your name is to remember the son he lost, I'll remember you, friend," Sean said and shook Cawil's hand and turned to go.

"Ok catch it all on tape we hold and watch, the McLoughlin's and the bank are the prizes, if we get the bank we get the whole rats nest," Pimm said, then saw Ruby emerge from her van and straddle across her motorbike parked behind, kick start it then take off toward the end of the park cutting the Somalian's off from their parked cars.

"Fuck it, this girl doesn't play well with others," Pimm said turning the dial on the screen and the wide-angle lens, hidden amongst the ladders and window cleaning equipment strapped to the roof, opened up. He watched the images of the ordinary people enjoying the park that morning, pulling the vision back he saw Ruby had skirted ahead of the group and was about to mount the pavement to re-enter the parks pedestrian path, returning back towards the fountain.

At that exact moment, a gust of wind caught Leon's newspaper, lifting it just enough for Musse to get a glimpse of the suns reflection of the gun in his lap. He pulled Cawil back by his shoulder, and seeing him raise his weapon, Sean reacted turning to see where he was aiming to shoot and began to unload his own shot as Leon dropped to the floor and twisted back behind the bench that was pelted with bullets. People in the park stopped what they were doing, there was the briefest moment when the air hung still while they tried to make sense of the sounds they heard and then as the Somalian's opened up again firing towards Leon a chaotic race of the innocent fleeing towards the nearest exits as the screaming grew in intensity, some running straight into Ruby on her bike, while others ducked to the grass.

"Jesus Ruby you picked a hell of a spot for a bun fight!" Pimm said as he watched Leon get hit in the shoulder then drop behind the bench.

Hearing the sound of the approaching bike engine and the screams as some of the civilians dodged out of the way of Ruby, the Somalian's and Klaus immediately turned their attention to her. With the first shell hitting the path in front of her, she leaned back dropping her motorbike on its side setting it free, letting it slide it tumble over, spilling fuel and oil towards the group of Somalian's. Her helmet took a glance from a bullet as she set two shells towards the tank of the bike and it erupted in a ball of flame and smoke injuring the nearest two Somalian's, but not fatally. Ruby rolled across the grass and clung to the back of one of the four square granite podium monuments set around the water feature, chips of its stone could be heard being nicked away as it was pelted on the reverse side by bullets.

Pimm watched as having pushed Nestlar down, Günther stood across him, and both he and Sebastian began an assault on the Mossad van, as the two other agents jumped out to assist Leon, while Ruby cut across to him as tufts of grass cut away inches from her feet caught by gunfire.

"In the car now!" Sebastian snapped at Nestlar, and for a moment the doctor was caught in his glare, then darted past him as Leon's bench disintegrated in a hail of bullets and Leon slumped forward dead.

"I thought London's orders were to sit this one out, Sir?" The Mi6 cameraman turned on Pimm as he reached for the door handle.

"They'll be slaughtered, you two get out of here." Pimm shook his head and pulled the sliding side door dropping to the roadside, hidden by their van. As he shuttered a bullet into the chamber of his revolver, the door opened again, and Collins joined his side. They took up positions at either end of the van as the Somalian's began to group around Cawil shielding him and began making their way back towards the far side of the park where their cars were waiting. Both Somalian drivers began to fire across the roof in the direction of Ruby pinning her down, preventing her from joining her colleagues.

With a blast from an Uzi that took out an innocent bystander in the street, Pimm signaled Collins, and they both broke cover. Crossing the road, they came upon the same side as the Mossad van and began shooting towards Günther and Sebastian's direction, through the water fountain that bronze figures chimed caught in the crossfire.

Günther dropped low now caught in the open and away from Sebastian and Sean, he took cover below the high lip of the fountain pool.

"Get the car ready, keep the doctor safe," Sebastian ordered, and Sean judged with the arrival of Pimm their advantage had altered as two of the Somalian's dropped to the floor. He caught a look from Cawil, and he shook his head as he was covered by Musse shielding him with his body as they retreated towards their cars.

Günther looked down at the woman praying as she lay across the pram, now on its side, covering her child hugging the edge of the fountain.

"Stay down, do not move, even when it's over," he told the women as the lip of the fountain was caught by Pimm's bullets.

Then everyone ducked low with the bark of loud gunfire unlike anything that they heard as significant chunks of stone were torn from the park's monuments including the fountains bronze statues that disintegrated as branches were slashed from the trees, one of the Somalian drivers had removed an M240 heavy machine gun from

the boot and began opening up across the park targeting anything that moved, covering the escape of Cawil and Musse.
Some shells tore unhindered through the steel rails of the park into the street traffic, and the sound of cars crashing to a halt as drivers were hit was mixed with the horns of confused drivers and screams of those cut down in the street, as loved ones were culled at their feet in the ensuing crossfire.

Klaus turned towards the Lake, then hesitatingly back looking at Nestlar now lying across the back seat of the BMW, shielded by Sebastian who began to cover Günther's retreat. As Ruby caught full sight of Klaus's back, she let off two rounds, catching him low above the buttocks and he fell forward to his knees. Within seconds blood appeared at his lips, he shouted towards the Mossad crew, cursing them, then taking a revolver from the hands of one of the fallen Somalian guards he began to shoot both guns, catching Ruby's driver who had joined in the attack. Pimm less than a metre behind Ruby let off a shot and hit the Somalian in the throat, Ruby looked back and gestured to him her appreciation, instantly recognizing him. Then they both began to target the driver with the M240 machine gun, within four rounds he dropped his weapon as sparks off the car roof sent fragments into his eyes and he ducked down on the other side out of sight, seeing Cawil and Musse climb into his car, he jumped behind the wheel. The Machine gun slid off the roof into the street as they sped off with both doors on that side open, the front was almost ripped clear by the next parked car. While the other driver stayed and continued to field the fire of the last two remaining Somalian bodyguards.
Pimm turned towards Günther, still pitched low behind the waterfall, and could see the legs of the woman crouched near him. Günther held one hand covering the head of the child as the mother pulled her close beneath the lip design of the fountain pond.
"Remember, don't move!" His husky whisper settled the women back and seeing Sean had now reached the driver's side of his car, Sebastian began laying down fire towards Ruby and Pimm, with along blast he leapt back towards the street and the nearest tree cover between himself and their BMW. Ruby could not see the woman with the child from her position and seeing Pimm reloading stood firing over his head catching Günther in the back of his right shoulder and then again in his right hip and watched him drop to the floor.
"Irish gun!" Sebastian shouted, and Sean threw him his Uzi over the car roof, then Sebastian sprang forward like a panther pushing a new magazine into his own gun and standing fully exposed, opened up with both machine guns obliterating the

meagre cover of Pimm and Ruby, Collins was struck immediately twice and rolled back, dead into the flower border.

Günther said nothing, his breath extinguished by the initial burn of the bullets entering his body, his hands pushed against the path and dropping his weapon he grappled to his feet, and as if in a rugby scrum barged forwards landing in the back of the car face down on top of the disheveled Nestlar. Looking back through the open car door he saw that woman who had been taking cover alongside him behind the waterfall, was now lying lifeless huddled over the pram in pool of blood. A mother's last heroic and desperate selfless act to save her child.

"Scheisse" Günther growled and buried his head into the cushion of the back seat, biting down on his forefinger as the pain from his wounds began to register and thousands hundreds of brittle fragments of the cars window glass scattered over his and Nestlar's body.

Outside, now alone, Sebastian continued to keep heads down, as he sprayed the air with bullets while walking slowly backwards towards the car. Feeling the door open on his back, he threw his guns to the ground and stepped into the passenger seat and before his door was closed Sean slammed his foot to the floor burning rubber as they mounted the pavement at points to escape along the traffic blocked main street, back across the bridge to the north side of the lake, passing police and ambulances coming in the opposite direction.

"Boat, now!" Sebastian ordered, and they cut back down into the underpass at the far side of the bridge, where they ditched the BMW and Sebastian had left Sean's rigid inflatable dinghy with twin outboard motors. As they crossed the lake heading towards the northeastern bank, Merill Nestlar watched a fireball plume erupted from the delayed incendiary Sean had left in the car.

"Do what you can for him, doctor," Sebastian ordered him pointing at Günther, as the blood from his wounds began to seep over the rubber walls of the boat and Günther slumped down, grimacing each time the bow of the craft buffeted the water.

"Hold him tight," Sean said as he drove the boat up onto a reclusive shale bank near Corsier, where they transferred Günther into Sean's VW Golf. Only four minutes to the French border, it was Sebastian belief f they were traced across the water, anyone tracking them would consider they had headed into France, instead, they casually turned south and headed back towards Geneva along the coastal road of Route de Thonon,

Stopping briefly in the hotel car park across from the mooring site of the Helena at La Belotte, while Sean picked up additional ammunition from the boat and the few medical supplies he carried, Sebastian had Nestlar treat Günther's wound, dumping the bloody rags he had used previously into the bins of the hotel and then they continued towards Geneva, but before heading directly in on the coast roast they turned west circumventing the traffic chaos within the city they skirted a prearranged route to come back into the city from the west and drop into the underground car park of their apartment, where Sebastian believed it would safer to hole up. It had taken them an hour and thirty five minutes since leaving the park and retrieving Nestlar, by the time they set the delirious Günther down on the bed he had lost nearly two and a half litres of blood and Sebastian's mind began to consider all possibilities with regards to getting him the right medical services and supplies as he watched Nestlar examining his wounds and Sean turned on Vince's portable Television and began to scan the stations for a news channel.

Less than a five-minute drive away Oliver Pimm walked the scene of the battlefield, while bodies still lay covered under sheets.
"So you took out this one, his passport says he is Klaus Ritter, You know him?"
Pimm looked sideways at Guillaume Lelt and gestured "No."
Lelt was the Senior Director of the FIS, *(Swiss intelligence service)*, knew Pimm was lying and raised his eyes.
With only a modest complement of twenty-five employees, for the most part, they monitored what other international agencies did on Swiss soil when those agencies such as Mi6, CIA and Mossad brought them into the loop, which was rare. That would all change since the massacre in the English garden, which was what the international press was calling it having mistaken the Jardin de Anglais initially as a British location.
It had come from the top floor of Century house, as one of the few surviving combatants Pimm was to offer all assistance to the Swiss, without divulging additional resources and personnel still on active service within Switzerland.
For Oliver Pimm having remained to assist saving the lives of those civilians caught up in the exchange, his cover was now blown. Soon after the first police arrived on the scene, a travel show film crew who were working on one of the yellow taxi boats, having captured some of the action during the firefight, once docked continued to film the aftermath.

His story was that he was there as an observer having traced the German's from Brazil. Control decided at his age to burn him as an agent in view that his actions had helped neutralize some of those responsible, and in remaining to assist with some of those that had been hit he had aided in saving lives, in particular, the film crew had captured his full headshot while he worked on chest compressions spattered to his elbows in the blood from a sixteen-year-old girl, the images were now being played on most global television news networks.

Pimm's personnel files in Department Drake had already hit the shredder and Berni Martin, and Bull Gordon both spent most of the afternoon with the top brass on the thirteenth floor of Century house being drilled down.
The only saving grace was the girl Pimm had worked on survived. Some French Newspapers would run a story the next morning calling him a British knight in shining armour. Pimm was finished as Sandman and Mi6 field operator at least that is what he thought as he looked out at the hordes of camera-wielding news crews baying behind the red and white police tape that sealed the park off, that afternoon. As he sensed Lelt's frustration he decided to relax, It was likely he was going to be fired when he returned to London, he knew that the least he could do was help the Swiss who had lost many people and if someone had to begin the healing process. Reluctantly he gestured toward Klaus.
"His real name was Henri Krause, The East Germans have said little, other than he was one of theirs, jumped the wall outside Berlin during an exercise on the border in 68. Since then he has been working within the Nazi Spider organisation. We believe he has been responsible for at least two other hits on industrialist's that either had become expendable or would not play ball with his people and of course you read my report Bull, Mr Gordon, passed to your governments concerning the loss of our agent in Rio and the Israelis."
Lelt looked around the park at the last remaining body bags being loaded onto ambulance trolleys as they walked towards railings.
"I understand that a car will take you back to your hotel, I may wish to speak again before you leave if your people allow it." His tone was cynical, resentful that he should have to ask approval to question Pimm on Swiss soil.
"Whatever you need, understand I did what I could to stop this," Pimm said respectfully.
"Yes, I am sure you did. Otherwise, we would not be talking out here." Lelt shook his hand.
As Pimm ducked his head to get in the car, he looked for signs of Ruby, but she had already been whisked away by her people.
Monday morning at the chateau Copeland had still not raised Carter-Wallis, he stopped trying as he watched as the news broke on CNN that an unconfirmed Pentagon source had leaked word of a story that was going to make Watergate look like a Doctor Zeus book.

Copeland began to make arrangements for his own relocation to a beachfront retirement safe haven he had in place on a remote Island on the Sulu Sea in the Philippines, a gift from a grateful ex-client Ferdinand Marcos, in his appreciation for Frank Copeland's mediation in a CIA arms shipment. Copeland had not visited the property once in six years and was aware it was little more than a shack, nothing like his chateau, he would need to additional recourse to live as he had in Geneva and so he decided to make a final stop at the FNIG bank before his departure.

"Bring the banker to the car Hong, we are going to make a withdrawal," Copeland said as he turned down the volume of the news program reporting the Jardin Anglais incident that had been playing all through the night.
"This is your fucking Irishman, you know that don't you, I should have had Hong kill him in the sauna," he stood to go "Well I blame myself, I have always been soft with you girls, now I will kill him myself, tell me where he is."
Suzy looked at the television, "How do you know this is him?"
Copeland snapped "Of course it's him! It's two streets from the fucking bank."
She went to protest, and he slapped her hard across the face.
"Where does he keep his boat?" he ground his teeth as he held her cheeks squashed together so that her lips puckered tightly and she screamed at him trying to pull free. Clawing at this his arm her long nails ripped into his flesh drawing blood from his wrist, but he did release her, she looked away expecting another blow to the face, but he released her as blood wept from her talons.
"No? You won't tell your dear old daddy, no matter the banker will know," he said as he let her go, and she slumped in her chair tears forming at her eyes.
Copeland looked up and smiled as Merryman appeared in the hall,
"Good Mr Merry-Merry, just in time to join the party, smarten yourself up and get in the car, we're leaving." The banker looked pale and disheveled, having been kept captive, all be it within one of the chateau's plush bedrooms, he had occasionally heard the angry ranting of his host coming over the past few hours and now considered if he could get back to the city he would try and make a break for it.
"Consider yourself grounded, young lady," Copeland said in a matter of fact way as he barged past Suzy's chair.
"These gentlemen are with me, Claude," Merryman answered the door security guard Claude Dennee, inquisitive expression as Copeland and Hong accompanied him through the revolving door of the bank, Hong held one hand at his back ready to pull his revolver as Merryman raised his hands gesturing the guard back off allowing them to pass.

"That's not necessary Francesca." Merryman told the receptionist when she stood to welcome them, "we are going to my office, is Mr Salter-Kingsley in?"
"He is in his office on a call, Sir, terrible news about the park" She answered, and gave Hong a glance as he removed his hand from his back.
"Yes yes, I saw very bad," Merryman answered, and Copeland gestured his agreement towards Francesca and smiled
"Don't say a fucking word!" Copeland snarled in a whisper as they approached the elevator and then gave a reassuring nod towards Claude who was still watching their progress as the lift bell pinged and doors opened.
On the third floor, Merryman took them straight into Salter-Kingsley's office, Miss Bishop stood, and Merryman made the gesture that it was alright and they marched into Salter-Kingsley's inner office. Salter-Kingsley looked up from his call, and his eyes held confusion at seeing Merryman walk in unannounced. Then about to protest, he held his tongue as he watched Hong close the door and pull his revolver.
"Panic button?" Copeland asked, Merryman gestured to the right of the desk of Salter-Kingsley's desk, "If you press it you are dead, so his he and so are all your staff, sit back take a breath Peter old chap and hang up, then tell your secretary to hold your calls no disturbance, nod if you understand." Copeland spoke in sharp, distinctive orders, and the banker nodded his head.
"I'm sorry Trevor something has come up, can I call you back later this afternoon, good, thank you." Salter-Kingsley leaned forwards slowly and hung up the receiver while keeping his eyes fixed on the gun Copeland had drawn. He pressed the intercom on his desk, "Miss Bishop, please hold my calls no disturbances, I'm in a meeting."
"Would you like refreshments for your guest Sir?" she asked, Salter-Kingsley looked to Copeland, and he frowned, then gestured, "yes, Earl grey" he said and then when Salter-Kingsley looked to them the American shook his head as he sat on the edge of Salter-Kingsley's desk, "my colleague is fine, Merryman is fine, sit Chas!" he ordered.
Salter-Kingsley was careful as he relayed the request to give no indication there was a problem, and as soon as he removed his finger from the intercom Copeland nodded his head to Hong, and he shot Merryman in the head, catching his body before it slipped from the chair, blood began to run from the exit wound soon his collar was bright crimson and his suit shoulder became darkly stained as it blotted with the bankers blood. Hong casually crossed the banker's hands over his lap as Merryman's lifeless head rolled back at an acute angle his mouth fixed open.

Peter Salter-Kingsley had only ever heard a silencer shot on the television, for a moment he thought one of the men had farted. Then he pushed back in his chair and began to hyperventilate as he watched Merryman's head flop back, his eyes crossed open as blood dribbled from a small hole in his forehead. Copeland did not turn to look and moved to sit on the edge of his desk and began to make a shushing sound.

"I know, stay calm, he's gone, now think only of yourself, you can do this you can live. Mr Merryman was stealing from you, did you know that and your clients?" Copeland saw the disbelief in his eyes, "that right, he was, so I have done you a service, so to speak."

Copeland looked around the office, his eyes, like so many before him came to rest on the certificate of membership to the Nazi party of Salter-Kingsley's grandfather. He examined it closely, then there was a knock on the door, and he turned, gesturing to Hong, who opened it, just wide enough to take the tray from Miss Bishop, from her position she could only see Merryman's leg and hand and Salter-Kingsley gestured all was ok, thanked her and she closed the door.

Copeland returned to sitting on the side of the desk and lit one of his Panther cigars, "So now that I have done you a service, I think it only fair you return the favour. You see this weasel of a man has cost my colleagues and me a great deal and I have to tell you on a personal note, he has caused staffing problems. it's not so easy to get reliable help these days, anyway, I digress, your first question will be what do I want, so we start there and hopefully, we can be out of your hair, and you can return to your call to clever Trevor."

Salter-Kingsley felt like he was taking part in some elaborate prank, Copeland's attitude was almost light with a cynical edge verging on crazy, then he looked again at Merryman as Copeland sipped his tea.

"Focus! Look at me, please Peter, look at me," he said with a smile,

"Ok first things first the recent disturbance you have seen in the news regarding the shooting in the tunnel, you may be aware it involved one of your clients and as I understand, two Irish gentlemen that you are acquainted with, I would like the contact details of both, now, the client and the Irish." Copeland replaced his cup in its saucer and watched Salter-Kingsley as he realised what was at the bottom of their visit and the death of Merryman.

Merryman must have been the inside man involved with both the attack on the container gold shipment belonging to Mubarak Ali Hassan and the attack on the Westerberg's, he leant forward and span his Rolodex.

"Merryman dealt with the security team, the Irish brothers, but this is the contact details Sean Byrne gave me. I believe they live on a houseboat or something moored on the lake. As for the client, I have a name, like most clients, it's probably a pseudonym, no contact address or number, we offer a private anonymous drop box facility within the Metropolitan hotel here in Geneva." Salter-Kingsley looked to see if Copeland believed him and was relieved when he took the card with Sean Byrne's details.

"Ok, good, so now you have a safe here in your office I expect, I understood from Mr Merryman you have many accounts that are never accessed, so please do not fall at this last fence, I am not a greedy man, but I will have some compensation, then you may go about your day." Copeland followed Salter-Kingsley's eyes to a wall cabinet.

Hong walked along the wall and pointed until he came to the large austere oil painting portrait of the John Morgan Kingsley and feeling along its inside wall edge located a catch, and the large painting hinged away from the wall revealing a safe.

"But of course, best to keep it in the family." Copeland smarted

"7 left, 11 right, 21 left, 23 right, 27 right, open the door with the key inside on the right, there is a button, it opens the money tray," Salter-Kingsley said with some degree of relief, realizing they had no intention to steal from the bank's main vault which would have made things far more likely to go wrong.

Hong did as directed, and an inner cabinet swung out from the wall safe, revealing deep built storage shelves, stacked with sealed blocks of money and smaller gold ingots.

"What about him? Now you will kill me." Salter-Kingsley asked.

"No, there no need, call the police, tell them there has been an accident, you confronted an employee he shot himself, I am sure an investigation will find Mr Merryman's private accounts were not normal, and a search of his home will uncover a significant use of drugs." Copeland handed Salter-Kingsley the phone, "first send your assistant outside to fetch for another coffee, that way, she will have a reason for not hearing the shot."

Salter-Kingsley realised the man he was talking with was no ordinary criminal

"Don't touch the stack on the bottom left!" Salter-Kingsley suddenly jumped forward in his chair, "it will activate a silent alarm."

Hong froze and looked to Copeland, who nodded "Do as he says."

Copeland sat down opposite Salter-Kingsley's desk

"I suppose you will need to get another skiing partner, I can always let you have the girl JoJo if you wish." He said patting Merryman's leg, realising the banker had finally begun to calm down as he watched him press his desk intercom and ordered his secretary away from her desk outside his office, as he watched Hong remove

from his safe eight 400 ounce gold ingots and approximately $150,000 in notes, in various currencies.
"If the police ask you can tell them we were an internal security team you hired, I don't know how you keep your books, but a smart man might use this as an excuse to get rid of any other discrepancies in accounting, that is up to you." Copeland stood as Hong removed his silencer and having smeared some of the blood from the back of Merryman's head on the barrel, placed it in his hand.
"Good, so have a pleasant day, perhaps our paths will cross again, it's a small world after all" Copeland sang the song from the Disney theme park adventure ride, "but let hope not, eh?" Copeland's word carried a definite threat, "I will look for Mr Merryman's obituary, goodbye, Pete."
Salter-Kingsley sat alone looking at Merryman's corpse for a moment with the phone in his hand then dialled for the police and reported his suicide.
He was just hanging up when the knock at the door was Miss Bishop with his coffee, on walking in she shrieked and dropped the cup, spilling the contents across his deep wine flock carpet, to which he tutted and then noticed the matted pool of blood at the feet of Merryman chair, *"Oh! Well."* he thought.
As immediately, other traders within the bank on hearing Miss Bishop's cries began to congregate outside his office. Salter-Kingsley rose and closing his door, tried to settled her down. Copeland and Hong were already stepping onto the street when Claude Dennee was eventually called to the third floor.
"Go tell Francesca in reception, the police are on their way and to send them straight up. They may wish to speak with you, and when they are done, you may go home early, this is a great shock I am sure." Salter-Kingsley looked across at Merryman and rather than thinking he had survived, he was considering Copeland's words and remembering accounts that Merryman had been involved with and which he could divert money from and blame on him, he didn't need Copeland to point out the opportunities that could be exploited from Merryman death.
With a member of the Swiss Guard stationed outside his door, Pimm was watching images of himself on the television in his hotel room, when the call came in from London.
"Is that an order?" Pimm asked Bull as he lay back on his bed and lit another cigarette, having just been told he was being recalled to London, booked on the 6.30 flight Tuesday morning and was to remain in the hotel until the car picked him up in the morning.
"Don't be like that old fruit, I've been taking shit loads of flack on this thing BP, and now the Yanks are pulling rank on the Geneva Bank. You know how it works now the cats out of the bag regarding Carter-Wallis everyone is trying to catch a picture

holding the winning catch, Tom Quinn will have his hands full just trying to get a mention, thankfully I dropped a word in Controls ear, gave him the heads up last week, so they are hard pushed to leave him out of the honours list over there, not that Tom can't handle himself. As for the rest of the circus on the top floor, between you and me there are few kidders that are letting it been known they apparently knew the CIA was grooming one of the senior executives for months, they've got as far as claiming he's Spanish, but none know his name, again yours truly hedged his bets last week before I sent you over there told Control the CIA had a mole they were harvesting an estranged son of whose parents who were mixed up with the Basque separatist movement, somehow they were listed as dead, turns out they were rotting in a cell in Salamanca. Courtesy of some imaginative intervention from Langley they have been reunited WITSAC have been keeping him on ice in Mexico, now he's landed they're going to put him into play, had already confirmed to Tom you boys were going to keep him out of the loop, in trying t catch the McLoughlin boys. In exchange as they'll have access to all the accounts, they have guaranteed they will pass on details of charitable donations made by US Irish patriots to aid the boys in Belfast, they'll be no chance of extradition, but no doubt we'll pick up some crumbs. All in all regardless of the poor souls caught in the middle we didn't do too bad, but unfortunately my old son it's over for you over there and I'm sure you probably have already guessed, seeing as your mug is plastered across every paper from Timbuktu to Tokyo, your field days are over. I'll see you in the office when you get back that is after the top floor is done with you, to be honest, BP it's a tossup between you getting a Knighthood and a serpentine dip with concrete willies, Bull hung up."

Pimm hung up and seeing he had drained his room mini-bar called reception to have it restocked, "May as well abuse it before you lose it...old fruit." Pimm raised a bottle of Holstein Pilsner to his own image, in the sideboard mirror as his phone rang again, it was Executive FIS Director Guillaume Lelt.

"We found the inflatable skiff, just outside Corsier about 30 kilometres beyond the headland, that side of the lake it's all old money, big houses, very big, they targeted an old couple, left them tied up." As the inspector spoke, Pimm looked at his map a found the location.

"Not much left but what was there had blood, a lot of blood, we have men at the hospitals and clinics, but I think they head to France, its two minutes to the border and Italy, Germany they could be anywhere by now, odd thing, they put in a call to the garage in Corsier, telling them where the old couple was, not what you would expect for those that caused all that shit at the park."

Looking at the area around Corsier, roads and number of buildings Pimm, considered they may have enlisted forced help, for whoever it was amongst their group that was injured,
"Just a thought, we had a man we were running down once, we cornered him in a veterinary surgery, on my map I show three within five kilometres, as you say old money they love their pets." Then he listened as Lelt expanded
"Well interesting, we will look into it, but I think those not injured are long gone, there was a report of an explosion, a boat that moored on the same side of the lake at the village of La Bellotte. I am heading out there now, there are reports of a body recovery, it could be the same man. It occurred to me you may be able to assist my enquiries, I can send a car if you wish?" Lelt waited for Pimm to respond.
Pimm looked to the door knowing there would be someone watching in the hotel reception from London, even if Lelt pulled the man from the door.
"I will find my own way, thank you, Inspector." Pimm hung up and then checked his spare gun magazine and threw on his Harrington bomber jacket. Leaning out of his bedroom window, he looked along to the bathroom window which had a large soil pipe feeding the toilets as there was knock at his door. It was the room service restocking his bar as the guard allowed the maid in Pimm removed one of the beers from the trolley cracked the cap off and handed it to the Swiss guard sat outside his door.
"Drowning my sorrows, here, it's a long night," he said and gestured to the empty bottles on his coffee table and once the maid had replenished his stock he took out three more bottles from the fridge opened the bottles and then having poured the contents down the sink placed two bottles along with the empties he had already drunk on the coffee table, so that anyone entering the room would initially consider he had drunk his fill and gone to bed. Then he placed blankets in his bed to make it look as if he was sleeping, he turned the lights off.
As he emerged, backing out of the bathroom window he was witnessed by the driver of a green Citroen 2cv, she turned the engine on as she watched him scale the wall then pulled up alongside him,
"On a night prowl Pimm? Get in." It was Ruby.
"I heard you were ordered back?" He said.
"Yer, I heard the same about you, good work with the young girl in the park." She said
"Well someone had to stay around and try and clean up that mess, shame we didn't save them all, I think my undercover days are over, probably have me in Mi6 mail room licking stamps when I get back." He sighed and then told her of Lelt's phone call and then gave her directions.

"Well if it's a consolation, I'm ordered back to Tel Aviv, I will be on a kibbutz next week picking oranges, Huh" She laughed and then informed him that like Mi6, Mossad had been warned away from the FNIG bank and Salter-Kingsley and that they had now received the full paperwork on Sean and Connor McLoughlin.
"Well, at least you got that shit, Klaus." Pimm
Arriving at the small dock in La Bellotte where Sean and Connor had moored The Helena, they were waved through by Lelt, two bodies laid on ambulance gurneys and the Director held a torch on the faces of the body of one as it was unzipped. Hong's face was bloated in death and was scarred badly from what must have been a blast from below as from the shape of his body bag he appeared to have nothing left below his stomach.
"I don't know him, I'm sure he was not in the park, he may have been in the car."
"The other is the woman from that hotel. She was found inside; double-tap to the head, professional." Lelt gestured over the street.
Pimm looked at Ruby, and they both gestured they had not seen them before then Pimm pulled down the zip further and noticed the six-inch nails embedded into his flesh and as he did both he and Ruby noticed the Yakuza tattoo on his arm, but Lelt did not.
"I think I know who did this, can we look at what's left of the boat." He asked as two heavily clad bomb disposal officers passed them by.
"It's clear Sir," one with a small spaniel dog on a lead said.
"Yes be my guest, anything to catch the bastards that did this today." Lelt waved the ambulance crew to take the bodies away.

Copeland along with Hong and another of his team had followed up on the information they had got from Salter-Kingsley and located Sean and Connor's boat. Unfortunately for them having picked up the supplies Sean had replaced his welcoming committee booby traps for any uninvited visitors. Having quizzed the hotel owner of what she knew about the Irishman and found the bloody rags in her bins Copeland had killed her.
Then he had made the mistake of climbing aboard the Helena, while he had moved stealthily to the front and begun to look through the overhead glass bulkheads to the rooms below, Hong had forced the latch on the berth stairs and begun accessing the hull by his third step he tripped one of Sean's booby traps, the IED shredded the timber berth and instantly disintegrated Hongs lower body. Outside on the deck, Copeland himself did not come away unscathed as a secondary device exploded within, sending a mixture of timber and glass shards upward into his face and body, one nail piercing his wrist as he shielded his face and was blasted over

the side into the water. Semi concussed Copeland's man dragged him out and drove him immediately back to his chateau.

"Director may I use the facilities in the hotel? The man, I feel quite ill." Ruby made an expression as if she was going to be sick, making an excuse at seeing Hong's mutilated body. However, Pimm knew she had an ulterior motive to leave them, she had seen worse than that.

Inside the hotel, she called her people from the hotel phone and received the answer to her question, "Who was Yakuza in Geneva?"

The answer given was like lighting a fuse, as Copeland's name filtered through the Mossad intelligence service and across the continent to America, as a name believed to be associated in some way with the massacre at the Jardin Anglais.

"There were two one got away, look here." Pimm pointed to the bloodstains on the remains of the deck where Copeland had been standing and then at the rope dangling free from the handrail, "I think whoever it was here, went over the side, you may have one still in the water, might be worth having your men check along the bank, see if he crawled out on his own."

Pimm looked at the nails that pierced wood and sails, and then as he went through the blackened room, he turned back to Lelt.

"Someone came looking for the men you hunt, the man I fought in the park and his friends, they clearly didn't know who they were hunting, this is the work of two Irish brothers that Six believed were taken out by their own people in London three years go. Get your people to look for pieces of coke or Guinness cans and the cord will be fishing line, that's as much as I can do, now I need to get back to the hotel, I'm on the first flight back to London in the morning" Pimm notice a bottle of J & B laying on its side and knew whose den he was in and became concerned the Swiss bomb disposal team had not made a complete sweep and began to back up,

"My advice Director, you keep your people off this until daylight and then have your bomb people look again if this is the boyo's I think they may have left other surprises."

Lelt froze and began backing up the way he came, "Can you give me a name between us?" He asked, expectantly.

"McLoughlin, Sean ad Connor, travelling under the name Byrne, I wish you well with your hunt Director, I am sorry we had to meet under such circumstances." Pimm saw Ruby coming back from the hotel.

"You done? I'll take you back, to your hotel," she said and thanked Lelt.

As he watched them drive away, he looked to the hotel and began to consider Ruby's absence, finding out she had made a call he called his office and had them trace the number, while waiting he looked at the ambulance crew, they had bagged the remains of Hong and were about to set off.
"Wait!" he called and climbing inside checked Hong's body again, this time seeing the Yakuza tattoo
Lelt knew where he had seen the red Koi fish pattern and gathered his team to go to the Senkin night club.

Chapter 20: The Breaker Zone

Geneva, Switzerland
May 1975

It was a little after midnight when Ruby and Oliver Pimm headed across from La Belotte to the Mossad safe house in Geneva from where she intended to locate Frank Copeland's whereabouts and pickup ammunition. In Sebastian's apartment, Nestlar with shirt sleeves rolled up past his elbows walked through to the kitchen and washed the blood from his hands and arms.
"It is a long time since my field surgery days gentleman, all I can tell you is I have done my best, lucky for him he is built like an ox, remarkable for his age and appears stable, the bullet in his shoulder went through, and I have this from his knee," he placed the remains of the shell in a glass, "But he needs blood, I cannot guarantee his survival." He looked at Sebastian, who sat at the kitchen table with a glass of vodka in his hand.
"It is quite remarkable, quite remarkable, especially for you Colonel" Nestlar gestured in a circling motion to his own face, his words were picked up by Sean as he poured himself a drink,
"I take it you two have got some catching up to do, I'll keep watch on the front Mr Westerberg," Sean said.
"Thank you, Sean, good work today, you can expect additional remuneration." Sean nodded.
"No bother, Just do'in what you paid for, but I would be grateful if you let me know how my brother is, soon as." Sean noticed how Sebastian appeared to be very cool around Nestlar.
"Of course, I will put a call in with our people, from the street phone box, just as soon as doctor here tells me what he requires for my father." Sebastian watched Sean walk through to the front room and sit on the balcony overlooking the lake in the dark and was surprised how comforted he felt, knowing the Irish man was the one watching out for them.
Nestlar's eyes raised at the word father and the years fell away, he remembered remarking to his RPA security henchman, Holts at the time that there was something familiar about Colonel Keplar's Adjutant Günther Brahn. His mind filled with questions, but it all came back to the same one how, how was it possible, that this man was Stefan Keplar?

"May I?" Nestlar moved forwards about to examine in closer detail Sebastian's facial features, but Sebastian recoiled with a snarl.

"Nein! I am no longer part of your experiment, it is for you to answer to me from this point on." Sebastian then noticed a few drops of blood had stained the doctor's crisp white shirt cuffs as he rolled his sleeves back down and calmed his tone.

"There will be plenty of time for you prove your skills when we return, especially concerning your knowledge of the workings of Dieter Myher's machine." Sebastian noticed the intrigue rise to Nestlar's eye's.

"Dieter Myher, another name I had not heard and takes me back, such a waste, truly a remarkable young man, you say you managed to obtain his finished pressure vessel, I am surprised, the pounding Berlin took."

Sebastian watched Nestlar pour himself a glass of water from the kitchen tap, it was almost as if he could hear the cogs of the doctor's brain spinning as he tried to work out what had happened at the end of the war and what role Sebastian intended him to play in the future.

"It seems like yesterday when I was removing that infernal chained case from your wrist, I am sure it was a tiresome affair for you at the time, and now, you have ...well you have hardly aged, can I ask how did you survive Sardinia. I say it again, it is quite remarkable. So long ago, my memories are probably not as good as yours, I recollect your Captain, visiting me in Berlin before the end, I remember he told me you were injured in an attack?" As Nestlar faltered in speech as he appeared to be trying to relive his past, Sebastian reminded himself that he was dealing with an old man, an old adversary.

"You mean how did I survive the assassin Holts, that you sent to kill us all. To speak of such things I believe would be a waste of my breath, let us just say, you are very fortunate doctor the man you see before you may appear to be the same SS Colonel you knew in 1940, but I assure I am not. I am well aware we all had puppet master's pulling our string back then, and the past cannot be rewritten. Moving forward you will assist me with my future endeavours as will those you serve today in your organisation. That said your man Holts did kill the Captain you spoke of, Count Leopold Von Stieglitz, my brother, there is no way you could make amends for such a thing, so remember this and concern yourself with ensuring I consider you an asset, you can start by fixing Günther, write down what you need I will get it." Sebastian had forgotten how much he despised Nestlar, but as he spoke, he was reminded of the purpose of securing him. Finding out what the encryption code key book was that the Nazi scientist's had used for protecting their information in the Vor Elle journal was the only reason to keep the doctor alive and

Nestlar was there to answer his questions, not the other way round. However, Günther came first and again, he needed Nestlar.

"He needs blood, do you know his blood group?" Nestlar asked.

"The same as mine." Sebastian nodded.

"Well that's a start, good, can you get some transfusion equipment, it is a simple process, but the sooner we act, the better." Nestlar went to light a cigarette, then Sean came back in the room.

"A car out front, three men, were you expecting company?" He pulled his gun and stood by the entry phone waiting to see if the image would appear on the entry phone screen, the buzzer sounded, and the small black and white screen illuminated showing a man hovering in front of the camera

"Mr Westerberg, we need to talk, my colleagues will wait downstairs. I am unarmed, as I stated in the letter, I am a friend of your father." Walter Thomas turned back and gestured to his bodyguards to wait in the car. Sebastian studied the image, there was something familiar about the man's profile in the dark when he turned side-on.

Sebastian leaned in and pressed the main lobby release, "Doctor sit, please." Sebastian gestured to the lounge and shut the door.

The apartment buzzer sounded, and Sean checked through the door spy hole then opened it with his gun muzzle pressed firmly against the door ready to fire through it, while Sebastian sat in the kitchen with his revolver on the table.

He watched the stranger enter and as he held his coat open and Sean frisked him as Walter held his arms up, then closed the door replacing the latch chain and double lock.

"Go through." Sean gestured, and as he walked forward, he removed his hat and Sebastian instantly recognised it was Walter, but Walter took some time to accept, that it was Sebastian before him.

"Huh Walter, I guessed as much, it is good to see you, Mr Byrne this is a very old friend, there are no concerns, please keep the doctor company,, keep him away from the windows."

"So, I got your letter," Sebastian held back his instinctive feeling to accept Walter as a friend, reminded that somehow he was involved with the planned attack in Sweden, it had been many years since Berlin, he may not have changed, but experience told him others had.

"I can't believe it's you, I thought maybe a son, I really don't know what I thought Stefan, tell me, Elizabet, your family, they are safe? You must know I had nothing to do with it." Walter's eye spoke the truth of his words.

"I believe you, my friend, sit, tell me how long have you known I was in town?" Sebastian asked.
"I don't know Stefan, maybe it's my age... I should have put two and two together when the woodsman game calling the first time with the gold, his name Lansford, I forgot about the housekeeper at the castle. Unfortunately, the people I work with have been complicating things, in particular, the man in charge responsible for the attack on your home. There are still some that believe you can conquer the world in a weekend and are willing to burn half of it to accomplish their plan...can I." he looked to the vodka bottle on the table, and Sebastian poured him a glass then offered him one of his cigarettes.
"No, I gave up, after...after I lost Grethe, I promised her for our children." Walter smiled and raised his glass,
"Old times, old friends, new dreams." they toasted.
"So where is he, I take it he is with you, Günther?" Walter looked around the room and noticed the bowl in the sink with the blood-stained cloth.
"He needs help, a transfusion, my blood will do it, but we need the equipment tonight." Sebastian gestured to the bedroom.
"That I can do, but we must talk. Things are just as they were in Count Erichh's day, those that believe they would be better sitting at the head of the table are less competent than the one that does and shouldn't?" Walter looked to the phone, "But that talk can wait first we fix him, may I use your telephone, I will only call those I know personally?"
Within minutes of Walter placing the receiver down, a van arrived with the equipment on Merill Nestlar's list.
"Take another one," Sebastian said as Nestlar went to plug the first pint of blood he had drained from his body.
"I hear sweet tea is good for that sort of thing," Sean said, and he filled the kettle.
Once Nestlar had connected a drip feed to Günther and cleaned his wounds again, with the better dressing Walter's people had supplied, he did as Sebastian ordered and began to take more blood. It was then Sebastian realised how subservient the doctor was around Walter, referring to him as *"Herr Director."*
"So now while we have this time, if you are up to it I need to ask what your plans are with the doctor and please understand my friend, if it were up to me, you could drop him from the balcony out there, but as I said there are others who require appeasement. You see, unfortunately, it is because you have laid claim to a substantial inheritance that they believed wrongly, would never be claimed." Walter said with Nestlar out of the room, "And to be honest Stefan if I had not seen it in the flesh, I would think you were a ghost." Walter studied Sebastian's face again, he

could not hide his astonishment or his emotions, with Sebastian's presence, he relived times that he had shared with Grethe, his wife.

Sean placed their tea in front of them and was still trying to work out the relationship between the two men.

"Well, Walter what can I say, here we are again. I am sorry to hear about Grethe, but maybe you will understand my task better. Whatever they did to me, and I think I now have a better idea, it has changed me, the blood he has taken from me is not blood as you know it, it's changed it has medicinal properties, but it will not solve my problem, I am not ageing and Elizabet is."

Walter's eyes lifted, "Again, I can only tell you, I was unaware of the escalation by the Chief Executive Director to ascertain your identity. I am so thankful that fool at the bank Salter-Kingsley was able to alert you about the men sent over by the CED. You should know, I have initiated a halt on any additional action with members of the Spider Executive Committee that I consider allies, it may hold until the meeting I have called, but unless I can convince the majority of the board the CED's actions will stand, they will simply send more men. The meeting has already been scheduled in Rome, you can appreciate what has occurred here in Geneva is a topic that will be discussed and the whereabouts of the doctor, I am not sure how much you know, but he was to form part of an agreement, this will need to be addressed, if there are not to be repercussions by those that had expected his presence. Can you give me something I can work with?" Walter looked to the room in which Nestlar still sat.

"For nearly ten years, we have been trying to establish what exactly the experiments in Sardinia did to my system and replicate its effects. Using my blood like today with Günther, we have synthesized a product which has proved to offer remarkable results, it helps with the rejuvenation of the outer layers of skin and to some extent muscle tissue, but it is not a permanent solution, and there is deterioration in the host's reaction to the product. It begins to accept it in increasing dosage with less reaction. Even working with some of the best people, I have exhausted our research. I need to replicate the doctor's experiments from the Vor Elle project, and I have the journals to do it. Unfortunately, the equations are encrypted, and I have no idea what the key book is, that is why I requested information from those that worked within the Kaiser Wilhelm Institute, people who worked in the RPA with Aktion T4." Sebastian refilled their glasses, and he could see Walter immediately understood why he had come for Merill Nestlar.

"You have Professor Heikkinen's work from the Sardinian facility?" Nestlar interrupted the two friends, entering the room and stood looking at Sebastian.

"I knew we could do it." He said, clapping his hands "Josef was so sure, he will be so very happy, Colonel, this will change our world, this is marvellous." Nestlar's exuberance was met with silence and a non-committal reaction.

Sebastian looked to the doctor, and he had to hold back a snarl, "Please take the doctor back into the lounge, Sean."

Sean sensed Sebastian's hostility and gestured for the doctor to move, Nestlar hovered for a moment then saw Walters look of agreement.

"You know, when I first heard his name, I thought of you, my people…our people, have been using him and others like him, what they learned in service for the Fatherland, nothing like what you have been working on, weapons. Like then as today, not everything that we do is as I would prefer, there are fractions that still believe a forceful will can overcome those that have discovered the strength of their own free will." Walter shrugged, "The world is as we made it, perhaps now you are here the wind of change will be as sweet and pure and sweet as the hearts of those two young me I once had the pleasure to drive to the youth camp in Habighorst." Walter held up his glass, "Meine Ehre heißt Treue, *(My honour is called loyalty)*"

"Meine Ehre heißt Treue, Leopold," Sebastian raised his glass.

"Leopold." Walter joined him in the toast.

"I am sorry Stefan, I am used to dealing only with figures and fixing problems on paper, so Elizabet is well, but you intend to use the doctor to give her what they gave you correct, it sounds risky?"

"Yes, but with great risk, as with great sacrifice, there comes great reward." Sebastian knew Walter would recognise Count Erichh's words, "and if I can crack it, Walter, then we will supply it to whoever is willing to pay and whoever I believe deserves it. As I said, we are already using my blood in natural products and have exclusive clients from all over the world, and with our wealth, we have been able to also carry out great charitable works. None know of the source of our product ingredients outside of our family and the site we have in Sweden is guarded well as your people now know. You say they will send more men unless you, we convince them to stop, I could tell you I will kill them and anyone that threatens my family, but the truth is you are right they must be convinced to leave me be and to that end my question to them would be who doesn't want to live forever?" Sebastian raised his glass.

"Well, it is certainly an appealing sell, as I said Stefan it is convincing the people that sit around the high table now. it is a real possibility that will be hard, especially with the resistance I can expect from the CED, at the moment you are an unseen threat, I cannot guarantee how he will react when he knows the reality of your origins." Walter began to consider how best to proceed within the Spider organisation.

"This is not for them to know, but my friend it is not just me, one of our daughters Lenora, she appears to have the serum running through her veins, and it does not stop there she smart, I mean super smart, they don't have computers that work as quickly as her. I just need that man in there to break the code the Professor used in the facility on the island, and I need a little time, can you give that to me Walter can you help me save Elizabet, if you can if your people can, you can tell them I can give you all the time you will ever need and a power that would bring the greatest leaders of the world to their door."

Walter scratched his head, "I can help, but I will need you to delay your plans to withdraw further funds from your account, I will speak with the banker myself, arrange additional funds through my own personal sources into the new account that I understand Günther set up, another five million to begin with, will that suffice, but in truth, I think this will not resolve the main issue, and that is the long term direction of our cause, it just might be that this thing of yours may be the answer, if you are willing once again to step forward for our Fatherland?"

Walter's question was serious as he explained that for some time he had been planning a coup of his own, to remove the more fanatical elements of the Spider network and how he agreed with Sebastian, the appeal to the elder members especially, that by supporting his actions he may possibly be able to provide a life-extension scenario through Sebastian's research, would assist his own purpose.

"You know some will not believe it, especially the CED." Walter looked up at Sebastian, capturing the image in his mind of the last time he saw him.

"Then we must convince them, as for your …Chief Executive, if he has no vision for a greater future, then he has no future. Take some of my blood, it has an effect on any small wound in its natural state, you will find it aids rheumatic pains, this will show you all is possible, I will not be the only one, first Katrina, Elizabet, then those that have a place in our future." Sebastian could see Walter realised there were opportunities that were now available to him to improve his status within Spider, but there was something else bothering Walter.

"You know there is a downside to this, some of the people may wish to own this, own you and your family, to get to the truth." Walter saw a glint of the attack dog in Sebastian's eyes as he looked towards the room where Merill Nestlar was resting.

"No one will be more dedicated to finding the path back, you can assure them of that as for my family we must impress upon them, I am as the Reichsführer made me, my honour is my truth, and my honour to my family is above all, it is the only thing I would burn the world for, to protect." His words held a hiss of his SS oath and a threat that was as pragmatic as it was true.

"Well, first we need to get you back to Sweden, if you are prepared to trust me I will arrange suitable transport, it will make things easier for Günther."

They spoke for a little over an hour more and then Sean showed Walter to the door as he was about to leave he turned to Sean.

"You work for Mr Westerberg?" Walter asked, looking back he could see Sebastian was fighting the tiredness from the ordeal of giving blood.

"Yes, I do sir." Sean, felt a strange affinity with Sebastian Westerberg, in hearing his own words, as if it was always so.

"Good, you should know it has been my honour also, please watch over him." Walter smiled, and one question kept coming to Sean's mind "How old was Westerberg?"

"What are using these days," Ruby asked as she pulled up and parked in a side street out of sight from the Mossad apartment in Rue René Jollien.

"Glock 17," he said and caught her smile.

"My gun?" She said, remembering him taking her weapon in Rio.

"No, I liked it so much I got my own, yours I keep in a spot at my home in London, just in case someone comes unannounced, it's there anytime you feel like popping over." He said, almost flirting with her.

"Huh, maybe I will one day, for now, I'll get you an extra Mag and silencer, wait here." She said and slipped out the door as he checked the rounds in the magazine of his gun.

A few minutes later she returned having received Copeland's home address from her handler, Pimm sensed she appeared somewhat frosty.

"There have been further problems with the bank today, do you know this?" her tone was accusational as if she believed he was holding information back from her, as she held back the extra magazine for his revolver and silencer.

"No I've been with you how could I" Pimm wondered if the American's had decided to wipe the slate clean as they had in Rio and burned anyone that they could be linked back to them, It just might be he and Ruby would find they had taken care of Frank Copeland themselves, that or they could be walking into a trap, the kind Lee Harvey Oswald fell into when agreeing to return some late library books for the CIA to the Texas School Book Depository in Dallas on the 22 November 1963.

"One of the senior bankers committed suicide, apparently in the bank itself, The Director Lelt must have known, but said nothing." She looked for a reaction from Pimm, but he just shrugged, as yet he had played dumb with both Guillaume Lelt and Ruby, that he already knew where Copeland lived, as far as he was concerned

this was no longer a retrieval mission, Bull had made it clear, If there was no way of getting Frank Copeland stateside, then he was to make sure he didn't get stuck in the crossfire of a CIA civil war, between Carter-Wallis and Tom Quinn
"Perhaps it is this man Copeland?" He said
"Perhaps." She nodded and handed him one of her spare magazines and the silencer.
"Seem's like every time we get on it I'm handing you ammunition, one day I just might ask for something in return." She smiled as she pulled away and they headed towards Saint-Prex and Copeland's chateau.
Parking up alongside the woods, pretty much as Sean had first done when he had tailed Suzy. Through the trees, they could see the house lights and Suzy's Mini and Copeland's black Mercedes set at the front. As they approached through the thick bracken, both Pimm and Ruby had drawn their revolvers with fixed silencers, they had only fought together once, in the park the day before but now moved like a team. Squatting low they watched how the silhouettes of the last four of Copeland's Yakuza house guards patrolling outside made clear targets of themselves, while one remained high on the outer stair landing in the shadows of the main front entrance.
Inside Suzy was aiding Copeland with his wounds in the kitchen as he swore, through clenched teeth, cursing Sean and Connor, whilst the dog Binki barked incessantly at his feet. Finally, he lashed out and kicked Binki across the tiled floor, the dog whimpered and for a second was quiet.
"What the fuck, don't take it out on my dog! Just because you and Hong fucked up." Suzy screamed at him and dropped the bloody rag she had been holding, turning her attention to the dog, just as Binki regained his feet and skipped back over and began snapping and barking again at Copeland.
"Get that fucking thing out of here, or I swear next time I'll kick it into orbit!" He reached for his gun, and quickly Suzy scooped up the little sheltie and whisked him outside, "Fix yourself, you already got Hong killed, old man, now you want to shoot my dog, I'm going to my club, fuck you!" Copeland raised his eyes and rattled his head back and forth, in frustration trying to ties hi bandage with one hand.
"Go to your fucking club then! And by the way, it's not your fucking club! it's my fucking club!" He yelled after her.
Like Pimm and Suzy the outer guard on the entrance stair had heard the commotion and turned back inside, as he did they swept forward and working themselves around the building in a clockwise direction, took out each guard in turn, returning round to the front to see Suzy jumping into her Mini and skid off down the driveway, spraying gravel in every direction, with the little dog sitting on the parcel

shelf yapping hard against the rear window as it saw Pimm emerge. The guard on the stairs, shrugged at seeing the dog and only had time to question where his colleagues were before he felt Pimm's slug hit him in the throat as he went down he let off a burst with his Uzi, and it sent a stream of bullets like a Roman candle firework from its barrel to his feet splitting shards of stone from the entrance parapet stone paving.

In the rear-view mirror of her mini Suzy's eyes caught something but she smiled seeing Binki still jumping and barking,

"Come Binki we'll leave that horrid man, sit, sit." she patted the passenger seat gesturing the dog come forward to calm him, but as she pulled up at the main gate about to turn onto the road she lit a cigarette, then in the approaching lights of another car passing by on the road saw Ruby's green Citroen, laying parked off the road in front of their private woods, she pulled her handbrake up.

Inside the Kitchen, Copeland heard the gunfire and dodged back and forth between the windows looking for signs of his guards outside.

"Fuck, fuck, fuck, are these your boys Benji come to clean house?" He swore, believing Carter-Wallis had sent a Seal team to take him out, as he skipped across the marble floor slipping in his open toe sandals he grabbed his revolver from the kitchen worktop and darted low back towards his study, where he kept an arsenal of weapons in a hidden wall cabinet.

Outside Pimm signaled Ruby to head around the side into the courtyard pool area, indicating he would go through the front and grabbed a handful of gravel as he began coming up the right-hand side stairs of the entrance parapet, and instinctively kicked the Uzi from the dead guard's hands.

Copeland had grabbed a 7.62 M60 and had just rammed in a back to back magazine and chamber the first shell when he saw the small green light belonging to the kitchen door zone on his security intruder alarm panel grid flash from to red, opened fire through the study double doorway towards the kitchen allowing the line of shells to rip through the wall across the hallway. With the sound of the machine gun Pimm struck low to the edge base on the outer threshold of one of the large entrance doors, as Ruby in the kitchen flung herself behind the units of central workstation island, while above her head, doors were ripped from the hinges of the fitted kitchen cupboards and all manner of pots pans and plates came crashing around her ears.

"You fucker's you're not Police, so let's make a deal unless you haven't had enough yet?" Copeland shouted then having reloaded let off another barrage of shells that took out most of the ornate balustrade and ripped through the furnishings on the ground floor.

Outside the entrance, Pimm decided a frontal assault would be suicidal as Copeland taunted again, "Had enough yet?"

"Ruby! Stay put, I'll come to you." Pimm shouted into the hall, deliberately drawing Copeland's attention and fire and threw the gravel from his hands across the floor of the hall.

"Ruby, nice name, hear that Ruby, Ruby, Ruby, Ruby your man's coming to save you." Squeezing a long burst of his weapon Copeland's fire now took in all of the far front windows of the study penetrating outside as far as the outer stair balustrade in the process disintegrated parts of the stone door frame and cutting across the door that Pimm had been shielding behind, if he had remained put he would have been dead, but by now he had moved low along the buildings outer wall and was working his way back round to the internal courtyard and swimming pool area.

Copeland began tapping in frustration at his house grid alarm panel, in seeing all the lights were now flashing intermittently because he had damaged the cabling with all his firepower. "Piece of shit!" he fired a round into the monitor.

Because the system was damaged, it did not pick up Pimm's entering into the long gallery between his study and the pool area coming in on the opposite side from the kitchen and hall. However, unfortunately for Pimm, outside there was the unmistakable sound of stilettos on a gravel path, as his stealthy approach had been observed by Suzy. Having found Ruby's Citroen, she had left Binki in her car blocking the entrance of the drive and drawn by the gunfire returned on foot. She took the gun from the dead guard at the front and began following Pimm. At one point Copeland heard her on the gravel outside the front of the study and mistaking it for one of his attackers opened up again with his M60 and as it spewed its last shell casing and he reached into his gun cabinet to take down his trusty M16 assault rifle, Pimm raised himself from his covering approach behind the glass doors that led from the study to the courtyard and shot him twice, catching Copeland in the shoulder and arm. The American dropped the rifle falling behind his desk as Pimm stepped into the room and hovered ready to shoot again, seeing Copeland's legs laying to the side he listened to his heavy breathing as he spluttered a sarcastic taunt, "Had enough?"

Pimm prepared to shoot him in his exposed leg when Copeland tore one of the loose rags from the wound to his hand, and with only, just enough effort waved it in surrender.

Pimm now considered Bull's instructions as he cautiously kept his aim and he peered around the desk, seeing both Copeland's hands raised and the American smiling churlishly, "This was one of my favourite shirts, I have them brought specially from the Island." He said as blood-soaked across the vivid pattern of his turquoise Hawaiian shirt.

Pimm ignored the comment, if he was going to end him, it needed to be now before Ruby joined them, he considered the news that one of the bankers had been killed at the bank, that Ruby had informed him on the way over there and decided the world would be better off with one less gangster with bad dress sense.

"Yep I'm done, time to call home, who do you guy's work with, I'm sure we can settle this." Copeland looked briefly to his own revolver but it was too far from his reach and rested back and in that split second Pimm saw Copeland recognised that he had decided to kill him, and as he gave a capitulating sigh and closed his eyes a fraction before he pulled the trigger, Pimm felt a pain in his lower back like someone hit him with an electric cattle prod, he buckled and dropped to one knee to see Suzy standing in the doorway, the pain spasmed as he felt for the grip of his gun realising he was caught as her eyes glanced across at Copeland, then as she appeared to raise the gun there was the sound of two separate light thuds, and she dropped forward, blood gurgling from her throat.

"Don't fucking move Yank!" Ruby ordered Copeland, and when he did slightly flinch his hand in the direction of his weapon, she shot him through the wrist.

"Fuck you, mother! Fuck it Ruby was that necessary, how am I suppose to have a wank now,!! Ruby" Copeland screamed and looking towards Suzy corpse lay back in capitulation.

"Another word it's your last, turn over face down, now! hands out front." She growled then turned her attention to Pimm as he slumped back against the desk, blood trickling from his wound like an open tap over his fingers and hand as he applied pressure to it.

"I'm ok, deal with him." Pimm groaned.

"No, you're not," she said and leaning over him picked up the M16 then slammed the butt of the rifle firmly across the back of Copeland's head knocking him unconscious.

"I'm not wasting time watching that fool we need to get you out of here." Ruby then grabbed one of the phones from the floor and finding it still working, made contact with her Mossad handler and issued an emergency evacuation order citing casualties.

She propped Pimm up against the back of the desk, and pulling up the back of his shirt, examined the entry wound, "I'm going to need to plug that hole." She said and seeing the collection of bottled of spirits on Copeland's sideboard, removed the cork from the bottle of Chivas Regal, she allowed Pimm a mouthful then felt him brace as she poured some of it over the wound and then pushed the cork stopper into the wound. She then looked the corpse of Suzy and ripped the fleece she had been wearing from her back, Pimm handed her his pocket knife and she cut one of the sleeves off it, then soaked the exit wound just below Pimm's left ribs, as she pushed the material into the open gash she could feel the sharpness of his shattered lower ribs, Pimm grit his teeth and moaned. "I can't" he gasped and slumped forward, "Stay with me Pimm." Ruby slapped him across the face, and his eyes opened again, and he gave a meagre smile as he fought the fatigue settling over his eyes as the blood drained from his face.

Ruby now focused on keeping his mind occupied, "I wonder who she was?" she asked, looking at Suzy, "I like her shoes."

Pimm knew what she was doing and nodded towards the bottle of Chivas, and she poured some into his mouth. Ruby checked Copeland was still out cold and seeing an open pack of his Panther cigarillos lit one.

The thirteen minutes it took for the Israeli helicopter to arrive and land on the back lawn felt like an hour to Ruby as she watched Pimm wane in and out of consciousness, she had done as much as she could and as she studied the Mi6 agents face, she felt drawn to him, more than the fact they were of a sort kindred spirits both working in a deadly profession. By the time she responded "In here!" to the call from her arriving colleagues, she realised that if Pimm was perhaps just ten years younger he may be someone she would consider, becoming involved with, his rugged features had an almost kindly softness as he sat calmly controlling his breathing and smiley eye wrinkles that drifted into the fine graying at his temples gave him an air of distinguished maturity, she imagined back in the day he would have been somewhat of a catch.

"Take him first." She pointed to Pimm, "I'll watch him, everyone else is dead."

As they cleared the shoreline crossing the Lake a number of blue flashing light could be seen arriving at the entrance to the chateau but were blocked off by Suzy's car.

"Get a dog handler for the mutt." Guillaume Lelt swore having nearly lost his fingers to Binki when he had tried to open the door of the Mini. "for now push it out the way!" he growled as he watched the disappearing flashing lights of the Israeli helicopter.

Inside Copeland was beginning to stir and immediately became chatty again, feeling some self-satisfaction in seeing Pimm appeared to be seriously injured as one Ruby's team worked on him, with gas and plasma fluids.

"Who the fuck are you guys, CIA, Mossad, don't tell me you're Brits, Cor Blimey Guv'nor, he put on an English accent like Dick Van Dyke in the film Mary Poppins.

"It doesn't matter to me, I've got enough cards up my sleeves Ruby for you me, and the Queen hearts herself."

"I swear old man one more word, out the door you go." Ruby snapped at Copeland as she noticed the look of concern on her colleague as Pimm lay motionless and obvious unconsciousness, and he called up to the Pilot to get them to the ground quickly if they were not to lose him and the Pilot immediately banked sharply right as they hovered only feet across the surface of the Lake to a waiting private ambulance on the French border.

Chapter 21: The Landing

Rome, Italy
1975

At around five-thirty the next morning, Sean McLoughlin stood guard alongside two of the security team Max Binder had enlisted to safeguard his master, outside the Westerberg apartment. Walter Thomas prepared to say goodbye to his friends as he watched as Merill Nestlar held a plasma bottle high, lifting the feeding line as another two of his men stretchered, Günther into the back of a lorry that was to be used to get the three men back to Sweden.

"Do you trust him?" Walter asked as he watched as Nestlar appeared to tut at the cramped conditions inside the wagon as he brushed the seat before sitting alongside Günther.

"No, but the doctor will do as he is told, beside's I think he knows, what I have in store for him is something he could only dream of being involved with, as he would put it, truly remarkable."

"Well I will remind him, his bridges are burnt with us, if anything it will focus his attention in serving your purpose." Walter said and went to step up.

Sebastian watched how attentive Max Binder was in helping Walter climb up to sit alongside Günther, who now lay on a makeshift bed hidden amongst the camouflage boxes of goods with Nestlar sitting at his feet, monitoring the plasma drip feed he had hooked up to the side of the truck wall. Suddenly Walter turned back to Max, "gun" he said, holding out his hand and Max reached into his jacket and handed him his own weapon.

"You will not need it, my friend, but I know it will bring you comfort. This man has protected my family for over twenty years. He will ride upfront and stay with you until you are safe."

Walter said as he placed the gun in Günther's hand, who could hardly keep his eyes own and said nothing but smiled up at his old friend.

"It's was good to see you, woodsman, rest now and be well, there will be time to catch up another day I assure you. Then perhaps we can share some of your wonderful goulash, yes." Walter read Günther's acceptance in his tired expression and in the confined space of the lorry it briefly brought back memories to the two men of a time when they sheltered within Count Erichh's wine cellar in the Berlin house during a bombing attack in 1943.

Walter eyes drifted to Nestlar as he raised himself and he stooped forwards gesturing the doctor to come closer.

"If he dies, so do you." he whispered into Nestlar's ear and then turned away.

As Max Binder again aided his masters decent to the pavement, Walter paused in stepping down, hearing somewhere in the distant streets the two tone sounds of emergency vehicles rushing by. They were headed to Copeland's chateau, summoned By Director Guillaume Lelt to deal with the aftermath of Pimm and Ruby's gun battle with the American. The Director had received word the helicopter he had witnessed leaving the property had dropped off the radar as it headed towards the Southern French border.

As the sound from the alarms faded, Sean stepped forwards to climb aboard the lorry.

"Ride up front" Walter gestured Max to the lorry drivers cab, "see my friends, onto the ferry and then return home, I will be fine with these men you have brought." Sebastian studied the man servant and realised he was reluctant to leave Walter's side as he went to climb up into the passenger seat alongside the waiting driver, *loyalty*, he thought and as Walter spoke briefly with his men Sebastian held out his hand to Max "Thank you for assistance last night and today, it is appreciated. Please, when he is asleep change it for this one." Sebastian handed Binder his own revolver.

As Walter prepared to say goodbye, Sebastian turned back to Sean, "you go with them I have unfinished business here, I have arranged for someone to meet you in Sweden, a police escort so to speak, so don't be alarmed, Günther will know who." as he spoke he saw the uncertainty in Sean's eyes, it had been a long time since he had trusted anyone other than his brother Connor, he looked to Walter, then towards the back of the lorry at Günther.

"Very good Mr Westerberg," Sean said.

"Sebastian or Seb, to friends, please, I have received word, your brother Connor and Vincent arrived and are safe with the rest of my family." Sebastian shook his hand and then pulled down the back of the concertina door of the truck, to the surprise of Walter, who had thought he intended to return with them.

"Now Walter, we need to talk and make plans. When I go back home, I go back knowing I need not look over my shoulder for signs of your friends, and there is only one way we can make that so. Your friends must become my friends, and they must learn to accept the power, the loyalty of true friendship brings to their table."

Three days later an extraordinary meeting of the executive board of the Spider network was convened at the bequest of Walter Thomas in Rome.

The eight other members sat in silence at the ten-meter long green marble table in blacked-out room, set at the heart of the secret modernised air-conditioned catacomb chambers hidden within the depths of the old Stadio Flaminio stadium, three kilometres northwest of the capital city centre. There were murmurs of discontent as some of the directors smoked while Walter played video news-reel footage of the scenes of the carnage of the massacre in the Park de Anglaise in Geneva and overlapped with images of the remains of Mengele's laboratories in Brazil, the news reports of the dead fish washed up on the beaches of Rio and other high profile headlines involving subversive activity that they all knew Spider had been involved with.

"Gentleman to operate at this level of indiscretion risks unnecessary exposure, and for what, the returns of such recklessness in becoming involved with fanatical individuals that share none of the elements and principles we originally pledged our oath to uphold will be the ruination of us all, as it has been proved in the past." Walter stood at the opposite end of the long boardroom table from the Chief Executive Director as he addressed the other members.

"I fail to see the purpose of you expounding your disagreement with my actions in the past. We are all aware of your stance to err on the over cautious… and such like." The Chief Executive Director's cynical reference to Walter's habitual phrase received a half hearted laugh from those sitting closest to the leader of the Spider organization and he continued to play to those members he knew supported his tenure.

"These matters have been dealt with through the judicial use of my power as Chief Executive Director and after consideration of the judgements of other Executive Directors, here present." he gestured to the other board members, "Some of you, including yourself Walter may not always have agreed with my strategy and the direction in which I have guided our organisation, but while I am at the helm it is my will that decides how best we should use our resources to achieve our ultimate goal. That said, each of you has the right to challenge my leadership, however I must remind you, should the challenger fail, then banishment from this Executive Directorship table is the least consideration that follows such a putsch for those involved. So as long as I have majority, my authority should be unquestioned to initiate operations I believe may assist our goal or protect our purpose and in using at my discretion any of our global enterprises or assets to whatever means necessary, Als Führer der Spinne ist dies mein Vorrecht!" *(As Führer of spider, this is my prerogative)* The Chief Executives Directors eyes glared out across at Walter from the dimly lit room illuminated by only the light from the television screens, his, tone held an abrupt sharpness to the challenge, being made against his authority.

"As with this incident in Geneva and the associated repercussions including the unfortunate loss of the operators I dispatched to Sweden," he appeared to calm himself as he continued, ignoring the images on the screen. "Walter, you should be focusing your attention in contacting the Scandinavian business contacts you have to ascertain the full identity and measure of those that are responsible for the abduction of Professor Nestlar. Our contacts in American and Israel have reported back, it was not the CIA or Mossad that were involved. Doctor Mengele has emphasized to me how important an asset Doctor Merill Nestlar was, and it has taken a great deal of time and effort, finding a replacement to satisfy the Somalian's. I have to make an open and frank observation that I must express to the other Executive Directors, to have wasted the committee time calling this meeting shows your lack of understanding of the nature of our commitments to the Africans. A collaboration that must be maintained strengthened and remains resolute so that we may, in turn, secure a permanent location to build our first new Youth training camps."

The Chief Executive Director then tapped vigorously with his index finger on a personnel file that lay before him, which Walter assumed carried details of his own family, and listened as his superiors next words were aimed at those he loved.

"Of all here considering your own beautiful kinder, I am a little surprised and I must confess disappointed with you Walter. That you do not accept the future lays with our youth as it once did, and only if they are given the strength and power to take up the reins of their forefathers. Without them we....you, are nothing." The Chief Executive Director sat forward into the light of the small table lamp in front of his desk position his words were clearly meant as a threat towards Walters own children as he looked for agreement from those to his left, and right he counted on being his most loyal supporters and took a sip of his water, then casually tossed the personnel file from the table, even in the dim light Walter could see the images of his children captured in photographs that slipped out from within its pages on to the floor.

Walter held his tongue and began to extract documents he intended to share with the other committee members, aware of what topic the Chief Executive Director would bring up next.

"But here we are, you have summoned us, and so first, I am sure like the rest of the committee I would like you to explain what have you done to resolve the problems with the unauthorized access to the Senior Statesman German account in Geneva you may appreciate we are all highly concerned at the potential loss of such financial assets and regarding the risk of a link to organisation through high exposure in the international news, of the incident in Geneva and the suicide of one of the Geneva banks senior accounts executives, this is all most disconcerting, but clearly in some way connected to these individuals that have attempted to steal from us, I sincerely hope you have safeguarded our interests."

The Chief Executive Director's tone now held an unmistakable threat of a pending action against Walter himself, and he noticed two of the guards behind him appeared to brace themselves awaiting a pre-planned order.

However, the faceoff between the Chief Executive Director and Walter had been brewing for some time, and now Walter had chosen the time and place.

"The suicide of the thief banker is of little consequence; our people have confirmed his addiction to drugs and his financial embezzlement of clients funds at the bank, I have been informed by the Chairman Peter Salter-Kingsley does not affect any our accounts including the one Mr Westerberg had accessed. It is as you say unfortunate, yes, but it does not affect the trading of the FNIG bank, any losses will be written off by the bank itself. However I must first respectfully correct the committee's conception of the illegitimacy of the individual that has accessed the account set up by General Von Stieglitz, who as many of you are aware I was honoured to serve for over ten years, allowing me the opportunity to assist in laying the foundations of the financial backbone of the structure that has become The Spider Network, including the purchase of this very building, but that is the past as you stated Chief Executive Director it is our future we must focus on." He then clicked a hand held sonic remote and two large wall projector screens dropped from the ceiling and immediately displayed images of Stefan Keplar head shot alongside extracts of his records and various images of him in his black SS uniform, that Walter had retained over the years some showing him alongside Leopold and the Count, but importantly one was forum that held the image of the Coliseum of Rome in the background, a Piazza very near where they now sat and showed Stefan receiving his first iron cross from Hitler himself.

"This gentleman is SS. SD. Colonel Stefan Robert Keplar commander of Einsatzgruppe 7339 in Sardinia and Gestapo Senior Inspector, promoted while serving in Berlin by SS General Lieutenant Heinrich Muller. I have known the Colonel personally through the house of Von Stieglitz for many years and served him whilst he was attached under orders from the Reichsführer to the Chancellery's special weapons projects in Berlin. His war record is exemplary, and as you can see, he was attached to the intelligence service prior to the war working within the Abwehr. During the time he spent fulfilling his duty to the Fatherland and our Führer he was wounded on a number of occasions, these our his medical records our people were able to retrieve from sources in Libya, which detail his injuries sustained during the North African campaign. The Colonel received the highest honour the Reich can bestow, from Reichsführer Himmler himself." Walter paused as he allowed the committee member to circulated duplicate folders containing detailing Stefan Keplar's military record and he acknowledged the committee sign of affirmation of the approval of Stefan's service to the Reich, until the Chief Executive Director cut in leaning forward once more with his arms crossed as he strummed at the marble table top.

"For sure, we all recognise the Colonel's war record but is that not the report listing that he was killed in action. What has this got to do with us at this time? Please explain and be brief."

Walter pressed a remote on the screen selector, and images of Stefan appeared as he appeared in his Swedish passport as Sebastian.

"Time is exactly what we are here for gentleman, something each of us has only what the gods, decide is our fair share. This is the man identified as Sebastian Westerberg, who accessed the Von Stieglitz bank account and by my word, he is the legitimate heir as the surviving ward of Count Erichh Von Stieglitz as detailed in his last will and testaments registered and held within the family strongbox that I placed inside the FNIG bank vaults in 1943, he is, Stefan Keplar." Walter displayed Sebastian's new Swedish passport.

There were gasps of astonishment, confusion and some words of challenging disbelief, especially from the Chief Executive Director, who stared up at the images of Stefan on the screen and then at the copy of Sebastian Westerberg's passport in his hand. "What rot is this Thomas, that man whoever it is may look like Colonel Keplar, but he is twenty years too young, this is preposterous. I have long since harboured a suspicion leaving such assets in the hands of a jumped up clerk was foolish, your position is only through ascension as Count Erichh's Adjutant and bookkeeper. This proves nothing if this man has stolen our money, we will deal with him appropriately."

Walter held his calm and laid a briefcase on the table, then removed polythene blood fusion packed of Sebastian blood.

"The Colonel once again is willing to bleed for his people for us. Our scientists have examined his blood sample it has the most remarkable properties, I have seen it at work, it is his blood. He said as the vacuum pack blood sample slapped down on the table, "It would appear the special project division scientist Reichsführer Himmler assigned the Colonel to, succeeded in their task. At the time the Colonel was willing to volunteer and sacrifice his own life so that the experiments would reach their fruition, unfortunately, there was a prolonged period of convalescence because once again the Colonel had sustained a battle injury, the details are incomplete, but his entire group including his adopted brother Leopold Von Stieglitz were all killed in Italy, it is my belief this led to the mistaken authorization of his death certificate, by the time the Colonel had recovered, Berlin had fallen."

The Chief Executive Director gestured that the blood package was passed to him for examination and the blood work documents from their own scientist as Walter continued, feeling all eyes were now on him.

"Although he has already begun in Sweden to recreate the process that he was exposed to as a volunteer of the Reich special project division and has expelled considerable resources of his own, with some success, he and a team of world-leading scientist's he has assembled have yet to identify the process completely. However, it is his belief Doctor Merill Nestlar has certain knowledge that he states will ensure his endeavours are successful. As for the SSG account in Geneva, although he is legitimately entitled to do so, as I have already explained, he has not removed any funds from the primary account, but has informed me to capitalize on his endeavours and bring an early completion date forwards, further substantial investment will be required and I have ensured him of such on our behalf."

The room was stunned into silence, as many of those present who like Walter were old men began to realize what was being offered to them.

"On our behalf, you overstep your place, Sir." The Chief Executive Directors blustered as his chair squeaked from side to side as he wriggled irritated by Walter statement and then tossed the blood pack across the table towards Walter.

But some of the committee members who already agreed of Walter assessment of their leader's helmsman ship had begun to speak out questioning what had happened regarding the Spider operatives that had been set to Sweden as there was the sound of boots marching on the stone floor.

"Gentleman it is my great pleasure to introduce Mr Sebastian Westerberg, SS SD Colonel and former Gestapo Senior Inspector Stefan Keplar."

Sebastian stepped into the light and almost with a sense of the theatrics removed his hat revealing the golden locks of his long kiss curl fringe which he brushed back from his forehead as he saluted, "Heil Hitler!" he called confidently, even though he thought it was ridiculous, but it got the response from the men at the table, except the Chief Executive Director, who shook his head grinning almost mocking. "Mein Gott im Himmel!" He slammed his palm on the table, "How are we to believe such a fantasy, I ask you, gentleman?"

"You have before you, Colonel Keplar's war record and this is a copy of his identity card as a Gestapo officer, with fingerprints."

Walter threw a card across the table towards the Chief Executive Director as some of the committees were still taking the word Gestapo in, while studying the dark suited man before them who most aged to be in his mid thirties, but from his record would have been fifty-eight, as he stepped forward of Walter placing his case on the desk.

"Those are the fingerprints taken from my hand in Berlin, unfortunately, shortly after my smallest finger to my right hand was lost in action in Italy."

The Chief executive shrugged, whilst the other committed member turned and saluted Stefan.

"I am who I say, as Walter Thomas has confirmed. Originally it had been my intention to continue with my quest to advance the fruits of a cause I have served all my life on my own and I had considered waiting until I was in a position to offer you a proposal that not even your Chief Executive Director could refuse, however, because of the importance of my work and the fact it required my undivided attention, the slightest possibility that your organisation may through lack of guidance and patience make a mistake and disrupted my purpose was something I was not prepared to allow, so having consulted Walter here I am, to once again prove my word is my truth." Sebastian looked up at the enlarged image of himself with Leopold, then turned back as he heard the first tones of a curt response from the Chief Executive.

"Welcome Colonel Keplar, if it is really true, you may appreciate with such an extraordinary claim if I suspend my acceptance place at this gathering until my own people have verified your identity. But if true, as I said, your record speaks of your valour, no doubt, but I must remind you, you were a Colonel, I was General of the Fifth Panzer brigade, there are four other Generals seated here that hold rank above yours and who have more authority. I admit there is no doubt in time if we had won the war you would have risen to join our ranks, but we are your superiors, we decide what actions should be taken."

The smirk across the chief executives face railed Walter to step forward, but he felt Sebastian's hand on his elbow and halted his own response

"Unfortunately gentleman the news is we lost the war?" Sebastian smiled, some of the committee members nodded in an almost sorrowful agreement, while a couple, including the Chief Executive Director, appeared to take offence to his candour.

"That was another time, like many here I did the best I could for my Fatherland my Führer and my family as I am sure many of you. Your time is of my concern now and although I am still determined as ever to succeed and honour my commitment to my oath, with such an individual guiding the process, this may not be possible and I will not allow the legacy of those that made the ultimate sacrifice for our

Fatherland be jeopardise with such leadership." Sebastian's eyes bored ahead his deep shallow eye highlighted his lean muscular nature, and his eyes glinted like a razor in the dark as the Chief Executive Director puffed out his chest and began to growl a vehement debunkal of Sebastian's statement, But Sebastian continued. "You sent men to my family, my home, men with orders to kill, my kinder, my wife, a woman who served, as a member of the Reichsführer's personal staff in chancellery and was trusted at the highest level with secrets of the Reich." His voice was as calm as it was cold.

"Yes, yes? Clearly an oversight on my part, but I was not aware of your true identity, If Walter here had kept me informed, or the bank?" The Chief Executive Director shrank back as other committee members looked towards him in discussed, many remembered the purges Hitler and the Reichsführer's instigated on loyal Officers of the Reich towards the end of the war. The CED blustered an apology as he stood looking to other members of the Executive committee at his side for their support.

Calmly Sebastian reached into the briefcase and removing a revolver shot the Chief Executive Director in the forehead, the back of his seat was bathed in blood, brain and skill matter as the room filled with the screech of chair legs as, stunned in horror, some members pushed their seat back from the table.

Then calm immediately descended, and they relaxed as Stefan placed the gun down beside his case, as the guards at the rear bristled forward while The Chief Executive Directors body slumped forward then fell from the table to the floor. "Remove that!" Sebastian ordered, then turned to the committee, "in the SS unacceptable actions of failure have no acceptable excuse, regardless of rank or motive, Meine Ehre heißt Treue that is written in our blood and the blood of those that shed theirs for our Fatherland, those that would wish to dilute and corrupt this oath by their own designs of greed and grandeur have no place in the Fatherland we will raise into the twenty-first century and no place at this table, but it will take time, that I can now offer you all and together we will see our Fatherland grow as once our Führer intended." With that, Sebastian slammed down a book on the boardroom table, one every Executive Director recognised and the key that he had come for that Merill Nestlar had informed him would assist his reading of Professor Heikkinen's equations, the codebook used by members of the RPA AND Aktion T4, Mein Kampf.

There was a murmur of acceptance with some members even tapping the table in agreement.

"So now gentleman, as the Reichsführer once told me, there is an order to things, first Walter if you would please." Sebastian turned to him as the guards, surprised by the boldness of his action, did as commanded and removed the corpse of the former, Walter turned to the committee.

"Gentleman it would appear there is a vacancy at this table I would like to propose Sebastian Westerberg to become the next Executive Director of Spider, do I hear a second" he paused as Sebastian placed his revolver back in the case as one of Walter's closest allies said "yes."

"All those in favour say I!" Walter then called the vote, and there was a resounding "I" from the committee.

"Excellent, thank you for your generous support, gentlemen. And so now for my first action as one of your members, I would like to propose the ascension of Walter Thomas to Chief Executive Director, all those in favour!" he gestured Walter to the vacant seat at the head of the table.

Chapter 22: The Rising

San Pantaleo,
Sardinia, Italy
September 1996

Known as a Medicane, in early September 1996, the first Mediterranean tropical-like cyclone storm Medicane of that year began, formed in the Balearic channel it was fed by low pressure driven up from the North African warm seas off the coast of Algeria and drifted east skirting the southern Aeolian isles of Italy before dissipating as far off as the Ionian islands of Greece.
As it would turn out this first storm would herald graver things to come and dark times for many of the inhabitants located on the Mediterranean island groups. Once considered infrequent meteorological phenomena of atmospheric disturbance, the third storm in October named by the NOAA as "Cornelia", revisited the region with greater ferocity and unfortunately for the islands inhabitants its path deviated dramatically towards Sardinia.
The unprecedented deluge would prove to be a storm, the like of which Sardinians had not seen for many decade and would come to remind all of the power of nature, that I the past, had sculpted the unique and unusual smooth pink megalithic boulders, synonymous to the islands its landscape.
During the first minutes as Cornelia began to break land, on the hills above the village of San Pantaleo, Olbia Tempio, Sardinia, already saturated though to his skin, even though he had forgone his routine of the last tour of the site that evening. The security guard Enrico Albani, looked back to Zanna Bianco, his little dog, as she continued to bark, while perched standing with her front legs on the dashboard of his 4 x 4 pickup watching her master set the heavy chain and padlock on the wrought iron gate, that blocked the road leading up towards the Cormorant Corporation freshwater pumping station.

"Abbastanza!" *(enough)*, Albani barked back, as his wet hands fumbled with the lock, while struggling to keep the water from his eyes as the rain lashed his face. Just as he felt the lock click firm a sudden heavy blast of wind down the inner track whipped the metal sign saying, **CHIUSO NO TRESPASS,** from the gate and before he could catch it, battered like a tin tray, the sign scuttered along the road before taking flight. Bracing himself with his back against the gate, Albani stood for a moment watching it disappear over the side of the hill, before making a run for his vehicle.

"I know, I know, it's a bad one," he said, calming Zanna and she curled into the passenger seat, looking up with a shiver as Albani started his engine.

He sat briefly watching the muddy rain funnel down on both sides of the road that led up to the pumping station, behind the gate he had just locked. Watching the night lights that had been recently strung for the construction vehicles, twist and spin on their cable lines.

"They won't be there in the morning" he whispered to himself as he gave Zanna a final pat before turning on the radio, then he backed up over the muddy mounds that were beginning to form on the road and set off for home, not stopping at his regular haunt for "*one for the road*".

With the private road on the other side of the gate that led up to San Pantaleo water plant, in recent weeks being subjected to a great deal of heavy traffic, the soil was already cut with the deep channels from the giant tyres of the construction vehicles and so the water gathered pace to a torrent. While above on the main terrace that had been cleared and made ready for the excavation of a new, replacement processing bottling plant and storage depot, the JCB's sat idle for the night like giant scorpions as the soil around began to shift and large pools of water formed on the loose overburden, like dams.

High up the same hillside, beyond the terrace walls amongst overgrown vegetation, beyond the chain-link fence of the Cormorant lands and where few locals now strayed, a lone light sifted in the dark, from behind the broken shutters of the old church villa. Inside, shadows stirred as the fire crackled from the occasional smattering of raindrops down the broken chimney.

With an almighty crack of lightning from a strike to land close by, the television picture fizzed with white noise and the images rolled on the screen of players taking part in the world cup qualifying match between Italy and Malta. The cacophony of thunder rode a cavalcade of air that made the roof timber creek as one of the shutters of the old villa ripped free of its rusted securing pins, violently clattering back on its hinges against the wall outside.

Thorn the grey whiskered Alsatian mongrel dog nestled at his threadbare socks, shot to her paws, ears raised and back, neck fur bristling she let out a low aggressive moan, baring a fang in the corner of her mouth. Her master let the paper on his lap drop to the floor and patted her calmly, stroking down her neck hair as he placed his coffee mug down. Then groaned as he lumbered from his chair to attend to the loose shutter. Pulling the outer shutter back he closed the inner window, locking the shutter in place to the internal frame with a butterfly hook which he wound tight until its rattling was silent.

"Just the Mistral winds girl, nothing to worry us, eh boys." the old man said looking at the three pups that lay in a knotted mass of comforting fur, almost on top of the stone fire hearth. The smallest pup, called Stella, tilted her head watching him return to the room, then licked the half stump of what remained of her right front leg she appeared to briefly acknowledge the sentiment with a raised eye, then snuggled down burying her nose deep into the haunches of her brother's side.

No sooner was Stella settled when the room was suddenly illuminated with another much closer lightning strike, which made the pans that hung in the kitchen clatter like goat bells, then within the next second the television and single table lamp went black and a great howl of air made the old man's ears pop as he heard the sound of glass smashing from behind.

With the fire lighting his only path in the darkness he went this time, towards his bedroom from where the sound had come. Another rusty shutter hook had broken free from its lock and peeled back, allowing the main window to slam inwards against the bedroom wall, shattering its glass.

By now all three pups sat up in the firelight, their eyes switching between the direction of their master and their mother who stood braced over them, staring down the narrow corridor towards the backroom as they watched their master's silhouette disappear from sight.

"Scheisse!" Cursing, the old man reached the window frame, wearing only socks he tried to avoid the glass on the quarry pan tile flooring. Using his shoulder he propped the window open as he stretched outside, battling with the wind to secure the shutter while his eyes stung by the lashing rain, may as well have been closed, as his hand felt in the dark along the wall for the timber edge of the shutter as it whipped back and forth.

With one hand on the window sill, he pulled with his full weight and as his nails gripped into the soft rotten timber allowing him to take a firm grip, he jolted back releasing his hold, shocked as another jagged blue streak across the sky briefly illuminated something outside his window. A man's figure that remained remote from the surroundings, distinguished by its glistening wetness, but darker than the darkness of the foreground only a few metres away it stood at the edge of the scrub and bracken in front of the villa, that dropped away in the direction of the main road. The old man squinted, and within the blink of the rain from his eyes, the image was gone. Even though he questioned his vision, he felt his neck hairs rise, and he arched himself high, to make himself appear more threatening to whoever may be out there.

"Hello! Who's there?" His bear-like roar disturbed the young pack to rise from the fire and stand forwards of their mother, upfront Stella the three-legged bitch pup snarled the most menacingly. Suddenly behind them, a heavy cluttering sound pulled their attention back to the fire as a loose brick from high up on the chimney, dislodged by the wind tumbled down the flue. With a heavy thud it hit the burning logs, scattering the two male pups from the warmth of the hearth, as the impact instantly showered the room and them in a cascade of hot embers and flaming charcoal, they whelped, whimpering ears cowered low as scuttled to safety beneath their mother who still stood firm, now with only her little daughter at her side, who turned and began snapping at some of the spark dust.

"All right, it's alright." The old man blustered, as he thundered back to the room and began stamping out the smoulderings that had already begun to catch lifting to flame from his tattered floor rug.

"Ah shiza!" he shouted with a twinge of pain to his foot, as some of the stubborn embers began to burn through the dry cotton of his socks.

Grabbing his newspaper he began beating the flames, but soon exasperated the situation as the thin pages soon ignited with flame lifting at the edge of the rolled paper wad. With the room lit up and seeing his mug he threw the paper down then doused the remains of his cold coffee over the newspaper. As the flames sizzled to a wisp of smoke, slightly out of breath, he let out an exhausted coughed laugh of relief, then shrugged at the pack of dogs with a cackle seeing six shiny eyes, like jewels set in coal and the pups, huddled against the wall in the shadows as the room briefly lit up again from the lightening of the storm.

"Look at you three, calm, calm, come on, it's over." he patted the rug coaxing them back to the fire as he threw the soggy paper into the hearth.

"That was something Thorn, eh?... Ja, Ja I know, you were right when you told me to fix the chimney in the summer, I know, I know, come on little girl, you're a brave one aren't you, braver the boys eh." He rubbed the little bitch's neck as he stared at the brick being roasted in the fire, then hearing a sound, looked for their mother and turned to the see her scratching at the door. His mind was drawn back to consider the image he thought he had seen outside as he felt a pain in his hand and realised some of the window glass had cut his palm.

He called to Thorn as he got up and taking from the draw of a wall cabinet a tea towel he wrapped it tightly, it soon crimsoned and now seeing his torch in the same draw he switched it on, checking the room, the air still held residue smoke from the paper burning as the torch beam scanned across the little room, .then settled on the dog still pawing at the door. His mind tried to make sense of the image he thought he witnessed outside, attempting to dismiss it as he lit candles that flickered wildly. "Leave it, Thorn, no one comes up here, especially not tonight," he told the dog, trying to convince himself it was a trick of the light as the pups ignored their mother and began to settle. He settled back in his chair and looked at the blank screen of his television and a flash of the image he thought he had seen outside plagued his thoughts, it appeared to have been a person with their arm stretched out, pointing? He looked to Thorn again, still standing before the door.

"Quiet, girl, there's nothing it's the wind and the imagination of an old fool, you stay in tonight, piss on the floor if you must." He said leaning forward and began switching the television on and off but nothing happened as Thorn persisted with scratching and biting at the edge of the door, that was heavily marked from years of abuse by past members of her family.

Finally, the old man scowled at her impatience and raised himself from the chair, "The town generator must be out" he whispered as he flicked the toggle light switch back and forth, "Thorn, enough!" he called to her patting his leg for her obedience, but she ignored him, suddenly launching high and with her full weight leapt at the door latch, it was dislodged and the wind outside did the rest, blasting it open, knocking the dog backward, almost ripping it from the hinges.

Candles were blown out as sodden twigs, grit and rain rallied inward, dancing around the open-plan room, as the Thorn raised herself and stood for a moment in the doorway snarling outward while the little villa filled with the clattering and ringing that broke out from the hanging kitchen utensils, pots and pans like an orchestra and the fire roared like a smithy's furnace back up the chimney then dulled so that the room was lit mainly by his torchlight, Thorn gave her master a quick glance then darted out the door barking. The old man span the torchlight onto the pups, "Stay!" he shouted at them, "Thorn! Get back here, Thorn!"

Grabbing his leather coat from the door hook he barged out, closing it behind him and immediately he had to brace himself against its back receiving little relief or shelter beneath the ramshackle, overhanging porch. He buttoned his jacket and as his torch slipped from his wet fumbling hands it rolled out, coming to rest near a puddle its beam cutting out across the yard, shielding his eyes he saw the searchlight had pinned the dog almost at the furthest edge of the clear yard, in a defensive posture standing between the house and the bracken that fell away into the hills below and beyond the trees and bush thrashed back and forth silhouette against the night, then the rain turned to hail and it's repetitive pelting for a moment reminded him of machine-gun fire, that he had once heard as a young man and he felt the presence of someone hiding in the dark.

"Thorn! back now! Who's there? come out! "" He shouted as he stepped forward to pick up his torch, but it appeared his voice was silenced by the eruption of the hail as it struck the leaves of giant palms and broadleaf plants relentlessly pounding the vegetation with marble-sized bullets of ice. At his feet, the soil was peppered and his arm and hand stung as if lashed by a whip as he reached down for the torch, but he held firm his grip. Then as he lifted the light again he caught the edge of the steps that led down the hillside where a dark image stood motionless and appeared unconcerned by the violent attack of the hail.

The old man went speak but found no words fall from his mouth as he watched Thorn back up towards him. Then as the figure took their first step forward the old man turned back to the villa's porch and grabbed at a hand axe set into the wood decking. Clasping it high shielding his head, he spun back as bullet-like hail ricochet off his body and edged forward coming up alongside Thorn, who continued to defend her territory and master.

"What do you want? Step out where I can see you." With a wipe of his eyes, the figure was gone again and he lowered the axe slowly as he scanned the edge of the brush. Seeing no sign of their intruder he reached down and fumbled for Thor's collar and began to tug at it pulling her back. "I have a phone I will call the police! Come, Thorn," he shouted out, It was a bluff he didn't and it was at his point he realized how cold his feet were, as he took a step backwards in his sodden threaded socks, his toes pruning in the muddy water.

All at once, he felt the ground beneath him slip away as the wind appeared to unleash its full force sending the pair tumbling back to the villa veranda, he slipped catching the porch decking and tripped, landing hard against the door which again ripped back open.

Thorn lay at his side, her legs partially over his with his hand still on her collar. Appearing as if she had been injured, she raised her head, looked at her master then lay it flat on the decking in submission letting out a low growl, as the old man propped himself against the door frame, partially dazed, trying to catch his breath. His hand reached out for the torch, but it was too far from his side still shining forward across the yard as the hail stopped as suddenly as it started. Now the hair on the back of the old man neck raised like the fur of Thorn, but again she shuffled and remained still as above the sound of dripping water they heard the definite slush and thud of heavy footfall, that he knew from its sound to be more than one individual and he pushed his hand out, searching for his axe handle, it was nowhere to be seen and looking up he saw to his horror caught in the torchlight, the legs of a group of people stretched out almost in a regimented formation across the yard.

"What the fuck! Who are you, I warn you I will let her go!" he shouted as suddenly Thorn mustered the strength to stand up, kicking her legs in the air to regain her paws, the old man felt her fearless strength and let her pull him to his feet, while by his ear he felt the breath of the three-legged bitch pup who had come forward first to protect her mother, she stepped past him and set herself at Thorn side, their fangs gnashing at the air leering a line of defence towards the intruders and before their master was able to raise himself he was brushed aside as the two brothers joined in, sensing their mother was hurt they stepped proudly beyond her, snapping and snarling, their pack instincts set to attack. Ringed by their protection the old man reached forward slowly and as he raised the torch up from the mud, he heard the words from the dark figure nearest him,

"Er Kommt!" *(He's coming)* it was almost a whisper, and even before his beam of light had struck the face of the spectre, the old man knew there was something unnatural, in those that had invaded his home. Anguish and fear gripped his face as his light rose to flicker over the Zombiesque face of the corpse that stood before him, he watched as the ghoul raised a hand and pointed back towards the steps,

"ER Kommt!" he cried out again, but louder, like the sound of a steam engine pulling into a platform and the shrill stripped leaves from branches to the wind and as the old man raised his torchlight following the creatures hand gesture it drifted hesitantly back and forth over the horrific supernatural scene set before him and the other members of the group, each just as grotesque in appearance as their leader. But something else made the old man's blood turn cold, sending shards of ice down his spine, even in the poor mudded light, he recognised the remnants of their tattered uniforms, a uniform he had once worn himself.

"Who are you?" He shouted, then his eyes cut to the heavens and with a crack of lightning, simultaneously his torch failed plunging the air into a darkness that hung like tar before his eyes.

He could no longer see or hear his dogs, with panic he groped at the torch, tapping the side and glass and suddenly it turned on, clutching it in both hands he thrust it round, and he froze with its beam set on a hideous face, as pale as the moon, less than arm's length from his face. It appeared to blot out the surrounding, hideously covered with lesions that were only obscured by the yellow and bloodshot green eyes, that once shone like the sun hitting the wave tips of the seas of Sardinia.

"Du hast uns verlassen, Jan!"*(You left us Jan)*

He could feel the foul breath of the ghoul on his face, as the words were spat by a man he hardly recognised,

"You!" he spasmed back, catching his hand on the splintered veranda decking, instantly he awoke in his armchair.

Jan looked to the fireplace, where there was no brick, nothing had fallen from the chimney and as the lights flickered on, the television sprung loudly to life, making him lurch as the onscreen commentator Andres Cantor roared out, ""Gooooooooal!"" Announcing the final goal of the match he had been watching before he dozed off.

Turning his head he looked to the door locked and bolted and his dry leather coat then his bare toe sprouting from his worn sock prickled back as he felt the warmth of Thorn sleeping at his feet. With another rattle of his loose shutters, he turned his head back still unnerved by the vision he had seen, still unsure it was a dream as the drafty room whistled and the flames of the fire were fanned.
Scratching at his arms, he looked for the wound in his hand, but saw only a fine blemish of a scar, all that remained from an accident, when in sharpening his axe the blade had slipped, almost severing his palm many years earlier.
Rubbing his palm with thumb, he stood shaking his head then stooped low, looking up the chimney as without moving from their huddle the pups eyes followed his progress and one let out a low comforting groan.
Still heavy from his dream-like state, he checked his reality, walking cautiously over to the window that he had battled with, in what he now realized was a nightmare. He opened it hesitantly but the outer shutter remained in place and he jammed the securing pins firmly, then closing the window he locked it.

"Just the mistral go back to sleep girl." He ordered Thorn who had now got the her feet intrigued by his stealth, and before he sat back in his chair, having reached for a glass and a bottle of his homemade Merto, he braced the door with its timber cross bar.
Having stoked the fire and added more wood, he poured himself a large measure of the thick alcohol and shrugged with an almost dismissive comical attitude at his sense of stupidity of fear, but as he settled back in his chair his thoughts turned to the images he had seen in his dream and memories of the youthful comrades he knew they represented, he raised his glass to the fire and then to the door.
"Mijn broers, proost... slaap lekker" *(my brothers, cheers, sleep well).*

The care and attention Sardinians lavish on the crops they tend in their gardens and fields is for some like a religious compulsion and so in October 1996 in the days leading up to that night there were those that welcomed the arrival of fresh rains, that brought the promise of rejuvenation to their sun-parched land.

However as they closed and latched their window shutters, just as they had done annually for centuries before awaiting the arrival of, Bentu Maestru, the Mistral winds, none could foresee the force of cyclone Cornelia and the rains, that fell as a continuous torrent for three days.
While most islanders remained sheltered within their homes sharing the warmth of a home fire with much of the islands electricity supply not functioning outside, the soft volcanic soil turned into rivers of mud, sweeping away ancient monuments, peasant farms and multi-million dollar holiday villas alike.
In the morning a state of emergency was declared as less than 20 kilometers from the village of San Pantaleo in the northern city port of Olbia, Mayor Gianni Giovanelli described the storm as apocalyptic.
When the winds finally ceased thousands of islanders had been made homeless and 16 people had lost their lives.

Amongst the devastation and destruction over the coming days that followed, it was soon discovered the sound of the thunderstorm that night masked a massive landslide on the hills below the old priest's villa, home to the hermit and his dogs, that sat beside the derelict church of St. Magdalena.
On that last night, with the rains subsiding, as the storm drifted back out to sea, the sky opened out clearing a path for the moonlight, which began to filter through the clouds settling on a recently excavated construction terrace, located just below the site of the old Smeralda Aqua water processing and bottling plant, built in the 1970s by the Cormorant Corporation.
This terrace was designated for the development of new replacement buildings, in the aftermath of the storm it now resembled the fields of the Somme.
With construction and heavy excavation machinery lying, tossed aside, like the toys of children discarded on a beach, pond sized puddles remained and reflected the giant orb and star-speckled dark sky with crystal clarity.

But most impressive was the eerily still surface of a large sinkhole, some fifteen meters in diameter, which had been created by the flash flooding. It was located on the far side of what was once an abandoned man-made plateau and marked the original site, where once a two-storey building had stood, now faded from the memory of nearly all but a few of the remaining soles that had witnessed its existence, in the 1940s.
A foul-smelling belch, sulphurous and stiflingly bilious in nature rippled across the surface of the sinkhole as gas bubbles rose from deep below its waters. Fed by the

main mountain water springs the pure fresh, life giving water that had travelled hundreds of kilometres along the ancient subterranean flumes of a long-extinct volcano. With tunnel walls breached and the washing away of soft material by the landslide, a cavernous magma chamber had opened and something dark and bloated was released, floating up from its deep-frozen crypt it stained the now untapped waters as it broke to the surface of the sinkhole with an oily smear.

While carrying out his perimeter check on the fences and assessing the storm damage on the 60-acre site a day later, it was the smell that led the little dog Zanna Bianco belonging to the security guard Enrico Albani's to a festering carcass that surfaced from the depths of the sinkhole. Believing it to be the remains of one of the indigenous brown boars of the Island, Albani looked for something to fish it from the water, the landslide had also uncovered a number of chunks of reinforced pale coloured concrete, Albani rocked back and forth on a long rusting iron ream rod until it broke away and as he stepped forward towards the water edge he was pulled back by Zanna who continued to snarl and pull at the lead showing an instinctive misgiving of his master actions. Albani was finally forced to tie him up to another metal rod, but Zanna continued to bare its teeth as Albani gingerly began to first prod the sodden ground to check it was solid under foot before stretching out, dangerously close to the fine edge of the bank of the sinkhole and began trying to hook onto the object.

After a few attempts, while trying not to vomit from the smell, he snagged the bar on what appeared to be a leather strap, his curiosity blinding his vision at one point he thought it was some sort of luggage case. It took all of his weight to drag the object from the water, while his boots lost their grip in the mud and as it drew closer he realised the leather strap was a belt. With a final tug one of sodden cloth loops that held the belt it in place, snapped and he slipped in the wet mud, exhausted he lay looking down past his boots and a panic made his feet scramble back as immediately now drained the cloth began to steam in the air and the smell became intolerable, choking for clean breath he clutch his hand over his mouth as he realized he was looking at the top half of the remains of a human corpse, wearing some sort of uniform with the chest face down into the mud. The clothing material ripped in the section around the arms and shoulders exposed strands of sinew and puce colored flesh not dissimilar to the texture and tones of a large jellyfish or coloured glass, while the hands were bloated like grotesque misshapen gloves, with fingers missing, eaten away.

Albani's head span with a lack of oxygen, his hearing was deafened by his own deep breaths and pounding heart, then as his senses returned he turned back over his shoulder,
"Calm Zan" he called to the little dog who continued to pull on the lead like some rabid creature as Albani used the metal bar to steady himself and slowly stood up, initially backing away studying the dark mass. Then with his first step forward he gasped in shock as the body appeared to move, and he held his breath as cowering, Zanna whimpered to silence and turned his back on the horror they had discovered.
Albani felt his jaw drop and he let the iron bar fall from his hands as again he retreated backwards, as the jacket the corpse appeared to be wearing began to rise and ripple with movement and then suddenly beneath the collar the head of a large brown eel appeared and it slithered out onto the soil.
"Figlio un cane" *(son of a bitch)* Albani spat "Mafankulo" *(Mother fucker)* he cursed biting his thumbnail, and kicked up mud ushering the creature on its way as it twisted over and over until it hit the water and disappeared into the deep. Albani stood for taking in the sight his eyes switched back and forth between the corpse remains, the landslide material and the sinkhole, and in his mind he began to make sense of what it is he was looking at, and images of what had once been built in that place and those that built it came flooding back from his childhood. He raised a hand across his mouth as he felt a strange grin grip his lips and he turned again seeing his dog shielding his head down buried in his tail.
"Perhaps we leave this to the bosses Zan." Albani said and slipped the knot from the dogs lead and backed away from the plateau, occasionally looking back over his shoulder as the wind appeared to pick up, throwing dust into the air as if driving him from the site of his discovery.

It would take days for Albani to get the stench from his nostrils and his discovery would eventually end his free range and reign of hunting in the area.
In the days that followed his report to his employers at the Commorant Corporation the site at first remained sealed off, initially guarded by the local Carabinieri.
All construction on the new plant building was halted and the local construction workers moved their equipment to the excavation of a site lower down the hill still within the Commorant lands, where a proposed hotel and villa complex was planned to be built. By now the corporation a major employer in the area, already owned a great deal of real estate on the island.
Following the site inspection by the Olbia council health and safety officer a full investigation of what lay below the sinkhole was ordered and the pumps of the

filtration system and existing bottling production ceased while the water valves that also serviced the nearby road stand taps and San Pantaleo village were capped shut.
For a while locals had to resort to getting fresh drinking water from Arzachena and Cali de Volpe while tests were carried out on existing stocks stored in the two giant vats, because of concerns of contamination to the spring water already pumped and purified. In a hot climate, a day without a regular supply of fresh water can feel like a week and adding to the animosity by some towards their employers nearly all workers were sent home.

However within less than a week, Enrico Albani and the villagers of San Pantaleo were informed the Carabinieri had finished their investigation and vacated the site. Filtering and pumping fresh water would recommence locally from the water supply already in storage, although the bottling side of the plant remained closed, with only a skeleton crew operating a single local emergency stand pump, located on the main road.

On the hill site an outer perimeter fence around the abandoned terrace and an inner cordon around the sinkhole itself were erected. Soon after a mainland Neapolitan private security team in two crew buses arrived, flown in from Rome, they were all armed and wore the same distinctive grey and green camouflage uniforms some still with the packing creases, as if they had just been purchased for the occasion.

Albani and the other local guards were expelled to dealing with the outer perimeter fence and main entrance, both of which were also soon upgraded.
What had once been a flimsy dilapidated gate that was rarely closed during the day and that in the past locals accessed without being stopped to visit the fresh water pump house and fill up their own water tanks became a two and half meter high electric heavy gauge steel plate gate with new surveillance cameras.
However things were not all bad, as the new entrance came with a new air-conditioned guard room prefabricated cabin, complete with a small kitchen and shower room, which Albani very much appreciated and was effectively under his domain.
As for the guards from Naples, they had their own on-site block of mobile homes and stayed much to their own, focusing around the main development site of the Hotel and villa complex that soon resumed construction.
Albani noticed they never visited the beaches near to San Pantaleo; all their weekly supplies came from Olbia. Albani assumed his employers had instructed them not

to mix with the locals, which they adhered to, even avoiding the local little petrol station of Marsino's garage.

So Albani gave them a wide berth when possible and remained wary of the interloping security team and especially their senior officer, he was careful not to make waves and ask to many questions, even though he resented being forced to work additional night guard shifts. He was just thankful that he was one of the few locals to remain employed and although pressed for answers by his neighbours and family, he had been warned to say nothing of what he had seen and nothing of what was to come so spoke with less than handful of very close confidents.

Of course he felt for those that had lost their jobs, many of whom he had known since childhood and he understood their frustrations and building animosity towards the owner of the plant, but he needed the work for his own family, and besides in truth he knew little, other than the corpse he had first discovered wore some sort of uniform. Privately he presumed the man was possibly a policeman, who may have been killed by gangsters and buried on the site some time ago, perhaps even by Mafia.

"You know as much as me, I sit in a box watching TV screens, unless it's in the paper, I have no idea." he told others, including his wife's family and remained tight lipped which was unusual for him, in their eyes, creating further suspicion.

While decision beyond his pay grade were made, at first the main water plant site resembled a ghost town, occasionally cars would arrive from the Corporation he would buzz them through and watch them pass by his window on the way up the hill to the main terrace and cordoned sinkhole. But it was rare; sometimes no more than two visits in as many weeks and he assumed his employers were investigating what was below ground and if it had caused problems with the fresh water supply. Privately with a close source within the carabinieri itself, he speculated the owner had paid off the local police, to keep things quiet and stay away and most of them did.

There was only one other local man that had access and watched with such intent as Albani, as things developed on the site. Hid amongst the scrub and bracken over the days that followed, the old man of the hill, known to the locals as Paguro *(The hermit crab)*, sat in the shade on a high rock outcrop vantage point along with his dogs, sometimes for hours, as below the area controlled by the Cormorant Corporation was sealed off, and specialised buildings were erected on an area he hardly recognised, the abandoned, overgrown terrace. Where little evidence now remained from its original construction as a Nazi facility and a building that he knew held secrets from his youth.

With ears pinned back, Thorn raised her head sniffing the air, as if catching the scent of an unseen danger and her master reached down calming one of her pups when the echo of a straining diesel engine brought a low growl to its lips. And as the hills filled with the bleating alarm signals of another crane lorry making its way slowly up the reinstated road that he had helped construct in the 1940's, Jan's eyes glistened with sweat and the emotion of buried memories, as he realised his world and the peace he had found was coming to an end, and he whispered, "Er Kommt."

Printed in Great Britain
by Amazon